Portrait of Fire

Edited by Tammy S. (Reedsy)
Typeset by Marta Dec (Reedsy)

Artwork by:
Cover Designer — @nskvsky
Chapter Heading Artist — @catherinedownen
Map Illustrator — @biblopolium
Additional Art Designer — @Sottiss

Connect Further
Website: tgclark.com
Bluesky: @T.G.Clark
TikTok: @T.G.Clark
Instagram: @T_G_Clark_POF

First Edition
Printed in the United States of America

ISBN:
E-Book: 979-8-218-81843-2
Paperback: 979-8-218-81844-9
Hardcover: 979-8-218-81845-6

Portrait of Fire

T.G. Clark

*For my grandmother, Betsy Benz,
whose love burns eternal in these pages.*

Book 1 of the
Portrait of Fire series

Jarbold
Isle of Fláimir
Calladen Sea
Aelfyrne
ELVES
CENTAURS
Hearthsea
Shiverloch Sea
GIANTS
God's End Ocean
The Empire of The Nine
Krithinia
Vaktzig
Knoxford
Eisvach
City of Battlebridge
HIGH NESS
Aberness
Dreadfjord
Toussé
The Heart Lake
Gothonia
Prophetenfyst
Isperia
Cilese
Valenzhard
Hammers Ford-En-Berg
Knights of the Reisonic Order
Imperane Sea
Illigois
@Saumyasvision
Kennessee
Mannenhalvara
Prophet's Crossing
Lyonnia
A'leyka Islands
The Holy Isle
Incendrium

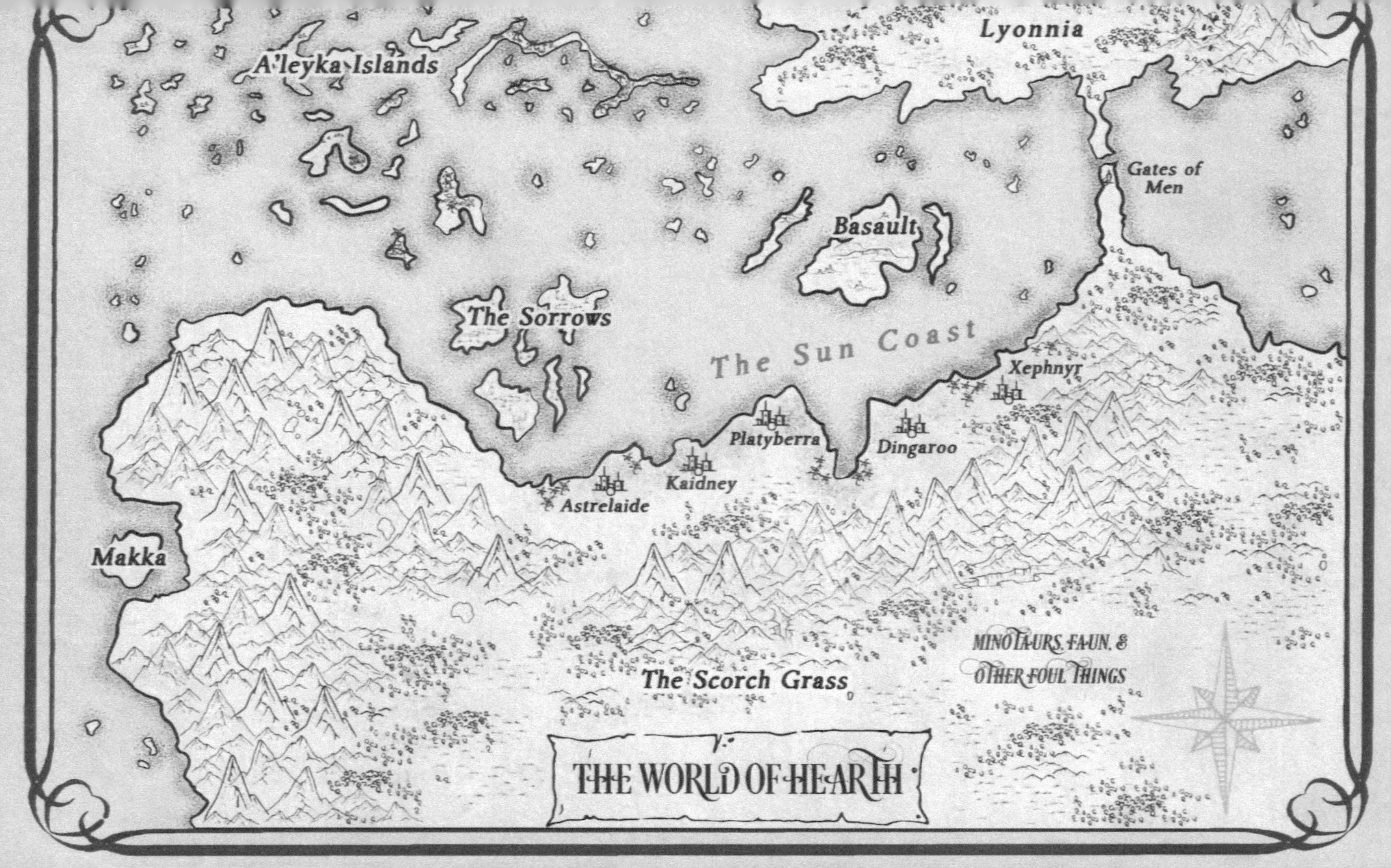

THE WORLD OF HEARTH
Lyonnia
A'leyka Islands
Gates of Men
Basault
The Sorrows
The Sun Coast
Xephnyt
Platyberra
Dingaroo
Kaidney
Astrelaide
Makka
The Scorch Grass
MINOTAURS, FAUN, & OTHER FOUL THINGS

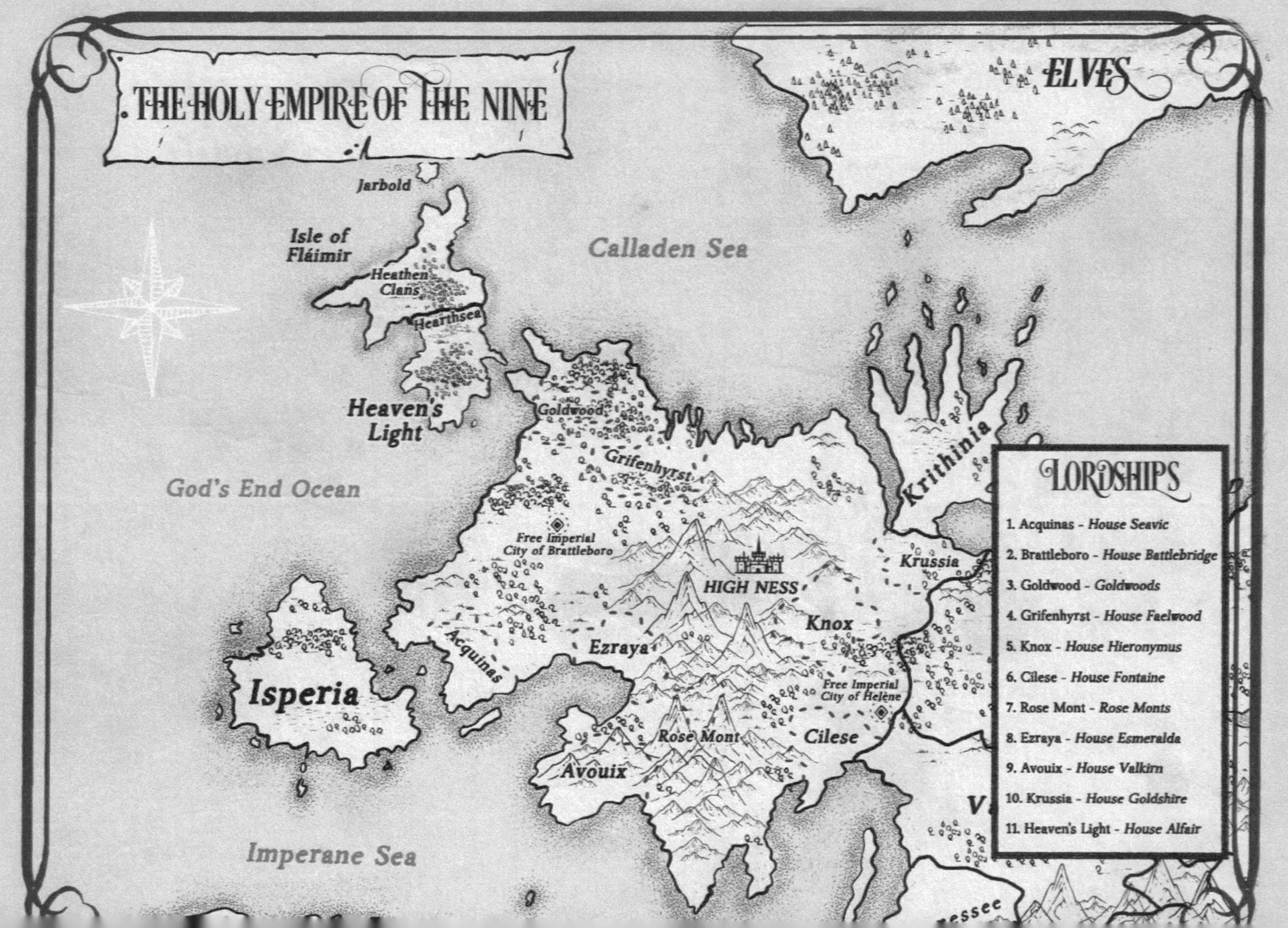

THE HOLY EMPIRE OF THE NINE
ELVES
Jarbold
Isle of Fláimir
Calladen Sea
Heathen Clans
Hearthsea
Heaven's Light
Goldwood
Grifenhyrst
Krithinia
God's End Ocean
LORDSHIPS
1. Acquinas - House Seavic
2. Brattleboro - House Battlebridge
3. Goldwood - Goldwoods
4. Grifenhyrst - House Faelwood
5. Knox - House Hieronymus
6. Cilese - House Fontaine
7. Rose Mont - Rose Monts
8. Ezraya - House Esmeralda
9. Avouix - House Valkirn
10. Krussia - House Goldshire
11. Heaven's Light - House Alfair
Free Imperial City of Brattleboro
Krussia
HIGH NESS
Knox
Isperia
Acquinas
Ezraya
Free Imperial City of Helène
Rose Mont
Cilese
Avouix
Imperane Sea

A Portrait of Fire

The Ash Fall

The end of the world had come.

The sky above turned molten, burning blood-dark and crimson red. Lightning crackled across volcanic clouds, their sickly masses twisting and writhing, spewing forth both magma and newborn rock upon the charred ground. Grand Master Ester Eisenhart gripped his cloak tightly, shielding his eyes from the fierce wind. Though it was the height of summer, the air was cool and thick with ash that fell like snow upon the world.

"Men and women of our holy order!" he roared through the pain of a raw throat. "Do I need to move behind you with the whip? We must find shelter! And with haste!"

Only a series of grunts and moans answered his call to move faster, but it was a response nonetheless. His knights were still alive behind him. *For now at least.*

"By God, no more deaths," he whispered, but the foul air caught his lungs, and the urge to cough threatened to overtake him. He constricted his throat, pulling his cloak tighter, doing his damndest not to let the other knights see.

Pass, damn you, pass! And aye, the urge did pass, but not without the taste of blood upon his tongue. He resumed walking, but not before a grim reality settled over him.

The air is killing us.

"Move it, you lot!" he barked. "We're knights after all!"

Obedient knights, he reminded himself. Men and women who were trained to defend humanity no matter the cost or threat. Ester glanced backward, eyeing his soldiers limping behind him. Three donkeys trudged alongside them, but their numbers had grown thin. Seven days had passed since their departure from their stronghold of Prophetenfyst, with eight horses and five donkeys to their ranks, but the horses grew weak and poisoned from the burnt grass, and once the black curtain of twisting ash revealed itself on the horizon, the beasts bolted in the night under the unnatural light of a blue moon.

The Demon Moon, his knights had whispered.

"Grand Master! What be it? Giants? Demons?" His second-in-command snapped him from his trance, sliding into a battle stance with a drawn sword.

Aye, a brave knight, and an old friend. Ester nodded, a single tear pooling in his eye. He and Trandler had trained since they were but babes, learning to hunt down herds of giants, donning both their knightly cloaks and taking their oath in unison. And when the time came, Trandler supported his bid for Grand Master. Now Trandler turned from him, scanning the horizon for an unknown threat, ash falling from the sky and peppering his white hair, at the ready to kill, *and die,* by his command.

"No, no giants… something other…" he answered, a biting tinge of regret walloping him from deep within his heart. He pushed down Trandler's raised sword, blinking hard as a gust of wind swept what felt like shards of glass upon his skin. His men looked at him, startled; the women, as strong as they were, choked back tears. This was no work of giants.

But why couldn't it be? The thought sent a violent chill through him. He knew how to fight giants. *It had to be them, just had to be! Otherwise...*

He didn't know how to fight the end of the world.

"What then? What do you see?"

"Nothing, you lot..." he spat. "We've fought giants our whole lives, what of it if it were? And as long as I have lived, ain't ever seen no demons." Ester whipped around and took a step forward.

He knew fear-mongering would get them nowhere, and without shelter, it would not matter what ailment struck the world, they would be dead soon anyway. He therefore buried the question, choosing to press onward through the rolling hills of the Giant's Rink. In non-apocalyptic times, the rolling, grassy knolls were painted in streaks of green and yellow, with splotches of red, violet, blue, orange and more from countless breeds of flowers.

A once beautiful land, squandered by a race of brutes! Now, only a sea of gray stretched beneath a burning sky.

"The Holy Five Warriors strengthen us, why couldn't this land be ours?" Trandler cursed as if he read his mind. "Look upon the ruination!"

Ester wanted to speak up and agree with him, but his lungs burned, and he had precious little energy left. He pushed his group farther, summiting more hills covered in ash, crunching dying grass beneath their feet. Each time they topped a hill, the glow of hell grew brighter in all shades of red and orange, with blue and yellow lightning, and an ash cloud as dark as night blanketing the horizon. The air whipped them hard, carrying shards of rock as it stung their skin and eyes. The temperature, too, began to dip, adding yet another bite to their miserable walk. *A once beautiful land, denied to humanity, now lost from the world forever.*

Finally, when Ester was sure he could push no farther for the day, as his calves ached and lungs burned and the taste of blood pooled in the back of his throat, he spotted a structure, its immense silhouette illuminated by the malignant glow of the ash cloud.

"Giants!" he barked, throat choked with ash. "Shelter even!" Tears stung his eyes, but by God, there could be respite from the Ash Fall!

He broke into a run, his knights quickly overtaking him as they charged the tower. His host, ten in total, unsheathed their swords, shouting as they made their charge. Lightning crackled overhead as they prepared to do battle for the structure. The donkeys followed behind them at a leisurely pace.

The immense tower teetered upward at a crooked angle. The giants were foul beasts, and the very thought of staying beneath their roof knotted his stomach. Yet their circumstances were dire, and he swallowed his pride.

"Forward, Knights of the Reisonic Order, and fear not pain nor death! Let us strip their heads from their bodies and claim this land in the name of men!"

The knights cheered and plowed through the ash, with Ester being the last to reach the tower. Panting, he stopped to look up upon the crude, stone behemoth of at least one hundred feet tall, constructed from rough-hewn stone and ancient trees. His knights looked frantically around, jeering at the tower, expecting a parade of stunned giants to come barreling out with their clumsy clubs and wooden swords at any moment, but not a soul stirred. Even in the dark, gargantuan windows, not a single candle or fire burned. Odd, given the growing cold.

Still bracing for battle, the knights took point on either side of a large door. Possessing neither the tools nor strength to ram it down, they instead banged upon its immense frame, demanding the giants come out and fight.

They never came.

Ester and the other knights eventually stepped back, devoid of breath. "A ruse?" a knight by the name of Hedrick proposed.

"Should they possess the mental acumen? No, I doubt such a thing." Ester dismissed him.

"Perhaps they have fled into the ash back to their homeland?" another knight, a young woman by the name of Sarah Tissabeth, countered.

"Craven, yes... that sounds like something a giant would do." Ester rubbed the base of his chin, thinking. Hedrick shot him a rude glance. "Knights! I know what we are going to do! Let us bust down the door and claim this tower as our refuge from this ash. We can cut around the lower hinges and pry open the base of the door. We should then be able to slink inside and refortify our position. At once, knights, at once!"

The knights set to work, hacking away with their swords at the base hinges of the mammoth door. Ester did his best to participate, but the wood was solid and the air thin, and quickly he had to recuse himself. He slunk along the base of the tower, avoiding the direct gaze of his comrades, and summoned all his willpower to not break into another coughing fit. Luckily, the other knights were in better health, and they broke through in no time. Hedrick was able to nudge the base of the door open by a few feet, wide enough to push the donkeys through. The knights then followed, except for Ester, who suddenly found it very difficult to stand. His vision blurred and he gripped his chest with a trembling hand. He uttered a prayer to the Five Warriors to save him, but the divine spirits had no such plans for him. Darkness overcame him and he toppled over.

He awoke sometime later within the structure, Sarah seated on the ground next to him. He tried to rise but found himself bundled tight in a nest of furs splayed across the floor. How much time had passed, he could not say.

"Do not try to rise, my lord," she urged him. "I found you unresponsive in the snow... er, I mean ash. We feared we lost you."

"Choking, covered in your own spittle." Hedrick appeared over him, shaking his head.

"Trandler... Trandler... where is he?" he rasped, tasting blood in his mouth. The sound of boots on stone answered him, and soon hands were on him, helping him to his feet. "Trandler... I need to speak..."

"He is up top," Hedrick finally answered him. A large man with large hands. His black beard ran damn near to his crotch, but not a strand of hair grew on his scalp. A reliable, if not blunt, soldier.

"Up top." Ester rubbed his head. He blinked hard as he struggled to stay on his feet while his vision slowly returned to him. "Sit, I need to sit. Find me a chair..."

"There are no chairs, least not those fit for humans," Hedrick answered.

"How do you mean?"

"We are in the giant's den and we did not bring a ladder to climb into their chairs." Hedrick shook his head. "Among other supplies if we are to persist here in this place of evil."

Ester looked sternly to him. "What is truly the matter?"

Hedrick did not answer. It was Sarah who spoke up. "Nester is gone. Where and when, we cannot say, for the ash has grown deep outside."

"Our holy work does not come easy," Ester bowed his head. He muttered a quiet prayer, and summoning his strength, he wobbled to his feet. Hedrick stepped forward, ready to catch him should he fall, but Ester waved him off. He managed to keep his balance, and blinking hard, tried to make sense of his surroundings.

A dark void towered above them, so tall that he was unsure if he was looking up at the ceiling or the dark night sky. A chandelier, crafted from bones, hung in the dark, larger in circumference than his own home back in the west. Astounded, he followed the line of sight downward to the sounds of japes and chatter from his fellow knights, who were perched beneath a table taller than his own head. Despite the loss of Nester, two knights danced a jig upon the table, amused at the absurdity of its size. Another knight sat perched in a chair, a makeshift rope of furs dangling from the seat.

He gasped. "A room for giants..."

"It would appear so." Hedrick beckoned him to stand beside a fire in the hearth at the center of the chamber. Ester approached, warming himself before flames that looked comically small in the vast space. The fireplace alone was larger than his bedroom at home. "We're burning one of their chairs. That wood alone should last us through the night."

"In all my years... I've never been inside an actual giant's... castle... home... whatever those creatures call it..." Ester stared into the flames, dumbfounded.

"Yes, and lucky us they were not home when we came to claim it."

"What! You mean to say we are not fit to fight those bastards? I've killed dozens in my day..." Though the warm air was comforting, it triggered another vicious coughing spell. Hedrick stood beside him, carefully watching him retch until the spell passed. More blood appeared in his spittle, staining the stone floor. He used his foot to cover the mess.

"Hedrick, tell me, how bad is our state of affairs?"

"Knights Cromster and Tendlev have developed a cough as well. Sarah has confined them to strict bedrest." Hedrick nodded into the darkness of the room. Beyond the massive table and chairs, he could see tents pitched along the far wall.

Comical. He smiled. *Even in the grandeur of the giant's watchtower, we still feel the need for shelter.*

"As for the others, aye, I say they are holding up. This shelter was a nice find."

"No losses then, aye? Good." Ester leaned back on his feet, closing his eyes, and enjoyed the warmth of the flames.

"Nester still remains lost to us," Hedrick answered grimly.

"Oh, yes..." He coughed again. "A good man... I suppose there is still a chance he could find his way to us." A silent, awkward tension followed as both men stared into the flames. "...And of the ash outside? Does it worsen? Tell me, how long have I been out?"

"Time flows eerily here, Grand Master. To what effect, I cannot say, but the moon is no longer visible, nor the stars. Still, I reckon a few hours. Day may have even come, but alas, the ash clouds have covered the sky, and we have no way of knowing it..."

"God be good." Ester coughed and closed his eyes. A few tears trickled down.

"The Five Warriors' blessings can still be felt." Hedrick nodded. "Our remaining donkeys seem to be in good health, and we have food and drink here to last a fortnight. Trandler and the others have scouted the structure, and there are two floors perched above us. One is lined with furs so large we could clothe an entire village, and on the top floor stands windows so tall we can see for miles around. The ash blows up there, aye, but it is not without its shelter. That is where Trandler is now. He watches the Ash Fall."

"I must go to him at once." Ester tried to rise, but again a coughing fit consumed him. "Water, please," he begged.

"Aye, and perhaps some meat? I will fetch these for you, Grand Master You must recover your strength."

Ester took the food and drink humbly, and for the first time in days, he could finally catch his breath. There was no ash here, no false snow, and his lungs rewarded him with full breaths of air. The coughing fits still came, but after some time, his strength returned to him, and he took up his exploration of the tower.

He knew his comrades were staring, but he paid them no mind. His leadership was earned not only through knowledge, but through strength and courage. Steeling himself, he placed a hand against the stone wall for support and stepped forward. Slowly, steadily, he moved along the length of the room, hand trailing the cold stone until he at last reached a massive staircase carved from the rock, spiraling upward into the darkness. He approached the first step, nearly a third of his own height, and threw himself upon the stair, rolling onto his back as he did so. He did this three more times before stopping to rest. He made slow progress but gradually fell into a methodical process his body could tolerate.

After some time, he reached the second floor: a dark and cavernous place filled only with the sounds of the wailing winds outside. A brother startled him as he emerged from a room, arms filled to the brim with looted furs.

"Careful, my good man! For I thought you may have been a brownie come to meet my sword!" Ester teased and the knight laughed. They parted ways smiling, but Ester's heart pounded. He did not feel safe here.

His climb resumed, but his progress slowed, and halfway up the staircase, he collapsed into another coughing fit. He coughed himself into unconsciousness, and when he awoke, found himself staring into a mousehole carved into the stone wall of the staircase. He looked inside, and wasn't it the darndest thing?—he thought he could make out a small bed and coat stand inside.

Ester ol' boy, you're seeing things! Queer things!

His skin prickled as he rolled to his feet and resumed his climb. He couldn't wait to be out of there.

Finally, he summited the final stair, coming up a landing awash with a fiery-red glow. A vista opened to the sky overlooking the Ash Fall. A black shadow stood against the evil, a long flowing cape fluttering in the wind.

"T-trandler?" he called out.

"Aye, Grand Master, it is me," Trandler quietly answered him.

Ester hobbled to his side. Trandler took a preemptive hold of him, for when he gazed upon the Ash Fall, his knees grew weak.

Before them, before God and his Holy Five Warriors, before the realms of men his father and grandfathers and forefathers had defended for generations, stood the edge of the world, torn asunder and in flame. There was no distinction between the horizon and the black ash, between the glow of hell and the crackling of blue lightning, the roar of thunder loud enough to even shake the great stone tower of the giants.

"By all that is good and holy, we are truly at the end of the world," Ester finally said.

"It appears so, my lord. The Ash Fall has ruined the Giant's Rink, and if my eyes are to be believed, even their sacred lake farther east."

"Their wickedness has caused this. I am sure of it."

"Grand Master, Ester, friend..." Trandler gently turned to

him as the red flames of the Ash Fall burned behind him. "I do not think this was the work of the giants."

"Nonsense, it must be. We've done our duty. For millenia we've killed the giants and worse to protect the realms of men. God wouldn't punish us... cause this... it can't be. We have not failed in our holy task."

"Yet the world burns the same. The ash blows west, my lord. It will cover the lands of men. This is beyond the works of giants or beastfolk. This is something else... His Five Warriors give us strength."

Ester worked his jaw, refusing to believe it. Yet the more he stared outward upon the ruination of the world, the more he came to the same conclusion as Trandler. This was the work of something far greater.

Lost for words, Trandler and Ester watched the world fester until his eyelids could no longer remain open. Ester retired downstairs to the quiet and emptiness of the second floor. There he pitched a tent beneath a giant's workbench, finding his accommodations warm and isolated. *As it should be,* he knew. He wanted no one to see the dark red stains filling his phlegm.

Time progressed and the ash fell. Ester's lungs worsened, and as the inevitable seemed upon him, he did everything in his power to keep morale high. He commissioned the artful ones to perform plays and recite poetry. Trandler juggled. They dressed a donkey in women's clothing and drank what little ale they had. Still the ash fell, and gradually their food and drink dwindled. They burned the remaining wood until the fire was extinguished and their bread turned stale. The tower became dark and cold like a tomb. Never in his wildest imagination did he imagine ash as deep as snow in the middle of summer.

Ester knew time was running low, until one morning (doing his best to judge the time of day) he awoke to find his pillow coated in a sea of blood. He gave a startled cry and tried to rise, but his arms trembled so badly from the cold and blood loss that he fell back into his own sickness.

"Trandler! Trandler!" he called in a hoarse voice.

At last, the knight came, shouting in shock to find his life-long friend trembling and coated with blood. Ester cursed himself for his display of weakness, but he no longer had the strength to care for himself. Sarah and Trandler tended to him that morning, washing the blood from his beard, and bundled him deeper beneath a mound of blankets. With luck, his trembling stopped, and so Sarah tried to coax him to eat, but the bread was dry and his lungs too inflamed. He could keep nothing down. That evening he summoned Hedrick to his side and told him of his final will.

"You are too kind," Hedrick answered him coldly.

"It is not about kindness. It is about the fitness of duty. Many are ill; they will need a strong leader to lead them home. And… for the coming war."

"War? How do you mean Grand Master?"

Ester shook his head, pointing a wobbly finger up at Hedrick. "That is your title now, with all its responsibilities. Mankind will need a new generation—a new line of thinking to lead us through this doom. If this is not the end of the world, and I pray to God it is not, then it will be up to us, the Knights of the Reisonic Order, to see mankind through this and exact our revenge on the foul races that brought this curse upon the world. Turn this doom into our blessing, Grand Master."

Hedrick, a stern man, nodded solemnly. "And what of Trandler? He will not accept this."

"Do not let our holy order fall to factionalism. Trandler is a faithful and loyal man. Use his advice and wisdom. You will need it when you return to the lands of men."

They exchanged handshakes as Ester lay beneath a mountain of furs. That evening, everything was packed up, and by the grace of God, a break in the Ash Fall came the next day. There was some hesitation from his knights, but in the end, all consented to return home. Ester would summon what strength remained to him and continue east with only a carrier pigeon to his person.

Trandler protested, refusing to go, yet the next morning he read Ester his last rites through tears in his eyes. "For your service to humanity. To the one true God of all creation. To our Five Warriors, the holy knights of protection and order, who will raise you into their eternal halls, and you will feast, and be warm, and be tended to by all the honor and valor you displayed in this life. We are the blessed, the chosen few of mankind, and your sacrifice shall live on in every babe born to a human mother. Amen."

"Amen," he answered. He then passed formal command over to Hedrick. The knights departed not long after.

Ester watched the knights and donkeys return west from the doorway of the tower. He stayed there a long time, only turning east once the last knight disappeared over a distant, ashy hill. He made for the end of the world, draping a blanket over his shoulders and wrapping a scarf around his mouth, hopeful to stem the flow of malignant air into his lungs. He used the last of his strength to trudge forward through ash that rose to his shins. The ruination stung his eyes and stained his clothes as well, but he did not relent from the matter at hand.

I am a knight of the holiest order, damn it! He steeled his nerves for his final act of service. He knew he was a dead man walking; this would be his final day upon the world of Hearth.

He pushed hard through the rolling hills of the Giant's Rink. Where grassy knolls once basked under a gentle sun, death and ash coated the dried and dead grass like cursed wildflowers upon the land. And there upon the horizon, as he pushed farther and farther from the civilized lands of man, he came upon the final black curtain—a twisting and chaotic thing churning in the foreground. Ash and lightning shot forth from the hells below, and a putrid stench, one of sulfur and brimstone, stole what little breath he could muster. Before the burning Hearth, he fell to his knees atop a large hill, knowing he could go no farther.

Facing the maelstrom of fire and brimstone, he uttered one last silent prayer and then removed the carrier pigeon from the cage strapped to his back. Ester quickly scribbled a final attestation regarding the Ash Fall, including a prayer for his fellow knights. He hoped they would make a safe return. Satisfied with his work, he cast the bird free into the sky.

He watched the bird go with a smile.

A coughing fit then came upon him. He heaved and blood spilled forth from his lungs. Once the spell passed, he tidied himself the best he could for his ascent to heaven and lay down upon his back, facing the ash wall to the east. His eyelids grew heavy as his lungs pooled with blood and phlegm, but he was content with his life of service. He readied himself to close his eyes for good, resting his arms upon his chest, when a flash of movement caught the last of his dwindling attention.

Upon the horizon, a figure walked along the lava plumes.

He forced himself back into a sitting position. *No, not just one!*—his eyes darted—*but thirteen!*

He tried to turn and scramble back down the hill. He inhaled, desperate for breath to call the bird to return, but there was no use. He collapsed back into a pile of ash, trembling as his lungs filled with blood. He rolled over one last time, watching the figures gather as dark wings spread behind them.

WARWICK I

He hoisted the pistol up, preparing to fire at his unmoving target. A hundred eyes watched him. His finger quivered, but he steadied his breath and pulled the trigger.

The bullet sliced through the air with a crackle of fire. He leaned back with a satisfied smile as it struck the target fifteen feet away, hitting the outermost ring of the bullseye. Applause erupted from the watching crowd.

The head of the imperial guard, Strammond of the Demonbreun, walked forward and congratulated him. "A fine display, my prince. Soon you'll be striking targets from a galloping horse!"

A soft mitten tugged at his shoulder, turning him around. It was his cousin, Catelyn, smiling warmly before she jumped on him in a great hug. He laughed, letting himself be pulled in, enjoying the feel of her against him. "Oh, I knew you could do it!"

"A fine shot. A steady shot," his other cousin affirmed. Derrick stepped forward and gently pulled him away from Catelyn. "You'll be the talk of the realm soon enough."

"In no time?" His face scrunched. "I am always the talk of the realm!" He jumped back and did a twirl, highlighting his fancy pantaloons, striped in yellow and red, and his pointed shoes laced with gold. He smiled, puffing out his chest, and dug his hands into his hips. The white ruff around his neck nearly obstructed his vision, but he didn't care. He could feel the wind pick up and carry the ribbon on the top of his plush hat. His arms were triple their normal size under the tunic. All the men and women of his court wore only furs and cloaks. A young girl of the court giggled at him and he blushed. He felt *princely*.

"Yes, Cousin, forgive me. Everyone in the south is sure to talk highly of you."

"The south? I am to inherit the whole realm."

Catelyn spoke up. "Oh my prince, forgive my stupid brother. You had a wonderful procession through the warm and pleasant princely states of the south. Don't fret over your younger brother…"

"Twin brother." Derrick rolled his eyes.

"… and his procession through the north. I know for a fact you are indeed the talk of the realm." She smiled and poked his nose.

"You mean it?"

"Of course! Derrick and I just came from Aberness, didn't we? And saw your brother, and I tell you, he does not have a single ribbon to his name. The northern lords only bestowed cheap mead and ugly daggers upon him." Catelyn put her hand on his shoulder and leaned in close. She cupped her hand and whispered into his ear. "And I hear there is a mountain of presents waiting for you too from those very lords of the north, but you didn't hear it from me."

He blushed as his trousers grew tight below the waist. Derrick stepped forward and pulled his sister back once more.

"It's only fitting—that I am to receive the most gifts. Don't forget who will be the emperor one day!" He announced this to his court but focused his proclamation on Derrick.

"Perhaps it is my turn then? Let us make a game of it!" Derrick jumped forward and snatched the pistol from him.

Derrick was older and stronger, pushing seventeen and past due for marriage. He easily stole the gun from his hands, sending Warwick into a huff as the crowd broke into startled whispers. Catelyn took a step back, also pouting, as Derrick, with his dark hair and muscular build wrapped tightly in a handsome dark cloak, lifted the pistol to fire. He steadied his gaze when Strammond took a step forward, only enough to catch the corner of Derrick's gaze, and then stepped back. Derrick's nose scrunched, followed by a pout. He closed his eyes and pulled the trigger. His shot missed the bullseye entirely.

"And the prince remains undefeated!" Warwick jumped, spinning in another circle. The court clapped as Derrick dropped the gun and slunk away. Catelyn clapped and beamed at him. He couldn't stop smiling. "Proclaim it far and wide, your prince's glory!" He started to laugh, but the unmistakable clink of steel and sword came from behind him. He turned and the court followed. Cutting through the snow came his personal guard and knight, Sir Wulford, a sour look upon his face.

It was Sir Strammond's turn to laugh. "And here comes your good knight, late for this momentous occasion. Well pray tell, Sir Wulford, where have you been to dare miss the prince's crowning achievement? Perhaps Prince Warwick should take another strike? Display for the whole court your immaculate training of your young squire and prince?"

A frown spread across Warwick's lips. He didn't like being interrupted. "What is the meaning of this?"

Wulford, a grizzly and traditional man from the lands of Esteria, frowned at the sight of the pistol. "My lord prince, a pigeon has just arrived from High Ness. Your father. If we may speak in private..."

"We are in the midst of a display of my pistol training, Sir Wulford. An artform whose training you denied me, or have you forgotten?" Warwick grinned to his courtiers. "I would dismiss you then, please, from my audience."

Strammond laughed as Wulford rocked back on his feet, yet defied the prince's command. "My prince, I am afraid it is of the most urgent business."

"I am to decide what is urgent business. Now be away with you for the time being, we can resume my training once I return to the castle. I am weary from my long travels."

"My prince!" Wulford's voice cut through the court, and Warwick did a visible double take. Many in the court looked away. Warwick forced a pretend smile, pretending not to hear the scandalized whispers of his courtiers.

Wulford stood before him, indignant. His brow furrowed, and despite the cold, he broke into a sweat. He took a humble step forward, but stopped himself, flashing his eyes briefly to Catelyn.

I am the crown prince, Warwick reminded himself, *the heir-to-be. I am in charge.*

Still, he bit his lip, thinking of what his father, the emperor, would say... but he hadn't seen him in over a year. No, he was sent on a grand trip of the realm to learn to rule and be adored by his subjects. He must find his own way. He noticed the scroll in Wulford's left hand. "The scroll to me at once," he commanded.

"This is not the best time, my prince..."

"The letter is from the emperor himself, is it not? You mean to disallow the prince from attending to stately business?" Strammond smiled.

"The scroll to me, Wulford. Now."

Wulford frowned but stepped forward. He handed the scroll over.

Warwick huffed and spun around, walking away from his knight and his court. He marched toward the bullseye marked with arrows and bullet holes, unfolding the scroll to read before the crowd like the southern actors upon the stage.

"To my beloved crown prince," Warwick started, beaming. The crowd nodded in approval. "It has been a year since I last saw you, and it has been a year for you to develop and grow into a strong man, fit for ruling the realm. I have heard many tales of your adventures through Sanguinia, and this has filled my heart with pride. You are a man now. The realm will soon belong to you."

Warwick poked his head around the outstretched scroll before him. The crowd smiled and a few applauded his impeccable reading skills. Wulford, however, silently begged him to stop. Smiling, Warwick continued.

"But it is as a man I must deliver the most dreaded of news. I must summon you back to the imperial court immediately. Pack your things and be quick. The realm will soon be in mourning. Your uncle is dead..."

He stopped reading as a sharp cry went up from Catelyn and Derrick. His small court broke into a frenzy. Cousins fell onto each other, frantic with tears. Courtiers turned and began the long run back to the castle. Strammond cursed. Wulford hung his head low. Warwick's court turned away from him, and with trembling fingers, he finished the letter. "He died valiantly defending the realm on the Isle of Fláimir. You will be among the first to hear this news. Be of the utmost caution. Return to me immediately. It is moments such as these that boys must become men. I know the tellings of your manhood from across the realm are true, but you must steel yourself for the coming trials. I look forward to seeing you before the moon turns. Your father, Emperor Bancroft Hieronymus." Below his father's signature, the two-headed phoenix of their house sigil was pressed into wax. He lowered the scroll fully to find only Wulford and Strammond remaining of his audience.

"Unbelievable..." Strammond shook his head. A tear fell from his cheek before he too turned from the crown prince and began the long walk to the castle.

Warwick, his fingers now numb from the cold, let the scroll fall to the snow. He turned back to the castle, abandoned. Wulford rushed behind him to snatch the scroll. "My prince," he called after him, but Warwick only lowered his head, kicking at the snow with his fine shoes. He walked slowly, keeping his distance from the wails of his court.

Above him, the ancestral castle of House Hieronymus stood high on a hill, bathed in warm light against the snowy drifts surrounding the countryside. Long ago, the pride of his house had led the stone walls to be demolished, and in their place, massive windows had been installed. Knoxford Castle had outgrown its role as a fortress, transforming instead into a testament of wealth, splendor, and unabated power. Massive square turrets rose high and mighty, burning brightly with countless chandeliers visible even from the bottom of the hill. Countless chimneys rose even higher, puncturing the white clouds above with plumes of black smoke. Even in the face of death, the ancient house of Hieronymus burned bright with life.

Warwick reached the castle last, followed only by his personal guard, Wulford. Knights of the Demonbreun Guard stood before a pair of great oak doors, nodding at his approach, but grunting curses at Wulford's passing. Neither Warwick nor Wulford acknowledged their open insubordination, instead focusing all their energy on ignoring the cries and tears coming from within the castle walls. In the parlor, his court had gathered as household staff peeled damp, cold clothing from his guests. He arrived just in time to see Catelyn fleeing from the room, followed by Derrick with tears in his eyes.

"The prince and proclaimed heir to the Crown of the Nine, Warwick Hieronymus, First of His Name…" Wulford announced but found his words cut short.

A great wail erupted from elsewhere in the castle. A cry of a mother outliving her child. The court grew quiet, and now all eyes in the parlor turned to him. Warwick winced, pulling at his frock, and looked desperately to the staircase on the other side of the room.

"A time for mourning, yes?" he said quietly to his audience. Looking from eye to eye, Warwick merely nodded to himself, finding not a single answer. "Right then."

He put his head down and pushed through his courtiers, winding his way like a snake through the court. A few trembling hands reached out for him, but he brushed them aside. He made for the staircase on the far wall, and climbing the curved steps, he stopped at the top, turning to face his audience, and found every teary eye trained upon him. He wavered on his feet, unable to stand, and gripped the handrail. Wulford placed a gentle hand upon his back and urged him up the staircase, away from the public view.

"The prince needs to grieve," Wulford apologized. They left among a sea of murmurs and cries.

Wulford followed close behind him as they ascended to the third floor. A long hallway greeted them, lined with the busts of countless ancestors. The muscles in his legs tensed as if his body wanted to burst into a sprint, but he restrained himself. He passed bedchamber after bedchamber, hearing muffled cries and shouts coming from within. They passed servants frantically running about, a few with tears of their own in their eyes. They at least had the courtesy to bow as he passed.

At long last they reached the family's private wing separated from the rest of the house by the family's insignia of the phoenix on a pair of oaken doors. A pair of Demonbreun knights dressed in their striped attire greeted them and pushed open the doors. A blast of warm, toasty air greeted them, followed by a grief-stricken wail.

Grandma'am. He swallowed. She resided in the grand bedchamber, the lady and castellan of the house. Warwick, though heir to their family's empire, had been delegated a smaller room overlooking the castle's snow-covered spice garden. When they reached his bedroom doors, the lump perched in his throat finally receded. He turned to his personal guard and demanded his departure. Wulford merely nodded and took position outside his chamber. Warwick narrowed his eyes and huffed. "That will do," before slamming the doors shut behind him.

"Unf," he pouted and threw his plush hat onto the floor. He stared at the ribbon, mulling his thoughts over in his head before he finally had to say it aloud. "My uncle is dead?"

Tears stung his eyes, but only for a moment. He wanted to cry and be sad. He wanted his court to see him weep and be heartbroken, yet in truth, he hardly knew his uncle. Besides, he was a man now, and shedding tears would make him seem childish… wouldn't it?

He pouted, looking about his princely room. A massive stone fireplace crackled in the center of the room, though it did little to fight the cold. Turning, he cast his gaze to his grand canopy bed, now fluffed and tidied since the morning. It now called to him with a long passion, and he wanted nothing more than to give into his wanton desire and curl up under a mountain of warm blankets, but he resisted. Instead, he turned his attention to his standing mirror, with phoenixes etched into the woodwork.

Manly, fitting for a king, he thought. He smiled and pranced to it, doing a spin in his dandy clothes. *The fanciest outfit in the realm!*

More content, he folded his arms and sat down on a plush chair near the fire. A servant had left an assortment of lemon tarts and roasted walnuts for his pleasure. He popped a tart into his mouth, wincing at the sourness, but drooling over the rush of sweetness at the end. That was how these things were best resolved—to allow the court to fight through the sourness of the day's news, and then rejoice later with a feast or hunting tour.

He popped another tart into his mouth, and then another. Soon nearly the entire tray had disappeared, and the tarts remaining made his stomach curdle. He put a walnut into his mouth, enjoying the taste of salt and butter, but a pain shot through his belly and he forcefully spat it into the fire.

Be of the utmost caution.

His father's words gurgled in the pit of his stomach. Father never spoke like that before.

And my uncle is dead. From battle.

He could nearly hear the clash of steel in his ears. Men swinging swords. Cavalry charging into battle. *Poison poured from the bottle.*

He leaped from his chair as the fire danced wildly behind him. He scanned his bedchamber, sure he heard the words, but he was alone. He looked down upon his remaining treats and slapped the tray, flinging the remaining walnuts into the flames.

Bang. Bang. Bang.

He yelped as his bedroom doors shook on their hinges. "H-hello?" he choked out. He knew he hadn't imagined that.

The doors burst open, swinging back to unveil a dark specter standing in the hall. He stumbled backward as if to faint, but he did not have a cushion in his vicinity.

"Heir to the throne and our family's legacy," the specter said.

"Grandma'am." Warwick wobbled as he regained his footing.

His grandmother, shrouded in black, floated into the room. Strammond and Wulford came after, the only indication this was real and not a nightmare.

His grandmother stopped before him and bent at the knee. Warwick gave a flick of his hand, indicating she could rise. In her old age, she struggled to stand as Strammond rushed forward to help her. Warwick stood still.

"Have you taught your squire nothing of chivalry?" Strammond cursed at Wulford. He took her under the arm as she steadied herself.

"That's enough, Strammond. My grandson, our heir, we must find somewhere to sit and talk urgently."

Warwick heard the words but did not move nor speak. He only looked into the black veil that shrouded his grandmother's face and clenched his teeth as his stomach did a somersault. Wulford coughed, however, rolling on his massive feet. The glint of his steel reflecting against the fire snapped Warwick from his trance.

He placed one hand upon his stomach and extended another to his grandmother. "Yes, Grandma'am, perhaps by the fire?"

"No!" she leaned in close. "This is an auspicious day in an auspicious time. Come, let us sit by your game set." She took his hand and pulled him forward, directing him to a pair of green armchairs in the corner of his room. She sat, extinguishing a small candle burning beside a game board, and did the

Tap of the Nine across her chest. Warwick sat, staring with a raised eyebrow as she muttered a prayer. He could only see the glint of her blue eyes through the black veil.

"Grandma'am, let me say I am so very sorry to have received word of Uncle…"

"Silence! Do you not know it is rude to interrupt someone when they are praying?"

His cheeks stung with the verbal slap. He pulled his arms together and fiddled with his thumbs. Grandma'am's blue eyes slid shut behind the veil as she finished her prayer. A moment later, they opened again, glistening.

"Wulford!" she barked. "Have you killed the boy?"

"My lady?" he asked. "I was not instructed to harm anyone…"

"Nonsense. You were hired to train my grandchild to become a knight. Trained in the art of chivalry, swordplay, and honor. The boy is fifteen. In a year he can marry. So why is it that I see only a boy before me?"

Strammond chuckled as Wulford shifted on his feet. "He has trained, my lady, for a year. On horseback and swordplay and archery."

"He can hit nary a bullseye with an arrow or bullet, let alone the broad side of a barn."

"Grandma'am, I hit the target today, honest, ask—"

"Had you been my ward, I would have thrown you in the stocks months ago. A year you have had. On the road, traveling from inn to inn, plenty of distance between the great families of Sanguinia. My grandson should have returned stout and strong, and yet I see only a boy so plump he's fit to burst from his linings…"

"It's designed to look that way, Grandma'am…"

"Still, you are my son's heir, and my son speaks with the voice of an empire, so I am in no position to dismiss you."

"Thank you, my lady."

"It is not a thank-you, but a curse," she hissed back. "My grandson goes now to court in a time of coming peril. My son is dead. My second born yes, but a son I loved dearly, and with his passing, who will command our armies? Who will fight for us on the Isle? This poor boy who can barely lift a knife? I think not.”

“The emperor doesn’t need to fight, Grandma’am. His knights and lords do it for him.”

“See! The boy is positively not right in the head.”

Strammond laughed, and in turn, Grandma’am turned her attention to him. “And you, a hundred years of your order protecting our family, and you haven’t instructed the boy a lick in the politics and order of our realm. You bear the failure as well.”

Strammond sputtered. “My lady… I am terribly sorry… but I have only just rejoined the prince. I did caution your lord son, the emperor, about appointing an Esterian knight over a trained member of my guard to train the boy…”

“That’s no excuse. At best you failed to educate the child out of spite, or as I would call it, high treason. Is that truly your defense?”

“No… my lady.”

“We sit here as four failures then. A boy who refuses to become a man. A knightly order so blind to justice it spared the lord who gave my grandson these pantaloons. A lame knight who has faltered in his sacred duty. And an old woman who has allowed it all to unfold. Well, I say… no longer! I have brought you something, Grandson.”

Warwick perked up in his seat as Grandma’am snapped to Strammond. He walked forward, producing an object wrapped in cloth. Grandma’am took it from him, and with trembling hands, pulled back the cloth. She unveiled a golden crown, topped with nine tips, and a two-headed phoenix branded into the metal.

“For you, my grandson. The family crown. Older than our empire. More ancient than even me. It has been in our family for centuries, perhaps millennia, for long has our family reigned, and even longer do the great deeds of our family go. Before the Ash Fall and the coming of the Makkan Empire, we controlled and governed these lands. It is time you take this crown for yourself and wear it proudly to court.”

"Oh, Grandma'am…" Warwick's eyes shimmered. He reached out to touch it but Grandma'am snatched it away. She tried to rise, but stumbled in her seating, so Warwick slunk to his knees and bowed before her.

"What is this? Why do you sink to your knees? Rise and receive the crown, lest everything we built crumble!"

Warwick felt the verbal slap again. He rose back to his feet, suppressing the urge to cry, and stared into the dark void of his grandmother's veil. "Kneeling is customary for a crowning…"

"This is an heirloom, not the emperor's Crown of the Nine. This is no crowning," Grandma'am shushed him, managing to rise to her feet. Warwick stood tall, very tall, but he did not buckle his knees for his grandmother's sake, not again. She rose to her tiptoes, and grunting, managed to lift the crown on top of his golden curls.

"You at least have the stature to be a king. Now tell me, Grandson, how does it feel?"

Warwick's eyes looked upward as if he could see his own forehead. The crown weighed heavy, pressing firm down upon his neck, but he did not wobble on his feet. In truth, he liked it. Butterflies sprouted where pit vipers had snarled in his stomach only moments ago.

"I love it."

"You will learn to hate it." His grandmother shook her head. "The weight of duty, of honor, of *serving* the realm. You will need to do great things, Warwick. Terrible things, yes, but great nonetheless."

"I am ready to serve my people!" he said triumphantly.

"No. You are far from ruling even a pack of noggins. You will need to go to the city of Aberness and find your twin brother. You will need each other at court. With the death of my son, how the scales of power swing away from our family."

"I will leave on the morrow. I shall show the realm, and my father, I will be fit to rule!"

At this Grandma'am broke into a suppressed chuckle. Even Strammond let a laugh slip through his tight demeanor.

Warwick frowned. He turned to scowl at Strammond, but the crown weighed heavy and threw off his center of balance. He stumbled on his feet, and Grandma'am had to grab his arm to steady him.

"Oh, by the divinity of Aethylios and his Nine Miracles, protect my family," she wailed.

"Surely you must come with us, my lady," Strammond urged.

"I will come to the capital, yes, but not yet. I must prepare myself and the household for the funeral of my... son," she whispered again. A sob broke from her lips a moment later.

"Come, my lady, I will escort you to your chambers." Strammond walked forward and took Grandma'am by the hand. In an instant, she transformed from the family matriarch to an ailing old woman. She hobbled from the room, guided by Sir Strammond of the Demonbreun. Wulford and Warwick watched them go and then locked eyes.

"Your Grace." He bowed, falling to one knee.

"Your Grace," Warwick repeated, running his fingers over the crown's ridges. He smiled and bid Sir Wulford to rise. "To my brother then, and onward, to my father."

"You have my promise, Your Grace, I will not let anything happen to you at court."

"And why should anything happen to me at court?"

Before Wulford could answer, he dismissed him with his hand. Wulford begrudgingly left the room as Warwick returned to his tray of sweets, fiddling with his crown and daydreaming of his future as he stared into the fire.

LEAWYN I

She looked down upon the body of her dead son. A tremor ran through her fingers as she reached out, brushing a lock of sandy-brown hair away from a gash on his cheek. The wound ran deep and red, even as the body gave itself to rot. But even for its size and stench, she knew this was not what killed him.

I will look. She steeled her breath. Slowly, she pulled back the layer of furs covering the body.

Her first instinct was to vomit, the second was to weep. A blast of rancid air greeted her, curdling her insides. *By the Hearth!* She gagged but did not let go. She forced herself to look.

A ragged wound split him open from pelvis to chest, his flesh gaping wide. The edges were brown with dried blood, his innards stiff and exposed, glistening where rot had not yet claimed them. Flies would come soon for him if she was not careful. She lowered the fur again. She looked upon her boy, cradling his clammy cheek in her hand. *My boy. My baby.*

Kaelin. She shuddered. A second child lost. Another fallen in the prime of his life.

"My brave warrior," she whispered, and leaned over to kiss him. She swept more sandy-brown locks from his forehead, pulling his head into her chest.

How many times had she held him like this before? When he was a babe, new to the world, his cries warm against her breast. When he had taken his first stumbling steps, moving away from her, never looking back. When had been the last time? The final moment before the years carried him beyond her reach?

A stirring at the entrance of the tent finally pulled her from her son.

"Grandma…" a little voice squeaked.

Leawyn turned, finding her granddaughter, small and frail in the gaping mouth of the tent, standing in the flaps, wrapped in a halo of light from the outside world.

"I told you not to come in, Arianwyn. Such things are better left unseen."

"I want to see him," the girl whispered. "I want to see Dad again… before he goes into the bog."

Leawyn sighed. "It is a hard sight, but come then." For the first time that day, tears burned behind her eyes.

Her granddaughter inched forward, at first unsure of herself, staring wide-eyed at the other corpses scattered about the tent. For a moment Leawyn thought she might bolt, but she instead brought her hands together beneath her chin, as if in prayer, and took a steadying breath. She walked up to the table, fingers interlocked, her gaze meeting her father's face at eye level. She stared at him for a long time while Leawyn cradled the back of her son's head, her fingers slowly drifting from his cold, matted hair to the soft strands of his daughter's.

"It looks like he is sleeping," Arianwyn said at last.

"He is sleeping… in a way." Leawyn nodded.

"How long… how long do I have to wait… until I see him again?"

Leawyn pulled her old, weary hands from her son's head and wrapped them around her granddaughter. She held her close, firm and steady, though neither shed a tear. "When the sun's light fades and the salt tides rise to wash the Hearth clean. When the moon climbs high and never wanes again. That is when we will see him again."

"And my uncle too?"

"Yes, and your uncle too."

Arianwyn hesitated. "And Granddad? Will I see him?"

"Of course, sweetling."

A longer pause. Then, softer still. "And my mother? Will she rise too?"

Leawyn sighed, pulling her granddaughter even closer. "Yes, we will see them all again. Your father will be placed into the bog, deep beneath the Hearth, where the waters are cold and still. There his body will rest through the ages of men and beasts alike. And when the moon rises high and outshines all the stars in the sky, he will rise again, born anew from the bog. And I will be there. You will be there. Your sister, your grandfather, your mother... all those who came before us."

She pressed a kiss to the girl's forehead.

"And the foreign soldiers?" The girl's nose wrinkled. "Them too?"

"No, darling, not them. They burn their dead. There will be no second life for them."

"Good," Arianwyn spat. "I don't want to see them—ever!"

At last her granddaughter broke into tears.

"Oh, shh, shh, young thing," Leawyn hushed her, rocking her gently. "It will all be all right."

"I don't want him to go down into the bog! I want him to stay right here!" She stomped.

"But don't you want him to go be with your mom? And his mother? And all his ancestors?"

"I want him to be here with me." Tears poured from her face.

Leawyn lowered herself to her knees with a groan, her joints protesting, but she bore the pain. She placed firm, steady hands on her granddaughter's shoulders, looking deep into her eyes. "Our people have only ever known loss. It isn't fair to you, and it isn't fair to me. But we have a secret, young one. A gift. We will rise again, together, as a family. We simply must be patient. Patience, my dear… for justice, and for those we love."

Arianwyn sniffed. "I know. Like when I had to wait for Layita to be born before Mom went under the soil too."

Leawyn held her granddaughter firm even as her nerves shook. "Darling, I think it is best we say goodbye to your papa, and that we go and find your sister."

"Must we?"

Leawyn stroked her hair. "Would you like a moment alone with him?"

"No. I want you to stay with me."

"Yes, my sweetling, I will stay."

Together, they stood for a few moments longer, grandmother and grandchild, looking upon their dead kin, until the air grew heavy with the stench of death, and both bid their farewells. They stepped out of the tent hand-in-hand.

They stood at the heart of their clan's camp, nestled in a muddy ditch beside a dense forest. Men moved back and forth through the gloom, many in good spirits, toasting the death of the Flaming Bird. But for every fistful of warriors lost to drink, another roamed the camp in silence, peering into the tents of the dead, searching for something that would not return for a long, long time. For this reason, Leawyn kept her granddaughter close, pulling her tight to her hip and keeping her gaze low. Some of the men were from her own village, others more distant kin, but all shared the same blood on the Isle of Fláimir. They drifted through the camp like ghosts, hollow-eyed and silent, their ties to humanity scattered like the ashes of the Outsiders.

"Really, little missy, you shouldn't have wandered off from our tent." Leawyn kept her voice low as they slid down the slippery embankment. A drunk man wobbled by, his gaze lingering on them with mild curiosity, but he said nothing.

"You told me not to be afraid of our people."

"Yes, *our people*." She shook her head.

They moved through more rows of tents, past campfires crackling in the evening air and heaps of crude weapons scattered on the ground. At last, they cleared the heart of the man's camp and stepped into a field of dead grass. The wind swept down from the north, cold and biting, but here at least, the air was cleaner, free from the stench of death and the sourness of drunken soldiers.

They continued onward, making their way toward another cluster of tents near the forest's edge. Other clusters dotted the land, but none belonged to their clan. Leawyn kept her head down, her gaze no longer avoiding dangerous men; but the women, old and shriveled, fixed their cold eyes on them from the doorways of their tents. Had they no courage to mourn their dead? A curse built in the back of her throat, feeling their scornful eyes bore into her skin, when a different thought washed over her. *Perhaps they have nothing to bury.*

She tightened her grip on her granddaughter as they reached a cluster of tents at the forest's edge. They made their way to the largest of them, where the banner of the Flaming Bird lay trampled into the snow-drenched mud. Snatched from the Outsiders in battle, its grotesque and twisted head stared up at them. Leawyn and Arianwyn both spat at the same time, their boots stomping the flag deeper into cold mud for good measure.

Inside the tent, the air was warm, thick with the scent of roasted meat. A fire crackled in the center, its flames licking the air, smoke rising through a small tear in the fabric above. A roasted pig turned slowly on the spit, its skin cracking and oozing grease, sending sparks into the fire with every drop. Leawyn pulled her granddaughter into a brief, gentle embrace before releasing her to wander. The tent was crowded with people who had come from far-off villages, all kin of clan Terrwoniwyn. Leawyn nodded at the faces she had known for a lifetime: Jahota, the baker; Lessawyn, the huntress;

Suthwyea, the crafter. Among this extended family, she found a seat near the fire, warming her hands against the flames.

"A peculiar power, don't you think?"

An old, weary voice spoke to her, and she turned to find her village's chieftain standing beside her.

"I am only a mortal, and my hands are worn and aged by time," Leawyn said softly, staring into the fire. "Strange that I need the flames for warmth when I know I'll find comfort soon in the cold waters beneath the Hearth."

The chieftain tugged at his withered gray beard.

"Hmm... Were it so. May there still be many days before we go under the good Hearth to rest."

"There is no time for rest," Leawyn replied, shaking her head. Her eyes flicked toward Arianwyn and her younger sister, Layita, sitting among a group of little girls, sipping from bowls of porridge. The chieftain followed her gaze, grunting, and slowly eased himself down beside her. His frail hands joined hers by the fire.

"Yes... there is no time for rest," he added.

They sat in silence, watching the flames dance before them. A lifetime together, from babes to old age, had woven their bond into something unspoken. He was her distant cousin, their blood entwined with the land, and the years had left little to say between them. Only the great mysteries of the world still held their attention. For the first time in a long while, Leawyn felt a question stir within her, watching the fire twist and crackle, its sound sharp like the stomp of a hoof. She thought of battle, and then of strangers, and fouler things.

"Do you suppose it is true—the centaurs, they do not produce flame?"

The chieftain let out a gravelly grunt, part laugh, part cough. "Would it be that I knew? Mysterious creatures keeping to their woods on the far side of the Isle. Our kind was never meant to mix with theirs."

Leawyn kept her gaze fixed on the fire, its heat and smoke making her eyes sting with tears. "Perhaps we should adopt their ways." She stared blankly. "Put out every fire. Live off berries and bark, like they do. Life without flame, closer to the Hearth. If not, then perhaps we're more like the Flaming Bird than we care to admit."

"I hope you would dare not utter such words beyond this tent," the chieftain warned, shaking his head. "The only thing I have learned in my advancing age is that I know little. What I do know is this: The people of the south, those of the Flaming Bird, are evil and wicked, with no love for the land or its people. This is our battle, our duty."

"To suffer before the long rest?" Leawyn finally pulled her gaze away from the flames. Her eyes drifted to her granddaughters across the tent. If they were boys, they would already have training axes in their hands.

"Our clan was called to serve, and our time is nearly at an end. The War Maker will send our warriors home, our few brave men and women, and other clans will take their place. That's how it has always been."

"Excuse me, Finn, but I've grown weary of the way things are."

The chieftain shifted beside her, his face twisted in disbelief. "You speak of such things after seeing the destruction the Outsiders have wrought? After the price we've paid?"

"We'll go home, we'll rest. The few boys will take their wives, more boys will be born, and the widowed women or brave-hearted women will follow them to battle, and the cycle will continue."

"I know your son has only just passed, and may the Hearth take his soul, but please, Leawyn," Finn said gently, placing a hand on her back. "you must keep faith in our people and the land."

"Our stolen land," she muttered.

Finn grunted, pretending to follow her reasoning.

"We've always shared this land. Long before the Outsiders came, since we rose from the Hearth itself, if you believe the stories. But where do the Outsiders come from? The centaurs?" Leawyn's voice hardened. "I do not fear death, my old friend, but I fear pain and misery. This war is a poison upon our land, and we cannot keep sacrificing our bodies and spirits to fight it." Her eyes narrowed as she stared into the flames until they burned with the ache of her thoughts. "Something needs to change. The legacy of the War Maker is a curse."

Finn burst into a coughing fit, brought on by her words. "Leawyn… such things…" He struggled to catch his breath. "I could not even imagine… let us… keep to ourselves."

Leawyn waited patiently, allowing him the time to compose himself. Once he had settled, she spoke again, her tone softened. "My chieftain, do you remember your grandfather?"

Still flushed, Finn managed to answer her, his voice steady but quiet. "Yes, I do… not much, though. He left for war when the ash still lingered in the air."

"I see." She nodded and looked back at the flames.

She felt the chieftain study her in silence, his weary eyes tracing the woman he had once played with as a child, the woman so full of light at the birth of her first child. *My sons.* The pain gripped her, her gaze shifted to her granddaughters, their innocent faces a living reflection of her lost children. Finn, noticing her gaze, whistled sharply, and within moments, the two little girls came bounding toward him, their giggles light as spring.

"There you two are!" He broke into a smile when they came with smiles and giggles upon their faces. "How was soup? Did you enjoy?"

"Yes, Chief!" Leawyn's youngest granddaughter, Layita, beamed. "And old Jahota gave me a berry after!"

"A berry? Well, by all that is well, do you know what is so special about a berry, young one?"

The little girl shook her head.

"A berry," he continued, "is the sweetest thing the Hearth can create. From all the dirt and decay, from the old, stubborn soil, the Hearth brings forth something pure, something sweet. Isn't that remarkable?"

Layita nodded with a grin. "Is that where my papa has gone? Has he become a berry?"

Finn observed Leawyn shift on the bench beside him. "No, not yet. We still need to send him below, where he can rest."

"And then... one day, I can see him again?"

"You will see everyone again, little thing. Your daddy, and great-granddaddy, and all those who came before."

"But I won't get to visit him before?"

Arianwyn, with her little sister's hand firmly in her own, leaned in. "We can go see him together, only if Grandmother says it's okay."

The two little girls turned to Leawyn, but she ignored them. She kept her gaze trained on the fire.

"Girls, we shall listen to your grandmother on the matter, but I should say yes, you will see him again before his rest."

"Can we see him now?"

"The sooner, the better, I reckon..." Finn turned toward Leawyn, and at last, she turned her gaze to him, her cheeks flushed red from the heat of the fire.

"Is that what you're about?" She sighed, her voice icy, but there was an underlying weariness to it. "Fine then. Very well. Let's proceed when the moon rises. We'll go into the woods, and you, Arianwyn and Layita, will kiss your father good-night... for his rest."

Her voice came cold, but her girls nodded happily. They scampered away in excitement as Finn turned to her, placing one firm hand upon her shoulder as he struggled to rise. "It will be for the best, Leawyn. There is no sense in waiting. I am truly sorry."

He lumbered away as she looked to the soil beneath her feet. She grew numb, like the dirt, like the Hearth beneath her, and cursed the flames. She prepared herself to bury her second child.

The time came early in the night. Snowflakes swirled in the air, yet the sky remained clear, the moon shining brightly. *A good omen, perhaps.* The men of their ranks hoisted the bodies of the dead on wooden stretchers. The families of the fallen walked beside them, their faces veiled in sorrow. Deep, methodical drums echoed through the night, a heartbeat in the vast stillness, as the procession was led into the forest. No torches lit their path, only the cold light of the moon to guide them.

Young Layita had been excited to see her father, but now, in the silent, solemn procession, she walked in eerie quiet, her small hand clutched tightly in her sister's. The stench of death, mixed with the bloodstained furs that draped her father's body, had stolen her words. She cast occasional glances at Leawyn for comfort, but found none. Leawyn's heart was heavy, cold with grief. She knew Layita's childhood was ending. It was better this way. She would learn the harsh truths of the world sooner than later.

The procession wound deep into the woods. Though all the land of the Isles belonged to them, their encampment near the front lines was foreign, unfamiliar to their clan. At the head of the group walked Finn, his body draped in painted furs, his head crowned with the great antlers of a slain aurochs. He moved in silence, his aging spine hunched beneath the weight of both years and antlers, his presence commanding silence save for the distant thrum of drums and the haunting wails of newly made widows.

Eventually, they arrived at marshy ground deep within the woods. All around them, bogs bubbled and gurgled, the sodden earth seeming eager to claim the dead. Men stood guard around massive gnarled trees, ensuring no one would slip too soon into the black waters.

Each family chose a different sinkhole to slip their dead into. Leawyn chose a spot farthest from the others, where wind whipped through sparser trees and moonlight fell clear and bright. The bog beside her feet gurgled incessantly, as if excited to take her son from her. She didn't want to do it—not so far from their ancestral village, but it would be cruel to let her son rot. When he rose again, someday far in the future, she wanted him whole. Not like this, broken and scattered.

Her son's body was brought to her wrapped in furs. Leawyn fell to her knees, her hands trembling as she turned to her granddaughter. "Are you ready to say goodbye to your papa?"

50

Layita stood frozen before the mound of furs, her small hands clasped tightly beneath her chin, unable to move or speak.

"It will only be for a little while, remember?"

Arianwyn's hand fell gently upon her shoulder. At this, Layita glanced at her, then down at the furs before her. After a long pause, she nodded. With a steady breath, Leawyn carefully pulled back the furs from her son's face. The pale light of the moon caught his features, and with the touch of death, he seemed to glow, his skin an eerie, ghostly white in the cold glow.

"Goodbye, Father." Arianwyn approached, gently tucking a wooden trinket into the furs around his chest. "It contains the soil of our village so that when you rise, you will be able to find your way home to us." She kissed him gently on the forehead and then stepped back.

Leawyn then looked to Layita next, but it took a gentle nudge from Arianwyn to get her to move. With trembling hands, she approached her father's body. Carefully, she placed a handful of berries upon the furs, her voice small but steady. "I will miss you, Papa. Don't wait too long now." Then, as if the weight of the words crushed her, she burst into silent tears. Arianwyn stepped forward and wrapped her in her arms, gently pulling her back from the body of their father.

Leawyn straightened her son's hair one last time as the chieftain came to her side.

"Is he ready to rest?"

"Yes, until we can meet again."

"Then he may take this blessing," the chieftain intoned. He uncorked a vial and poured nightshade, a flower that blooms only under the moon's light, onto her son's chest. "He is anointed with the flower of the moon, of this land, blessed by his chieftain, for his selfless acts in defense of his children, his clan, and his land. May his rest be peaceful, and when he rises, may he rejoin his family."

"Amen," the gathering answered.

With careful hands, he shifted her son's body, placing his feet gently into the bog. Leawyn prepared herself for the final act of sending him beneath the waters when Arianwyn's voice broke the silence.

"WAIT!" She sprinted forward, throwing herself onto her father's body. Leawyn's heart clenched as she moved to pull her away, but before she could, Arianwyn bent over her father's head, pressing a soft, final kiss to his forehead. Leawyn froze, momentarily paralyzed by the sight.

For a long, quiet moment, Arianwyn lingered there, until with a shuddering breath, she rose of her own volition.

They stood huddled together as a family, Finn standing respectfully beside them as Kaelin's body slipped beneath the cold waters of the bog. His pale skin quickly disappeared into the murky brown water, his entire life marked only by a few gurgling bubbles. Leawyn stared at them for a long while, the chieftain eventually guiding her grandchildren away when they grew restless.

Leawyn remained, standing over the resting place of her second son. She had buried her father and mother, her husband, both daughters-in-law, and her two children. Soon, she hoped, it would be her turn.

She waited for the other mourning families to disperse; only then did she move to say goodbye. She closed her eyes and took a step toward the bog when a crack in the woods froze her midstep.

A large shadow loomed at the edge of the tree line. She felt eyes upon her, and slowly, she took a step back from the bog. Only then did the shadow turn, trotting away with the sound of hooves.

WARWICK II

Wulford refused to remove his hand from his sword hilt. A surge of humanity pressed against their parade route. Shouts and cries of men, women, and children in mourning pressed against the knights of the Demonbreun, waving handkerchiefs and tissues, bidding the prince's favor. He obliged from atop his carriage, blowing kisses to the crowd. Catelyn sat beside him, arms folded and head bent, dressed in black. The crowd shouted her deceased father's name, desperate to share in her grief, but she kept her gaze solely upon the passing cobblestones beneath their carriage.

"This is a time, is it not?" Warwick beamed, rising next to his cousin to stand tall atop the carriage. Adorned in his striped tunic with the Crown of Knox resting heavy upon his golden curls, he cast a slow wave for all to see. Banners of the two-headed phoenix flapped in the cold winter air as rose petals rained down from citizens who crammed themselves onto banisters and rooftops. Warwick bowed and waved to his audience, grinning ear to ear, as Catelyn turned away from him.

Behind their carriage, her brother Derrick rode one of his father's prized warhorses from the imperial stables, a flowing black cape flapping in the cold wind behind him. The massive sword strapped to his belt drew the attention of the crowd.

"Hail to the fallen Master of War! Hail to the protector of the realm!"

Derrick gave solemn nods to the peasantry as he passed. The citizens looked upon the imperial procession, mourning with the grieving family as a building roar began to sweep the city. Cannons, crude and loud weapons, split the chill air, fired from the city walls. The crowd, consumed by grief, pushed forward, their decorum lost like a noggin near food.

Strammond rode forward, his horse adorned in the colors of his order, and barked a command to Wulford. "We need to move faster. Tell the crown prince to take his seat. We will ride quickly to the palace!" He yanked hard on the reins of his horse and sped off to the front of the procession. Derrick rode after him, much to the irritation of Catelyn.

Wulford rose from the back seat of the carriage. "My prince, a winter storm is blowing in hard from the east. We will need to ride hard. Please take your seat."

"My seat? Are you ill in the head? My people wish to see me!"

"My prince, I do not wish for you to tumble and fall..."

"I do not wish to hear of it again. I will greet my people as their ruler should. Tell the caravan master to keep his steady pace. Rain or snow, they must see me..."

"Sit. Down," Catelyn snarled, and before Wulford could act, she rose and placed a heavy hand upon Warwick's shoulder. His rump collided hard against the cushioned seat, and his crown tilted, slipping to cover his eyes. At the same time, the horses pulling the carriage cried with the crack of a whip. They jolted forward and Catelyn fell backward. A cry went up from the crowd, but Wulford steadied her.

"Are you all right, my lady?"

"I want to be out of here. Now," Catelyn answered. Her lower lip wobbled as she retook her position next to the prince. Not a cloud hung in the sky.

"Really? That was uncalled for," Warwick huffed. He fidgeted with the crown, hoping to have it level. "Nevertheless, I do suppose it is time to see my brother. It has been over a year, you know? I hope he has fared well without me. I'm sure the news of my uncle has hit him hard…"

"I do think you should save your princely voice," Catelyn shot back. "There is a sharp chill in the air. We can't afford for you to fall ill."

Warwick looked to her with a furrowed brow but relented, sliding back into his carriage seat. *Good point,* he thought.

They hurried down the Phoenix Arcadia, and soon the dense clusters of city buildings opened up into a vast promenade, the grand circle spreading wide before the Sun Palace. The imperial caravan looped gracefully around the circle's edge, where at its heart stood a towering statue of Thermon the Devout, a long-ago ancestor of their house who had conquered the city a millennium past. Warwick looked upon the head of his progenitor and spied the stone carving of the Crown of Knox. *My crown.* He smiled as the gates of the palace sprang open.

They rode forward toward a palace of unrivaled opulence. Constructed of white stone and marble, the building glistened under the winter sun and stretched into perpetuity in either direction. Hundreds of carved two-headed phoenixes adorned the pale stone, each figure uniquely crafted from sunstone and amber, their fiery red and orange colors a stark contrast against the winter-white marble.

A small army of guards spilled from every doorway and corridor as they passed under a central archway of pure marble dividing the outer wing of the palace in two. They reached the central courtyard, an intimate space reserved for esteemed guests and the imperial family, and a small string band started up a somber note. Warwick rose in his seat, swelling with pride as they approached a set of white doors so large a giant would marvel at their size.

"ALL HAIL PRINCE WARWICK, PROCLAIMED HEIR TO THE CROWN OF THE NINE. ALL HAIL LADY CATE-LYN AND LORD DERRICK OF THE LATE THANE HIER-ONYMUS..." An imperial herald boomed their arrival as the carriage halted before the towering white doors. They swung open with thunderous force, a gust sweeping outward as though the palace itself had gasped at his arrival.

"Mother..." Catelyn cried out beside him. In a flash, she gripped the side of the carriage and dismounted over the side, hitting the marble platform below with a loud *clack*.

A cold figure emerged from the palace doors. *Auntie,* he knew, as he took Wulford's hand to dismount the carriage. Catelyn ran forward to greet her mother, throwing herself into her arms and sinking to her knees in a sob.

"There, there," his aunt cooed softly, but Warwick eyed her with suspicion. She, too, wore black—a color he was beginning to despise enough to consider banning from the realm—though her ears gleamed with oversized pearls, and a net of diamonds sparkled over her tightly bound hair.

So much for mourning. He rolled his eyes and stepped forward, only to feel Wulford's massive hand pull him back.

A moment later, Derrick dashed past him, gripping his warhorse's reins and rearing it onto its hind legs with a sharp whinny before he dismounted. "Mother!" Derrick called, strid-ing over. His aunt extended an arm, and he nestled his head against her neck while Catelyn continued to sob.

"Brother! Sister!" came more cries from behind, as two small children, Warwick's younger cousins, rushed forward to join the family huddle.

Warwick stood back, feeling Wulford's firm grip on him. Auntie coddled all four of her children, a touching spectacle, but he was ignored, alone before his family's palace. "And where is my brother?" he said to Wulford. "Where is my greeting?"

"Walk forward, my prince. Announce yourself by presence alone. Authority needs no call to attention."

"Hmph," he replied, shaking off Wulford's hold. He marched ahead, fists clenched, toward a set of marble steps leading to the entryway. Derrick's warhorse, however, lingered stubbornly before the imperial family. Warwick had to wait for a guard to come and fetch the beast before he could finally reach the base of the steps. With his hands on his hips, he stood there, awaiting recognition.

His aunt, Lady Elizabeth, was lost in the solace of her children and did not notice him. It wasn't until the imperial herald, shifting uneasily on his feet, finally called out once more to announce Warwick's arrival that her head snapped away from the tender scene.

"Prince Warwick! I bid you welcome to the palace."

"My lady." He nodded, offering a small courtesy out of respect for her loss.

"Children, please, we will have all the time in the world to be together." She nudged Catelyn softly with her hand, who turned her head from her mother's bosom and looked to Warwick with a snotty, red-faced glare. She rose from her mother's feet and took her side by Derrick, pulling her youngest sibling, the Lady Dalia, onto her hip. Derrick took charge of his younger brother, the young Lord Manford. His auntie walked forward, putting a few feet between her children, and broke into a deep bow. The diamonds in her net rattled, giving Warwick a reason to smile.

"Thank you, Aunt Elizabeth, the lady of Aberness, beloved wife of the late and great Thane, brother to the emperor of our holy empire, and my dear and beloved uncle."

His auntie rose, her head slightly twisted, her eyes glistening with tears. "Thank you, my prince, for those kind words."

"We are a family. And a wonderful family, are we not?"

"Y-yes, of course. I thank you for making this journey. I understand you must be weary after your long tour of Sanguinia."

"I am weary, thank you, but the desire to be with one's family can be a powerful driver, and it is with this longing in my heart I have made this trip. Pray tell, my good aunt, in this hour of grief, where is my good brother? It has been a year since we have last seen one another and I miss him dearly."

"Yes, where is our good cousin, Mother?" Derrick joined his call.

Lady Elizabeth swallowed uneasily on the steps before Warwick. She cleared her throat. "Well, my prince, your good brother has chosen to ride to High Ness at once to be with your father the emperor in this time of grief."

Warwick turned his cheek as if slapped. "He is not here then?"

"No, my prince."

"And he has gone to the emperor prematurely?"

"Yes."

"Ahead of the prince-heir?"

"Yes, my prince."

Warwick's fingers trembled as he brought them into fists. "That... that—!"

He stomped, his voice cracking and squealing before the court, and his crown slipped from his head, landing on the cobblestones with a loud clatter. Wulford rushed forward as Warwick turned as red as a beet. In a heartbeat, his aunt swept sideways, gathering her children and ushering them inside. The knights of the Demonbreun rushed forward too, clambering to his side.

"My prince! My king? Are you all right? The crown! Has it cracked? Call the smithy! Does he need rest? Warwick?"

The calls and concerns of his knights and guards meant nothing to him. His world grew woozy, made worse when Wulford placed the heavy crown back upon his head. A fainting couch was brought, and he was laid upon its silk cushions and carried through the palace. The massive doors slammed shut behind him, leaving guards, courtiers, and servants to whisper in the cold silence.

Warwick lay still on the fainting couch, ignoring the voices around him. Carried through the hallways, he stared up at the vaulted ceilings of his family's palace. Old paintings moved slowly above him like a quiet procession. He found some comfort in their stories: robed pilgrims walking toward a distant light, a humble cabin growing into a great hall, then a fortress. A sword rose from a sea of fire. Cavaliers clashed on bloodied fields defending a new city. Brick by brick, a palace took shape, its walls spreading until a city surrounded it and bannermen marched under a two-headed phoenix.

At first, the images pleased him, until the paintings showed a menacing snake curled among the rafters of the great hall. It was coiled among swords and pikes, two great fangs rising from its head, which was covered in a rainbow of feathers. Fire rained down on both warriors and beast alike. The unholy feathered serpent of Makka.

He closed his eyes, placing a hand on his belly. The flash of images hurt his head, and his guards carried his fainting couch like a fishmonger's wife steering a ship through a maelstrom. "Oooooh," he moaned, placing a hand on his head, feeling as though his soul may slip from this world. His party continued onward, but with their prince indisposed.

When he finally awoke, he found himself alone in yet another unfamiliar bedchamber. Sitting upright on the velvet couch, he stared absently around the room. Another canopy bed, another roaring fire. He looked up at the vaulted ceilings, so high that he could have been laid to rest in a cathedral. He puffed, rubbing his eyes.

Where am I? Which castle? Which land? Which lord?

He stood up, wobbling on his feet to a window. Outside, he found a garden, frozen in the dead of winter, but ornate nonetheless. A maze of lifeless shrubbery still painted the shape of his household sigil. He winced, gritting his teeth as if a knife stabbed his belly. The family palace, but with no family to be found.

Tears stung his eyes. He tore away from the window, finding his trunks from the journey placed neatly about the room. He rushed forward and kicked one with a silk slipper. He yelped, hobbling onto one foot. Now he cursed, prying open the chest and throwing lumps of clothing across the room.

"Damn it all!"

He marched back to his fainting crouch, finding his crown resting upon the silk. He snatched it up, running his hands over the metal.

A crack. His heart dropped. The metal chipped from where it hit the cobblestone. *Before his court. His family.*

"Brother," he said aloud, a sob lodged in his throat. "You were supposed to be here. For me. And now I have no one!"

He threw his crown down upon the fainting couch. It bounced off the plush silk, flying onto the floor with another loud *clank.* He yelped and rushed forward, snatching the crown again. *I can never do anything right.* He wept for his father and his father's father, for the unbroken line of men who had borne the ancient symbol of the two-headed phoenix. Through the Ash Fall. Through the fall of the empire. Through persecution and past troubles, his family had never been extinguished, like the phoenix.

And now it has fallen to me.

Trembling, he placed the crown back on his head, standing still for a solid minute, too scared to move lest it should fall again. A knock on his bedroom door negated this caution.

He jumped, and the crown fell, but this time he caught it in his hands. He had just enough time to place it back upon his head before his bedroom door opened.

"My prince?" Wulford called.

"Yes, what is the matter, Wulford?"

"Oh good, you are awake. Are you feeling better?"

"Very so. Now, what is the matter? Why have you entered my bedchamber without permission?"

"Forgive me, my prince, I have only come to check on your person. The lady of the house, your good aunt, also sent me to see if you are fit for dinner. The family and court gather in the dining hall for a feast. They hope to see you join them."

A feast? And I receive a late invitation? His cheeks burned.

He detested the thought of appearing before the court tonight as some spectacle.

"No, Wulford, I will not be joining them. Not with the prince ill disposed..."

"Very well, my prince. Shall I ask that a plate be brought to your room?"

He stamped his foot. "No one shall be feasting tonight! Not with my uncle fallen in battle, my health at risk, and my twin brother... *departed*. No. There will be no feast, not tonight, nor during this moon. The court will depart for my father as soon as the caravan master can prepare for the journey. I trust you to deliver this message, yes?"

Wulford hung in the doorway to his chamber. Shadows danced across his face from the crackle of the fireplace. Outside, a cold wind howled. "Of course, my prince."

"Very good. Additionally, tell the staff I will take my dinner in the study... our *founder's* study. That is all."

"...It shall be done." Wulford bowed and backed away from the door.

Warwick waited, listening closely until the faint clank of steel armor faded down the corridor. Only then did he slip into the hallway. He needed to move—standing still felt unbearable. Lysander had gone ahead to court. They hadn't seen each other in over a year. What game was he playing?

With a brisk pace, he rounded corners and descended stairs, growing more disoriented with each step. The palace was too damn large, a maze of endless twists and turns, filled with stately rooms even for the most mundane purposes, all clouding his already troubled mind. *Think. Think. Think,* he urged himself. It had been years since he had roamed the palace of his own volition. Back then, he had been a child, playing with Lysander, lost in the funhouse of the estate, with servants desperately chasing after them. Now he avoided the help, darting in and out of rooms and corridors, chasing memories of his boyhood.

Lost in thought, he came upon a pair of massive double doors, their dark mahogany wood carved with the family sigil of the two-headed phoenix. He stopped, racking his brain for memories, when he realized he had finally stumbled upon the study of his great-great-grandfather. He moved forward slowly, stepping cautiously into what felt like a mausoleum honoring the family's legacy. Ancient treaties lay sealed beneath glass, and portraits of ancestors older than the palace itself lined the walls. Their unblinking eyes seemed to follow him as he passed. He carefully sidestepped suits of armor, some still bearing dents and ancient bloodstains from his family's ancient conquests. The dim hallway grew heavier with shadows, and the study doors loomed darker still, surrounding him with a growing sense of being watched. Gathering his resolve, he pushed the doors open, but a sudden wave of unease made him spin around and slam them shut.

Panting, Warwick turned to find a portrait of his thrice great-grandfather above the crackling fireplace, shadows from the flames animating his painted scowl. *The liberator, the warrior, the forger of an empire,* Warwick thought as he met the cold eyes of his ancestor, bitterness rising at how one man could hold so many titles. *I have to fight for everything!* He wanted to scream, but a sudden chill swept over him, and he felt a fool. He raised a hand to his crown, testing its weight upon his head.

Your crown too, he thought, nodding toward the portrait, but the firelight only deepened the frown on the Phoenix King's face.

Shivering, Warwick let his gaze drift to the grand mahogany desk before the fireplace. *The Forge.* His breath caught, and he stepped forward. He marveled at the dark wood, almost black in places, polished smooth where countless hands had rested over centuries. Phoenixes, their wings spread wide, soared across the rim of the desk, their beaks grasping swords and shields as they clashed with knights in full plate armor. The knights, proud and valiant, were captured in midstrike, their faces frozen in expressions of grim resolve. Their swords gleamed with the luster of polished wood, though worn by the years, as they fought alongside kings in flowing mantles, crowned and armored, standing tall against their enemies. In the wood, these battles came alive, and Warwick stepped closer, drawn to the artistry. His fingers traced the edge of a knight's sword, then lingered on the fierce outline of a phoenix, its wings sweeping upward, rising from the flames of battle.

He stepped behind the desk, behind the glare of the Phoenix King, and took his seat. The weathered leather chair creaked beneath him, and its stiff embrace did little to soothe the chill that clung to the room. *This is where it all started. This is where an empire was forged.* Sinking into the embrace of the chair, he traced the faint, worn groove left by countless pens, quills, and knives that had sparked revolutions and shaped history. This was the birthplace of the empire, where the House of Hieronymus had risen through the Phoenix King. He turned toward the portrait, now seeing himself reflected in the cold. The same golden eyes, same crown, same hair. *Hell, even the same strong chin!*

"My prince? Warwick?"

Warwick jumped, snatched from wandering thoughts. A shadow slipped into the room. Another specter, just like Grandma'am.

"Auntie?"

"Oh, it is you, child. I became so worried when I heard you did not wish to feast..."

"I am not a child."

The specter hung in the doorway of the study, then stepped fully inside, allowing the door to close quietly behind her. "Yes, I suppose you have grown into a man during your tour of the realm. I struggle the very same with my oldest."

"You wouldn't call Derrick a child before your liege lord, my father and *emperor* of the realm."

Again, the specter hung heavy in her spot. "No, I suppose not, but we are a family, my prince."

"I am not keen on the family at the moment." The words slipped from Warwick's tongue before he fully registered them. The fire swirled with a blast of cold air, yet strangely, he did not feel the chill. Instead, heat surged through his veins, his blood simmering close to the boiling point.

The specter drew nearer, and in the glow of the fire, his auntie emerged, dressed in a flowing black gown. She bowed her head. "I understand, my prince. This is a difficult time… to care for others deeply."

"I see the feeling is mutual then."

"You're upset about your brother, aren't you? I would be too, my prince."

Warwick pushed back into his seat. *Finally, someone said it out loud.* "It is against tradition… against the very crown even to depart before the prince-heir. I do not understand it…"

Aunt Elizabeth nodded, her own eyes filling with tears. She placed one hand on a plush chair before the desk. She nodded to it, inviting his permission. He nodded, and she took a seat. "It was a questionable decision. I cannot say I agree with it. He left in the morning with nothing but a small party of knights riding horseback. A dreadful way to travel at this time of the year, especially in the mountains. I suspect the emperor, your father, will be wroth."

"Then perhaps there will be some sort of justice."

"Justice…" She nodded. "Justice, yes. That is the most important role of a ruler—justice. It is what separates us from the animals and monsters of this world."

"And you had nothing to do with his early departure?"

Auntie leaned back into her chair. A few tears fell from her eyes. "My husband is dead!" she said with a suppressed roar. "My children have no father now! Our family has suffered a grievous defeat on the Isle of Fláimir. Other lords of the realm will look to this as weakness. You may not realize it, but our family has been grievously wounded. I have much more important things to worry about than a petty insult to you, my prince. We are all in this together. We are a family."

Warwick leaned forward, bringing himself to drum his fingers along the table. He sat upright, feeling princely. "Family and justice. Two very hard things to reconcile, don't you think?"

"They don't have to be."

"And... how do you mean?"

"It is not my place to step between you and your brother... or even the emperor for that matter, but justice can be dealt now. My husband was the lord of this palace, this city, and the surrounding lands. It is only right that my son Derrick be confirmed in this station."

"You come to me with a favor?"

"I come to you in a time of grief! In a time of great need. My young prince..."

"I am no longer young..."

"Then open your eyes, Warwick! Our enemies will crowd around us, gathering to pick at the carcass of my late husband for their selfish desires! Perhaps when you were a boy at court you did not see the dangers of the realm, but you are about to come of age, and you can no longer deny them, lest you be a fool."

His aunt paused, and Warwick met her fierce gaze, his fingers still drumming steadily on the table. Neither of them was craven enough to break eye contact. "The court is cutthroat," she continued. "Lords and ladies will come to you seeking every favor imaginable. The realm will fracture. Your father will be more vulnerable than ever. And the family... the greater family... I daresay they may not be true allies."

"I know of our cadet branches... the Rose Monts and the Goldwoods..."

"Then confirm my son now! Before the snakes of the realm deny our family our dues. Justice, Warwick, justice! We are a family, and we are loyal to each other. I cannot say so for our distant relatives, nor for the other great families."

"I can... consider your proposal..."

"Oh please, my prince, consider hastily. I know you mean to leave for your father shortly. Please, consider it for me, or poor Catelyn. She is beset by grief, but I know your generosity to her beloved brother could steady her heart."

"Catelyn, aye?" Something stirred within him. His aunt had

made a great many points, none of them wrong. The fire crackled behind him, its heat biting at his neck as he mulled over her
words. "Okay… very well, you have my word then. Derrick
shall inherit his father's titles. I will personally confirm it."

"OH!" His aunt sprang from her chair. She threw herself
upon him, hugging and kissing him relentlessly. Warwick recoiled, embarrassed. "Oh, thank you, thank you!"

"Enough!" he grunted, pushing her away. Already, he regretted his decision. But it was done now.

Before he could regain his composure, the door swung
open. A pair of servants wheeled in his dinner, breaking the
moment of chaos.

"That is enough, please. I have done a great deal for our
family, remember that. Now leave me. I am still feeling ill, and
it is past time that I ate."

His aunt stepped back, offering a deep bow. "Bless you, our
future emperor, Warwick Hieronymus, First of His Name."
With a final nod, she retreated from the study.

Warwick sat idle, twiddling his fingers where his aunt had
stood a moment ago. Around him, the servants plated his food:
roasted goose, garlic potatoes, minced meat. Though the rich
aroma teased his senses, his stomach churned with unease.

"Away with you all, now!" he commanded, and politely
dropping their serving ware where they stood, the servants
quickly departed the room.

"Emperor… First of His Name…" He chewed the title over
in his mouth. *Yes, I like that, but…*

"Father," he said aloud.

His heart dropped, and with it, his stomach.

*Father must be truly ill if I am already being fawned over
for favors. If Lysander has pulled such a stunt…*

With a balled fist, he grabbed a fork and stabbed into the
roast goose, dashing grease across the storied desk. *Take me
for a fool already?* Tears welled in his eyes. He hastily turned
the chair, testing the limits of its antique frame, and gazed
upward at the portrait of the Phoenix King.

My legacy will be mine to build, he swore. *For Father, for my family... for Catelyn's hand.* He turned sideways, pressing his right hand against the cool wood of the Forge desk. His thoughts drifted to the Phoenix King, to the lineage of Hieronymus men who had ruled before him, to his uncle slain in battle.

He would have Catelyn, his crown, and his cake too. *They think me weak or a fool, but I will not be bought.*

JAE I

The minotaur towered above him, reeking of filth and hatred. The beast took one half step toward him, quivering on its hoofed feet. The monster looked down upon him, the whites of its eyes flashing wildly, and all the breath was pulled from Jae'eli's lungs. The minotaur roared, and he felt all the world could hear it.

Crack!

The sound of a whip sliced through the holding pen. Jae'eli winced, shrinking into the muddy floor. The minotaur bellowed and lurched forward, straining against the great iron shackles anchoring the beast to the wall. The dusty wood panels of the slave pen groaned under the pressure as another lash tore through the air. The minotaur let out a broken moan, fresh blood matting its dark fur, and collapsed to its knees only inches away from him as flies swarmed its wounds. Jae'eli trembled but did not look away as the creature's breath came hot and heavy upon his face. The beast's dark, heavy eyes darted back and forth, quivering, before tears streaked down its face. Without realizing it, Jae'eli extended his arm, when another crack of the whip sliced the air above his arm, and the warm coating of the beast's blood sent him reeling to the back of his stall. The minotaur relented, crawling back into its own stall as blood poured from the gashes torn across its gargantuan back.

Jae'eli watched with his knees pulled tightly to his chest, dreading another crack of the master's cruelty. Yet no further punishment came. The minotaur lowered its massive head to its chest and closed its eyes, muttering quietly in a language Jae'eli did not understand. It almost sounded like a prayer.

"Zovaesys!" The word sliced through the foul air of the pen worse than the crack of the whip.

Jae'eli winced as the word wormed its way into his brain and his body hummed with a strange compulsion. *The master's tongue*, he realized, lifting his gaze to the dark-skinned man with golden eyes who stood on the wooden platform overlooking their pen.

"Zovaesys!" came the cry again.

Jae'eli lifted his hands, wishing to cover his ears, but they would not rise, whether from his own fear of the whip or the power of the word, he could not say, only that he hated the sound of the word. The master's language existed solely to inflict pain and suffering.

"Zovaesys!"

The word was called for the third and last time. Around him, zombies slowly rose to life. Men and women covered in their own excrement, caked in mud and sand, bruises and cuts. Mothers, shackled to their children, burst into muffled cries. The children stared absentmindedly into space, perhaps knowing what awaited them, perhaps not. Jae'eli knew how they felt. He lost his own mother and father a long time ago.

Heeding the master's wicked tongue, he dug his feet into the feces-crusted mud and stood up. The iron shackles around his feet and hands wore heavy on his starved muscles, but the fear of the whip motivated him to stay on his feet. The minotaur was the last to rise, but even the beast recognized what was happening to them. They stood together as an odd clutch of creatures, most of whom had at some point been human, plus a minotaur.

The sound of a heavy bolt gave way to the slave pen door opening. Their pen was a crude circle with nothing more than flimsy wooden panels delineating each "stall" from the next. Hot air blasted sand from the outside through cracks in the wall, where bright light pierced and carried the heat of the region's broiling sun. This had been Jae'eli's pen for only a night, but it absolutely beat the slave drives through the humid marshlands and sands outside the city. His pen had almost felt like a home, but like with everything in a slave's life, comfort was fleeting, and the Thorned Men had come to steal his peace.

A wooden door burst open. Sand and heat blasted into the pen. Jae'eli resisted the urge to flinch even as his eyes stung. Two dark figures emerged from the blinding sun, clad in black metal chain armor, their faces, except their yellow eyes, were concealed behind black masks. The Thorned Men walked silently to the center of the pen, clutching long metal rods. Jae'eli's heartbeat shot to his throat as the mother stifled her daughter's cries, and even the minotaur slowed its putrid breath.

"At attention!" A voice from above called to them. A man dressed in white looked down upon them from the safety of a raised platform. A scowl spread over his lips. "Do not incur their wrath."

Jae'eli stood straight as an arrow, the chains linking his feet and hands to the wall pulled taut. The Thorned Men began their work, reaching behind each slave to free them from the wall. Each slave saw the tip of the iron rod brush past their face, an icon of both discipline and despair. Jagged metal teeth, stained red from years of use, were crafted to rip flesh without delivering lasting wounds, and they hovered before their eyes as the Thorned Men went about their grim work. They released each slave, though no man, or beast, gave a sign of relief. Everyone stood still and silent, only the muffled cries of desperate slaves from afar and the shifting of hot sand to break the silence.

Jae'eli was the last slave to be unshackled. He held his breath as they worked on his chains, but he was a good slave, and it took only the click of a key from one of the Thorned Men to release his taut chains. They fell with a heavy clink into the mud, though he gave no sign of relief. He stood firm, unmoving, unhuman.

"Zovaesys!" the word came once more, and the slaves, even the minotaur, trod obediently from their holding pen.

The slaves moved slowly, heads bowed, not daring to meet the gaze of their masters, or worse, indicate any sign of dignity, except for one. A man from their pen, with golden sandy hair and a slight plumpness to him, looked wildly around him. He had all the hallmarks of a new slave, someone who could still taste freedom in the hot wind versus those who could only smell the overbearing perfume of their robed masters. Jae'eli swallowed hard at the man's half-muted mutterings, speaking in a language foreign to him, but the intonations of fear were there in the man's voice.

Inhuman fear, he heard the masters sometimes remark. Human fear was civilized; it kept your master happy and yourself alive. Inhuman fear was the mark of the beast: wild and untampered. A human feared for himself and his kind, but not a beast. A beast would trample his own herd without hesitation. Jae'eli silently prayed that the man knew better.

Their small group was filtered out of the pen into a new holding area, surrounded by more miserable holding pens all around them. Hundreds of muffled cries, some human and some of beasts and creatures from far and foreign lands, filled the air around them. Above them, mammoth wooden pillars served as the supports for the tent's girth. Wooden catwalks crisscrossed the slave pens on the ground floor, and lookout nests, like those he had seen on the great ships of the sea, were nestled at the very top of the tents where the pillars and cloth exterior met. Here in the dark crevices of the tent's roof, more Thorned Men watched over them, looking for the smallest sign of disobedience. Jae'eli could feel their harsh gaze upon him now, digging into his back, even as he kept his neck down as the Thorned Men shepherded them toward the exit. Light poured in through flaps blowing in the wind.

False light, Jae'eli knew. The sun offered no salvation. Only further misery lay outside the tent. He hoped the new slave understood this, or else the whole flock would be punished. A thin stream of urine trickled down the leg of the man before him. The troublesome slave spoke again, his voice rising with the strengthening sunlight, and tension coiled through those pressed against the dirt floor. When the man dug in his heels to bolt, Jae'eli watched a Thorned Man raise his weapon. They would all be punished.

He squeezed his eyes shut, bracing for flesh to be torn from bone, when the minotaur behind him rumbled a deep, guttural curse at the rebellious slave.

"Zovaesys."

A moment later came the scissoring sound of metal teeth biting through leather hide. Jae'eli gritted his teeth as his stomach lurched, the metallic stench of blood flooding the air. Their small group shuffled toward the tent's edge, the rebellious slave now silent, the minotaur having made his point without uttering a single cry of pain.

They emerged from the tent into blazing sunlight that baked the cracked hearth and seared their eyes. The Thorned Men herded them forward, halting before large vats of murky brown water. "Bathe... and quickly," one of them barked.

Jae'eli did not need to be told twice. He bathed himself with the filthy water as if it were a desert oasis, washing the mud from his person, and felt the heat evaporate from his skin. The others did the same, both man and beast enjoying a moment of respite after being corralled in the tent. Between splashes of water to his face, Jae'eli enjoyed the kiss of sunlight on his skin, staring upward at the broiling sun and the sandy white cliff faces that loomed over them like a crashing wave. With the splash of water running down his body, he almost felt like he was back home on a distant island, playing with siblings along the ocean shore.

"Enough." The order came too soon. His memories of home quickly disappeared like a mirage in the desert. "It is time to move. Come."

They were led away from the mammoth slave tents. The moans, cries, and smells of the slave quarters quickly dissipated, and in their place came the rising circus of shouts and cheers. Great wooden structures appeared before them, emerging from the hazy heat like great desert dunes. Jae'eli's stomach somersaulted at the sight of them, his throat constricting. He knew of the barbaric slave fighting pits: bloody arenas where man and beast were ripped apart for the master's enjoyment. He swallowed hard, his heartbeat speeding up, adrenaline pouring into his veins. He prayed he would be assigned to fight the minotaur—his death would be quicker that way.

The Thorned Men yanked their chains forward, pulling them not into a dense crowd filled with desperate slaves and gladiators but into a crowd of perfumed and robed men. These men walked in fine linens of red and gold, green and blue, shades and hues he had never seen before, flaunting jewels and fine leather sandals. All were unarmed. Jae'eli swallowed, quieting the gladiator battle occurring within his own stomach. No freeman would walk these grounds, surrounded by desperate slaves, unarmed. Whatever awaited him, it wasn't a fight to the death. At least not yet.

The Thorned Men quickened their pace as the dirt path gave way to scorching brick, burning the soles of their feet. The slaves hobbled forward, but before the pain could fully set in, they were ushered into the cool shade of a massive wooden structure. As they were herded into a narrow wooden tunnel, the air around them buzzed with the shouts and footsteps of hundreds of men and women. Prodded forward by the dark-skinned guards, they came to a halt before a man clad in a white robe waiting at the tunnel's end. Beyond him, sunlight blazed with intensity, but his face remained shadowed, a dim grimace etched across his lips.

"Listen you lot. You will do as I say and you will do it without protest. If you present yourself well, you will find yourself in new homes and with noble professions, fed and cared for as God wills it. If you do not, you will be escorted back to the pits, condemned to wallow in your own filth. There shall be no bold actions today. You will not be the first to show pride through defiance, nor will you be the first to be killed even today for that matter. Do right by me, and do right by yourselves. Am I understood?"

The slaves nodded in unison. The master's lips curved upward. *"Zovaesys."*

Jae'eli felt his muscles lock, his spine straightening against his will. The master didn't even look back. He merely turned away, snatched up a golden whip, and marched into the light. The Thorned Men prodded the group forward into the sun's glare.

They were led onto a raised wooden platform, encircled by wooden risers filled with slavers, their eyes coldly scanning the human and beastly wares for sale. Orders were barked, and they were told to form a straight line, single file. Jae'eli found himself positioned between a mother and her daughter on his left, and a hulking minotaur on his right. The beast's rancid stench assaulted his senses, his eyes watering, but he willed himself not to show it. Along the line, the Thorned Men moved silently, adjusting the slaves' postures with cold, precise touches of their iron rods, the metal tips as hot as embers.

The little ginger girl beside him whimpered, and Jae'eli closed his eyes. A Thorned Man stopped in front of her, and Jae'eli's pulse quickened, though he held his breath and maintained composure. He now realized they were in the midst of an auction, and knew all too well the consequences if *zovaesys* was not maintained. A shadow fell over them as a rare cloud drifted across the sun. The tension thickened. Even the minotaur's breath grew ragged, its massive chest heaving, sending swarms of biting flies scattering into the air.

Jae'eli felt the weight of eyes falling on their line. The world seemed to pause, waiting.

The girl whimpered again, frightened by the Thorned Man, and buried her face in her mother's leg. The mother's hand shot out, yanking her child to face the crowd once more. But it was too late—the snarl from the Thorned Man sealed their fate. Iron flashed in the dim light, and a scream pierced the air. Jae'eli resisted the urge to look but felt the warm spray of blood on his face. Despite himself, his eyes snapped open.

The little girl still stood by her mother's side, crying. But now, the minotaur's massive arm trembled, its outstretched hand split open by a vicious wound running from forearm to shoulder, blood oozing in dark, pulsing streams. The Thorned Man snarled in fury, wrenching the iron rod from the beast's flesh with a sickening tear, preparing to strike again.

"No, that will not be necessary," the man in white interjected. As he spoke, the cloud drifted away, and the sun's harsh light returned, glinting off the golden whip at his side.

"We do not tolerate defiance," the Thorned Man growled. "Punishment is in order." He raised his rod, ready to strike again.

"I will not repeat myself," the man in white said calmly, hands clasped before him, the iron rod just inches from the minotaur's dark, fur-covered flesh.

A tense standoff followed. The minotaur's arm remained outstretched, shielding the girl, who wept silently. The iron rod hovered over its torn flesh, while the slave master stood unmoved before the scene. Around them, silence cracked into murmurs of discontent, rising into excited shouts. The slavers erupted, all in favor of the Thorned Men, their voices wild with rage. They rose from their seats, shaking their fists under shaded canopies, foaming at the mouth, their fury fueled by the scorching heat. Cries for death and blood echoed through the arena, chanted in more tongues than Jae'eli could count.

Yet the man in white remained calm. The mother beside

Jae'eli whispered a plea for mercy, though Jae'eli knew there was none to be found here. Mercy held no power in this place. Power was gold and the golden whip at the man's hip ruled these grounds. The minotaur, Jae'eli thought, represented too much gold to be squandered so easily.

"We don't need more of this, not today. We need them. Lower your weapon. The livestock always squabbles," the man in white said softly.

The Thorned Man, his face obscured by dark leather, grunted in response and slowly lowered his iron rod, followed by the minotaur's massive furry arm. A brief moment of peace settled over the platform.

Then the biting flies returned, nesting in the minotaur's open wounds. The beast grunted, snorting in agony, a sound that seemed to satisfy the Thorned Man. He nodded curtly before disappearing behind them, his iron rod always inches away, lurking just out of sight. The man in white also nodded, turning to speak quietly with his fellow slavers, who were preparing for the auction. Their group of eight—seven humans and one beast—stood like stone on the platform, exhaling a collective sigh of relief, even as the sun beat down mercilessly and slavers in the stands hurled foul insults, threatening to grow into a full-blown riot.

Shouts erupted around them, and then a commotion to their left drew Jae'eli's attention. He dared not move but cast his gaze to the far side of the platform. There, he witnessed a young man, shackled by chains, tackle another man in white to the ground. Blood splattered across the slaver's pristine robes, followed by a horrifying spray as a Thorned Man promptly severed the rebellious slave's head from his neck.

Screams and sobs of slaves filled the air, mixing with shouts of alarm from masters in the stands and the frantic calls from the slavers surrounding them. The crack of a whip sliced through the chaos and more slaves were herded past, a mix of humans and creatures that took his breath away. More minotaurs grunted at their passing, a sound filled with an instinctive, animalistic awareness. The sight disgusted him, but one quick jolt reminded him of his station. To the masters, he was not a human. He was a commodity, just like the minotaur.

"Witness! Witness all, good ladies and gentlemen! Wise masters and their servants!" The man in white beamed radiantly, raising his arms joyfully to the sky. "Look upon these good slaves, obedient and still, eagerly awaiting masters such as yourselves to serve them. See here! See here!" He flashed a toothy grin, revealing gold teeth that glimmered in the light, drawing the audience's attention to the line of captives before them. "Raw power, untamed, yes—but powerful nonetheless! The right master can teach restraint, bend this beast man to your will, and reap the rewards! How many slaves does it take to drive your oxen? They cannot steer themselves! But this beast… an abomination from the Scorch Grass could bring you immense profits!"

The man in white grinned eagerly at the crowd even as frantic commotion continued among the slavers. Thorned Men darted across the auction blocks, some carrying the dismembered remains of human slaves.

Then came the most dreaded sound, slicing through the air like a wicked symphony.

Crack! Crack! Crack!

The smell of blood and urine followed as the minotaur fell to one knee, panting and choking through fat bovine tears. "Behold, my patrons! A steel whip!" The man in white raised his cruel instrument high, catching its metal glint in the harsh sunlight. "No ordinary leather could tame such a creature! His hide is thicker than any human's—weathered against sun and steel alike. He'll toil endlessly in your fields, or once broken properly, stand sentinel against others of his kind!" The auctioneer's voice boomed across the crowd. "And see how he bears the lash! Such endurance! Such discipline under stress! Let me hear fifteen hundred to start the bidding!"

A few bidding paddles shot into the air. Jae'eli stood transfixed, his mouth unknowingly agape, while the minotaur trembled beside him. Warm blood from the creature splattered against him, attracting a swarm of biting flies that buzzed around them both. He winced as the pests gnawed at his flesh, coming in droves.

"Seventeen hundred! Can I hear eighteen?"

More paddles shot up, and the flies dug in deeper. A single tear, not from pain but from frustration, slipped down Jae'eli's cheek. He felt paralyzed, unable even to swat the foul creatures away. Casting a glance at the minotaur, he found himself boiling with disdain for the beast. He had seen only a few of these imposing creatures before. The first slave ship that had come and stolen him from his family had carried a few of these beasts, locked away in the sub-decks, chained and fighting for space in their cramped cages, uttering horrifying cries that were half-human, half-animal. No one spoke kindly of them, even when he worked side by side with them in the fields, yet here one was, trembling beside him. Overcome with a mix of sympathy and grief, Jae'eli broke from the line, stepping forward to swat two flies from the minotaur's wounded shoulder.

Gasps rippled through the crowd as the minotaur's head twisted around to meet Jae'eli's gaze. They locked eyes—a human and a bull—both caught in a moment of mutual confusion. The beast roared and pounded the floorboards, rising steadily above him. The crowd erupted into a cacophony of jeers, hollers, and cries of both fear and intrigue as the beast man towered over Jae'eli, snorting through its massive nostrils.

"Human…" The creature spoke, its voice so deep it reverberated in his chest. The minotaur extended a furry, leathery hand, twice the size of his own.

Jae'eli stumbled back, staring upward at the beast, sweat stinging his eyes, yet he could not look away from the minotaur's intense gaze. Just then, the crack of another whip sliced through the air, yanking the beast backward, sending it tumbling from the wooden stage. The crowd of slavers erupted in wild cheers.

The man in white was momentarily at a loss for words. The minotaur roared but quickly disappeared into a swirl of dust and the crack of whips. The crowd clapped and cheered, bidding paddles flying into the air.

"Two thousand! Twenty-four hundred! Three thousand!" The sound of money clinking in rich men's pockets, coupled with the erasure of personhood, snapped the auctioneer back to reality. He darted forward, rushing to Jae'eli's side, and thrust his arm into the air.

"Wise masters! Ladies and gentlemen! The bravery, the valor of this item! Where soldiers must be taught courage and rangers instilled with discipline, I present to you this young specimen—a perfect to add to your household, to win glory in the pits, or to protect your daughters and wives from the very monster you just witnessed! Four thousand! Nay, let me hear five thousand! Do I have five thousand?"

The bidding raged on, a chaotic blend of paddles, shouts, flailing arms, and curses in tongues from across the globe filling the auction plaza. Behind him, his fellow slaves, chained to him by their feet, broke decorum in excited whispers. "You'll have the pits, a chance at your freedom!"

"Are you kidding? He'll be sold to a cowboy, shipped out to the frontier, driving those beasts from human lands."

"Guard duty, for sure. And who could complain? When was the last time you ever saw a skinny guard? Once he's trained, he'll be fed for life..."

Jae'eli ignored them, as did the mother and child beside him. The heat of the day was rising, suffocating them all in the oppressive atmosphere of an impending sale. Each of them was about to be bought and sold, forever condemned to a life of servitude. It made no difference to him. His small act of defiance had been the only taste of freedom he would ever know.

"Five thousand seven hundred! Sold!" the man in white proclaimed to an ecstatic crowd. The Thorned Men returned, but this time did not point their metal rods at him. He was no longer their property.

"Zovaesys." The man in white winked. A golden toothy grin consumed his face.

"Zovaesys," Jae'eli replied coldly, his heart heavy as he was led away from the auction stand. The other slaves smiled happily for him, except for the mother and daughter, who stared vacantly into the distance.

A Thorned Man guided him to a shaded stall, away from the prying eyes of the crowd. In an instant, his life circumstances shifted dramatically. The stall was lavish, adorned with deep red carpeting and sumptuous drapes that enveloped him in a false sense of luxury. The Thorned Man stepped forward and unlocked his shackles, freeing both his hands and feet. For the first time in what felt like an eternity, Jae'eli rubbed the raw skin beneath the metal restraints, savoring the sensation of liberation.

"Boy, look here," a voice snapped at him.

Jae'eli turned to see another man in white, flanked by a quartet of men approaching. Two household guards clad in brown leather stood at attention beside a man draped in extravagant red and yellow robes.

"Your new master," the man declared.

Jae'eli bowed to the man he would now call Master. The man scrutinized him with an appraising gaze.

"Boy," the man said. "you may address me as Master Aeksilor."

"Yes, Master Aeksilor."

His new master seized Jae'eli's wrists, examining them for wounds and other signs of mistreatment. "Very well, he is in fine condition. This transaction is complete. Come!" With a sharp clap, Master Aeksilor turned, striding away with his guards.

Beside his new master, a boy with striking green eyes offered Jae'eli a coy smile. "You're very lucky," he whispered. "House Aeksilor is a great house to serve."

Jae'eli tried to smile, but behind him he heard the auctioneer call up the mother and daughter for auction. *Separately.*

Jae knew there was no luck in this world, only servitude.

Leawyn II

It was the screams of men that woke her, but it was the smell of smoke that got her moving.

She slipped from her bedroll, rising in tandem with the other women of their tent. The fire at the center had been extinguished, leaving the adults to stir like specters in the dark, blindly fumbling through a world they could not recognize. Leawyn, dazed, stumbled into a pile of pots and pans, sending them clattering to the floor. A child cried out in the dark. Someone tried to strike a match, but failed.

Backpedaling from the mess, Leawyn collided with one of the poles that supported the tent's roof. It groaned but held steady. Another match sparked, but before it could catch, the world outside began to glow. Shadows darted against the canvas cover.

The sun rises? Good, Leawyn thought as the fire in the center of the tent ignited.

With the firelight, she could finally see, finally emerging from her dreamlike daze. The tent was in full disarray, both from their days of packing in anticipation of returning to their village and the rising chaos of the dawn. Outside, screams and shouts mixed with the distant sound of a war horn. Smoke seeped in through the flaps of the tent.

"Grandma?" her youngest grandchild, Layita, cried out.

"Yes, baby, yes, I am here." She went to her, taking her from her bedroll and hoisting her onto her hip. Her joints popped with the action, but adrenaline numbed the pain.

Arianwyn rose beside her from her bedroll, drool coating her cheek, sleep still flush in her eyes. "Wah? What is happening, Grandma?"

The question greeted her like a slap in the face. She blinked hard and turned haphazardly to look about the tent. Women scrambled to rise, children shrieked, and the chieftain stumbled from a private section, the only man among them, clutching his sleeping britches. The sounds of frantic movement filled the air. Screams, shouts, and the distant thrum of war drums. Leawyn didn't know how to answer her granddaughter, so she chose the only truth she could.

"I don't know, but quickly, rise and dress yourself. You too, Layita." She set her upon the floor, but the young girl only sat still and trembled. Already exasperated, Leawyn fumbled as she tore into the sack of clothes, flinging furs, mittens, and boots aside in haste. Layita struggled to dress herself, still frozen in shock. Leawyn, teeth clenched, rushed to help, but her own hands betrayed her, her aching fingers stiff from the cold. She couldn't get the drawstring to tie on her fur coat.

"Focus on yourself, child," she at last whispered to her granddaughter. She slipped on her boots as a woman finally tore open the tent flaps. She let out a shriek.

Like a rock thrown upon a hornet's nest, the occupants of the tent burst into a fury. Leawyn, sensing the growing beat of drums in the distance, grabbed their rucksack containing their very meager belongings, snatched Layita's hand,

and barked a harsh order to her half-dressed granddaughter. "LET'S MOVE!"

A stampede for the exit occurred. They tramped through bedrolls and sacks of supplies, spilling food, garments, and trinkets upon the floor. A poor older woman, too slow to move from her bedroll, was stepped on. The snap of her arm bone was only barely mitigated by the sound of her shriek.

These were her clanspeople, her kin, but that did not seem to matter now. They were beneath a tent, and Leawyn knew the danger of chaos and fire under a burlap roof. She burst out into the dawn clutching her youngest, waiting desperately for Arianwyn to emerge. She came a moment later, barefoot, wearing only a coat and her undertrousers.

"Grandma?" Her voice trembled, but once again, Leawyn had no answer.

"To the hill by the forest," she managed.

She turned, taking the brunt of a woman slamming into her as she desperately scrambled away. She was discombobulated, unsure of where the hill lay. Smoke curled in the air, thickening around them. She searched the sky, hoping to use the rising sun to orient herself, but the orange glow in the distance was not the break of day. It was the fading light of the waning moon, still high above. It couldn't have been more than an hour past midnight.

That is no dawn.

The beat of the drums grew louder.

Bum de dum dum, dum de dum dum.

The beats were slow, methodical, and dismal. These weren't the rhythms of her people. The Outsiders had come, attacking under the waning power of their sacred moon.

"Leawyn!" Their chieftain appeared beside her. He was panting, draped in a massive fur overcoat, yet trembling already from the cold. Upon his head, he wore his antler battle helm, something she had not seen outside ceremonies in decades.

"Finn, surely you do not mean to join—"

"Listen to me," he cut her off. "Take your girls and climb the hill. Slip into the forest and await the dawn. Should you hear the horn of our people, you may return. If not, flee. Flee all the way back home to our village."

"Of course," she said at once. "but you must come with us!"

Arianwyn tugged at Leawyn's leg, urging her to move.

"I may be old, but I will not be shamed. I will join the other boys and defend our land. Better die in battle than sickly in my bed. Now go!" He slapped her on the back so hard she nearly dropped Layita. With a final glance at him, Leawyn dug her heels into the cold, muddy soil and ran.

Arianwyn took the lead as they dashed through the throngs of frantic people. Women were running, clutching children, or helping the elderly limp toward the forest. Yet through the chaos, other women emerged from their tents, bows and arrows carried in their hands, dashing toward the battlefield. If she weren't burdened with her grandchildren, Leawyn might have joined them.

They pushed through the scattering crowd, heading for the hill that rose toward the forest's edge. A tent to her right ignited, flames licking the air. But Leawyn didn't stop. She couldn't afford to wonder if anyone was still inside.

She ran until she reached the forest's edge, then paused. Leawyn needed a moment to catch her breath. Turning, they looked back toward the encampment. A wall of orange flames roared from the wooden huts and fortifications, casting long shadows in the smoke. Dark figures darted among the flames, and behind them, the shadow of the enemy emerged. Foreign men, their battle cries sharp and cruel.

"Grandma!"

She felt a tug on her leg. She looked down to find Arianwyn trembling.

Leawyn didn't want to move. She wanted to stay and watch, even strike up a bow for herself and loose arrows from the hilltop. Yet Layita trembled in her arms, and the cold gnawed at her hands, stiffening her fingers. She knew she wouldn't be able to pull a bowstring or loose an arrow. Reluctantly, she placed a hand over Layita's eyes to shield her from the sight of the flames, and followed Arianwyn into the dark embrace of the forest.

They scattered into the trees like insects fleeing a flame. They followed the haunting cries of children, until Leawyn's legs could carry her no farther. Her knees throbbed with each step, and Arianwyn, barefoot, was slowing them down. They stopped and found refuge at the base of a large, gnarled tree, its twisted roots offering a small shelter from the cold wind sweeping through the bare branches. Here she slipped off her fur coat and wrapped it around Arianwyn's feet and legs, hoping to stave off frostbite. The cold gnawed at Leawyn too, and the thought of surviving the night felt too distant to hold on to. In the end, she was ready to surrender to the cold.

The Outsider war drums grew louder. Leawyn knew they were advancing. Nestling her granddaughters close, she squeezed them tight, her gaze lifting to the waning moon. She wondered if the stars above looked the same as the bog holes beneath the Hearthsea.

"Is all lost?" Arianwyn said to her at last. She looked sad and tired, perhaps a mirror of Leawyn herself, wrapped in her fur coat, a bead of snot frozen halfway to her lip. She didn't have the heart to answer her.

The beat of the drums continued to grow louder, and with them, more shadows darted through the trees. Women were picking up their young and old and fleeing deeper into the forest. Leawyn's heart leaped, and suddenly, she found herself rising, wishing for nothing more than to run—run all the way back to her village to where her firstborn, and her husband, and her parent's parents all rested, so she may join them, and her granddaughters could be raised in the safety of her kin.

DUM DUM DUM DUM DUM.

The thunderous beat of the drums grew so loud, they chased away her dreams. The Outsiders must be coming through the trees!

Layita screamed, throwing her hands over her ears as a tidal wave washed over them. A thousand hooves stamped through the forest, stampeding mere feet from their refuge among the tree roots.

Centaurs.

Leawyn had never dreamed of their numbers. Half-man, half-horse, they moved with lightning speed, darting through the darkness, bows and swords gripped firmly in their hands.

She stood still, watching with her mouth open as they swept past, racing toward the forest edge, down the hill, and onto the open fields of frozen grass to wage their battle. Trembling, she slowly took a seat among the roots again, finding comfort in the warmth of Layita as she flung herself onto Leawyn's chest. The heat was a small but welcome reprieve. Arianwyn, too, scooted closer, pulling the fur coat over all three of them, doing her best to shield them from the biting cold.

A sight of horror greeted them on the hillside. A quarter of the tents had burned down, along with most of the few possessions her clan's people had brought with them. On the horizon, the wooden barricades and defensive structures of their warriors were burnt or burning, and across the entire plain, innumerable footprints encircled the entire encampment, the centaurs long since vanished.

They lay there in silence, save for Layita's quiet sobs, until just before dawn. The horn of victory sounded throughout the still air, echoing across the hillside. They rose, nearly frozen in the first rays of morning, and slowly made their way to the forest's edge.

Cries and moans of the survivors echoed in the distance. Women, the young, and the elderly emerged from the tree line, slinking back toward the ruins of their tents. Leawyn and her granddaughters followed, their steps slow and heavy, as though in a waking nightmare. The bone-chilling cold was a constant reminder that this was no dream.

Among the surviving tents, little had changed. To their blessing, the tent of her clan was still upright, and the survivors were already tending to repairs and cleaning the remnants of the camp. A herald bearing a deep wound on his biceps ran by, sounding the cry for any available help to tend to the soldiers and ruins of the front line. Leawyn passed off her two grandchildren to Jahota, much to Layita's dismay, and followed a small procession of women to the front line.

The stench of smoke filled her nostrils as she approached. The ground beneath her feet was uneven, marked by the heavy hoofprints of the centaurs. Leawyn carefully navigated the uneven turf, reaching the first line of burning buildings, and braced herself to find the dead.

More for the bog, she thought, but to her surprise, the cold silence of death was not what she found. Instead, the shrieks of the living pierced her ears as rows upon rows of men were laid out on the uneven soil, grunting and shouting in pain from their wounds.

"By the good Hearth," she whispered under her breath.

She moved between the rows, her heart heavy with their suffering, but as the first light of dawn broke over the horizon, warmth began to seep back into her body. It was as though the rising sun had breathed new purpose into her.

I would have given anything for my son to be among them. These men have a chance.

Without hesitation, she set to work. She found a shaman among the wounded, distributing healing supplies. Leawyn knew the ways of treatment well, even if she understood that many would not survive. Decay and infection were inevitable companions in war. But their survival, the fact that they still had men to treat, meant they had won a surprising victory, and she would not let their struggle or sacrifice go to waste.

She didn't know where to begin, so she simply dropped to her knees beside the first man she saw. He had a deep sword wound across the base of his back, and she worked quickly to clean it, packing the wound with herbs. The man uttered a thanks, his voice weak, and she moved on to the next. This one bled profusely from the left side of his face. His ear hung by a single flap of skin, and she knew he wouldn't last much longer. She held him as he sobbed, his cries desperate for the comfort of his mother. Leawyn stroked his hair, as though he were her own son, offering him what solace she could until, in his delirium, his cries fell silent. His body shuddered, then stilled, and Leawyn closed his eyes gently with her fingers.

She moved to the next, pulling the shaft of an arrow from a man. He wept at first, but once the shaft was removed and the blood paused, hope returned to the man.

"Bless you, miss, bless you!" he thanked her.

"No, it is you, strong warrior, who deserves thanks for your duty and bravery." She fell silent for a moment, focusing on his wound, but then felt a deep need to add. "And for holding the line."

"It was a battle, fierce as any I've ever seen, and they took us by surprise. Cowards!" The soldier turned his head and spat into the dirt. "Had they met us in true battle, we could have held them, I'm sure of it."

"But you did hold them, did you not?" Leawyn's voice came colder than she intended, but her fingers were warm with his blood.

"Yes, miss, but wouldn't have if not for the centaurs." He let out a breath, shaking his head. "They came flooding from the forest at the peak of the fight, just as our makeshift lines were starting to crumble. Damn near shat myself, I did!"

Leawyn did not have the heart to tell him that, judging by his smell, he had indeed shat himself.

"They came from all sides, charging through our ranks and filling our gaps. They secured our flanks, and then, before you know it, in the enemy's rear as well! I've never seen the Outsiders routed so fast. The centaurs chased them right to the far forest edge and, damn if I didn't see it, followed them right in too."

Leawyn packed his wound with herbal ointment, grabbing a sewing needle and thread to sew the flesh back together. She let the man talk, engrossed in his words, but she said little, only reaffirming the man's bravery when appropriate. When she finished, she bid him farewell and moved on to the next man, and the next. Before long, she had held a dozen as they slipped from this world, and closed a hundred other wounds. Each told the same tale of victory, though spun in countless ways: drums that had summoned centaurs from the Hearth itself, warriors leaping onto centaur backs to ride through battle, and axes splitting enemy skulls in sprays of blood and bone.

She finished her work by midday, when her back and aching fingers could allow her to tend to no one else. She returned to her tent, finding the girls fast asleep, and to her great relief, her old friend the chieftain resting by the central fire. She ran over and kissed him upon the cheek.

"You old fool!" She gripped him by the cheek like a scornful mother.

He chuckled, his facial muscles tightening into a weary smile. "It was nothing," he said, though a cough soon betrayed him. "I held the rear guard. I was never in real danger."

She sat beside him, snatching his hand into her own, grateful for the warmth of his fingers and the fire. "I have heard nothing but tall tales all day. Please, you must tell me how the battle truly went."

"Fair enough," he said, settling deeper into his seat. "Those fools thought it wise to attack us in the night, bah! Cowards. They must be desperate after we killed their leader. They needed a victory, but we handed them none."

"But the battle, you old fool, the battle!"

"Yes, yes, quite right." He tugged on his beard. "They loosed fire arrows first and tried to blind us with smoke. Damn near set everything ablaze, those bastards. Foolish ones at that, for wood can be replaced, but men cannot. That gave us just enough time to form ranks. Our archers took the hill, and damn if those women didn't stand their ground. They loosed their own arrows in return, cutting down the first wave and buying us precious moments."

He paused, taking a deep breath. "Then the real fight began. The men held formation, waiting for the shield wall to crash into us. When it did, the ground shook. They pierced our ranks, damn near broke them clean through. I came this close," he held his fingers an inch apart, "to joining the fray myself, just an arm's length from burying my hatchet into an Outsider's skull." He stopped, shaking his head with a wry chuckle. "And then, before I knew it, we had won. The enemy was swept from the field."

Leawyn's fingers slipped from his hand, and she furrowed her brow. "You mean to say nothing of the centaurs? I have heard all day of their plunge into battle."

"Oh, eh? What's that? Those beasts from the woods?" He waved a dismissive hand. "Yes, I suppose they were there, riding down soldiers on the flanks. How many, I couldn't say. Perhaps no more than a few dozen."

"A few dozen?" She scoffed. "I saw them myself! A whole herd plunging through the forest!"

Finn let out a gruff chuckle. "Now, my old friend, you sound like an old soldier, spinning his tales from battles long past!"

She stiffened. "You mean to discredit what I've seen? The actions of the battlefield? My girls and I are alive and you still draw breath because they kept our lines intact."

Finn gave a low laugh before breaking into a harsh coughing fit. Leawyn waited for him to regain his composure, and when he did, his voice was low and gravelly. "Now see here, what occurred last night among the pitch of battle and the moon, that is not for us to say. Only that our warriors fought bravely, that is all that needs to be said. Our time on the front is nearly at an end."

Leawyn did a double take at her old friend. "Were you conked in the head, old man? We would all be dead right now if it wasn't for them. If only we had treated with them earlier. They could be allies!"

"Now, Leawyn, don't go causing a scene…"

Leawyn shot to her feet, drawing every eye in the tent. "I have buried two sons and a husband because of these Outsiders. Death and battle are all we have known since the People of the Sails first came. But now we may have an ally and a chance to end this war once and for all! We must speak of them! We must name them! So that when my girls marry, my bloodline does not clog every bog in this land!"

Finn grunted as he rose from his seat, rising to meet Leawyn's eyes. "That is not our place to say. If you truly seek peace, then please, take your seat, and fill your mouth with porridge rather than talk. Soon we will all be back home, and this nastiness of war will be behind us. Your girls will grow into women—not warriors."

Leawyn stared at him, her jaw tight, her hands trembling at her sides. She searched for the right words, something sharp enough to cut through his weary resolve, but they did not come.

Finn too looked back upon her, his once green eyes faded to gray, the wrinkles cut deep into his flesh. He was a weary man, who too had lost father and son, kin and cousin to war. Spittle dribbled from his mouth, and she could spy his chest heaving as he suppressed another cough. He would not be long for this world, she knew. He just wanted to go home.

"So be it," she finally answered him. She took his advice, filling her belly with porridge and warming herself by the fire. Then she lay down beside her grandchildren, closing her eyes for what should have been a long, dreamless rest.

But when she woke deep in the night, the camp was still.

Quietly, she packed a bag, slipped from the tent, and vanished into the forest.

JAE II

A knife pressed cold and sharp against the base of Jae'eli's neck. The brute behind him twisted it just enough to break the skin.

"Tell me, boy, do you know how to run?"

Jae'eli swallowed, feeling the blade bite deeper. "Only if my master were to command it," he replied, his voice barely above a whisper.

His new master rocked back on his heels, a slow smile creeping across his lips. The green-eyed boy beside him mirrored his master's expression.

"And tell me, *boy*, what is your name?"

He'd been called many things before—worm, dirt, trash. The masters named him however they pleased, and sometimes they didn't bother naming him at all. In the vast, desolate fields of the Sorrows, there was little use for names, and it was only this saving grace, a nameless thing in a sea of worthless men, that allowed him to retain his God-given name, *Jae'eli*. But he knew better than to ask to keep it. His eyes flicked toward the man, trying to meet his gaze despite the harsh sun glinting off the blade and his master's bald head. "I have no name unless my master wills it."

The master's smile widened. The green-eyed boy nodded approvingly. "Good. Very good. Luke, remove your blade." A snap of the master's fingers, and the knife withdrew, leaving a thin trail of blood trickling down Jae'eli's neck.

Luke, the massive brute of a man with fair skin burned red by the sun, sheathed the knife without a word. He towered over Jae'eli, his muscles straining against the leather straps of his armor as his cold gray eyes stared down at him. "Remember, boy," Luke said, his voice low. "Don't run."

"Oh Luke, must you always be so unpleasant?" Aeksilor clapped his hands together. "Today is a marvelous day! My lady wife has been in desperate need of new protection for our fine manse, and I've acquired this '*slayer of bulls*' at a fine price! A very fine price indeed!"

Luke took a step back with a frown, but the other two guards with Aeksilor, redheaded twins by the looks of it, broke into toothy grins beneath their leather helms. "A wise choice, Lucien," one of them said, nodding toward the green-eyed boy.

Lucien, however, shrank back a little, his smile slipping as he glanced at Jae'eli. Aeksilor broke into a frown, jabbing his finger into the sky.

"Lucien, bah! It was all me! I'll do anything for my lady wife—especially when the price is right," Aeksilor boasted, rubbing his fingers together with a glint in his eyes. "But onto more important matters. Boy!" He snapped his fingers sharply, and Jae'eli flinched, his neck tingling with the memory of the knife. "Listen here," Aeksilor continued, puffing his chest. "I am a good master of this fine city, as my father was before me, and his father before him. For a thousand unbroken years, my family has ruled, and do you know why?" He paused as if expecting Jae'eli to answer. When Jae'eli said nothing, Aeksilor grinned. "Tradition. Honor. That is what has kept us in power. You'll notice I give my slaves their names back. Yes, indeed. They've served me well, and so I restore what was taken. Serve me well and your name will be returned too."

Aeksilor stroked the beard on his chin, eyes scanning his new slave like a merchant sizing up goods. "And who are you to be? The bull slayer?" Jae'eli's heart leaped at the name, but Aeksilor must have sensed this, for he shook his head immediately. "Ah, nothing is more obscene than a prideful slave." His tone darkened. "No, you will be humbled as you should be before a great master. Whatever foolish bravery made you face that beast doesn't matter to me. You play with fire, boy."

Aeksilor's voice grew thoughtful as he mused. "Yes... a moth, a pitiful creature drawn to flames. A sickly little thing—fluttering in the dark, only to be burned by the light it chases. Perfect!" He stepped back, clapping his hands, the rings on his fingers clinking like coins. "Wilted Moth! A fitting name, don't you think, boys?"

"Yes, Master Aeksilor," his slaves echoed in unison.

Jae'eli held his expression firm. "A fine name from a fine master," he said, his voice steady. "Thank you."

Aeksilor's tongue flicked across his lips as his dark eyes drilled into Jae'eli's. He stepped forward, lifting his arm to trace stubby fingers along Jae'eli's smooth skin, muttering to himself. "Olive skin, large hands and feet... You'll make a mighty guard. The sun won't burn you like it does like my other slaves from the far north." He gestured toward his men, and Luke's gaze dropped as if struck by an invisible blow. "Yes..." His voice grew softer. "You'll be a fine guard. A fine purchase. A very fine purchase indeed."

Jae'eli exhaled slowly as Aeksilor stepped aside to speak with Lucien. He hadn't realized he'd been holding his breath. His new name, Wilted Moth, felt oddly fitting. Despite the scorching sun overhead, an unsettling chill filled him. He glanced upward, squinting into the blazing sky, but the sun's rays offered him no comfort.

"Listen up, all of you!" Luke's voice boomed like thunder. "We're heading back to the city proper. You know the drill. Except for you." His brow furrowed as he locked eyes with Jae'eli. "You—new one. Follow behind the master. If you run, I'll cut you down. *Zovaesys*, remember." Luke, a fellow slave, used the word of the masters, but it didn't sting Jae'eli the way it should have.

Aeksilor's dark eyes narrowed, and he shot Luke a sharp glance. "That's enough. Unless you want the Thorned Men to cut out your tongue, leave the speeches to me."

Luke, already sunburned, flushed an even deeper shade of red, but he said nothing more.

They fell into formation, preparing to leave the Slave Quarter. Luke took the lead, with Aeksilor just behind him. Jae'eli followed closely, feeling the green-eyed boy, Lucien, hovering so near that he could feel his breath against his ear. The redheaded twins fell into step behind them, sealing Jae'eli in.

"Hurry up, I wish to be home to see my good lady wife," Aeksilor commanded.

Luke did not need to be told twice. They approached a wooden gate manned by a contingent of Thorned Men. Jae'eli instinctively dropped his eyes, sure to feel their iron rods upon his flesh as they passed, but they kept moving, and no pain ever came. In fact, pleasantries were exchanged between Aeksilor and the Thorned Men, their words unusually pleasant and nonanimalistic. They passed through a wooden gate with ease, and at once, the reek of the Slave Quarter disappeared, replaced by the sights, sounds, and most noticeable of all, the *sweet* smells of the city.

"You smell that, boy?" Aeksilor's voice rang out, thick with pride. "That is the aroma of Astrelaide, the city of flowers! What a fine life I've given you, free from the stench of that pen." He waved a hand in front of his nose, theatrically ridding himself of the slave stench, as the gates slammed shut behind them. The ginger twins giggled behind him.

Jae'eli's bare feet left the grime of the Slave Quarter as he stepped onto a smooth yellow-bricked street. On the streets of

Astrelaide proper, the crowds were thick, and though Jae'eli was accustomed to crowded, deplorable conditions, he was not accustomed to the sheer number of people, nor the roar of commerce and city life. Among the crowds, tiny shops bustled with activity at the base of towering white apartment blocks. Merchants sported colorful stalls filled with exotic rugs, animals, wines, and clothing, shouting over a thousand footsteps and languages exchanged on the bustling streets. Only the cooks and chefs remained quiet in this sea of exchanging gold, for the smells of their shops, cozily embedded at the base of multistory apartment blocks, drew in their patrons. Familiar scents like saffron and mint wafted from their shops and bakeries, and suddenly he was thinking of his homeland—of the ocean and dense, lush green forests. His feet felt lighter too, almost as if he were swimming...

He quickly shot a glance through a narrow alleyway, catching a glimpse of the blue sea and the tall masts of distant ships. He contemplated, wildly, for the first time in many months, how easy it would be to slip into the crowd and go unnoticed. He did not have a collar to designate his slave status, and he was dressed in only rags, still coated in dirt and probably feces, and spoke the native language with a thick tongue. He knew it would never work. He could see Luke ahead of him, one hand always clutched on his sword hilt. Yet seagulls squawked overhead, and he caught a whiff of sea salt. His leg muscles twitched, pulled like a siren or the rumored mermaids of his homeland. He could run straight to the ocean—to them, and together they could be pulled under the tide. At least then he'd be free...

A soft fist dug into the base of his spine, pulling him from his trance. Lucien leaned in close, his breath warm against Jae'eli's ear. "We're in the Ivy now," he whispered. "See how the buildings seem to creep along the shore? This part of the city—it traps you if you move too quickly, like it was built to ensnare." The boy licked his lips, breathing softly into his left ear. "Yet look how the people move for our good master. The name Aeksilor commands respect here. How lucky we were to find you."

The boy's hand twisted slowly into the base of his back until Jae'eli swallowed and nodded. Only then did the boy pull away. Jae'eli lowered his head as thoughts of the ocean receded like the tide. The Ivy, for its namesake, crept onward along the shoreline of the city, boxed in by the sharp rise of a massive cliff face that surrounded the entire city. Slowly, he raised his head, rubbing his arm as he took in the winding streets of whitewashed homes seemingly carved into the rock. His eyes followed the path upward toward the summit, where grand white palaces stretched like a string of pearls beneath the largest of all bluffs—the Stone Master.

"The Rose." Lucien's hot breath returned to his ear. "That's where Aeksilor lives."

Jae'eli's gaze lingered on the looming stone cliffs before it was pulled back to the streets by a new commanding sight. Like the Stone Master above, another monumental structure rose from the Ivy, emerging over the cluster of whitewashed homes like a tidal wave. It was a grand stepped pyramid, larger than any building he had seen in the city. Its stone walls dominated the skyline, and atop it, a massive brazier blazed, rivaling the brightness of the sun.

"Luke! To the plaza, please. I wish to pay my respects!" Master Aeksilor called out loudly when he caught sight of the structure too.

Jae'eli's curiosity was piqued, and his eyes locked on the imposing structure. They followed Luke's lead, weaving their way toward the Plaza of the Masters, and with each step, his awe deepened. The plaza itself was vast, its wide expanse paved in smooth white brick that surrounded the red-stoned pyramid at its center. Though less crowded than the narrow streets of the Ivy, the plaza was alive with activity. For every twenty human slaves, other strange and fiendish creatures were paraded between their masters.

Jae'eli's time in the fields had introduced him to the beast-folk, like the hulking minotaur, but here he encountered creatures beyond his understanding. Noggins, small doglike beings waddling on short legs, were bound together in long chains. Greejees, terrifying apelike creatures with thick fur-covered forearms, short, devilish snouts, and demonlike green eyes, were led through the plaza in chains as if they were pets. Yet, even they paled in comparison to the worst of all—the satyrs. Jae'eli knew their kind well; their stench preceded them, a foul odor he had come to associate with misery. His stomach dropped as he spotted one, a goat-like beast of human size with ragged fur and twisted horns.

A crowd had gathered around a miserable satyr strung up on a plinth. Jae'eli's horror deepened as he watched a Thorned Man step forward, hammer in hand, driving nails into the creature's extremities. The creature's agonized cry pierced the plaza, bringing the bustling activity to a brief, chilling halt.

"Oh by the sun above, not another one." Master Aeksilor shook his head.

The stench of blood filled the air, overwhelming Jae'eli as he stumbled back. The satyr's scream sliced through the streets of Astrelaide with its agony. Lucien bent over, plugging his nose, and Jae'eli felt a moment of opportunity overtake him. The dark spectacle had drawn every eye as he backed away slowly, heart pounding in his ears. The fields were rough, but he had never seen anything like this...

Jae'eli collided with something hard. He froze in his tracks.

His eyes darted to Lucien, who stared back with wide, terrified eyes. Hot breath poured over Jae'eli's neck as a large, meaty hand closed around his neck. Before he knew it, his muddy feet were kicking wildly in the air.

"What is this? A slave without a collar? Did you think you could evade the sun's gaze, here of all places?"

The voice that came from behind him was deep and thunderous. Jae'eli squirmed, stars dancing in his vision even as the midday sun blazed overhead. Finally, Aeksilor, distracted by the satyr spectacle, turned at the sound of the voice. His eyes widened in shock, and he rushed forward, dropping to his knees before the figure behind Jae'eli.

"High Priest, Your Holiness, I do beg your pardon, that is my slave..." Aeksilor pleaded, his forehead nearly touching the ground.

"Aeksilor," the voice thundered. "I was not privy to your arrival. Why does a good master of this fine city drop to his knees before me? A humble priest?"

Aeksilor scrambled to his feet, his face flushed. "Of course, Your Holiness. It is merely a matter of respect. The House of Aeksilor is known for its piety, after all."

The High Priest did not release his grip. Jae'eli gasped desperately for air, the day slowly turning to night. Aeksilor's attention slowly drifted to Jae'eli, his fingers twitching as if counting imaginary gold coins.

Jae'eli hit the brick floor of the plaza with a sudden thud. He sucked in air desperately, his windpipe nearly crushed. He thrashed about on the ground as more hands were laid upon him. He wanted to scream, but his throat simply wouldn't cooperate.

"Master Aeksilor, how pleased I am to know you are acquiring slaves once more."

Jae'eli was brought to his feet. Luke had one fist tangled in the back of his tunic, while Lucien supported him under his arm. He still couldn't breathe.

"Only the finest for my household. I am sure you can understand." Aeksilor winked. "I found this one at the auction block challenging a minotaur upon the stage. 'The Bull Slayer' they are calling him! A brave soul, I will give him that. Once trained, he will make a perfect guard for my wife and family."

Jae'eli finally had the strength to look upon his attacker, but when he did, it felt as though the breath was stolen from him all over again. A human man, but *monstrous* in stature, stood before him. He was not a fat man, but hefty, and his fingers seemed to swell around countless golden rings. A noisy series of golden chains clanked around his neck as he shifted on slippered feet, and his yellow and white robe glistened with enough gold to balance the city's budget for a year. Atop his head sat a grand golden hat emblazoned with the emblem of the sun, adding to his already great height, and in his hand, he clutched an ornate golden scepter crowned with a dark ruby, seemingly smoldering in the light of the sun.

The High Priest leaned over as Jae'eli stared helplessly up. He stared directly into Jae'eli's eyes as Jae'eli clutched his bruised throat, still struggling for air. "A minotaur, you say?" the priest mused, his voice dripping with amusement. "I don't see it in those skinny arms of yours. But that's the thing about pride, isn't it? You don't always see it on the outside." He straightened, his gaze drifting to the tortured satyr strung up on the plinth, before turning his attention back to Jae'eli. "The Bull Slayer, aye? Tell me then, boy, what is your true name?"

A lump formed in his throat. "The Wilted Moth..." he squeaked out.

"No, boy, I asked for your true name." The High Priest leaned in.

He tried to swallow the lump in his throat. He couldn't tell if this was a trick or not. He braced himself like he was to be hit and let his name slip out. "Jae'eli."

"Hmm, of the A'leykan Islands. A fine name, for a man... but you are no man, yes?"

He nodded feverishly.

"Good," the High Priest snarled. "Men and beast have pride. And see here what pride gets you..." Aeksilor and his slaves turned to follow the High Priest's gaze, though Luke had to lift to turn him. They stood in silence as the satyr's goat-like screams filled the plaza, thick as a curse in the air, until Aeksilor, visibly uncomfortable, shifted on his feet and muttered, "Another runner? If they were quick about it, they could cut down on the stench..."

"No. Not a runner." The High Priest smiled. "That filthy creature dared raise a hand to its master and nearly killed one of our holy Thorned Men. A disgrace. A sign of what's rotting in our great city." He shook his head, as though mourning the fall of civilization itself.

"Oh..." Aeksilor shook his head. "I could never imagine... such a thing is usually unheard of... especially in my manse..."

The High Priest cut him off with a chilling laugh. "Yes, your manse. Word has reached me, good master. I've heard troubling things. You've sold off most of your slaves. And here you are, walking through the streets on foot instead of in a covered litter like the other masters. And your slave, daring enough to challenge a minotaur, pfft! He oozes with pride," the High Priest looked to him. "Have you taken his true name?"

Aeksilor stumbled on his words. "I-I gave him a slave name."

"A half-measure. Take his true name, and with it, his pride."

Jae's blood flooded with fear, but then so did Aeksilor's. His new master stepped forward, breath frantic, where he commanded, "say after me, boy." Jae'eli could only nod. "Khazan. Me'Giv, *Jae'eli*."

The other slaves looked away. Aeksilor waivered. Yet the High Priest grinned, staring at the two of them. *"Zovaesys."* He did as he was bid.

"Khazan. Me'Giv, *Jae'eli*."

He recognized the sounds; the chest grinding nature of the words of the Old Tongue, the very same that bid him to obey. He said the words, and as he did, a pain ripped at his heart and a fog settled over his mind. His name, his true name, became lost to him.

"Perfection," the High Priest growled. "No pride, only fear. And a powerful thing, isn't it? Look how the citizens of our great city skirt around the beast, afraid of such a lowly creature even before the power of our holy temple of the Sun God. There is much to be done if we are to protect our city and preserve our traditions. Yet I cannot do it alone, not without the power of our Sun above, and the good masters, who, I pray, are also not stricken with fear..."

"The House of Aeksilor has stood for a millennium, through the Ash Fall and foreign empires aplenty. Why, fear, bah! I would never fear my own!"

The High Priest's smile twisted into something darker. "The enemy within, my good lord, is often the most dangerous of all. They could be in your very walls..." His voice trailed off into a low, ominous whisper, before he tapped the base of his golden scepter upon the pavement. Aeksilor's troop flinched. Jae's eyes widened as a Thorned Man appeared from the base of the pyramid, stepping toward Luke. With a simple nod from the priest, the Thorned Man sliced a chunk of flesh from Luke's arm without hesitation.

"Let us all remember," the High Priest continued, looking to the sky, "that the Sun's light touches everything. There is no escaping it. It sees all." He leaned in, nearly touching noses with Jae. "*Zovaesys.*"

Jae flinched, the pain in his throat roaring back at the word. The High Priest straightened as he clasped Aeksilor's hands and shifted effortlessly into pleasantries. Their conversation turned to empty words, but Lucien, still holding Jae upright, tightened his grip, steadying him as he struggled to catch his breath. The weight of the moment would not lift from Jae's neck.

Finally, Aeksilor summoned Luke. He stepped forward, his face expressionless despite the blood dripping from his wounded arm. Without hesitation, he led the group away from the plaza. Jae, eager to leave the nightmarish scene behind, fell in line behind Aeksilor, relieved to put distance between himself and the red pyramid, the Thorned Men, and the pitiful, fading bleats of the satyr.

Luke led the troop through the lower city. No further incidents occurred, for a foul mood seemed to have gripped the denizens of this ward, and all hung their heads low. In a public square, near a row of crumbling water fountains, three slaves hung lifeless from crosses, their bodies beaten and bloody. No one had bothered to remove them, the stench of decay mingling with the heat. Severed heads were also mounted on spikes, leering from the edges of a market street, and many buildings wore the scars of recent unrest.

Charred brick, shattered windows, and dark splatters of dried blood marred the white plaster walls, blemishes among the city of flowers.

Jae's mood further soured as they approached a long white wall that separated the Ivy from the steep slopes of a fancier neighborhood rising above the crowded streets. Thorned Men stood at the gates, scowling at all who passed. Jae gulped, looking around Aeksilor's bobbing bald head, spying the bleeding gash in Luke's forearm.

He swallowed hard, and sensing his unease, Lucien leaned forward, saying into his ear. "The gates to the Vanilla. They keep out the riffraff, so to speak. Don't worry—they won't harm you, not with Aeksilor by your side."

Jae had a hard time believing him though. He braced himself for a slice of their rod.

But the Thorned Men barely glanced their way, and they passed without incident. Beyond the wall, the yellow bricks curved steeply upward, and Jae found himself leaning forward as the path sloped sharply beneath them. The street wound through more serene quarters carved into the cliff side, where lesser nobles strolled at a leisurely pace past shops and cafés. Glassware and jewels were displayed openly, shimmering in the sunlight, and only a few slaves, quiet and cautious, slipped between their masters with downcast eyes.

Occasionally, litters carried by slaves passed by, bearing higher nobles, who grew soft and frail atop their cushioned thrones. Aeksilor nodded and greeted these men and women with deference, pausing only for brief conversations. Lucien kept a light hand on Jae's back, guiding him with subtle pushes and pulls to match Aeksilor's movements as their master darted in and out of shops, exchanged pleasantries with other nobles, and, oddly, even acknowledged the slaves with a few polite words.

They continued their climb, winding through narrow roads and alleys, until the ground finally leveled out at the top of the cliff. Another set of Thorned Men stood guard at a golden gate nestled between opulent white mansions. These guards did acknowledge them, bowing to Aeksilor as they passed through the grand entryway. Jae's head spun, for they had climbed a long way. The day had been long, the Thorned Men bowed in his direction, and he was tired of climbing. Yet once they slipped through the golden gates, the terrain flattened, and Jae may as well have been on top of the world.

The whole city of Astrelaide unfurled below him. The city gleamed in the sunlight, rows upon rows of white houses with their adorned rooftops—some with yellow tiles, others draped in red, yellow, or white canopies. Dotted along the distant horizon were countless ships, their white sails billowing as they ferried goods and slaves into the harbor. From this height, the docks appeared like streaks of brown wood he could cover with his thumb, and the sea never appeared so far away.

Up here in the upper city, Jae found himself in a strange and new world. Magnificent palaces lined its hills, their towering mansions guarded by gleaming white walls, each family vying to outdo the other with extravagant displays of wealth and art. Manicured gardens overflowed with lush greenery, and pathways were adorned with flowers of every shape and color. The air here was fragrant, sweet with the scent of blossoms, and the clamor of the lower city seemed to melt away, replaced by the gentle trickling of fountains and the soft chirping of birds.

Then his gaze shifted to the far left of the city, where the Slave Quarters lurked, carved into the very cliff side they had ascended. The area seemed to fester with a dull, putrid brown that Jae swore he could smell even from here. And beyond that, the city's left gate stood, a wall of white brick guarding the short distance between the cliffs and the sea. This was the very gate through which Jae had been driven just days ago in the mass of slaves. Now, from this new vantage point, he realized he had never truly left his cage. The cliffs that encircled the city on three sides held them all in place, while the distant sea taunted him with a false promise of freedom. Jae's focus then turned at last to the Stone Master, the cliff face that still cast its shadow over the world below. Jae's heart sank. Even here, where the rich basked in luxury, the ever-present watch of the masters remained.

Lucien's hand suddenly wrapped around his waist as he skipped forward from his place in line. "This is the Rose," he whispered as Luke started them down a path carved from white marble. "You won't find any of those Thorned Men here."

The twins also broke from formation, their tension dissolving. One of them even tousled Jae's hair as he sprinted past, laughing loudly. Jae managed a halfhearted smile back to Lucien, his cheeks blushing as they walked among a sea of roses and blooming flowers.

Their formation dissolved as they continued down the quiet path, passing no other slaves, freemen, or masters. The air was serene, untouched by the chaos of the city below. Jae enjoyed the peace and quiet, walking alongside one of the redheaded twins as he broke into a whistle. Soon, the artisanal walls of a magnificent palace came into view, seemingly built directly into the side of the cliff. To the right, the bare yellow cliff face stretched high above them, and to the left, immaculate white walls adorned with intricate yellow and red tiles rose imposingly. A golden gate swung open with a quiet creak after Luke applied a key, and they entered a vast courtyard.

At its center, a marble fountain gurgled softly, a carved mermaid perched in the middle, her stone hair flowing like the water around her. Lush green grass blanketed the courtyard, and as Jae stepped onto it, his calloused feet sank into the soft earth, a rare comfort. Flowers of every imaginable color lined the walls, and the air buzzed with butterflies while birds chirped a cheerful melody.

"This shall be your home," Aeksilor declared, turning to Jae with a wide grin. "Have you ever seen such beauty? No, I imagine not. I've taken you from the dirt, and now you stand in one of the wealthiest and most noble houses in all of Astrelaide." His voice was grand, dripping with pride. "You will guard my family and possessions. You will be seen but never heard. And for this, you shall be rewarded. You'll eat well—duck and tarts, beer and wine on festive nights—and you'll call a comfortable bed your own. For this is the House of Aeksilor, and you, a humble servant."

"Thank you, Master," Jae replied. He half meant it this time.

"Very good!" Aeksilor clapped his hands, satisfied. "Let the duties begin!"

Aeksilor turned to a pair of large, carved mahogany doors. Luke and Lucien approached, and together they pushed them apart, welcoming their master into their home. Aeksilor strolled inside, Lucien gently nudging Jae to follow.

"Wife! Wife! Where is my darling?" Aeksilor called out. He did a spin in his foyer, nearly tumbling into yet another marble fountain.

Jae stepped into the mansion, his breath catching in his throat. It was, without a doubt, the finest place he had ever seen. While the heat in the lower city had been relentless, here a cool, damp breeze welcomed him as he crossed the threshold into the grand foyer. Bronze and marble tables lined with priceless artifacts and even more flowers filled the entryway, and from there, hallways branched off into elaborately decorated rooms. Yet Jae's attention was drawn to a grand balcony ahead, its doors thrown open, offering a view that seemed to lead directly into the sky.

"Husband?" A soft but irritated voice froze Jae in his tracks.

"Yes, my dear. Please, come! Come! I have brought us a new gift."

A younger woman emerged from a side doorway, tall and slender, her white gown flowing like silk over her form, shimmering with the light of the jewels at her neck and ears. Her beauty was undeniable, her eyes the color of bright sapphires and hair the color of rubies that flowed to her pronounced collarbones.

"Wilted Moth, come." Aeksilor beckoned Jae forward, waving his hand. Jae hesitated but obeyed, his steps tentative. "Boy, this is my wife, Lady Aril. You will show her the utmost respect at all times. And, my darling, here is the new guard you asked for! Someone to protect our precious family.”

Lady Aril approached slowly, her lips pursed, scrutinizing Jae from head to toe. Her gaze was sharp, assessing him like one would appraise livestock. “He smells terrible and is much too thin. How is he to protect anyone?” She spoke to her husband, though her piercing blue eyes remained fixed on Jae. Her accent was rich and refined—yet foreign. Perhaps another outsider, or once a slave herself?

“Stenches can be removed, my darling, and wait until I tell you of his bravery today... It was such an act of bravery...”

Lady Aril sighed and her husband ceased his rambling. “Very well. Lucien, take him at once to be bathed in the help’s quarters. Luke, you may begin training him at once come the morrow. Tonight I want the boy to rest and to be well fed.”

Aril’s gaze lingered a moment longer on Jae before she turned and slipped away, her white gown trailing like mist behind her.

Aeksilor clapped his hands loudly. “Now, you fools, make it quick!” he barked before chasing after his wife.

Lucien took Jae’s hand gently. “Quickly, now,” he whispered with a wink.

He pulled Jae to a hallway where a gilded wooden door stood. Lucien opened it without hesitation, unveiling a narrow and dark staircase. They flew down into the dark, coming to a dark room lined with benches and shelves. Baskets, tools, swords, and shields, everything needed to run the household had been assembled here, but Lucien did not give him time to pause. He led him down another hallway into a bathing room. A large tub was erected in the center with a window to the outside casting it in a bright glow.

“The water will be cold, but clean. Go ahead.” Lucien nodded and then stepped back from the room.

Jae took a moment and stared at the tub. He had never taken a bath before.

With a deep breath, he instinctively slipped his head beneath the surface. For a moment, everything was still. The sounds of the world above faded away, and he was back to his childhood, floating freely beneath the waves, where nothing could reach him. His eyes closed, and a soft smile spread across his lips. He let his body drift, weightless, as a lifetime of grimness slowly melted away. He could hear the ocean, smell the salt, and hear the faint voice of his mother, calling to him.

"Jae..." he heard her say, but that wasn't quite right. He squirmed under the water, trying to recall her voice, his name, but it wouldn't come. Slowly he came up out of the water, forcing his mind to remember, his tongue to speak, but his mouth could only produce broken syllables. He could neither say nor even think of his god-given name.

That was how Lucien found him, staring absent-mindedly in the murky bath water. He brought with him a set of simple brown cotton clothes in one hand and a dark metal collar in the other. "I've brought you these. We can burn your old clothes if you'd like," he said quietly.

Jae stared at him from the water for a long moment before nodding.

"The collar can go on last," Lucien added gently.

Not saying a word, Jae stood up from the bath, shivering. Lucien handed him a towel, which Jae accepted with a quiet nod. He dried himself quickly and then dressed in the simple brown garments. They were nothing special, but the soft cotton was the most comfortable thing he had ever worn. He almost smiled, but Lucien held the slave collar before him. Unlike those of his past, this one was golden, engraved with the name *Aeksilor* across its iron clamp.

"Are you ready?" Lucien said quietly.

"Yes," Jae replied, but not before touching the bare skin around his neck one last time.

"I'm sorry," Lucien said. Jae only nodded.

The metal collar clasped shut a moment later.

WARWICK III

A blizzard descended upon the mountain pass, sheathing the world in a swirling white maelstrom that hissed like a living thing. Warwick sat in his carriage, swaddled in a heavy fur cloak, shivering. He didn't think they were going to die, but his trembles came from more than just the cold.

He glanced at his cousin, Lady Catelyn, who sat rigidly beside him, cocooned in a thick coat. Unlike him, she remained still, offering neither a word nor a glance. Throughout their journey, she had steadfastly ignored him—shunning his attempts at conversation during every inn stop and or feast held by minor lords. Even locked in the carriage in the biting cold, she refused to look his way.

For two whole days we've been trapped in this carriage, by the Nine! He shook his head. *Women! She is likely the one who summoned this storm with her icy demeanor.*

"You've done a great deal for her family," Wulford had

told him after a particularly scornful rebuke of his affection at the last inn.

"But I am the prince! How many women of the court have beckoned for my hand? I could make her the most powerful woman of the realm! If she would only have me…"

Warwick had blushed, followed by Wulford's chuckles. "Do not worry, my prince. Many princes and kings before you have had greater trouble managing their wives and betrothed than they have the realm. Let Catelyn be the first of your trials with their sex."

But it was as if a bell had been placed over Warwick's head and rung. "Betrothed?" he whispered. "Do you think she would go for it?"

"As you have said, my prince, you could make her the most powerful woman in the realm, but… if I might add, the courting of a woman is a very delicate process, requiring many talents. You can't simply expect her to fall for you just because you are the heir-to-be, not if you want a happy relationship. You need to win her heart as well."

Warwick frowned. "We've known each other since we were children. We've gone hunting and feasting and played lawn games together. What more could she want?"

Warwick and Wulford had both turned at this time to stare at the Lady Catelyn from afar. They were stopped by a traveler's inn, preparing for the steep climb into the mountains. Catelyn spoke with other ladies of the court, all of whom continued to wear black in mourning for her father.

Black. He was sick of it! Yet a genius idea hatched inside his princely head. He had asked Wulford to produce a black cloak, perfect for the cold weather in the mountains, to publicly display his mourning. Underneath he could still wear his striped pantaloons for his arrival to the court. *Perfect.*

The blizzard struck just hours later, and for two days they lurched along the treacherous mountain road, neither castle nor city of High Ness in sight. Only a sheet of white hung beside the mountain road, and frustrated, Warwick stretched his legs, leaning against the frost-covered window as he peered down into the steep gorge, where the depths vanished beneath a shroud of swirling white clouds.

"Gods! Will this storm ever end?" Warwick exclaimed, slumping back against his cushion. He stole a glance at Catelyn, who merely rolled her shoulders, her gaze fixed on the rock face outside as if the mountain's steadfastness could shield her from the tempest within the carriage.

Warwick sighed, pulling the cloak tighter. How deeply he wanted to go to her and pull her close. *She is so beautiful in the cold,* he thought, as her cheeks and nose turned bright red to match the color of her hair. They could join their body heat together, cuddled beneath a sea of furs. But no—she had spurned him, the prince. He let out another sigh and flopped back against the cushions, pouting like a child denied a toy.

"This weather, I'm sorry, my lady, it has me all cooped up..." But then the magic words hit him. *I'm sorry.* He turned to Catelyn, this time forcefully taking her hand. She tried to snatch it away, but he held his grip firm. "And, my lady, if I may, I should *apologize* for my behavior before. I have not properly expressed my condolences regarding my uncle, your father. He was a great man and the realm owes him a great debt. I am sorry for your loss."

Warwick held her hand, staring intently at her as the carriage rocked back and forth over the stony, snow-covered road. Catelyn kept her gaze trained out the window, but for a split second, her eyes darted to him. Though she remained silent, she did not pull her hand away. A smile tugged at his lips as he returned his gaze to the frosted landscape, and they sat there, hand in hand.

They rode in silence for several more hours, and in a peculiar fashion, the winter storm that had haunted them for the past two days began to clear. The white clouds dissipated, allowing bursts of sunlight to stream down upon the mountains. A smile spread across his lips as he gazed upon an ocean of whitecaps stirred as if by a storm. He even caught Lady Catelyn leaning across in her seat, looking over his shoulder at the view. They were almost to court.

True to his prediction, their carriage train rumbled by an outpost of the Demonbreun Guard. They stood by a stone structure etched into the mountainside by the road, their color garments covered in thick furs. They stood at attention as Warwick's carriage train passed, and his heart fluttered.

I return to my kind of people. He beamed, and then his heart leaped with the cry of Strammond from afar.

"All halt!" came his cry, and the carriage came to a stop.

Warwick gave a toothy grin to Catelyn, who blushed in return. She began to gather herself as a flurry of footsteps erupted from outside the carriage. Warwick had waited over a year for this moment.

The carriage door swung open. Wulford stood on the other side, his steel armor glinting in the sunlight and his white cloak whipping in the wind. "My prince," he held the door and bowed, "we are nearing the township of High Ness. It is time for the procession."

"Splendid!" He beamed. He reached for the door of the carriage when a sudden thought halted his reach. "Wulford, I can't possibly go first, not when this procession is in honor of my uncle…" He hesitated, a flush creeping up his cheeks as he cleared his throat. "My cousin, Lady Catelyn. She must go first—in honor of her father."

"Very good, my prince," Wulford replied with a nod. He extended a hand toward Catelyn. "My lady?"

Catelyn stepped out of the carriage, her cheeks rosy with a mix of embarrassment and pride. Warwick followed closely behind her, feeling a surge of warmth as he watched her emerge into the light, the winter sun glinting off her hair.

Wulford helped the pair climb to the top of their carriage. The ice and snow had been cleared away and a wolf pelt laid down to aid their bums. Ahead, a knight led the way on horseback, signaling the start of their procession, while behind them, a long line of carriages awaited to carry the rest of the imperial family and court. His aunt and smaller cousins rode directly behind them, and farther back, Derrick climbed aboard his carriage with a contingent of laughing knights and other young men.

"Where is the respect?" he muttered to himself. He looked to his aunt, dressed in a mound of black furs, who looked at him with a stern frown, before darting her eyes to her daughter. Warwick gulped and slid back around to face the front of the procession. He tried to take Catelyn's hand again, but she shooed him away.

"Not before the crowds," she said without looking at him. "It would be most scandalous."

"So? Who among the court doesn't like a little intrigue?" he joked back, but she scoffed and turned an icy shoulder to him.

"I'd sooner be at court," he huffed silently to himself.

The procession began again, and as the carriage train rounded a mountainside, his wish came true. The township of High Ness came into view, and farther behind, perched on the very side of a mountain, stood the grand castle.

"Oh! We're home!" he squealed to himself.

The horses moved swiftly, as if eager to return to court. High Ness loomed ahead, situated atop a natural plateau and surrounded by steep canyons on all sides. A single gate afforded entrance into the city, guarded by walls of pristine white brick. Each home, a quaint mix of stone and timber, nestled snugly against the mountain, its snow-dusted eaves like frosted icing. The land's geography naturally confined the city, driving every home to rise upward with sharp, sloping rooftops mirroring the surrounding mountains, while taller chimneys released ribbons of black smoke, curling against the blinding white of the snow-covered peaks.

And yet, Warwick's gaze was drawn upward, through a throng of turrets and towers built for the city's most elite, to the shining white castle built into the very side of Mount Ness. The Crownhold, its white brick blanketed in fresh snow, jutted upward into the cloud layer above so that the tips of its tallest towers were lost to the heavens, praise be to Aethylios. This was the seat of the emperor, the home of the Opal Throne and Crown of the Nine. A tear welled in Warwick's eyes; after a year of travel, he was finally home, where no minor lord's castle or estate could compare.

Catelyn gasped beside him. "It's so beautiful." She suddenly scooted closer to him, gazing upward at the towers lost to the sky.

Warwick ignored her, however, his heart full of wonder as the gates to the city swung open, splitting a carved mountain flower, the edelweiss, in two. They rode beneath the gatehouse, the twin turrets rising high above them like watchful guardians.

"All hail the prince!" a voice called from high above.

On the other side of the wall, a battalion of the Demonbreun Guard awaited them, resplendent in their traditional garb of pantaloons of red, black, and gold, their heads adorned with plush hats. They wielded long ceremonial spears. It was a vibrant sea of color, a striking contrast to the monotonous white of their journey. As Warwick's carriage approached, the ranks parted as if by divine command, the guards stepping aside to line the avenue. Many raised brass instruments from their sides, ready to herald the prince's arrival.

"All hail the prince!" answered the roar of the guard, followed by a blast of music from trumpets and horns. The Demonbreun knights welcomed their prince back to court.

Warwick beamed, offering small, enthusiastic waves as his carriage rolled past. Wulford walked alongside the carriage, accompanied by a contingent of the household guard, but all proceeded with calm dignity, their welcomes subdued. High Ness was a city of the court, where only those of distinction were permitted: the guard, royal courtiers, traveling nobles, and diplomats. Even the working class consisted of artisans and musicians of notable wealth, their talents earning them a place within imperial society.

The contingent of Demonbreun fell away as the procession entered the city proper. There could be no place safer than this, nestled high in the mountains and sheltered beneath the Crownhold's shadow. High Ness possessed only one avenue worthy of an imperial procession, and even that was narrow, compressed further by the gathering of the city's residents. Bells tolled throughout the city, announcing their arrival, and citizens poured from narrow alleyways to press against the towering buildings as the imperial procession passed.

An outpouring of grief accompanied them, with torrents of black handkerchiefs waving in the hands of the mourners. Warwick waved to them all, dividing his attention between the residents on the street and those leaning from windows high above, showering rose petals down upon them in a fragrant tribute.

Lady Catelyn, caught in a rainstorm of flowers in honor of her father, broke into tears. Noticing Warwick, she leaned over and offered him a brief hug. He could almost hear the gasp from his good aunt behind him, but he didn't care. A roar of sorrow surged from the crowd, and a nod from Wulford confirmed that he had made the right move. His subjects welcomed him home.

Their procession proceeded through the Way of the Emperor. A few women cried as others openly called his widowed aunt's name. Weeping courtiers held portraits of the late prince high in the air, chanting his name. More extended their arms, reaching respectfully for Lady Catelyn, crying out for her as she waved back with teary eyes. For once, Warwick did not mind the sharing of affection; he sighed and relaxed his shoulders at the sight of the crowded streets and alleyways. His brother's premature arrival had not dampened the outpouring of support, and his own princely return would surely be the talk of court.

The workings of the imperial court would be everything in the coming weeks, and the Crownhold carved into the very side of a mountain could not, and would not, be forgotten.

And so, Warwick's gaze drifted upward as they neared the end of the Way of the Emperor. The avenue culminated at another massive white gatehouse, the last formidable line of defense before the castle itself. Banners emblazoned with the two-headed phoenix of his family fluttered in the wind, welcoming them home. Another resounding blast of horns and trumpets announced their arrival as they approached the gate.

Their carriage slipped beneath the iron gate and continued onto the White Bridge, a grand arched structure that spanned a vast mountain gorge. Perched on top of his carriage, Warwick's head spun as he glanced over the side of the bridge. He could not see the bottom, and he desired his fainting couch as he spied Wulford walking precariously close to the edge beside the carriage.

"My prince?" Catelyn finally spoke to him, placing a gentle hand on his shoulder.

"Wah?" he mumbled, shaking off the dizziness. Turning to Catelyn, he sought comfort in her presence, but the roar of the crowd behind them echoed against the mountainside, a reminder of the great depths below.

"You are nearly home. Steady yourself... for your father and the court," she urged, her voice steady and reassuring.

"My father? Oh yes..." He blinked rapidly. He looked away from her, staring ahead at the base of the castle before them. He could almost feel the weight of the palace above them, pressing into the rock.

He tugged at the frock beneath his cloak, feeling the pressure too tight around his neck. Truthfully, he had not thought of his father, but rather of his desire to impress the court with his travels, and to outshine his brother, *whatever he may scheme.* He lifted his hands upward, feeling the family crown upon his head. It weighed heavy and true, just as the White Palace did over their heads. They passed beneath yet another portcullis, arriving in a domed cavern beneath the castle.

"By the Nine!" Catelyn gasped beside him.

High above, an enormous chandelier hung from the cavern's vaulted roof. Thousands of candles blazed among rows of intricately carved glass, casting their light over a mural unmatched in size anywhere else in the known world. The mural stretched across the smoothed rock like a painted chronicle, illustrating the power and conquests of the fallen empire of Makka, the original rulers of the castle, as they subdued the native houses of these lands—House Hieronymus included.

Inside the domed chamber, Catelyn gasped, clutching his hand. High above, a gargantuan feathered serpent stretched across the ceiling, its coiled body a symbol of the fallen Makkan empire's former strength and dominion. Over the generations, the House of Hieronymus had worked to redo parts of the mural, though it was too vast to completely erase. The serpent still coiled, ready to strike, but the scene had been transformed. Now war banners displayed the symbols of Verope's nine noble houses, with the two-headed phoenix of House Hieronymus most prominent among them. Opposite the snake, the people and armies of Verope, once depicted in humble submission, bore swords and raised banners in defiance. Above all, including House Hieronymus, nine stars glimmered for the Nine Miracles of Aethylios, a divine sign over subjects-turned-liberators.

"It just never gets old," Catelyn whispered.

"No, it doesn't," Warwick said with a smile, though his gaze wasn't on the mural. The carriage procession had come to a halt in a grand circle beneath a chandelier, where a magnificent fountain gurgled in tribute to the founder's legacy. But as a prince, Warwick's carriage bypassed the fountain entirely, pulling directly up to the marble columns that rose seamlessly from the stone floor to the vaulted ceiling above. A contingent of officials and courtiers awaited him, but his brother, and more notably, his father, were absent.

"All hail the prince!" Strammond's voice rang out from the front of the procession.

"All hail the prince!" echoed the assembled court.

The carriage stopped before the towering white columns. A marble platform lined with intricately carved braziers, their flames flickering in the cavernous light, greeted him, alongside a host of bowing courtiers.

"I do believe this is where we depart." Warwick turned to Catelyn. He grinned from ear to ear. "Perhaps you can join me later this evening, for supper perhaps?"

"Go forth, my prince, and take up your duties as heir. Though, I suggest we keep our distance these next few days; your display of affection in the city will undoubtedly stir talk among the court."

"But... my lady..."

"Shh." She pressed a finger to his lips. "Go. Assume your place, and wait for me to come and kneel before you in honor."

Warwick furrowed his brow and nodded. "Yes... yes... a marvelous plan."

"My prince," Wulford appeared. "Shall I assist you in dismounting?"

"Yes, Wulford, that would indeed make a show of it." Warwick turned from Catelyn, his neck warm under the weight of her touch, and took Wulford's hand. He dismounted slowly, and when his booted feet finally met the marble floor, he sighed audibly. "Ah, it is so good to be done with these travels!"

A gaggle of girls, all dressed in their finest gowns, giggled and blushed at his declaration. "The prince looks most regal in his cloak!" one courtier called out with admiration.

Warwick, feeling the heat of their attention, did a quick turn, letting his heavy fur cloak sweep around him in a flourish. The young women broke into another chorus of giggles.

"You see? This is what I'm talking about!" Warwick turned to Wulford with a grin. "People here who appreciate me. *My* people."

"You look very comely wrapped in your furs, aye it is true. The last these women would have seen of you, you were not nearly fourteen, and just a boy. They see now that you have grown into a man—large and powerful. Your servants were wise to dress in the fashion of the wolf."

"Yes, wise indeed, but not wiser than their prince, for I always have a trick up my sleeve." He gave a confident nod. "Come, Wulford. Escort me up the steps to the castle doors, and I shall astonish the court even further!"

Wulford looked at him questioningly. "My prince?"

But Warwick placed a firm hand on his back, urging him forward. Amid the arriving carriages and bustling courtiers, with the gathered crowds watching from within the castle walls, Warwick ascended a short flight of marble steps. His wolf cloak trailed behind him, its fur rippling with each stride, while Wulford, his knight, walked beside him in his cloak of the wolf, his armor clinking in step with the prince's.

They climbed the steps, coming before a set of towering golden doors hung open on their massive steel hinges. Knights and suitors, courtiers and cousins, artists and musicians, dignitaries and diplomats all poured from the castle or filled the marble staircase just inside the door. A round of applause rose around him, hundreds clapping in his honor, though many were dressed in the somber black of mourning.

"My court, my court," Warwick called, halting just before the doors. He glanced up, smiling, for while the golden doors loomed large above him, they did not outshine his splendor. With a flourish, he undid his fur cloak, letting it fall in a soft *thud* to the floor. He spun once, unveiling his prized attire from his travels in Sanguinia: a striking set of black-and-white-striped pantaloons paired with an oversized tunic. Completing his spin, he threw his hands into the air, his chest heaving, drawing all eyes to the Crown of Knox upon his head.

He awaited another round of applause, yet only silence greeted him.

"Well?" He stood posed, his voice echoing off the cavernous walls. A member of the court coughed, and Warwick felt his confidence waver as he began to lower his arms, heat creeping into his cheeks. A thousand eyes were upon him, most filled with scorn or confusion. It was Wulford who finally broke the silence, bringing his hands together to spark a round of applause. A few moments passed, but the rest of the court soon followed.

"Unbelievable they do not applaud the prince," his father's castellan shook his head. A grievously old man, he hobbled forward to bestow a greeting. "My prince, it has been some time." He tried to lower himself, but nearly toppled over. Wulford had to rush to his side to steady him.

Is this the state of the realm? Where the court knows nothing of culture and sends forth this fossil to bestow a greeting?

Nevertheless, Warwick forced a smile. "Rise, Alden. It has indeed been a while. I have traveled far and returned the wiser for it. Perhaps many of my court should consider doing the same."

"A very wise observation, my prince," Alden croaked. "It is an honor to see that you have grown tall and strong since we have last seen each other. It seems as if only yesterday you and your brother were but babes—"

"Yes, my brother," Warwick cut him off. "Pray tell, where is my brother? And my father, for that matter?"

"They have gathered in the throne room. Your father, the emperor, has summoned you at once."

The crown summons me. He swallowed hard.

"Very well, let us proceed at once."

Alden beckoned him inside, but cast Wulford a suspicious glance. Warwick entered the main antechamber and stared upward at the grand staircase, instantly flooded with memories of his boyhood spent racing up and down the many flights within the castle. Now, as he faced the marble steps, his legs felt heavy with reluctance—months of travel had withered his calf muscles and added inches to his waistline. He managed to ascend only halfway up the staircase before he had to pause, catching his breath.

"My prince, shall I fetch your fainting couch?" Wulford asked of him.

Warwick paused, turning to look at the pitiful progress behind, but only found the tired eyes of Alden behind him. *Damnable old man,* he grumbled.

"I do-o not ne-ed a couch..." he tried to declare, but the words came out as a wheeze. A curse formed in the back of his throat, but one look at the remaining flight of stairs stole the breath from his lungs. The castle was simply too huge to be wasting precious air—and the antechamber, a gargantuan room of vertical splendor, towered upward hundreds of feet. A chill breeze at least whistled through the chamber, carrying cold air from the numerous cavernous hallways that each branched into entire wards of the castle. The lengthy windows that lined the staircase unveiled an unmatched view of the world beneath them.

"I am the prince," he panted. "I will not be made to look the fool."

Yet below, courtiers gathered to ascend the staircase behind him. Though they pretended to ignore him, he was impossible to overlook. The imperial caravan had begun to disperse outside, and hundreds waited to climb the stairs to their chambers. A cold gust from the mountain swept upward, ruffling the sea of black below him like a dark curtain fluttering in the wind.

Warwick leaned over the banister, desperate to catch his breath, feeling the oppressive weight of the void gaze upon him. The realm was watching.

"Okay… I am ready…" He grunted, and they resumed their climb. Warwick pushed forward, driven if not by the gaze of the realm, then by the incessant wheeze of Alden, his father's right-hand man, beside him.

Together, a chubby boy of five-and-ten and a living corpse of a man ascended to the top of the grand chamber, and there before them, at the end of another long marble hallway, the golden doors of the throne room, brazen with the symbol of the two-headed phoenix, awaited him.

Warwick, numb from the chill, released his grip from the banister, letting his feet carry him toward the sigil of his house. It was only muscle memory guiding him now, as weak as those muscles had become.

WARWICK IV

The golden phoenix doors of the throne room slammed shut behind him. A draft coursed through the vast hall, rattling the tall windows that lined the right wall, their glass panes groaning against the howling wind outside. Warwick looked to the vast expanse of dull gray sky for miles, hearing the wind howl, and his teeth broke into a frigid chatter. No sunlight reached here; the mountain and stone cast a shadow over all.

The cold wind stole his breath, and soft, elusive whispers tugged at his focus, drawing his attention to a pale glimmer at the far end of the room. *The throne. My father. And ultimately, the crown.*

His heart leaped as he stepped forward, entering a maze of marble columns, each one so massive that it would take a dozen knights hand in hand to encircle a single trunk. Childhood memories often exaggerated spaces, but not here. The throne itself seemed to have grown—the cavernous ceiling above dark and shrouded, hidden in shadow as if there was no such ceiling, but only an extension of the sky.

The throne room was a world unto itself. Here, the wind coiled through the cavern, slipping into the ears of courtiers like threads of rumor and intrigue. It snaked through hidden passageways in the mountain, setting the ancient stone to creak and sigh—a low, ancient chant cementing men and women with pride, so they became immovable in their positions. This was the court of the Opal Throne, locked in a ceaseless struggle of pride and callousness. Such were the politics of the realm. And such was the emperor's burden to balance.

Warwick approached the base of the throne, looking up at the vast marble seat, its polished white dulled beneath the overcast sky. The man seated upon it seemed smaller than Warwick remembered, swallowed by a throne built for a giant.

"Father," he said, bending a knee as custom demanded.

A cold voice answered him. "Rise, my son."

Warwick stood and, balancing on his toes, offered a courtly bow, grinning to draw attention to his new attire: extravagant pantaloons from the sunny southern courts. Yet his father's face remained impassive, unreadable. The emperor's shoulders seemed to sag, his arms bent at odd angles to rest upon the throne's oversized armrests, while his feet dangled nearly an inch from the floor. An aged man, overcast in shadows, whose long golden hair had weathered into gray, matched by the wilting of a comely golden beard gone to silver. He let out a heavy, weary sigh as their gazes met, and Warwick noticed the vibrant blue eyes he remembered had dimmed, cold and steely.

"So, the stories are true." His father shifted uncomfortably on the throne. "You have not grown into a man."

Warwick took a step backward, turning his cheek aside as if slapped. "Father, are we not well met? Look upon my garment and see the fruits of my travels. The lords and ladies of the south have bestowed upon me their finest. This is their mark of loyalty to the crown… and to me. You will see I have grown and seen and studied much in Sanguinia."

The mountain groaned beneath their feet, and his father's voice added to the aches of the mountain. "I believe you have grown much, but it seems you are still the same boy I sent away all that time ago. Has Wulford taught you nothing? Or the hardships of the road?"

"The road has taught me much, Father. I studied among the best artists and was entertained among the best playwrights. I speak the languages of Sanguinia fluently and have trained in the warrior's way. With a bow and arrow, or even the pistol, I can show you my ascent into manhood..."

A cough from the shadows interrupted him. Warwick cocked his head as if mistaking the sound for the wind, before a figure emerged from the shadow of the throne, one hand resting on the hilt of a sheathed sword.

Warwick's chest tightened. "B-brother?"

The man who stood before him could not possibly be his twin. Lysander, who had once been his lesser, now looked down on him, a full two, perhaps three inches taller. His frame had thickened with muscle, his arms and legs solid beneath a fur-lined tunic that seemed almost rustic yet dignified. Dark stubble shadowed his square jaw, and his brown hair fell artfully across his face, casting half his expression in shadow.

The man gave a slight bow, as custom required of those standing before the heir-to-be, but there was a glint of amusement in his eyes. Warwick scoffed, taking a step back, eyes widening.

This cannot be my twin. He struggled for words. "Lysander? Truly?"

"The northern climate and diet has been good to me." Lysander smiled. He slapped his flat stomach for good measure, finally releasing his hand from his sheathed sword. "And Big Wick, I see the Sanguinia courts have been good to you."

Warwick's cheeks burned bright red. He reached up and plucked at the collar of his costume, the fabric suddenly too tight. "Yes, indeed, Sanguinia was very good to me. I studied and feasted and jousted with the best of the realm..." But his words faltered as if struck by a northern blizzard, the chill of doubt settling inside him. "Yet it was Grandma'am who was the highlight of my travels. She bestowed upon me our family crown, no less—her grief was immense... I only wish you could have been there with us."

Lysander's expression softened slightly. "I trust Grandma'am is well. I sent a carrier pigeon with my condolences some time ago." He shifted slightly on his feet, expression unreadable. "Though forgive me, Brother. I've seen much and heard more on my journey through the north. With the death of our uncle, I knew I had to return to court immediately. There is much you don't know."

Another slap, another gut punch. How tired he was growing of his family accusing him of not jousting when every family conversation was combat. "Then it is your duty, as a loyal servant of the realm, to inform your crown prince of all that transpires." Warwick's tongue flicked, joining the howling of the wind as his shoulders drooped under the weight of the throne's shadow. "How else am I to rule as emperor..."

Warwick's voice trailed off as his hand moved to his brow, steadying himself as if struck by some sudden revelation. He looked again at Lysander's poised hand, resting firmly on the hilt of his sword.

"Empyrean Flame."

Lysander drew the sword from its sheath and stepped forward. He lifted Empyrean Flame into the air, catching the dim light of the outside world. Even among the dreariness of the throne room, the sword seemed to shimmer.

"Y-you have bestowed the family sword... to him? Before I even arrived."

A heavy sigh came from his father. "My son, my heir-to-be, I am glad you have returned, but you must understand the precarious standing of our family. Like this castle, teetering on the edge of Mount Ness, so too does our power... and inheritance. Your uncle, and my dear brother, has fallen in battle, and to the heathens no less..." He gripped his chest and gave a pained moan. "And despite his sacrifice, it seems we are still to lose territory on the Isle of Fláimir. Never before has our family suffered such a loss. We have maintained the crown only through the perception of strength and the blessing of the one true God. And now… Warwick…" His father moaned.

"Yes, Father," he whispered back.

"Look upon my crown."

From the edge of the Opal Throne, his father gripped the armrests, pushing himself forward with effort. Lysander lowered his sword and moved toward the marble throne, but his father waved him off weakly, sinking deeper into his seat. At that moment, the Crown of the Nine, the true symbol of imperial power, emerged from the shadows, its gleaming form catching the dim light and scattering it into a rainbow of colors.

Warwick's heart leaped. His gaze locked onto the crown, his inheritance. At its center, nestled within the gold, lay a ruby of immense size, its crimson glow pulsing like a living flame. The legend of the gem was known to all. Said to have been taken from the prophet Aethylios himself, blessed, and given to charity. Over time, it had become the sacred emblem of House Hieronymus, the imperial house that had ruled for five generations.

Yet, the ruby was not the only gem that adorned the crown. Woven into its ornate framework, eight other stones gleamed, each representing one of the electoral houses. A sapphire, deep as the sea, for House Fontaine, masters of the trade routes. An emerald, as green as spring, for House Esmerelda, the masters of fruits and luxuries. A diamond, clear and resolute, for House Faelwood, the heart of the empire and home to the Kaesnfolk. Other stones sparkled alongside them, but Warwick's gaze drifted upward. He looked to the very apex of the crown, and there, rising from the arched rim, sculpted like a gilded flower, burned a golden flame, its tip shaped like a candle's blaze. It was a tribute to the prophet Aethylios and his Nine Miracles. A reminder, both to the ruler who would wear it and the Electors who chose him, that dominion was not simply a matter of politics or power, but of fate, will, and divine right.

"This is the Crown of the Nine," his father affirmed. "And one day, Aethylios willing, it will fall to you, Warwick. Yet, I cannot guarantee it. The family Crown of Knox rests upon your head. That is your birthright. But we live in an empire of powerful vassals, of cities and lords with deep alliances and ambitions, all of whom vote for the one who wears this crown. For five generations, our family has held it." His voice faltered. "I pray I will not be the last."

"Yes, Father." Warwick bowed out of respect for his father. *He is aged—he is not the strong man I remember.* Warwick rose, looking upon the limp form of his father, seemingly dangling from the throne's edge, to the crown, and then at last to Lysander, still clutching the unsheathed sword.

"… But as heir, am I not entitled to all our family's possessions?" He took a measured step toward Lysander. "Though I am confident the south will support my ascension, if our family's position is as fragile as you say, then should I not be the very symbol of strength the realm demands?"

A scoff escaped from Lysander, but he caught himself, and immediately stepped back into the shadow of the throne, sheathing the sword. Above them, their father sighed.

"Our founder—my great-great-grandfather—bore three sons. An eldest male heir and a pair of twin boys. Ah, a pair of second sons! What a curse from the gods." Father shook his head. "We descend from the eldest, a clear heir. But what did my great-great-grandfather do with two second sons? He thought himself wise marrying them off to minor families, yes, but those with vast resources."

"The Rose Monts and the Goldwoods." Lysander nodded.

"And for generations they have plotted against us. Now within our weakest hour, they come to court to pay homage to my brother, and to plot and scheme."

"Then let us meet them as a united front. Bestow the family

sword upon me. Let the court see their future emperor with all the symbols of his birthright, his strength."

Father sighed again, followed by a deep cough. "My good son, that would be an unwise decision."

Warwick huffed this time, his hands balling into tight fists. "I have done more for this family than you know! You speak of divides, I speak of bridges. With the south, and our cousins. Don't name me to be so lame!"

Father rose from the throne. He took a step down, slowly descending the white marble steps until he came but an inch from Warwick. Now, face-to-face, father and son, emperor and heir, boy and man.

"Sit on the throne."

"Father?"

"Your emperor commands it. Sit. On. The. Throne."

Warwick looked upon his father—the deep-set bags under his eyes and the lines carved into his face. More than a year had elapsed since they last met, and where before Warwick looked up to his father, now they stood on equal footing, as his father's shoulders began to slope, and he swayed faintly on his feet, as if weary.

Warwick broke his stare from his father, turning to the throne, and with a deep breath, climbed the first marble stair. He rose above his father. He rose above his brother. The marble throne seemed to glow in the dim light, hurting his eyes like the shine of fresh snow upon the field. He mounted all nine steps, his gaze shifting between the throne's gleaming surface and the golden bands arching above like the pipes of a towering organ. Slowly, he turned, looking from the gold and marble upon his audience chamber. The massive columns appeared shorter, as if he could glimpse the top of an ancient forest, and he gained clarity over the terrain. Below him, Lysander took his place by his father's side, and together they bowed. Warwick took his seat, finding the throne so cold and hard it snatched his breath away. He struggled to find his words until a cool breeze whispered to him, drifting downward from the dark ceiling above.

"You may rise," he commanded.

And so his father and brother lifted from their bow. Lysander struggled to meet his eye, but his father's brow narrowed and he met his eyes with intent. "Will the prince be counseled? Will he hear the good advice of his court?"

Warwick stiffened his back and placed firm hands upon the cold marble armrests of the throne. "The prince cherishes the advice his councilors bring. Do not hold your tongue; speak your wisdom before the future emperor."

"The family sword is not fit for you. My father, your late grandsire, made the same decision for me. I bore the family crown, and my brother bore the family sword. I ruled from the throne, and he led the realm's campaigns. A good ruler knows his strengths, but a better ruler knows the strengths of his realm. Lysander is fit to wield the sword, and by the Nine, he shall swear it to you, carrying the strength of our armies into battle."

"Aye, Brother," Lysander said, stepping forward, his hand resting on the hilt of Empyrean Flame. "I will be your sword. I shall brandish it in your name."

Warwick looked away from them, staring dead ahead to the far end of the chamber as the wind howled through it. An echo from deep within the mountain gave his heart a jump, and he shivered. "Very well, I understand the nature of our family. Lysander shall bear the family sword and be a champion for both myself and the crown. Though I should request, as the heir proclaimed and future head of our house, such decisions are shared with me in advance."

A moment of silence stretched as Lysander shifted, mouth opening to speak, but a slight flick of their father's hand silenced him. Warwick noted all of this.

"How my heart is relieved, my son, to see the weight of the crown comes naturally to you. A fine request, a *reasonable* request," his father stressed. "that the heir to the throne is knowledgeable of the family workings. Yes, you shall inherit the throne, the family crown, and the ancestral family home of Knoxford. As your grandsire arranged, I and my brother each inherited our own legacies, so too shall you and Lysander. Lysander will hold the family sword and, as is proper, inherit the seat at Aberness. Thus, the unity of our house is ensured."

A tremor rippled through the Hearth and Warwick felt it pulse through the marble beneath him as a boulder crashed into the valley below. His heart leaped to his throat. "Wait... Lysander is to inherit the city of Aberness?"

"Aye, and to seal the bonds of union between my brother's family and our own, he shall be betrothed to your first cousin, the Lady Catelyn."

"I shall take her to wife, and together we will forge a lineage that will command the respect and fear of the realm. The Electors will see the power of our house united."

Warwick broke into a tremor, feeling the mountain move beneath him. The words formed on his lips, the desire to share the news of his conversation with his good aunt—of his confirmation of Derrick's inheritance of Aberness, but the news of Catelyn shattered his heart.

He drew in a breath, desperate to speak, to reclaim the blade and the hand of the woman he loved, but words failed him. His body sank into the throne, powerless.

Could anyone be more pathetic than me?

JOSEPHINA I

Josephina stumbled from the woods with a bundle of firewood in her arms. She stepped into the clearing of her homestead, a cold wind sweeping downward from the surrounding snowcapped mountains. The chill sent a shiver down her back, but it was the sight of her mother in the yard that froze her to the bone.

She halted abruptly, dropping a few logs into the freshly fallen snow.

"Curses." She quickly bent over to pick them up. If the logs became damp, Mother would have a fit.

But Mother is always having a fit. The thought flew into her head. *Oh, please be kind today!*

Before her, Mother stood as a crooked scarecrow in a field of snow. She wore only a black cloak, removing any trace of her human shape. Josephina bit her lip and forced herself forward, her stomach sinking. She detested it when Mother behaved this way. She had vivid thoughts of her childhood, of Mother standing this way in the moonlight, sometimes not speaking for hours, or at worst, for days.

Josephina inched forward. She stepped uneasily over flower beds and unplowed fields buried beneath her in the snow. In the spring, the fields would explode with a variety of fruits and vegetables, and Mother would come home with strangers, men and women with vacant eyes, their pupils faded to white, who mumbled incoherently as they tended the fields. Josephina would be locked away in the house, permitted only to leave at night to tend to her chores. The strangers, Mother's guests, would be locked in the barn.

She shivered at the memory, pulling her cloak tighter. *At least for now it will just be Mother and I,* she thought. *No strangers. No scary knights with swords. No monsters from the woods.*

Mother's body jerked. Josephina froze again.

Mother stood with her back crooked, arms positioned broken and bent into the air. Her mouth hung open and she stared absentmindedly up into the white sky above. Josephina gulped.

I should go around.

She turned to go around Mother, sidestepping her to reach the back of the house, when an explosion of caws erupted from the forest. Josephina whipped around, eyes wide. A dark mass of birds erupted from the treetops, a black cloud swirling above the bare branches, their wings even darker than the forest floor.

Heart pounding, she forced her legs to move, kicking through the snow. She dropped a log, and then two, as she did her best to break into a run. Yet her stubby legs failed to gain clearance over the snow. She fell, face-planting, her logs spilling everywhere.

She looked up, face coated in snow, gasping as a flock of crows swarmed the homestead. "No! Shoo! Shoo!" she cried. Many landed next to her, staring with their beady eyes, cawing incessantly. Tears filled her eyes. "Go! Get away from me!"

She broke into a sob, pulling herself into a ball in the snow. The crows cawed and screamed. Wings fluttered all around her. She thought she heard something crash in the woods. She closed her eyes and hugged her knees, and when she opened them again, a dark shadow stood over her, a crow perched on her head, left shoulder, and right hand.

"Josephina," it said.

"Mother."

"Just what on this Hearth are you doing down there?"

"I saw the birds. I thought they were mad at me."

"Mad at you? And why would they be mad at you, silly girl?"

"I..." She looked away from the shadow. "I wanted to go away so they would talk to you and not me."

"Hmm," the shadow said. "Well you were very wise to think so."

Two white hands emerged from the shadow as it tossed back the top of the black cloak. Josephina looked upon her mother's face, trembling. Her mother's dark hair, peppered with gray, hung down upon her sunken face. Her nose, thin and entirely too small, burned red in the cold air. And her eyes, one iris green, the other black and twice as large, stared down at her. Josephina knew better than to look away. She was ugly too—as mother loved to remind her, but Mother was far more self-conscious.

"I'm sorry, Mother."

"Sorry? Ah my dear, there is nothing to be sorry for!"

Her mother extended a pale hand. She reached out with trembling fingers and let herself be pulled to her feet. The crow perched on her mother's head cawed at her—midnight black except for a single white feather in its coat. A smile spread across Mother's thin, cracked lips.

"I am sorry, Mother. I am so very sorry."

"Stop it, Daughter. There is no need to apologize. For everything has gone according to plan. My little friends here bring great news. Oléfur is on his way back."

Ice cracked on a distant mountainside. An icicle broke from the roof.

"*No.*"

"Yes, and he will be here sooner than we know it!"

Josephina looked away from her mother. Tears came back to her eyes. She started to breathe fast and heavy. It was suddenly too hot.

"Josephina, darling, what is the matter with you? I swear you are such an awkward little girl. Every time a stranger or friend comes around our farm, you have to go and get the heebie-jeebies, *as ugly as you are*." She sighed. "Just what am I going to do with you?"

"I'm… sorry… Mother…" she said through tears.

The crow on her mother's shoulder cawed three times and Mother smiled. "They are excited. Why can't you be?"

Josephina only cried.

"Well then, if you're going to have a fit about it, then perhaps you can make it up to me. Go into the woods to Oléfur's hut. Ensure that it is cleaned and entirely up to his liking. Stock it with fresh firewood." Mother looked down upon the scattered logs. "Return home when you are done. We'll need to make preparations."

Josephina cried more.

"Josephina." Her mother's voice grew dark.

She looked upon her face, grateful the tears half blinded her. "Y-yes, Mother," she answered.

"You need to behave."

"But… is he going to take from me again?" The words spilled from her lips before she could stop them. A bitter wind swept down from the mountains.

"I am sure he will demand payment, but if you are a good girl, and do as I ask, I am sure he will make it less painful this time."

A long sob broke from her throat.

"Josephina! Stop this at once. We all make sacrifices in one form or another. It isn't easy hiding you from the world and keeping those self-righteous knights at bay, but hear me, daughter of mine." Mother leaned in close and placed her fingers below her chin. "All of that is about to change. I'll make you a princess!"

Josephina blinked heavily. "I can't be a princess! I am a monster."

"You're not a monster, Josephina, just horribly malformed. And that won't even matter when Oléfur returns. We'll finally have a power over these lands so that no prince could ever deny your hand! Wouldn't you like that? To marry a handsome prince?"

Josephina sniffled but nodded.

"Then, silly girl, *why* are you just standing here and not getting to work?" Mother slapped the side of her head. The crows exploded from her body, followed quickly by the whole swarm.

"Yes, Mother." She wiped the snot from her nose and stumbled past Mother, heading back for the woods.

"Faster!" She heard her mother call from behind. "Faster! You must work faster!"

The swarm of crows joined her mother's screams.

She ran through the snow, the sound of her mother and the crows growing louder and louder in her ears, until she broke through the tree line and tripped over an exposed root. She hit the frozen ground with a thud, knocking the wind from her. She rolled onto her back, panting, sucking in cold air, and thrust her arms in front of her face. She screamed, expecting the swarm of crows to attack her, but they never came. Slowly, she lowered her arms, staring upward at the bare branches crisscrossing the sky. White fluffy snow clouds were slowly giving way to darker gray clouds. The forest darkened around her.

She crawled onto her knees and hacked up some spittle. She gave herself a moment to catch her breath and rose to her feet, finding the forest quiet and still. Snow littered the ground but only in light drifts. Dark patches of frozen soil peered out from around gnarled tree roots. She found the path easygoing.

Oléfur stayed in a small house not far from the homestead. Normally, she did everything in her power to avoid this part of the forest. The trees were older, ancient, and mangled. Trinkets hung from dark branches, twirling from hair and twine. The ground rose and the trees caught more wind here. The forest whispered with voices. Darkness lurked behind every tree, and Josephina could never shake the feeling that something was watching her, even when Oléfur was away. Here his hut nestled at the base of a massive tree, its hollow trunk transformed into his home. A thatched roof covered the entry, and a single glass window stared out, speaking of only darkness within. The red door, worn and weathered by ice and snow, stood crooked against a white snowbank. Arriving, Josephina sighed and bit her lip. She would set to her work and be quick about it.

She dropped to her knees, shoveling away snow from the entrance, ignoring the trinkets swaying above her and the strange symbols carved into the ancient wood. Once the door was cleared, she knocked. No answer.

Hesitant, she knocked again and pressed her ear to the door. Only the rustling of nearby trees answered her.

She gulped, pinching the doorknob with her pointer finger and thumb. The door slid open with a creak and she poked her head inside.

Quiet and still.

She wormed her way inside. She was only twelve, yet she could hardly fit. The hut fit an elf comfortably, but as a human, she had to pull her knees to her chest to sit comfortably in the center. She took a moment to let her eyes adjust to the darkness and took a look around. A fireplace hissed quietly with the passing of the wind against the chimney. In the corner, a small bed was tucked away, adorned with two feather pillows no bigger than her palm. A desk with a quail feather and thimble of ink stood next to the window. Dry herbs knocked against her head from above. She breathed out, finding herself completely alone.

She took to her work. First, she fluffed the blankets and pillows on Oléfur's bed, pleased to find no spiders or critters lurking between the sheets. Next, she wiped the glass window with her mitten, carefully clearing away dust, snow, and grime. Shuffling halfway out the front door so her legs rested in the

142

snow, she straightened a small dining table, arranging the tiny silverware just as she did at home. Finally, she picked up an armchair no larger than her head and set it beside the empty fireplace. Taking a moment, she admired her handiwork.

No way Oléfur will be mad. I have done a good job.

But a snap in the woods sent her head banging into the roof of the hut. Her hand instinctively shot to her head, knocking over the dining table.

"Curses!" she screamed. She frantically put everything back into place and threw herself out into the snow. She looked wildly around but saw nothing between the darkness of the trees. Quickly, she scrambled to her feet.

"Firewood!" She darted around the base of the tree, scooping up small twigs scattered across the forest floor. Her hands moved quickly as she circled the massive trunk, gathering kindling, until her foot suddenly plunged into a hidden hollow. She pitched backward with a startled cry, yanking her foot free—and a small, yellowed bone tumbled out with it, clattering against the roots.

She stared at it, panting. A crow flew overhead. With a trembling hand, she picked it up, dangling it in front of her as she approached the hole. Holding her breath, she lowered her hand into the darkness, carefully placing the bone back where she found it. Glancing inside, she spotted countless more bones, some animal, some...

She shook her head and dropped the bone. She scrambled backward, kicking as much snow into the hole as she could.

He won't notice. He won't care.

But did she believe that? She snatched up all the dropped twigs and forced her way back into the hut. She intricately placed the twigs into Oléfur's fireplace, tears streaming down her cheeks. The twigs wouldn't stand the way she wanted and she knocked the table over again by mistake. Her body wouldn't listen to her. She couldn't stop shaking.

Frustrated, she flipped the table back upright and repositioned the tiny silverware for the third time before rolling out into the snow. She gently closed his door and shot to her feet, but in her haste, she smacked into a hanging wooden trinket. It exploded into a mess of pieces.

"Curses! Curses to all!" she screeched, gathering the broken pieces and yanking the string from the branch above. Without a second thought, she broke into a run, not stopping until she reached the homestead.

She came barreling from the forest but stopped only when she remembered she needed firewood for Mother as well. She snatched a few branches from the edge of the forest and returned to a run, her lungs and legs screaming, then burst into their house. The ground floor of their home only had two rooms: the parlor and the kitchen. She entered the parlor, where a fire had shrunk pitifully small. She threw in the logs, including the broken remains of Oléfur's trinket, and turned wide-eyed to the kitchen. She could hear Mother gently singing to herself from inside. Her shadow danced in the doorway, churning something in a great pot. Josephina bit her lip but considered herself lucky. Mother was working.

At the center of the home, an ancient tree trunk rose upward, supporting the house and dividing the kitchen from the parlor. A rickety wooden staircase snaked its way upward around it, disappearing into a dark hole above the kitchen. Josephina ran toward it, neglecting to take off her wet galoshes, and pounded up upstairs. She ascended to the second floor—*Mother's room*—and dashed through it. She ignored the empty cauldrons and stacks of forbidden books. She ran for a crude wooden ladder next and climbed. She pushed open a trapdoor and slid into the attic. *Her room.*

She broke into fresh tears. Her room, the top of the home, burned warm, but she shivered all the same. She lit a candle, undressing from her cold and wet clothes, and wished desperately to crawl into her warm and safe bed. She needed to dry before she could though, so she turned to a window overlooking their farm. Her footprints were visible in the yard. Her thick forehead, dull eyes, untamed black hair, and pudgy nose stared back at her, taunting her...

He knows. He knows what I did.

She tore herself from the window, shaking.

I did a bad job. I always do a bad job!

She could feel the gaze of the forest on her back. Night would fall soon. She didn't like the woods at night. She didn't like what watched from the dark.

She dove into bed, pulling the covers over her head, and found her only comfort in the whole wide world: a mangled lump of stuffed cloth she had sewn herself as a young girl. With two heads and just three buttons for eyes, he was a peculiar companion, complete with a claw for a hand and a stubby left foot. Mishie was, in truth, little more than a tattered piece of fabric that barely resembled anything human. A broken creation from a broken creature.

"Did I do a good job? Do you think so, Mishie?" she whispered to him.

Mishie, unlike Mother, unlike Oléfur, unlike the world, embraced her. She held him tight, feeling his warmth again.

BANCROFT I

She stood with her back to him, fingers tracing over the porcelain with a light touch. "My dearest," she said quietly, and in turn, the cruel world answered with a flash of light. The urn glowed for the briefest of moments, life momentarily given to their dead child, only to be snatched away again. A thunderclap followed so that not even her sweet hymn could be heard.

"My love?" his voice came gentle from behind her.

She jolted in surprise, turning to look upon him. He stood at the far wall at the entry to the sitting room, nestled between the two wings of their separate bedchambers. "My liege," she replied through a lump in her throat.

"You don't have to call me that... you of all people, not here."

She lowered her head, her fingers fumbling with the diamond necklace at her throat. Tears pooled in her eyes. "I'm sorry... I'm just... reminded of failed duty."

Another lightning strike bathed the room in a flash of light. Their castle turret stood so high in the air, nestled among the mountain, the clouds swirled against their window, casting untold shadows, some real, others false, against the walls. Bancroft rubbed his eyes, stunned by the flash, chilled by the sight of his wife, pale as porcelain, standing at the far end of the room.

"You have failed no duty. You have served me and the realm beyond faithfully."

A small sniffle escaped her, followed by the sharp, steady rhythm of rain against the windows.

"You have been a terrific mother. To my boys, and the realm. Please, my wife, do not dwell on what could have been. It will only lead to more sorrow, and the Nine know there is enough sorrow in the world." This time his voice wavered, nearly breaking like the creak of the tower against the wind. His knees wobbled and his chest felt full to bursting.

His wife looked at him, dropping the necklace from her restless fingers. "Oh Bancroft," she whispered, and like a magnet, he was drawn to her, flying across the room and wrapping her in a tight embrace, followed by a series of wet kisses.

"You will tell me, yes, my love, if I have been a bad wife?" she said at long last, only when the kisses stopped, and the roll of thunder pulled them from their wet embrace.

"An emperor could ask for no better wife." He held her tight.

She closed her eyes and leaned against his chest. When she opened them, a flash of lightning again illuminated the room, and not one but three porcelain urns glowed from their resting place.

"Oh Bancroft!" she squealed, again burying her face in his chest. "It is so hard! To look upon them and think what could have been. What lives they might be living! Would they like art? Or ballroom dancing? Or would they be swift with the sword, eager to cut down our enemies!"

"Hush, my good woman, for you will drive yourself to madness, wondering. There will come a day, yes, when we are joined with them, but I pray to Aethylios that day is long off."

Her fingers clutched the fabric of his tunic, her voice trembling as she spoke again. "Your heart beats so fiercely, my love. What troubles you? Is it your suppressed tongue, wishing to lash out at the Nine for taking our children?"

The wind beat hard against the windows, and Bancroft swayed—or was it the tower that leaned? He cursed inwardly, his chest tight with something darker than sorrow. "I worry not for the children that never were, but for the two I have now."

"Do not say such things!" She hit his chest, rearing up to look at him. "Do not say they never were!"

"I do not have it in my heart to worry for five children, when two already threaten my well-being!" Bancroft cursed and spun away from his wife. "What hope did I have in sending them to opposite ends of the realm to build unity for the crown?"

"Nothing has gone awry, love, the children do not quarrel…"

"It is not the children I am worried for, Nine be damned!"

"Bancroft!"

"It is a curse I say upon our house! What ruler desires male twins? It takes but only a whisper to send the realm to chaos! Aye, look upon the founder. Three boys, two born as twins after the eldest, and the realm suffers still a century later."

"Look upon the boys we have raised, Husband. Tell me, truly, do you see it in their hearts, they would mean to tear the realm apart? Or would succumb to others who would? They are bonded, inseparable…"

"Maybe for a time, aye, I would agree with you. But I in my pride and cunning pulled them apart, flinging them to opposite ends of the continent. Warwick the sensitive, I thought he would find common ground among the artisan princes of Sanguinia, and Lysander, more abrasive, eager to fend for his brother, a natural fit for the north."

"It was a good tour. You have heard how the lords speak!"

"An emperor hears how they speak, aye. With the courtesies and courtly processions, it would be treason to say otherwise. Don't lie to me, you know the castle is large and the court eager to whisper. You have heard the true tellings… Warwick the fool, the glutton, the showboat. Oh, how he arrived to me, dressed like a jester ready to pop!"

"The fashion senses of Sanguinia are queer to us, aye, I do not deny this…"

"It is not fashion, my dearest, dearest wife." He turned back to her. They were only an arm's length apart, but all of the realm may have well stood between them. "It is the whispers… the mere idea of a *better choice*."

"Warwick is your firstborn. He is a male. He bears your family's crown. There is no other choice. You have proclaimed it. Never mind Lysander's premature arrival—he was only worried for you."

"And in Warwick's absence, I awarded him the family sword. Both of us weakened his claim, whether we intended to or not."

"You are the emperor. Take back the sword if you must or proclaim him your heir-apparent yet again. Your word is law. Do not present it as a choice."

"The realm is held together only by the idea of choice. The Electors will make the final decision, not me, not a hundred oaths. Oh!" Bancroft wavered on his feet.

Melinda scrambled, fetching a wooden chair and quickly placing it behind him. "Sit! Sit, my husband! You must rest. You worry yourself sick!"

Bancroft allowed himself to sit, resting his head in his hands. Melinda squatted beside him. "I would be a terrible emperor if I did not worry so," he muttered, his words muffled by his hands. "The whispers of Warwick's ascension have grown into shouts with my brother's death. And what of me? Given no time to grieve. This is the weight of my crown."

"Then grieve now, husband! Grieve here and now within the safety of our chambers."

"I cannot grieve my brother without suffering the consequences of his death. Elizabeth sits in this very castle, and yet we have not spoken privately. My condolences go unsaid, as do my intentions to pass the claim of Aberness onto my own son, not Derrick."

"You are the emperor, Bancroft. She must listen," Melinda

replied, her voice steady. "And if it eases your burden, I can speak to her as a woman. Let me formally propose the betrothal of Catelyn to Lysander."

Bancroft let out a long sigh. "Its more than just Catelyn's betrothal. I... I just cannot send Lysander off to war. To lose another so dear to me. The Isle is a curse, and yet one we cannot lose. Derrick is some much like his father, my brother... he would be better fit for war. And that, I'm afraid, would destroy all semblance of family unity. "

"You do not need family unity," Melinda countered. "At least, not at the cost of putting too much weight on Elizabeth's thoughts and feelings. Our household is but one of the nine votes to become emperor. In the end, Elizabeth will have no say in the vote. And husband, blessed be the Nine Miracles, there will be plenty of time to smooth over the difficulties of inheritance."

Bancroft listened to his wife, but ultimately shook his head, dismissing her claims. "Our lineage knows better than anyone the importance of family unity. I lost my grandfather in the Diet of Blood, and the toll it took on my father..." He sighed again, his shoulders slumping as he let his head drop freely. His body folded in on itself, as though the weight of his thoughts had become too much to bear.

Melinda crouched beside him and kissed him upon the cheek before moving to a nearby serving dish left by a servant and pouring a glass of wine. The sudden flash of lightning startled her, momentarily blinding her as she turned back. She stumbled, nearly tripping over a footstool, and shadows darted along the chamber walls.

"Drink," she said, returning to him. She held the glass under his nose.

"You would have me turn to drink?"

"I would have you turn back to happiness, or at least for the moment, aloofness."

"Aloofness would be the death of us."

"Take a drink and see."

Bancroft slowly lifted his head, taking the goblet of wine. He gave a silent toast to his wife and took a swig of the nectar. He let the tart sensation rest on his tongue. It helped, if only a little.

"If only I had been born the second son, then I could go off to war, and my enemies would be clear and clean-cut. I could swing my ax by day and drink my fill by night," he said with a great heaviness in his voice, but Melinda snorted, before breaking into full-blown laughter. He turned to her, a twinkle in his eye. "Are my desires and weariness so funny?"

"Husband, I have seen you with an ax. It is truly outstanding that you do not carry the title of drunk already—the way you flail and stumble on your feet!"

Bancroft smiled, snorting himself, and took another swig of the wine. "Perhaps that is my problem then—a curse passed to Warwick. A father and son doomed to fail at the sword."

"You wear the sword well," Melinda replied, her tone teasing but affectionate. "And I daresay that's all that matters. Better you give the impression of a knight than a tyrant. Perhaps that's all Warwick needs as well."

"I gave him a personal knight to oversee his training," he reminded her.

"From a lesser house in Esteria of all places! Wulford and his brother do not possess the training of the Demonbreun. You should have known how Strammond and his knights would feel. They have always been our protector."

"Yes precisely, and so I was hoping both boys could learn a little bit of ruggedness while securing our border holdings with Krithinia. Aye, I did," Bancroft moaned. "and with my gamble I nearly lost the allegiance of the Demonbreun."

"Don't give yourself to doubt," Melinda said softly. "The realm adores you. And so does Strammond."

His wife's assurances did little to ease his burden. He sat beside his wife, staring into the shifting shadows, words trapped somewhere between his throat and the wine's creeping numbness. Outside the castle walls, the storm raged on.

Melinda's fingers found their way through his thinning hair, a gentle touch before she broke the silence. "Winter retreats at last," she said softly, as thunder rumbled overhead. "The first spring storm has come upon us—a time for renewal and warmth. A good omen, if I have ever seen one."

"You should know better. The Nine Miracles, the Five Warriors of the East, the… *whatever*, how fickle God seems to be. How many ways can an omen cut? See what the lords of the realm say as they descend upon us like butterflies drawn to the blossom, only to find the spider disguised within the petal. Spring is the time for roots to take hold. A time for life, aye, but also a fight for life."

"The seed is spread in the fall, not the spring, my husband. You did your job a season ago. Now it is time to tend to your flowers and nourish them as they sprout. Let us go to our boys and nurture the vine of our family."

Bancroft snorted again, shaking his head. "You will find the family vine tangled and unruly. Perhaps I should add a master gardener to my court."

Melinda rose from her chair, standing before her husband. "This isn't about Lysander and Warwick. This is about the Rose Monts and Goldwoods."

"Aye, ever it is so. They come to court, eager to sow their seeds of distrust and jealousy."

"By your own words, they have planted nothing. Neither side of the family possesses a vote for the emperor. We can blunt them at court and dispatch them as necessary. The bond between brothers is strong, do not let your mind turn to flights of fancy on dying branches of the family tree."

"I wish I held your optimism."

"Bancroft." She took a gentle hold of his jaw. She raised his head, forcing him to look upon her. Quickly, he set down his goblet of wine and rose, brushing past her bosom, feeling the wine, and more, take hold of him. "You are my source of optimism. Fate has been cruel to me. I have lost three children in the cradle or to miscarriage. It has only been you, and those boys who have accepted me as their mother, who have given me any joy in this world."

"Fate is cruel to us all, my love. The boys and I have loved you since the beginning, and you have been the only mother they have known since their own passed in birth. Perhaps we should take greater counsel in one another, for we both have suffered, and our optimism stems from only one another..."

The passion of the wine, and the moment, could no longer be ignored. Bancroft took her then, right there, lying on the floor. Their union was quick but no less passionate, and their shouts rang out so loudly that not even the distant rumblings of thunder could mask them. When it was over, Bancroft rolled onto his back, panting, his body slick with sweat.

"I should give you more wine in the future." Melinda panted, giggling to herself.

"Perhaps you will bear fruit for me now?" He lay next to her, taking her hand.

"Oh love, I am much too old now, and my body has already produced disappointments."

"Dearest, do not such say things!"

Melinda sat up, her expression soft but firm. "We shouldn't cling to false hopes, Bancroft. Instead, we should embrace what we have. And what we have are two handsome, eager young boys, probably cross with our tardiness on this most holy of days."

Bancroft grumbled, slowly rising from the floor. "Oh, the Equinox—the first day of spring. I can only imagine how Warwick must feel, starving for his dinner."

The two broke into fresh laughter. Bancroft helped his wife fully rise and allowed her to freshen herself, and together, arm in arm, they walked from their bedchamber, descending a few floors to the family's private dining hall. Here they found Lysander and Warwick waiting. True to his character, Warwick was standing with his arms crossed, scowling as he muttered to himself that the main course had yet to be served. Melinda and Bancroft smiled to one another, laughing quietly to themselves, and joined the boys for a meal.

They were served a main course of roasted duck and seasoned vegetables, and through playfully tossed peas and carrots, growing outlandish tall tales of the boys' trips through
the realm were told. Wine was poured, though the boys were
allowed only ceremonial sips, which did little to dampen their
moods. For the first time in over a year, Bancroft sat with his
children and second wife, his heart swelling with laughter
and love.

Leawyn III

The forest reeked of death.

Spring was fast approaching, but the trees gave no sign of life. Their gnarled branches stretched overhead into a dense, lifeless canopy. Leawyn walked beneath this roof of decay, careful to watch her footing. Thick roots crisscrossed her path, twisting like grasping fingers, making each step a battle. Age had stolen the swiftness from her limbs, and the cold gnawed at her joints, biting at her fingers, knees, and elbows, until every movement became an ache.

She had no guide save instinct. Even the moon had abandoned her, blackened by its waning cycle and offering no light. Only the stars offered their distant glow, faint and uncaring. She navigated purely by intuition, allowing the forest to shape her path. The gnarled trees and dense, dead brush underfoot gradually gave way to soft, gooey ground. The Hearth itself seemed to call for her, grabbing at her feet so that the mud sucked at her boots with each step. From here, the trees became sparser and the canopy of branches overhead lessened to reveal large patches of dark sky. She spotted a dark bird in the sky, the only other life she came across.

Her knees began to buckle as the soil dissolved into patches of standing water, then stretches of gurgling bog. She watched her footing carefully, knowing one false step would send her under permanently, until the day came she would be called to rise again. Above, a lone crow wheeled through the darkness and gave a single, distant caw.

But this was not the song of the land. No, the true voice of the Hearth lay beneath her feet, rising in putrid whispers, bubbles that broke the black water's surface, carrying omens from the depths.

Is this where my boy lies?

She halted in a clearing, the bogs gurgling around her like creatures stirring in their sleep. The air was thick with rot. Her stomach twisted at the stench, the sharp tang of decay slithering down her spine like cold fingers. *My boy rests,* she told herself. *It cannot be him.*

She pressed on until she found the source of the rot.

A hundred bodies from the previous night's battle, draped in furs and cloth, laid out to be offered to the preserving waters. Blood and pus and other foul substances oozed from beneath their coverings. She dropped to her knees, retching upon the soil, and desperate for air, she inhaled the stench of death.

She shrieked, giving life to the still forest, turning her throat raw as she gripped the frozen soil. Yet even in this frozen hell, a tinge of hope overcame her. An icy sweat poured from her brow as she launched herself onto her haunches, dribble oozing from her mouth as she crawled to the nearest body and ripped the covering from it.

A boy with red hair and green eyes. *Human.* An old man missing an eye. *Human.* A young woman, pierced through the neck by an arrow. *Human.*

She frowned, looking through the mass grave, searching for any sign of *them*.

Did they suffer casualties? Did they bury their dead?

She stared blankly at the field of dead before her, letting her body go numb. Only the burning heat in her lungs gave any sign she was not a ghost herself, hopelessly awaiting the day of reunion.

Reunion. The word struck her like a battle-ax to the skull.

She snatched at more blankets and furs, tearing the coverings from the dead. She worked frantically, her eyes darting across every face: boys and girls, women gashed across the face, and men... The men she paid special attention to, looking carefully at their faces in the dim light.

Red hair... He had red hair! Just like his father!

No tears came, no feeling whatsoever, except for the pounding of her heart, which she figured must be a mirage. She was trapped in purgatory, for some reason unable to rest.

I have to find him! I have to find my boy!

She searched relentlessly for her oldest. She found a boy with red hair, but when she pried open his eyes, they were blue instead of green. She found another with the same curls, but he had both his ears, and Nukhta, the name of her eldest, had his right cleaved off in battle. She tore a sheet from a body, caressing each of the bodies, searching... She would not lie down to rest until she found him.

It was a coughing fit that finally brought her back to life. It started as a heat in her lungs and brought her to her knees. She heaved onto the cold, boggy ground, sending spittle, snot, and tears across the soil.

"Damn it!" she cried aloud.

She was still alive.

When the fit passed, she forced herself back to her feet. Her legs trembled beneath her, and though her lungs still burned, her body had grown ice cold. With what little strength remained, she moved with slow, deliberate care, re-covering the bodies she had disturbed. She tucked them in once more, smoothing the furs over their still forms, preparing them for their long rest. Then she turned, hobbling blindly back into the forest. She had no destination, no path to follow—only the distant caw of a crow echoing from deep within the wood

Her pace slowed considerably. It took her well over a minute to climb over a single tree root. Her shoulders were hunched and her spine was bent. She coughed relentlessly. She continued this way, pushing deeper into the wood, knowing that if tired and wounded soldiers could drag the bodies this far, her old bones had made little progress.

She walked all night until the sun's rays peeked through the bare tree branches. Her lungs burned and her body ached and she understood it was her time to die. She found a bog, isolated by a circle of trees, and made a nest of furs beside the pool. She chose not to slip into the cold waters herself, for she prayed somebody would come across her body and perform her last rites. She closed her eyes, content to know the next time she opened them, the world would have ended, and she would be with her sons again.

When she opened her eyes, she was with them.

Her world was hazy and her chest cold. She sat up, finding herself topless, and warm mud coated her chest. She tried to rise but didn't have the strength. She gave in, resting, staring upward at the blurry glow of multicolored lights. She knew the new world had come.

Laughter bubbled in her throat, weak and breathless. She giggled, rocking herself back and forth. She rolled to her side, but before she could move farther, a hand caught her waist and held her still.

She stilled.

Her breath hitched. Slowly, she turned her gaze downward, expecting, *hoping*, to see the familiar grasp of her son, but the arm was coarse and hairy.

Her blood ran cold.

Her gaze traveled upward, and when she met the face looming over her, she screamed.

The creature stood tall over her, towering and bare-chested, covered in thick, coarse hair like that of a man's, yet below, instead of human legs, she saw those of a horse's. He bent down toward her, his face strangely human, yet his teeth, large and square like a horse's, betrayed his true nature. A scraggly brown beard adorned his chin, and messy brown hair spilled over his forehead. His ears were pointed, and his eyes... his eyes were green and welcoming, just like her son's...

"Nayhuetta kovaeysiz."

Leawyn rubbed her eyes, her mind struggling to process what she was seeing. This couldn't be real.

Her body felt heavy, and she propped herself up on her elbows, disoriented. The creature extended a hand to her once more, but she recoiled, confused and afraid.

"No, please," is all she thought to say. She tried to look around the room, but her head was swimming and her vision blurry.

"You must rest, Old Bird," the creature said, his voice ancient, foreign, and thick, yet oddly human. "You were found in the forest, close to death."

Leawyn lay back down, a tremor ripping through her. Only then did she realize that she was completely naked. A surge of embarrassment rushed through her, and she instinctively folded her arms across her breasts, consumed with the urge to cover up, though the beast above her stood naked.

"You shiver," he said. "I shall fetch you some tea."

She watched him go with suspicious eyes, spying him stop before a cauldron gurgling over a low fire. The creature poured a thick green liquid into a small cup, then made his way back to her, lowering his front horse legs as he bent down to offer the drink.

She reached out with a trembling hand and took it. "T-thank you."

"You are most welcome. It is nettle tea... great for curing whatever burns inside of you."

She hesitated for only a moment before bringing the cup to her lips. The tea burned as it slid down her throat, sharp and bitter, but the warmth spread through her body, and the tremors slowly subsided. The beast stood patiently, watching her.

When Leawyn finally felt some strength return, she sat up slowly, her gaze sweeping around the room. She found herself in a large circular hut made of wood, the roof low and flat overhead. The floors were barren, marked with scattered hoofprints. The walls, however, were adorned with a variety of trinkets and artwork. Woven mats and tapestries, crystals, rocks, and cages filled with glowing beetles that flickered in hues of red, purple, blue, and green. Despite the beast's strong scent of horse and something wild, the air was rich with the fragrance of burning herbs and incense, filling her lungs with soothing warmth.

For the first time in a long time, she felt she could breathe. A long, shuddering sigh escaped her, and the emotion she'd been holding back finally spilled over in the form of tears.

The creature's voice broke through her thoughts, soft but heavy with concern.

"Old Bird, I found you lost in the woods, so far from your kind, near a sacred pool. I thought you meant to slip under, but when I tended to your body, you rolled away in your doze. I felt compelled to bring you here. Does your song mean to continue, or have I dishonored you?"

Leawyn, naked and covered in dirt, looked upon the beast, and most peculiarly, she broke into a bit of laughter. The centaur cocked his head, ears fluttering like a faun's.

"It appears I have caused some offense. I will fetch a blade to aid in your transition into the Hearth…"

Leawyn laughed louder, her giggle rising into a mad, childlike cackle. "I've chased death for so long, only for it to slip away at every turn. And yet, when I finally set out to find you, He would come to me instead!"

The centaur's right front leg stamped the ground. "Old Bird, I am afraid I do not understand your meaning. You sought to find me? Or is it my blade you seek?"

"I seek your blade, yes, but not for me."

The centaur cocked his head as his horse tail flicked beside him. "The fever, I see, must still rage within you. I shall fetch your furs, it did not occur to me... you would not sleep on your feet. The ground must be cold for you."

Leawyn rubbed her arm as she realized just how cold she was. "Yes, that would be nice."

The centaur nodded and stepped out of the tent. Leawyn sat on the ground, staring at her wrinkled feet, a dull, burning pain creeping from the edges of her toes, like frostbite. She glanced at the fire, its warmth a small comfort, before her attention was drawn to voices drifting from outside. They spoke in a language she couldn't understand, and the unmistakable clop of hooves was impossible to miss.

A moment later, the centaur returned, a bundle of furs and her clothes in his arms. As he carefully laid them down upon the Hearth, a flash of waning light from outside caught her eye. A frown creased her brow.

"How... how long have I been out?" she asked.

"It has been a day since I brought you here," the centaur replied. He set the furs and clothes down, and Leawyn, not wanting to dress herself in the mud, scattered the furs to make a comfortable nest. The shame she once felt at her nakedness had all but disappeared. After all, it was a beast, not a human man, who stood before her.

"Has there been word of the outside world... beyond the trees?"

"You mean of your kind?"

"Yes, I suppose so."

The centaur's tail flicked whimsically as he regarded her with curiosity. "Why have you wandered so far into the woods? This is not the land of humans. We do not trespass on your cleared lands, nor fill your sacred pools with our dead."

Leawyn tilted her head, eyeing him with suspicion. "That's not true, though. The other night, your people stormed from the forest and slaughtered the Outsiders. You saved our soldiers and our camp."

"Ah," the centaur said with a low chuckle, "so that is why you have come. Well, there is no thank-you necessary. We are the offspring of this land, you and I. It is the wish of our people not to see these 'Outsiders,' as you call them, encroach deeper into our lands, cutting our trees and defiling the soil."

Leawyn's gaze hardened. "Well that is why I've come to find you. To find you... to put an end to this. The Outsiders... the death..."

The centaur snorted. "Such a thing is not possible."

"But we are of the Hearth, you said so yourself."

"Old Bird, though the snake and the lizard hunt the rat, they are not friends," he replied. "One slithers beneath the brush, the other scampers in the trees. That is how they live in harmony."

Leawyn frowned, her jaw tight. "A difference of four legs, nothing more."

The centaur snorted again, this time with a smile tugging at his lips. "Old Bird, I am merely a scout for my herd. Such a thing has never been done..."

Before Leawyn could respond, the flap of the tent suddenly whipped open. Both she and the centaur turned, their eyes meeting the imposing figure of another centaur. A larger glaring female entered, gripping a bow in one hand, an arrow in the other. She sized up Leawyn, snorted, and stepped into the hut. They spoke in their tongue, leaving her to stare, dumbfounded, at them both.

The two went back and forth, the female stamping her hooves multiple times as the younger male stood his ground. At last, the female centaur turned back to her. She had long silver hair, reminiscent of Leawyn's own, and a black-and-white fur coat covering her horse body. She snorted, wiggling her long ears.

"Our chieftess," the young male replied.

"An honor." Leawyn rose in an attempt to bow, but her head went dizzy, and she toppled over, landing on her hands and knees.

The chieftess bucked backward, snorting. She shouted in her native tongue.

"Tell her I am sorry… I'm just…" Leawyn placed a hand to her forehead. She was warm, and her stomach… *When was the last time I ate?*

The young centaur fired back in their language.

"She is angry that I interrupted your death rite," he explained to Leawyn. "She wants you returned to the sacred pool of your people, far from our lands…"

"No!" Leawyn blurted out, falling back onto her rump. She looked upon the chieftess, locking eyes with her. "I have come as a diplomat. So we can drive these Outsiders out… together."

The young male fell silent for a moment, but turned to translate her speech. The chieftess listened intently, then snorted, her stance growing even more hostile. With a sharp motion, she hoisted her large intricately carved bow, her intention clear.

"She believes your tribe will blame us for your disappearance," the young male explained. "She promises you a swift death, Old Bird, one befitting an honorable creature of this land."

The chieftess raised her bow higher, but Leawyn was quicker. "Then tell her this! How many of your kind have been dishonored in death by the Outsiders? We are all at war here. Fighting for our people, for our land. Whether you, she, or even my own people realize it, we've already worked together and achieved a victory. Tell her…"

The chieftess's expression darkened, her patience wearing thin. "I speak enough… *your* tongue!" she roared. Her bow remained raised, but her tail flicked back and forth just like the male's.

"Then hear me. I fear we have all become too comfortable with death. I alone have buried most of my family, perhaps your own people can relate. I do not wish this to continue… I do not wish…" But just as she was finding her strength, the burning in her lungs returned. She doubled over, coughing violently, as her body shook with spasms. The chieftess watched her with a cold, almost disinterested gaze before speaking again.

"A crime," the chieftess shook her head. "imagine to hunt and only wound the doe... to create suffering." She slowly sounded out the words, her cold blue eyes never leaving Leawyn. "You must finish your hunt!" With that, she bucked her legs wildly into the air, and flew from the hut.

The male centaur moved quickly, gathering herbs from various jars and packing them into mud. He heated the mixture over the fire as Leawyn continued to cough and wheeze, her body trembling. Once the mixture was warm, he gently applied it to her chest.

"Tell me..." Leawyn rasped between coughs. "am I finally to die? Or will my message be heard?"

The male frowned. "The will to live comes from deep within us... not from strangers."

"Hmph," Leawyn snorted. "Then I am Leawyn of Clan Terrwoniwyn, and you?"

The centaur only looked at her with a sad look. "I am Omnageddenon."

"Om," she said softly. "then we are well met, and no longer strangers."

But Om only shook his head. "You must heal, Old Bird, should you choose. I will return to check upon you by nightfall. If I find you cold, I will lay you to rest in your pools, as your people do."

Leawyn turned away, her eyes focusing on the thatched ceiling above. "Thank you, Omnageddenon. That will do."

JAE III

The sheen of the metal sword glistened in the hot sun.

Jae dodged right, but Luke anticipated this and swung hard with his sword. Jae's practice blade, nothing more than a slag of steel pulled from back storage, flew from his hands with a *clank*. He yelped, though he tried not to. His hands trembled from the clash of metal.

"Again," Luke commanded.

"Of course." Jae retrieved the sword, enjoying the crunch of grass beneath his feet. He had been gifted a pair of sandals to wear by his master, but when he trained in the front yard for guard duty, he preferred to go barefoot. It reminded him of his time in his homeland running barefoot through beach sand. Now lost in a new world, the grass on his bare feet was a small consolation prize.

"Don't drop it, no matter how much it stings," Pate warned.

"You'd be dead, gone to the wind, a feast for the birds, bones turned to ashes, turned to a pile of dung by a…"

"Pate, enough," Luke snapped.

Pate, another member of the household guard, leaned against a post nearby, watching with feigned interest while munching on an apple. "What?" he smirked, taking a loud, exaggerated bite. "You think in real combat you'll fight in peace and quiet? In this city, there's always an audience."

"Fair point."

Luke swung his sword hard for Jae. Jae pivoted on his feet, slipping behind Luke as the blade whistled past. Though well-fed since being purchased by the House of Aeksilor, Jae remained thin and agile. He knew better than to face Luke's brute strength head-on, so he danced around him, finding an opening. His practice sword nudged lightly against Luke's back.

"Have I won?" Jae almost allowed himself to smile.

"No," Luke whispered.

Jae leaned in, straining to hear, and that was when Luke struck—an elbow slammed into Jae's hand, followed by a swift, full-body twist. Luke's sword flashed, and Jae stumbled backward, losing his footing. Before he could recover, the tip of Luke's blade hovered inches from his neck.

Luke's eyes narrowed into a vicious glare, his brow dripping with sweat that matted his dark hair. His pale skin, unaccustomed to the searing sun of this land, was flushed a deep red, with his arms and legs baking under the relentless sun. Reluctantly, Jae met Luke's gaze and found his training master was no longer there. Instead, Luke had become someone else, his sword inching closer to Jae's throat. Luke's arm trembled, his eyes fixed on a point beyond Jae, lost to the moment, while blood still oozed from the wound the Thorned Man had left on him. His lips moved, muttering something under his breath in a language Jae didn't recognize.

"Luke, my friend, that is enough! You've nearly sliced him from ear to ear!"

Luke blinked, as if shaking off a trance. His gaze finally settled on Jae, and with a startled sigh, he lowered his sword, stepping back. "All right, that's enough for today," he muttered, pulling a handkerchief from his belt loop to dab at his forehead. Sweat drenched his brow, but Jae didn't think it was from the heat.

Jae rolled over, picking up his practice sword, and slowly raised it back to Luke. He liked the way his reflection shimmered in the steel. He decided to tease the bull. "Why didn't I win back there?"

"Excuse me?" Luke replied distantly. Nearby, Pate chuckled.

"I had the sword to your back. You should have called it," Jae pressed, pushing his luck.

Luke, drenched in sweat, looked him over. "See me well, boy," he said, breathless. "I'm wearing nothing but cloth for your training. Aeksilor, or any master worth his salt, would blindfold you and starve you for a week if you joined him on patrol with anything less than leather armor. In real combat, maybe your sword would've struck true. But if your opponent's in armor, it would've glanced off the metal, and you," he paused, jabbing a finger at Jae. "would be flat on your back like a bug, waiting for me to squash you."

Jae frowned, considering the words before shaking his head. "But you weren't wearing armor. I attacked based on the situation. Your answer is minotaur shit."

Luke stood upright and turned to stare at him with disbelief. Pate broke into hysterical laughter.

"Son, you certainly enjoy poking the bull, don't you? Well of course you do, I guess that's why you're here. Fine. We'll call it a draw if it makes you feel better. But let me give you a warning: Never speak such foul words around the master, or worse, his wife. She'd have you whipped. And speaking of the lady of the house, clean yourself up. You're dripping with sweat, and you know how she feels about filth."

"I got your sword, *Wilted Moth*!" Pate cackled, wiping tears from his eyes. "You've made my day!"

Jae let his practice sword fall into the grass and seized the chance to leave. He slipped away toward the servants' entrance at the back of the master's estate, moving along a hedge-lined path. He wasn't allowed to use the front doors anymore—those were reserved for the master and his guests. He was confined to the narrow, winding passageways reserved for the household staff.

In the slave quarters, he cleansed himself in the cold bathwater. The water was slightly grimy from a previous occupant, but he didn't mind. Bathing had become an almost daily ritual for him, something that had never been afforded to him before. The cool water felt like home, and when he closed his eyes and dipped his head beneath the surface, he could almost hear the crashing waves of his homeland...

But such memories weren't meant for lingering. A slave's life was never idle, and he didn't stay in the water for long. He dried himself off quickly and slipped into a fresh set of clothes: a simple cotton tunic that felt like a gift compared to what he used to wear. The thrill of fresh clothes hadn't worn off, and he hoped it never would.

Bathed and dressed, he felt his stomach rumble. He smiled, for he had been given unbridled access to the kitchen, where he always felt welcome. He slipped on his sandals, for the lady of the house detested bare feet in the house, and slipped into a hidden passageway. A dark and narrow staircase carried him up onto the main floor of the estate. He emerged directly into the kitchen, where a wall of heat immediately hit him. The large white room was alive with activity—rows of dough and freshly baked bread lined the counters, pots bubbled on the stoves, and the scent of rising loaves filled the air. It was hotter than the sun in here, thanks to the ever-burning brick fireplace, where a great cauldron simmered endlessly above the flames. Smaller ovens blazed along one wall, casting a golden glow and the sweet smell of baking bread throughout the room.

At the center stood a well-worn wooden island, and at it toiled his favorite person—Old Mother Berona. Her wrinkled hands worked tirelessly kneading great lumps of dough. The blue headscarf she wore had turned nearly white, dusted by the flour that hung in the air like mist. But today, her usual toothy grin was absent, replaced with a look of quiet worry.

"Berona!" Jae called out eagerly, his heart lifting at the sight of her. "Old Mother, how are you this day?" He flashed her his best smile.

She glanced up, her greeting curt. "Moth," she said, her voice almost a hiss. Jae's stomach dropped at the use of that name. He had grown accustomed to her calling him Jae in private, but now something felt dangerously off. "Your daily ration of bread is on the far counter."

Puzzled, Jae turned to see a stale loaf from the master's previous dinner laid out for him. Heat rose to his cheeks as tears pricked the corners of his eyes. He had learned long ago not to expect too much, but this stung. What had he done wrong?

"No pie today?" he asked, his voice small. "I thought the good lady wished for me to continue…" He paused, catching Berona's sharp, warning gaze. Her eyes darted quickly aside before she returned her full attention to kneading the dough.

"It has been commanded that you switch to proper rations," she said flatly. "The bread will suffice."

Jae swallowed the lump in his throat and nodded, fighting back tears. It was his fault for growing attached to even an ounce of motherly love. "No more sweets... I understand."

And then he saw her—a flash of black hair by Berona's side. *Sirene.*

"Is it sweets you're after, *slave*?" A small but fierce face appeared from behind the kitchen island. Jae felt a jolt of panic, as if Luke's sword had struck him a thousand times harder.

"Lady Sirene, I…" But no excuse would do. He shut his mouth and quickly dipped into a customary bow. The girl was young, but unusually perceptive. He feared he'd already said too much.

"Sweets are for the family—*my family*. Slaves are not meant to eat sweets. Daddy has cautioned against it. You will forget your place!"

Jae slowly released his bow. He dared not speak. Despite his olive skin, he was sure he was as red as a beet.

"Hmm? You won't even say sorry? Daddy will hear of this, or can you not speak? You Islanders. Dumber than rocks. Everyone knows so." Sirene coiled her arms across her chest like a snake. Small, but very venomous.

"I offer my most humble of apologies. I am but a lowly moth," Jae answered.

To his surprise, Sirene laughed. Old Berona kept her head down, hands busy with the dough, but Jae could feel her gaze. "And moths deserve to be squished!" she exclaimed gleefully. "But Momma has different plans. Momma is the daughter of a great ship lord, you know? That makes me his granddaughter! Momma says I am as speedy and fast as his corsairs, so she sent me to tell *you* what to do! Daddy needs you. He is going into the city."

"Of course, my lady."

"Lady Sirene, darling," Berona interrupted gently, her voice tender and full of warmth. "This little moth here is your father's newest guard. He needs his strength to protect your good father. Please, let him eat before such an important task."

Sirene unfolded her arms, looking to Berona with a scowl, but her little foot was tapping on the tile floor, and her eyebrow was cocked. "Very well. Daddy's health is very important. Eat you bread, *Moth*, but I shall stand guard and watch. The rules must be upheld!"

"Of course, my good lady," Berona affirmed.

"You are most wise. I thank you, my lady." Jae bowed again.

Sirene huffed and then skedaddled to a wooden stool in the corner of the kitchen. With some effort, she clambered up, folding her arms tightly across her chest, her gaze fixed on Jae and Berona, now their self-appointed warden.

"Well? Go on, then!" she shouted impatiently.

Berona bent her head, breaking eye contact, and Jae quickly moved toward the bread. He tore off stale chunks, using a basin of water to help him choke it down. Sirene's gaze bored into his back, watchful and sharp, so he hurried, knowing the day ahead would be long and hot, and he would need every ounce of energy. As he snapped up another piece of bread, something unusual caught his eye. A small slip of paper hidden inside the crust. His chewing halted for a brief moment.

He could almost feel Berona's anxiety from across the room and heard the faint creak of Sirene's stool as she shifted, inspecting him with hawklike intensity. But Jae was quick. Without drawing attention, he nudged the paper to the edge of the table and finished his bread before slipping the note into his pocket as he turned around.

"I am finished, my lady," he said, bowing low.

"Good. Be away with you," she replied, hopping down from her stool and scampering off, satisfied.

Jae didn't dare open the note in the kitchen, for the heat was high and Old Berona looked near to passing out already. So, in the safety of the slave quarters, he opened the note. He couldn't read, but scribbled on a small piece of parchment was nothing more than a crude drawing of the sun. *Her sunshine,* he knew at once. He smiled and tucked the paper into his straw mattress.

Jae's attention then turned to the equipment Luke designated for his guard duties. A leather torso and legs, alongside arm braces and a leather helm. He had no issue with the leather body coverings, but the helm had given him pause. It was not unlike the helms of the Thorned Men. Luke had been patient during the early days of training, but the master's expectations were clear. They had to be met. With a deep breath, Jae donned the helm, his world narrowing behind the two eye slits. His hands trembled as he grabbed a sword and knife, fearful of what he may be asked to do, but like a good slave, he sheathed them both.

He stumbled from the slave quarters, his vision still adjusting. Emerging onto a side path that scaled the far side of the manse, he avoided the gaze of his master's family. The sun blazed down, and after the darkness inside, it was blinding. His pupils contracted, and from nowhere, a demonic creature appeared on the slopes of the estate—a half-man, half-goat leering from the shadows.

Jae shrieked, stumbling backward on the loose rock of the path. He fell with a thud, landing on his back. Scrambling, he sat upright, blood oozing from his scuff marks. Above him stood the monstrosity, a creature of stature no more than five feet, including his dulled horns. His upper torso was humanlike with pale skin and coarse hair across his chest. Shaggy brunet hair swept down across his face, matching the short goatee on his chin. The beast looked down upon him with sickening slit eyes, and in his hands, he wielded a hammer.

"Beast..." Jae choked out and tried to pull himself to his feet, but he stumbled, uneasy on the slanted, loose rock.

"He can understand you, you know." The sharp voice, but human, flew at him from behind. Luke would curse him for not watching his back.

Uneasy, he pivoted on his side, digging in one foot on the slope for stability. Behind him, a fellow slave emerged from a patchwork of berry vines. *Petra,* he realized, and lessened his guard, but kept one hand clenched on his sword for the goatman above.

"You know of this creature?"

"Know of him? Simply look upon him and see the collar clasped around his throat. Tell me then you do not know of him either." Petra glared at Jae with defiant eyes. They were blue, a rarity in this part of the world, and filled with contempt. She was a pointed individual, someone whom he rarely crossed paths with. They worked separate chores around the house, only passing one another for sleep. "He's called a faun, by the way."

"I did not see it... nor realize such a creature was employed here..." Jae stammered.

"Are you angry it is not another minotaur for you to slay?" she asked sharply. "His name is Hex, and he's a faun—a slave, just like you are. Or have you forgotten already, now that you carry a sword and wear armor?"

174

The creature turned his gaze to Jae and spoke. "Hell-*oh*." His voice sounded oddly human, but with the unmistakable trace of something *other*.

Jae stared at the beast, slowly lowering his guard. This faun, Hex, stared nervously down upon him, his grotesquely human torso contrasting with the goat-like lower half that trembled as his small tail wagged back and forth.

"You must forgive me," Jae said at last, sheathing his sword. "I did not realize the good master employed other creatures besides men. I was startled and it was an honest mistake."

"I understand," Hex replied. He cast Jae one last nervous glance before scampering away.

Jae watched him go with fascination, his little hoofs working wonders in the steep, loose terrain. He disappeared into a small hut where the master's white wall of the manse met the cliff side.

"That is his home," Petra said sharply, her gaze fixed on the goatman's retreat. "He's not allowed to sleep in the master's house, nor even in our quarters. But you wouldn't know that, would you?" She gathered her basket of berries, shot him a pointed look, and slipped into the same entrance from which he had just emerged.

"Oh," was all Jae thought to say, but no one was around to hear him say it. He burned red, but the helm would never show it.

He stumbled up the path and made it to the courtyard where Master Aeksilor's troop waited. Pate, and his twin, Pete, were already in attendance. Luke had opened a nearby pavilion housing the master's covered litter, though Aeksilor never requested it. Lucien was also present, adorned in a green tunic and brown trousers with his black hair tied neatly into a bun, save for two strands that framed his face. A messenger bag was also slung across his shoulder, indicating his role as the master's courier. He hailed from far northern lands where people were literate and skilled in counting, making him well-suited to manage the master's affairs. Lucien had even taught him to read a few words in the master's tongue, though Jae was hardly interested. Masters changed, and languages came and went. Besides, the flickering candlelight and complicated words often made his head ache, and his muscles already hurt from training. Most nights, he opted for sleep instead.

"Hear, hear! The bull slayer approaches!" Pete slapped his leg, laughing, while Pate's eyes sparkled with amusement. Now Jae was grateful for the helm, for his face burned even brighter.

"Your reputation precedes you in the city, Jae'eli." Lucien smiled, whispering his true name.

Butterflies engulfed his stomach at the mention of it. Yet the moment the word left Lucien's lips, it dissolved in his memory like sand swept away by the tide.

"My reputation is of no concern to me, only that the master is happy and my back has not been whipped."

He eyed the three of them cautiously. Pate and Lucien stopped their giggling, but Pete couldn't contain himself. Jae ignored them and walked toward the central fountain, dipping his hand into the cool water. He gazed up at the marble mermaid's face, wishing her siren call could beckon him out to sea, far from this place.

Lucien trailed behind him. "The master is late. He always is. Probably instructing the guards on how to properly protect Lady Aril." When Jae kept his attention fixed on the clear water, Lucien hovered quietly beside him. "Do you never wish to talk?"

Jae splashed a hand in the fountain.

"The master isn't here," Lucien pressed. "Nothing of concern can happen."

"That is a lie," Jae pushed back. "Something terrible can always happen."

"You must have more faith than that. I thought you people of the Islands were meant to be a happy people? Dancing and singing and whatnot?"

Jae looked up at him with a raised eyebrow. Lucien was pushing his luck today.

"I only meant... look at your skin, the color of olives, perfect for this sun. Mine burns even on the cloudiest of days." He stuck his arm out, placing his pale white arm against his own. "See!" he laughed, their skin brushing. Jae smiled, but pulled his arm away.

"Let us go! Let us make haste! I am behind schedule, you fools. Blast that damnable guard... that... what's his name...?" Master Aeksilor came flying out of the manse, slamming its great brown doors open wide in dramatic fashion. Today he wore a long and oversized robe, burying his body beneath its gold-and-red trim. Jewels dangled from his fingers and neck, and a small white hat covered his otherwise bald head. He hurried toward them, and Luke ran to greet his master. Pete, Pate, and Jae snapped to attention, while Lucien merely cast a sly smile, turning to face the master.

"Oh whatever his name may be, that guard sure gets my lady wife riled up. Now onward, into the Vanilla District below. There is much business to conduct!"

Pete and Pate rushed forward to open the golden gates to the outside. Luke eyeballed Jae to move it, but before he could take a step, Lucien leaned in and quickly whispered. "Watch and learn from the master. He is great at what he does. He walks where others ride. He listens when others talk. And above all, he is very shrewd." Lucien winked to Jae, then spun away, chasing after the master.

Jae fell in line, surrounding their good master as they made their way down from the Rose into the Vanilla. His heart pounded as he left the safety of his master's manse, a max of excitement and fear taking hold of him. The perfumed halls, the cold baths, and the sweet treats—he wanted to cling to it all, but he also dreaded returning to the lower city. *Back into shackles near that wretched creature.* He shook at the thought of the minotaur. Its stench, its bulging muscles... its red, hateful eyes. And yet, he owed a lot to that beast. He knew he wouldn't be where he was without it.

A slave, yes, but a member of the powerful and most

prestigious house of Aeksilor. He placed a hand on his sword hilt whenever they passed another slave in the streets. He detested this necessity, but he would fight for his privileges. *I've earned this,* he told himself, swelling with pride like overripe fruit.

Yet as they approached the gates to the lower district of the Vanilla, guarded by a contingent of Thorned Men, the mere sight of their iron rods punctured his rotten ego. He deflated on the inside, ready to face their wrath and insults, but they passed without incident. The Thorned Men even nodded to him, peering out from behind their slitted helms with their eerie yellow eyes.

Astrelaide, he was quickly realizing, was a city of many layers, much like the sweetcakes Old Berona baked in her kitchen. The bottom layer, the burnt and ashy crust, was all that he was accustomed to. On top lay the sweet icing, coveted by all. Yet now he understood there was more to the city of Astrelaide and the slavers' society, a filling to the cake. His stomach rumbled. The Vanilla, teeming with cheerful minor lords and freemen, lived up to its name. The air was thick with the scent of vanilla and sweets, the yellow-bricked streets were pristine and free of clutter, and every windowsill spilled over with blossoming flowers.

Among this scene, Master Aeksilor was in his element. He paraded through the streets, stopping at every other bakery, café, or shop to exchange hellos and pleasantries, shake hands, and conduct business. Jae and the guards were relegated to stand outside, for very few slaves were permitted in the freemen's and minor lords' homes and places of work unless they had business. For this reason, Lucien, however, followed Aeksilor everywhere, ducking into shops, shaking hands with the slaves of various households, and even sampling a sweet or two once the master had indulged in enough samples.

They traveled from shop to shop, winding their way down through the bustling streets to the lower wards as Aeksilor conducted his affairs. His good master even took the time to greet other slaves conducting business for their masters. Collared and overworked beneath the sun, each would blush and bow in the presence of such a high lord. Some muttered desperate apologies for simply stepping in his way, while others glared daggers at Jae. Inside the narrow slits of his helm, Jae began to burn hot, and not just from the heat.

Lucien, however, seemed unbothered by his fellow slave's indignity. He drifted effortlessly through the day, always surrounded by smiles and gifts from slaves and masters alike. He met with other slaves in private, exchanged notes and whispered greetings, all while their master stood only a few feet away, oblivious or uncaring.

Jae's frustration simmered as the day wore on. He vowed his pride would never grow so large, even with his precious baths at stake. He bore the glare of the other slaves with quiet resolve. All the while Aeksilor conducted his business and Lucien played master from the shadows.

This routine continued throughout the afternoon until, at last, they descended to the foot of the Vanilla and passed through the gates that marked the boundary of the lower city. "Only one more thing to tend to, my good slaves." Aeksilor stuck one boisterous finger into the air. "And it is the most important of them all."

The art of guarding their good master became a lot harder back in the lower ward. They were forced back into a single-file line among the bustling streets, Luke naturally up front and Jae in the rear. They marched without incident through the sea of men and sometimes beasts until they came upon a crowded public square. With determination, they pushed forward, maneuvering through rowdy citizens toward a large wooden stage erected in the center of the square. A booming voice resonated from somewhere above the plaza, but Jae couldn't discern the words until they reached the front, where he nearly stumbled over his own feet.

Before them, a large stage had been erected in a public garden. Jae glanced around, enjoying the sights of the flowers. The roses, the lilies, even the worms...

No, not worms, he realized in horror.

Upon the stage, wiggling like caterpillars in the garden, slaves squirmed in the ropes of gallows. Jae's mouth dropped open.

"Ah, we are just in time!" he heard his good master cheer, but it was hardly more than a whisper over the roar of the crowd.

A large fat man, ordained in a brilliant blue-and-white robe, with every finger lined with a sparkling diamond and ruby, stepped forward. He raised a horn to his lips and bellowed, his voice cutting through the clamor. "And behold! That no slave forget his station—you are commanded, not merely by me or the good masters of this city, but by the laws of the very Sun above, to toil and serve! Shall we tolerate further insults to our Sun God, to this great city, and to the noble masters who lead us, lest another horror like the great Ash Fall befall our great society? I say unto you all, nay!"

The crowd roared back. "Nay!"

Lucien, who had been silent beside Jae, leaned in with the slightest whisper that only a mouse could hear. "Master Balon, another of the ruling families." Lucien paused as the crowd settled and waited for the fat man to shout again.

The crowd's chants rose again as Balon continued to preach, but Lucien's words held Jae's focus.

"Did you observe as I asked?" Lucien asked in a near-silent breath.

"… Both slave and freeman must be vigilant to protect our values!"

"The flow of information. How Aeksilor stays on top. He watches and he talks… to everyone."

"… Our people, free or slave, have suffered greatly. Great beasts roam beyond our walls, threatening each and every one of us within our great city…"

Lucien wet his lips, his gaze distant as he whispered. "And so do I."

The crowd erupted into a thunderous roar as Lucien took a step back. The slaves in their nooses dropped from the gallows. Jae didn't look away, however. He watched, just as Lucien said.

He watched his good master cheer.

JOSEPHINA II

Mother pressed the reins of the donkey firmly in her mittens.

"Please, Mother, don't make me go. I don't want to go!"

The wind whipped her mother's dark cloak. Against the freshly fallen snow, she scowled like some dark thing in the forest. Even their donkey side-eyed them both uneasily. She had a sinking feeling about this.

"Josephina, take the bag of coins. Do it!"

Josephina lowered her head as tears filled her eyes.

"Why! Why must you tempt me every time?"

"Because I don't like to speak their language... They make fun of me for it, and I am a monster... They'll ask me questions... I don't know how to lie to them. Please, Mother, do not make me go!"

"You speak their tongue just fine, but as to your appearance, yes..." Mother paused, considering her words. "I do see your point. They will be frightened and disheartened by your disturbing appearance, and so, because I am such a wonderful mother, I will cast a spell on you to disguise your deformities."

Josephina sniffed. "Really?"

"Yes, just a moment, dear…"

Mother left her, bounding through the forest like an animal. Snow covered everything: the ground, the trees, and the trickle of the creek beneath an embankment. Josephina shivered, tugging her fur coat tightly around her misshapen body, watching Mother dart through the gnarled tree roots of the forest. Her donkey wore a shawl, and she even wrapped Mishie, her little stuffed plush, in a napkin secured by a bobby pin. He was to help accompany her through the forest.

Mother came hopping back a few moments later. She carried in her arms a few twigs and a bundle of leaves pulled from the forest floor.

"Now, child, I am going to cast my spell, and when I am done, all will see you as a perfectly normal little girl."

"Y-you mean it?"

"I do. I really do. But!" Mother cackled. "You will only have a day and a half, maybe two, before the spell wears off. You must be quick, Josephina, or the knights will take notice."

"Only a day and a half?" She broke into fresh trembles.

"That is plenty of time, child. The trek through the forest will take you the longest. Ensure you are back to me before the spell wears off. Now, stand still, and I will work my magic upon you."

Mother lifted her arms, spinning the twigs between her fingers. Josephina shut her eyes, knowing better than to look upon Mother when she worked. She heard words she did not understand and Mother's hot breath on her face. Her heart hammered in her throat. Finally, Mother stopped, whispering to her. "*Zakaenys.* Open your eyes, Josephina."

Josephina's eyes popped open. Mother stood with arms crossed, tapping her foot in the snow.

"Is it done? Am I different?"

"To others, yes. A mirage has been cast."

"And will they see me as pretty?"

"Do you doubt my ability, child?"

"Did you do it with the Old Tongue, Mother?" Josephina looked down at her mittens, turning her hands over with wonder. Her cheeks blushed with excitement. *Will the others see me as pretty?*

"Of course. That is where the most powerful magic is found. Now, enough talking, you must be going..."

"Will you ever teach me the Old Tongue?"

"Josephina!" Her mother's voice resonated through the forest. Twigs cracked in the dark and ice fell from trees miles away. She looked upon Mother's face, watching the mist rise in the mountains behind her. "We are nearly without food. Do you want to starve or die? Do you?"

Josephina shook her head.

"You must go now. Take the money bag." Mother shoved it into her hands. "Go into the nearest town, purchase what we need and no more."

Josephina took the sack of coins from Mother. She jostled them in her hands, marveling at the weight. "Potatoes, carrots, onions, meats... What about a sweetcake, Mother? Could I please buy one?"

A wide grin spread across the lips of Mother. "Well, darling, this damnable early spring blizzard has probably taken a toll on everything and everyone, so prices are likely to be higher. I suppose, hmm." Mother tapped her chin with her finger. "I suppose if you also bring back something of equal value, I could allow that."

"What else could I bring, Mother?"

"Knowledge."

"Mother?"

"When you arrive in town, go about your duties quickly. You have packed your tent, but I worry about you in the cold. I know you dislike the tavern, but you must go there, Josephina. Rent a room for the night, but before you head to bed, you have my permission to buy a sweetcake. Wait for the tavern to fill with life and then find a spot you won't be noticed. Listen, my sweet thing. Tell me what the outside world is talking of and I will not punish you for your obsession with sweets."

Josephina gulped. "That's okay, Mother, I can sleep in the woods, I don't need to buy a—"

"Nonsense. I cannot let a daughter of mine sleep in the freezing woods. Go now and you'll make it by nightfall. Go!" Mother shoved the reins of the donkey back into her grip.

Josephina stared wide-eyed at her mother before stowing the sack of coins in one of the donkey's satchels with a shaking hand. "Are you sure you can't come with me?"

"Oh no, darling, I must wait for Oléfur here. He is bringing me a very special gift, unless, of course, you would like to wait for him in my place?"

Josephina pivoted on her feet and pulled at the donkey's reins. She started to yank, pulling on the reins as her feet slid out from under her as she slid into the snow.

"I swear, Josephina, you are the curse for what I do." Mother shook her head and spanked the donkey. It let out a sharp cry as it bolted for the woods. Josephina held on to the reins, her cheeks blushing as the donkey led her, not the other way around.

"Tah tah!" Mother called from behind. "Hurry now, my dear! Oléfur will return soon. Remember, great things are in the works!"

The mere mention of Oléfur sent a jolt through her, and Josephina dashed ahead of the donkey. Mishie perched on the donkey's back, one head peering forward while the other twisted backward, watching their trail with a single cold button eye.

The trek to town was long but straightforward. Josephina walked alongside the snow-covered creek, its icy waters gushing through the forest. All she had to do was follow the creek to a bridge about a day's walk ahead, then turn right and follow the road into town. The instructions were simple enough—until the donkey decided they were far enough from

Mother and came to an abrupt halt. Josephina yanked and yanked on the reins. It didn't budge. She smacked it on the ass, and still it didn't budge.

"Curses!" she cried in the forest. She sat down on the cold forest floor for several hours until the donkey decided it would move again.

Once they were back on their journey, they made good time following the creek. The sun climbed to its midday position, offering some relief from the biting cold. Josephina wrapped herself tightly in her cloak, using it to shield against the wind that whistled through the trees. She even placed a spare mitten on one of Mishie's heads, the one facing forward. She slid it down over his button eyes to make it stay, but she kept his other head bare. He needed to keep watch behind them.

Despite Mishie's vigilance, she shuddered, and not solely from the cold. As the midday sun dipped toward evening, dark shadows crept through the woods. Twigs snapped ominously from behind trees, and birds shifted uneasily in the branches. The donkey quickened its pace, straining her small legs to keep up. Anything could lurk in these woods, and she recalled Mother's stories. *The knights aren't what they used to be.*

Evening finally crept upon them. She pulled the donkey along (or it pulled her), eager to make it to the bridge that marked civilization, but the donkey suddenly stopped again. "Curses!" she screamed aloud and pulled at the creature, yet it wouldn't obey. Instead, it started to backpedal, retreating back toward Mother. "Curse you all!" she yelled again and pulled at the donkey.

Mishie's one button eye stared back at her, dark in the low light, when it sparkled. She heard the crack of a twig behind her. She whipped around just in time to see three brown creatures with long, spindly arms emerge from the trees. Their noses stretched for miles, and puffy patches of fabric bulged from hastily sewn shawls draped around their heads, necks, and torsos. Even stranger, large, bulbous sacks weighed heavy on their backs. *Monsters!* She froze in her tracks as the largest of the creatures raised an arm to her, its large cat eyes moving rapidly back and forth, a grin on its hideously large lips.

"Curses!" she screamed and threw herself onto the donkey's back. She punched the donkey in the head with all her might. The donkey bolted, quick when it wanted to be. They flew through the forest as she held on to the donkey and Mishie for dear life. A brown flash darted through the underbrush, and she instinctively turned the donkey. Snow cascaded from a nearby tree, and she punched the donkey again. An inhuman voice called out from the shadows, but she refused to listen. They rode hard, and when the donkey began to slow, she leaped from its back, yanking it forward as they sprinted together toward the main road.

Josephina emerged from the forest in such a rush she did not see the old woman and her cart. A horse reared up and screamed, and the old woman shouted as her donkey yanked her back. Josephina fell into the cold snow, shaking her head furiously, trying to comprehend what had just happened.

"What in the five hells are you doing, little girl? You could have gotten yourself killed! What were you doing in the forest like that?"

A barrage of words flew from the old woman. Josephina, dazed, did her best to catch their meaning in a tongue not natural to her. The old woman climbed down from her cart and soothed her frightened horse before turning to her. She stuck out a wobbly old arm and helped Josephina climb to her feet. Josephina tried to smile and say thank you.

"Tante kon."

But the old woman didn't respond. Her gaze fell on Josephina's face, and she began to back away. In horror, Josephina realized her hood had slipped down. She quickly pulled it back over her head, tightening it to conceal her features, but it was too late—the woman had already seen.

"Abomination," she whispered in her tongue.

Josephina understood that word too well. The old woman, now trembling and cursing under her breath, hastily climbed back into her cart and snapped the reins. Josephina backed away as a wad of spit landed at her feet. Tears poured from her eyes.

Mother lied to me again. She pounded at the sides of her head for being so stupid. *I will always be a monster!*

"Abomination!" the old woman cried again from down the road.

Josephina, sobbing, pulled on her cloak as tight as she could, concealing everything but her nose and just the corners of her eyes from the outside world. She could hardly see, but she could make do. She grabbed her donkey and pulled it. It obeyed this time and together they set off toward town—opposite the direction the old woman rode.

Once again, Josephina found herself alone, shaking and trembling. The sun hung low in the sky, casting long shadows, while the wind howled down from the surrounding mountains. Snow choked the roadway, muffling the sound of the old woman's horse and cart until they faded into silence. She tightened her cloak further, glancing between the dark forest and the distant town.

Tears froze on her cheeks. *I could sleep in the woods... I have a tent... The donkey could stand guard...* Desperation clawed at her as she dug into her mittens, instinctively trying to tear at her own flesh. Biting down hard on her lip, she tasted blood and let out a piercing scream. In a fit of anguish, she pounded her fists against the sides of her head, great lumps of nearly frozen snot falling to the ground.

"I have to help Mother!" she screamed, her voice cracking. "Curses!"

Josephina arrived in the town of Guttenburg just after sundown. A hundred stone homes and wooden shops sparkled with torchlight, creating a warm glow against the backdrop of the snow-covered mountains. Reluctantly, she guided her donkey to a cobblestone bridge that spanned a babbling stream, its waters glimmering under the fading light. The town lay quiet, the cold and wind her only companions, but Josephina hesitated at the bridge's edge. The bridge led onto a tight corridor of shops. Multistory homes and shops towered over the narrow street, and above her, anchored to either side of the stone bridge, the black banner of the knights whipped in the wind.

"Come, Mishie, we must be brave… *for Mother.*"

She crossed the bridge with her donkey in tow. Though the streets lay largely deserted, voices, shouts, and laughter echoed from tightly shuttered windows and doors, languages and a people she did not understand. Torches and lanterns burned outside storefronts and she found herself stopping before each one, desperately trying to sound out the foreign language. She moved slowly from sign to sign, keeping her head down whenever someone passed her on the narrow street. She could always feel their gaze, and each time, she pulled harder on the strings of her cloak, only to find they wouldn't tighten any further.

Finally, she came upon a large, crooked building towering over the narrow street. Each level had been haphazardly stacked atop the one below, giving the structure a menacing tilt. Looking up, blinking through the falling snowflakes, she glimpsed the twinkle of a few burning candles flickering in the rooms high above.

Like my room, above Mother, and my trapdoor…

My trapdoor! A small smile spread across her lips. *I bet they have a heavy bedroom door here.*

Slowly, she stepped forward and pressed her mittens against the sturdy wooden door of the inn. It creaked open, and a blast of warm air rushed to greet her, accompanied by the lively tune of a strummed violin. She watched as a group of men twirled in front of a grand fireplace, their feet tapping in rapid succession. She stepped farther inside, her eyes darting back and forth as she followed their rhythmic movements, mesmerized by the way they threw themselves into each other's arms, twirling and shouting before spinning back to resume their jig. She bit her lip, never having seen such a dance before, and felt the floorboards creak and bend beneath her, even from halfway inside the door.

"Look, Mishie, look! These men know how to dance!"

Mother danced only occasionally, and that was only to make the fire talk. She hid in her room when that happened.

She pushed farther in, the donkey following closely behind her. Together, they watched as the men spun faster and faster, while the violinist twirled in a trance of his own making. Her heart raced, her foot tapping along with the beat of the floorboards. Suddenly, all the men stopped, thrusting their fists into the air. "Hurra!" they cried as the music came to an abrupt end.

The donkey brayed at their performance, sharing in their excitement.

"Aye, you! Get that beast out of here! Stable is out back. And shut the damn door!" a woman from behind the bar shouted.

She stumbled back on her feet, and now the men were looking at her, breathing heavily with drunk, sloppy smiles on their red faces.

"Y-yes, Mother!" she squealed. She shot back outside, letting the door slam shut behind her.

Mother? Curses!

Quickly, she pulled on her donkey, but the creature refused to budge. It nudged its head against the tavern door as another lively song began to play inside. "No, curse you, creature!" she shouted, pounding her fists against the donkey, but it only stood there stubbornly.

"Excuse me, young lady, would you like some help with that?"

A deep voice came from behind her. She yelped and shrank deeper into her cloak.

"Erm, young lady? Hello? Do you need help?"

She heard the words, but her mind was slow to translate them.

Don't speak with an accent, never! Mother had warned her. *The knights will know you're not from here. They'll see your malformed face, hear the foreign sounds on your tongue, and then what will they do? They'll chain you up in their forts, or worse, they'll come looking for me! And then Mother will have to hurt them. You don't want to watch Mother hurt people again, do you?* She shook her head at the memory. *Good, now practice in their tongue once more…*

"No, sir, I don't need help," she squeaked out.

"Nonsense! I insist on helping a young woman in distress." She watched as a large ungloved hand—thick and monstrous, bulging with veins—reached out and seized her donkey's reins. With a firm tug, the donkey came willingly, while Mishie, perched on the donkey's back, gave her a troubled glare with his one button eye.

"Thank you, sir." She turned, following the man… but no, he wasn't just any man; he was a knight of the order, sworn to slay anything deemed inhuman.

Curses!

JOSEPHINA III

The knight led Josephina deep into the dark. He took her donkey by the reins, pulling them from the safety of the lighted cobblestone street into a narrow back alley. Snowflakes drifted softly from the dark sky, blanketing the ground in silence; the light of the moon was also hidden from her as she gave chase to her donkey and Mishie.

"Oh little lady…" The knight spoke with a slight slur. "A young woman like you shouldn't be out on the streets at this hour. You never know what might be lurking in the dark so close to the forts…"

The faint scent of whiskey mingled with the biting chill that enveloped them. Mishie looked back at her, helpless atop the donkey. She pulled her cloak tighter around her shoulders, pressing on despite the chilling dread that settled in her stomach. The knight's sheathed sword caught the faintest glint of light, casting an eerie glow in the night—its length nearly matching her own stumpy height. A squeal echoed silently in her mind, but she steeled herself. She would not abandon Mishie.

The knight's armor creaked with his uneven steps as she walked beside him. He towered above her, the tallest man she had ever seen, with a billowing cape that flowed behind him like a pair of dark wings. His voice was dark but not unfriendly, but she did not trust the smell of liquor on his breath. She had heard stories about men and their love of drink from Mother.

"You're a trader…" he swayed on his feet. "Awfully young for this line of work."

She did her best to translate the knight's speech. "Yes, sir."

"Sent out all alone, huh? I understand. The blizzard has been merciless." He chuckled. "I suppose that explains the shortages across the entire county. Your family must be counting on you to return safely."

His words chilled her more than the night air as he guided her toward a stable tucked behind the inn. She followed, silent, as he tied up her donkey with the same detached efficiency as if he were restraining a creature far less gentle. Her eyes flitted to the other animals, to the horses draped in black cloth bearing the emblem of his order, each as dark and still as the night itself. She wanted nothing more than to grab Mishie and bolt.

She took a cautious step forward, slipping her belongings from her donkey as it whined beside her. *Be gentle,* she wanted to say to the donkey, the poor thing tied too tightly to the stall. The horses, large and cloaked in black, were frightening it. Still, she had a job to do. She sucked in an icy breath and grabbed Mishie, turning to the knight, when he snatched him from her.

She wanted to scream.

He turned the doll over in his gloved hands. "Well, well, what a hideous thing. You ought to get a new one—monsters like this belong in fires, not in the arms of young ladies."

Josephina felt her breath catch, a fierce tremor running through her limbs as his gaze held hers.

"Oh, did I frighten you?" he asked, voice softening only enough to make her flinch. "But that's how it is here on the edge, isn't it? These woods crawl with things worse than what you can imagine, things we knights hunt down and keep from prying little eyes like yours." He dropped the doll back into her hands, his stare still fixed on her, as if daring her to tremble even more.

She clutched her doll to her chest, heart racing, unable to shake the feeling that his words were more warning than reassurance. The knight's eyes flicked over her trembling frame, and suddenly a sorrowful look fell over his face.

"I'm sorry, I didn't mean to scare you. Just terrible things, inhuman creatures live in these woods, you understand. We always have to be vigilant, you understand. I'm sure if you're out on these roads alone… We're the brave ones… you and me. The humans that live so close to the edge of civilization, but you have nothing to fear… not with us watching." Josephina had pulled her hands to her chest like the wings of a chicken, shaking. The knight stopped himself, finally noticing her trembles only worsened. "Oh sweet thing, you must be absolutely freezing! Let's get inside where it's warm, shall we? You can meet all my friends. And don't worry, I'll protect you from any monsters."

The knight placed a firm hand on her back. He guided her back inside the inn as silent tears tracked down her cheeks. She kept her gaze firmly on the floor, hoping no one would notice her trembling.

"Helga!" the knight barked as they stepped back into the warmth of the inn.

Josephina's cheeks flushed hotter as a few heads turned her way, but only for a fleeting moment. The laughter and clinking tankards resumed, and the men returned to their jig, filling the room with rowdy cheer. The knight kept a steady hand on her shoulder, guiding her to the tavern bar, where behind the counter, the innkeeper looked up—a towering woman who matched the knight in size and severity. Her thick arms were crossed tightly over her chest in a stance that could wither lesser men.

"What is it now, Franz? Half my beer stock's not yet recovered from the last ruckus you caused here."

"A pleasure as always, miss." He gave her a wry smile. "I bring coin this time, and my young friend here needs a room."

His hand on Josephina's back urged her forward. She stumbled slightly, scrambling for the right words. "A room, please," she managed, her voice thin as a whisper.

Helga's sharp eyes raked over her, brows pinched beneath a small, dented cap that divided her blonde hair into two thick braids. The innkeeper's voice, a low and steady rumble, was even harder than Franz's tongue to translate. She was unable to understand the stern woman's response.

"One bed?" Josephina pleaded, trying again with a simple phrase. The innkeeper only shook her head.

Reluctantly, she pulled at the drawstring of her cloak, finally loosening the cloak wrapped firmly around her head. She relaxed it only a few inches, enough for her top lip to stick out. She tried one more time. "A bed, please, *sir*." Josephina watched as the woman's eyes went wide and a scowl spread across her one brow. Josephina closed her eyes and blinked, prepared to be struck as Mother surely would, when she heard the woman sigh, and when she opened her eyes again, the innkeeper held her palm open.

"Give, give," she understood clearly this time.

Josephina quickly produced her bag of coins and handed them over. The innkeeper pulled out a few coins and rolled them in her palm. For good measure, she bit into a few of them, and seemingly satisfied, grunted with approval. She produced a key and placed it firmly into Josephina's hand.

"THANK YOU," Josephina replied much too loudly. She turned, eyes searching for the stairway, when her mother's voice echoed in her mind: *Information, sweetling.* Another thought swiftly followed, more tempting—*sweetcakes.* The room key in hand, her nose finally noticed the smells of roast duck, bread, and honey in the air. Her stomach growled.

She paused, looking about the tavern. A group of men was finishing yet another jig as the violinist strummed away, one foot plopped onto a table, lost entirely in his music. The warm

194

glow of the massive stone fireplace at the center of the room drew her in, its flames crackling beneath a twisted, grotesque creature mounted on the stone wall above. Elsewhere, bar patrons and travelers were scattered about the rows of tables and benches, dining and drinking below three chandeliers dripping with candle wax. In the corners, green plush chairs invited coziness from the shadows, and she found herself longing for the comfort of not being seen, but she thought about Mother, and her questions. She could lie, but Mother always knew when she fibbed. Besides, she wanted a sweetcake, and the knight who guided her donkey had already invited her to sit with him.

"Curses," she mumbled to herself, but the smell of pastries and meat baking in the kitchen convinced her otherwise. She turned and placed another coin upon the counter and miraculously ordered a sweetcake with no language trouble. Holding her head low, she shuffled over to the knight who had brought her in. Thankfully, he glanced up and motioned for her to sit.

"Gentlemen, look here!" he announced with a flourish, his arm snaking around her shoulders. "I've found a special young guest! Come, girl, have a seat. Tell us your name." His grip tightened, and Josephina sank deeper into her cloak. She barely caught the meaning of his words.

"Josep—" But she stopped herself. *Your real name? Are you stupid? What would Mother say! Curses, you fool.* "Yo-rina. Yorina, thank you."

A knight across the table let out a chuckle, his tone just shy of mocking. "By the Five, Franz, she's young enough to be your own daughter."

Franz's arm tensed around her, but he gave a dismissive laugh. "Oh for the love of mankind, I'm just being friendly is all."

Another knight, older and gray-bearded, leaned forward, his eyes sharp. "Friendly? Don't let that 'friendly' spirit get you in trouble, Franz. My own daughter's learned how to handle a sword, after all. A woman with a blade is a dangerous thing."

Josephina kept her head down, but she could feel Franz's arm flex around her before he finally pulled it away, his knuckles rapping the table hard enough to make her flinch. "Trouble, Wilhelm?" Franz scoffed. "This one couldn't even lift a sword, but a *knife*?" He looked to her with a wicked smile, eyes moving from her face down to his trousers. Franz winked and his compatriots rolled their eyes with a groan.

"Careful, Franz, a woman who knows her way around a knife is far more dangerous."

"Bah, what do any of you know? She's wrapped up so tight in that cloak, and when I found her, she could barely keep herself upright in the snow. Well? Where's my reward for all I do for this world?" Franz waved his hand as his arms slipped from her. She tried to untense herself, but then Franz pounded the table, loud and insistent. "Well? Where are our drinks?"

Moments later, the innkeeper arrived, balancing four large tankards in her thick arms. "No trouble this time, Franz. Understood?" Her voice carried a warning that made Josephina's stomach twist.

"Trouble? Can't a knight on leave from the Eisvach Fort enjoy himself in peace?" He grinned, glancing down at Josephina. "I've earned this drink, don't you think, girl?"

All eyes turn to her. She lifted her gaze from the table to find them staring, some smirking, others watching with hard, scrutinizing eyes. Across from her, an older knight with a pointed goatee looked upon her the hardest.

"This isn't the order, Franz. I rule here." Helga crossed her arms and Franz's stature deflated. If there was to be a fight, Josephina would put her money on the innkeeper.

"Yes, yes." Franz dismissed her with his hand. Helga went as Franz's face hardened. "Damnable woman. She has no idea of the creatures we face out there. The things we see…"

Creatures? Josephina bit her lip.

The knights raised their tankards high, their collective sigh thick with bitterness as they toasted. They came crashing down a few seconds later. "To your new friend, then." Another knight turned to her. "I'm Gerald, of the Knight's Order. This is my town, and the rest of these good men—you'll find no better fighters this side of the Five Forts—the Fist of Men."

The men all thumped their chests, their eyes still on her as though she were some rare thing dropped into their midst. "Any human who respects our work is a friend of ours."

"I-I'm from here too," she replied, her voice small. The knights roared with laughter.

"From here?" scoffed Gerald. "Listen to that accent!"

"Accent? I mistook it for a wisp?" Wilhelm laughed.

The older knight leaned in, smirking. "Tell me, young one, do you even know how to handle a sword? Or a knife, perhaps?" He chuckled, letting the question linger as though it were the start of some private joke. "You're in the land of the order, girl. Everyone here trains. Everyone learns how to defend themselves. You are a sweet little thing, but if you want to survive alone in these parts, you'll need to lie a bit better than that. A trader girl from the port city of Vaktzig, perhaps. But *here*? Among our bloodlines?" He shook his head as if the very idea amused him.

Wilhelm leaped up, shouting. "Dance the Cavalier's Trample! Crush their skulls—giants, brownies, or the turncoat gargoyles. Whatever comes!" He banged his tankard down, grinning, and the others followed suit.

"Here! Here!" Gerald raised his tankard high, and the knights all drained their cups, slamming them down on the table, empty. Leaning back with a satisfied groan, he patted his stomach. "A fine ale. A damn good one. May it not be my last for a long while."

Franz shifted beside her, his movements making the bench creak. Josephina's heartbeat thundered in her throat, her pulse quickening with every side glance he shot her way. "I'll drink to that." Franz sighed. "Being pulled from Eisvach, I still don't understand it. A thousand years of our order and look how far we've sunk since the Ash Fall. Civil war between knights, brother turning against sister—what kind of curse is that, eh?

Kin killing kin." Franz shook his head as a somberness over-took the table.

"The dark days are behind us," Wilhelm muttered.

"Oh? You think so?" Franz replied, raising an eyebrow. "Our bloodlines have grown thin. So many of our own lost to those fools from Gothonia when we went to war—Five bless me! I've lost more aunts, uncles, and cousins to human knives than those beasts beyond the mountains... It's enough to drive a man crazy." Franz shook his head, once again looking to her.

Gerald leaned forward, voice low and conspiratorial. "Sir Franz of the Knights of the Holy Reisonic Order, you know there's a simple way to remedy that, don't you?"

"I've found there are no simple remedies in this life. So speak your lies."

"Why... my dear Franz... you go and make babies!" Gerald thrust his hips toward the table with a bawdy grin. The knights exploded into laughter, their fists pounding the table, some howling loud enough to draw stares from the other patrons.

The innkeeper approached, carrying another round of tankards, her lips set in a hard line as she slid them down onto the table. She placed a small sweetcake before Josephina without a word, her gaze flicking to the men with a scowl. Josephina tried to smile at the treat, but the lingering gaze of the older knight with the goatee caught her eye, his expression flushed from drink and something more. His fingers idly tugged at his beard, his eyes still fixed on her as he muttered something under his breath. He worried her more than Franz.

"To the glory of our order!" Franz declared, raising his tankard before taking a long, messy swig, ale dripping down his chin. "And aye, to the glory of mankind," he added, slamming his cup down. His voice dropped, bitter. "We've been wasting our blades on each other, by the Five." He spat on the floor. The innkeeper shot him a sharp glare, which he ignored. "Fighting ourselves, wasting men on those damned Gothonians—and now, we're pulled from the sacred forts to take up this fool's crusade? Fine then. Let's take Gothonia; let it be ours. But let us *never* forget the true enemy to the east."

"Beasts and worse," Wilhelm muttered, shaking his head.

"Aye, but who's seen any of them in the flesh?" Franz scoffed. "Maybe my grandpappy did—he'd talk of giants, claiming he saw them right after the Ash Fall."

"They live, I'm certain," Wilhelm nodded. "dying off slowly on that cursed island in the Shiverloch."

"Nay, I've seen one myself, I swear it," Gerald cut in, his eyes glinting. The table erupted in laughter, tankards raised and sloshing.

"Gerald, you're full of wind." Franz snorted. "Bet the next round you're lying!"

"Not a word of it!" Gerald rose from his seat, stumbling slightly. "I saw it with my very own eyes, I tell you! And if you don't believe me—look there!" He pointed with exaggerated drama at the mounted head over the fireplace, a twisted, monstrous thing with leathery skin stretched taut across its face, its jaw hanging open in a permanent, grisly grin. "A giant right there!"

Franz squinted at the head, smirking. "And *this* is why I never gamble," he muttered, his face splitting into a grin as laughter broke out around the table. They raised their tankards again, reveling in the warmth of the fire and the strength of their drink.

Amid the uproar, Josephina's stomach growled, the sound almost drowned out by the raucous toasts. Quickly, she pulled down the edge of her cloak and broke off a piece of her sweetcake, tucking it into her mouth. Bliss overtook her as the icing and honey melted on her tongue, her small respite from the knights' coarse jokes and laughter.

Relaxing slightly, she leaned back against the bench, letting herself enjoy the moment. But when she looked up, her gaze locked with the same knight as before. He wasn't drinking. He was staring directly at her, his expression sharp and unblinking. Josephina stiffened, the sweetness turning to ash on her tongue.

The tankards of his compatriots finally hit the table again, empty. The knight with the goatee finally spoke up. "What did you say your name was again?"

The knights' heads were swimming, their eyes bleary, but they all turned to her, grinning sloppily.

"J-Jorina," she answered, her voice small.

"To Jorina!" Franz bellowed, raising his mug once more. "Here! Here!"

But the knight narrowed his eyes, his smile gone. "That's not her name," he said, his voice low and chilling.

"Eh? Leave the girl in peace, Alfred," Gared pleaded, though his voice was uncertain. "There's more drink to be had."

Josephina felt the sweetcake churn in her stomach as all eyes fixed on her. She reached for her cloak, desperate to disappear again beneath it, but froze. Would hiding make her look more suspicious? Curses! What would Mother tell her to do?

Alfred leaned in, his voice a slurred but harsh whisper. "Look upon her face! She's a monster—or at the very least, some foul abomination!"

The sloppy smiles of Franz, Gerald, and Wilhelm vanished as their gazes fell on her, their expressions hardening in dawning suspicion.

"Oh… my…" Gerald muttered, his drunken cheer evaporating.

Alfred rose from the bench opposite her, his hand moving to his sword. "She doesn't speak our tongue. She lies about her name. And look at her face—marked and unnatural! A spy from the east? A curse from the western woods?" He looked to his fellow knights. "Or perhaps she's the witch they speak of. She needs to be questioned… *extensively*."

Franz shifted on the bench beside her, and in a flash, she was gone. Josephina flew, young and nimble, faster than the large drunken knights. Behind her, she heard the music and dancing of the men come to an abrupt stop. A bench crashed against the floor and the innkeeper screamed.

Josephina didn't know where she was running, only to run. The key to her room jangled in her pocket, and instinctively, she raced for the stairs to the upper floor, pounding up each step. But as soon as she reached the landing, tears broke free onto her cheeks—she'd cornered herself like a trapped animal.

Spittle flowing from her mouth, she shot down the first hallway she came to. She sprinted, hearing the heavy footsteps on the stairs behind her, and burst through a random doorway. A woman nursing a babe screamed, but Josephina didn't pause. Without a word, Josephina bolted past her, eyes fixed on the small window. She shoved it open, seized the ledge, and clambered through, tumbling to the ground below. Her feet hit the cobblestones with a sharp jolt that drove the breath from her lungs, but she forced herself up, gasping, and ran.

She fled behind the inn and ducked into the shadows of the stables, spotting a large hay pile in the corner. She dove in, burrowing deep into its scratchy depths as she heard the clang of steel and the shouts of knights spilling outside. Her body shivered with cold and fear, and she clutched her knees, hardly daring to breathe as their voices grew closer. One of the horses stamped its hooves and whinnied, but the knights didn't linger. The smell of drink was strong on them, and as the snow began to fall again, she heard them curse and retreat back into the warmth of the inn.

A sob escaped her, muffled in the hay, and her body relaxed with exhausted relief. Curling tighter, she drew Mishie from her pocket and hugged the little doll close, his button eyes staring back in silent companionship.

"I love you, Mishie," she whispered, the words barely reaching her own ears. In the bitter cold, she drifted into a fitful sleep, the ache in her stomach gnawing deeper.

She awoke at first light. The temperature had dropped again during the night, but the hay kept her relatively warm, though she woke with a tingle in her throat. She knew she had to act fast to escape the village, yet she also knew better than to disappoint Mother. Quietly, she poked her head from the hay, and to her relief, her donkey was still there. Not wasting a second, she spilled from the hay and snagged it.

"Do not be difficult with me now," she pleaded. The donkey snorted and shook its head, but thankfully it obeyed as she freed its reins.

She led them quickly away from the inn, sticking to a narrow alley behind the main street. The hour was young and the day cold, but commerce must flow, and so sleepy people emerged from their homes to begin their day. She pulled her hood tight again and made her way to the market square. An elderly woman had been the first to set up a food stall, and much to her relief, she was able to purchase sacks of potatoes, onions, carrots, and a few pounds of salted meats with only a pointed finger and a few grunts.

Her stores replenished, it was time to hightail it from town. She led the donkey back into an alleyway and placed Mishie upon its back again. "Your eyes and ears," she whispered to him.

She led the donkey from the alley and in a wide arc around the village, setting out into the snowy fields to draw as little attention to herself as possible. The snow had fallen deeper here, and her head grew woozy with fatigue and sleepiness. Still, she pressed on, growing nauseous as she rounded the village and found her way back to the main road. Yet she couldn't bring herself to move forward. She paused, stomach flipping with hesitation as she looked back toward the village. She felt the prickling warmth of the sweetcake she'd left behind. She never got to finish it.

She led the donkey off the main path and tied it to a lone tree. "You stand watch with Mishie," she whispered, patting its neck before dashing back toward town, keeping close to fences and back walls. She dodged between coops, animal pens, and sheds until she was back at the inn's stone walls. Breath tight in her chest, she pressed herself against the outer wall, inching forward and scanning the street for any sign of the knights. Men, women, horses, and carts tumbled in the street out front. None of them knew her. The day was too early for the knights to have risen. She could get her sweet back.

Licking her dry lips, she slipped into the street and kept her head down as she approached the inn's door. It swung open with a faint creak, and she slipped inside, glancing into the familiar tavern room. The fire had burned down to embers, and the room felt cold and hollow. Helga was nowhere to be seen; instead, a bald man with thick muttonchops was wiping down glasses at the counter. He raised a brow, but she held up her room key, and he gave a brief nod.

Safe for the moment, Josephina scanned the room, disappointment washing over her as she saw her sweetcake was gone. However, two knights were slumped in the corner, fast asleep. Butterflies danced in her tummy.

She crept forward, finding Franz and Gerald sleeping soundly in two of the plush chairs. Any food or drink they may have had from the night before was long gone, but Franz's belt lay spilled out on the floor. Josephina, eyes gleaming and tongue working its way across her lips, snuck forward and snatched a long knife from the belt. She held it up in the air, seeing her eyes sparkle in the steel blade.

"Hey! What are you doing?" the new innkeeper shouted, but Josephina was already halfway out the door.

She burst into the village street, knocking a woman to the ground and sending a horse cart veering into a stack of barrels. She flew back down the alleyway, through the inn stables, over a wooden wall, down a dirt path, into a chicken coop, and sprinted through a field of snow. She found her donkey waiting for her, Mishie's button eyes coldly welcoming her back.

"I know, I know," she said to him, fervently untying the donkey. "But I paid for a sweet!"

Together, they galloped away, avoiding the main road and cutting through the snow toward the safety of the forest. They didn't stop until they were deep among the trees, riding parallel to the road until Josephina found the babbling brook that marked the path back to Mother's. There, she paused to catch her breath and tore into a piece of salted meat. A giddy laugh escaped her as she allowed herself, for once, to indulge. She broke off chunks of meat to share with Mishie and passed a few carrots to her donkey. By the mountain creek, the three of them feasted on their stolen spoils.

With her stomach finally full, she pulled her cherished prize from her coat pocket. It was a long dagger that glowed white in the snowy light. She held it up to her eyes and admired the sharp sheen of the blade. Along the handle were five sockets, each once meant to cradle a jewel for the five holy warrior prophets. Two still held red stones that gleamed in the cold light. The other three sockets were empty.

Marveling at her prize, she laughed, slicing the blade through the air, in awe of its power. The donkey neighed nervously, sidestepping away from her. She cackled again, feeling the reassuring weight of the weapon in her hand. "I can protect you now, Mishie."

Mishie didn't answer her, only the cawing of birds breaking the stillness above. Dark in feather, they finally broke her trance, squawking in the midmorning sun. In the distance, she thought she could hear the trotting of horses along the stone bridge.

She sheathed the blade, storing it in her coat pocket. Turning quickly from the road, she led the donkey deeper into the forest, no longer afraid of what may lurk within. The sun shined brightly through the tree branches, and with her newfound *sweet*, she headed home to Mother.

BANCROFT II

Warwick knelt before him, holding the Crown of the Nine, its weight heavy, its brilliance blinding. Nine jewels circled its rim, each representing an Elector, with the central ruby glowing red, the proud symbol of their house. Bancroft gently lifted the crown, his fingers brushing the cool metal before lowering it onto Warwick's golden curls. It settled into place with ease, a perfect fit. A blessed omen.

Warwick had worn the Crown of the Nine as a boy, but this time was different. He met his father's gaze as he rose, his fingers testing the weight, eyes narrowing slightly. "It's heavier than the family crown," Warwick admitted.

"Much heavier indeed," Bancroft agreed. "A ruler must always remember the weight of power. The Opal Throne—grand though it is—does not give us power. It is rooted to the mountain, immovable. But this crown… it passes from emperor to emperor. Be it with our house, or another."

Warwick nodded, the weight of the words settling on his shoulders. "Your tutelage has been everything, Father. If I am to rule justly, it is only by your grace."

Bancroft took a long, quiet look at his son. His eyes traveled from the golden slippers that adorned Warwick's feet, up past the silk tunic that clung to his frame, to the gleaming two-headed phoenix embroidered on his chest. Even in the dim hallway light, the design shimmered with the pride of their house.

Father and son locked eyes, standing nearly the same height. The boy was a man now, and Bancroft's heart stirred with a mixture of pride and sorrow. He opened his mouth to speak, but the words faltered, caught in the tightness of his throat. He looked upon his son, seeing much of himself.

"I know, Father." Warwick patted his hands softly. "I know."

Bancroft held his grip for another minute or two, then let it drop. With a gentle nod, Warwick placed the imperial crown back onto his father's head. Bancroft, with slow reverence, retrieved the House of Knox's crown from its velvet cushion and placed it upon Warwick's head. "Shall we ascend?"

They left the private chamber behind the Opal Throne and made their way through the chilly corridors that were alive with the bustle of servants and the arrival of lords and ladies from across the realm. Their progress was slow, interrupted by endless greetings and courtesies. Guests had traveled far to High Ness to express their condolences for the loss of the emperor's brother, and in turn, expected an audience for their grief. After what felt like ages, they finally stood at the base of a towering staircase, its white marble steps leading into the shadows of the Tower of the Castellan.

The staircase spiraled upward. Through the tower's windows, the city of High Ness and the rising roof of the throne room grew smaller with every step. The day was cold and clear, the mountains in the distance shrouded in fog. Father and son climbed in silence, their footsteps echoing softly in the stillness. Bancroft moved with determination, though each step sent a sharp pang through his chest. He lagged behind Warwick, who surged ahead, only to falter and fall back. The rhythm of their ascent was a quiet dance until they reached the top of the tower.

At the entrance to the Council Chamber, two Demonbreun Guards awaited them. One stepped forward to assist Bancroft, but the emperor waved him off with a grunt. "No need," he wheezed, steadying his breath. Beside him, Warwick, panting and looking as if he might collapse, cast his father a quick glance. In that moment, they were almost mirror images of each other—two portly men, set apart only by the silver creeping into Bancroft's hair. Warwick wanted to smile, but a dull ache settled in his stomach. They were too alike, and that thought worried him deeply.

"Warwick, come." Bancroft's voice was firm as he beckoned his son, leading him toward a nearby window. Unlike the narrow slits along the staircase, this one opened to a sweeping view of the castle and the sprawling lands beyond. "What do you see?"

Warwick stood silently, considering the question. After a moment, he replied slowly. "Our realm?"

Bancroft shook his head. "You look too far, my son. The big picture is often important, aye, but sometimes it's what's just beneath our feet that matters most." His gaze drifted downward, and Warwick followed it, his eyes flicking from the distant mountains to the city of High Ness, then down to the roof of the throne room directly below. Warwick's eyes narrowed.

"We are above the throne."

"Precisely."

"… and yet, we're headed to the High Councilmen who sit above the throne?"

Bancroft removed his arm from around his son. The corners of his lips flinched with a smile. "And why do you suppose that is?"

Warwick's brow furrowed. "Because we lack the absolution of thrones like Isperia or Gothonia?"

Bancroft chuckled, a small, dry sound. "The Electors of this empire do not bend to the throne. They demand appeasement—any one of them could raise a claim to my crown. Yet it is our family that has stewarded this realm for five generations, and I intend for you to be the sixth."

Warwick straightened. "I will bring them to my favor, Father."

Bancroft gave him a long, assessing look, then nodded. "I've no doubt." With a firm, but gentle grip, he guided Warwick to another window. The guards shuffled behind them, keeping their distance. "Now... what do you see?"

Warwick looked out the window, spying nothing but the castle above and below. "Our courtiers?"

"Look up."

Warwick's eyes glanced up but soared past the towers to the top of Ness. "The mountain?"

Bancroft sighed, but deep down he was relieved. "No, my son, the towers. The towers of this great castle we have claimed for our own. Yes, the Tower of the Castellan may rise above the throne, but it is our family's towers that rise above all. Do you understand what I am saying to you?"

Warwick swallowed and looked upon the towers.

"I have sent Lysander away for the day—to treat with a few knights of the realm."

Warwick studied the towers, letting the meaning settle in, then turned back to his father and nodded. "Shall we greet our councilors?"

"Aye. And bring the realm to heel." Bancroft's voice dropped to a lower register, and he signaled to the guards. With a creak, the oak doors swung open, and a chorus of voices poured out. An assortment of noblemen turned to face them, but it was Strammond of the Demonbreun Guard who brought the room to attention. "Presenting His Grace, our emperor, Bancroft Hieronymus, First of His Name, and his son, Warwick Hieronymus, proclaimed heir to the crown!"

The men in the room bent low in deep bows—all but Alden, the realm's castellan and Bancroft's most trusted advisor.

Bancroft's heart clenched as he watched the old man struggle, gripping a chair to support himself as he barely managed a nod.

"All may rise," Bancroft proclaimed. The men straightened, and as if a spell had been lifted, laughter and jests filled the room.

"I cannot recall the last time I bent so low, except perhaps to tend to my late wife," Edwin Battlebridge, the treasurer, crowed, drawing a round of chuckles.

"Aye, let it be known that no tower in the castle is tall enough to muffle the cries of a good tongue flick!" came a quick retort from Graham Fontaine, Admiral of Ships. Even the High Priest of the Nine chuckled, tipping more wine into his half-full goblet. But not all joined in the merriment: Alden remained silent, as did Wulfnoth, the emperor's Confessor Lacius, and a young cupbearer named Gael.

"Perhaps this council has forgotten the decorum due before the crown," Bancroft declared, and a sudden hush fell. He surveyed them, his tone heavy. "Or have we all forgotten the dark cloud that hangs over my family and thus the realm? Or does the tragedy of my family not concern the lords of the council?"

Wide eyes spread across the realm's most powerful. It was the priest, a man of proclaimed faith and chastity, who cleared his throat and begged the council to begin their work. The men did so without hesitation, taking their seats around an immense circular marble table. Bancroft took his place on a gilded chair, ordained with jewels and the symbol of his house. To his left, Castellan Alden sat, formally surrendering his seat to the right of the emperor to the heir proclaimed. Bancroft watched with a smile as Warwick took his place by his side.

The other lords filled in the seats of the table, and each produced a carved marble piece of an eagle, placing it before them upon a carved wooden base resembling a nest. Only the emperor did not produce such a token, instead revealing a carved phoenix made of pure amber. He placed it upon his own nest of carved wood encased in gold and called his flock to order. "It is with the gravest of attention I call this council to session."

Bancroft let his words rest. Many were seated around the table, though one chair sat empty. The position of Master of War stood vacant—a reminder that not every bird had come to roost.

Warwick leaned forward, elbows upon the table, a break in decorum that earned him more than a few raised brows. But he held his stare directly on Osbert, the High Priest. "Words, then, for my uncle?"

The High Priest, lips stained red from wine, seemed momentarily flustered. He shifted backward in his seat, and his immense jewel-studded hat slipped askew. A trembling hand rose to steady it. "A fine call indeed, my prince," Osbert replied, adjusting himself before speaking again. "Let us bow our heads.

"O heavenly divine," Osbert began, his voice assuming a solemn tone. "We are gathered here today not only to mourn Your most devoted of sons but to pay homage to his selfless acts in service to Your realm. Thane served this land with honor and left behind a family, a wife, a brother, and a nephew. Grant us the courage to carry on in his image, as we strive to live in Yours. By Aethylios and the Nine Miracles, we honor Thane and deeply mourn his passing. Amen."

"Amen," answered the High Council.

Bancroft had closed his eyes during the prayer, and when he opened them, he found his eyebrows raised and attention turned to his son. Warwick sat back in his chair, arms crossed, a small smirk on his mouth, and the High Council at attention.

"Thank you, Osbert, for those kind words concerning my family and late brother. I know the realm feels the same for my brother, who died valiantly fighting for his realm against the savages of Fláimir. It is my deep hope we can bring forth an end to this conflict swiftly and without further bloodshed."

"A tall order, a brazen order," sniffed Dymtrus, Master of Laws. "Your Grace, forgive me, but the people of the realm are not ignorant of such affairs. Ours is a collection of lands, of many tongues and customs. And it does not bode well, my lord, when the Fláimirish rebels can rise up and claim the life of the emperor's own kin. Such an image is difficult to contain, to say the least, and it cannot simply be... hoped away. This is surely no easy task."

Next came the voice of Graham Fontaine, Grand Admiral of the Realm. "A fair point, I do agree with you. But this is only one small setback, there is no need for alarm. Our navy is strong, and though my expertise may be of the sea, I daresay our armies fare no worse."

"Of course, you may say such a thing," Dymtrus shot back. "The Fláimirish of the Isle have no fleet, and as to the state of our armies, who knows? Thane led our forces, and the intricate knowledge of our armies may have died with him."

"That is precisely why we are gathered here today. I intend to name a new Master of War—a lord who will carry our empire's banner with neither pause nor hesitation. I therefore beseech the High Council for advice and nominations for this position." A heavy silence fell over the council. Bancroft's gaze swept the room as his council shifted uncomfortably. His cupbearer approached with wine, but he waved the boy off. The silence tightened around him. The most self-serving of the realm, who were quick to speak on any other matter, now held their tongues. Dymtrus, of course, bristled but said nothing. Wulfnoth, Secretary of the Realm, met Bancroft's gaze but offered no counsel. His cousin and governor of High Ness, Milton, absently brushed his fingers as if batting away a fly, while Norbert, the herald who normally wielded words with finesse, only stared at the table, seemingly wishing to disappear. Finally, it was his confessor, an ancient yet wily figure, who leaned forward and spoke with quiet deliberation.

"Perhaps, Your Grace..." he smiled, "the nomination should come from within the family?"

Warwick stiffened beside him. Murmurs spread around the table as councilors exchanged wild glances. Bancroft's chest suddenly tightened. "Surely no one means to send my son, the heir to the crown, to fight in a land of monsters and heathens a thousand miles away?"

"I do not think that is what the confessor had in mind," Dymtrus answered where others would not.

Slowly, Bancroft's eyes went wide. "You mean to say Lysander?"

"Well, I would daresay, what better purpose for a second son than to lead the banner for the family?" answered Edwin. Osbert, Norbert, and Dymtrus nodded in approval.

"Simply out of the question," Bancroft answered.

"That was, after all, your brother's role—a second son," joined Milton.

Bancroft's eyes shot to his cousin, who himself appeared surprised the words came from his own mouth. Bancroft stared with an open mouth. Heat flushed his face. This was not the direction of conversation he had wished.

Lacius, his confessor, cut in, his voice a rasp, almost reptilian. "I see the heir sits at your right, a fine place of honor. But where is Lysander now?" Bald and dressed in only a simple white robe, he looked as if a lizard had crawled into a man's body.

"He is preoccupied with matters not of state," Warwick answered.

"Such as?" Lacius hissed.

"He trains with knights, and aye, I see the council's point," Bancroft lamented. "Though I must say at once, there are other plans in store for my second son, and this matter should be put to rest at once."

"Such an appointment could reassure the realm, Your Grace. Lysander carries the family sword. He has all the legitimacy..."

"Did I not order such a command!" Bancroft slammed his fist upon the table. The statues of birds jumped from their nests, sending all but Wulfnoth's and Alden's from their roosts.

In the aftermath came the hoarsest of voices. It was Alden, bent with age and visibly in pain, who finally broke the silence. He leaned forward, rasping. "If it pleases the council, I may have a suggestion of greater relevance." He coughed, gesturing to the young cupbearer. "Young man, bring me a cup of water." The boy scampered forward, carrying a goblet of fresh water.

"Thank you, young man. Now, ehh, pray tell me, you are new to your position, yes? Remind me your name."

The young boy looked upon the old man and then flashed his eyes to the rest of the council. All looked upon him. "G-gael," he answered.

"Ahh, but that is no formal name, now is it? Are you not proud of your family name?"

The boy straightened a little, clearing his throat. "No, sir. My name is Gael Alfair."

The High Council rocked back in their chairs, nodding in approval. "An Alfair, indeed! A-ha! A noble name... a powerful name!" Dymtrus grinned. "And from the Isle, no less. Your father commands one of the nine votes for emperor, does he not?"

"Aye, sir, he does."

Bancroft exchanged a subtle smile with Alden, who gave a conspiratorial wink. "Tell me, as a son of Fláimir who understands the threats these savages pose, would you say your father is strong enough to lead?"

The young boy snapped to attention as if called upon by a commanding officer. "My father has dedicated his life to protecting the empire's holdings on the Isle!"

"And do you think, ehh pray tell, he would be willing to lead the charge against those who would threaten even your family's holdings?"

"Without hesitation, sir."

"Then, ehh, my council, I see that we have an appropriate name for a nomination to fill the vacant position—Thane Hieronymus rest in peace—for Master of War."

"A noble fitting." Bancroft nodded. He looked to his son, who stared intently at Dymtrus.

"Remind us, lad, what is the name of your father?" Alden asked.

"Hereward Alfair."

"Ah, a name for a position," Alden announced, collapsing back into his chair as if the effort had spent all of his energy.

Bancroft's smile widened. He winked to Warwick, whose scowl finally broke from Dymtrus. "Must we vote on the matter, or shall my endorsement be sufficient?"

"A fine name, a fine recommendation," Wulfnoth finally piped up. "I see no reason that I nor anyone else at this table should reject the motion. I second the nomination."

"While I believe the merit in the nomination of a family member to serve, I will not oppose. I support the suggestion as well," Milton answered.

"Then I see no further grounds for discussion on the matter." Bancroft brought down his hand in finality, just as Dymtrus appeared poised to object. "Wulfnoth, as the secretary of this council, please be kind enough to send a pigeon at once to the House of Alfair requesting Hereward's affirmation of the position of Master of War."

"It will be done, Your Grace."

"Very good, then." Bancroft settled back into his chair, feeling a rare sense of satisfaction. The major hurdle of the day—and perhaps of the realm—was cleared. Just as he let himself relax, Gael, the young cupbearer, let out an unexpected whimper. Bancroft turned, and so did the rest of the council, to find the boy's face streaked with tears.

"What troubles you, son?" Milton asked.

Gael only trembled, clutching the goblet he held.

"Can't you see? He's worried for his damned father," Dymtrus muttered, rolling his eyes.

Bancroft sighed. "There's no need for concern, child. To serve the High Council and the realm is a noble calling. Your father will be safe, especially now that we understand the true threat these rebels pose."

"I... I hear they ride with monsters..." the boy whispered, barely audible.

"Monsters?" Bancroft asked, brow furrowing.

"Centaurs," Wulfnoth replied gravely. Some members of the council groaned, yet Wulfnoth remained unmoved. "Perhaps we've grown too comfortable in our towers and cities, forgetting the old threats. The Knights of the Reisonic Order keep vigil in the east so giants and worse do not corrupt our lands. Perhaps, we have grown complacent behind their forts."

"The centaurs haven't left their bogs in centuries." Dymtrus scoffed. "To think they'd join humans to fight our forces is laughable."

"A curious idea, but not impossible," Wulfnoth replied. "As Secretary of the Realm, I hear stranger tales. Rumors from the far south even speak of minotaurs rebelling alongside men to break the chains of their oppressors."

"Harr harr! If true, then the slavers get what they deserve!" Norbert laughed.

"This council strays from its purpose!" Bancroft shouted once more, shutting the curtain on revelry. "The boy weeps still, and to him, I will say this: Gael, it is indeed an honor for your father to serve the realm. Just as you serve me here at council, would you not wish him to return to court as a hero, by your side, when the war is concluded?"

Gael sniffed and wiped away a tear with his free hand. "Aye, but…"

Bancroft raised an eyebrow.

"H-he councils my brother to rule. He will inherit our lands… I don't want them to fall to the monsters!"

Bancroft's understanding crystallized as he gestured for Gael to come closer, drawing the boy onto his knee. Gael, composed but trembling, rested his head against the jeweled two-headed phoenix of House Hieronymus.

"You fulfill the duties of a second son well, young man of House Alfair," Bancroft said. "My own brother was a second son; he gave everything to support me, the emperor. It is the role God assigns men of your birth."

"God knows best," Warwick interjected coldly. "A second son's role is servitude, nothing more."

From across the table, Osbert slurred through his wine. "Servitude, indeed. And you, boy, will counsel us on the affairs of your father's realm."

Gael nodded, wiping his face as Bancroft released him. At the far end, Lacius licked his lips. "And should your elder brother fail, you will inherit your father's legacy."

A pang struck Bancroft's chest, anger swelling within him as though Mount Ness itself quaked. But as his rage grew, a sharp, unexpected stab of restraint deflated him. "Alden, please take my cupbearer to your chambers and have him draft a letter to his father. It may relieve his conscience." Bancroft's voice was strained.

"Yes, Your Grace," Alden replied, taking Gael's small hand and leading him from the room. The oak doors shut behind them like a gavel.

In the now too-hot Council Chamber, Osbert whispered. "Ill omen, speaking of death."

Bancroft glanced at Wulfnoth, who nervously tugged his collar. "On such a subject, perhaps we should discuss your brother's progress, Your Grace?"

Bancroft slumped back in his chair. "And what of my late brother's journey?"

Silence fell as Wulfnoth cast a pointed glance at Fontaine, who sprang from his wine-induced stupor. "Yes, well... your brother's... um, body has left the Isle. It is being escorted south by the Hieronymus fleet."

"South?" Bancroft interrupted. "I instructed it be sent directly to Aberness, then here."

"That remains the plan, Your Grace." Fontaine reddened. "The fleet honors your brother's memory across the realm."

"The emperor has already lost his brother's life. Shall he lose his body too?" Wulfnoth snapped.

"No one would dare harm the fleet," Fontaine insisted, though his gaze avoided the emperor's. "Your Grace, though our customs differ, we honor you and your family."

"You stole the emperor's brother's body for a parade!" Wulfnoth spat. "A display for your own gain!"

Bancroft shook his head. "Would my brother have sacrificed himself if he knew his body would be made a spectacle?"

"A morbid question," Osbert muttered.

Fontaine cleared his throat, mumbling. "The fleet has rounded Isperia and will reach Aberness shortly."

"Isperia," Dymtrus whispered.

"An evil land, heretical land." Osbert shuddered.

"My brother's body sails off the coast of Isperia? We may as well have surrendered him to the Rose Monts, or better yet, the Goldwoods!"

The council froze again at the mention of the cadet branches of House Hieronymus. Bancroft's head was spinning when Warwick broke the tension. "Too much has been said of the second son when a second cousin, or further, strikes greater fear in the realm. We, as a council, must not be ruled by fear. We as a council should learn to fear words less, for we are mortals, prone to sin, who can… misspeak from time to time…" Warwick paused, giving weight to his words. "The division that stirs among us mirrors that of my family. Names like Rose Monts and Goldwoods, branches of our tree that cannot be pruned, are nothing but words. And now we learn of my uncle's funeral procession, possibly lost to the waters of Isperia, how terrible, for he was a good man who served his realm in a foreign land. We should choose to honor his memory through unity, not division." Warwick removed his crown, holding it to his chest, and closed his eyes. He held this pose in silent prayer.

"Good words for a good man. Our lord would be proud." Osbert nodded.

Bancroft took his son's words to heart. "Indeed, we must unite, not splinter further," he said, glaring at Fontaine. "The emperor's word must not be twisted for personal gain."

"Aptly put, Your Grace." Wulfnoth nodded.

"Words are fickle; action speaks louder." Lacius curled his lips.

Bancroft turned his glare to him, but it was Edwin, silent for too long, who hit back. "Such a statement from the Confessor of the Realm. Aye, whose whole role is to hear the words of the emperor."

"It is true I merely listen, but on behalf of Aethylios, who as we all know is capable of great action." Lacius smiled, turning to Osbert.

The High Priest jumped in his seat, suddenly aware the attention was now turned to him. "Yes... yes, indeed," Osbert stammered. "The Nine Miracles were powerful acts of faith, but words have power too, aye."

"By the Nine, are we here to have a philosophical debate?" Dymtrus shouted. "This council has been idle too long. Now, with the heirs returned and war on our doorstep, do we crumble so quickly? We should be a council of action, not words."

Warwick returned fire. "The heir has come home to roost. What action would you have of me, my father, and the council then? A brave man to utter such talk, you speak boldly, but it is still words that drip from your tongue."

"Ever the poet." Dymtrus smiled. "Pray tell, your journey through Sanguinia went well, my prince? I have heard much talk, words further, of your deeds. Your feasts, your poems, but not much of action, aside from draining Lord Fontaine's honey stores."

At his mention, Fontaine turned red again and burst into nervous coughing.

"Your brother, it is said, went north with a sword in hand to temper the cold hearts of the Kaesnfolk. *Your supposed kin.* And how their lords grumble now as the heir-to-be goes south to win votes from men of a different tongue, while the second son—a man set to inherit little and thus speak for even less—takes audience with their concerns. Meanwhile, it is I, a lord of the west, who receives nothing at all."

"Is that what you will have? Petty jealousy? Neither boy crossed to the Isle of Fláimir, yet those of us in the east do not grumble. We follow, with honor and with duty," Wulfnoth fired back.

"Aye, and who flanks the prince's sides, if not two boys from Esteria, whispering in their ears far from court?"

"Their personal knights were chosen to strengthen ties between the east and the crown, and to guard against Krithinia.

Let us not forget they were allied to Isperia not but a moon's turn ago," Wulfnoth replied calmly.

"And your people are content, while mine go neglected," Dymtrus growled.

"These petty insults must end…" Bancroft started, but Warwick raised a hand, and the council fell silent once more.

"Tell us, Lord Dymtrus of Acquanis, what is it your people desire?" Warwick asked quietly. "What would bring them peace of mind?"

Lord Dymtrus, a man of dark hair and dark complexion, sat upright in his seat as if finally recognized for the first time in his career. He fluffed his tunic, pulling at the creases, and cleared his throat, before folding his hands and placing them upon the marble table. "My people, we are the only Vayerns within the realm. You may hear treason when I say this, but know I speak only the truth. The Spider Queen of Isperia has united all other Vayerns under her yoke, except those of us within your borders, Your Majesty. My people feel ignored, or worse, tempted by the promises of Isperia and common kin. We receive no imperial processions and fewer political appointments. We maintain a crucial border of our great realm, yet I fear too little is seen of us."

"Then, pray tell, how might the realm be guided to see your people?"

"I have a daughter," Dymtrus said, his voice smooth as he measured each word. "Fourteen years, learned, and comely. She should wed into the imperial family, binding our blood to yours. It is past time for your boys to marry."

Bancroft could not have been more grateful for the placement of the High Council Chamber, for perched high in the sky, saturated with crisp, fresh mountainous air, he gravely feared the men of the room would have exhausted the air supply of any other castle. The High Council gasped, including himself, except for Warwick, whose face froze, wiped of all emotion.

"A grand… proposal…" Warwick calmly answered. "And one the crown will consider."

There was much commotion afterward, but little registered with Bancroft. The remaining words and actions of the council registered as a blur for him. Warwick sat beside him, equally frozen, but nodding along with the lords of the realm, before at long last the men of the high table began to rise and depart from the room. Only when the last footsteps faded and the chamber fell into silence, except the howl of the wind outside the tower, did Bancroft's chest finally unharden, and he turned to his son.

"Your first council meeting," he said to his son.

Warwick didn't meet his glance. "It seems I am to be married soon."

"My boy... soon to be a man with an heir of his own," he tried to joke, but neither of them laughed.

Leawyn IV

She wished to trade her walking cane for a bow and arrow.

Her health had taken a turn for the worse. Wrapped in furs, she lay for days upon the floor of the centaur's hut, naked, caked in dirt and herbs. Fever racked her body, pulling her between delirium and oblivion.

Om, the scout, tended to her often, brewing her tea for her throat and tossing water upon hot coals. The hut effectively became a sweat lodge, though her body still trembled, and in the night, she rose screaming, finding the specters of her dead sons and her husband lurking in the shadows.

"WICKED THINGS!" she cried, dashing forward and flailing her arms to banish them from the tent. The chieftains and shamans spoke of the dead returning one day, but not like this. These were not her beloved; they were demons come to drag her from the Hearth, far from the bogs where her family lay. "I WILL NOT HAVE YOU!"

A ruckus kicked up outside the tent. A torrent of shadows and beasts stormed along the walls. She lifted her arms up to the thatch roof and screamed just as Om burst back through the door, followed closely behind by the chieftess. The chieftess screamed, kicking her front legs up madly, brandishing a blade between her humanlike hands. Om dashed before her, shouting again in a tongue she did not understand. In her madness, she cackled madly, shouting babble at them as sweat poured from her skin.

The chieftess struck first. Her hoof collided with Om's chest. He staggered back, swinging at her face. Then the blade came down. Blood spattered across the dirt floor.

Everyone froze.

Leawyn panted, her lungs thick with phlegm, the sound rattling in the hush. Beyond the walls, the stampede froze, as if holding its breath. The chieftess stared at Om, her eyes wide, her blade dripping. Om trembled, clutching his arm where crimson poured freely. Then, in a flash, she seized him by the throat and dragged him from the tent. The centaurs beyond the walls went mad. Leawyn fell into a giggle, collapsing back into her furs, going into the long black.

When she finally awoke, it was due to the sound of stirring from within the lodge. Om had returned, his arm bandaged and packed with herbs. She rose, finding her throat healed and fever gone, but her arms trembled, and she was terribly weak.

"Old Bird." He came to her. His voice sounded sad. "I feared the worst for you, but you have made it to this day. I see you have found the strength within you."

She let him grip her arm and attempted to rise, but only collapsed back onto her furs with a grunt.

"Do not be discouraged," he reassured her. "You have eaten little and fought a brave battle. Your body will catch up to the strength inside you."

He returned with a bowl of greens and berries. She devoured it eagerly, and he prepared another bowl for her. She longed to request roasted fowl or strips of deer meat, but from what little she knew of the centaurs, one fact stood clear: they did not hunt, except when pursuing foreign men.

The next day, he brought her a staff to help her walk. At first, she hobbled clumsily around the tent, but when exhaustion overtook her, she would sit and trace her fingers over the elegant carvings. It was a beautiful piece, its handle shaped into the form of a vicious viper.

Days passed, and slowly her strength returned. By the time she could stand without trembling, she had become intimately familiar with each grooved scale, knowing exactly where her fingers could rest comfortably between the serpent's fangs. She traced the carved scales with a calloused finger and finally voiced the question that had been growing in her mind. "So is this what you think of me? A snake?"

"No," he replied curtly. "You're an Old Bird, and it is known the snake eats the bird."

She broke into a laugh. "Is my age such a muse for you? Tend to me more, a hundred years! And we shall see what creations I inspire for you." She tossed the cane between her hands, grinning.

"I am enjoying your company, Old Bird, but there is wisdom in knowing when it is your time as well."

"Is that your subtle way of telling me to leave?"

His smile lingered. "No. I will not cast you out until you are ready."

"You think that as an old bird, I should have learned by now when to take flight."

"A fledgling would be ignorant of such wisdom."

"Hmm." She looked down upon her staff, running her fingers over the carved snake. "It's beautiful."

"It is a cherished relic. I requested it from our shamans further east."

More centaurs. The thought excited her. "And you, my new friend? Does your arm fester? Have I caused strife within your herd?"

Om glanced at his bandaged arm as if only now remembering his wound. "All things in the forest exist as they are. *In balance.* The beetle eats the leaf, the bird eats the beetle, the hawk takes the bird in the end. I was wounded, yes, but as the forest provides, so too has it afforded me the opportunity to remain with you… rather than return to my duties scouting your people."

She studied him. "Was it you I saw that night? When I slipped my son beneath the waters?"

His ears flicked. "Yes," he answered.

"Then tell me, new friend, you know of the strife of my people, and perhaps of the strife of all native clans across this isle. Surely the centaurs have felt the ax of foreigners, too? Why can't we find common cause to defend our home?"

Om's ears flickered as he struggled to collect his thoughts. "The decision does not lie with me. As I have stated, the forest maintains balance. We live in the west, among the dense woods and bogs, and your clan to the east, where you have cleared patches of the forest for your gardens. While mutual respect can be found, I do not see an allyship in our path."

"We do not disrespect the land as the Outsiders do," she said pointedly, but when Om didn't answer her, she pressed. "So with no forest, there is no common ground?"

Om stomped the ground with his forefoot. "Yes, it is so."

A slow, bitter frown crept across Leawyn's face. She studied the cane a moment longer, then cast it away.

Om took a step back, ears flicking in what might have been offense.

"You are an excellent artisan and healer, new friend," she said, voice steady. "Your staff has served me well, but it will not serve me in the battle ahead. I came here prepared to pass beneath the Hearth and rest, but you," her breath hitched slightly. "You have given me the resolve to continue. Do not deny me the chance to try. We have a common cause."

Om's ears flicked again. "As I have said, such a decision does not lie with me."

"I understand."

She hobbled closer, resting her weight against him. Though she barely reached the ridge of his equine back, she still managed to drape an arm around his torso. He stiffened in surprise, glancing down at her.

"I need a bow," she demanded. "Any will do."

"My herd has plenty, but I do not understand. Do not attempt to hunt on our land. We do not eat meat..."

Leawyn dismissed his concern with a wave of her hand. Her gaze drifted to his broad back. Gently, she reached out, running her fingers along his side. His coat was unexpectedly soft, well-groomed, and clean.

"You call me Old Bird..." she whispered, "and you speak of flight. I am old, yes, and human. I have never possessed wings, but I do know a feeling close to flight. On horseback."

Om reared violently, throwing her to the mud. She barely had time to react before he kicked out, striking the air in warning. His teeth were bared, his nostrils flared, and his eyes flashed with animalistic fury. "You would show me such disrespect?" he snarled.

"I did not know..." She held up her forearms as he rose again, leaning back on his two hind legs. "I'm sorry..."

But the blow never came. Om snorted, falling back onto all fours. "I shall fetch you your bow, Old Bird, but remember this," his ears flicked sharply, "even a fledgling, in its naivety, knows when to take flight."

With that, he turned and stormed from the hut.

Leawyn sat frozen, her breath shallow, her limbs trembling. Her cheeks burned with humiliation. She glanced toward the wooden wall, to the very spot where, in the depths of fever, she had seen the twisted shadows of her dead family. The memory still swirled in her mind. Not in clear images, but in hazy, shifting colors.

She had made a fool of herself, but she had come too far. Twice now she had nearly died from her own hubris. A third time did not scare her.

Om returned minutes later, a crude wooden bow clutched

in his arms. He thrust it toward her. "Take it, and be about your business."

Leawyn accepted it carefully, reluctantly trading the staff for the bow. "Thank you... new friend."

He snorted at the words.

"Tell me," she continued, gripping the bow. "where may I find your chieftess?"

Om exhaled through his nose, rolling his eyes. His tail flicked, impatient. "She has gone for her morning prayers."

"May I speak with her?"

"If you value your life, I would not recommend it."

Leawyn held his gaze. "So where may I find her?"

Om snorted, his tail flicking once. "Follow the stream through the forest. You'll find a grotto."

She bowed her head in gratitude. "Thank you."

Om did not return the gesture. Instead, he pulled aside the fur flap, revealing the world beyond. She hesitated, waiting for him to say something more, but when no words came, she lowered her head and stepped past him into the open air.

Outside, a strange and foreign world greeted her. Towering trees, the largest she had ever seen, loomed overhead, their gnarled branches already budding with new life. Though the air was still sharp with winter's chill, a whisper of spring wove through the wind, warm and fleeting. High above, delicate blossoms had begun to emerge, dotting the canopy like pale stars. From the bare limbs of the trees, unfamiliar trinkets dangled: carved runes she did not recognize, swaying beside ribbons, banners, and lanterns in a dozen colors. The sight struck her still. How long had she been indoors? How much of the world had passed her by while she lay feverish in the hut?

A snort behind her broke the spell.

She turned and found the gaze of a dozen centaurs, who had stopped in their tracks. Some clutched baskets, others axes, one a bow, and yet another a strange flutelike instrument. Their gazes flicked over her, wary yet unreadable. She met their eyes one by one, but none held her stare for long.

A sudden breath of warmth against the nape of her neck sent a jolt through her.

She spun around to find Om standing just behind her. He did not acknowledge her reaction, nor did he look at her at all. When she turned back, the centaurs had resumed their tasks, moving with quiet efficiency, pointedly avoiding her presence.

"Thank you." She bowed again, knowing it would go unacknowledged.

She set off toward the brook, its soft babble weaving through the heart of the centaur encampment. It was a settlement unlike any she had known. Life here seemed to revolve around the forest itself. Goats and sheep wandered freely among their shepherds, unmarked by bells or enclosures, while wooden shelves suspended from ropes served as makeshift tables between the trees.

Most dwellings were cloth tents strung at the base of massive trunks, much like those of her own people, though a few wooden structures stood scattered throughout the dense woodland. Yet these buildings were small, more akin to horse stalls than proper homes, barely adequate even for humans. There were no fences, no pens, no rigid boundaries of any kind. Only hooved creatures and their caretakers living together in quiet harmony, beset only by a babbling brook.

She followed the brook beyond the centaur encampment, deeper into the dense woods. Tiny shoots of green pierced through the thawing soil, and birdsong rang wild in the branches above. Spring was indeed on the way, and with it, a spirit of rejuvenation and rebirth. A time for new beginnings.

It was in this spirit she found the chieftess at the base of an enormous tree. Its trunk alone could have swallowed ten men whole, and who could say how many centaurs? At its roots, a small pond fed by the brook shimmered in the daylight, its surface rippling where the water flowed toward a dark, yawning hollow beneath the tree. The place was magical even in winter. She could only imagine the beauty once spring arrived in full.

She approached the chieftess locked in silent prayer, her head bowed and arms folded before her. Leawyn tried to approach cautiously, stepping on every branch and dead leaf she could to signal her approach, but the centaur gave no indication she heard her. She got close, but stopped just on the other side of the spring, eyeing the half-human before her, looking over her peppered coat, which she now realized in the sunlight was masked with wisps of gray. Her hair too upon her humanlike head was long and straight, falling past her shoulders to the base of her horse body, completely silver, just like her own. On her head, she wore a twisted crown woven of branches, and in the center lay a green gemstone.

"It's beautiful," Leawyn said quietly, nudging a pebble into the stream with the toe of her boot.

The chieftess did not stir.

Leawyn took a deep breath in, and uttering a silent prayer to keep her balance, she placed one foot upon a stepping stone and vaulted across the stream. She was now just a few arm's lengths away.

"Your Chieftess," she tried again, appealing to her title. But the centaur remained unmoved, her head still bowed, her face turned away.

Leawyn scrunched her brow, but decided it best to not prod the creature again. Instead, she turned her attention to the large hole at the base of the tree and ducked her head inside. At the center stood an altar, hewn from stone, draped in a shawl of deep teal and green, surrounded by multi-colored jars filled with glow beetles. And there, resting upon the stone slab, lay a human skull.

Leawyn gasped and staggered back, her foot catching on a root as she tumbled onto her elbows.

"You should not have come here!"

The chieftess appeared above her, terrifyingly tall, her silhouette blocking the light. Leawyn scrambled to her feet, breath uneven. The centaur did not offer a hand.

"I... I have made it my intention to leave," Leawyn stammered as she got to her feet. "I do not intend to overstay my welcome."

"You were never welcome to begin with." The chieftess snorted.

Leawyn was on her feet now, but she barely rose above the creature's horse body. The centaur's cold green eyes still peered down at her from high above.

"You don't understand. I have to try."

"Try?" The centaur snorted again, her eyes darting back and forth as if contemplating the word.

"It means to..."

"I know enough of your tongue!" She spat upon the ground. "You are strong. Death should have taken you... yet here you stand, in one of our most sacred places."

A chill swept through Leawyn at the chieftess's words. The centaur began to circle her, slow and deliberate, studying her with an unreadable expression. Leawyn's eyes, however, drifted back to the altar.

"Tell me," she said quietly, her gaze locked on the skull. "Who was he?"

"That does not concern you."

"If it is one of my people, then I say it does concern me. The skull should rest beneath the Hearth. Or if it is one of the Outsiders, then I say, let us smash it together and be done with their presence on our land."

"You are a fool," the chieftess answered.

A tinge of hatred shot through her chest, and before she knew it, she had raised her bow, a hand instinctively reaching for an arrow. The centaur reared up, and her arrow loosed prematurely, striking the wall of the grotto inches from the skull.

"You devil of the woods!" the centaur spat. A string of words in her language quickly followed. "I would have your throat slit and your body thrown into your bogs!"

"Do I not deserve the honor of resting upon your altar then?"

Leawyn shot back. The two locked eyes, the centaur's powerful muscles twitching just beneath the skin.

"You are not of my race. I would never place you in such a sacred place."

Leawyn's eyes went wide. The chieftess had played her well.

In a flash, she dropped to her knees, bowing her head, trembling in rage for herself. "I am sorry, Chieftess. Forgive me. I... I... know little of your people or your ways."

"The ignorance... the blatant trespassing. Humans have always imagined they know best. The land has grown weak under your care. Forests cleared and soil raped. See here the sum of your actions. The skull of my son, slain in battle, and you insult me!"

The centaur rose up, dancing delicately upon her two hind legs. Her two front hooves dangled just above Leawyn's head.

"Slay me then. I have grown tired of this world and its suffering. Let me join my own sons in the ground. It is long overdue."

The centaur's hoofs came down. They missed her head by a hair, smashing the bow she still held within her hand. Leawyn stared at the wreckage.

"I know of your loss, human. Om made his case for you."

"And I am afraid I have lost his goodwill as well," Leawyn lamented.

"Then everything is as it should be. You have come to me with nothing but insults. Look upon your bow, your pitiful show of strength. Is this the light of your kind? An old crone who has wasted the resources of my people? Who has caused me to spill the blood of my own?"

Leawyn had no answer.

The chieftess's voice hardened. "Go in your suffering. It is well overdue."

Leawyn stared at the shattered remains of her bow. She had never felt more the fool.

"Chieftess, I came with the best of intentions, but I know I have failed. Our land deserves no more spilled blood from its people. So I thank you for sparing me and not poisoning your sacred grotto with my blood." She exhaled a bitter, tired breath. "I will return to my people, where death surely awaits—as it does for all who oppose the Outsiders."

The chieftess snorted. Then scoffed. Then dashed backward, kicking her legs wildly in the air as she reared up like a wild stallion. "Humans!" she screamed, her voice thundering with the weight of her horse body behind her. "You are all the same! Do you think I do not wish to cleanse the land of those tree-fallers? This is your war, not mine! I will not sacrifice more of my kin! Nor do I have the power to!"

"We all have the power to fight," Leawyn interrupted, ready to take a finishing blow from the creature. Her answer, how-ever, only sent the chieftess into a greater chaotic rage.

"I lead my herd! But the Great Shaman, she speaks for all the centaurs! Ignorance! Fool! Beastly, foul thing!" More words followed in her native tongue. Then, with a final furious kick, she spat. "Go, now! Spill your blood far from my grotto, far from my woods! And do not take the coward's way out. Fall in battle! See for yourself the cost when one chooses war!"

The chieftess bucked and kicked, shouting in her tongue, before leaping over Leawyn and making a mad dash into the forest. Leawyn sat upon her knees, trembling, looking upon the dirt, before her eyes finally rose, looking upon the skull on the altar.

"Thank you for your sacrifice," she said aloud. Then she rose and began her journey back to the centaur tribe. She would gather her things and slip back into the woods. The chieftess was right.

She needed to slay an Outsider for herself.

Melinda I

Melinda knelt before the altar, her fingers steady as she lit the twin incense candles. Two flames flickered to life, casting a soft glow over the polished marble. With a careful breath, she extinguished the flame of her match and placed it gently into a porcelain urn. All flame, no matter how small or fleeting, she considered sacred.

The small room stood still, save for the faint hiss of the burning incense. Melinda rested her elbows on the cool stone, bowing her head toward the portrait of the Phoenix King that stood steadfast on the altar. His painted eyes bore the weight of command, and the fiery crown her husband now wore was a reminder of the divine authority granted to mortal blood. Yet her gaze wandered past him, settling on the vast, swirling portrait of God above. Painted centuries ago by the mad artist Lorenzo of Lucardi, its many all-seeing eyes sent a shiver through her. Trembling, she dropped to her knees, and seeking His warmth, began to pray.

"Dear Lord and the Holy Flame,

"I give thanks for Your many blessings. For the health of my family and for the safe return of my boys, Lysander and Warwick, whose journeys across the realm You have protected. I thank You for the love of my husband, a love I cherish as a reflection of Your own."

Her faith faltered. The gratitude in her heart clashed with a deeper ache and she opened her eyes, her gaze locked with the portrait of God. Her lips parted as though to speak but she found no words. Instead, she lowered her head again, trusting the Nine.

"Yet I ask for Your continued favor of my family. My husband, Your humble servant, bears the weight of grief for his brother, Thane, Your warrior. His heart grows heavy with the burden of loss, even as he strives to uphold Your will. Please, Lord, grant him Your strength. And if it is within Your will, may Your prophet Aethylios extend Your blessings to our household."

Her hands tightened in her lap. The ache came again, sharper now, as her fingers grazed her abdomen. It was a pain she had learned to live with, though it never softened. A silent wound that time refused to heal. Tears prickled at her eyes as she lifted her head toward the Phoenix King's portrait, his stern, painted visage offering neither comfort nor reprieve. The frustration surged like a wave, and before she could stop herself, she seized the frame and slammed it down onto the marble. For a moment, she simply stared at the fallen portrait, her hands trembling, her breath shallow. The lump in her throat swelled, and when she finally looked upward again, it was toward the portrait of God. Her voice broke as she spoke, raw and trembling.

"What do You want from me?" she whispered. "Have I not been faithful? Have I not given everything? I raised the boys You gifted me. I have served this realm with every breath. Why must You take and take?"

She waited for an answer as the incense curled around her, its smoke soft and indifferent. She clenched her fists, her voice rising in anger.

"Speak to me!" she cried. "Please. Give me something."

Slowly, she lowered her gaze back to the altar, her hands instinctively returning to her womb. The dull, persistent ache still lingered. A cramping that would pass in time but never truly leave. She was too old now; the dream of a child would never come to be. Her head bowed, and she exhaled a long weary sigh. The candles flickered but did not go out.

She reached forward to turn back up the portrait of the Phoenix King. A crack ran down the glass that ordained his portrait, and this time a pain of regret hit her in the stomach. She sat back down on her knees, ruffling her dress as she stared into his eyes.

She was the empress and inheritor of all he had built. Yet, no matter how fiercely she tried, love could never bind them, not truly. She loved Bancroft's boys as her own, but deep in her heart, she felt the Phoenix King, Manton, even in death, despised her for failing to carry forth his bloodline. His ashes rested in his sacred urn, his body long burned and ascended to heaven, but his judgment loomed heavy over her.

Melinda's hands trembled. She was a daughter of the House Esmerelda, not of the ancient and royal bloodlines of Lyonnia like House Hieronymus. Nor was she of the Kaesnfolk, whose common blood made up most of the realm. Even her voice betrayed her origins; no matter how diligently she suppressed her native Travesian tongue, she still spoke with a slight accent. She would always be an outsider, she feared, to both her realm and her family. That is why God punished her.

"I surrender my pride to You," she whispered at last, her gaze falling to the cold marble beneath her. "It was an ill-fated marriage, wasn't it? Arranged not by divine will, but by the Trickster... or worse, by my own foolish pride."

"The duty to love is a duty to suffer."

The words came in a pair of twin whispers, soft as a breeze yet sharp enough to make her flinch. Her head snapped up, her wide eyes locking onto the portrait of God.

"Lord, yes, do you mean to speak with me?"

But the painting was silent. The mouth of God did not move, though a voice did come from behind her.

"I am not the Lord," said a familiar voice. "But I do beseech a moment of your time."

Melinda spun around, a gasp escaping her lips. Hastily, she gathered her skirts beneath her and rose to her feet. Standing at the entrance to the solar was Elizabeth, her arms folded neatly before her.

"A-auntie," Melinda stammered, her words stumbling over themselves. "Or... Lady Elizabeth... cousin... dear. Why don't you come in and sit with me?"

Elizabeth regarded her with a cool gaze before replying. "Only if I am not interrupting."

"Nonsense! There is always time for family. Please, come!" Melinda gestured warmly toward a pair of red wingback chairs near the altar.

Elizabeth stepped into the room with a nod and settled into one of the chairs. Melinda seized the moment to fetch a small pot of tea from the nearby sideboard. Pouring two delicate cups, she handed one to Elizabeth before taking the other chair herself.

"Why thank you." Elizabeth gave a half smile as she took the tea. She took one courtesy sip before placing the cup down. "But truly, my empress, if this is an inopportune time, do not hesitate to dismiss me."

"There is no such thing as an inopportune time for family. I was just finishing up my morning prayers. Tell me, is this room not remarkable? It was the personal solar of the Phoenix King when he took up residence, driving the Makkans from the realm."

Elizabeth's gaze wandered across the room. Her eyes lingered on the portrait of the Phoenix King before drifting to the imposing image of God above the altar. The many eyes, flames, and abstract shapes of the divine visage seemed to unnerve her; the corners of her mouth twitched, and a faint flush rose in her cheeks. She quickly looked away, her focus returning to Melinda.

"Truly impressive… yes," she said, her voice but a whisper. "Though I may add, the Sun Palace is where he ruled long before coming to High Ness. I'm afraid I've grown rather accustomed to our founder's style and presence… wishes and desires… back in *Aberness*…"

Melinda's smile remained steady, though a flush crept across her cheeks. She swiftly steered the conversation onward. "Oh, how foolish of me! Nestled here in the mountains, I forget the world beyond. It's been far too long since I've seen a true city. Perhaps, when all is settled, we could travel together. When Warwick," she paused, crossing herself with the Nine, "inherits the crown in the Lord's time."

"Aye, I pray for the same," Elizabeth replied with a nod, yet her words rang hollow. "As any good wife or mother would." She leaned forward, placing her hand gently on Melinda's, her smile faint but sincere. "And like any good mother, we do what is best for our families."

"That is what gives us our strength, does it not?"

"Indeed," Elizabeth answered, her smile fading. She turned away slightly, her gaze falling to the floor as she withdrew her hand from Melinda's. "And yet it also limits us so."

Melinda looked at her with concern. "Elizabeth, darling, whatever is the matter? Tell me, does this concern your late husband? If so, allow me to once again offer my sincerest…"

"It is not just his death!" she snapped but did not lift her eyes from the floor. "It is everything that surrounds such an awful affair." Her fingers clenched, and she took a sharp breath, as though restraining herself.

"Elizabeth… I…"

"Let us pray Warwick does not inherit the crown anytime soon, but promises have already been made to me, and a mother must remain vigilant." She took a deep breath and let it out slowly. "The inheritance of Aberness is undecided, unconfirmed. That title, with its tangled history, is prone to change with the whims of politics. And your husband, Bancroft, avoids me in private as though I carry some plague." She scoffed, shaking her head in disbelief. "It seems he means not to confront me, his grieving sister-in-law, over the matter that now supersedes even his own brother's death."

Elizabeth fell silent, but when Melinda said nothing in turn, she raised her head and narrowed her brow. "Derrick must inherit Aberness," Elizabeth said firmly. "I want Bancroft, the emperor, to confirm this long before the day the crown passes to Warwick."

"Oh dear Auntie, how I see the pain in your heart." It was her turn to extend a hand and lean in close. She forced tears into her eyes, though if they were truly genuine, she could not say herself. "I can promise you Derrick is highly regarded by my husband, and his station is under consideration."

"Is it so?" Elizabeth answered coldly.

Melinda cocked her head. "I am afraid I do not follow."

"The realm has always been a place of scandal and whispers, and the death of my late husband has been no different. I have heard talk and backroom whispers that an invitation to fill my late husband's role has been extended to Hereward of Fláimir."

"Oh, is that so?" Melinda forced her smile to remain steady. "You will excuse me if I do not mind every rumor that swirls within these halls..."

"But the emperor is your husband," Elizabeth pressed. "Surely he would know of such a matter."

Melinda chuckled lightly, withdrawing her hand to rest it on her neck as she laughed. "Oh! The day my husband speaks to me of the High Council's affairs..."

"Whether or not you know of such a matter is an entirely different thing. Still, if such a tale were true, it paints a dire situation for my son."

"Auntie, Elizabeth, dear sister..." Melinda tried to soothe her, but Elizabeth raised her head, as if preparing to be slapped, and silenced her.

"If Hereward is to be considered for Master of War, what station does that leave Lysander? Now I see the writing on the wall. He would stand to inherit Aberness, and then what of my son? What of me and my family? I am of the Isles myself, I know what horrors lurk there."

"My dearest, please, I understand you are in mourning, and your grief weighs heavy. But you must trust my husband to bring comfort not only to you but to the realm. He will make time for you, I promise. Still, you know the nature of this court. How it teems with whispers and serpents..." Melinda paused, her gaze drifting to a peculiar charm hanging from Elizabeth's neck. It was a flame, enshrouded by a web, with a half-open eye glinting at its base. "... It takes time for the court to settle. And besides, I promise you directly, Derrick will have a fine marriage, and so will Catelyn. I will see to it personally."

"That is hardly sufficient." Elizabeth's voice trembled as tears brimmed in her eyes. Tears, Melinda suspected, that were as practiced as her own. "Aye, it seems without a man by my side, all the realm, even a fellow wife and mother, shall cast me aside. I fear I have no agency, for the protection of myself or the legacy of my children."

"Elizabeth, I beg of you, place your faith in the crown. You shall see, Catelyn will be given a station of great importance, perhaps even empress." Melinda nodded, and found that a small smile appeared on Elizabeth's face. "And as for Derrick, there is every chance he could find a role befitting his lineage. Through marriage, yes, or perhaps even as a general or commander, taking up the mantle of his father..."

"NO!" Elizabeth shouted and jumped from her chair. She paced wildly to the center of the room, fiddling with the necklace around her neck, before at last turning back to Melinda, true tears pouring down her face. "No! I will not tolerate my son being sent to war! I will not have it!"

"Elizabeth, Auntie... I'm sorry," Melinda said quickly, rising halfway from her seat. "I didn't mean to upset you. I only meant to suggest... there is much respect and prestige to be found in such a station..."

"You know nothing of my station," Elizabeth scowled. "Of the many lonely nights, with no husband to tend to me. To wear a wedding band in name only. To have children who barely know their father!"

Melinda rose from her chair and tried to approach Elizabeth, but she twisted away sharply.

"My youngest, Manford, did not even recognize his own father when he last returned home! Such a thing..." she whispered. "And then, when you are given precious time with the one man in this whole world you love and gives you comfort, he breaks into a sweat and a fever, and so even in my own home, I am robbed of my bed with him. And his fever grows worse, and the doctors, oh! When I saw the cuts upon his body... after a lifetime of war... such sinister acts committed by savages and beasts the realm could hardly imagine—I grew sick. Yet for all my ailment, Thane ailed worse, and in the middle of the night, he screamed for me and I came, and with fear in his eyes and sweat on his brow, the bravest man of the realm you see brought to such terror and fear told me of a vision, where the phoenix did not rise from the ash rebirthed, but instead clawed at its own feathers, ripping them from its own body, so that the bird no longer possessed the spirit of fire, and died, and rotted, as he saw his fate to be."

Melinda stood still as Elizabeth sobbed quietly, as the scent of incense curled around them. "Elizabeth... dearest, please, you do not make any sense. We were unaware of any ailment that befell Thane during his last leave to Aberness, but I thank you profoundly for bearing the weight of his duties on behalf of the realm. I am fortunate to see my husband every day, and aye, this past year has been among the hardest of my life with my boys traveling the realm. It was but a year, mere peanuts compared to a whole marriage, yet my heart ached every day without them. I can only imagine the suffering you have endured."

Elizabeth straightened, wiping tears from her face, her dark gown mirroring the stormy expression that replaced her grief. "I do not weep for myself," she said, her voice sharp. "I weep for Thane, the love of my life! And for the misery he endured, both known and foreseen."

Melinda arched a brow, unsure how to navigate this revelation. "Surely, you don't mean to suggest his dream was anything more than a simple fever?"

"No," she said coldly, insulted. "He was gravely ill, but I believe the terror that lived within his mind. A lifetime of war, can you imagine? And so, the day he was scheduled to depart... for what would be the last time, he did not take the family sword to war. Imagine, such an action, inspired by such terror, to leave a symbol of our house behind."

"So... is it you who desires the sword?"

Elizabeth turned away, her fingers brushing over the altar as she picked up the cracked portrait of the Phoenix King. She ran a finger along the fracture in the glass before setting it down with care. "It is as if you've heard nothing."

"Elizabeth, understand that I play no role in these decisions. You come to me in grief, speaking of visions and inheritances. Reflect on your own words: As women, what agency do we truly possess in such matters? If these rumors of the Master of War nomination are true, what power do you think I wield to sway them?"

"Your husband is alive, is he not? Sway him."

"I shall speak to him. I have promised you this."

"I want more than promises, my empress. I want justice and safety for my family. The realm is a fragile place—the Diet of Blood taught us so two generations ago. I cannot leave my family's station to chance or goodwill."

Melinda drew herself up, her voice gaining a steely edge. "I have listened patiently to your words in this room, and aye, as they have been spoken before God, I shall honor the secrecy of this conversation. But know this: I will not entertain talk of a weak realm or suggestions of my interference with the High Council, or God forbid, that accursed crown succession. My husband and your emperor, the holy anointed ruler from God, bears the burden of an entire realm, not just one family. As Thane sacrificed, so too does Bancroft. I honor your late husband's service, as I honor Derrick's potential and

Catelyn's maturity. A path will be laid for all, that much I am certain of."

Elizabeth twisted the chain of her necklace around her fingers, her eyes locking with Melinda's. The room fell into stillness, broken only by the tendrils of smoke rising from the altar's candles. At last, she lifted her chin, her voice measured but laden with warning. "Perhaps I have spoken out of turn. Forgive me, for I am a widow in grief. The realm is vast, and many considerations weigh upon you and your husband. I will bide my time, for now. But know this: I will fight for my children, as the Lord commands all mothers to do. I pray we do not find ourselves at odds. When conflicts arise, as they did during the Diet of Blood, when violence threatened to topple us, clarity emerged in the vote of the Electors. I trust the same will happen again."

A lump formed in Melinda's throat at Elizabeth's rebuke. She opened her mouth to respond, anger flaring in her chest, but Elizabeth turned on her heel and swept from the room without another word. Melinda stood rooted in place, realizing only then that sweat beaded on her brow. With a deep sigh, she pressed a hand to her forehead and turned her gaze to the portrait of the Phoenix King.

"I'm sorry," she whispered to him. The mention of the Diet of Blood was a grim curse in a holy room, a period when the Electors dared to challenge the primacy of the eldest male heir of House Hieronymus, plunging the family and the realm into chaos. Brother turned on brother, cousin against cousin, and the blood of nobles stained the very foundations of their house. She did not want history to repeat itself but knew she could not yield—for Warwick and Lysander alike.

"Fire does not choose what it burns."

A wall of incense hit her nose. She spun around on her heels, but found no one.

"Oh my." She patted her brow and shook off her jitters. She hiked her skirt, and following in Elizabeth's shadow, fled from the solar as well.

JAE IV

The faun scaled the hillside leading to the estate, his hooves sure-footed on the uneven rock, unfurling a long banner as he went. Jae watched from the safety of the manicured grass, holding the other end of the banner. Petra, assigned to kitchen duty, found every excuse to watch, her head frequently popping out from the slave passageways. She didn't trust the so-called slayer of bulls around the faun.

Jae, however, pretended not to notice her. Petra reported directly to Old Berona in the kitchens now, and he couldn't risk jeopardizing his relationship with the estate's head chef. Not just for the constant supply of cookies and pies that Berona baked in abundance, but for the warmth and affection she gave so freely. The old woman reminded him of his grandmother— only a blur in his memory now, a sweet figure buried beneath the waves, but there was still a lingering sweetness in the way Berona's presence filled that void.

"No, no, no! This simply won't do!" Aeksilor appeared from nowhere. "The Balons have unfurled twice as many banners, twice! This is an outrage! What will the good people of Astrelaide think when they look up and see my magnificent home with no honor and respect for the occasion? There will be riots I tell you! I'm not spending good coin this year for nothing. More banners! Everywhere!" He snapped his fingers, and just as quickly as he appeared, he vanished.

Jae found his heartbeat in his throat as looked to Hex for guidance. The faun hopped along the cliff face, his small tail wagging as he hammered an iron stake into the rock, securing the far end of the streamers. Jae, gripping the opposite end, began to step backward as Hex bounded back toward him, moving effortlessly across the uneven stone.

"No," he said firmly, holding up his hairy arms.

He refused to pry the banner from Jae's grasp, his expression one of polite insistence. Jae furrowed his brow but handed over the banner, a string of triangular red flags adorned with embroidered yellow suns in the center. Hex looked up at him—barely reaching Jae's chest save for his horns, which glinted at eye level, dull and rounded, more ceremonial than dangerous.

"I'll take it," Hex huffed. His short legs shuffled backward as if preparing to bow, but then he shot up the side of the estate, his hooves finding natural grooves in the white walls, as though he'd done this a thousand times before. With ease, he clambered onto the roof and fastened the banner in place.

"Does it look right?" Hex called down, his tail wagging in the light of the early afternoon sun.

Jae shielded his eyes with his hand. "Straight, yes," he called back. "but Master Aeksilor was just here. He wants more banners."

Hex sighed. "I understand. I'll find more." The faun looked to the cliff-side ridge, where other homes of Astrelaide's elite perched precariously on the hillside. Streams of banners, mostly red, but some a blend of rainbow hues, dotted the ridgeline of the Rose like a colorful web from an enormous spider. "More," he sighed again. He hopped down from the roof, landing in a cloud of dust before him. "Leave it to me."

"For the good master," Jae added quickly. He didn't want Hex to think this was his doing, but the faun made him no further mind, scampering off to fetch more supplies. Jae watched him go, when a sharp voice cut through his thoughts.

"You there!"

Jae jumped for the second time that day and turned to find Petra emerging from the small opening that led to the slave quarters carved into the hillside.

"Oh, no, I wasn't, no… I wasn't bossing him around."

"You have been requested, come with me." She stamped her foot. She was flushed, her fair skin dotted with freckles, and her dark brunette curls clinging to her face, damp with sweat. She had been working in the kitchens. "Come with me, *now*."

"The kitchens?" he asked. His stomach growled.

"No, not the kitchens. Hurry," Petra snapped, vanishing back into the dark opening.

Jae hesitated but followed, ducking into the cool, shadowy space of the equipment-and-storage room. Only narrow, high-set windows allowed thin shafts of light to break through, casting pale beams that illuminated drifting dust motes like falling ash.

"Petra, I didn't mean to—about Hex, it wasn't my…"

"Shush," she hissed, grabbing his arm and pulling him deeper into the quarters.

They moved quickly through the storage room, past racks of tools and supplies, and into a narrow hallway that led to the bath chambers. But instead of stopping there, Petra steered him down another dark passage that led toward the sleeping chambers.

Their quarters were carved directly into the cliff side, the walls transitioning from cheap plaster and stone to bare, solid rock as they moved deeper beneath the estate. The slaves' sleeping areas were segregated between men and women, and the hallway forked just beyond a single large candle that flickered dimly outside the chambers, marking the divide.

Petra grabbed the candle without hesitation, its weak flame barely lighting the path ahead. "Wait in the dark." She pointed to his chamber. "I will be quick."

He did as he was bid, slipping into his chamber. It was nearly pitch-black, only a trickle of light managing to reach this deep into the basement. As his eyes adjusted, he could make out the rows of wooden beds lining the walls, each stuffed with straw and covered in rough, cheap cotton. Small chests were scattered between the beds, holding what little meager possessions his fellow slaves owned. Jae ran his fingers over the coarse fabric of his own bed, still in disbelief that it was his… Lucien insisted on the first night that Guard move across the room to free up the bed beside him.

"Here." Petra materialized beside him, thrusting a red tunic into his hands. "I hope this is acceptable to the slayer of bulls."

"Petra…"

"Be quick about it. Meet me at the bath when you're done." She vanished as swiftly as she had come.

Frowning, he inspected the red tunic. It was silky soft but heavy. It would be a magnet for heat. Jae sighed, removing his clothes. In the dark, he felt over the tunic, trying to ascertain the opening, running his hands over it, and trying to slip it over his head. It went with some difficulty when Jae realized it had been fetched from the woman's chamber. It barely slid over his torso as his growing muscles and new weight resisted the cloth. "Ironic," he muttered. He waddled around the room, arms squeezed to his sides in mock indignation. "I thought moths were meant to be kept away from nice clothes." And to his surprise, he laughed.

Smirking at his joke, he waddled down the hall and to the bath, where he found Petra drying her freshly washed hair, her face clean.

"Petra, this tunic is for a woman—"

"None of that now," she cut him off. "Clean your face, quickly."

Reluctantly, he obeyed, scrubbing his face in silence. When he finished, Petra had another humiliation waiting.

"Perfume," she commanded, producing a small bottle. Without waiting for his response, she doused him in the foul odor.

He coughed and batted the air. "I don't think the good lady of the house would like us using her—"

"Don't tell me what she likes," Petra snapped. "Besides, it's from the good master." She circled him, spraying more, then spun him around with such force that Jae nearly lost his balance. The tunic strained at the seams.

"You've gained muscles," she said, finally stepping back with a satisfied look. "No longer the skeleton from the slave pits. You could slay a dragon now." She smirked, and before he could protest, she pulled out a small ornate handheld mirror, gilded with jewels.

"Hold this," she commanded, thrusting the mirror into his hands.

Jae raised it reluctantly, and a shock ran through him. His face had changed—his once sunken cheeks had filled out, and dark stubble spread across his jaw. He would have to start shaving soon.

"I would never let Luke shave my head even if my life depended on it." Petra finally cracked a joke, tugging at his short, dark hair. "Not much to work with, but… there." She yanked the mirror away. "Satisfied?"

He looked down at the red tunic, its fabric stretched taut across his chest. A large gilded sun was embroidered at the center, its stitches straining against his growing muscles. It was hard to believe, even seeing it… *feeling it*, for himself. He was growing stout, and his biceps, once nothing more than skin on bone, now swelled.

"This is for girls," he muttered at last, though a smile tugged at his lips. It was the first time he'd ever seen his reflection in a mirror.

"If it was for girls, it wouldn't be tight on your chest," Petra replied, shaking her head. "Besides, the good masters don't pay for gendered clothes unless you're a pillow girl. Now listen—Old Berona has prepared a modest feast for lunch. You're going to practice serving. Walk with grace, be calm and steady, and you'll do just fine."

"Serve?" Jae's face twisted in disbelief. His whole life, he'd eaten with his fingers. Old Berona had only recently introduced him to a spoon and taught him the complex maneuvers of the fork and knife. "I cannot serve. I'm a guard now."

"You are whatever the good master says you are," Petra snapped. "Now listen." She brushed up against him, her chest pressing against his own. "Aeksilor is a very shrewd and fearful man. This manse once swarmed with slaves, and only I and the others survived his culling. You will not disappoint tonight, understand? Neither one of us is going back to the auction block. Not now, not ever." Her eyes burned as she pressed her point. "Enough complaining. Upstairs, let's go. You have much to learn before tonight."

She grabbed his arm again, as if he couldn't follow simple instructions on his own, and practically dragged him up the narrow staircase. They emerged into the kitchen, where Old Berona was rushing about, a whirlwind of motion. The rich smells of stew and roast duck hit him like the blunt force of a sword, but his appetite didn't stir. Petra's words had left him cold, draining the hunger from his stomach.

"This is not for you, love. There is much work to be done." The old woman did not so much as look upon him, as she was so furiously stirring a pot of stew above a crackling fire. "Valeana is in the dining chamber now, making preparations. You should join her."

"Yes, ma'am." Petra nodded.

"And *Moth*," Old Berona added. "keep them well-fed with duck, stew, and bread. Merry and drunk, and there may be a sweet or two for you before the night ends."

Jae smiled and nodded, but Petra rolled her eyes and grabbed his arm, dragging him from the kitchen.

They entered a large hallway, lined with red tiles and

adorned with vases and exquisite artwork. "Not for your untrained eye." Petra scoffed, tugging him along.

She pulled him toward a grand set of mahogany doors that opened into a magnificent room. Jae gasped as they stepped inside, his gaze drawn to the towering arched ceilings anchored by two dazzling chandeliers, sparkling in the sunlight that filtered through the half-enclosed space. White archways framed stunning views of the sky, opening to a mezzanine along the cliff side. The view plummeted to reveal the sprawling city below, alive with vibrant preparations for the festival. Distant sounds of trumpets and drums drifted upward from the streets, promising a grand celebration ahead.

"Did you bring me him?" came a dark, jaded voice from across the dining hall. A massive table stretched the length of the room, capable of seating a hundred guests with ease. It was already set with golden goblets, vases filled with red flowers, extravagant porcelain from distant lands, and gleaming silverware, including the illustrious fork and spoon. At the far end of the table stood another slave, Valeana, furiously polishing a box of silverware.

"He is all that is available," Petra answered. She nearly had to shout to be heard a continent away.

"Then he shall do. Quickly, he must be trained before tonight, and before I am called back to…"

"VALEANA!"

The shriek pierced the air, causing Petra to release Jae's arm, though he wished she hadn't. It was the most terrifying voice he had ever heard.

"Valeana!" The shriek echoed again as Sirene's tiny head appeared among one of the archways. "I need help with my braids, now!"

Petra and Jae snapped to attention, bowing, but Sirene paid them no mind. She simply watched Valeana put down the silverware and begin her long march toward them. With a roll of her eyes, Sirene disappeared with an annoye. "hmmph!"

Valeana shuffled quickly, her breath coming in short gasps. Though still a young woman, years of servitude to Sirene had left their mark. Strands of gray crisscrossed her dark hair, and deep lines etched into her face told stories of fatigue. She wore the same red tunic as Jae but halted before him, her heavy-lidded eyes locking onto his. "Do not mess this up."

"Come on." Petra grabbed his shoulder as Valeana sped off. "I'll show you the ropes."

The afternoon was spent attending to the most useless rules and procedures Jae could ever imagine. The placement of forks, varying only slightly in size, was deemed of utmost importance. Drinks had to be poured from the right with one hand. Handkerchiefs were to be artfully arranged beneath the utensils and in carefully folded stacks at the center of the table. A golden goblet held wine, while a glass cup held water. Servers stood along the walls, one arm folded in front, the other behind. Eye contact with guests was forbidden unless summoned. Petra instructed him on their silent signals for what Jae thought were needlessly complex tasks. Food was food to him; he could tear duck with his hands and drink soup straight from the bowl. Wine could come straight from the bottle and water from the tap, but these were not the ways of the masters—*of civilized people.*

"I can't possibly remember all this," Jae eventually lamented to Petra. They were busy placing the utensils on the far side of the table. "Why did the good master choose me?"

"Because Lucien is busy running errands for the master, and the other guards are too brutish and old to attend to the good masters and their ladies. You will do fine; there's simply no other option. Besides, tonight will be just for the family."

Jae froze and stood upright from the table. He looked upon the rows of seats, his temple pounding with the drumbeats of the lower city. "They won't even fill all the seats?" he gasped, breathless.

"It is customary to prepare for unexpected guests. Now back to work!"

He looked to Petra, watching as he micro-maneuvered the placement of a spoon and fork, her eyebrow wincing from the posture of her bent back. They came along Hex, straddling the outside balcony of the dining room's mezzanine, a roll of solstice flags clenched in his mouth as he dangled over nothing but open sky. Jae didn't think it wise to complain further.

So his training continued until the sun dipped below the cliff face and cast the city into shadow. Streamers decorated the house as the ruckus from the city below took on a new life. The relentless beat of drums and even the boisterous laughter of drunken revelers reached all the way up to the master's manse. As Petra finally deemed their work complete and the masters prepared for their solstice eve meal, Jae found a rare moment to himself. He leaned against the balcony railing, gazing out over the city and into the evening air.

He smiled, taking in the energy of the night. A cool breeze greeted him, carrying the familiar scent of salt air from the ocean. *Home.* He gazed at the sea of lights twinkling below as torches flickered to life, and far out at sea, a thousand ships appeared on the horizon, their lanterns sailing toward destinations unknown. In an instant, he felt himself falling. He gripped the railing for dear life, his heart racing as the floor beneath him seemed to tremble, but with a firm stamp of his foot, he found it steady beneath him. Tears pricked at his eyes, and his stomach twisted into a knot.

The sea stretched out before him, the very same sea from his childhood—the sea that held memories of his mother and father, his brothers and sisters, the crystal-clear waters of his home, and his beloved pet coconut crab, Coco. But it was also the same sea that had brought marauders, fire, and destruction. Even in his memories they pillaged, bringing their rattling chains and collars. Slowly, he lifted a trembling hand to his throat, feeling the cold collar clamped above his breastbone. There would never be an escape.

"Jae," a soft voice called to him from behind. He jumped at the use of his true name, finding it strange and foreign upon his ears. The word began to fade from his thoughts even as he turned to find Old Berona standing in the shadows. "It is almost time to begin, child." Her voice was soft. She looked so small in the dim light.

"Thank you, old mother," he replied, walking toward her.

She took him by the arm, and together they made their way to the kitchen. To his surprise, he found Pete and Pate hoisting a monstrous crate onto the center island. Dark wings jutted out from the top, and a massive scorpion tail dangled from the back. Jae did a double take, but Old Berona quickly turned him away. Petra and Valeana were waiting, and the old woman had no time to dwell on the creature in her kitchen.

"All right, you lot, let's see to it. Treat our good masters well and perhaps there will be duck on the bone and a tart filled with jelly waiting for us come midnight. Let us move with haste!" The old mother clapped her hands, and like a swarm of bees, they unceremoniously began their work.

Jae transported jugs of water and wine into the dining hall, where the good master's family had gathered. At the head of the table sat Master Aeksilor, with his good lady wife, Lady Aril, at his right hand. Next to her sat their sole daughter, God bless her, Sirene, and across from them were Aeksilor's two sons: the eldest, Luthor, and the younger, Boros. Only Luthor resembled their father, with black hair, tan skin, and dark eyes. The youngest neared plumpness, while the older leaned skinny. Together, they occupied only a fraction of the grand table, and to Jae's astonishment, wore clothing selected simply for the act of dining. They wore red and gold robes dripping with jewels, primarily of rubies for their dark red hue. Jae had never seen such extravagant clothes, even here in the upper city. He guessed each robe was worth the life of a slave at least.

The first course began with an endless parade of small dishes: plates of spiced potatoes, bowls of loaded hummus, salads mixed with feta and dates, and peppers, vegetables, and exotic foods Jae had no name for. Petra, Valeana, and Jae carried out Old Berona's handiwork with efficiency and speed before taking their places along the back wall. Behind the good masters, the night sky twinkled with stars, pulsing to the rhythm of the drums echoing from the streets below.

The family stuffed themselves for an hour, and once the first course was finished, Aeksilor gleefully tapped his knife to a goblet of wine and rose, one hand firmly supporting his bulging and overstuffed belly. "My good family, I am so… grateful, to have you all gathered around this table. This past year has not been easy, and perhaps I have been neglectful in my duties as a father and a caring husband to you all…"

"Daddy, no! You are the best!"

Aeksilor smiled at his daughter, a slight belch escaping his lips. "… but I thank you all for your patience and belief in me. I carry the name of Aeksilor with pride, though it is a heavy burden, and soon, someday, my boys, Luthor and Boros, will shoulder the same weight. I can only pray that the burden will be lighter on your shoulders. For that, we must pray, for the solstice is a celebration of the Sun Father, the almighty one, the blazing fury in the sky who provides us with sustenance and comfort, and scorches those who neglect their duties. Sun Father, honor us further; pass your blessings onto my children, so they may marry well and have bountiful offspring. We give our thanks to you."

"Amen," echoed the family. With that, Aeksilor raised his goblet high, downing the drink in great gulps. Luthor lifted his goblet under the watchful eyes of his mother, taking only a cautious sip. Lady Aril, her back to the twinkling stars of the night sky, took only a sip of her wine.

The master's family began their celebrations, breaking into rapid conversation and gossip. Boros brought out a series of spinning tops and dice, and the children, along with Aeksilor, broke into frantic laughter, gambling their future desserts or daring each other to unveil ridiculous truths. Only Lady Aril did not play. She only poked at her soup with a troubled expression and occasionally sipped her wine.

"Next course!" Aeksilor announced, still riding high from a particularly robust defeat at the hands of his daughter.

Jae, Petra, and Valeana swooped in, swiftly clearing the picked-over bowls of soup and salad. Jae hurried back to the kitchen, where Old Berona worked alongside Pete and Pate to pull a large, roasted creature from the oven. But this was not his role, so he returned to the dining room with a sparkling jug of water, making his rounds to refresh the family's drinks. They barely acknowledged him, engrossed as they were in Aeksilor's drunken tales of his youth, including one particularly ridiculous story about wrestling a faun. Only when Pete and Pate appeared, hoisting the great roasted manticore between them, did the family finally turn their attention away from the stories. Luthor and Boros burst into applause.

The roasted body of the beast was set on the table. Jae looked on, astonished, as the body had been dismembered: the head, with its eerily human face, had been removed, and the scorpion tail was nowhere to be seen. Only the great wings of the beast, roasted and seasoned, remained as testament to the creature's former terror. Master Aeksilor greeted the meal with a toothy grin and eagerly delegated the role of carving the monster to his eldest son, who, with a large smile, no doubt in part from the wine, took a great knife, carved with the image of this people's Sun God, and sliced open the manticore.

Petra and Valeana returned with an endless array of sides: baked and mashed potatoes of every variety, roasted onions glistening with grease, and seasoned locusts skewered and fried to perfection. Roasted peppers in every hue were arranged in colorful rows, flowing from the kitchen like harvest bounty. Old Berona's handiwork was evident as the family carefully selected the most succulent roasted vegetables, the butteriest slices of bread, and the richest cuts of manticore.

Jae stood at attention, frequently called upon to serve, dishing out water to quench the thirst of the good masters as they indulged in the spicy, salty delights of their meal. Petra and Valeana worked diligently, scrutinizing the masters' plates with a meticulousness that bordered on scientific, adeptly gauging when a dish had lost its appeal and needed to be cleared away. The kitchen was a whirlwind of activity, even with the main course served; plate after plate of half-eaten meat and vegetables returned to Old Berona for disposal—or, more hopefully, for their bellies to enjoy past the midnight hour. Far below in the city, the tempo of the drumbeats matched their frenzied footsteps.

Finally, Master Aeksilor leaned back in his chair, one hand resting on his belly, and grunted with pleasure. His sons mirrored his posture, the eldest clearly intoxicated, while Lady Aril remained an island of indifference, her lips pursed in quiet satisfaction. Beside her, however, a wicked grin spread across Sirene's face.

"Daddy! Is it time? Is it time, Daddy!" She leaned over the table, her palms pressing down so that the silverware clinked with each eager syllable.

"Oh sweety, of course it is. But who will you choose to break the wing with you?"

"Boros, because I am stronger than him!"

Boros leaned forward with the same toothy grin as his father, but the master had other intentions. "Nonsense, sweety. Junior, you should break the wing with your sister. You are almost of age now, and I would be remiss if I did not give you a chance to wish for a great lady wife like my own!" The master burst into laughter. Lady Aril did not.

Luthor jumped at the opportunity. Sirene smiled and climbed onto the table, shattering a priceless dish before her mother. She positioned herself beside the manticore roast, grasping one of the beast's seasoned wings. Luthor mirrored her actions, grinning widely as he leaned over the creature's carved body, its bones and spine exposed, grease still glistening on its hide.

The master leaned forward, grease dripping from his pointed beard. "Are we ready?"

"Do it, Daddy!"

"Then we take this dark beast's wings on the day of our Lord to celebrate the eternal Sun. May His great rays shine forever, casting good judgment upon the land, and may evil, which shall always find defeat, be vanquished. By the power of good, we mock the manticore's wicked ways. May the winner find great fortune!"

Luthor immediately yanked at the wing, tearing ligaments from the roast. But Sirene, ever the crafty one, dropped to her knees and clasped her hands around the base of the adjacent wing. Before Luthor even realized what was happening, she yanked hard, pulling the wing from the roast and falling backward on the table. Laughing, she held up the wing, larger than her own body, triumphantly in her hands.

"I did it! I did it!"

Lady Aril looked on in dismay as Luthor frowned, staring down at his feet. The good master laughed heartily and jumped up to applaud. Jae pretended not to watch, stationed along the wall, but the sound of the wing tearing from the body made his stomach churn.

"And they say dark wings bring dark tidings." Aeksilor roared in laughter. "What did you wish for, my vanilla bean?"

"Daddy, you know I cannot say!" She giggled. She jumped down from the table, the massive wing still in her hands. Lady Aril looked away in revulsion. Sirene began to run around the room, pretending to fly and snap at her brothers, who squealed with laughter, ducking to avoid her imaginary claws.

"Children, now really..." Lady Aril rose from the table. "This is not how we show decorum on this day..." But her voice trailed off, her head cocked to the side. Jae noticed it too. The drums and music from the city below had fallen silent. The night air was thick with an eerie stillness.

Lucien stood in the dining room. Lady Aril's eyes widened as if she were staring at a phantom. Aeksilor, his smile fading at his lady's reaction, followed her gaze to the slave courier. Lucien's hair clung to his face in damp clumps, and he was breathing heavily, sweat pouring down his body. The children froze, adding to the silence of the night.

"Well..." Aeksilor grumbled, his eyebrows lowering into a frown. "Speak then, damn you, to interrupt our festivities."

"Murdered!" Lucien choked out. "The good Master Balon, murdered in the streets."

Sirene, across the room, dropped the dark wing.

MELINDA II

Melinda looked up at the coiled serpent. She swallowed hard, fighting the urge to flee. She did not fear snakes, but this one was simply massive, towering over the entire room.

"Melinda? Please, answer me!"

A hand pulled on her arm, begging her to move, but she did not. She looked upward upon the legless monstrosity, cursing the symbol of the fallen Makkan Empire. The snake, fit to eat a hundred men, bared its fangs over the banquet hall. A thousand colored feathers, each the size of a person, crowned the creature's head, doing little to mask its hideous nature. Her mind wheeled, eyes quickly darting through the startled women of the chamber. The tail of the beast wrapped along the far wall, before at last a forked tail with two golden rattles hung over the hall's doors. It rattled now, drawing the guests' attention. *Fools.* Why turn your attention from the beast's fangs?

"... and announcing her daughter, the Lady Torralin Hieronymus of Rose Mont!"

With a faint roll of her eyes, Melinda joined in the polite applause, her hands barely touching. Her guests, a hundred ladies of the realm, watched her reaction closely. She would not let this turn into the day's scandal.

Two women stood at the forefront of the banquet hall. Beneath the golden rattles of the feathered serpent, the women of House Hieronymus's Rose Mont cadet branch offered deep curtsies. They wore magnificent ball gowns, and already gasps and whispers of amusement and disdain, intrigue and fashion, swept through the crowd.

"A choice, to be sure," Jayne Hieronymus whispered as the applause died down.

Lesser courtiers surged forward to greet the cadet branch of the family tree, but Melinda made no such effort. She was the empress—they would come to her.

"Indeed," Melinda said, lifting her teacup with a bemused smile. "Let us see how this rose fares in a garden of snakes."

"My husband Milton be praised, nothing goes on in the city of High Ness without his knowledge."

"The shamelessness of it all," Ruby of House Landstride tsked. "To come to court and interrupt *your* tea party!"

Melinda smiled, looking to her friend, a minor noblewoman with a penchant for court gossip. "The road to High Ness is long and winding, and in late spring, I'm sure it's a muddy, miserable affair. I imagine they arrived with the best intentions."

"In good faith? I heard the whispers too! They arrived last night in High Ness, and still, they chose now to make an appearance!"

Ruby, true to her namesake, turned bright red. Melinda merely shrugged, taking another sip of tea.

Undeterred, she turned to the final woman of their small group. "Arrianette, please tell me you find this development most unwelcome?"

Arrianette had her attention trained on the Rose Mont women. Flocks of lesser courtiers were squawking for their attention, while those of higher standing bided their time. A cousin to Graham Fontaine, an Elector and filthy-rich lord of the realm, Arrianette, Melinda noted, kept her eyes solely trained on the dresses and jewels of the Rose Monts.

"Arrianette?"

"Do you suppose there is a scandal on the horizon?" Arrianette said at last.

"On the horizon? A scandal is already here!" Ruby cried.

"Ruby, dear, perhaps more tea would soothe your nerves?" Jayne placed a gloved hand on Ruby's trembling wrist.

"Tea? Tea? Oh yes, tea, that would be nice, yes..."

Jayne snapped her fingers to summon the servants. Meanwhile, Arrianette kept her gaze fixed on the Rose Monts, a faint smirk tugging at the corner of her mouth as gasps of excitement rippled through the cluster of ladies surrounding them.

"Arrianette, do you suspect something is the matter?" Melinda asked.

Arrianette possessed cold blue eyes. Her beauty was known far and wide, and with pale skin and dark-red curly hair, she looked more like a doll than a person. Lesser ladies whispered that her allure masked a false heart, but Melinda knew better. Arrianette's intuition was sharp, honed by a lifetime of sidestepping scandals. If there was a game at play, Arrianette would see it.

"Look, my empress, how the women of the court crowd the Rose Monts. Chiefly, the daughter." Arrianette touched the corner of her mouth with a gloved hand.

"Flies drawn to manure."

"Observe how she glitters in the sunlight," Arrianette continued. "She turns, and her jewels cast a dazzling array across the room. Yet... perhaps that's not why they're so taken." She lifted a gloved hand to her mouth, hiding the faintest smile.

Melinda frowned. She lowered her teacup, her focus now fully on the girl at the center of attention. "Her dress... yes, it's finely crafted, well-embroidered… but do you notice the frills along the hem? And those flowers stitched into the lace? How… last season."

"Everyone knows swirls are the fashion of the summer," Arrianette replied, tapping her chin thoughtfully. "No, it's not the dress. The true attraction must be…" Her voice trailed off, and her eyes widened slightly. "Ah. Yes."

"What? What is it?" Melinda leaned forward, rising on tiptoes to catch a better view.

A murmur rose around her, and a courtier to her right noticed her sudden interest, sparking a wave of whispering and gloved hands rising in the direction of the Rose Monts, as ripples from a sugar cube dropped into a teacup. Realizing the stir she was causing, Melinda quickly looked away, shifting her focus to Arrianette's composed expression.

"The girl is engaged."

"Engaged!" Ruby squealed, her voice echoing across the banquet hall. In seconds, the entire room was abuzz.

"Dearest." Melinda simply smiled at her. "Let's endeavor to exercise a little restraint, shall we?"

Ruby flushed an even deeper red, while Jayne patted her hand consolingly. "Do we know who the unfortunate soul might be?"

"Unfortunate, perhaps, but a fool?" Melinda's eyes stayed trained on the growing spectacle as more ladies peeled away from their groups to gawk at the Rose Mont girl. "Let's not be too quick to judge. Whoever he is, he's already secured the court's full attention."

"For what it's worth, they have already made themselves the talk of the court."

"The *scandal* of it," Arrianette said, finally breaking her intense gaze from the Rose Monts. She lifted a delicate hand to her forehead. "Oh, the utter tragedy!"

"Arrianette!" Melinda clucked, immediately playing into her game. "Are you light in the head? Quick, summon a fainting couch at once!"

"Yes! I am overcome!" Arrianette leaned dramatically against the table at their center, her expression a mix of feigned horror and delight. "I just feel... such sorrow."

"Whatever for?" Ruby squeezed Jayne's hand, squealing with real horror.

"What times we live in, when all decorum is tossed to the wind!" Arrianette declared, waving her hand. "I remember when visiting dignitaries would first pay homage to the host of the hall—never mind the *empress*!" She looked to Melinda, batting her large eyelashes. Now it was her turn to burn red.

Their theatrics were working; courtiers around them began shifting their attention from the Rose Mont girls back to their circle, as servants scrambled to bring a fainting couch. With a dramatic moan, Arrianette pressed a hand to her forehead, letting it brush a glass, which tumbled to the floor and shattered.

"An insult as plain as daylight! Come, ladies, we must demonstrate the empress's grace," Melinda announced, gripping Arrianette's arm with faux concern. "The day shall end at once—I'll instruct the guards to dismiss—" But before she could give the order, the hooligan Harriet Hieronymus gave out a sharp cry, and at once snatched the attention of every last lady.

"My lady!" Harriet cried, pushing through the circle of ladies that had gathered around her and her daughter. An audible gasp rippled through the room as all eyes turned toward the far end, where a figure shrouded in black had emerged from a hidden doorway, slipping out beside the giant feathered serpent.

The hall was silent, save for the rattling of the serpent's gilded tail. Harriet herself froze in place. The guards, caught in the tension, hesitated, torn between decorum and the duty to fetch fainting couches for the swooning ladies.

"By the Nine!" Jayne rasped. The veiled figure glided forward, crossing the hall in eerie silence. Melinda's stomach twisted as she realized who it was.

"Announcing... announcing..." a member of the Demon-breun tried to call out, but he too was as shocked and confused as the ladies. The rattles of the forked serpent's tail shook, dousing the room in chaos, and the ecstasy of scandal at court reached its peak. A path cleared for Harriet, who hiked up her great dress and ran with a distinctive *click clack* of her shoes across the tiled floor.

"Why... why! I know exactly who that is... It's... It's..."

"My sister-in-law. The widow of Aberness," Melinda answered.

The shadow figure pulled back her veil, unveiling Elizabeth for all the good ladies of the realm to see.

Harriet ran forth, very unladylike, and gripped the widow in a tight hug. "Oh, when I heard what those savages had done, I cried for a fortnight!"

A collective sigh of awws swept the room. Even young Torralin—the Rose Mont daughter whose engagement had moments ago stolen the spotlight—pressed her hands to her chest, eyes filling with sympathetic tears for her distant, distant aunt.

"That *bitch*!" The word escaped Melinda's lips before she could stop herself.

Ruby, in shock, turned to Melinda with a face red as a beet, lifted her arm in a final gesture of horror, and fainted dead away onto the floor.

Oh, what a day at court!

Several shrieks echoed from the ladies of the realm, and guards rushed forward as Melinda stood frozen, wide-eyed, watching her friend and vassal sprawled on the floor. Jayne dropped to her knees, frantically fanning the incoherent Ruby.

Taking a measured step back, Melinda allowed the guards to lift Ruby and carry her out, with Jayne clutching her hand and waving desperately at Ruby's flushed face. Meanwhile, Arrianette merely smiled, flicking her wrist with practiced elegance, reclaiming the room's attention as eyes shifted back to their circle.

"Right then, very good," Melinda murmured, more to herself than anyone else. She felt a prickling heat rise in her cheeks and a strong temptation to follow after her fainted friend and escape the banquet hall's intensifying atmosphere. But she held her ground, keenly aware that a plot was unfolding. The timing was too perfect.

"Excuse me, my dearest," she said to Arrianette, dipping in a graceful curtsy, before turning with fierce determination masked by regal composure. Melinda strode through the throngs of ladies, every step deliberate, every glance directed. She felt the eyes of the room settle heavily upon her. Ahead, Harriet and Elizabeth froze in their embrace, looking up at her with expressions hovering between apprehension and something close to disdain.

"Elizabeth." She curtsied before her sister-in-law. She also bit her tongue, well aware Elizabeth had scarcely worn black since the day of her arrival. "And Harriet, oh, what an auspicious day of your arrival. The day grief resumes its place at court!"

"Grief, yes, oh it is very so!" Harriet gripped Elizabeth's hands. "My husband Charles and I came at once—the very moment we heard the news! An attack on one of us is an attack on us all, is it not?"

Elizabeth dabbed at her eyes, though her lips pressed into a slight suspicious purse that Melinda did not miss. A shiver ran down Melinda's spine.

"Indeed," Elizabeth said softly. "In times like these, we need family more than ever."

"There's not a single day that Bancroft and I don't grieve. He is... utterly bereft without his brother," Melinda replied, reaching for Elizabeth's hand. She scowled at the gesture, but Melinda's fingers closed firmly around hers, securing her in place.

"I appreciate your words, both of you, though I must confess, what I desire most is the emperor's presence." Elizabeth's voice softened, though her fingers tensed. "My late husband and I loved him dearly, and I feel lost without the comfort of his counsel."

"I am sure an arrangement can be made shortly." Melinda smiled, squeezing Elizabeth's hands in turn.

"Oh, I'm certain an arrangement could be made soon enough," Elizabeth replied with a saccharine smile. She dabbed another tear from her eye, her gaze sweeping across the court as though overcome with grief. "Though... perhaps this isn't the place for me to burden the ladies of the realm with my sorrow. Pray, might we go to Bancroft now, so we may mourn together? Where might he be, my sovereign?"

Melinda turned her head, a fake smile taking hold of her lips. *Why play this game now? Catelyn is to have a bright future ahead of her.* "I'm afraid he's... otherwise occupied," she replied smoothly.

"Oh?" Harriet interjected, feigning surprise. "Some matter of state has arisen, perhaps?" Her voice lilting with amusement, she continued. "I'd heard rumors of a small tourney today, and you know, my Charles simply can't resist displays of valor. The moment he heard steel would clash on steel... why, he nearly drove our horses to ruin in his haste."

"Your husband intends to joust?" Melinda asked, masking her surprise.

"Oh, heavens, no—my Charles's days of swordplay are behind him," Harriet replied, her smile twisting into something more pointed. "But my son James? He lives for it. And who knows? Perhaps young Lysander and Warwick might even have the pleasure of facing him."

Melinda's carefully held smile faltered. "The needs of boys and their lust for conflict." Her voice softened to a chill. "As if this realm has not seen enough bloodshed already."

"Oh, enough! I cannot bear talk of violence; it's all too much!" Elizabeth looked around at the gathered ladies, her expression artfully pained, each woman in the crowd seeming to hold her breath as she spoke.

Melinda forced her polite smile back into place, attempting to withdraw her hand. But Elizabeth held firm, her grip tightening until her nails pressed sharply against Melinda's skin.

"Come now, ladies, let us speak of cheer instead," Melinda suggested, trying to redirect the gathering. "Elizabeth, you've borne enough grief. Perhaps we may meet Torralin, so we may delight in our family's good news?"

"Ah, my daughter?" Harriet remarked with satisfaction. "Why, yes. I've heard rumors of much merriment to come." She gave a wave, and her daughter came bounding over—a petite young thing with her mother's large green eyes, raven hair, and an air of youthful exuberance. Harriet smiled broadly, pleased to present her. "May I introduce my daughter, Torralin, just four-and-ten, and newly betrothed to a most promising gentleman," Harriet announced, her voice practically a squeal.

Torralin curtsied before the queen, her expression bright and adoring. "It is a true honor to meet you, Your Majesty," she said with a gentle smile.

Melinda inclined her head in acknowledgment. "The honor is mine, young lady."

"And Elizabeth, my lady, what a horror I understand you and your children have been through. Thane and your family have lived in my prayers every night since the news reached our household."

"What a pretty young thing indeed," Elizabeth cooed, appraising Torralin. "My grief aside, I do cherish seeing young love. My late husband and I shared such love ourselves. You are very fortunate, my dear."

"Fortunate, indeed—but more than that, blessed by God alone," Torralin replied with a happy sigh. "Well… aside from the empress's blessings, of course." She dipped into a bow, her smile as guileless as it was sweet.

Melinda's pulse quickened. A calculated remark, and yet somehow the girl seemed entirely unaware of its implications.

"Oh, I hadn't realized the empress had blessed—or arranged—this betrothal," Elizabeth added, her tone perfectly polite, yet laced with pointed intrigue.

Melinda recoiled as though struck by the serpent above her. Her eyes flickered to it for a split second, just to be sure.

"To my knowledge… I'm afraid the empress did not play a role in this holy arrangement—no, it was fate, and of course, love!" Harriet proclaimed.

"Then pray tell, does the realm, or even the empress herself, know of such an arrangement?" Elizabeth turned toward Melinda with a wide, knowing smile.

Torralin, her face lit with unrestrained joy, burst out in a squeal. "None other than Casimir of House Valkirn!"

Melinda's decorum faltered. She swayed, stunned by the revelation that the betrothal was not to some minor lord, but to one of the only families in the realm absent from both court and the High Council—an Elector family, no less! Elizabeth's gleeful release of her grip and her ensuing squeal was all that kept Melinda standing as the room broke into scattered applause and murmurs.

"I know!" Harriet replied, and she and Elizabeth took hands, practically bouncing as they squealed together, drawing the court's eyes back to them.

Melinda forced her expression into one of glee, but her heart tightened with each shared gasp and giggle. How she wished now that she'd fled with Ruby!

"We are honored, truly honored, to share the news with you, Your Majesty," Harriet swiped a dramatic tear from her eye. "This, after all, is what life is truly about: family, children, marriage, and most importantly, love. It is a woman's power to cultivate love, to continue the family line, and ultimately, to shape the very course of the realm."

"Your words speak true, though they pull at my heart." Elizabeth released her grip from Torralin.

The young girl, a whimsical smile still on her lips, turned from their huddle, and without a curtsy or bow, skedaddled to the nearest group of ladies, eagerly presenting her betrothal to them.

"The talk of the realm," Melinda said.

"Such a young, pretty thing too." Elizabeth sighed, her eyes fondly following the girl. "Why, she's younger than my Catelyn."

"Who is…six-and-ten… if I recall," Harriet answered. "It is hard to believe a girl of such renowned beauty and station within the realm has not yet found a match."

Melinda's smile grew thin, her fingers tightening on her gown as she managed a response. "Well, the best matches are often worth waiting for," she replied, letting her gaze settle on each of them in turn. "I have no doubt her future will be as illustrious as she deserves."

"Is it true your son Derrick is to inherit Aberness? That would place him near the center of the realm's attention—though, of course, not above Lysander and Warwick, who are nearly of age themselves."

"And of course there's no talk of either young prince taking a wife," Elizabeth replied smoothly. "Perhaps Lysander found his adventures up north more… engaging than marriage. He is rather comely, after all. From the talk I hear, he has all the build and nature of a knight. I could think of no better figure to lead the realm in war."

Melinda's composure cracked, her smile faltering. "Dearest, what you suggest could be… treasonous."

Elizabeth waved her hand dismissively. "Nonsense! You misunderstand. I came to know the boy while he stayed with me in Aberness. I only meant you may fill the role of Master of War—a role I daresay I came to be familiar with."

Melinda's throat constricted as if the feathered snake itself had sprung to life. Her eyes shot between Harriet and Elizabeth rapidly, the sweat on her brow now streaking down her forehead. Both women looked intently upon her. "Lysander is too young for such an appointment… and regardless, the decision will fall to my husband and his council."

"Both boys are nearly sixteen," Elizabeth said, leaning closer. "And we know how young men act once they get a taste of power."

Melinda swallowed. "Meaning?"

Elizabeth clasped her hands gently but firmly, forcing Melinda to meet her gaze. "Your influence as a mother is waning. Derrick grows restless without a father's guidance, and Catelyn is well past the age for betrothal. Let us turn this funeral into a celebration. I propose we join Catelyn and Warwick, formally."

Harriet gasped—a well-practiced reaction, Melinda noticed with growing suspicion. She pulled her hands from Elizabeth's grip. "I'm afraid I must go... my friend Arrianette—"

"Oh, won't you allow a grieving widow this small joy?" Elizabeth's voice rose, drawing curious glances from nearby ladies. "Warwick and Catelyn belong together. Let us wed them!"

Harriet squealed, clapping her hands. "A splendid proposal!"

Melinda felt the walls closing in. *This is a trap—such things aren't done like this!*

Whispers rippled through the room. "A betrothal? Warwick and Catelyn, cousin to cousin?"

Melinda's head spun. Elizabeth looked at her, eyes wide and tear-brimmed, her gloved fingers pressing into Melinda's hand.

"The Master of Laws has already proposed a match..." Melinda said faintly, her composure crumbling.

Elizabeth released her grip as if burned. "Dymtrus? Of House Seavíc? Warwick is to wed a... Vayern?"

"...The proposal is under review," Melinda murmured.

Elizabeth's expression hardened, all traces of gentility vanishing. "Bancroft would choose Seavíc blood from Acquanis over our own? To a *Vayern*? I hadn't been informed of this. I've heard terrible things of those people..."

Harriet's smile grew sharp, her eyes glinting with amusement as she placed a hand on Melinda's shoulder. "We mustn't allow prejudice to divide our realm. Allow me to ease such fears." She gave a flick of her glove, and the faint rattle of the feathered snake caught everyone's attention as the herald's voice rang out.

"ANNOUNCING THE ARRIVAL OF THE... LADY VIPRA, PRINCESS OF ISPERIA!"

Melinda's eyes widened as she whirled, etiquette forgotten, to see the latest cause for gossip entering the hall. Slender and poised, with dark olive skin and hair like midnight, the Isperian princess glided into the room, her deep yellow gown revealing both her ankles and her décolletage. Gasps filled the hall.

"What is a princess of Isperia doing here?" Melinda whispered.

Harriet's smile didn't falter. "Why, I invited her, of course."

Melinda turned back to Harriet, barely containing her anger. She opened her mouth to unleash a retort when Elizabeth cut in, her expression as bewildered as Melinda's.

"Harriet... was that wise?"

Melinda paused, realizing Elizabeth hadn't known either. Harriet Rose Mont had played them both.

"Your late husband's influence extended further than you may know," Harriet said smoothly. "Now, come—allow me to introduce you." She took Elizabeth's hand, missing Melinda's as she glided toward the princess.

"I'm afraid I must decline. Give her my regards." Melinda forced a polite smile, then turned and slipped toward the exit, relief flooding her as the room's attention shifted to the foreign guest.

God above, she thought, *this is no longer a matter of prayers—I'll need more than Nine Miracles to navigate this.* She straightened her shoulders, her heart heavy. A betrothal to secure, and a future to shape.

Forgive me, Warwick.

JOSEPHINA IV

A shadow darted between the trees. A tree branch cracked in the woods. Someone or something stalked her. Josephina's breath grew quick and rapid as she unsheathed her knife. The donkey whined, sensing the same danger. Mishie, her lone watchman, remained vigilant.

She broke into fresh trembles but did not give herself to tears, at least not yet anyway. Her blood ran hot and sweat coated the inside of her cloak. Mother's house was close; she could feel its pull like a whirlpool of shadow and dread, but it was home nonetheless.

Have I been gone too long? Has Mother wroth with me? A tree groaned in the dark forest. She held the knife out in front of her, slowing her pace to a crawl. The snow underneath her galoshes clung to her calves, half-melted. The spring blizzard was losing its bite, and all around her, the forest was coming alive with melting ice and snow.

"If that's you, Mother, it wasn't my fault! The snow's too thick. I had to sleep in the woods!" she whispered to the dark trees. She kept the dagger ready in her hand, knowing Mother wouldn't recognize her. Not like this.

A breath. Too close. To her right.

The donkey brayed, dancing nervously aside. Josephina spun, her heart hammering, but saw nothing but the deepening shadows. The sun was sinking fast. She was running out of time.

She yanked the donkey's reins and they broke into a run. They dashed along the mountain stream, pushing for their house. Wet snow splashed on her shins as melting ice dampened her coat from above. They ran faster and faster as a shadow in the trees kept pace with her every step, until she finally burst from the forest's edge and saw her mother's homestead. She tumbled forward, crashing face-first into the snow. Gasping, she rolled onto her side, the knife still clutched in her hand. It had punctured her coat, slicing the fabric, and drew a line of blood from her skin.

"Curses," she whimpered, staring at the red trickle spreading through the snowy folds of her cloak.

An explosion of birds from the treetops jolted her to her feet. The donkey bolted instinctively toward the barn, and she rushed forward, snatching Mishie from its back. Together, she and Mishie sprinted for the house, and at last, she burst through the front door, the warmth washing over her as she slammed it shut behind her. With a shaking hand, she finally sheathed the knife back into her cloak.

"Mother? I'm home!"

She pulled off her wet galoshes and socks. Her bare feet were soaked and nearly frostbitten, but the house was so warm. She sighed as she wiggled her toes, finally pulling back the hood of her cloak as well. The fire in the parlor burned brightly, crackling to the tune of snapping bones. *Home*. She smiled.

"Mother?" she called again, louder this time. "I've brought your supplies."

She walked toward the fire and pulled the mittens from her fingers. She strung them over the mantel and warmed her hands, closing her eyes to listen to the crackle of the fire.

The bird grows a third head. The bull bucks the man. A serpent enters the ocean.

She heard the words as goosebumps shot up her back. She thought it came from the kitchen. The fire hissed.

"Mother?" she whispered, inching toward the kitchen. Through the flickering light, she could see small shadows dancing on the walls. The hairs on the back of her neck stood on end.

"Mother, are you here?" She slunk into the kitchen. The fireplace glowed with red-hot coals as Mother's pot rested among them. A lid covered whatever strange potion she was brewing. Josephina scrunched her nose at the smell. It reeked of sulfur and brimstone.

A gurgle in the corner of the kitchen. A living shadow. The elf had returned.

Josephina threw herself backward, smashing into a kitchen cabinet. She raised one trembling hand to her throat as if to claw it open. She couldn't breathe.

The elf smiled, stepping out of the shadows with a wicked grin stretching across his small, twisted mouth. Josephina wanted to cry, but no sound escaped her throat.

"Jo-sep-hina," his voice squeaked, dripping with darkness. His voice mirrored the dark twinkle in his black eyes.

"N-no!" Josephina dropped her hand from her throat, desperately searching for Mishie. She grabbed hold of him, squeezing him for dear life.

"An o-o-o-o-oath has been swo-o-o-rn," the elf answered. He stepped forward. He barely reached her knee, but his shadow swallowed the room.

"Never again." The words formed on her lips, but she couldn't bring herself to say them.

"Pro-o-o-mises must be kept," the elf crooned, eyes gleaming.

"Never again," she squeaked. Tears sprang into her eyes. One hand clung to Mishie; the other inched toward her knife.

The elf watched, his tiny nose twitching as he sniffed the air, his black-on-black eyes fixed on her every move. Josephina felt as if she were falling, her body crumpling from within. She pulled the knife from her pocket, extending it shakily in front of her.

The elf's grin widened, his nostrils flaring. The blade was stained with her blood from the fall outside. He licked his lips.

"A t-a-a-a-ste?"

She saw a row of tiny razor-sharp teeth flash. His fingers twitched as he drummed them together, taking another step closer.

"For m-m-me?"

"Never!"

Josephina held the knife out, but her hands shook so violently that the blade trembled in the air. The elf took another step forward, now just an arm's length away. Oléfur reached up with his tiny fingers, standing on tiptoes to press down upon the blade. Josephina felt her arms lower, sweating as the elf brought the knife level with his mouth. His tongue emerged and moved like a serpent over the blade, licking it clean. She heard his tiny stomach rumble.

"A debt is owed to me," he growled.

"And a debt you shall be paid."

Mother appeared in the doorway. Josephina didn't know how long she had stood there, only that she was flooded with relief. The elf hissed, taking a step back, and spat something in the Old Tongue. The house trembled and the windows rattled. The floorboards groaned as though the very wood was twisting in on itself. The sound clawed at Josephina's mind, squeezing her lungs until she struggled to breathe.

"I keep my word. You will be paid," Mother answered.

The elf looked from Mother to Josephina, eyeing them both. Josephina's arm wobbled, the knife still extended. Blood and spittle dripped from the sides of her mouth.

"A blood oath is always paid… in one way or another." The elf nodded. He slunk away from Josephina.

276

"And you, young lady, is this how we treat our guests? Put the knife down, now."

Josephina didn't register her mother's request. Her eyes were still fixed upon the elf.

"Zakaenys. *Now!*"

Her knife hit the floor with a crash.

"Ah, now isn't this better? Maybe we can all get along now? As a family, perhaps?" Mother snickered. The elf hissed and Josephina sobbed. "Well, we certainly act like one big family. We are joined by *blood* after all."

Stepping closer, Mother patted Josephina on the head, then used a handkerchief to wipe the spittle from her chin. "Much better. Where would you be without me to take care of you?"

Josephina sputtered as if trying to talk.

"And what's this?" Mother stooped down to pick up the knife. "Josephina, darling, I didn't raise you to have this." Mother turned the knife over in her hands, tutting pitifully to herself.

"I... I... did the errand..."

"Yes, and how was your trip? Did you get everything I requested?"

Josephina tried to talk, but her ribs burned and her tongue throbbed. She only nodded instead.

"And maybe, perhaps, a little bit more?"

"M-m-mother, I..."

"Completed your task, and then some, or am I wrong? Do not worry, Josephina, I am not cross with you, only... worried. Yes, that is it, worried about your well-being. A little girl shouldn't play with such weapons, no. Or even *pay* for such weapons, do you disagree, Josephina?"

She shook her head no.

"Then tell me, young daughter, how did you come to have such an object?" Mother jostled the weapon in her hand, feeling its weight. The elf stood by the fire, watching Mother, and the steel, with glinting eyes. "This is the knife of the knight's order, is it not?"

"Y-yes, Mother, I f-found it..."

"NEVER LIE!" Josephina was thrown backward by Mother's fury. The elf snickered from the corner, but Mother's hand flinched, and a hot coal shot from the fireplace, striking him squarely on the forehead. He hissed and darted for cover.

"A dangerous gambit you have played, girl. Never in a million years did I think you would be capable of theft, let alone from a knight! A simple task, that is all I gave you. Buy supplies, eat a sweetcake, eavesdrop on the town gossip, and instead, you come home with this!" Mother threw the knife at Josephina, embedding it in the wall beside her head. "You are one stupid, stupid little girl."

"A monster, in the woods. I saw one, brown and..."

"The only monster you ever need to concern yourself with in these woods is me. These trees are mine. I see all, I know all, and what I know is you have done me a favor, as lucky albeit stupid as you may be."

Josephina choked on her fear, struggling to form words, but they wouldn't come. Mother glared at her, then let out a heavy sigh of disappointment.

"You left tracks in the snow straight into the forest. Though the sun's warmth may usher in the changing of the season, it does little to bless us. The knights will follow the stream, track our donkey's bowel movements, see your campsite in the woods, and it will lead them straight here. Here! Josephina, to our home, our fragile, fragile little home..."

Something strange flickered in Mother's eyes as she spoke. Tears welled up, and her voice softened. She recoiled, pulling her hands close to her heart. "For something truly magical has blessed us, young Josephina. A child. A baby! Growing among us, nestled safely in the heart of our home. See now." She gestured toward the covered pot simmering in the coals of the fire. "New life is growing. New life will join our precious little family."

"The heat is too low. It will never hatch," the elf hissed.

"Nonsense. The coals sustain life. While the sun has done its best to damn us, it empowers the fire, so we must be patient, my dearest family. The summer solstice is only a few months away, and our youngling will hatch under its full strength."

"Blood is binding. I am o-o-o-owed. Your daughter withers. You pro-o-o-mised me."

Mother sighed, twirling in her black coat. "Does nobody ever trust dear old Mother? Even you, little Oléfur? How many years have we worked together? Josephina, though stupidly as is her fashion, has inadvertently done wonderfully, luring a fine group of young men to our doorstep. We are going to feast, Oléfur. Do you understand? Carrots and onions, meat and potatoes..." Her smile widened. "Mere appetizers for what is to come."

The elf started to snicker, then burst into laughter. Josephina remained pinned to the kitchen wall, trembling. At last, Mother turned back to her, tossing the knife to the floor, where it slid beneath a cabinet. Josephina watched it disappear.

"Now for you, stupid little girl." Mother flew forward, her finger pushing against the bottom of her chin. "You're lucky I don't let Oléfur drain you dry for your stupid actions. You hear me? I could make your life a living hell. If it weren't for your lucky break in fortune that I need these men, you'd be more sorry than you'd care to know. Now see here!" She unpinned her finger and pointed to the fire. "I don't want to see you anywhere near that pot! ANYWHERE!" she screamed. "I'll boil you alive if I catch you near my unborn child. Now show your manners to our guest! Oléfur will be with us until the baby is ready, and I won't have either of you at each other's throats. Am I understood?"

Josephina nodded as Mother released her from the wall. Tears blurred her vision, and with her heart in her throat, she choked out. "Sorry, Oléfur. Welcome home."

"Good. Now get upstairs. Oléfur and I have a feast to plan."

Mother turned, and Josephina bolted up the stairs, racing through her mother's room and into the attic. She collapsed onto the floor, sobbing so violently her stomach roiled, nearly forcing her to vomit. Kicking her feet, she slammed the trapdoor shut and pushed a large chest on top of it, using the last of her strength.

She climbed into bed with Mishie. She lay there, sobbing until her tear ducts ran dry, and finally curled up under the blankets with him. Mishie didn't have to say anything, she knew he loved her too.

JAE V

Jae hid awkwardly in the hallway. Across the way, Valeana stared at him with wide eyes, raising a finger silently to her lips.

"What do you mean you are taking Luke? You are so selfish. Selfish, I say!"

Lady Aril's voice echoed through the marble and stone corridors of the manse of Aeksilor. Not a creature stirred. Even Aeksilor, whom Jae glimpsed for a brief moment around the corner, stood completely red-faced, his bald head burning red-hot like an iron. Only Sirene dared to move, dangling and spinning in circles from her father's arm.

"My good wife, my love, please. I assure you, you have all the protection you will need..."

"You don't know that! You can't possibly know that!"

"You are in the Rose, my darling. You could not be any safer..."

"Safe!" Jae heard Aril spin on her heels and fly across the

room. "And who will guard the manse while we are away! Who!"

"Dearest, my love, I promise you are being completely irrational…"

Valeana's head fell silently into her palms as Lady Aril's heels struck the floor in a harsh rhythm. The slap that followed echoed like thunder through the halls.

"This is your doing! This is your fault! All of you… proud 'good lords' of Astrelaide. Look around our dearest manse, dear husband. We are like ghosts haunting a ruin!"

"Daddy!" Sirene's voice rang out, the only force powerful enough to counter the wrath of the lady of the house.

Silence followed, then Aeksilor's voice, low and gravelly. "Surely you do not mean to blame me for the death of the good lord, Palo Balon."

Jae heard Lady Aril snort and exhale with the power of a lioness. "No, my good husband, I do not. For our household is nearly to ruin. The hallways are empty. The servants' corridors gather cobwebs. You sold off every last slave we had! You claimed it was shrewd for the market, ha!" Her cackle sent ice into Jae's veins.

"The dress and jewels you wear now, my good wife, came from my sense of business. From my family's legacy, which you now insult in our ancient halls."

"Oh, I am very sure you made a good bargain, my good lord. Our coffers fill with gold, but at what cost, Cato? At what cost have you sacrificed our safety? You and the other proud lords act as if nothing is happening, but I see that you are afraid, my shrewd husband. Very afraid. So do not ridicule me when I say I am afraid too. And worst of all, you leave not just me but your very children with those oafish twins for guards and that twig who barely speaks our language…"

Jae jolted, knowing Aril just mentioned him. Across the hallway, Valeana stared at him, attempting a wry smile, but it did little to comfort him.

"The boy is brave, and his muscles and training improve every day," Aeksilor said, his voice a practiced calm. "Please, my dear wife, take my word when I say you will be safe. It will be good for you and the children to be out of the manse, to interact with the other families of our great city. Take the twins, the 'bull slayer' if you will, and Valeana. All will be well."

Aril snorted again. "I can take a sword to the belly. And I will! If it means my children survive. But be wary, my good lord. These are your heirs, the legacy of the House of Aeksilor. You reap but what your slaves sow."

Her heels clacked sharply as she stormed from the room, eyes brimming with heated tears. She appeared before Jae and Valeana, her expression a tempest barely contained.

"Well? What are you two waiting for? Fetch my boys and those two buffoons! Now!"

Jae had never heard Lady Aril yell before, and he prayed he never would again. He spun on his heels, darting down the corridor. He slipped between two marble walls into a cool, shadowed passage, his footsteps echoing softly as he descended into the basement of the manse. There, he found Pate and Pete cutting up with each other as they lazily sharpened swords. Without a word, he grabbed both by the scruffs of their necks and tossed them into the armor stands.

"Oy! What's the meaning of this?" Pate cried out, struggling to untangle himself from a heap of leather.

"Enough. We're going out with the good lady of the house. Be prepared to leave at once." Jae's voice came harsh and low, projected with a power he didn't know he had. His chest swelled.

The twins grumbled as they pulled themselves from the armor stand. "Looks like we got a new Luke…"

But one sharp look from Jae shut them up. The twins were taller than him but lanky and lean, their years of guard service having done little to harden them. Jae felt certain he could box circles around them.

"Let's go."

They emerged into the grand foyer of the manor, where Lady Aril waited with her two sons, Boros and Luthor. Valeana stood off to the side, balancing a precarious load of a blanket, picnic basket, and umbrella on her slim shoulders. Jae stepped forward to help, but one look from Valeana told him to back off.

Lady Aril's scowl twisted like a living thing. "Remember, you are not serving the House of Aeksilor out there. You are serving *me*."

Jae's blood ran cold. He prayed Pate and Pete also got the message.

The twins heaved open the grand doors, and sunlight poured into the house foyer. Luthor strode forward, nearly a man grown, his posture straight and proud. Boros, on the other hand, clung to his mother's hand, whether from fear or because Lady Aril's grip was too tight, Jae couldn't tell. Either way, the boy's pudgy face was a mix of frustration and helplessness.

Out in the courtyard, Jae glimpsed the good Master Aeksilor dipping away from his manse with Lucien and Luke, off to conduct some business in the Vanilla. Aril huffed in frustration at the sight of him.

The day was oppressively hot, and the sun blazed brightly overhead. It wouldn't be until much later that the sun would dip behind the Stone Master: a towering stone cliff that loomed even over the Rose neighborhood, perched high above the rest of the city. Even here, nearly among the clouds, where the sunlight reflected harshly off the blue sea stretching to the horizon and the wind whipped fiercely, sending the city's fine ladies into frenzies with their hair, the air remained stifling. With no desire to burn, Lady Aril commanded they be on their way.

"We can't even afford servants for a litter." She tutted.

Outside the manse, Jae immediately clacked his heels together and straightened his back. "To the gates!" he commanded.

Pate and Pete moved at once, their long limbs a tangle as they hauled the massive gates closed. Lady Aril raised an eyebrow at Jae, but it was Valeana's expression that unsettled him. A look of surprise, perhaps even approval. His cheeks burned, and he was grateful for the heat of the day, hoping it hid his embarrassment beneath the flush of his olive skin.

Jae didn't want the attention to linger on him any longer. Once the gates were closed and secured, he snapped the twins into action, positioning them behind Lady Aril and Valeana, whose arms were full. He moved to the front, his strides purposeful and precise, a few steps ahead of Luthor. While Luthor strolled at a leisurely pace along the sunlit road, Jae's hand remained on the hilt of his sword, ready to draw. His eyes darted between the few travelers on the road. The high lords were wrapped in silks and velvets, their shadows stretching long across the golden bricks. Their slaves and errand boys scurried behind, bundles of parchment and silks weighing down their backs. Jae dared not raise a sword to a good master, but not so the slaves he eyed with suspicion.

He marched them along the Primrose Walk, a winding path of sun-kissed yellow bricks interspersed with mosaics of crimson and coral tile. The tiles formed delicate patterns of creeping vines, spirals of flame, and the crests of noble houses. On either side, high white walls lined the road, carved with reliefs of mythical beasts and ancient heroes. Iron gates, wrought in twisting shapes of serpents and ivy, guarded the entrances to these homes. Through their iron rails, sprawling mansions rose, their rooftops red as blood, and columns veined with marble. Roses bloomed in shades of crimson, ivory, saffron, and a rare, translucent green climbed the walls and wound around golden lattices. Marble fountains too stood at the forefront of many properties, their waters flowing from the mouths of carved manticores. The cool streams glittered in the light, crystal clear, but he knew they were forbidden to touch. They were not for drinking or bathing, but beauty alone.

Jae could barely believe his newfound life. From behind one white wall, the strum of a harp curled through the air. From another, the low hum of voices rose in a language he did not understand, seemingly singing alongside peppy songbirds. Somewhere, a young woman laughed, followed by the applause of an audience from a lawn game he didn't know how to play. Though he was barred from all these activities, to simply be here swelled his chest with pride. No longer did he break his back under the burning sun, sickle in hand. His muscles, once wiry and brittle, had grown thick with strength and nourishment. The leather straps of his armor bit into his broadening shoulders, and his tunic hugged the lines of his chest. Dark curls flopped over his brow, a mop of hair left to grow wild where once it had been shorn to a harsh scalp to fend off lice. A wiry beard, dark and defiant, had begun to claim his jawline.

And with all these newfound privileges, he led the House of Aeksilor through the heart of Astrelaide's most privileged neighborhood. The path terminated at the Vhaldrīvāzma, or Park of the Sun Drinker, though few still used the old name for this sanctuary perched just below the sunlit face of the Stone Master. That great yellow cliff dominated the skyline, and from its shadow, the city sprawled beneath them in a cascade of terra-cotta roofs and white stone towers. Beyond the rooftops, the sea stretched toward the world's edge, its blue expanse scattered with merchant sails and the slender hulls of pleasure yachts.

In the park, only masters and a select few slaves were permitted. It was a world within a world, a hidden oasis in the savannah where the grass shimmered a deep emerald green, trimmed and combed into perfection. Jae had never seen anything like it. Rows of white marble fountains bubbled with cool water, their basins shaped like seashells and dragon scales. Flowers exploded from carefully cultivated gardens, growing in every shade, tangled with vines and statues, their petals open and greedy for the sun.

In this world, Luthor took the lead as their formation broke. Jae strolled along helplessly, following the park's winding path through archways of twisted stone and color tiles. Every piece of infrastructure was an art piece. Even the benches were made of smooth mosaic tile that snaked along the park's edge, their backs swirling with the shapes of mythical beasts and ancient kings. Each tile was a different color, a jigsaw of blues, greens, and molten oranges.

Jae's heart swelled simply to be present here, among these splendors, and to escort Lady Aril and her family (minus the terror of Sirene, thank God) to this small slice of heaven. The sun burned hot and clean above, and beneath its harsh light, for the first time in what felt like ages, Jae felt at home.

Upon stumbling upon a vast patch of grass, Boros turned to Aril. "Can we eat now, Mother?"

Aril cupped his cheek. "Of course, my boy."

Aril wandered among the manicured grass, taking her sweet time as Valeana struggled behind her. Aril finally decided upon a spot next to a fig tree, where the babble and refreshing breeze of a fountain were nearby, and none of the screaming children of the other masters' families could bother her. Valeana quickly set up shop, throwing down the picnic blanket, planting the shade umbrella, and setting out the picnic basket.

"That is all, you four are dismissed." Aril's command was curt and dismissive, and the quartet did not waste time scattering under the hot sun.

Jae's sense of decorum in the park, however, was lost. The park was a world of open spaces and bright light. There was nowhere to hide, no shadows to slink into. Dazed and sweating, he followed Valeana's casual stroll over to the nearest fountain, where, slinking from Aril's view, she rested upon the marble rim and even splashed her hand in the cool water.

The twins took it a step further and began to splash one another with the cool water. Inside, Jae wanted to scream. He thought of barking orders, but he couldn't bring himself to disturb any of the noble families. Aside from the casual squeal of a child, there were no crowds or shouts or even the sound of chatter, only the chirp of birds and the splashing of the fountains.

Frustrated but resigned, Jae leaned against the fountain, his posture casual but his muscles taut. Valeana cast him a coy smile, and he forced his focus elsewhere. He kept his eyes on the family. Luthor had kicked off his shoes, his britches rolled up as he stretched out on the grass. Aril and Boros sat under the umbrella, feeding each other berries and bread dipped in oil. They giggled madly to each other from their blanket, though Jae couldn't hear them. He kept his gaze sharp and ears trained for danger, but in time with the passing of the clouds and the splashing of the water, he began to lose himself, and his gaze shifted to the expanse of blue stretching out beneath the park's tiled walls. From his vantage point, the city of Astrelaide didn't exist, only the white-capped waves of the ocean, and when he closed his eyes, he felt like he was on top of the tallest of them all, riding the crest on his board as the wind whipped his hair. The sun burned his shoulders, but it was a good heat, a reminder of life. He rode the waves out to sea, to his people, to his mother, to Coco the coconut crab, and…

"JAE!"

A sharp pain bit into his arm. Valeana had pinched him, her nails digging deep.

He jolted upright, his hand already on his sword hilt. Aril stood across the lawn, Boros at her side, her foot tapping impatiently against the blanket.

He rushed to her at once, Valeana close behind.

"There you are," Aril snapped. "If you had taken any longer, the food would have spoiled."

Jae started to open his mouth, but Valeana took the heat. "Pardon, my good lady."

Aril's scowl tightened. "The food will spoil soon under the sun. Eat it if you wish, but I do not want flies or the smell of rot following us home. We are off to play croquet on the lawn. Do not disturb us."

Aril departed with a stiff upper lip, leaving Valeana and Jae to exchange stunned looks. Once they were sure Aril was serious, they immediately plopped down upon the blanket, shielded from the sun, and tore into the remaining bread, oils, nuts, and fruits left behind by the good family. Once Pate and Pete noticed they had food, they came running too. The four of them feasted, crumbs and laughter spilling over the blanket.

Jae had never eaten so well. Valeana giggled, pointing to Jae's beard, where bits of bread and honey clung stubbornly. His cheeks burned as he swiped at the mess, suddenly conscious of the scruff covering his jaw. He was becoming a proper man, and with that realization came a strange embarrassment.

"You poor thing," Valeana cooed while Pate and Pete laughed, and she leaned forward to clean his beard for him. For a moment, he looked into her green eyes, feeling a stir in his stomach, when his thoughts turned to Lucien...

He gently pushed her hand away, his voice light. "If the bees come for the honey, so be it."

The others laughed, and soon enough, they settled into lounging. The afternoon stretched long and lazy as they watched the boys play. Even Aril joined in, and for once, Jae thought he heard her laugh, but as the sun sank behind the yellow face of the Stone Master and shadows swept over the park, the change in Aril was unmistakable. The stiffness returned to her posture, and her laughter faded, her lips settling back into their habitual scowl.

Sensing it was time, Jae sighed, the spell of the afternoon breaking. "Well, this has been a fine day." He rose to his feet and brushed the crumbs from his tunic.

Yet strangely, the others didn't move. Pate instead yawned, sprawling across the grass. "Just strike me down here. I'm fine with it."

"Agreed," Pete added, barely awake.

You idiots, Jae wanted to curse, but even Valeana didn't stir.

"Relax, boy. They're probably going to the stage. She'll summon us when she's ready."

Jae, confused, watched Aril take Boros's hand as Luthor ran ahead, walking toward a covered pavilion nestled among a dense patch of trees in the back of the park. He wanted to follow, not wishing for the good lady and her family to be without his protection, when a strange glimmer from across the lawn caught his eye. Nervously, he turned from Aril, watching her take a seat in the grass before the stage, joined by the other good masters and their families, not a slave in sight. He didn't want to disturb the good lady, and the glare...

He bit his lip and turned, headed toward the light.

At the center of the park, surrounded by a cluster of unremarkable rosebushes, sat a single rose. Its leaves were an unnatural shade of purple, curled upward on themselves. Most peculiar, though, was the glass dome resting over it, with only tiny golden ornate holes for wind and air to pass through. Something about it drew him in. He bent down, his curiosity piqued, and inhaled deeply. The gentle scent of its nectar filled the air and gently, with a single finger, he tapped the glass.

"The Desert Rose, young boy," an old, scraggily voice said from over his shoulder.

Jae jumped backward, nearly bumping into an old woman. His heart raced in his chest.

"I'm sorry, good master, I didn't realize..." He stopped, breathless, as he realized the woman, haggard and hunched, wore a metal collar like his own. *A fellow slave.* Anger surged within him. "What do you think you're doing, sneaking up on a guard like that?"

The old woman didn't seem fazed. "It's a precious thing, that flower. It only blooms at night, opening its petals to the light of the moon. A wondrous creation. It grows in the heat and light of the desert, but it only offers its beauty to the moonlight. So strange..."

The woman reached out with gnarled hands, as if to touch the glass. Without thinking, Jae swatted her hands away.

"I don't think we should touch it," he said firmly.

"No... no, of course not. The flower isn't for me." The old woman pulled back, a sly grin creeping across her toothless mouth. "But you, 'Bull Slayer,' our guiding moth, the flower will open for you, when it is time."

His temper flared. He balled his hands into fists. He bumped the old woman back with just his chest, standing tall over the shriveled creature. "I serve the House of Aeksilor," his voice trembled. "You must be mistaken."

"As I serve the House of Balon, yes," she said with a strange satisfaction, licking her lips. "Yes, that's the strange thing about the Desert Rose. The people of this city hold it sacred because it always knows... just when to open."

As she spoke, she reached up with a bony finger and tapped the metal collar around his neck.

"To hell with you, old woman!" Jae shouted, careless of who might hear him. He stormed away, his feet pounding the ground. He didn't know where to go, but his eyes were drawn to the vast expanse of the ocean beyond the limits of the city.

He walked to the edge of the park, where a low stone wall overlooked the city. The breeze from the cliff was cool, carrying the smells of the city below and the salt of the ocean. Jae breathed deeply, closing his eyes. The wind tousled his hair, and for a moment, he let it all wash over him. He looked out to the horizon, where ships came and went, then turned his gaze downward to the city. From his vantage point, he could see the vast fields stretching out beyond the east and west gates.

I have earned this, he told himself, thinking back to the brutal days spent in the swamp lands near the Sorrows—driven like cattle, enduring the biting flies and the crack of the whip. The fear, *the constant fear*, not just of the masters, but of far worse things lurking in the savannah...

I have earned this, he repeated, the words steadying him. *Better them than me.*

But then his eyes drifted downward, away from the ocean, to the Slave Quarter of the city. The rancid, stinking squalor, splattered with brown, among the otherwise beautiful city of flowers.

His stomach dropped. Quickly, he turned his head, unwilling to look any longer. His fingers reached up and brushed against his collar. The heavy, cold reminder of his place in this world. Despite everything he had achieved, no matter how high he rose in this city, he would always remain beneath the gaze of the Stone Master.

WARWICK V

The clash of steel rang out through the halls of the castle. It was time to prove himself.

The armory teemed with activity. Soldiers, courtiers, knights, and green boys, too young to fully lift a sword, swarmed the racks of swords, shields, and spears. Experienced and aged men relaxed comfortably before combat, exchanging jugs of ale, jostling and tussling with one another before giving way to the sword. Others, like Warwick, slunk into the armory, sulking in the shadow of their sword master.

"I don't see how this will prove anything. I am the prince, not a soldier of the rank and file."

"Mind your tone, squire," Wulford, his personal guard, warned sharply. "Today, you are no prince, but a knight in training."

"Then let me be knighted already," Warwick snapped back. "This pomp and fuss are pointless."

Yet despite his japes, he followed behind Wulford's flowing cloak like a child clinging to his mother's skirts. The clash of steel rang in his ears and rattled his teeth. This was no place for a prince, yet his father had been resolute. With nobles from across the land arriving at court, Electors included, his ascension was at stake whether the combat was ceremonial or not.

Wulford strode into the armory, Warwick all but hidden in the wake of his master's cloak.

Warwick braced himself, expecting a flood of salutations. But silence greeted him. The knights and squires hardly spared him a glance, carrying on as if he were invisible. For a moment, he stood still, stunned by their indifference.

"Oh, Father," he muttered under his breath, pressing a dramatic hand to his brow. The air was thick with the smell of men and boys, straw and sweat, tinged with blood—a nauseating mix. And he, cursed by the season's change, could barely smell a thing through his clogged nose. "Of all days," he lamented. "on this fine day of spring when new life emerges from the soil!"

"Life doesn't merely emerge," came a voice behind him. "It claws its way out, fighting for a place."

Warwick jumped, not realizing anyone had heard his pitiful poetry. Derrick appeared beside him, followed closely by a knight of the Demonbreun, Sir Lyfford.

"Oh, I had not realized…"

"Save your breath, Cousin. You will need it today in the tourney."

"Tourney?" Warwick's stomach dropped. "I agreed to no such thing."

Sir Lyfford smirked, clearly amused by Warwick's discomfort, while Derrick shook his head, draping a reassuring arm around him as he steered him toward the rows of swords and helms.

"Look, dear cousin, my mother has told me of the promise you have sworn to her regarding my inheritance. I am truly grateful, but mistake not my words or actions, for today we will have much to prove. I, the inheritor of the greatest city in the realm, and you, the crown prince, to take the mantle of the throne under your own... padded throne."

Warwick turned red. "You would insult me after I've pledged you a great prize?"

"I do not mean to insult you, but take heed of my earlier words. The knights and courtiers of this realm do not need to see you as a prince today. They need to see a warrior—a man who can beat down anyone who may challenge his claim."

"No one would challenge me," Warwick muttered through gritted teeth. "That would be high treason."

"Good, Warwick," Derrick said, watching him intently. "Hold on to that fire. Grow angry. Bring your sword down on me, strike with everything you have. I'll yield to you, but only if you bring your best. I, too, have something to prove."

"But I do not wish to fight!" Warwick's voice cracked. The anger in his voice dropped and his knees were suddenly wobbly. Derrick stopped, releasing his arm from around his shoulder, and stared him squarely in the face.

"You must." Without warning, Derrick shoved him backward into a rack of shields.

The shields clattered to the floor with a deafening crash, drawing laughter from the nearby knights. They raised their tankards of ale, jeering. "The prince drinks the good ale!" Warwick's face burned as he gave an awkward wave before scrambling after Derrick.

Though imperial privilege was in short order today, a section of the armory had been roped off, secluded for only the imperial family and their escorts by a row of partitions. Warwick followed Derrick within, positively boiling on the inside, ready to strike him back. He came within an inch of striking him back when he spied his brother, and the family sword at his belt.

"Brother," Warwick said, stopping in his tracks.

Lysander turned, shirtless and grinning. A shadow of a beard had formed along his jaw, and his chest was dark with hair, muscles taut beneath his skin. His stomach was as hard and flat as an ax blade. "Good morrow, Warwick. It's a rare day indeed! No more blunt practice blades, but real steel, eh?"

Warwick only stared at him, his mouth working but failing to produce any words. Derrick strode forward, pulling off his shirt in one swift motion, and clasped Lysander's outstretched hand in a firm brotherly handshake. Muscles and hair coated Derrick's chest too.

"My prince."

A deep, resonant voice broke through his daze. Warwick turned to find himself face-to-face with a figure cloaked in long black hair and a thick, mangled beard. It was Dyrebane, Lysander's guard and Wulford's brother.

"Sir," Warwick answered, though it took all his will. Something was terribly wrong here. He was the prince, yet he had never felt smaller.

"I'm eager to see you in the field today. I trust my brother has trained you well?" Dyrebane nodded to Wulford.

"The boy's eager to hold a sword, don't worry." Wulford clapped Dyrebane on the shoulder, answering for Warwick. The two brothers exchanged a fierce grin before slamming into each other's chests in greeting.

"A fine day, an excellent day for sparring!" Dyrebane proclaimed. "Let's get the pups into their gear. Aye, Lyfford, what say you? Can your boy fight?"

Lyfford broke into a scowl. "Of course my boy can fight. He has been trained in accordance with the holy order—the *proper* order."

Dyrebane let out a booming laugh. "The only 'proper order' is victory. That's the only outcome that matters in battle."

"And what of chivalry? Or honor? I fear much with your placement, but alas I trust the emperor knows his business…" Lyfford paused, looking to Warwick. An older man, Lyfford still boasted toned muscles but lacked the raw physical strength of the two brothers, Dyrebane and Wulford. Still, he possessed a powerful scorn and two beady eyes that inspired terror in his chosen victim. Warwick did not keep his gaze.

296

"All shall come to head today." Lyfford nodded. "The Rose Monts have arrived."

"Aye," Wulford replied. "Then let's suit the boys up, for if there's one thing we all agree on, it's loyalty to the line of Hieronymus."

"Say aye," Lyfford answered.

Derrick and Lysander were quick to jump into their armor, but Warwick limped to his gear stand. Wulford helped him undress, though Warwick made the process difficult. He kept his back turned to his brother and cousin, suddenly very keenly aware of his size. His belly hung inches over his waistband, and though he sported light blond stubble on his jaw, nothing coated his chest but a rolling layer of fat. Derrick and Lysander appeared almost as brothers, twins themselves, both muscled and dark of hair, both taller than himself, though Warwick was not short by any means. And so, given Warwick's immense girth, Wulford struggled to find the appropriate gear, for while plate armor existed for the big and tall knights, it did not exist for the big and tall and wide. Warwick yelped like a pup given a nip for the first time as Wulford yanked and pulled on straps, entrapping him in a case of metal that pinched his fat with every movement of his body. Warwick could no longer keep the pain and anger and belly from spilling out.

"This is unacceptable!" he barked in a harsh whisper. He gritted his teeth, sucking in tears as Wulford tried to secure leg plates.

"You must be still! Otherwise, these will never be secured!" Wulford tugged.

"How was this not accounted for earlier?" Warwick demanded, voice strained with anger and embarrassment. "You're making me look the fool."

Wulford paused, then let out a hard sigh, dropping the leg plates. Rising to meet Warwick's gaze, he said firmly. "Had you listened to my repeated requests for training, this wouldn't be an issue."

"You are my knight and I am the squire. Do you blame the dog who nips at the guest or the master who refuses to scold such a beast?"

Wulford yanked a final strap tight, making Warwick yelp. "You blame the master, yes, but only with an eye fixed on his shadow. There'll be no Strammond here to whine for you and spare you from practice today."

"At least Strammond understands when a break is needed..." Warwick muttered.

"Strammond understands nothing but undermining me simply because my brother and I are not of the Demonbreun. Well, must I club you over the ears like a proper knight? Perhaps that shall rattle your brain and clear your sight. This is a momentous day for you and myself. For my homeland, Esteria, too. It has been a great honor to serve you, as obstinate as you can be. Now pray tell, you remember how to hold a sword, yes?"

"If I am obstinate, it is only because I am the future head of the realm, and I must be accustomed to standing my ground in a realm of a thousand demands. And yes, I can hold a sword."

"Good. Today, you must be ferocious. Nothing less," Wulford replied coldly.

"And of honor and chivalry? Strammond would argue otherwise."

Without warning, Wulford clubbed his ears. Warwick's vision blurred as his ears rang out. "I told you to be a warrior, not a jester!" Warwick opened his mouth to return fire, but a single raised fist from Wulford made him bite his tongue. "I will give you this one last gift—my cloak."

"Your cloak? Will that not slow me?"

Wulford gave him a measured look. "My liege, you're already slow. Besides, it'll bring honor to my house and hide the *lumps* in your armor."

Warwick glanced down, raising his arms in frustration like a bird struggling to take flight. His flesh bulged through the gaps in the armor, a discomfort that soured his expression even further. He scowled as Wulford draped the white cloak over his shoulders, fastening it with care.

Am I a prince or a puppet? And as if reading his thoughts, Wulford whispered to him. "Better to be strong than strong-headed today. Use your anger, Warwick. This is no court; it's the field."

With that, Wulford offered nothing more than a firm nod and a thump to his chest. Warwick rolled his eyes but brought his own fist to his chest, producing a metallic clink that resonated through him. The sound, to his surprise, excited him.

He joined his brother and cousin near the opening of the armory. They peeked through a curtain, watching knights practice dueling in the yard. Warwick fully expected them to jape, but to his surprise, they pulled back from the curtain with a surprise. Warwick stood tall, and though shorter in stature than his kin, the clink of his armor and breadth of his cloak gave him the appearance of a lumbering giant. Warwick's sullen shoulders and sword clutched in a single hand, dangling inches from the floor, added an intimidating edge, like a knight weary of play-shenanigans.

"Damn Big Wick, you play knight well."

"Big Wick?" Derrick smiled, but a quick rise from Warwick's sword wiped it from his face.

"No, not you. Only him," Warwick said crossly.

Derrick's eyes widened, but his cousin's smile did not disappear. "As my prince commands. Now come see, you must watch the practice."

"Hmm?" he said aloud. Another leap in his chest. He stepped forward, shouldering his two cousins aside, peering through the curtain.

The tourney yard was no mere yard—it was a vast, artificial dirt field set atop the castle's rooftop. Towering turrets and watchful towers framed the space, with distant onlookers craning from windows, straining for a view. Around the field lay a ring of marble bleachers, while one edge of the rooftop plunged open to the sky and the mountains beyond. A true, deadly boundary. Though rarely employed, it was a lethal affair, and speaking of lethal affairs, Warwick spied a man near his father who sent a lump skyrocketing into his throat.

"Charles Rose Mont," he said aloud, peering upward into the audience.

"Yes," Derrick replied, his tone sour. "Arrived within the hour."

"Poor Father," Lysander growled. "You can smell the stink of the man's treachery even from here."

Warwick eyed his father, who looked visibly displeased. Seated to his right was Warwick's stepmother, but to his left the bane of their esteemed house whispered into the emperor's ears.

"The father of bastards schemes even now. Look how his eyes are turned only to my father's crown—" But he paused as he found their eyes suddenly locked. Warwick's blood ran cold. Charles looked directly at him.

"The father of bastards, aye? Care to back your words with your sword?" a voice challenged from behind him.

Witchcraft? The thought flared as Warwick spun around, his heart racing, only to find himself face-to-face with James Rose Mont, a distant cousin bearing the same piercing Rose Mont glare. Behind him, Strammond came panting up, casting a wary glance between them.

"I-I... w-what are you doing here?" Warwick stammered.

"I've come to mourn the loss of family," he answered and shrugged his shoulders. "Because you fight for family."

"You are hardly family," Derrick interrupted, stepping firmly between Warwick and James.

"Says one cousin to another." James sneered. "Careful now, before the pastry chef with a sword casts you aside as well."

Strammond, struggling to catch his breath, finally found the words to say. "My prince... Lord James Rose Mont... has arrived... with his family. He wishes... to participate... in the practice today."

"A duel, is it?" Derrick growled. "Would you rather fight with poison and pit vipers?"

"An insult? Only a brave man would hold such a fierce beast."

"Then learn your family history, Rose Mont," Lysander fired back. "We destroy snakes, we don't take pride in their filthy ways."

Wulford, Dyrebane, and Lyfford noticed the commotion and came running. "What is the matter? What is the meaning of this?"

"The boy... means to fight... the prince..." Strammond did his best to answer.

"I understand this is a family practice," James explained himself. "I wish to participate."

"Surely you do not mean to challenge the crown prince?" Lyfford gasped.

"I am a cousin, I will take the prince. Derrick is a cousin, he may take the heir's brother. By the Nine, a fair deal I say."

"You would use the Nine for your vile intentions," Dyrebane growled. "An outrage, I answer you in return."

"You are not to fight the prince," Strammond answered definitively, finally finding his voice. "By the voice of the Demonbreun Guard, I forbid it."

"The voice of the Demonbreun then? Then what of the prince? His voice is the true power of the realm, is it not?" James smiled, turning to Warwick, who only moments ago felt large in stature. His muscles started to tremble, and surely his armor would have rattled if his flesh did not abound from every gap.

"I... I say as the crown prince... I am to listen to my guard. As an emperor should."

Wulford thumped the side of Warwick's head lightly with his fist, offering a crooked smile and a silent nod.

"A coward's choice," James answered.

"I will fight you," Lysander said in return. "Let us go, here and now, onto the field."

"Then the realm will see the prince's cowardice, and aye, the whispers of the *better choice* will go louder." James snickered. "I will meet you in the field, aye."

Better choice?

A torrent of shouting broke out, but none of it reached Warwick. His mind was elsewhere, tangled in his thoughts. Lysander thumped his chest with pride, Derrick slapped him on the back, and Dyrebane bumped fists with him. The cheers from the crowd were muffled, drowned out by the rising beat of his pulse.

Then, the sun hit him.

A burst of bright light flooded the field as the first true rays of spring reached the castle. The mountains in the distance remained capped with snow, their bases awash in the first green of the season. Here at the castle, the air remained crisp, and though many of the court complained of sore throats and congestion, the cool wind felt refreshing against Warwick's skin.

But none of it mattered as the crowd's excitement surged. A cheer erupted when Lysander and James charged into the center of the field, their swords raised. Knights who had been sparring scattered, and the emperor, sitting front and center, rose from his seat with his wife at his side. Warwick's eyes flicked to Charles Rose Mont, seated near his father. Their eyes locked again for a brief, unsettling moment, and Charles smiled at him.

Lysander and James exchanged a few words, too distant for Warwick to hear, their voices drowned out by the calls of Dyrebane beside him, shouting for Lysander's victory. The two cousins, both in their late teens, were clad only in plate armor over their chests and shins. With a final nod to one another—custom in this ritual—the fight began.

The clash of steel rang out.

James moved swiftly, aggressively pushing Lysander back with each strike. Lysander, to Warwick's frustration, kept his guard high and his body low, blocking each blow but never countering. He seemed to retreat farther, his back now nearly pressed against the emperor's raised seating.

"James is pushing hard." Derrick shifted on his feet, struggling for a better view. "Why isn't Lysander attacking?"

Warwick studied the show, biting his lip. He looked to his father, who clutched his chair with great angst. James was driving the fight right toward them.

"What are you doing, boy? Fight back!" Dyrebane's voice cracked through the air, harsh and unyielding. "Counter! You know how to do this!"

It clicked in Warwick's mind a moment before Lysander made his move. His brother had been backed to the edge of the fighting area, just below the railing that separated the combatants from the crowd above, where the emperor and Charles sat in the front row. With swift precision, Lysander dropped to one knee and rolled behind his cousin, his movements fast and calculated. James's sword struck the metal railing with a sharp *clank*, and Warwick could almost feel the reverberation of the impact in his bones from across the yard.

James tried to spin around and regain control, but Lysander was already upon him. The strike came like lightning, a blur of steel in the air. James staggered back, now forced to defend himself, but Lysander pushed forward relentlessly. Then, with a final brutal strike, Lysander sent James's sword flying, the sound echoing sharply across the yard.

"Do you yield?" he heard his brother yell.

The crowd gasped. A second later, James dropped to his knee and the court broke into cheers. The emperor himself jumped to his feet, applauding furiously. Charles frowned, yet rose to his feet regardless and clapped.

"A show! A jolly good show if I've ever seen one!" Dyrebane screamed.

Lysander took a dramatic bow before the crowd, a smirk of triumph on his face. Warwick watched as Catelyn squealed with delight in the stands, her hands clutching her mother's. It was like the world was moving in slow motion, the noise fading into a distant hum.

Warwick blinked as if waking from a daze. It felt as though his hearing had been muffled from Wulford clubbing his ears again. He glanced at his knight, who mouthed something to him, followed by a firm nod. He turned to Derrick, who, too, nodded, his expression serious.

The better choice.

The words blocked out all the noise, except the beat of his heart. He pulled Derrick out onto the field.

Warwick did not hear the crowd gasp, though he felt the wind rush into their lungs. He walked with his head down, carrying his sword with one hand, marching to the center. Derrick rushed to his side, finally slicing through the quiet, whispering into his ear. "You should face the crowd. Let them see their prince."

Warwick swallowed hard. "No. I do not wish to see them."

"Very well. Remember our deal. I shall go easy if necessary—I am honored to have your blessing for my inheritance of Aberness."

Warwick only nodded.

Warwick's back was to the crowd, his gaze fixed on the distant mountains, their jagged peaks silhouetted against the bright sky. Behind him lay the unprotected edge of the practice field, the wind pulling at his cloak. Derrick, on the other hand, turned his face toward the crowd, offering a broad, confident smile and a wave. Warwick raised a hand too, though he held it low and waved it. Derrick looked to him with pity, and at last, Warwick raised his head to stand at full attention. The one thing he excelled at was pageantry and being the center of attention. Derrick was none the wiser.

They faced one another. They raised their swords in customary fashion and locked eyes. Then the swords fell and the first blow was struck.

Derrick swung first. Warwick raised his sword to meet him. The impact struck him as if his bones were about to shatter. He gritted his teeth, feeling them shake against the clash of the steel. Again and again, Derrick raised his sword, and each time Warwick met the blow, blocking his cousin's attack. Warwick took a step forward.

The clash of steel rang out. There was nothing but this moment, though he could feel the weight of the crowd's gaze as he advanced. He did not know any fancy parries, he did not even know how to properly swing the sword, but he did know how to be *heavy*. He did not have muscles, but he had weight, and so he pressed it to his advantage. Derrick swung and he answered. Warwick watched as Derrick's eyes widened as he found himself on the backfoot. As he attacked, a rush unlike any Warwick had ever felt consumed him. Derrick tried to sidestep, moving to the left, but Warwick was already there, blocking him. Derrick stumbled, his footing unsure. Warwick's sword rose high, a heavy arc that caught the sun. The sound of steel crashing against steel filled the air once more.

Back and back, Warwick drove him, each step heavy with the rhythm of battle. His body jiggled within his armor, but it didn't matter. The sting of each strike, the clashing of swords, made his hands and bones numb, but still he pressed on. Derrick, stumbling and desperate, tried to parry around him, but Warwick was relentless. Again and again, he blocked his cousin's every attempt.

They neared the edge of the field now, the wind picking up mightily as it rushed over the mountain's edge, a gust that carried the sharp scent of snow and stone. The ground beneath them teetered away to nothingness, the sheer drop only feet away.

"Stop! What are you doing?"

Derrick's eyes screamed, but Warwick ignored his silent plea. He could hear the faintest tremor in his cousin's breath, the fear clawing at him, but he did not stop.

It was only when Derrick's legs began to tremble, the edge of the mountain so close he could feel the wind beneath him, that the words came. "I yield!"

Derrick threw down his sword.

Warwick, however, had already raised his sword. He let it fall, and with it, dared to squash any whispers of a *better choice*.

LEAWYN V

Om guided her to the resting place of her people, but no farther. Their journey was long and silent, and his departure cast a shadow over their future. She walked with her head bowed, following the heavy stench of death back to her people.

By the time she reached the forest's edge, the sun had begun to fade, casting a waning light across the sky. A warm breeze struck through the open fields, causing the previously dead grass to sprout in bright shades of green. It would have been beautiful, had her people still been there to witness it.

Her stomach churned, her feet rooted to the spot. Atop the hill, she stood motionless, the forest at her back, her gaze sweeping the horizon. The tents of her clan were gone. The makeshift battle ramparts were gone. Only piles of mud marred the ground, but at least there were no bodies. A battle had not taken place in her absence. Her people had likely moved the front line, and her clansfolk had returned to their homes.

Leawyn exhaled slowly, though she wasn't sure why the emptiness surprised her. She shuffled down the hill into the barren field. Rings of mud and withered grass marked where the tents once stood, and fading footprints in the fresh grass confirmed her suspicion. She knelt, letting her fingers brush the delicate new shoots, then dig into the soil. She closed her eyes, feeling the pulse of the Hearth beneath her palms, hoping for guidance. When she opened them again, a decision had been made.

She walked in the opposite direction of her clan and village, toward the scorched earth of the previous battle. She passed between the charred ramparts, fingers grazing the splintered wood, and approached the field where the Outsiders had clashed with her people. The ground was trampled, the fresh breath of spring slow to take root here, the Hearth still scarred and muddied. She moved carefully, her footsteps muted by the soaked ground, indifferent to the bloodstains but pained by the occasional hoofprint that marred the soil.

She passed beyond the battle, nearing the distant tree line where the Outsiders had retreated in the face of a unified charge by the centaurs. Like a ghost reliving the past, she slipped between the trees, venturing farther south than she ever had before. The trees were alive with new leaves of tiny pink, green, and white bulbs nestled among the branches. In the midst of so much death, she became lost in the rebirth of the forest. Without the sun to guide her through the gnarled roots of this ancient wood, she relied instead on the footprints of her people's warriors etched into the soil. They became her compass, her only light. She hoped her grandchildren could forgive her.

She continued into the dark, clambering over trees and jumping over babbling brooks. After her stint in the woods and her battle with the fever, nothing seemed impossible to her, and even her old and aching joints could do little to stop her spirit. She figured she was making good time, stopping to sip from a stream and eat from a collection of hardened bread

Om had given her. It was here, munching her bread upon a log, she noticed something peculiar. Among the fading light of the day, protruding from behind a large fallen log, a single hoof stuck up into the air. She rubbed her eyes, unsure of what she was seeing, before curiosity finally compelled her to rise and confirm what her eyes were telling her.

Behind the log, she found the twisted, mangled bodies of both a centaur and an Outsider, their forms locked in a final brutal struggle. The stench of death hit her like a physical blow, but she pressed on, holding her nose as she forced herself to look. A spear had pierced the belly of the fallen centaur, while the Outsider lay trampled beneath the weight of the centaur's body. With a sigh, she bent down, running her fingers along the auburn hair of the centaur and closing his left eye for peace, finding the right devoured by some creature of the forest.

"Rest now, for your time will come again," she said to the creature. She then looked to the Outsider, a man of dark hair and a gaping mouth filled with maggots. She spat upon the corpse, wishing him nothing but ruin.

She would have burned his body, denying him his right to rise after this world would come to an end, but she did not have the strength to remove the centaur from atop him. The best she could do was kiss the centaur upon the forehead, and when she rose, she spied his bow and arrows flung into a brush pile not far from his corpse. She lifted the bow, finding the wood intricately carved, and slung the arrow quiver over her shoulder. She would continue the centaur's work.

That night, she rested in the forest beneath the shelter of a great tree, wrapped in furs. The cold seeped into her bones, and as morning arrived, she woke with a cough, but as she began to move and the sun pierced through the trees, her lungs cleared. She pressed on.

Another day of travel brought her deeper into the country of her people. She had never ventured this far south before, and the landscape gradually became increasingly hilly and dotted with scattered fields. Here among the hillsides, the scars of abandoned mine shafts remained from where the Outsiders had once plundered the Hearth. She stopped to peak into one such shaft, a cold, wind wafting up from far below. She thought of venturing in, but she spied a long forgotten banner of the flaming bird lost in the rubble, and at the same time a foul taste swept up from deep within in the shaft. She ran, and lost in her hatred, nearly stumbled off a cliff face overlooking a quarry partially filled with foul water, where invaders had carved away a massive chunk of stone from the world. She spat into the stagnant pool below, then immediately regretted it. This was still her land; she should treat it better.

On the morning of her third day, she broke free of the last patch of trees and came upon an abandoned village nestled in rolling green hills. Little of the settlement remained, yet she recognized it as once belonging to the Outsiders. Hate immediately consumed her, but her stomach rumbled, and cooler thoughts prevailed. She paused for breakfast in the ruins of a great hall, a long wooden building that had once hosted dances, feasts, and important gatherings. Now it sheltered only a family of pigeons nesting in the rafters. Whoever had once lived here, it had long surrendered to nature and peace. She ate slowly, savoring the stillness, then left the hall as quietly as she had entered. Under the full moon's glow, she moved through the hills, her dark furs blending into the night.

The next morning, she was awoken by the sound of a war horn.

Battle. Her heart leaped. Rising to meet the late morning sun, she quickly grabbed a snack, packed her things, and dashed in the direction of the sound.

Smoke churned in the sky, yet she did not find herself dashing toward an open field, but back into a patchwork of trees. She moved as quickly as her old knees would take her, hoping she could make it before the attack ended, when a man came stumbling past her.

"Hey! Good brother! Is there battle? Tell me!" she shouted, but the soldier didn't stop. He merely glanced at her, war paint streaking his terrified face, before yelping like a dog and fleeing deeper into the woods.

A deserter?

"Coward!" she shouted. She gritted her teeth, hatred bubbling within her. You do not turn from your people. *You do not turn from your land.*

She pressed forward, making a mental note of the man who fled. But as she moved, two more men streaked past, fleeing the battle.

Is it a rout? Have we lost?

The thought ground her to a halt, and she took the opportunity to rest upon a tree, panting. *How can we be losing?* But she stopped that thought. They had been losing for a long time. The Outsiders came from a faraway land with seemingly endless children... and before them, the men of dark skin, again with their men and women, boundless in number to be thrown away...

She removed an arrow from her quiver.

She did not create life only for them to be thrown away. Her children mattered. The future of her isle mattered. Defeating these Outsiders *mattered*.

She released her grip on the tree, finding the resolve to move forward when she heard a man crashing through the underbrush, heading straight for her. Swiftly, she ducked behind the tree. As the soldier neared, she stuck out her foot as far as it would go, catching him as he tried to vault over a root. He hit the ground with a grunt, and before he could react, Leawyn planted both feet above him, locking her bow in place. The man turned, eyes wide, only to find an arrow aimed between them.

"Coward. Deserter," Leawyn growled.

The man's eyes flicked between the tip of the arrow and her face, struggling to focus.

"How could you abandon your own people? Do you have any idea of the sacrifices that came before you?"

The man lifted his hands up as if to surrender. "P-please, you don't understand. They have brought with them... evil!"

Leawyn's laugh was sharp, bitter. "Are you new to the front, boy? Or even to the isle? Of course they brought evil."

"You don't understand. They don't fight with honor. They point their metal rods and… the whole first row… my clansmen… gone."

"Many have joined the war. Many have fallen. But you, you're a deserter! A coward!" Leawyn shouted, pulling the drawstring of her bow back with force. "You dishonor them all."

"Don't be so quick to name me a coward, old crone!" the man spat and broke into a mad giggle, trembling on the ground. "You do not know what it means to fight these Outsiders with their evil weapons!"

Leawyn nodded. "You're right. I've never fought like you. But I've loosed an arrow or two in my time. Tell me, is the battle lost then?"

"The line is smashed, but my clan fights, I am sure…"

The man noticed her gaze shift to the side as she thought of battle. In a flash, the man rolled to his side, knocking her off-balance and sending her to the ground as well. Her arrow loosed, striking the man in his fur armor, pinning a piece of wolf fur to the soil. Before she could regain her bearings, the man was on his feet and lost to the forest.

Let that be a lesson to you. She gathered herself and climbed back to her feet. Her ankle throbbed, sore but not sprained. *I'll need to be more careful. If I lose my ankle, I may never walk again.*

The sound of war drums still pounded in the distance, telling of the battle still raging. If she hurried, she could still make it.

She broke into a light jog, careful to not test her luck further with her footing. She scrambled onward, and soon the smell of smoke began to fill her lungs, along with a bitter taste within her mouth. She could not place it… a strange stench that filled both her nose and tongue.

Could this be the evil the soldier spoke of?

Perhaps, for a wave of soldiers appeared through the brush. *More deserters?* Her heart dropped, but no… these men were still fighting, joined by throngs of women archers, dashing into the trees, holding the line. She was nearly upon the battle.

She rushed forward, coming upon an archer slumped within the roots of a tree. The woman was panting heavily.

"You there, speak quickly! How fares the battle! Is all lost?"

The archer looked at her with surprise. "We've lost the field. They smashed the men up front. They've brought horses and… something else…" She stopped, a tear gleaming in her eye. "I don't know how else to explain…"

Leawyn looked at the woman, feeling both sorrow and contempt. These people weren't her clan. She could hear it in the accent of their speech. Her people… *Terrwoniwyn*… they had struck down the Flaming Bird's commander, but these warriors… she shook her head. They needed a lesson in bravery.

"Where is the War Maker? Is he with your ranks?"

The woman shook her head. "He has gone farther down the line to a different clan."

Leawyn nodded. *This could work to my advantage.* "Very well. Stay here and hold the forest. I will set out and bring their leaders to heel. Be ready to follow."

She set off, leaving the woman staring with a wide-open mouth. She clambered to the edge of the forest, passing throngs of soldiers and archers embedded within the trees. The clash of steel and the sound of… *thunder?* pulsed from just beyond the tree line. More of their warriors were slipping into the woods. Not a terrible strategy, Leawyn thought, but one that lacked the force to claim a true victory.

From beyond the trees, a final line of her people held back the Outsiders, clashing with steel. Farther beyond, a huge clump of fallen men lay scattered across the battlefield, and beyond that, two square formations of men marching with barrels upon their soldiers, approaching from either side. She did not know what this meant, only that they must be routed. She turned to face her people hiding within the trees, timing her shout between a gap in the war drums.

"CLANSPEOPLE OF FLÁIMIR. LET US FEAR NOT OUR FIRST DEATH! THE LONG REST COMES REGARDLESS AND I FULLY INTEND TO EARN MY SLEEP! DAMN THEIR EVIL, IT WILL NOT STOP ME. RALLY TO ME! RALLY TO YOUR LAND!"

She screamed, feeling a hundred eyes upon her, but she didn't expect anyone to answer. She knew better. She would have to earn this victory first or finally meet death.

Incidentally, Death came riding.

A quartet of horses approached, ridden by Outsiders dressed in pompous outfits upon gilded seats, flying the banners of the Flaming Bird. Each man held a silver barrel, and with a flick of their hands, Leawyn saw them unleash thunder, dropping several of her people in unison. She did not understand this power, but she would not fear it. She stepped forward from the trees, moving across the field toward the thundering horses. As she did, she dropped to one knee, drawing her bow. The men didn't seem to notice her yet, but one horse whinnied at her approach, its ears flattening.

Smart creature, she thought, smiling grimly.

She drew back the string and released the arrow. It struck an Outsider in the shoulder.

Damn, Leawyn cursed, but her aim had not failed her. The man arched back and toppled from his horse. His comrades shouted in horror, quickly turning their thundering horses toward her. Leawyn nocked another arrow, but the horses were coming too fast. She saw one man raise the silver barrel in her direction.

She loosed the arrow, not aiming for the soldier, but for the lead horse.

The arrow struck above the right leg of the beast. The horse reared, sending its rider tumbling from the saddle. The creature hit the ground, then scrambled to its hooves, dashing off madly into the forest.

Leawyn ran, knowing she could never outrun a horse, let alone two. She expected a sword to cleave her in half or a bolt of thunder to send her into the soil, but it never came. She looked upon the forest edge, spying a legion of the archers and soldiers emerging from the trees. They stared at her, watching her sprint, though they did not yet join her in battle.

The foreign soldiers did not come for her. Instead, down two in number, and facing archers from the forest, they rode their horses hard, fleeing past the encroaching men with silver barrels pressed to their shoulders. Leawyn, upon realizing she was not about to die, stopped in her tracks, panting hard, and looked not to the two Outsiders wiggling in agony upon the ground, but to the horse of her first victim, kicking wildly, evidently overwhelmed by the stress of battle. She went to the beast.

Leawyn had seen horses before. Her people had even ridden them and owned them in the past, but with the centaurs milling around in the woods, their captivity never seemed to last long. She approached the massive pure-white creature with calm confidence. It snorted and stamped its hooves, its wild eyes flicking toward her, then back to the chaos of the battlefield, unsure of what to do.

"Shh, shh," she cooed when she was close enough for the stallion to hear her. It stamped its hooves again, but Leawyn didn't falter. More eyes were watching from the forest, and the foreign soldiers were closing in. Patience would not serve her now.

She got close enough to reach out a hand. The horse kicked and whipped its head, but Leawyn caught the reins. The beast jerked its body, threatening to tear her arm from its socket, but she held tight and planted her heels. It whipped its head again side to side, but she stayed calm, cooing softly to the creature. Overwhelmed, perhaps sensing her steadiness, the beast began to relax.

Leawyn had ridden before in her youth, but her people didn't use saddles or reins. Still, she was in foreign territory now and did what felt natural. She glanced at the horse's back, whispering. "Sorry about this, new friend," before slipping her foot into the stirrup. Without hesitation, she hoisted herself up and swung her leg over the saddle.

She sat atop the horse.

With a gentle hand, she stroked the creature's mane. "Let us go to war then, new friend." She dug her heels into its side, as she had learned to do as a girl. The horse jolted to life, eager for direction, and they were off. She steered the beast up the embankment toward the tree line, raising her bow high into the air. Her gray hair whipped in the wind behind her.

"FOR THE ISLE! FOR THOSE WHO REST! AND TO FEAR NOT OUR FIRST DEATH! BUT PITY FOR THOSE WHO WILL NEVER RISE AGAIN!"

Her voice rang out, and the charge began. She rode along the tree line, her heart beating hard in her chest, as the first square formation of Outsider soldiers marched toward her people's battle line. A clash of steel and iron rang out as the soldiers met in battle. She didn't know what power these silver barrels could unleash, but she knew this… *evil* would not win the day.

Her people felt the same.

The archers came first. Women, swift and deadly, emerged from the trees behind her with bows drawn. Leawyn jerked the horse to a stop several hundred feet from the marching Outsiders. She gave her archers time to catch up, calculating the seconds that were slipping away. Fifteen, maybe twenty archers. Time was running out. The Outsiders were removing their barrels, pointing them toward her.

Leawyn turned, her eyes catching the red-haired girl from the forest standing among her fellow archers. The battle was about to take a darker turn, but they would not surrender.

"Aim your arrows high into the air! Save our boys on the front line! Shatter their ranks! LOOSE. AT. WILL!"

A string of arrows soared into the sky, Leawyn's among them. From horseback, she released an arrow, not expecting it to find its mark. Yet, where her arrow landed in a puddle of mud, twenty others struck true, cutting through the ranks of the Outsiders.

"LOOSE AGAIN! AND AGAIN!"

The Outsider formation faltered. There couldn't have been more than fifty of them, and no more than five hundred across the field in total. *We could do this.*

Another volley of arrows flew high, and the beat of war drums followed in time. Beside Leawyn, a man marked with war paint appeared, breathing heavily. He gave her a nod, rallying twenty soldiers behind him. They surged forward, shields raised and iron blades drawn. Leawyn's eyes caught a figure breaking from the front line—the chieftain, a massive aurochs antler helm atop his head.

They charged, but then came the thunder. The sound of the barrels and her people crumpled.

The Outsiders released their unnatural terror. The horse beneath her whinnied and bucked, but Leawyn kept her grip on the reins, digging her heels in as the chaos unfolded. The Outsiders, shaken by the arrows, were still not ready for the soldier's charge, yet their numbers were overwhelming. *Two to one.* Leawyn needed to act.

"WOMEN OF OUR ISLE! DAUGHTERS, WIVES, AND MOTHERS OF THIS LAND! WE SHALL NOT STAND BACK AND LET OUR MEN BE SLAUGHTERED! LET US TAKE THE FIGHT TO THEM! DRAW UPON YOUR BLADES, SISTERS! BRING THEIR FIRST AND ONLY DEATH TO THEM!"

Leawyn charged, the archers behind her. She pivoted her horse, bringing it around their ranks, grabbing a small knife stashed in her boot. She knew it wouldn't do much from horseback, but who would follow her lead if she didn't show them?

Into the fray she rode, the horse galloping hard, cutting through the Outsiders' line. She ran one man down, her knife flashing, before breaking off again. The archers, with fury in their eyes, joined the charge. Women, old men, everyone who could fight, came alongside her, knives drawn and war cries ringing through the air. And from the forest, warriors found their strength. Together, they charged.

The Outsiders did not last long. Cut down by arrows, charged by a horse, stricken by rejuvenated men and women, and without the power of their silver barrels, they fell quickly. The left flank of their front line was secure. With that, their chieftain, a middle-aged, lumbering man with a dark beard, came charging over, his eyes wild as blood dripped from his helm.

"Who called for you, Old Maid? These are not my commands! Was it the War Maker who sent you?"

"Chieftain, now is not the time for words but for action. Let us summon the newfound courage of our people and drive those Outsiders from our land. We will lead them in a charge behind their lines. They will collapse, and the day will be ours! Ya!"

Leawyn whipped her horse, sending it rearing into the air with a whinny, and took off toward the front line—but not too quickly. She gave the chieftain space to rally his troops. A man of his position would not suffer the insult of being overtaken by an old woman on horseback.

His troops followed, their charge a force of pure will. Together, they plowed into the Outsiders' front line from the side. Leawyn surged through the thinning ranks of her own people, rallying them with the forest warriors flooding back into battle. The rout of the Outsiders came swift. Their line quickly collapsed as the Outsider formation to their right, armed with their dreaded silver barrels, managed only a single volley before they turned and fled. They scattered across the field, retreating toward the distant trees.

"Well fought! You have made your ancestors proud!" Leawyn cheered as she rode through the ranks. Soldiers raised their shields and swords in response, but even in their triumph, the battlefield bore the heavy weight of loss. Scattered across the field were the fallen, bodies marking the price of this hard-fought battle. In a single day, this clan had been pushed to the brink of extinction.

Leawyn's eyes scanned the soldiers before settling on the chieftain. She made her way toward him, dismounting as a sign of respect. Her hand, however, remained firmly gripped on the reins. This horse was hers now.

The chieftain met her with a scowl, but, after a long pause, he removed his helm in kind. A sign of respect, albeit reluctant. Leawyn studied him: a man still in his prime, but already carved by war. His face was a map of battle. Half his teeth missing, blood and dirt streaking his features, and countless cuts crisscrossing his battered body. His shoulders sagged under the weight of it all, as if the very burden of war had physically crushed him. She recognized it. She'd seen this weariness too many times before.

"Chieftain." She offered a small bow.

He studied her for a long moment, eyes narrowing, before he spat a wad of blood onto the Hearth. "Old Crone," he muttered. "my people say it is you who brought us victory today."

"I rallied their spirits, no more, Chieftain."

"Spirits, huh?" The chieftain's lip curled slightly. "Then tell me, Old Crone, are you not a spirit yourself? Some wraith risen from the forest? You summon women to your side, command beasts with a wave of your hand. What sorcery is this?"

She stepped closer, unwavering. "Is it sorcery to have pride in your land? To banish fear? I am but an old crone, and no longer do I fear the time when I'll step into the Hearth to rest. This war has taken my family from me. I do not wish for it to take more. So I have come."

A small chuckle came from the chieftain. "If you have been summoned, then I suppose you can be banished too."

Leawyn looked to the throngs of eyes watching them from afar. "I am the spirit of this land. Tell me, is that what you wish to banish?"

The chieftain looked over her with a suspicious glance, then plunged his battle-ax down into the ground. "Be curt with me, Old Crone. I have lost many great men today. What is it you want?"

"I have told you. Victory, no more, no less."

The chieftain's gaze flickered, weighing her words as his eyes darted between his men, the women, and finally, back to her. A small laugh escaped him, softening the tension in his posture.

He placed both hands on his belly, his tone shifting. "Perhaps the Great Rising is upon us. You remind me of my grandmother, reborn." He paused, considering. "Very well, Old Crone. Stay among us. I'll alert the War Maker of our victory. I'll mention the spirit of the land, though he'll likely think me a fool. Let him! I've been outwitted by an old woman."

"We seek the same goal, Chieftain," Leawyn replied coolly. "But let it be known: This is your clan, yes, but this is my land. This is my cause."

Before he could answer, she jumped back into the stirrups of her horse and rode off.

JAE VI

The master's manse lay in dark silence. A waning moon hung in the night sky. It was the only light Jae had to finish his chores.

He tidied the dining hall, careful to avoid extra noise. The good masters had retired to their rooms after a long day of mourning. Sirene's quiet sobs could be heard from down the hall. Aeksilor was in her bedroom with her, offering whispered assurances that all would be well.

In the depths of the house, the other slaves rested as well. The day had been long and heavy for all, and Jae too felt ready for rest. He finished setting the table for the master's breakfast and returned to the kitchen. Cast in a deep shadow, he moved carefully to avoid knocking into any pots or pans. A sliver of moonlight trickled through a window, illuminating the counter just enough for him to place a tray of extra utensils down. As he did, he noticed tiny mouse tracks pressed into the loose flour and made a mental note to mention it to Berona in the morning.

He opened the hidden staircase leading to the slave quarters and stepped into total darkness. It was only at the bottom that the moonlight filtered through narrow windows, allowing him to see again. Just then, a shadow darted down the hallway and vanished outside. His curiosity piqued, he followed, emerging onto the pathway where the faun had once frightened him. Above, a trellis covered in vines trembled as if someone had just shimmied onto the roof.

"Hex?" he whispered. No one answered. Jae turned to the faun's hut, spying a single candle burning in the window. "Hex?" he called out again, his voice a bit louder this time. "Is that you?" Again, no answer.

His heart rate quickened, his mind turning to the murder of Master Balon, and a terrifying thought gripped him. *An assassin? On our roof?* He shook his head, grabbing a hold of the trellis. He refused to believe it. He climbed silently up onto the flat roof, finding a shadow seated on the edge. He cursed himself for not bringing a knife from the kitchen for protection. "Hex... is that you?"

"Are my legs that stumpy?"

"Oh, I wasn't sure..." Jae replied, relief flooding through him as he recognized the familiar tone.

"No, come sit." The shadow beckoned, patting the ledge beside it. Green eyes looked to him. "I could bleat for you if that would help."

Jae complied, taking a seat on the roof ledge beside the shadow. Their arms brushed together.

"Some night," Lucien said, gazing out over the dark city.

"Some day," Jae answered.

"You were outside the temple all day, right? Baking in the sun? I'm sorry for that."

"I imagine the good masters could have been more *severe...* given the circumstances."

"A good master dies, and we bear the burden." Lucien shook his head, eyes distant. Not a cloud hung in the night sky. "They didn't let you into the temple, did they?"

"No." Jae shook his head. "We stood in the sun. Fitting, I suppose. The Thorned Men were there. We were forbidden to even touch the temple's ground. The Thorned Men flogged a few household guards too for no good reason—not that they've ever needed a reason before. The funeral felt endless, and the heat was stifling. I'm surprised, though. I thought the good master would have taken you with him."

"No slaves were permitted inside the temple," Lucien replied, his voice low. "The masters are scared. Terrified, actually."

"Terrified? Of what? Us?" Jae shook his head in disbelief.

Lucien remained silent, his gaze lost in the shadows. Below them, only a single light flickered in the entire city. The Temple of the Sun stood as a dark, shadowy prism, save for a single solitary brazier burning atop the structure. Jae's eyes fixated on the distant yellow dot of the brazier, and he couldn't help but smile, laughing softly to himself.

"What?" Lucien laughed back at him.

"The moon wanes and yet it glows brighter than their pyre. I'm afraid it's stolen the dead master's glory. The great dark one. The enemy of the Sun God."

"Dark wings bring dark tidings," Lucien replied, his smile vanishing. He turned his gaze away, and Jae's stomach sank as he focused on the funeral brazier.

"What do you think will happen, Lucien?"

"It's hard to say," Lucien replied thoughtfully. "The world is brimming with revolutionary spirit. More often than not, though, it fails. Men get grand ideas in their heads until the first blood is shed, and then all their courage melts away."

Jae didn't buy Lucien's response. "They already shed our blood and tear families apart. What else is there to lose?"

Lucien turned back to him, his eyes glowing green in the moonlight. "You've had it worse than me, I suppose. I've had it too good here for many years. I've forgotten what it is like in the slave pens below. I've never been in the fields, either. In some ways, I'm scared—scared that when talk finally turns to action, the consequences will become all too real."

"Were you always a slave? You know so much—how to read, write, and count. I've never heard of a slave who hasn't worked in the fields."

Lucien turned his gaze away, gently kicking his legs over the roof's ledge. "No, I haven't always been a slave. I was born free in a distant land called Lyonnia. My father was a merchant, not highborn. But we managed well enough, or that's how I remember it."

"Lyonnia? I've heard that name before. How did you end up here?"

"Through tragedy," Lucien replied, his voice somber.

Jae sighed, frustration creeping into his tone. "That's not an answer. That's how we all ended up here."

"Fair point," Lucien admitted, voice dropping. "After the Ash Fall a hundred years ago, when famine swept through the land and countless people perished, we lowborns grew restless. There were too few peasants to work the fields and too few men and women to exploit. Taxes increased to make up for lost revenue. My father became enraged, as did the other peasants—rich and poor alike. We rose up, but I've learned that rebellions are fickle things. They thrive on division. Turn one man against another for the language he speaks, and it's all over. Your father's head rolls, and you're sold off to recoup the damages. But I'm educated and thin, with fair skin. I'd never survive in the fields. I suppose I'm lucky in that way."

"I'd say so... Our master's manse beats anything I've ever seen outside the city."

"Even in your homeland?"

"My homeland?" Jae leaned back as if struck in the chest. "I don't think about my homeland, or my time before... all this."

"Is it that you don't remember, or you try not to?"

Jae slid back into his memories. "It's all a blur, like trying to look at the sun from underwater. I remember my mother's smile, my two older brothers, and my younger sister. I had a coconut crab named Coco who slept with me and would chase me for food. And then..." His nose scrunched up. "My memories always end the same. The smell of the boat, the ring of steel in the air, the cries from my village, and the look of fear in my sister's eyes—chained just feet from me on the boat, already a world apart. Then, at the next port, she was gone, and I was in the fields."

"I'm sorry to hear that. Your story is the story of millions."

"Yeah, I guess so…" he played with his thumbs. "Say, you don't think that creature can hear us?" He glanced suspiciously to the side. The night was filled with shadows; anyone could be listening.

"No, Jae, I don't think so, and he is a *faun*. Please don't tell me you're falling for that bull slayer nonsense that's taken on a life of its own, are you?"

"What? No!" His voice rose, but Lucien held a finger to his lips. "No… no, of course not. I've just never seen a faun before. The slavers did not have them out west…"

"Good," Lucien interrupted, shaking his head. "It's been a pain to temper down your reputation. It's spread through the city, you know? And I'm trying to build unity."

"My reputation? And unity?"

"The master wanted another slave to serve in his guard, and at the time you did not fit the bill. Just skin and bones…" But Lucien paused, watching Jae flex his arm as a counterpoint. Jae smiled as Lucien leaned over and squeezed his muscle. "But I saw you on that stage next to that minotaur. The way you rose up and fearlessly swatted those flies away from its bleeding wounds—that was something, really something. I knew right then you would be perfect for the master, and your reputation could bridge the gap between man and beast…"

"But why? Why would I need a reputation?" Jae lowered his arm. "I don't even want to be known as the bull slayer!"

"Quiet!" Lucien grabbed his shoulder, glancing around. "I know. It's just the masters and those idiot twins, Pete and Pate, who call you that. But believe me, in the lower city, your reputation is spreading. They call you the True Moth. Many know of you now. Only those in the Vanilla need convincing you're not one of them... a good master, full of hate toward the minotaurs and other beasts of this city."

"But why? Why is all this happening? And the master... that's so close to my slave name, and if he makes the connection..." Jae shook his head. "I don't want to be known throughout the city. I don't want to be the Bull Slayer! Or the True Moth. I just want to be me. I want to be..." He paused, his heart in his throat, tongue desperately trying to recall his real name, but he couldn't.

"...I just want to do the master's work and receive tarts from Old Berona. I have soft clothes and sleep under cotton sheets. You don't know what it's like to sleep in dirt and mud. I like it here."

"You don't really believe that." Lucien answered him. "And can you honestly say you'd never like to see your homeland again? Or what of your sister? She could still be alive, or your family!"

"My mother, father, and older brothers were killed. There would be nothing to go home to."

Lucien did a double take, clearly not expecting that answer. He lowered his voice again. "It's the same story everywhere. The high lords divide and conquer. It's how they rule in my homeland and how they control the fields of Astrelaide. Everyone will need to unite. Everyone! A figurehead who can lead all to the light, a leader who treats all creatures equally, is a powerful rallying cry. Someone who doesn't harbor hate for man or beast..."

"I'm not hateful..." But Jae's voice betrayed him. He paused, frowning as he gazed into the black abyss below the roof ledge. "On the islands, we only had coconut crabs and whispers of mermaids in the sea. Then I found myself in the fields of the Sorrows. Minotaurs and other beasts raided our work camps, attacking even their enslaved beastfolk. Yet still, they care not for us, and we for them, even as we were both shackled and driven farther west like cattle. I've never known a minotaur to care for a human, and vice versa."

"That is changing," Lucien said, turning to him earnestly. "And it's changing fast. With the fall of the western slave fields and the legacy of the Ash Fall looming over us, the power of the masters is waning."

"I do not want to hold prejudice in my heart, but you have lived among the roses for too long. Terror lived in all our hearts as we fled field after field, the monsters of the savannah always right behind us. Many good slaves died at the hands of beasts, and they are still out there. I want to believe in what you say, but a part of me can't forget..."

"And still, with that trauma, look what you did! Your compassion for the minotaur!" Lucien's voice rose. He leaped to his feet.

"Lucien, please, you're shouting..."

"Let the whole world hear! You are proof that any animosity in this world can be forgiven and forgotten. We can tear this all down—beast and human together!"

"I want to believe you, but I fear for your tongue, Lucien. Terrible things can happen to all of us."

"Stand with me." He extended his arm, and Jae looked up at him, Lucien's green eyes glowing in the moonlight. He placed his hand in Lucien's and was pulled up. Their eyes met, noses nearly touching, hot breath against one another.

"How can you always know what you're doing?" Jae whispered.

"I don't." And they kissed.

They held their embrace as the world stood black and empty, the moon their only witness.

"Am I a part of your plan now?" Jae asked.

"Maybe." Lucien took his hand. "Fate, at least, has brought us together."

"Is it fate now?" He smiled.

"One man cannot possibly plan for everything."

"The good masters seem to think so." Jae laughed, but Lucien tightened his grip on his hand.

"You'll need to be careful, Jae. We've struck a match, but I can't control which way the wind blows the flame."

Jae stared into Lucien's green eyes for another moment, then turned for the trestle. "Come on, let's head to bed before we are missed."

Lucien nodded and followed him downstairs.

In the night sky, dark brushstrokes moved across the full moon.

WARWICK VI

The dagger hung but an inch from his right cheek. Warwick's hand closed around the hilt, muscles taut as he wrestled with the blade, but still, it inched forward, closer. He closed his eyes, bracing himself for its bite.

"MY PRINCE!" The shout cracked through the room. The knife tumbled to the floor. Warwick's eyes flew open just as Wulford lunged, wrapping him in a fierce grip and kicking the dagger across the stones. "What madness has taken you, boy?"

Warwick's cheeks blushed as he squirmed within Wulford's tight grasp. "It was nothing… only practice…"

"Do you mean to take your own life? Oh, foolish child! Tell me!" Wulford shook him, but Warwick wormed his way free. He scampered away, back turned to his personal knight.

"I meant to do no such thing, just perhaps, only leave a little… scar."

"A scar? A scar! Upon your princely face!"

"Battle-tested... fierce... *justified*..." He hunched his shoulders.

Wulford stood at the back of the prince, mouth open, panting like a dog. "How do... I can't... *oh*." He paused before breaking into a laugh. Warwick felt the floor rumble underneath him as Wulford thundered to him, snatching him back up into a bear hug. "My prince! Why didn't you tell me you were nervous? Pray tell, you know you don't have to kiss the fair lady on your first visit? Or do you worry you do not know how..."

"What!" Warwick burst from his arms, spinning around. "Certainly I of all people know how to kiss a girl. Need I remind you of my tour through the Sanguinia states and the ladies who fawned over me?"

"Yes, my prince," Wulford replied with a grin. "but I never did see you..."

"Respectfully, I kept my affections behind partitions, hidden from the eyes of jealous knights. I know how to show a lady my interest."

"Well then, if you aren't nervous for your visitation, why the knife?"

Warwick froze, his face paling at the question he hadn't expected to hear again. He crossed his arms, cheeks warming. "It's my first public appearance since... the duel. I thought if they saw me with a scar, they'd see me as... battle-tested."

Wulford's expression softened as understanding dawned. "Oh, my prince..." He knelt, gazing up at Warwick. "Your cousin Derrick is fine. He will live."

"This does not discount the rumors and whispers within these walls. Have the Nine cursed me so as to win a duel only for tales of wickedness to supplant my victory?"

"Yes," Wulford said gently. "there were few witnesses, and so tales have grown in the dark. But Derrick is recovering, your father is not displeased, and, best of all, a fair lady of the realm awaits your company."

Warwick glanced at his knight. "She... longs for me?"

"She does," Wulford assured him, standing. He looked at Warwick with a warm smile, barely eclipsing the growing boy's height. "She's in the gardens, eager for your call."

"Hmm." Warwick tapped his foot. He turned to his mirror, eyeing himself and running his fingers along the smoothness of his cheeks until his fingers dropped to his new tunic. He pinched the cloth between his fingers, tugging at the looseness of the threads, and couldn't help but smile. Despite the trouble with his cousin, the court had been quick to praise his stature under Wulford's protection, flooding him with fresh attire. His coattails draped over burgundy britches, and a neat row of buttons and a cummerbund sat snug over his immense belly. This look wasn't quite the fashion of the south, but he could no longer be mistaken for an overripe pear beside his brother.

"You look comely, my prince. Shall we go to her?"

Warwick nodded, giving himself a final spin in the mirror. Wulford led him from his chamber to a waiting fainting couch, where three Demonbreun Guards stood ready. They saluted as Warwick climbed aboard, then lifted the couch, bearing him down from his high bedchamber—itself a section of the imperial family's chambers. Warwick rested carefully as they descended flights of steps, bypassing Lysander's chambers, passing no one else but guards and servants.

The descent was long and twisting, and their venture only ceased when they reached the base of the imperial chambers. Warwick here departed the couch, snatched a sweet from the imperial dining chamber, and was led into the castle proper. Wulford and the trio of Demonbreun Guards formed a loose circle around him, maneuvering through the bustling corridors. The palace was alive with nobles and dignitaries: lords and ladies of every rank, alongside wealthy merchants, artisans, and foreign dignitaries. The castle swelled with both sorrow and splendor; such was the nature of death with the imperial family. Most guests wore black, though some flaunted lavish attire, pushing the boundaries of the latest fashions.

Warwick felt torn, both wishing to draw the eye of the court and hide in the recesses of the castle's passages until a new, more scandalous development swept the whispers of the realm. He dared to think the worst as guests took notice of him, but few whispers or looks of disdain found their way to him. Lords and ladies alike bowed at his passing, and still others called his name, eager to make their presence known. Warwick acknowledged them as best he could, though the tension from the crowd was palpable, mirrored in his guard's vigilant watch. They allowed no one to approach too closely.

"I am their prince! The realm wishes to see me. Let me oblige them!" he eventually pleaded to his guard, growing impatient with their relentless pace.

"Aye, my prince, you are indeed—and that means attending to matters of grave importance, like not angering your lady-in-waiting!" Wulford assured him with a grin.

The explanation worked; Warwick broke into a smile and kept his pace with his guard, his worries forgotten. Wulford looked upon the happy boy, thinking of the knife poised to strike upon the boy's gentle cheeks only moments before, then looked upon the crowd of court guests. For every four courtiers seeking the prince's favor, a fifth stood tucked into a corner or shadow, watching with a blank expression as the heir-to-be passed, and those weren't even the ones he truly feared. He looked to the prince's audience, those clawing for his attention, and dared himself to think how many concealed daggers beneath their cloaks. He moved closer to the prince.

A sound strategy, until the prince saw something he wanted.

They made good time to the gardens until a group of guards halted their path, revealing Lady Catelyn within their protective circle.

Wulford gave a quick nod. "Apologies, my lady," he called out. In a flash, Warwick slipped from his protection and approached his cousin.

"Lady Catelyn, a fine day, is it not?"

"Perhaps for a man who rides high on his victory. For others, we have much to worry over."

"My lady?" Warwick ventured, but Catelyn only tossed her crimson hair over her shoulder, brushing him off with a dismissive wave.

Wulford had to go to the boy, pulling him back under his wing as Warwick only stood frozen to the spot, a twitch working in his cheek. "My prince?" he asked softly, noting the boy's clenched fists.

Warwick only grumbled under his breath. "Let's just get this over with."

They continued to the castle gardens, a secluded space perched on yet another rooftop. Warwick's eyes instinctively drifted upward, drawn to the peak of Mount Ness towering high above, still capped with snow even in spring.

"You will find the good lady waiting for..."

"I know where I will find her." He batted away Wulford. "Wait for me here. I doubt I will need your help with courtship."

"I sincerely pray," Wulford muttered to himself. He placed a hand on the hilt of his sword, ready to spring just in case the worst should happen.

Warwick did not share Wulford's concerns. The gardens were deserted, cleared by his guard in the morning. The only occupants were the hatchlings of butterflies and caterpillars swarming the rows of hedges and blooming flowers. He pouted as he walked, swatting flowers in his way and even spitting into a sparkling fountain carved in the shape of a young maiden.

"Reprehensible thing." And suddenly his cheeks became wet. A dull roar began to overcome him, filling his chest like the growl of a lion. Looking up, he caught sight of a waterfall escaping from a cavern high above on the mountain of Ness. The waterfall plummeted through the open air, disappearing in a misty veil near the castle's edge. He moved closer, breathing in the fine mist, and felt a tremor in his chest. The tears weren't even his, yet he wanted to cry all the same.

A single sob escaped before he swallowed it. Beyond the misty garden's edge, his suitor awaited, seated beneath an arch woven with fine hummingbird vines. The waterfall crashed just feet away, vanishing into a bottomless cavern shrouded in mist. She rose at his approach.

"My prince." She did a small curtsy, pulling on the bottom of her dress. Warwick stopped, spotting her exposed cleavage pushing against the bosom of her dress. The proximity to the falls had dampened her and she was positively slick with moisture. Even her strawberry-blonde hair was becoming undone by the power of the falls, and a few stray hairs clung loosely to her face. Something deep within Warwick stirred.

"My lady," he replied with a princely bow, circling the arch to take her hand. He lifted it to his lips. "The pleasure is all mine."

"You are charmed, I'm sure," she said coolly, pulling her hand back. Gathering her dress, she took a seat on the bench beneath the archway, her gaze drifting to the mist-filled chasm below.

"My lady…"

"You may address me by my given name—Polina, if it pleases you."

"Polina…" he started. He looked to the falls as well, an invisible handprint burning into the side of his cheek. *Twice spurned in a single day.* He hiked his britches and took a seat beside her, grimacing as his trousers became wet with the dew of the falls. "Polina. A beautiful name—not of the common tongue, certainly."

"And does this displease you?"

"Displease me?" He chuckled. "I have spent the last year being treated from castle to castle along the warm, foreign lands of Sanguinia. Aye, where the wine is bountiful and the fruit is aplenty."

"I see. You've certainly… absorbed the culture well." She cast a brief, pointed look at his midsection.

Warwick looked away from her. They both stared, wordless, into the mist of the falls, the roar of the falls filling the quiet between them, until a frown found its way on his face and he felt compelled to stand. Extending his arm as if to speak to some unseen maiden, he delivered his own verbal retort.

"How the fair maiden treads water
Belly swollen, a lamb for the slaughter
Her lover calls to her from ashore
Yet to duty she shirks, 'nevermore'"

He delivered his lines in Monteclecian. He paused after the delivery of his lines, hand still extended, feeling the moisture in the air wrap around his fingertips. In the roar of the falls, he could hear the shout and cries for an encore, and with a smirk, he straightened his trousers and plopped back down beside his maiden. He leaned back, plopping one leg over another, and let the mist kiss his face in place of a thousand fans.

Polina plucked at the necklace about her neck with her fingers, and ever so quietly over the Falls of Ness, she answered him. "I did not know you spoke the tongue of Sanguinia so fluently."

"There is much the court does not know of me. Everyone is fixated on my brother and his skill with a sword. But it was I who learned the southern tongues of Sanguinia, who tasted their strange foods and embraced their customs. I traveled to the farthest reaches of our empire, listening to the grievances of lords and smallfolk alike. And yet—none of that seems to matter, least of all when I pick up a sword and win. Does the world know nothing but cruelty?"

Polina twirled the necklace around her finger. She still did not look at him. "How many tongues do you speak?"

"I know the language of the Kaesnfolk, naturally, and its sister dialects well enough," he replied, his pride tinged with bitterness. "And Sanguinian languages of Monteclecian and Lucardi well enough. I can also read and write in the Old Tongue, as well as some Lyonnian and Makkan too."

"That is most impressive."

"Aye, I have tried. It is my duty to speak the languages of the realm and those of great antiquity."

"Aye, but do you not speak the tongue of Acquanis?"

Warwick frowned and leaned forward. "No, and now it seems my words may have spurned you."

"Your words have spurned me no more than the rest of the realm."

"My lady?" he asked, trying to understand.

"Yes?" And finally she turned to him, looking upon him with large blue eyes.

"Is this your first time to court?"

"No, my prince, it is not."

"Then you must know—this is no place for pleasantries or fairness, even for a crown prince."

"I am afraid I have learned this far in advance. My time has been split between my homeland and foreign castles, and though I thank your father for the greater honor of my father's position, it has done little to elevate the acceptance of my people within the realm."

"Then speak to me," Warwick urged, his voice softening. "As heir to this realm, I can listen, and perhaps—pray I may understand."

"It is very good… to hear that you will listen. I had heard stories…" Polina paused, returning her fingers to the necklace.

"Aye, as I have heard stories of the Vayern people…"

Polina flinched, as though struck. "Perhaps this world would be better if we were all slower to judge." She sighed, dropping the necklace, and looked to the waterfall. "Acquanis is the only Vayern holding in all the realm and we are treated as if we are dogs. My father's position on the council is granted only because our land is needed to secure the realm's borders from Isperia. Your father is wise to avoid giving Vipra a formal audience. Nothing good can come from her being here.""

"I assure you, my lady, your father's position is a great honor…"

"It is an honor in name only. We are treated merely as a threat to be contained."

"I know the Spider Queen of Isperia has united her fellow Vayerns through tyranny. Her sister, the princess Vipra, will have no audience here. You are no threat. What a silly concern..."

"I thought you said you were here to listen?" she snapped at him.

Warwick jumped back, touching his hand upon his cheek. "I came here to listen," he cut in quickly, but his voice softened. "Forgive me, my lady."

Polina's glare simmered before softening into something close to a smile. "They are common people to me, my prince, and how deeply I long to be among kin. Were it not for my father's station, and his vote, would I even be welcome at court?"

"Well, my lady, allow me to say that you will be most welcome in my court," Warwick replied with a tender smile.

The sincerity in his voice made her glance down at her necklace, blushing. Warwick's eyes lingered on her hands, and he, too, reddened. Polina caught his look, smiled, and then, realizing how close they were, scooted back upon the bench.

"Please forgive me, my prince. I am unaccustomed to the styles and ways of High Ness. I am afraid... we are alone in the garden. I would be remorseful to think anyone should get the wrong impression."

"We are protected by my guard and the roar of the waterfall, my lady. I daresay there is no safer place in the whole castle to speak."

Polina's eyes shifted uneasily. "It's not words I fear, but the eyes that linger... and where eyes go, hands often follow." She folded her arms, rising from the bench and glancing up at the vine-draped arch as if watching for hidden observers.

"My lady!" Warwick also rose to his feet. "Please do not go with such great haste. We have barely become acquainted with one another."

"I have waited in the garden a good while. It was you who arrived late as I recall."

"It is said a prince never arrives late. The court only arrives early." He smiled, trying to jest with her again, but there was no flicker of her lips this time.

"I must say, my prince, much of what I've heard of you has proven false," Polina replied. "though tales of your lack of humility ring rather true. Now I really must go—"

"My lady!" Warwick called again, reaching for her hand. She deftly stepped back. "If you wish to test my humility, perhaps I should command you to stay."

"I would not abide," she answered. "for I recognize an even greater authority."

Warwick's face flushed. "My father's, perhaps? Or even— my brother's?"

Polina stopped, turning back on her heels to him. "No, Warwick, for there are greater things in this world than crowns and princes."

"The Nine?"

"Precisely," she replied smoothly. "And I am overdue with the confessor. I fear that while I may overlook tardiness, he surely will not." She turned, quickening her pace, but Warwick followed a step behind.

"My lady, when will I see you again?"

"Perhaps in the pews at the next congregation, my prince," she replied over her shoulder, then hurried on, leaving him alone in the mist-filled gardens, damp and slightly dazed.

"Oh Aethylios, bless me," is all he could think to say. He slunk slowly out of the gardens, finding Wulford waiting for him at the entrance.

"Ah, my prince, how did you fare?" Wulford's grin betrayed his amusement.

"Better than I'd hoped, though she's off to confess her 'transgressions' to the High Priest now, or some such…" he grumbled, accepting a towel from Wulford and rubbing it over his damp face.

Wulford chuckled and gave him a hearty slap on the back. "Do not tell me, my prince, that you inspired such deep emotion that she must rush off to confess it to our Lord?"

Warwick wobbled, frowning though his face lay buried in a towel. "Is a woman even worth the trouble if she is so pious?"

"Aye, is any woman ever worth the trouble?" Wulford laughed again.

Warwick withdrew the towel, scowling, his hair wild. Wulford stuck out his hands to gently comb Warwick's princely hair back into place.

"Were it so, my prince, the land of Acquanis is the only Vayern land that reveres the Nine Miracles. Religion is near and dear to them—as well the only thing binding them to our realm."

"It appears so…"

Warwick allowed himself to be groomed before stepping back into the castle. A gaggle of ladies awaited him here, giggling wildly as he passed with Wulford. He smiled, doing a bow for them, but strangely, felt a hollow emptiness in him for the first time. He told himself it was hunger, but something deeper stirred, turning his steps away from his private quarters and toward the guest chambers nestled within his family's wing of the castle.

"My prince?" Wulford called, noticing the sudden change in direction. "Has something happened?"

"I have shifted one heart today; perhaps I can sway another," Warwick replied, picking up his pace. Without further word, he began to ascend the stairwell, leaving Wulford scrambling to keep up, panting as he trailed behind.

"My prince?" he called again. "If it is lunch you seek, it is not yet served!"

Warwick ignored him, emerging on a landing barricaded by a line of Demonbreun Guards. They parted at once at his arrival but gave Wulford a scowl. Warwick sauntered down the hallway, arriving at a pair of large oaken doors. Only a serving girl awaited outside.

"My prince," she squeaked, eyes wide. "The Lord Derrick has requested to be left alone…"

But Warwick paid her no mind. He slipped in through the doors, leaving his guard and the serving girl behind a barrier of imperial privilege. He tiptoed into his cousin's bedchamber quietly, rounding a bend to find his cousin resting in his bed, shirtless, with a sling wrapped around his arm.

"Warwick?" Derrick's voice was a faint slur. Propped against his pillows, his skin pallid, he looked up with a drowsy frown. "What... are you doing here?"

"I have come to apologize..." But he stopped in his tracks. A woman emerged from behind a partition near his bed. She had olive skin, and dark, flowing hair, with a dress adorned in ruby-red jewels.

"You are no serving girl," he said at once.

The woman smiled, lifting a bowl of dark liquid that gleamed like oil. "Aye, that is correct, Your Grace." She spoke with a heavy accent, not unlike Polina.

"I am your prince, you will address me as such. Now, who are you, and who permitted you into my cousin's bedchamber?"

"Warwickkk... am I in my own cashhtle yet?" Derrick slurred.

Warwick's eyes went wide. "Do you bring harm to my cousin?"

At that accusation, the woman laughed. "Oh my poor boy, such an accusation from an attempted kin slayer."

Warwick turned hot. "Should I name you a witch? Skulking about the imperial chambers."

The woman turned from him, walking over to Derrick with deliberate calm. She tugged on his sling, revealing the raw, jagged gash that ran along his forearm. Warwick's heart pounded as he rushed forward, his breath catching. "Do you smell it?"

Warwick's heartbeat was in his throat. "I... I..." But his words failed him. The smell was there, stinging his eyes as he witnessed what had become of his cousin.

"The wound festers," the woman said coldly, her hands deftly working around Derrick's injury. "And if I am to save this poor boy's life, I must work without interruption."

"I... I..." Warwick stammered again. "I do not trust you!" He looked to his cousin, wallowing on the bed, sweat dripping from his brow.

"It would seem trust is in short order in this family."

Warwick looked to the exotic woman but found her head turned, tending to his cousin. Instead, he glanced behind him to find his aunt poised to strike.

"Auntie..."

"Who permitted you within these quarters?" she demanded.

"I am the prince?"

His aunt's scowl deepened. "You say it as if it were a question—as if you lack the authority to command."

Warwick took a step back, his body tingling from the day's bruises. "Auntie, I have only come to express my sorrow to my cousin."

"Well, you'll find words in short supply," she retorted, pressing forward. "Now is the time for action, which is why I've asked Lady Vipra to tend to my son."

Vipra? The wheels turned within his head. He knew that name... that it stemmed from royalty. *Vayern* royalty. "A princess of Isperia?"

The woman, revealed as a foreign princess, smiled warmly at him. "I arrived some time ago, my prince."

"Does my father know of this?"

Now his auntie took a step back, a wicked grin spreading across her face. "Bancroft avoids me at every turn. He must be truly ill to avoid me *and* a foreign princess at every turn." Warwick said nothing, his unease mounting. His auntie sighed, clearly tired of the game. "So tell me, my prince, when will he confirm my son's inheritance of Aberness?"

The pieces finally clicked in Warwick's mind. His jaw clenched, and he raised his chin, ready to withstand his aunt's verbal blows. "The funeral is his priority. The realm demands his attention. Perhaps his silence speaks to the certainty of Derrick's inheritance."

"Is that so? For whispers have been heard at court."

"Whispers are always heard at court," Warwick fired back.

"Even inklings of a... *choice?*"

Warwick's gaze hardened. "I gave you my word."

"And now my son lies gravely wounded and unlanded. If you are a religious man, my prince, then you will take note of God's disdain for violence against a family member—and broken promises."

"Worry not, Auntie, for you shall find my reign filled with neither. As it were, I am on my way to see the confessor, but I felt it best to express my grief and regret in person, rather than hide behind a confession box."

His auntie's lips pursed as she chewed on a response, but Warwick didn't give her the chance. He bowed to his cousin, whispering a quick apology, and brushed past his aunt on the way out of the chamber.

As he exited the chamber, he found Wulford waiting in the hall. "My prince? Is something the matter?"

Warwick brushed past him with tears in his eyes. "Am I so cursed?"

JOSEPHINA V

The homestead blossomed with new life. Grass as lush and green as Josephina had ever seen burst forth from the freshly turned soil. Butterflies and bees filled the air, and flowers of every variety took over the surrounding mountains, only limited by the snowcaps of faraway peaks. Spring had finally arrived, warm and pulsing with birth and renewal. And yet, in the yard, dressed in white with her hands raised skyward, Mother prepared to mock the season of life.

Josephina tried to busy herself with chores, tasked by Mother to gather stones for a grand fire pit in the field. Day after day, she ventured into the woods, collecting stones, only to bolt back in fear whenever Oléfur made his unsettling appearance. A rift was growing between him and Mother. Oléfur wanted his payment now. Josephina could sense it—her blood growing thin in her veins at the mere sight of him. Yet Mother promised a bountiful feast, and to Josephina's growing dread, today was to be the day of reckoning.

A sudden burst of caws shattered the quiet as a flock of crows erupted from the forest. Startled, Josephina dropped the stones she had been arranging and froze. Hundreds of black wings circled the homestead, forming a tightening spiral above. Then, in a coordinated frenzy, they dove toward Mother.

Josephina could only watch as the swarm engulfed her. Through the chaos of feathers and shrieks, one crow broke from the frenzy and landed gently on Mother's outstretched hands. It hopped to her shoulder, then to her ear, snapping its beak and rustling its wings, a single white feather among its black coat. At once, the rest of the flock scattered.

Mother turned to Josephina, the lone crow perched on her arm. "It's time," she said calmly. "Prepare yourself, Josephina."

"Yes, Mother." She dropped her remaining stones and ran, heart racing up to her room. Through her window, Josephina spotted Oléfur and his pointed hat emerging from the forest, dread pooling in her stomach as she gulped. His inhuman speed across the grass fields sent shivers down her spine. If today did not go as planned, she knew she could never outrun him. He would claim her blood one way or another.

Trembling, she moved to her trunk and dug through it. At the very bottom, carefully hidden away, lay the dress Mother had instructed her to wear—a garment specially sewn for this occasion. It was the finest thing ever bestowed upon her: short sleeves, a red embroidered neckline, and a hem that barely brushed her thighs. It was a beautiful dress meant for a beautiful girl, fashioned in the spirit of spring to cultivate fertility. She hated it. Just holding it sent her into full-body shakes, her teeth gritting together, with tears gathering in the corners of her eyes. She missed winter. She missed the season of cloaks and mittens. She missed going unseen. Slowly, she worked her thumbs along the seams of the dress as if to rip it in two, but then the kitchen door downstairs slammed shut. She knew Oléfur had arrived.

"Curses," she said with silent tears streaming down her

cheeks. She removed the droopy frock she currently wore, and with a deep sigh, pulled the spring dress over her. It barely fit, exposing her bosom, along with most of her legs and arms. She crossed her arms and hung her head in shame. Slowly, she shuffled to a window, glancing at herself in the reflection. Her skin glowed whiter than a ghost. She looked almost naked in the white dress. A horrible, stumpy mess in the reflection. The monster she was meant to be.

"Josephina!"

"Coming, Mother," she replied too quietly for anyone to hear. She made her way slowly downstairs.

Mother stood in the kitchen, now dressed in black from head to toe. Oléfur, too, had shed his clothes for dark attire, and together they seemed to hover in the dim light, little more than shadows. Josephina couldn't bear to look at them.

"Josephina," her mother growled.

"Y-yes, Mother."

"The time is at hand. The knights are nearly at our homestead. Are you prepared?"

"Yes, Mother." She kept her head down.

"Then tonight we shall feast, and our family will grow stronger. Plans within plans, Josephina. Your simple mind may struggle to comprehend, but greatness is upon us."

A snicker escaped Oléfur, woven into the dark tapestry of shadows.

"Yes, Mother."

"Josephina…" Mother called to her.

Dread coiled in Josephina's stomach, and she hesitated to raise her eyes. Her cheeks burned with shame.

"Josephina, here," Mother urged, her tone more insistent.

Trembling, Josephina slowly lifted her gaze from the floor, meeting her mother's ghastly visage—a creature only vaguely human. A dark hand extended toward her, shadowy fingers revealing the glint of steel. Josephina's heart raced. *Her knife.* She snatched it from her mother's grasp.

"You are not to use it, do I make myself clear?"

"Yes, Mother." She nodded eagerly.

"Make sure they see you with it. It will drive them into an angry frenzy."

Josephina held up the knife to her eyes. She could make out her reflection in the steel, but somehow she didn't feel as ugly.

"Oléfur and I will go into the woods. Let us begin."

The kitchen door creaked open, revealing the fields beyond. Oléfur slunk from the house, moving as an obscure shadow, even in the light. Mother followed behind, her feet seemingly never touching the ground. Josephina came last, watching the two of them glide over the fields and slip into the forest. Crows squawked from the treetops.

"I wish you were here, Mishie," she whispered. She glanced at her reflection in the knife one last time before sheathing it in a small loop sewn into the side of her dress. Its glint would betray her even from a distance. With a sigh, she stepped away from the house, taking a moment to gaze up at her bedroom window where Mishie lay.

Though clouds hung heavy in the sky, they began to part as she walked barefoot through the fields, and sunlight poured down. Josephina strolled along, twirling in the sun, a genuine smile spreading across her face as she laughed, feeling the rays kiss her skin. Mindfully, she twisted and turned as Mother had instructed, extending her arms wide before spinning again. Her dress flared up, and the weight of the knife pulled it tight around her midsection.

Ugly, ugly, ugly. The thoughts echoed in her mind, but she twirled anyway, letting out a giggle. She had the knife. Mother lurked in the woods. She hated the knights too. Could she, for once in her life, grasp a bit of justice?

The sound of barking dogs served as her answer.

She stopped, her heart pounding once more, but the sun shone brightly and warmly, igniting a spark within her. With a burst of joy, she twirled again, laughter spilling forth like she was a genuinely happy child. The crows took flight from the trees as if sensing the shift in fate.

Four knights emerged from the trees, leading two large barking dogs on leashes.

Josephina stopped as if frightened and pulled her hand to her chest. "Oh my!"

"You there!" one knight called from a distance. "Halt in the name of the Reisonic Order!"

The knights left the tree line and marched toward her. The dogs barked furiously from their leashes. Behind them, the forest groaned.

"We are in search of a dangerous creature known to haunt these woods. Do you know of such a beast...?"

The knights paused, their attention shifting. Josephina turned toward them, arms outstretched. She smiled at them— not because Mother wanted her to, but because she genuinely felt the warmth of the sun and the thrill of the moment. The lead knight froze, his eyes widening in recognition. She spotted the familiar ginger hair peeking out from beneath his helmet. *Franz.* He saw the glint of his knife from her hilt.

"You! The monster child! In the name of the order, in the name of humanity, I place you under arrest!"

The knights unleashed their dogs. Josephina watched as a bead of sweat slipped from her brow. They came barreling toward her just when a tree snapped in half behind them.

The knights whipped their heads around, hands instinctively reaching for their swords. The dogs skidded to a halt halfway to her and then arced back toward the woods, their barks and howls growing louder, spit flying from their jowls. They went barreling through their masters, knocking one knight to the ground, and disappeared back into the trees.

"Heel! Heel!" A knight ran after the dogs, but it was no use. Their barks echoed through the forest, followed by two sharp yelps.

The knights stared into the forest.

Slowly, the knights withdrew their swords. Two of them moved cautiously toward the forest, but Franz thrust his sword out to stop them. A sound escaped Josephina's lips, drawing his gaze back to her. She didn't realize it at first, but she was laughing.

"You stain on humanity! What have you done? Who do you work for?" A fellow knight placed a hand on Franz's shoulder, whispering something in his ear, but he shrugged him off, his fury palpable. "Surrender now! Your death will be swift, and I will ordain you to be blessed by the Five. Your soul may yet find peace!"

The sun's rays grew brighter and hotter. Every bird within miles took to flight. Josephina took a step back, withdrawing the knife from her waist. She held it out, allowing the steel to glint in the sun's light. Franz only grinned and came running.

Josephina spun, digging in her heels and ran. She sprinted, knowing these fields well, and flew through the grass. She could hear Franz behind her, his armor clanging as he struggled to keep pace. But he was much bigger, and her stubby legs could only carry her so fast. She passed the house on her right, veering toward the barn and ultimately the woods. She wondered what Mishie thought, watching from the window.

She ran as fast as she could but Franz was gaining on her. The other knights raced just behind him.

Josephina hit the tree line just as Franz caught up with her. His hand clamped down on her head, but she was barefoot and light on her feet; she pivoted on a tree root, shaking off his grip. They both fell hard onto the forest floor.

"You damnable girl! You abominable monstrosity," he coughed. "Do you know what I am going to do when I catch you?"

"Nothing worse than Mother," she found herself saying. She spat dirt from her mouth and clawed away from Franz. A cold hand gripped her ankle and she screamed.

"And I think I'll start with your hand. The thief's punishment," he sneered.

Josephina's eyes went wide as she realized he had her. He grabbed her other ankle and dragged her backward. She tried to crawl away, but he flipped her onto her back. He pinned her to the dirt as he reared up over her, snatching back his stolen knife from her clutch. She screamed, but Franz only laughed. Her cheeks flushed with humiliation as he glared down at her, his expression twisting into a scowl of pure disgust.

"There are giants and brownies and worse in the woods, and then there is you. Your scalp shall hang on the main road so all will know of your deeds." He pressed the knife to her wrist, letting Josephina feel the pressure as he broke the skin and blood pooled. The smell of iron hit her nostrils and a shadow broke behind her. It came as a flash and then Franz fell to his back, frothing at the mouth. Josephina immediately flipped to her knees and crawled a short distance away, before turning back to look. Oléfur stood over Franz's shaking body, forked tongue hanging from his mouth.

She ran from the woods. She ran from the other screams of the knights. She ran back to the house, up into her bedroom, and slammed the trapdoor shut. She pushed the chest back on top, panting, and ripped the dress from her body. She tore it to shreds, letting it fall to the floor in clumps. Ignoring the bruises and cuts that marred her skin, she pulled on her frock and collapsed onto her bed beside Mishie. Instead of crying, she found herself laughing—a wild, manic laughter that echoed in the silence until Mother returned home.

"Josephina!" Mother's fist struck the bottom of the trapdoor. She leaped from her bed and pushed back the trunk. Mother emerged from below, bloodstains coating her dark cloak, hood drawn back to reveal her face. "What do you think you are doing?"

Josephina felt the slap even if it was not physical. "Did I not do my job, Mother?"

"In the field, yes. You did excellent. What I fail to understand is your laziness. Is the day over? Has all been completed on the farm?"

"Mother, I don't understand…"

"Josephina, there is a child on the way. The day is quickly approaching in which he will join us. I have many, many woes to care for, so my patience grows thin with you. There is much to be done."

"But what about the knights? Are they dead or...?"

"Now, young lady!"

"They were mean to me! Will they suffer? I want to help..."

"This minute, Josephina!"

Josephina frowned and marched past Mother's scornful eyes, descending with heavy footsteps down the ladder.

"Honestly, with such attitude?" Mother sighed.

Josephina stormed her way through the whole house and back into the field. The stone fire pit lay only half-completed. Many more days and nights would be needed to complete it.

She set about her work, stacking and preparing the stones. She wanted to cry, but instead of tears, her blood boiled. As she piled the rocks together, she glared daggers at Mother, who emerged from the house with Oléfur. They ignored her, making their way toward the barn. Frustrated, Josephina hurled the rock she was holding to the ground. Huffing, she decided to follow them. She made it halfway to the barn when a piercing scream filled the air.

A chilling wind swept down from the mountains, rustling through the trees, which groaned under its weight. More muffled sounds came from the barn, and Josephina stepped back, biting her lip.

I am brave. I am strong. I want to see. I want them to see me!

She took a step back toward the barn when an unnatural, bloodcurdling scream cut through the air. Josephina turned and bolted. She ran all the way back to her assigned task and set about doing it quickly, the sound of her hammering heartbeat drowning out the knights. She worked harder and harder, running to the woods, hauling rocks, keeping the dull thud in her ears roaring as the sun dimmed on the horizon. The screams grew louder, and soon the moon emerged above their humble homestead, shining brightly. She started to throw the rocks hard against each other, anything to break up the sounds coming from within the barn.

She craved revenge. She wanted to be strong. Yet deep down, she was relieved. It wasn't her this time.

"Curses," she mourned quietly for the knights.

JAE VII

"The Ghost Bull..." Pate squeaked, his voice muffled beneath his mask.

"The Specter of the Scorch Grass!" Pete squealed back, and the two of them dissolved into laughter. Jae marched beside them in silence, his jaw clenched.

"Look at our little bull slayer. Boy, don't you know? You could say anything to those beasts. I doubt they can even understand us!"

"Of course they can, you just have to speak like a cow. Moooooooooo-ve your fat arse."

"They understand us." Jae's voice cut in, low and steady. "Very well."

"Hmph! Well then, do they understand a fool's gambit? Because that's the mess they've dragged us into—we're knee-deep in a cow pie."

"A ghost minotaur? Really? That's the kind of idiocy only

beasts could believe." Pate scoffed, then hesitated, as if realizing too late who he might offend. "No one's coming to save us... them," he muttered, quieter now.

Jae broke the silence that followed. "Things are different beyond the walls. Endless plains. No barriers, just fields stretching to the horizon."

"... Do you miss it?" Pete asked.

Jae's gaze hardened. "No. It's a false freedom. There are chains in the plains, just as there are in the cities. Shackles heavier than steel, and the persistent fear that the minotaur on the horizon isn't there to plow your fields, but come to kill you. Besides, I eat better under our master's roof."

Pete and Pate exchanged glances, letting his words sink in, before bursting out laughing again. "Old Berona, damn that woman can cook!" Pete said between chuckles. "She wouldn't last a day in the wilds with minotaurs and raiders roaming about. And ghosts, apparently."

"Ghosts..." Pate shook his head. "Probably just some albino minotaur wandering around. There's a whole clan of 'em out in the deep deserts if the stories are true."

"You'd fit right in," Jae punched back. "Pale as ghosts, red hair like the devil. You'd be their king."

Pete and Pate howled with laughter.

"Ah, what would Luke say, knowing the lessons his prized pupil's learning from us?" Pete grinned.

Pate launched into an impression of Luke, puffing up his chest and deepening his voice. "Boy! Your stamina's worse than an elf's, and your stance? Hells, it's worse than the old mother's. What you need is discipline. Diligent, diligent discipline."

"Old Berona, now she knows things, I tell you," Pate muttered. "Ever seen an old lady work in the dead of night? Always leaving those treats for her 'sweetlings.' I'd hate to end up on her bad side."

"Don't talk bad about her," Jae grumbled, his tone dark.

Pete shot him a glance through the slits of his helmet, brow furrowed. "Geez, kid, we didn't mean anything by it."

352

"Yeah, no need to go telling the old mother, all right? I need those sweets," Pate added.

"I think it's best we all keep quiet."

Pete nudged Pate. "Oh, I think we've upset the kid... haven't we..."

"Oof!" Pete doubled over as Pate's elbow landed hard in his side, cutting him off.

Jae straightened, his grip tightening on his sword as they neared the towering yellow walls of Astrelaide. The Thorned Men stood in rigid formation, spears in hand, eyeing the approaching crowd with indifference.

"No jokes now," Pate muttered, his tone serious for once. "We've got orders from the good master."

The eastern gates bustled with activity. Donkeys, horses, and even a few minotaurs lumbered through the throng, hauling wagons loaded with fruits, vegetables, and other goods. The air was thick with the sounds of haggling and the clatter of hooves on cobblestones.

"The minotaurs don't shit on the roads," Pate whispered with a grin, leaning toward Pete. Naturally, a chuckle followed from the idiot as Jae tightened the grip on his sword even more.

Ahead, the flow of traffic at the gates slowed to a crawl, like water pressing against a dam. Slaves with permission to leave waited in stalled lines while the Thorned Men scoured every paper. Above them, higher even than the thick yellow city walls, the Stone Master loomed like a sentinel, its golden face lit by the morning sun. Around the crowd, guards laughed and bantered, much like Pete and Pate, until the Thorned Men drew close. Then, as if on command, the laughter faded and silence settled over the gates.

Jae, Pete, and Pate joined the other household guards in line, inching forward as the Thorned Men scrutinized and ridiculed each document presented to them. Discontent brewed in the fields beyond the city walls, and the good masters were volunteering their own household slave stock to keep the field-workers in hand. The Thorned Men were extra vigilant today;

only those deemed capable of beating down fellow slaves were getting through. Jae didn't want to go, but disobeying Aeksilor wasn't an option.

"Do you have it?" Pate whispered to Pete.

"Yeah, I got it, I got it," Pete muttered, nodding, but his frantic hands betrayed him as they searched his pockets in a panic.

"Well?" Pate stressed as the Thorned Men approached. Their privilege of working for Master Aeksilor meant nothing now—out here, they were no better than dirt.

And by the sun in the sky, why did the good master entrust these fools with his signature?

"Papers," one of the Thorned Men rasped, his voice low and guttural, like stones grinding together.

Pete fumbled harder, his movements desperate. The Thorned Men exchanged glances before stepping apart, their hands moving to their weapons.

"I have it, yes indeed, my good lords," Pete stammered, finally producing the scroll bearing Aeksilor's seal. He surrendered it with a shaky, sweaty hand. One of the Thorned Men snatched it from him, scanning the letter before grabbing Pete's chin with a filthy gloved hand. He yanked Pete's head back and forth, inspecting him with hateful yellow eyes.

"Your master claims he sent three honorable guards, but I see only two—and his fool," the Thorned Man sneered. "If your master needs better eyesight, perhaps he should visit the lens crafters of the Vanilla." With that, he shoved the scroll hard against Pete's chest, causing him to stumble. "Do your duty, fool, and be back by nightfall. The gates will be sealed then, and any guard still outside will be considered a runner. Do you know what happens to slaves who are runners?"

"... Yes, sir," Pete choked.

"Then you are less a fool than thought. Begone." The Thorned Men waved them by, and Pete trembled as Pate stole the master's scroll away from him.

"Honestly," Pate said exasperated, and pushed Pete through Astrelaide's Honeysuckle Gate.

354

Jae followed close behind, his eyes drawn upward. The gate-house loomed like a cathedral, its archway swallowed by the vastness of the yellow-stone walls. Honeysuckle vines spiraled along the seams of the masonry, thick and golden, their scent rich in the sunlit air. His fingers twitched faintly at his side. *How cruel,* he thought, *that something so sweet go untasted.*

The squadron passed through the gatehouse, a cavern in its own right, with towering, ancient ceilings, and thick, imposing walls. A soft breeze lingered here, shielded by the sun, as if they were to transgress deep into a mountainside. The walls of the city were immeasurably thick, ancient, and battle-tested. Birds flew through the cavern overhead, and below, ingrained into the very foundations of the walls, scars of long-ago sieges were worn into the brick. The walls of Astrelaide were a barrier, and as a border in their own right, the moment they passed beneath the yellow bricks of the defensible city, a new world, one strange, foreign, and hostile, opened up before him. The polished streets and sculpted courtyards gave way to dirt roads and slanting huts, sun-bleached and wind-worn. A few free-men beyond the walls had tried to imitate the city's gleaming facades, but without the shelter of the cliff or the fortification of stone, the wind had stained their homes with dust and grime.

Yet Astrelaide and her surrounding lands were full of sur-prises. The squad marched swiftly, leaving behind the scattered huts clinging to the city's edge. Soon, they reached hills burst-ing with color, for Astrelaide was the city of flowers. Hilltops swayed in a gentle breeze, rippling in shades of purple, red, green, and yellow. Flowers stretched across the horizon—roses, lilies, and countless others, some polka-dotted, others striped, painted the landscape.

"This is nothing, kid," Pate said, catching Jae's distracted gaze with a gleam in his eye. "It's summer. They're focused on bringing in the wheat and vegetables now. You should see spring—when it rains nearly every day. The fields stretch lush and alive, from the sea to the horizon, with colors you can't even imagine."

Jae believed it. The sweet fragrance of roses and love filled the air, mingling with the fluttering of butterflies, their vibrant wings as numerous as the petals around them. Before long, the delicate creatures settled on the squadron, their pink, white, yellow, and purple wings adorning the men's drab leather armor like living jewels. Pete and Pate giggled at the sight, but Jae only frowned, feeling robbed as they tickled his skin. *Where were these butterflies when I was in the fields?* In the west, the skies had only buzzed with flies and mosquitoes, thick over the putrid bogs and saltwater marshes. And here too, slaves in wide-brimmed sunflower hats carefully tended the roses.

"What a gig, huh?" Pate mused, shaking his head. "They get those silly hats to keep the sun off their backs. The good masters think sweat's bad for the flowers. Too much stink and all that."

"Some people get all the luck," Jae grumbled, just as a butterfly landed on his lips as if to shush him.

"Luck's subjective," Pete muttered.

Their troop continued marching through the vibrant hills, while the city of Astrelaide slowly shrank into the distance, leaving only the towering bluffs behind. The morning sun hung low in the sky, casting long shadows.

"This is nothing," Pate continued. "I've worked rice paddies filled with monitor lizards—*poisonous* ones, some as big as your leg. You can thank them for the slave shortage."

"Would you prefer lizards or minotaurs?" Pete quipped, glancing over his shoulder. Behind them, a guard from another household whooped and hollered, followed by muffled laughter. *Great, they have an audience now.*

"You're asking the slayer of bulls." Pate laughed. "This'll be a piece of cake for him."

Ahead, a stone watchtower loomed atop the final hill, its silhouette cutting into the sky. Jae couldn't see what lay below.

"I never slayed the beast..." Jae started, but his words trailed off. As their troop crested the ridgeline, the view ahead unfurled before them. A row of dark-clad Thorned Men stood at attention, gazing out across the horizon. Surprisingly, they nodded in approval as the armored slaves marched into the vast domain.

Beyond the ridge, the dirt path sloped sharply downward, revealing the great grasslands of beast country. A tan haze stretched to the horizon, broken only by the patchwork of wheat fields sown in the dry soil. Slaves moved through the fields like specks, bobbing in the early morning light, their bent forms resembling flies on dung. Wooden watchtowers dotted the landscape, with Thorned Men roosting above, their gazes fixed not on the horizon but on the laborers below.

"Let's see if the three of us can't land a job in one of those towers." Pate nudged Jae and Pete. "We'd be safe from the sun up there."

"Aye." Pete chuckled. "And we'll get the first look at the Ghost Bull when his phantom army shows up on the horizon."

"That Ghost Bull eh?" A new guard appeared from behind them. He bumped Jae out of the way, draping his mammoth arms around Pete and Pate. Jae scowled but said nothing. Those buffoons were always getting into trouble.

"I heard he's some kind of sick albino, mad as the heat itself," the guard said, pointing toward the shimmering horizon, where the sun's early rays already blurred the edges of the land. "You see those stone watchtowers? They're not just for scenery. They're looking for him—or anything else wandering out there. Minotaurs, dwarves… even packs of rabid noggins."

"Yarr harr!" another slave guard shouted, hamming it up like a sailor. "They call the savannah to the south the Scorch Grass, but I say it's a sea of beasts. And further still, could things become even worse, lie the lands of the fallen empire of Makka. I'd wager my meager savings those Makkans are out there now, building a fresh fleet to rise again. They'd come for us in a heartbeat if we let the Ghost Bull, a rogue troll, or even a rabid noggin tear a hole in our ranks!"

"And we'll wallop them too!" the first guard bellowed, tightening his grip around Pete's and Pate's necks. "For we are the city of Astrelaide, and we protect our own!"

"For the city of Astrelaide!" a dozen guards roared in unison, slapping their chests. "We are the flower in the desert! Beware our thorns!"

The guards slapped their chests again. Slaves in the fields looked up from their positions, watching them march past. Jae looked behind them up to the ridgeline. The line of guards continued to pour forth, but their numbers appeared to him like ants swarming a garden. *We don't have the numbers to...* But he stopped himself. *They don't have the numbers to monitor these fields.*

"All right, you boisterous lot, listen up!" their appointed captain called to them. He pulled them from the main path, trampling into a field of wheat. A few slaves scattered at the sight of a trio of Thorned Men approaching them. "I see your hearts swell for the city of Astrelaide, and I say good, for it is for the *people* of this city that we do our good work here today. The good masters have asked us to keep order in the fields. Well, I stand with the great Master Balon and his legacy. Wild rumors swell among these men, women, and beasts—tall tales of ghosts and bandits lurking on the far horizon. The threats are real. The beasts are real. Fanning the flames of fear among our fellow slaves, and we all know what fear can do to a rational mind..."

A Thorned Man approached their captain and laid a gentle hand on his shoulder. His voice melted away. The Thorned Man spoke quietly. "Let us ensure you are not here to entertain such farfetched delusions as an invasion of spectral beasts from the desert. Leave that security to us. You are here to maintain order in the fields, nothing more. Remember your station, as you say, for the great city of Astrelaide. You are slaves meant to fulfill your duty, and that duty is to maintain order, even among your own ranks. You will obey our commands, or you will be punished. You may feel free beyond the walls of the good masters, but know their reach is just as terrible here."

The Thorned Man paused, his yellow eyes gleaming at them through the narrow slits of his helm. "You will break into patrol groups. Listen for the sound of whistles; this will mean we summon you for a task. You will work all day until we dismiss you for the closing of the Honeysuckle Gate. There will be no questions."

The Thorned Man finally lifted his hand from their captain's shoulder. "I will divide you into patrols. Now." With no regard for their households, he forcefully splintered the guards into random groups. His companions barked orders, and Jae was abruptly shoved into a cluster of guards, instructed to head into the fields immediately. He left, glancing back to see Pete and Pate watching solemnly, each placed in separate groupings.

As the sun climbed higher, the day grew hot, and Jae mindlessly strolled along the rows of crops. Rows of slaves labored around him, their movements steady and practiced as they tended the wheat. Most of them were human, thin and weathered, their faces marked by the harsh realities of their lives. Among them, minotaurs worked as well, their massive forms dragging carts or hauling heavy loads with ease. He eyed each of them, looking over their fur coats that came in a hundred varieties, from tan to white, brown to black, some spattered with dots on their bellies and backs, some with horns that reached three feet into the air. None of the minotaurs looked familiar to him, however, and none so much as cast him a glance.

He was lost in thought, his feet carrying him forward without purpose, when something familiar caught his eye. A flash of ginger hair, dull from dirt but unmistakable. His heart skipped a beat. *The little girl*—the one he had seen separated from her mother at the auction, her tiny frame now bent under the weight of the scythe she wielded to slash at the wheat. She looked even more fragile than he remembered.

Jae broke into a run. He was smiling and he didn't know why. He ran, cutting through the waist-high wheat, waving his arms as she looked to him startled, when he lost his footing and hit the ground hard, taking the little girl down with him. He coughed, rolling onto his back as the wind was knocked from his chest. He blinked hard, looking around him for the little girl, when a hideous creature appeared above him.

Jae screamed, kicking backward and flipping onto his back before springing to his knees, sword drawn, facing… a creature? A demon? The slave girl, also knocked to the dirt, looked up at him with wide, terrified eyes.

"Don't!" he heard her whisper, but the damage was done. Thorned Men were coming.

Jae kept his gaze on the creature, however. It stood no taller than five feet and was completely green from head to toe, with long, spindly arms, legs, and fingers. Its nose was nearly a foot long, and its enormous yellow eyes, with slitted green pupils, darted nervously in his direction. Even its hair, a mass of squiggly tendrils, sprouted wildly from its head and clung around the base of its neck, all pure green!

"Are you hurt?" he asked of the slave girl, never taking his eyes off the monster. It looked at him shyly, shifting seeds between its long, spindly fingers. "What is this thing? Did it hurt you? Did it attack you from beneath?"

The monster smiled at him, panting.

"They are coming," the girl whimpered. "Do as they command."

"Huh?" But he didn't get an answer. Two Thorned Men arrived quickly.

"You, slave," they snarled through gritted teeth. "sheath your sword. Immediately."

Jae, his eyes locked on the creature still, found his muscles unable to move.

An iron tip pressed into the side of his neck. "You were ordered to sheath your weapon, slave."

A wad of spit hit him in the face. Jae flinched, only then noticing the slave collar tucked beneath the creature's neck fluff. *What have I done?* He trembled, quickly sheathing his sword.

The Thorned Man did not remove the point of his weapon, however. "What do you think should be done?" he asked his companions.

One of them stepped forward, locking eyes with Jae before glancing at the creature. Jae's patrol comrades, lacking any loyalty, had already scattered.

"Gardener, return to your duties at once," the Thorned Man commanded. The creature wasted no time, diving back into the field and disappearing among the wheat tops.

"Foul creature," the other Thorned Man hissed. "but worth its weight in gold."

The tip of the iron pushed harder into the side of his neck. "What about this one? A slice? Or a punch?"

The one not brandishing a weapon stepped before him. They locked eyes, Jae staring into the yellow snake eyes underneath his mask. The Thorned Man looked over him, chewing something in his mouth. He held this stance for what seemed like an eternity before he grunted, spitting a foul substance to the side, and looked at the girl.

"He will discipline the girl. No sense of solidarity between these two. Be about it, boy, strike the girl, and then return to your patrol."

Jae found the iron tip removed from his neck. He looked down at the girl, who met his gaze with unwavering eyes. He wouldn't do it.

"Do it, boy. Or we take flesh from the both of you."

The girl rose to her feet, staring blankly at his chest. She couldn't have been more than eight or nine. Quickly, Jae hit her in the ribs. She fell without a cry back to the ground.

"Again," the Thorned Man commanded.

Jae leaned down and struck her once more.

"And again."

He obeyed, each hit tearing at his resolve. The girl curled into a ball, whimpering softly.

"Satisfactory. As you were." The Thorned Men nodded, their iron rods whipping through the air as they turned to leave. Jae remained frozen in place, breathing heavily down upon the little girl, and tears began to fall from his cheeks.

The little girl unfolded herself and looked up to him. She

had a black eye and a bloody nose, but she did not cry. Instead, she pulled herself back to her feet, nodded to him, and then grabbed her harvest basket and walked away.

Jae watched her go as blood dripped from his bruised knuckles, his gaze trailing after the little girl until she was swallowed by the field. He lowered his head, about to turn away, when he felt a hundred eyes on him. To his horror, every slave had silently witnessed it all.

One of them, a man not far from Jae, straightened from his work. His skin was dark and olive, not unlike Jae's own, glistening with sweat from hours under the heat. He held his sickle loosely, then lifted it in a small but deliberate gesture of acknowledgment. Their eyes met, and the man gave a firm nod, before returning to his work.

Jae swallowed hard, picking up his sword as Lucien's words echoed in his ears.

The slaves were due for a ripe harvest.

Melinda III

The grand chamber echoed with the call of a hundred trumpets.

Lords and ladies of the court gathered beneath the painted rock dome of the grand entry hall of the castle. Melinda stood chief among them, dressed in her finest garb, a massive golden dress that consumed her body, matched by the magnificence of a golden tiara, her hair laced with diamonds, and her neck dressed with more gold. She truly looked like an empress, and today, she was going to need it.

"Do they mean to displace half the castle?" Lysander shrugged, watching as a seemingly endless train of carriages rumbled up to the base of the great stone stair.

"She is an electoral lady of the realm," Melinda replied evenly. "You would do well to remember that."

Lysander hesitated, then asked. "Will she even remember me?"

Melinda placed a gentle arm upon his shoulder. She was

not his real mother, only stepmother by marriage, but she saw him as her own blood, and that was all that mattered.

"She will know you. Everyone in the realm knows you, my prince." She smiled at him, but Lysander pulled back slightly, unlike him. She saw him shuffle on his feet.

"Grandmother and grandfather didn't… at least not at first. They knew my name, my status, sure, but not me. I was a stranger to them."

Melinda's heart melted as she forced herself to smile. "My boy, when your mother…" She stopped, sucking in her breath, having almost said his real mother. "when she married your father, it was quite the scandal. She came from a wealthy merchant family, yes, but not nobility."

"And why should that matter?" Lysander shot back. "Edwin is a merchant and he's Treasurer of the Realm!"

Melinda kept her composure cool, even though she felt as if she may shatter. She knew who had banished Warwick and Lysander's maternal family from the imperial court. She was arriving just now. She didn't have the heart to tell him, and not that she would have to. Instead, she cast Lysander a warm smile just as the crowning jewel of the procession appeared: a gilded carriage drawn by white horses, their saddles and harnesses intricately worked with gold-leafed leather. At a silent signal, a retinue of the Demonbreun moved forward in perfect formation, one stepping ahead to open the carriage door.

A herald inhaled deeply, steadied himself, and then, his voice ringing through the cavernous space, proclaimed. "WELCOME TO HOUSE ESMERELDA, THE GOOD LADY LAYANA, AND HER SON AND HEIR, LORD ERNEST."

Trumpets erupted again. Lords and ladies erupted into polite applause. Lysander joined them. Melinda did not.

From within the carriage, a gloved hand appeared first, awaiting an escort. A guard stepped forward, offering his arm, and then, at an almost agonizing pace, her mother emerged.

Time had shrunk her. The once commanding woman was smaller now, her figure wrapped in a gown of deep emerald, its jeweled fabric glittering even in the cavern's dim light. She climbed the stairs with a grace untouched by age as the symphony swelled to greet her. Melinda did not blink. At her side, Lysander whispered. "Grandmother is magnificent."

Melinda's response was swift, quiet. "Do not call her that at court. And hush."

Lysander fell silent, shifting uneasily, his hand dropping to the hilt of Empyrean Flame.

Behind Layana, a second figure emerged.

Ernest.

Melinda swallowed a laugh before it could escape. *By the Lord of Flames, he has grown fat.* A thick belly swelled beneath his emerald cloak, and what little hair remained atop his head had gone entirely gray. He gave a quick bow before the court, waiting for his turn to ascend the stairs. Unlike his mother, he moved without grace or ceremony and, despite his stature, caught the auspicious wink of several young ladies-in-waiting. He climbed behind his mother, and as he did so, the music crescendoed. Some of the court were moved to tears by the music, but Melinda remained statuesque. Lady Layana, *her mother,* would expect nothing less.

At last, the symphony reached its peak, and as the echoes faded among the vaulted stone ceiling, Layana came to a halt, a single step beneath Melinda. The chamber fell into silence.

"My empress, I grieve for the loss of our Master of War, and for the death of a member of the imperial family. You have my heart, and my loyalty." A pause, followed by a deep bow. Her mother's old joints creaked faintly, yet she did not falter as she extended one gloved hand toward Melinda. She hesitated, feeling the last of the symphony's echoes die within the stone chamber, and then finally took her mother's hand and pressed upon it a gentle kiss.

"Rise, good lady of House Esmerelda, and be welcome at court. Your words touch me deeply, as I know they will please our good emperor—"

"Long may he reign," the court responded in unison.

"—and the realm's proclaimed heir, Warwick of House Hieronymus."

With a flick of her wrist, Layana straightened and stepped aside, allowing Ernest to step forward. He grinned broadly.

"Hey there, Sis." He seized her hand and squeezed it hard, bowing with a jarring lack of grace. "Long road, but we're here now."

"Welcome… Brother," Melinda answered smoothly, retrieving her hand before his sweat could linger.

Ernest, oblivious, turned immediately to Lysander. "Aye, lad. You must be one of them Esterian knights guarding the princes. I'm a fan of the ale from your region. Simply incredible!" He elbowed Lysander with a laugh. His mother sighed.

Lysander did not react. "Uncle," he acknowledged curtly before turning his attention to Layana and bowing with impeccable form. "Good lady, be welcome. It is an honor to have you among us in mourning."

Ernest flushed crimson as Layana gasped. "Warwick?" she proclaimed as she broke into a deep bow. "What an honor it is to stand before you!"

Melinda almost broke into a chuckle. "Be welcome here in the presence of Lysander, brother to proclaimed heir, Warwick of House Hieronymus."

Layana shot up, shooting a scowl to her daughter before turning back to the boy. "Lysander? Truly?" With a firm but precise gesture, she shooed Ernest aside and lifted her gloved fingers beneath Lysander's chin, tilting his face upward. "I have not seen you since you were a boy. Your hair was lighter then. You have grown into a man. A strong man," she said with a touch of almost grandmotherly affection, but just as she did, she stepped back as a frown overtook her lips. "And where is Warwick? Where is the heir?"

Melinda's voice, when she answered, was cold. "Mother, the emperor and the proclaimed heir await you in the throne room. Come."

At her command, the Demonbreun fell into step. Lysander

moved to escort his grandmother, and together, they passed beneath the grand doors into the castle proper.

Lifting a single hand, she gave the order. "A traveling couch for the good lady. At once."

They were ready. Guards swiftly produced a gilded seat, and Layana allowed herself to be transported without question. Melinda, too, took her place upon a litter, her golden robes spilling over the sides like molten ore. She detested the act, feeling less like an empress and more like a slave lord of the Sun Coast.

They ascended the grand staircase and stopped before the phoenix doors of the throne room. Melinda turned, awaiting her mother, who arrived a moment later upon her couch. Her brother followed much later, red-faced and huffing, with Lysander walking solemnly beside him. The guards were dismissed, and at last, the family was alone.

"Mother." She smiled, reaching toward her.

Her mother recoiled. A look of sheer horror crossed her face. "Melinda! *Decorum.* Not before the emperor!" she hissed in their native tongue.

The training of a lifetime took hold. Instinctively, as if hearing the crack of the whip from her childhood whipping maid, Melinda withdrew her hands.

Ernest snickered, answering too in the Travesi language of their homeland. "Yes, decorum, Sis!"

"Yes." Melinda ignored him, straightening her dress. "Of course."

Lysander stood clueless, unable to follow their tongue.

"Lysander, Son, please then," Melinda asked, switching back to the common tongue. Lysander nodded and stepped forward, pressing open the grand doors to the throne room.

A cold blast of air greeted them.

Lysander held one of the doors open as Melinda, her mother, and Ernest passed through. Together, they stepped into a marble forest, where towering columns stretched into the darkened heights of the throne room like trees stripped bare by winter. The sun, veiled by thick clouds, cast the chamber into deep shadow, leaving the hall in a brittle chill.

They walked the length of the marble hall. At the far end, serving as their guiding light, towered the Opal Throne, flanked by two braziers casting a flickering glow. A slouched figure sat upon it, and by its side stood Warwick, a mere speck against the throne's immense marble weight. In escort with her mother, Melinda's heart swelled with pride. Her mother had tirelessly crafted her destiny, shaping her into a proper match for an emperor. Though her mother's demeanor could be cold, it was a privilege to bring her forth to the pinnacle of the realm's power.

Until Bancroft's coughs rang out through the chamber.

Melinda's heart fell. She broke into a brisk walk, forcing her family to keep pace. Her golden dress, a burst of color against the pale marble, caught the few rays of light in the room, making her seem like a falling star.

The Nine hear me, I pray this goes well!

Slowly, the Opal Throne grew to tower above them, and as they arrived before the seat of imperial authority, they fell into an orderly line. Melinda stepped forward first, curtsying before her husband. She then did the same to her son, Warwick, who nodded approvingly. Lysander followed, though Warwick granted him only a brief, dismissive nod. Ernest stepped forward next. And then, at last, her mother.

The lady of House Esmerelda performed a deep curtsy, only rising at the voice of the emperor.

"You may rise, Lady Layana of House Esmerelda."

"Thank you, Your Imperial Majesty. I am honored to stand before you and the Crown of the Nine." She turned her gaze to Warwick. "And you, the prince of the realm. House Esmerelda extends its well-wishes to the heir-to-be."

"Thank you, dearest grandmother," Warwick answered in the language of their homeland, his accent thick and heavy, but his gratitude apparent.

Layana rose, turning her attention back to Bancroft. "It is with great remorse that I speak of the loss of Thane of House Hieronymus. A tragic loss, especially at the hands of those savages who do not seek the light of Aethylios. It is in his honor that my husband,

368

who, by God's light, is unfit for travel, has commissioned a new church to be built in Toussé to bear his name. There was no greater servant to the realm in this world or the next."

From atop the throne, the ruby of House Hieronymus gleamed, the brightest jewel in the imperial crown. Melinda caught the way her mother's gaze lingered on it, eyeing more than just the ruby itself. There was an emerald, deep green, set engrained within the crown's rim.

Among seven others.

"My dear son, and the future of my house, has come today in place of my husband. Ernest." She bowed, beckoning Melinda's brother forward. Ernest, ever the rapscallion, returned only a half bow before rising with his signature toothy grin.

"A pleasure, *Brother.*"

Melinda saw her mother stiffen, a gloved hand flying to her throat in a silent gasp.

"What?" Ernest's voice was light, teasing. "We are family, yes? Hieronymus and Esmerelda, bound by blood. You are my nephews, are you not?" He turned to Warwick and Lysander, casting each of them a wink. "Let us speak as a family, then! Bancroft, Your Majesty, the loss of Thane was a true tragedy. Were I not the head of my house, I would gladly see justice done for him on the Isle myself! And as for you two boys—especially you, Warwick, House Esmerelda will lay down its life and legacy to ensure the crown passes to you. Aye, I swear it upon my name."

Layana's eyes were wide, petrified even, as if she might keel over at any moment. Melinda silently glided toward her, placing a gentle hand upon her shoulder. She looked up at the throne, frozen.

"Ernest, Layana, I am so grateful..." Bancroft suppressed a cough. "It is so refreshing, in a court of snakes, to have family, *warm blood*, come to pay homage to my brother and his sacrifices."

"And for your support, dear uncle," Warwick interjected

smoothly. "I will not forget your words, nor the loyalty of House Esmerelda when I take the crown."

"Of course." Ernest smiled.

"I look forward to hosting you," Bancroft continued. "I will arrange a dinner for us all at once. You must be... you must be..." He faltered, breaking into a harsh coughing fit. Lysander stepped forward, climbing a few steps toward the throne, but Bancroft shooed him away. "You must be tired after such a long journey. Please, have full rein of the castle. As an Elector and the mother of the empress, you will find your chambers most com... comfortable..."

The coughing resumed, harder this time. Lysander shot Melinda an uneasy glance. She met his eyes and nodded, granting him silent permission to act. From the side, Warwick rolled his eyes.

"Mother, Brother, thank you both for your kind and warm words," he said smoothly. "The loss of Thane, and the cold winds of the mountain, have taken their toll on the emperor. Please, allow Lysander to escort him to his private chambers. There is much business that requires his attention."

"Oh my! Of course," Layana exclaimed. "My emperor, Your Imperial Majesty, forgive me if I have caused you any inconvenience." She bowed deeply. "Do not worry for me, nor for my son. The burdens of your duty are great, and by the flames of our Lord, I wish you strength and good health."

"Thank you, Layana." Bancroft accepted Lysander's firm hand as he descended the marble stairs of the Opal Throne. At the base, before he was led away, he turned to her one last time. "I don't believe I have ever truly thanked you for bringing her here," he said. Then, with a smile at Melinda, he added. "She has been a great comfort to me, and the court."

"Why... of course." Layana blushed, a sly smile creeping onto her lips. "House Esmerelda serves the imperial court. We serve you."

Bancroft nodded once more before allowing Lysander to lead him away.

An awkward pause followed, where Layana, Melinda, Ernest, and Warwick stood uncomfortably before the empty throne. Warwick, the Crown of Knox resting upon his head, stepped onto the stairs of the throne and turned to his grandmother. "May I interest the good lady in some tea?" he asked smoothly. "Or perhaps a treat? Fruit or lemoncakes?"

Ernest broke into a harsh laugh, drawing the ire of his mother. He strode over to Warwick, standing on his tiptoes to sling an arm around the boy's shoulders. Wiping a tear from his eye, he grinned. "Oh, what a good one, boy! Don't worry," he giggled. "The formalities of court are over with. Say, why don't you show me where the ale is stashed? Or where they keep the imperial pistols? I've been dying to shoot."

Warwick looked to his mother helplessly, but for once she was glad for her brother's nature.

"Why, I think that is a fantastic idea, Ernest. Warwick, be a good host and show your uncle the castle."

Ernest didn't need to be told twice. "Come on, boy!" He roped Warwick in like a steer, dragging him off the steps. Melinda and Layana stood still, waiting until the distant slam of a door confirmed they were alone. The throne room was silent, save for the wind howling beyond the high windows. Taking her mother's hand, Melinda placed it upon her own shoulder and pulled her into a firm embrace.

"Mother! It has been some time. Much… seems to have changed." Melinda's voice cracked.

"The world is always changing, Melinda. I thought I raised you well enough to know that."

Her mother's answer was curt, and she pulled back from Melinda's embrace. The two women stood apart, their gowns worth more than a single petty kingdom, as a single ray of light broke through the clouds outside.

"I have handled the trials of the imperial court better than you may know," Melinda countered, her tone sharpening. "It is not easy raising twin princes of the realm."

Layana seemed to take that as a slap on the cheek. "You know your brother has always been... willful."

"That is to put it mildly, Mother."

"Nevertheless, he is meant to inherit a vassal subjugate to the imperial throne. That is his birthright. You, on the other hand, were owed very little as a woman, and yet, look at what I have given you." Her mother turned, looking from the throne, sweeping her gaze across the entirety of the chamber, seemingly chasing the echo of her voice through the columns.

"I am not ungrateful."

"Nor did I claim you to be."

"Then even now, standing before the empress, *your daughter*, you will not speak plainly?" Melinda demanded. "Even Aethylios, bless him and his Miracles, would speak as candidly to a king as to a peasant."

"I am not a miracle worker, Melinda. I am a mother. And a concerned one at that." Her voice softened slightly. "What of Warwick and Lysander? Even in my distant court of Toussé, I have heard whispers of the succession. And there should never be whispers, Melinda. *Never.*"

"You have come all this way, Mother, after shunning me for how many years, only to tell me the most basic truths?"

"No. I have come to see you, the revered empress of a vast realm, and do my duty as the representative of our family to ensure Warwick's ascension is not threatened, and..." she paused, finally looking upon Melinda with an ounce of care. "Do a mother's duty as well."

Melinda rocked back on her heels, though her gown hid the motion. "I appreciate the thought."

"Now tell me, Melinda," Layana pressed. "Is there hope? Have the realm's finest tended to you?"

Melinda lowered her gaze, placing a gentle hand over her womb.

"No," she admitted. "That wish died a long time ago. Warwick and Lysander are my children. They have known no other mother and treat me as no less."

Her mother studied her with stern eyes, though they glistened faintly. "I raised you to be an empress, and that duty included motherhood. I know you think me strict, but I see now that my efforts were not in vain. Those boys are yours, if not by blood, then by spirit."

Melinda let her hand fall from her belly. "Thank you, Mother. They have treated me well... I just wish they would treat one another the same."

Layana's brows fell. "So it is true, then? The boys feud?"

"Aye," Melinda admitted, "though not for the crown, but for the hand of a maiden, I fear."

Her mother closed her eyes, nodding as if she had expected nothing less. "Hmm. For the girl, Catelyn. A great beauty of the realm, or so I hear. I can think of no better reason for blood to spill."

"Mother?" She put a hand to her throat.

"Melinda, I do not like it here... Alone, I mean, among the columns. Any serving girl or peasant could be listening. Take me somewhere private where you and I can converse as empress and lady, or as mother and daughter, I am sure you would prefer."

Melinda, suddenly short of breath, agreed. She stuck out her arm, taking her mother in her arm. "Right away, good lady of House Esmerelda." They walked together from the throne room, their dresses dripping with jewels, clacking together as they went.

Beyond the chamber, the castle was alive with energy. Lords and ladies from across the realm had descended upon the capital, eager for the season's social scene. Whether they had secured lodgings within the Crownhold or not, they flooded the halls, their chatter buzzing with scandal, scheming, marriage pacts, and the daily dose of tea sweeping not just the empire but the world itself.

"Did you hear? A ghost bull has swept the Sorrows of the Sun Coast? What foolish things those mongrels believe."

"Mongrels, my dear?" Layana leaned casually into the conversation, the ghost of a smirk on her lips. "They say they lie with beasts. They are far lower than any mongrel bitch pup begging for scraps outside a tavern. Ha!"

Melinda stiffened even as she increased their pace, mindful that without the Demonbreun at their side, the lords and ladies would soon descend upon them like vultures, though her mother seemed not to care. This was her element, an entire castle, nay, the whole city of High Ness, isolated far from the riffraff and lower classes of the world. The Crownhold was an entire city teeming with only the most noble, except for the serving staff relegated to their shadows and dark corridors.

"Look, oh dearest," Layana cooed, suddenly stopping before the Lady Jocelyn, nothing more than a minor vassal under some greater lord of Valkirn. She smiled, ruffling the fabric of the young woman's ruby-red gown between her fingers. "Ah, the color of Aethylios himself. I hear they wear it well upon the Holy Isle. *Marvelous*, darling, *marvelous!* Find me at tea, I simply *must* know the designer!"

Lady Jocelyn blushed, turning as red as her dress.

Layana turned away, laughing, though her voice carried well within earshot. "Did you hear what I said? *Red!* In fashion among the priests of the Flame? They'll call me a riot!"

Melinda sighed. "Really, Mother. This castle already carries enough whispers. I would rather not add the *rudeness* of the imperial family to them."

"Rudeness?" Layana paused dramatically.

At once, they were surrounded by noblewomen in puffed gowns, bowing politely, eager for even a scrap of attention. Layana's gaze landed sharply upon one of them.

"Was it *you*?" she demanded.

The woman, already powdered white, paled further. "A-apologies, my good lady, but I-I do not..."

"Was it *you* who just broke wind? Or do I merely smell the brimstone of hell in these halls, for someone dares speak ill of Warwick's handling of a sword?"

The young lady trembled.

"No? Not you? *Good.* For if one had such lame words to speak, they would not stand pale as a ghost but shriek like a banshee!"

With a sharp tug, Layana pulled Melinda back into motion, leaving behind the flustered courtiers in their wake.

"Mother!" She cursed as soon as they were free of the last crowd.

Layana merely laughed, shaking off the reprimand like dust from a fine cloak. "You are the empress, Melinda. *Not* a queen, *not* a lady, an *empress.* Your word is *law.*"

Melinda sighed, wondering if Warwick was having as much trouble with Ernest. "I can assure you, Mother, my word is *not* law. Our realm is far too complex for such absolutes."

"Nonsense. Take me to some tea and biscuits, and I will tell you what the realm is really about…"

She stopped midstride.

Beyond the row of guards, standing at the foot of the imperial tower, was Elizabeth. Dressed in black, she stood motionless, her arms folded neatly, obstructing their path.

Melinda felt her mother's arm go rigid.

"E-Elizabeth… is that you?" Layana called out, her voice suddenly brittle.

Elizabeth did not move, save for the slight tilt of her head. "Lady Layana," she said coolly. "It is I. How nice of you to finally grace us… for my husband's funeral."

Melinda opened her mouth, but before she could speak, her mother untangled their arms and took a measured step forward. With practiced elegance, she dipped into a curtsy.

"When I heard the news, my heart shattered," Layana answered, her voice as soft as silk. "Such service is beyond commendable. It is *holy.* A fight for the Lord of Flames. A fight for the realm. I cannot begin to express my gratitude. My daughter and her husband, the emperor, will do everything in their power to ensure…"

"The emperor?" Elizabeth cut in. "He must be the most grieved of all, for even he will not grant me an audience."

Layana stiffened. Her eyes darted—only once—from Melinda to Elizabeth, and though her face betrayed nothing, Melinda heard the edge in her voice.

"I *just* saw the emperor," she said carefully. "And only for a moment. He is ill, aye. It is true. I speak it plainly, good lady. Just as my own husband was too ill to travel, the emperor too remains confined, but he *sends his regards*." She inhaled softly. "Grief is a powerful thing, my lady. As an imperial woman, I know you understand this well."

Elizabeth did not speak right away. She only regarded Layana in a way that made the space between them feel smaller. Then, with a slow curl of her lips, she exhaled.

"Yes, my good lady. I do understand the power of grief. And loss." Then Elizabeth stepped forward. Not around them, but *between* them, brushing past both their shoulders. "And what we all wouldn't do for family…"

They stood in silence, watching her disappear down the corridor. Layana's fingers twitched at her skirts. Then, without a word, she linked her arm through Melinda's and turned them both toward the staircase.

The stairway spiraled high into the castle's secluded heights, and they climbed faster than usual, though neither acknowledged it. Their skirts skimmed the stone, the sound swallowed by the hush of the corridor. No lingering courtiers. No servants scurrying about. Only the rhythmic echo of their footsteps, winding ever upward.

This time, they did not bother with a litter.

Layana, for all her huffing and puffing, never shied from a challenge, and they made good time. The statues that lined the walls seemed to watch as they passed, their carved faces unreadable in the dim light. Still, they climbed, higher and higher, until they reached the base of a great turret jutting hundreds of feet above the private gardens, and at last stood high in the heavens. With the view of the cascading Falls of Ness nearly at eye level and the castle sprawling far below, she let out a breath and settled onto the balcony's ornate seating, *alone.* A pristine tea set awaited them, cucumber sandwiches already prepared.

Layana reached for a cup, her hand as steady as ever, and said as if nothing at all had happened. "Now, where were we?"

Melinda, huffing, did not move at first.

"Sit, darling, I insist," her mother said, patting the chair beside her.

Melinda hiked up her dress and obeyed.

On the balcony, her head swam. They were perched hundreds of feet above the next roofline, and above them, only the open, cloudy sky stretched endlessly. Nestled in her chair, she couldn't even rest against the white stone of the tower, which still rose behind them, disappearing into the mist above. Her mother, meanwhile, sat comfortably, unbothered by the dizzying height, delicately choosing which cucumber sandwich to bite into first. She looked utterly content, as if not a soul, save perhaps an eavesdropping raven, could hear them.

"Perhaps… Mother… we could enjoy the snack indoors. I've never been one for heights."

"That will not be necessary. You sit atop the realm, and you have handled that with grace, my dear."

Melinda swallowed, trying to focus on smoothing her dress, which had billowed through the iron railings and rattled in the wind.

"I understand, Melinda. Perched here among the clouds higher than even our family's holdings, I sense the challenge. Allow me to speak now as a lady of the realm, not as your mother, but as an Imperial Elector."

"Ladies rarely get to speak, Mother. It is a station we both know well."

"Then let me speak as your brother, Ernest, perhaps." Layana slid a cucumber sandwich into her mouth.

"Mother, he is a fool! Do you not remember the antics he got into as a child? Or as a young man? By the Nine, half the church's gold is from his indulgences…"

"Precisely, Melinda, precisely. Your brother is a fool, and

soon…" Layana sighed, briefly looking up at the sky. "By Aethylios himself, and I take no happiness in saying this, your father will pass, and Ernest will inherit our lands and titles, including the title of Elector."

"The Nine help us."

"Yes, indeed, the Nine help us." Layana pointed a half-eaten sandwich at her, much against decorum. "That is what the realm is composed of: fickle men with fickle ideas about how power works."

"They are the power, Mother. We sit in our ivory tower, but nothing in this castle is our right by blood. Ernest can be a fool, but no matter his behavior, he is a firstborn male, destined for his birthright. The Crown of the Nine has no birthright. It is different here. I am empress, aye, but not through blood."

"Indeed. That is the genius of it." Her mother shrugged.

"Oh, Mother." Melinda shook her head. A flock of birds passed beneath them.

"It is moments like this that we are truly free, Melinda. Look around us, look above us." Layana's voice softened. "Aye, I have never seen such beauty… so close to the clouds, the sun. Even in our homelands, with their fields of green and flowers aplenty, nothing compares to being so near to God himself." She smiled—a rare feat. Melinda wasn't sure if it was her own dizziness or the altitude affecting her mother. "Hear me well, my darling. The Phoenix King, he was a genius. A masterful tactician who united men who hated one another, who spoke in tongues that once wagged with only insults from castle to castle. He cast off a foreign oppressor, *and* this, Melinda, is the real genius of it! He kept the realm together. Do you know how he did that?"

Melinda indulged her mother. "The Electors."

"Indeed. The *illusion* of choice. There is nothing more powerful. The realm believes itself to possess free will. It does not."

"That does not resolve the rumors. The very real possibility of—"

"Any lord of meager standing can dream himself emperor," Layana cut in. "but when reality strikes him on the head and he whispers in his liege lord's ear who to select, and the Elector, say,

378

your father for example, considers the transfer of the crown, what do we all crave?" She leaned forward. "Stability. The chance to *pretend* we have a say in the matter. *That* is genius, my daughter."

"That did not stop the Diet of Blood from happening," Melinda replied coolly.

Layana paused, chewing the last of her sandwich. In an instant, the seemingly free-spirited woman evaporated, replaced by the cold, stern figure Melinda had known all her life.

"Even *that* was an illusion," her mother said flatly. "Blood was spilled, aye, but it sobered the lords and ladies of the realm. It reminded them of reality. That no one but a *Hieronymus* keeps the crown. The *right* Hieronymus, too."

"And who, pray tell, Mother, do you think is the *right* Hieronymus?"

The slap across her cheek echoed across the mountainside.

"Do not *ever* say such a thing against your house, Melinda! It is Warwick. *It is always Warwick*. Scream it from the mountaintops if you must! By the Nine, I will do it myself!"

Melinda held her cheek, stunned. A lump rose in her throat, but she swallowed it down. Slowly, she looked up at her mother.

Layana, heaving, wiped away a loose strand of hair from her face. "Melinda... I am sorry. This is what happens when we break decorum. When we descend to the level of peasants and lesser folk. We *must* keep the illusion, my daughter. That is all that matters."

"I am not a magician. I am an empress."

Layana studied her for a moment, then sighed. "Leave it to me then. I earned you this role, I will help you keep it, a mother's duty at least. Are those wretched Rose Monts and Goldwoods here yet?"

"The Rose Monts, aye."

"Hmm. Expected. But it is *not* who is here that speaks greater volumes."

"Cornwallice Faelwood," Melinda muttered. "The voice of the Kaesnfolk. Should an Elector's vote matter the most, it would be his."

"Indeed." Layana worked her jaw before returning her gaze to her daughter. "You can afford a few defections, but too many and the mirage shatters." Her voice darkened. "And that Elizabeth… I suspect there is more than grief behind her veil."

Melinda hesitated. "Mother?"

"Not to worry, darling." Layana smoothed the cuffs of her gloves. "Mother is here now, and I just happen to have a few tricks up my sleeve." She rose gracefully. "I will gather the Electors soon. Once the audience is set, I will, with a wave of my hand, pass the crown to Warwick, just as I passed imperial authority to you."

Then, with a sly smile, she turned and disappeared into her chambers.

LEAWYN VI

The war camp of clan Laehosha teemed with life. Across the field, tucked away in the forest, Leawyn could only watch.

She stood at the tree line, her gaze sweeping over the throngs of men and women attending to their duties. The burned tents and fortifications were torn down and were slowly coming back to life. It had not rained since the battle, and the field still bore its bloody imprints from the deaths of hundreds. In the custom of the Outsiders, their bodies were piled high and set aflame, but not before their armor, weapons, and worldly possessions were looted. Many of the soldiers now sported their war trophies—gold chains and silver trinkets, but Leawyn had forbidden such acts to her band of followers. She only permitted them to help slip their dead beneath the Hearth.

As she watched, lost in thought, the snap of a twig behind her broke the silence. She instinctively gripped the nearest tree branch, the memories of that fateful night flooding back when she stood above the cold bog of the Hearth and saw the eyes silently staring back at her from the trees. Then his smell, and all the curiosities of living within their camp…

"They are rebuilding quickly." Saralyn joined her, looking upon the battle camp.

"Your clan works fast," Leawyn said, her voice heavy. "But I wish we could leave this place behind."

"No one is here by choice."

Leawyn turned to face her, defiant. "I'm here because I want to be."

She looked at the woman. Saralyn was young, at least compared to herself. Her hair, once fiery red, had grown into a tangled nest of gray, streaked with a few stubborn remnants of its original color. Yet she remained strong and agile, and her piercing blue eyes could still command discipline. She had been among the first to come to Leawyn after the battle.

Saralyn didn't flinch at the contradiction. "Of course," she said. "Few among us would willingly choose this life for their people, let alone for themselves. I am still in awe of you."

Leawyn looked away, returning her gaze to the camp. She spied their chieftain walking among the men, his tall antler helm easy to identify. Her eyes narrowed at the sight of him. "Thank you, but… I only wish others felt the same."

"Chief Hunta is a good man, but like all men, he is stubborn. His pride has been dragged through the mud by an old woman." Saralyn placed a hand on Leawyn's shoulder. "Do not worry for him. In our songs, we know the folly of a man wrapped in the cloak of his own pride."

"Yes, but one man… one man who could help turn the tide of this war. Him, among many others…"

Saralyn removed her hand and snorted. "You have a following. Men, and women, committed to your ideas. You should return to them, before the glow of your victory seeps below the Hearth as well."

"The War Maker comes. We all stand to make a difference," Leawyn replied, but even as she spoke, the words felt hollow. She lowered her gaze to the ground.

"That did not stop Gaelyn and Luhoka from returning to Chief Hunta this morning."

"I know. I watched them go."

Saralyn's tone softened. "You old bird, don't make me lose faith as well. I cannot carry the weight of this alone. I can't maintain morale without you. You must stop focusing on those who didn't believe in your cause or those who've turned against us. They've made their choice."

Leawyn swallowed hard, her gaze still fixed on the ground. "It's not them that troubles me. It's… my horse." Her cheeks flushed as soon as the words left her lips.

"You cannot be serious."

"Your chieftain took it from me."

"A trophy is what distracts you from your people? An Outsider's mount?"

"No," Leawyn said defiantly. "An omen I hope to see fulfilled."

Saralyn's face twisted in confusion, but Leawyn didn't give her a chance to ask further questions. "Come, let's return to camp."

She led Saralyn to their encampment, a dense sprawl of tents and makeshift shelters tucked between towering tree trunks and the thick forest canopy. The camp was a practical blend of nature and necessity. Limited in supplies from the main military camp, it also reflected Leawyn's newfound connection to nature. Cloth tents were strung up between the trees, though many of her followers chose to sleep beneath piles of furs, taking shelter under the dense green canopy above.

Leawyn's shelter stood apart from the rest, a modest wooden structure nestled at the base of a massive tree. With three wooden walls and a thatched roof, its open side faced the camp, offering an unbroken view of her people. Inside, she had crafted a simple nest of furs, a tree stump doubling as a table where half-melted candles flickered softly. Wildflowers and decorative cloth brightened the space, while red and blue mushrooms from the deep forest lined the structure. By day, butterflies flitted through, drawn to the blooms; at night, moths settled quietly on the mushrooms.

Leawyn surveyed her followers, a varied group of Laehosha women both young and old, along with a handful of men, most of them elderly. The few younger men, barely of age to be warriors, had already gained a reputation for cowardice, something she intended to correct. Though her people were deeply attuned to nature, the boys needed toughening, just as she had been hardened by her own ordeal: sick, freezing, and near death in the forest. Now they slept in simple sacks beside the campfires that burned day and night, while tents were reserved for the very young and the very old. As matriarch, Leawyn kept a vigilant eye on the herd, quick to discipline any who strayed from order.

Crossing the camp, she stopped briefly at a boiling pot to sample the stew. A fellow widow looked up at her with quiet pride, and Leawyn thanked her. Smiles were growing rare in camp. Too much time had passed without meaningful action. It was time to hold court.

She nestled into her furs, turning to face the camp. Though she hid it well, her knees creaked and her joints ached. But she maintained her composure, gesturing for Saralyn to join her. Saralyn promptly whistled, summoning Takoda to their side.

Takoda, for all his years and wisdom, commanded great respect among the camp's inhabitants. Like Leawyn, and like so many others, he knew war far better than peace. He approached now, wobbling slightly, his long beard turned white, his scalp spotted and bald, marked with the lines of toil and grief. Together, they represented the storied wisdom of their clan. Yet more importantly, they both understood the necessity for change.

Takoda settled beside Leawyn, sitting cross-legged on the edge of her nest. Today he wore paint smeared across his forehead and cheeks, customary for his clan's shamanistic traditions. Butterflies fluttered around them.

"Wise Mother," Takoda greeted her.

Leawyn nodded, but frowned. She wasn't sure how she felt about that title. "And how are we today? Has the mood further soured?"

Takoda's neck bobbed as if he'd swallowed a bug. "Soured? No, no, my wise mother."

Leawyn's voice grew cold as she stared at Takoda. "Gaelyn and Luhoka left this morning." Takoda flinched, and Leawyn met his gaze. "I don't need you to lie to me. We're all disappointed, I assure you."

Takoda sputtered, as if struck in the gut. "As I said, no... we have not soured. Impossible, really, as if our mood were not already sour from the start."

Saralyn nodded in agreement. "You are too harsh on yourself, Leawyn. We all came to you for a reason."

Leawyn looked down, her eyes tracing the ancient lines in her hands, as though searching an old map for something she couldn't find. "And now they leave for another reason. We are camped in the woods, awaiting what, another man? Bah."

"Wise Mother, we beseech your wisdom. Our clan has rested these past few years by the shores of the Calladen Sea, growing our families, tending our sheep, and most importantly, biding our time. Like cattle, like sheep, we were put to pasture, and for a season, times were nice. But only for a season. We all know it's coming. We're bound to be culled sooner or later."

Leawyn lifted her gaze, but her eyes didn't meet either of them. She stared past Takoda and Saralyn, her focus drawn to the slow, endless movements of the camp behind them. There her gaze lingered, a distant sadness in her eyes.

"Let us not forget, my good friend," Saralyn patted her friend's leg. "We are only here because of Leawyn. You have delayed the culling. You have saved us. A woman, a *grandmother*, of another clan. Your time was up, your desire to return home strong, and yet you came to us and saved us. Had you been born a man, all our warriors would have flocked to you."

"Pffft!" Takoda snorted and rose quickly for an old man, sweeping his hand in an arc for emphasis. "We are of the isle, regardless of tribe! Man or woman, we all answer the call to defend our land and ancestors! You have men and women, girls and boys here. It's easy for the weak to waver between camps, even though we fight for the same cause. Let them go! Their bellies will lead them, not their hearts. The ones you have here are good." He thumped his chest. "The men may not be in their prime, but they came for a reason. And the women are fierce, if not fiercer than any man with an ax."

Leawyn didn't turn to him, but she heard his words clearly. She only shifted when Saralyn gave a soft chuckle, her gaze catching Takoda, who was winded from his outburst, and Saralyn with a wide grin on her face.

"You old fool. We're thirty archers, maybe ten ax-wielders left. Hardly an army to be feared."

Takoda sucked air in through his ancient lips, ready to rail again, when another touch from Saralyn silenced him. "But your courage is admirable, dear shaman, as is Leawyn's. Our people were surely for the slaughter, especially when they marched with those..." Saralyn's smile faded. A flash of darkness crossed her face, and she turned aside to spit upon the Hearth. "Their metal rods. Their bottled thunder. Disgusting. A crime against nature. It grows worse each day with these Outsiders."

A long pause lingered between. Leawyn herself looked up, her eyes following the distant gaze of Saralyn, staring through the tree branches and leaves toward the open sky as though searching for storm clouds.

"However they have done it... I do not wish to know the price the Outsiders paid for their wickedness. Thank you both for your words." Her voice softened with weariness. "I am an old woman and my time on Hearth is limited as is my patience. It seems for every move we make, the Outsiders redouble their vileness and pillage our land."

"They can be killed though; they can be stopped. You've shown us that." Saralyn nodded.

At last, a small smile formed on Leawyn's lips.

"Death is a wicked thing to speak of… but perhaps I am nearing my final days myself." Takoda coughed. "Yet I'm not afraid. We have the Hearth, the cold bogs, and the waters of preservation. What do the Outsiders have but their heretical fires for their dead? Imagine," he laughed. "how many of them died and were erased from this world during the time of ash? My good ladies, I say it will be glorious, whether tomorrow or a thousand thousand years from now, when we emerge from the cold ground and find we have the Hearth to ourselves, with the Outsiders long since burned away."

Saralyn broke into a toothy grin. "To the new dawn. To our ancestors."

"And to our kin." Leawyn nodded. "To our youth."

They held their breath in prayer, Leawyn's words lingering in the air, mingling with the fluttering wings of the butterflies around them. For a moment, there was peace—a fleeting connection to the trees, the birds, and the Hearth. But, as with all things on the isle, war and battle marred the landscape. From the Laehosha clan's battle encampment came the blare of a war horn.

All eyes and ears turned in the direction of the sound. Leawyn's heart leaped in her chest. She was ready to rise and grab her bow, but a moment later, a second, then a third blare followed, and she relaxed her muscles. *A training exercise, nothing more.*

"The soldiers drill," Saralyn said, nodding in understanding. She too sank back down, releasing the tension in her body. "Perhaps the chieftain will finally come to speak with us."

Leawyn shook her head. "He has nothing to say to me. As long as we sit here idle, he has already won his battle for your clan's hearts and minds. We have no direction… no plan. That's what we need. We shall see if the War Maker comes to us. We'll see if he gives us the numbers we need."

She looked down again, twiddling her thumbs, the weight of failure pressing on her chest. Even after their great victory, a soul-crushing feeling lingered. The exhilaration of wind in her hair, blood on her tongue, the gallop of her horse beneath her. Those moments of power and freedom now felt distant, as if they'd been nothing more than a brief, fleeting taste of ecstasy. A taste that most men never knew.

Her gaze shifted to the side, and she dug her fingers into the cool dirt beneath her, feeling the Hearth's embrace against her skin. Both of her sons were down there. But had Kaelin already passed when the Outsiders' chief fell? Had he felt the same surge of triumph and wrath? Or had a blade already found its mark, tearing him apart before he could taste the victory she had?

She heard the blare of the training horn again and rose, her two companions following suit, though she paid them no mind as she strode out into the open of the camp. Her eyes flicked to the woods, scanning the dense underbrush and shadows for any sign... A hoofbeat. A whinny. The loosing of an arrow. Or the crackle of fire through the trees.

Oh please, give me a sign, she prayed to the world, when a shadow darted between the trees, sudden and quick. Leawyn gasped, the sound escaping before she could stop it. Her companions turned to her with confused looks, but before they could ask, she blushed in embarrassment and stormed into the forest with balled fists. Saralyn followed behind her, and Takoda hobbled after them.

Rowan. A boy, barely sixteen. Lanky and tall, with fiery-red hair and pale green eyes. He could barely loose an arrow, let alone hold a sword, and had been mocked relentlessly by the other men of his old camp. *Craven,* Leawyn thought, her eyes narrowing as she stared down into the boy's daring green eyes—eyes wide with fear, especially at her hands gripping his throat. Fearful of *her,* an old woman. She pinned his throat against a tree.

"W-wise Mother, a m-message," the boy choked out.

Takoda hobbled up beside her, his old eyes narrowing with concern. "Has something happened?"

Leawyn didn't answer, only tightening her grip around the boy's throat, digging his neck into the rough bark.

The boy looked at Takoda with helpless eyes. Leawyn's gaze followed, meeting Saralyn's scowl, and Takoda's confused, weary expression. With a frustrated sigh, Leawyn released the boy, letting him crumple to the base of the tree, rubbing his neck.

She looked down at him. Part of her wanted to throw a punch into the boy's face, to force him to toughen up. But then something inside her stirred, a familiar ache. A chord had been struck like a song played deep within her, one of pain, one of misery, laden with a lifetime of the same look. A boy who feared war and death. *This* was who she was trying to save.

"You were saying," she said to the young man.

Rowan looked up to her with watery green eyes, and when she thought he might break into tears, his brow furrowed, and a tone of disgust filled his breath. "I came to warn you... He's coming. Chieftain Hunta."

Leawyn immediately turned her gaze to Saralyn and Takoda, who stared at her with equal curiosity.

"The war front has shifted? Or the War Maker, he comes to us? Well! Which is it, boy?" she persisted.

"Perhaps he has come to drag us all back to camp," Rowan muttered, shaking his head. "At least the chieftain doesn't strike his own." He rose, still rubbing his neck, and shot Leawyn a glare as he stumbled away. But she didn't notice. Her mind was reeling.

"Finally," she said to her companions. "He brings news."

"Good or ill tidings, we don't know. We must be careful what we wish for now," Takoda cautioned.

"It is the standing still that is eroding our support. Change, direction, one way or the other," Saralyn added.

"If I am to have my head taken from my body today, so be it. I'm old. I cannot continue to sit and wait. No more than my camp and followers, I do not like having my fate outside my own hands. I will meet him now, and hear what he has to say."

"Away from the camp?" Takoda asked.

"For the best," Saralyn agreed.

Leawyn nodded, then stepped between the two of them. With surprising speed for her age, she rounded the camp, walking briskly to the edge of the tree line. There, she saw his shadow, a large and hulking figure befitting a chieftain in the prime of his life. He moved through the trees with force, his antlered helmet snapping branches aside as he approached. They stopped a few feet from one another.

"Chieftain."

"Old Bird."

"A pleasure to have you finally come see our camp."

"My camp," he corrected. Leawyn arched a gray eyebrow, poised to respond, but he continued, cutting her off. "My people, my clan, my army. I have allowed them to take up residence here. To listen to your words, to hear your guidance. For you are indeed wise and brave," he said, his eyes narrowing slightly. "But I will not be so prideful as to think you've taken my kin for your own."

His voice was low, rough with exhaustion. He looked as if he hadn't slept in days.

Leawyn pressed her advantage. "We have the same enemy. We are the same people. Whether of Clan Laehosha or Terrwoniwyn, the Outsiders will come for us both. All I want is victory."

"Then go home, or better yet, listen to the advice of those who know the battlefield."

"The battlefield?" Leawyn scoffed. "You mean the same war that has been waged for hundreds of years with no end in sight? The same war that cost me my father, his father, my husband, and two sons? Notice how the seasons change; the animals, the creatures of this land adapt and evolve as the Hearth does. I am old, yes, and maybe wise, maybe a fool, but if I learned one thing in this life, repetition is the means to failure."

"You got lucky," Hunta answered.

"Perhaps," she admitted, tilting her head. "But maybe all we needed was a change in tactics."

Hunta stayed rooted in place, hulking within the shadows of the trees.

"The Outsiders have brought change. This war… this *invasion*, has raged for countless generations. Every child believes they have seen the worst of it, but what did we witness on the battlefield? Thunder captured in a bottle. A crime against nature. Whether or not you accept change, the Outsiders surely do. They come with horses and metals whose forging is lost to us. There must be change, my chieftain, or the cold Hearth will beckon us all."

Hunta stood unmoving, his dark beard and deep eyes swallowed by shifting shadows overhead. When he finally spoke, his voice was softer than before. "I am sorry for the losses you have experienced in your life."

"Thank you." Leawyn nodded. "And I am sorry for the losses I know you, and your clan, have undoubtedly experienced as well."

Hunta let out a breath, shaking his head slightly. "That's a funny word, isn't it?"

She frowned. "Which word?"

"Loss."

Leawyn cocked her head. "Forgive me, but I do not understand."

Hunta stepped forward, emerging from the shadows, his massive frame draped in a thick fur cloak despite the warmth of early summer. His voice was low, almost contemplative. "Loss. A strange word, is it not?"

Leawyn parted her lips to answer, but he shook his head, silencing her before she could speak.

"Tell me, do you know where your sons rest? Your father? Your husband? Or did the Outsiders burn their bodies, as is their wicked custom?"

A lump formed in Leawyn's throat. She forcefully swallowed it. "My husband, yes. But my father and sons… somewhere. Lost to me, but not to the Hearth. Scattered across the isle."

"Hmm." Hunta closed his eyes and nodded. "On the isle. Within the bogs. In the Hearth. Not lost. They will rise again."

"By the moon herself, the reflection of our world, my children, your clan… all our people, we will all rise again. Someday."

"Amen," he answered. "And thus, they are not lost but simply given to the Hearth, resting, as you and I will do, when the time comes."

Hunta again fell silent, his broad shoulders rising and falling with a heavy breath. Leawyn studied him. He was still young, perhaps no more than five-and-thirty, but time and sorrow weighed on him. His thick black eyebrows were furrowed, his beard long enough to brush his chest, and scars marred both his face and his heavy, calloused arms. He should have stood proud as a warrior in his prime, yet the burden he carried bent him. Even the great aurochs crown upon his head was stained with dried blood.

"You came with a message, Chieftain. I see it written across your face."

He did not answer directly. "Where is your clan from, again?"

"The north," she answered. "Nestled between the rolling hills of the Taeng, surrounded by the forests and the bogs and lakes of our isle."

"Hmm," he groaned, placing a thick hand to his beard. "Inland. Well protected by the Hearth. The Outsiders haven't struck that far north in ages."

"No," she answered curtly. "And not that it matters. We have lost all the same."

"No," Hunta fired back, voice deep and rapacious. "You have not. You have not known loss like I have. Like my people." He took a step forward, fists clenched at his sides. "When the Outsiders come and burn your dead, that is one thing, a horrible, wicked thing. But know, Leawyn, our world is vast and strange, filled with many strange creatures and peoples. More Outsiders come by sea, bearing no sign of the flaming bird, but bringing creatures and lands stranger and far crueler. You know where your dead lie, buried deep beneath the Hearth, untouched by their flames. But until you have lost a son, a brother, to those who bear chains of sun-cursed metal, until you have watched your kin stolen, dragged across the sea to a land from which they will never return, he stepped so close she could see the bloodshot veins in his tired eyes. "Until then, Leawyn… you do not know loss."

Hunta studied her, searching for an answer, but she had none. Words tangled on her tongue, grasping for a retort that would not come. There had been whispers, yes, of the Sun-Landers creeping inland, but they had never plagued her people. She had never tasted the salt of the seas that surrounded their land.

"Your struggles have not been told to me," she finally answered.

"Few would speak of it. Even fewer would dare to imagine it."

Leawyn lowered her head as if shamed. "Our world is strange and full of terrors. I do not deny that, Chieftain. But never forget the moon is our mirror and the reflection of our world. No matter where they are, our people will find their way home…" Her voice fell to a whisper. "Unless they burn."

Hunta grunted low in his throat, his gaze heavy on the forest floor. Leawyn stepped closer, barely reaching his shoulder, and wrapped her arms around him. She cradled him as a mother would a child.

"Tell me, Son. What plagues you? Does the War Maker come at last? Does the enemy move against us?"

Hunta rolled his shoulders as if gently trying to shrug her off, but she held on. "No, Old Bird. The War Maker does not come, even if you saved us all that day, for there is much across this land that requires his attention. And certainly not for some old crone."

Then, at last, he lifted his eyes. Dark. Wet. And on his reddened lips, he spoke the words that struck her through the heart.

"A messenger came to me this morning. Your chieftain is coming. Astonished that you have risen from your rest."

Leawyn drew back, caught off guard. The War Maker would not come, but Finn would…

My clan could swell our ranks!

A spark of hope filled her chest. She even started to smile, until Hunta continued.

"But I am also told your granddaughter, the youngest, fights for her life. A sickness has overtaken her."

Leawyn turned her head as if slapped, but Hunta held her gaze.

"Know the difference between loss and death, Leawyn," he said softly. "Know them well. Return to your family. Let us resume the war. Your chieftain comes to take you home."

BANCROFT III

Edwin Battlebridge pushed the ridges of the abacus back and forth. Sweat formed on his brow as he turned red. "Well, now see, that's just not quite right."

The members of the High Council sat around the high table. A few, like Dymtrus, nodded off in their seats, while Osbert looked longingly at an empty goblet of wine. Even the emperor's cup-bearer, young Gael, rested against his serving table, desperate to keep his eyes open. The day had grown late, and with the warm afternoon glow of the sun, Bancroft feared he too might find himself asleep like his castellan, Alden, who snored gently beside him.

"It must be seventeen hundred... I am sure of it," Edwin finally declared.

"Not even close." Warwick rolled his eyes, head resting on his chin. Edwin shot him a sour look but held his tongue.

"I think not. It is seventeen hundred and six silver, no higher, no lower."

"It is compounded interest, you're not tabulating it correctly," Warwick responded again.

Edwin ignored him again, crossing his arms and leaning back in his chair as if to pout. Bancroft worked the numbers over in his mind, but stopped short, also finding a bead of sweat on his brow. Mathematics was not his strong suit.

"The crown prince names you a fool." Strammond snorted. He appeared the only council member truly awake, bathed in the light of the sun streaming through the window. Bancroft had to wince at the glare coming from his bald head. "Our treasurer can't even do basic math."

"I assure you there is nothing basic about calculating interest..." Edwin pulled at the collar of his shirt.

"Give me the abacus." Warwick stuck out his hand.

Edwin did a double take. He searched about the table for backup but found only bored, longing faces. He at last turned to Bancroft, who merely waved his hand to support his son. Edwin, with a lowered head, slid the abacus down the high table. Warwick took hold of the counting device and quickly set to work. Whisking the wooden rings back and forth, he quickly came up with a formal answer. "They owe seventeen hundred and twenty silver, not your total, Sir Treasurer."

"And how can we be sure of it?" Edwin huffed.

"The math is here before you."

"You would have shorted the crown its due," Strammond said dryly. "A mystery—how your house rules over the richest city in the realm."

Edwin looked to the abacus and then to the High Council. Beads of sweat poured from his brow as his tongue worked in his mouth, spittle forming in the corners of his mouth. "I won't sit here and let my work be branded as treason... not while I'm mocked as if I weren't a good lord of this realm!" He shot to his feet, snapping every head toward him.

Bancroft's heart thudded as he glanced at his furious councilor—and, crucially, an Elector. Edwin's eyes bulged, one hand twitching toward his hip as if reaching for a sword that wasn't there. His tongue darted to and fro, wetting his lips with quick, snakelike flicks.

A burst of pain gripped Bancroft's chest, but he resisted the urge to flinch, and instead, he slowly rose from his seat, head swimming with dizziness, and sucked the poison from his councilor. "The day grows late, my good lord. Perhaps we are nearly ready to break for the day..." But he stopped, stars lining his vision. It gave him time to think, especially of Edwin's serpent tongue, and he wished to contain the spread of any further discontent. "Aside from the final plans for my brother's funeral, Aethylios bless his soul, today's session has served us well. Edwin, you've done your duty here. Take your leave and rest. We'll not discuss the realm's finances further today."

Edwin looked to him, burning red, his mouth still working. He looked to the council, and though they sat at attention, he found no safe harbor. "Very well," he whispered. He spun on his heels and quickly fled the room.

Bancroft watched him go, and once the council doors slammed shut behind him, he placed his hands upon the high table and breathed a deep sigh, finding his feet numb beneath him.

Wulfnoth seized the chance to shift the focus away from the tense silence. He cleared his throat, shuffling a pile of papers. "With the lord treasurer's departure, we shall adjourn the discussion of financial matters," he said, his voice firm. "I'll ensure the owed tax amount reaches the lord of the Breakwater..."

"The *correct* tax amount," Strammond interrupted, winking to Warwick.

"... the correct tax amount, thank you." Wulfnoth shuffled his papers again. "With legal and financial concerns out of the way, this council shall now turn its attention to matters of diplomacy."

A sudden coughing fit seized Bancroft. He felt Warwick rise beside him, steadying him with a firm hand on his shoulder. Bancroft allowed himself to be lowered back into his chair, the coughs racking his chest as sweat dampened his brow. Warwick produced a handkerchief, standing by his side. He took the handkerchief but motioned for his son to sit. He didn't need the extra attention on him.

"I fear this council session runs the risk of pushing us all into fits of madness," Dymtrus said. He rubbed his forehead, grimacing as the sun slowly shifted to shine upon his face. "Perhaps we call this session to end. We have accomplished much today."

"I'm afraid there is still much to discuss…" More coughs erupted from his chest, though he did his best to speak, fearing Edwin's presence just beyond the door. "There is… still the matter… of my brother's funeral…"

"A fair point." Wulfnoth nodded. "Graham, may you provide an update on the progress of the late Master of War's journey?"

"The emperor's brother has arrived safely ashore in my holding of Cilese. His arrival and procession were met with great sorrow, but honor and praise as well. The name Hieronymus is held with great esteem among the Monteclari people. Assuming the crowd sizes do not detract from the speed of your brother's progress, his body may arrive in the capital in as little as a fortnight."

"Had you followed your true instructions, the late Thane wouldn't have had to sail around the whole continent and we could have been done with this whole mess." Dymtrus patted his forehead.

"My father and I are appreciative of the opportunity for our citizens to grieve my uncle and his grand sacrifice," Warwick said. "After all, he fell in the line of battle, protecting all of us in the realm." Warwick smiled at Graham.

The tightness in Bancroft's chest loosened a little, allowing him to catch his breath. Warwick was healing the stain of his character, just as he prayed Derrick's wound would heal.

"My brother has returned to us safely; that is all that matters," Bancroft managed, finding his breath. "Let us proceed to discuss the funeral arrangements. Are they progressing well?"

Wulfnoth nodded. "Aye, the purchase requests of goat and

lamb, pork and duck, potatoes and carrots, foods and drink of every accord have been placed."

"The wine shall flow strongly on my accord. The vineyards of my homeland have been most productive, and not at all at a cost to the crown, in honor of your brother." Graham grinned.

"And every inn and spare room in High Ness is nearly full," Milton added. "The city is prepared, Your Grace."

"Aye, and I have doubled the shifts of my guard around the city and castle. I do not expect much trouble, though I hear talk that the city already runs dangerously low on ale and wine," Strammond confirmed.

"A fine problem to have," Bancroft replied with a rare smile, his breathing finally steadying.

Just as calm settled over the council, the chamber doors creaked open, and a Demonbreun Guard slipped in. The High Council pretended not to notice, but Bancroft's gaze followed the guard as he moved directly to Strammond, leaning close to whisper in his ear. The guard left as quickly as he'd come, while Strammond's expression remained impassive.

"... and your late brother will lie in state in the city of Aberness for three days. Though not for the holy nine, the distance of your brother's travels has led Osbert to assure me and this council that it will satisfy our lord's judgment."

Osbert stirred, adjusting the jeweled hat on his brow as a smug smile spread across his face. "Yes, Your Grace. After much prayer, I received a vision from our good Lord. Though your brother will not rest for the holy nine days in his home city, his deeds and journey have earned him the holy three. It will be enough in the eyes of our faith."

Strammond took this declaration to rise from his seat. "Apologies to this council and Your Grace. A matter of the guard calls for my attention, please excuse my absence."

Bancroft sensed this coming. He waved his hand in a quick dismissal, but the pain in his chest, always seeming to linger, returned once more. He just wanted this funeral, and appointment of the new Master of War, over with.

Strammond left in a quiet hurry, yet his absence caused a stir nonetheless. The realm's High Council, Bancroft included, were weary after a long day of deliberations, and with two councilors now absent, the rest grew visibly on edge. Still, he would not dismiss his council.

Let Edwin drown his indignation over my son's actions in wine—or better yet, in the bed of some whore or adulteress within the castle walls. Bancroft's stomach twisted at his own ill thoughts. He knew Edwin was too devout and upright for such vices, though he almost wished the man would fall prey to them, just once. Intoxicated, he might reveal himself, or at least be easier to silence. Bancroft's gaze drifted to Lacius, his confessor, who sat silently at the high table. Lacius met his eyes for a brief, knowing moment, a faint, sly smile playing on his lips as if he'd sensed the emperor's musings. Bancroft quickly looked away.

"I am glad to have the High Priest's blessing on the matter." Warwick took the opportunity to pull from Strammond's absence. "It is matters of faith that keep this realm together. I know it was a guiding principle that drove my uncle to give himself selflessly to this realm. That, and his honor and love for family."

Bancroft smiled at his son's words, even as his cousin, Milton, dared to scoff. Again the council fell to silence, and Bancroft, for once growing numb, found his jaw clenched as the weight of his crown pressed down upon his brow. "Perhaps it is my fault for allowing this council to forget its place. It was a tourney—injuries occur, and I will not have it whispered Warwick is a wicked kin slayer. He is either not of the sword or too intimidating of a knight. Whispers are a natural, accursed part of the realm, but know I will not tolerate words, or worse, actions of *treason*, especially from family."

"Very aptly put," Dymtrus nodded.

Yet Milton, seated between Osbert and Lacius, took the emperor's words like a slap in the face. "I worry for nothing more than *our* family."

"I regret the actions that befell my cousin from my sword, and aye it was my sword," Warwick immediately replied. "I do not run from what happened, but I did not intend for such an action to happen. I love my cousin as I love my family."

"Fine words from a fine boy," Osbert affirmed. "He confesses and acknowledges the sin."

"The boy has committed no sin!" Dymtrus snapped. "As the crown prince has said, it was an accident. Have any of you ever wielded a sword? Such things happen! He will recover."

"Sin does not have to be intentional, Lord Dymtrus." Lacius's body uncoiled, slithering forward to lean onto the high table. "It lives in all of us and can drive us to wickedness, whether intentional or not. None of us at this table are above it."

"Did none of you hear my words?" Bancroft tried to cry out but found his voice hoarse and muffled.

"In the face of sin, what can one do?" Lacius continued, undeterred. "By our divine prophet Aethylios and the Nine Miracles, the answer is clear: to be absolved, one must confess."

Warwick started to speak, but Bancroft shot a hand out onto his son's knee, silencing him. A toothy, sly grin spread across Lacius's face.

"Eh... what a day... when the court does not... eh, heed the word of the emperor..." Alden muttered, having woken up midsentence. His voice, thick with sleep, barely carried, and a spot of drool hung from his lip.

Oh, damn it all! Bancroft mentally face-palmed himself. He knew his castellan meant well, but his words came as yet another insult to the crown.

"I will not hear of this matter any further, nor will I tolerate it spoken. By the authority of my crown..." Bancroft paused. There was a commotion outside the doors to the chamber. The councilors looked to one another in confusion as the scuffling grew louder, and then the doors to the chamber suddenly burst open. Strammond appeared, red of face and panting.

"... Your... Grace..."

"What is the meaning of this?" Bancroft demanded. He placed his knuckles down upon the table, pushing himself up with a grunt. *A mistake.* His head spun as the world went woozy.

"It is my honor... and privilege... to welcome to the council chamber... the good lady... Sylvia of House Hieronymus..."

Bancroft's head spun as the name washed over him. *Did I hear that right?* He turned to his son, who shot to his feet, as did each of the High Council members, as Warwick called out. "Grandma'am?"

At the top of the stairs outside the chamber, two Demonbreun Guards appeared, carrying a gilded chair. Seated on a white velvet cushion was a frail yet commanding woman, her jeweled attire accentuating a scowl as sharp as the gems themselves. *Mother.*

The guards carried the chair forward and gently set it down at the edge of the High Council Chamber. The council members rose and immediately bowed as the matriarch of House Hieronymus rose from her seat. She gathered the edges of her black dress and managed a trembling curtsy, her piercing gaze sweeping over the council, lingering on her son and grandson.

"It is with much pleasantry I see the high lords of this realm still remember basic decorum in the presence of royalty." His mother broke her curtsy, clasping her hands before the High Council. She stood no taller than the shortest man's shoulder, yet she commanded every eye. The room stood in awe, her spell of reverence broken only by Warwick's startled words once more.

"Grandma'am?"

"Yes, darling, it is I in the flesh, not the spectral ghost many in the realm name me to be."

"Mother..." Bancroft's voice faltered as he struggled to draw breath. "We did not expect you at court so soon."

"My good son, you must forgive me, for I am a mother in grieving, and I miss my family." His mother raised a hand, placing it over her heart as her voice cracked.

"Well, Sylvia, if I may, allow me to be the first to express my sincerest sympathies to you on behalf of House Seavíc and myself for the passing of your son. The realm has truly lost its finest." Dymtrus moved quickly, rounding from his place to her side, bending down to one knee and lifting her free hand to kiss it.

"Ah, such a welcome, and with kind words too," his mother raised her hand from her heart to her head. "It is so good to return to court and find such wholesome and loyal men working for the good of the realm. I hear such dreadful rumors back in Knoxford, but I know they're nothing more than idle gossip, spread by lowborn ladies and scandal-mongers!"

"Very aptly put, my lady!" Graham chimed in, springing from his seat and eagerly stepping past Dymtrus to take Grandma'am's hand. He bowed deeply, pressing a reverent kiss to her knuckles, further satiating the old woman.

"Oh! A Fontaine! A most welcome name, and ally to court! Do my eyes deceive me? That must be Graham!"

"Yes, Sylvia, yes!" He rose with a smile. His mother took her hand and cupped it under his chin, smiling upward into the southern man's eyes.

"Ah, the southern spirit shines bright in you, my boy," she laughed. "My grandson and I cannot thank you enough for organizing his procession through Sanguinia. He returned with so many gifts from his travels that I feared the entire city of Aberness would overflow!"

"It was nothing for the proclaimed heir and House Hieronymus, of course!"

"And how my heart races! Is that my dear nephew?" She turned to Milton, who smiled, shoulders rising in a shrug as though he were once again a child caught sneaking treats. "Oh, I remember when you were small—trouble keeping you out of the honey pots in the servant kitchens."

"Grandma'am," he laughed sweetly. "Such a pleasure to have you at court again."

Her eyes then landed on his cupbearer, the young Gael. She beckoned him forward with a bony finger. The boy, usually so self-possessed, approached shyly, his cheeks burning as he folded his hands behind him. Grandma'am leaned down to pinch his cheek. "The tales of your father's bravery," she said with a knowing smile, "are second only to your own in this realm. When your time comes, you'll make a fine knight—and who knows, perhaps a Master of War."

The boy beamed, his words stammering before he scampered away at the release of Grandma'am's bony hands.

Next, she turned to Wulfnoth and thanked him profusely for securing the allegiance of the houses bordering Krithinia. "Only the Demonbreun rivals the two knights you've selected to train my young grandsons. You've raised good stock in your lands. Job well done."

Norbert she thanked for his loyal service before bending over to whisper a scandal into his ear. Bancroft watched as his imperial herald turned a shade of white and cried out. "No!"

"Yes, the very same!"

"But who knows? Who can know!" he cried.

"Why, I would suspect the whole realm of course. Just keep tight lips about who told you." Grandma'am winked.

At last, she turned to Osbert, who rose to greet her, bowing low as he took her hand. But to everyone's shock, she dropped to her knees, bending almost to the floor. Bancroft gasped, watching Strammond's urgent step forward as if to steady her frail form, but she moved with surprising purpose, crawling the final steps to Osbert's feet and kissing them. The High Priest laughed, a look of pure joy spreading across his lips, and he nearly clapped.

"Oh my dear lady, such an act is unnecessary for one of imperial blood!"

"Nonsense," Grandma'am grunted, allowing Strammond to help her back to her feet. "All serve the crown, but the crown serves the Nine, though we sometimes forget."

"Humbleness—a trait rarely observed among the noble families."

The wind howled outside the tower. A cloud moved before

the late afternoon sun. Lacius grinned, also dressed in a holy man's robe.

"You will find none more humble than I," Grandma'am responded. The two locked eyes. His confessor licked his lips, a sly smile spreading across them.

They broke into laughter.

Grandma'am extended her hand, allowing Lacius to kiss it. They exchanged another chuckle before she leaned in, her voice just loud enough for Bancroft to catch. "You'll stick close by, won't you?"

"I live to serve the imperial family, and the Nine, Your Grace."

"Atta boy." Grandma'am patted him on the back.

Turning to the council, she spread her arms wide, a wistful warmth softening her stern countenance. "Ah, my grandson and my firstborn! Such fine men, indeed. It warms my heart to see you both so well cared for. How I wish for us to reconnect, and perhaps, to share fond memories of your brother and uncle." An achiness returned to Grandma'am's voice as a tear pooled in her eye. At once the High Council became nervous, bouncing into one another as they struggled to gather their things.

"Thank you, gentlemen. Let's give the emperor and prince some time with family, eh?" Strammond suggested.

The council rose and departed, though not without a final barb from Dymtrus. "Are you suddenly family now too, Strammond?"

Strammond's response was immediate. "Your daughter does not yet bear a ring."

Dymtrus broke into a scowl, but a quick play from Grandma'am settled the matter. "Now, now, matters of the heart can be addressed later. Dymtrus, I expect you and your daughter for tea tomorrow. But please excuse us; Strammond has protected my family his entire life. I trust no one more."

Dymtrus nodded, though it was hard to miss his scowl as he exited the chamber. All else followed, except Alden, who remained by Bancroft's side.

"Yes, even the emperor's castellan. Out with you!" Strammond commanded.

"Nonsense! Strammond, can't you tell who is family and who is not?" Grandma'am beamed and walked over to Alden. They embraced, kissing each other on either cheek. "Well, he may as well be family. He's served us long enough."

"Not servitude, my good lady. For it has been my honor, and a joy, to help your house prosper."

"Do you see, Strammond? Family."

Strammond rolled his eyes and closed the council doors.

Bancroft exhaled a deep sigh, crossing the chamber to face his mother. "Mother..."

"Son," she said, and the two flew at each other, burying each other in their arms.

"How I have missed you. How are you feeling? Are you all right? Are you well?"

"Right as rain now that the cold has passed."

"I am glad to see you again, Grandma'am." Warwick inched forward, carefully.

In an instant, her hands flew up, boxing Warwick's ears with surprising strength. "What did you do to your cousin? Are you ill in the head? Or has the whole realm simply gone mad with rumor?"

Warwick stumbled back, stunned. "Grandma'am—"

"Mother, please." Bancroft tried to calm her. "It was an accident."

"An accident? So the boy has learned to hold a sword. Well, thank the Nine he's learned as much instead of holding a fork. But your cousin? Truly?" She turned back to her grandson. "Do you have any idea the ill omen it is to strike a family member? I had to kiss that apostate of a priest's feet just for starters!"

"A grand gesture. One a prideful man like the High Priest is likely to share with every ear in court," Alden added.

"Yes, well, it's something I should never have had to do in the first place. Truly, with the death of my son, and your uncle, and your brother!" She flew to Bancroft, eyes wide. "Do you have any idea the danger we are in? What words now fly with the death of your brother and the actions of your son!"

"We are mending the situation as of now, Mother..."

"Don't you dare interrupt me, boy!" She shoved a finger into his face. "You are lucky the servants at Knoxford think me deaf, lest I learn the real truth that goes on in this country."

"Mother..." Bancroft tried, but his mother turned to him with a wrath that silenced him.

"Did you not hear me? Or have you too gone deaf? Danger, that is what we all find ourselves in. Do you feel the weight of the crown upon your head, boy? Do you? Because without it, we may as well lose our heads. This castle, that ugly-ass throne, means absolutely nothing without that crown. And why is it—*how is it*—that an old, old woman, who should be mourning her son, is now responsible for saving our family, the realm, and her fat grandson's ascendancy?"

Alden took a step back, clearly unsettled by her ferocity. Bancroft, however, remained rooted in place, steeling himself. "Mother, if I may, there is none who may contend with Warwick's claim."

"Lysander's name is spoken often enough, and I fear such words may go to the boy's head. I suspect it was enough to sweep him away from under my thumb at Aberness before Warwick could even arrive. Nevertheless, I do not believe the boy to be evil."

"My son is not evil." Bancroft shook his head. His heart ached, if not from physical pain, then from the act of defying his mother.

"I know the boy is not evil! I know that!" Grandma'am turned and broke into a pace he had not seen her walk in twenty years. "It is not him I fear, but the schemes of our enemies. It was on the road to High Ness I learned the Goldwoods would arrive earlier than myself. Knowing this, I jumped from my wagon, climbing onto the back of the fastest knight's horse in my entourage, and commanded him to ride hard. We overtook them, just barely, so I could deliver you this warning.

Vipers have come to nest in this castle. Warwick's claim is in danger of being challenged."

Bancroft refused to believe such. "Not a lord will dare challenge our family."

"Open your ears, child, lest we repeat a civil war. Even I have heard such talk at our very ancestral home, damn the Nine!" Grandma'am's voice cracked, sharp and biting, as she looked from Bancroft to Warwick.

Alden gasped, his breath catching in his throat, while Bancroft stumbled backward, his mind reeling from the weight of his mother's words. Warwick stood frozen, too stunned to act.

"We have deluded ourselves into thinking the real war was across waters... The Isle of Fláimir burns, and I fear soon an ember shall land on our shores and set the whole realm alight. Such events already occur in the south, where queer stories of man and beast fighting together come from. Talk of war is contagious; it spreads like wildfire. Our enemies—every lord of importance—will be under one roof. We must not underestimate this moment. Warwick must be seen as the heir, no matter the cost."

Bancroft stared at his mother, her tears fueling his own. He opened his mouth to speak yet couldn't find the words. The crown weighed heavy on his head. A crown forged by his great-great-grandfather. A crown passed down between father and son. A crown he planned, *hoped*, to pass down to his own son. The thought of it going to someone else made his stomach churn.

Strammond gently spoke up. "Your Grace."

"Speak," Bancroft answered, his voice barely above a whisper.

"One of my guards has just slipped notice. The Goldwoods have arrived."

"They are here so soon?" Grandma'am's words were clipped and heavy. She glanced sharply at Bancroft, then at Warwick. "They are here. With the Rose Monts—who are now engaged to the Valkirns. One vote down. We can only lose three more."

"We will not lose another," he answered firmly, though the uncertainty in his chest pained him.

Strammond, ever the dutiful servant, didn't pause. "Your Grace... they tell me they have gone to the throne room to seek an audience with you."

"You see? They seek audience with me, their sovereign."

"... I am also told Lysander has greeted them."

"Oh by the Nine," Alden croaked.

"Family betrays family." Warwick looked to the floor. " A tradition—it would appear."

"Well then, let us go to them," Grandma'am declared.

Bancroft refused to believe it. If not the sudden arrival of his enemies, then the tear streaking down his mother's cheek.

WARWICK VII

The sun dipped behind the mountain, shrouding the castle in a veil of shadow. The hallways buzzed with chaotic life, souls trapped in purgatory, lost and confused among the dying of the light. Intrigue filled the corridors, though no voice dared to rise above a whisper for fear of shattering their perturbed reality. The castle, and thus the realm, teetered like a boulder on the mountain's edge, ready to come crashing down at the slightest breath. Warwick moved quickly, but dark words had a habit of moving faster than a man's feet.

Down he flew from the council tower, feet working so quickly he nearly stumbled a time or two on the narrow, twisting steps. He reached the bottom first, outpacing even the guards, and found himself leaning against a white stone wall, breathing hard as his head spun. The world tilted, and he fought a wave of nausea. Grandma'am's words had cut through him like a knife—he didn't want to admit it, but he had grown to fear his brother. He swallowed hard at this realization, closing his eyes to bring the spinning to a stop. This made him feel better, and he fluttered his eyes open, breathing slowly to quell his racing heart.

I don't need to rush, he told himself. He looked upon a pair of oaken doors down a short stretch of hallway. Beyond them lay the rest of the castle, and thus, the realm. Courtiers and nobles, merchants and singers. It hit him like a punch to the face. *Every step is a battle! Every smile is a treaty.* He would need his grandmother; he needed his father. He couldn't stop Lysander with a war, it had to be decorum.

"Warwick… son!" His father came panting down the staircase a moment later. He was positively red in the face, and upon reaching the floor, began to claw at the collar of his shirt as if mad for air.

"Father!" Warwick barked and rushed forward, placing an arm around him to assist him to a nearby bench. Bancroft accepted the help, allowing himself to be placed down with a *thump.* "Father, are you well?"

Bancroft wheezed and threw his head back, desperate for air. The crown flew backward, but Warwick's hands caught it in a flash. His fingers clasped around it, filling in the grooves between the jewels, and he marveled at its weight. It strained his arms to hold it steady.

"It's heavy," his father whispered to him. "So heavy."

Warwick stared down at the crown, twisting it slowly in his hands. "You do not need to bear the weight alone."

Bancroft's breath came in ragged spurts. "I sent my two boys away… only to have two men return. One in my brother's place, dead… and my sister-in-law baying at my throat, with distant kin slithering through these halls."

"Family should not be the enemy."

"No, it shouldn't. Yet none are as dangerous as our own blood. A poison runs in it, with no purpose but to ruin our line."

Warwick felt a strange impulse to place the crown on his head, yet he knew what such an act would imply. More so, he already wore the ancestral Crown of Knox, and a tinge of sympathy ignited in his stomach before a crash of rage filled him. Here he stood, with his father the emperor, in possession of not one but two crowns. Lysander would never have either. Twin brothers, raised in opulence, denied not a want, Warwick felt the jealousy that must burn within his brother. And yet his father coughed, growing to hack and wheeze, while Warwick slowly turned the Crown of the Nine in his hands. *While he's off playing his games, I bear the weight of the realm. This crown would crush him.*

"Your Grace!" Strammond called at once. He and his guard placed Grandma'am safely upon the floor and then rushed to his side. "Are you ill?"

"No, no." Bancroft batted away his guard. "I am quite all right. I have just had it with surprises today—and stairs."

He helped his father back into a sitting position and placed the crown back upon its true owner. A second later, Demonbreun Guards led by Strammond arrived with Grandma'am upon her gilded chair, with Alden hobbling and wheezing down the stairs behind them.

"This whole damned castle is filled with stairs." Grandma'am hobbled over. "It is a curse. The Makkans knew what they were doing when they built this place. Our ancestors should have never chosen this place as their seat of rule."

"Perhaps my boy can rule from Aberness." Bancroft tried to laugh. "Fewer stairs, friendlier people."

"And have me perceived as weak?" Warwick answered. There was no joke in his tone.

Grandma'am, Strammond, and his father looked to him with an intensity he had never seen before.

"Very well then," Bancroft replied. "The reality of our realm. We must make for the throne room. Strammond, send your guards ahead. Find Lysander, check on the Rose Monts, and keep an eye on whom the Goldwoods mingle with. Block anyone who tries to enter the throne room unless they're *family*."

"Right away, sir."

"Let us proceed then. We will go slow as if not a concern in the realm plagues us."

"My hips will see to that." Grandma'am nodded.

"Let us go, as one." Warwick nodded.

The Demonbreun opened the doors separating the base of the council tower from the rest of the castle. An eerie time of day, the castle hallways existed between a time of light and dark. Servants moved through the corridors, igniting torches and candles, but the process was only in its infancy, and the imperial family glided through their own seat of power like shades, strangers to their own home.

They were not completely invisible to the patrons of the castle, however. Like the blessing of the Nine Miracles themselves, the lords and courtiers of the realm could not ignore their presence. Many greetings were shared, courtesies and handshakes, bows and pleasantries, and for every guest they greeted, two more would emerge to take their place. Warwick fumed but did not break from his composure, even as the hour shifted later into the evening and his stomach began to grumble. A salacious idea occurred to him. He pulled Strammond aside, pointing to a servant passage, and instructed everyone to follow him. With reluctance they followed, stepping into secret and unseen passages of the castle, running into only surprised servants, who, balancing laundry or trays of food, were at a loss for how to bow within the narrow confines of the space. Warwick bulldozed past them, however, using his nose, and the ache in his belly, to trace his way to the kitchens, a route he knew well from his childhood of sneaking sweets, and then reoriented them toward the throne room. Finally, they emerged into a corridor just as the final rays of sunlight hung on the horizon.

"An excellent gambit for time, my prince." Strammond nodded to him. They were mere feet from the entrance to the throne room.

"Your Grace! My prince!" Two guards snapped to attention, startled by the sudden appearance of the imperial family.

"At ease," Strammond instructed. "Have you seen Prince Lysander? Or any of the arriving family—particularly the Goldwoods?"

The two guards looked to one another as Warwick's heart soared. It pummeled against his chest as he saw a wave of agony wash over his father's face. Seeing his pain, Warwick did his best to swallow his rage, even if he was prepared to drive a sword into Lysander's back.

"… Lord Strammond, the crown prince entered the throne room some time ago, followed soon after by Charles Rose Mont and his kin. The Goldwoods arrived only moments ago."

"And you let them in?" Strammond roared.

The two guards looked to one another again, eyes wide and faces twisted in confusion. "We didn't know otherwise, my lord. We were told only family were permitted within…"

"Strammond, please." Grandma'am placed a gentle hand on his shoulder. "They've done no wrong."

"Enough talk, let us uncover their schemes and be done with this." Bancroft walked through the guards.

Warwick didn't need to be told twice. He followed his father, and approaching a large, mahogany door bearing the two-headed phoenix of House Hieronymus no less, he took the liberty to shove it open, slipping inside the throne room first.

There were no ceremonies scheduled for the day, and unlike the rest of the castle, where fires and candles now cast their glow, the throne room grew darker by the minute. Warwick stepped inside, immediately grabbing a hold of either shoulder with a shudder. His teeth nearly rattled, for the throne room was *bitterly* cold. Summer was only weeks away, though it may as well have been the dead of winter in here. The wind howled from outside.

"Father, look there," Warwick whispered as the family gathered close. They had slipped into the throne room not from the grand entrance but through a discreet side passage reserved for the imperial family and guards.

"Do you hear that?" Strammond turned his head. The wind rattled against the towering windows, and a faint hum seemed to resonate through the floor as if the castle itself were drawing breath from the mountain beneath it.

"Yes, I hear it too." Warwick frowned.

"I don't hear anything, ehh… anything." Alden strained his ear.

Warwick slowly crept from his position, sliding like an alley cat between two pillars. His family and Alden followed behind him as he struggled to see. Before him, standing before the white throne of the castle, a collection of specters gathered. A crescent moon, thin and sharp like a knife, rose in the background, pouring in only the faintest hints of light. Warwick gritted his teeth, suddenly afraid, suddenly angry. His father breathed over his shoulder, also staring into the dark. *We are the imperial family and we're too afraid to approach our own throne!*

"Wait, who is that?" Strammond called out.

Warwick inhaled, the cold, steely air of the chamber stinging his lungs. "Someone sits on the throne," he answered.

The imperial family all bunched together, even Strammond and Alden pressing themselves together as they all struggled to peer through the dark to a distant, dark figure atop the throne.

"Who would dare?" Alden moaned.

"Those bastards," Grandma'am hissed. "Strammond, call your guard! The very action is treason!"

"No… wait…" Bancroft strained his eyes. "I know who…"

But Warwick needed no confirmation. Without a second thought, he launched himself from behind the pillar, heart pounding, fists balled. His footsteps echoed off the marble walls like boulders crashing against the mountainside. He knew who sat on the throne, his character nothing more than a shadow.

Warwick gripped his side, suddenly wishing for the family sword. *Another insult, another robbery.* No more *better choice*—no more choices, pure and simple. The crown and the throne were absolute. Let the realm and every scheming relative witness it.

The collection of shadows at the base of the throne turned at his approach. Slowly, they gained shape, revealing a collection of seven individuals huddled in the dark. Warwick's entourage followed quickly behind him.

"Ah, and here comes my brother and father now," the shadow on the throne announced. The shade rose as Warwick and Bancroft approached.

"Make way for the emperor, Bancroft the First of House Hieronymus, accompanied by his son, the proclaimed heir to the throne, Warwick, and the good mother to the crown, Sylvia Hieronymus," Strammond's voice called out.

Warwick came to a halt in the middle of the crowd, his father breathing heavily beside him. To his left, he recognized his distant cousins, the Rose Monts. Charles and Harriet, accompanied by their son, James. And to his right, a collection of four individuals he did not recognize, though he assumed them to be the Goldwoods.

"Hail to you, Father, Brother, and Grandmother," Lysander's voice rang out from the throne. The figure bowed, and his kin followed, their heads inclining in a courteous display.

This courtesy did nothing for Warwick. "Brother!" he barked, fists clenched at his side.

"My son," Bancroft barked. "The crown has need of the throne."

"Of course, Father, Brother," Lysander replied smoothly, stepping down from the throne's platform. "I merely took the liberty of welcoming our guests with the authority of our house."

As he descended, the shadows fell away, revealing his face— dark hair, dark eyes, and the family sword hanging at his side. Warwick at once reached for it, but Lysander moved quickly, brushing past him and dropping to his knees, taking his Grandma'am's hand and kissing it.

"Oh Grandma'am, it brings me joy to see you here in such good health."

Grandma'am appeared genuinely taken aback, looking hysterically from her son to her grandchild. "Well, yes, child," she replied, her voice softening. "A few winding roads would never keep me from seeing you and setting this court to rights."

An interrupting cough came from Charles Rose Mont, who leaned against a stylish walking cane, grinning in the low light. "Speaking of setting the court right, perhaps it is time to welcome our newest guests, hmm?"

Bancroft turned alongside Grandma'am to the figures gathered by the tall windows, backlit by the faint glow of evening. "Alexander, Hollace," Bancroft intoned, extending a hand. "Welcome to court."

The two figures stepped forward, bowing and pressing his hand in a customary show of fealty. Warwick's gaze shifted to Lysander, who had now settled himself between Grandma'am and their cousin James. *Traitor,* he thought, his hand itching to reach for the throne's armrest.

"Cousin, Your Grace." Alexander nodded as he straightened. "It has indeed been too long since we last met. And to the esteemed matron of the realm," he added, inclining his head to Grandma'am. "My wife and I offer our deepest condolences for the loss of your son and our Master of War. There are far too few who can say they've fallen in true service to the realm."

"A tragedy, and at the hands of those godless savages across the water," Hollace interjected bitterly, her face twisting in disgust. "Our hearts broke when we received the news."

Warwick took another step closer to the throne as Grandma'am moved forward, her eyes softening as she regarded Alexander. "Is that truly you, little Alex? I haven't seen you since my late husband reigned on this throne. What was it, some twenty years ago? You were just a boy then! Come, give this old woman a hug!" She opened her arms, and Alexander stepped into her embrace, though a bit stiffly. She then turned her gaze to Hollace, her face lighting with recognition. "And this must be Hollace, yes? I nearly wept when I heard that the young boy I knew had taken a wife. What a sight it is to watch a child grow into a fine man."

Hollace returned the hug with polite warmth, patting Grandma'am's shoulder. "Yes, well," she replied, a touch wryly, "these things do happen, don't they?"

"And your children?" Grandma'am inquired, glancing at the two younger figures lingering behind them.

Hollace stepped back, gesturing proudly. "May I present two of our children to His Imperial Majesty," she said, motioning them forward. "My daughter, Makepeace, and our youngest son, Emerson." The children stepped forward, bowing uneasily under the gaze of Bancroft and Grandma'am.

"Welcome, young ones." Bancroft smiled to the children. "It's an honor to have you here. I remember my youth when your father came to squire under a knight in these very halls. The scrapes we got into, sneaking through the castle, stealing cakes from the kitchens, and terrifying the guards at every turn. I hope you, too, find such joy within these walls."

Warwick listened to the exchange of formalities, but his focus was elsewhere. Keeping a careful eye upon James and Lysander, he inched toward the throne until he was close enough to reach out and touch it, whereas his stomach ignited with butterflies, and he lunged for it. The cold touch of the marble took his breath from him, but he did not care. He clambered onto the throne, falling back into the deep seat and kicking his legs out, gripping the solid marble armrests as if the throne were a dragon, ready to take flight.

"So strange, isn't it..." Alexander mused, glancing around. "To return after all these years, and now to think my children will wander the same halls seized from the late Makkan Empire by our forebears. Such glory, wouldn't you say?"

"Our family name liberated a continent," Bancroft affirmed.

"And now those savages across the water threaten it all," Hollace spat. "They trample upon the name of House Hieronymus with the feet of monsters. Have you heard the rumors? They use half-man, half-beast creatures."

"Centaurs, to be sure," Alden added.

"It fills me with horror," Hollace continued, "and that is why, dear cousin, we've come to offer an olive branch of peace."

"Peace?" Bancroft took offense. "Were we at war?"

"It is no secret our branch of the family has feuded with

your own for decades. Indeed!" Alexander waved his hand as if batting away a fart. "We have much bigger foes and threats to not only our family name but the realm as well."

"We have nothing more to gain from court whispers and wagging tongues," Hollace added, her tone resolute. "Our children are a testament to that. Makepeace is soon to be wed to Wallace Faelwood, and our eldest, Fielding, remains at home, promised to a wealthy merchant's daughter."

"The Faelwoods?" Lysander interrupted. "I treated with them in the north. I did not know Makepeace treated with their son, whom I have come to know well."

Alexander stepped into the moonlight, his face lit as a wry grin spread across his lips. He brushed a finger over his thin pencil mustache, his dark eyes matching his short, slicked hair black as midnight.

"Then I suppose congratulations are in order," Bancroft said, his voice unusually calm even with the sudden loss of an Elector family. "Or is there something else you're hinting at?"

"My children, with the exception of my youngest son, are already betrothed. You have no daughters left, your brother has fallen, and beasts press on our borders. The only path forward is family unity under the blessing of the Nine."

The wind howled outside the throne room. A string of clouds passed before the moon. Shadows darted in the corners of the room.

"That is... a most noble of requests," Bancroft eventually answered.

"Noble? Oh, how many of our ancestors wished to hear such words?" Grandma'am clasped her hands together. She flew forward, throwing herself upon Alexander. He patted Grandma'am's back with a bewildered expression, gently shooing her off him.

"Yes, indeed." He straightened his attire. "We have come to pay our respects to your late brother and, if it's not too forward, to discuss a possible match for my youngest, Emerson."

"A delightful proposal!" Harriet exclaimed. "The empress

and I are well acquainted with the eligible young ladies of the court. Why, my own daughter was just recently betrothed!"

"Yes, I heard, and to the firstborn of House Valkirn, no less." Hollace smiled, twisting slyly on her feet.

"Cousin, we have not had the pleasure to meet, but I am James," he said, stepping forward with a slight bow as he crossed from the Rose Monts to the Goldwoods' side. Placing a hand on young Emerson's shoulder, he steered him toward the exit with a smile. "I know all the fairest young ladies in court. Do you know how to handle a sword? A fine skill to have—the girls will be at your feet in no time."

"Look at that! Our boys, fast friends already." Charles chuckled. "Lysander, I'd be disappointed if you didn't join them. If they're speaking of swords, then surely the prince who bested my son in the play tourney should be there to advise young Goldwood!"

Lysander looked to his father for approval. "I suppose I could…"

"What a turn of events. Perhaps we can bury the hatchet." Bancroft raised a handkerchief to his forehead, dotting away beads of sweat.

"You must be exhausted from your travels. Have you been assigned a room yet?" Grandma'am took hold of Hollace's hand.

"We are weary, indeed," Alexander replied with a weary sigh. "The wind gusts were fierce as we crossed the mountains. And the clouds… I feared we might crash straight into the castle! A hot bath and a glass of mead would be a cure for my malaise."

Grandma'am looked to Alexander with an inquisitive glance. "I'm sorry, I don't understand. I heard you were on the road just this evening…"

"Oh, Sylvia, I do hope you didn't hurry on our account," Hollace chimed in with a light giggle. "We traveled by balloon, not by road."

"Balloon?" Bancroft and Grandma'am said as one.

"We're anchored to a castle tower," Alexander said, a smile tugging at his lips. "What an age we live in, with such innovations that let man take to the skies."

Grandma'am tilted her head at the news, her eyebrows twitching before she clapped her hands together, forcing a bright smile as she released Hollace's grip and bent down to Makepeace. "And you, dearest! Would you like something sweet from the kitchens?"

Warwick could see the girl shrink from Grandma'am. *Coward*. "Yes, ma'am, thank you."

"I will see to it that my guard has your belongings delivered appropriately. Come, and let me escort you myself, for this castle is a maze if anything," Strammond instructed. Warwick's family turned, following Strammond from the chamber.

"I do recall that from my boyhood..." Alexander's voice trailed off as the group exited, leaving Warwick alone in the vast chamber. He sat alone, listening to the howl of the wind, feeling the mountain breathe from underneath his feet.

"The Nine be damned."

His voice echoed across the vacant throne room, his words becoming lost and entangled within the web of shadows of the room. His brother had commanded an audience; he, only ghosts.

He rose, reluctantly loosening his grip from the cool marble. He stepped down from the throne, turning to look back at the white marble, its shine and sparkle seemingly diminished. It looked like nothing more than a comically oversized chair, fit for a monster like a giant... or perhaps the realm's fattest prince. He looked down, gripping his belly through the oversized tunic he wore, designed to hide his girth, as a tinge of pain hit his stomach.

"A sweet," he choked, lowering his head.

He slunk out of the throne room, startling the two guards who had been stationed outside.

"My prince! We didn't... how foolish of us... had we known you were still here..."

But he ignored them and made his way back toward the servant passage he had used to guide his family. He did not wish to encounter another soul. All he wanted was to sneak into the kitchen and find comfort in an assortment of sweets.

He ducked into the passageway, finding it dark and cool. He traced his fingers along the crude stone walls, spying only the occasional torch, but otherwise walked in near total darkness, allowing his nose and memory to guide him. He was a child of this castle, after all. Every nook and cranny was as common to him as the rotation of the guard. His nanny had once told him he was more of a nuisance to the staff than the rats in the walls. A tear welled in his eye at the recollection of that. *The only thing I am good at.*

He sniffed, and right before a surge of tears overtook him, a whisper tickled his ear. He stopped right before a turn in the passageway.

Voices, urgent, but hushed, drifted from just ahead.

The hour was late and the passages vacant. Slowly, he poked his head around the bend, finding two figures huddled together in the dark, and a yelp nearly overtook him.

"Perhaps they are serious," one whispered. "The Goldwoods have nothing to gain. Their marriage pacts are sealed. There is no path forward for them."

"Surely you have not become the fool in your late years, old man. You have served the imperial family longer than all. You know what they are capable of."

"Forgive me then, ehh, for trying to find light at the end of the tunnel. My time on this world is coming to a close. Let us do our best to see that an era of peace follows when Warwick ascends the throne."

"Are you growing deaf? Do you not hear the words of the court? Warwick's claim grows weaker by the day."

"You do not need to insult me, I hear, ehh, just fine."

"Then it is your eyes that fail you. Open them and see the truth before you."

"The truth, and may Aethylios damn me for speaking such a thing... is that the emperor's health is failing faster than my own. Let us indulge in pleasantries, build some real common ground, and make strategic marriages. The crown may pass to Warwick sooner than we think.”

“Warwick will not have the crown if things continue as they are!”

The second voice all but shouted and Warwick gasped, darting his head back behind the wall. A long, dreadful pause then followed, the silence cut only by his heartbeat pounding in his ears.

“Did you hear that?”

“Your ears play games with you, old man.”

“I am tired of being insulted. For a man of your station, you speak only of treason.”

“Treason?”

Warwick’s breath hitched as he heard a scuffle from around the corner, followed by a pained groan.

“Ow, you’re hurting me!” the second voice yelped.

“Listen, you old fool! It’s been over a month since word was sent to the Isle for Hereward Alfair to take up the mantle of Master of War.”

“The flight is long… the bird may have grown… ehh… tired…”

“Messages have nearly stopped between the capital and Fláimir. Do you not find that suspicious?”

“Well… I… uhh…”

“The flight path passes directly over Goldwood land.”

“You don’t mean to suggest…”

“Think of it!” Warwick heard one man press the other man hard against the stone wall. “Which is worse for the realm? Either the Goldwoods have intercepted our messages on purpose, or Hereward, an Elector for the crown, has declined the role of Master of War. Neither possibility brings any comfort, does it?”

“That is… that is enough! Ehh… you must produce more evidence before uttering such words! Especially with the boy so vulnerable.”

“Someone must say it, and not before the emperor. He grows more foolish and senile with every passing day, unable to

424

rein in his secondborn son while doting on the enemies of the crown."

"Surely you do not mean to suggest I present such a thing to him?"

"You are on your way to the family's chambers now, are you not?"

"…I was simply turned around, ehh yes, lost in the corridors…"

"Listen to me, old man, and listen well. When you find your way to the old woman's chambers, you plant the seed, understand? She's the last competent one left in the whole family!"

"I'm sure… positively… no idea what you're talking about…"

"Be away with you!"

There was another scuffle from around the bend followed by the hasty sounds of footsteps disappearing farther into the labyrinth of tunnels. Warwick held his breath, standing still in the cool dark, waiting for what felt like an eternity, listening for any sound of life before stepping out from around the corner.

He was a fool.

A dark figure waited for him, smiling from the shadows. "Come see me sometime." Lacius winked to him. He then turned and disappeared into the dark.

JOSEPHINA VI

Josephina woke to find Oléfur standing by her bed, his beady black eyes just visible over the mattress's edge. A tiny hand reached for her blanket, tugging at the fabric. She squealed, clutching Mishie to roll away.

"Jo-seh-phii-i-i-na, it's t-i-i-i-me. Your m-o-o-o-ther's child is ready."

Oléfur clambered onto the bed, his pointed shoes jingling with each unsteady step across her blankets. A green pointed hat nearly doubled his height, and around his torso, a green jacket, black belt, and striped trousers also jingled with the ring of bells.

"Do you l-i-i-i-ke?" he asked, twisting his arms and kicking his legs in unnatural directions, sending the bells into a chaotic frenzy.

Josephina blinked, half-asleep, half-convinced that this was some terrible nightmare.

"This is your m-o-o-o-ther's work. She doesn't tr-u-u-u-st me, I ba-a-a-rgain. But things will ch-a-a-a-nge. Your br-o-o-o-ther wakes. Power stirs in his d-a-a-a-rk heart. And Mother..." he grinned wider than seemed possible. "she will be cr-a-a-a-zier than ever. Blood magic is d-a-a-a-rk, little girl."

Josephina's brow furrowed as she sat upright. "You're afraid, aren't you?" she said to him as her straw mattress shifted under the elf's feet.

He lost his footing and tumbled to his rump in a heap of jingles. A hiss escaped his lips. "Yesssss, and if I am afra-a-a-aid, you should be terrifi-i-i-i-ed."

Josephina rubbed sleep from her eye. "No. He will be my brother. We will be a family bound by blood."

"Am I not f-a-a-amily? Are we not... bound by bl-o-o-o-d?" A smile spread across his lips again.

Josephina looked upon him, and squeezing Mishie tight, she smacked the elf straight off her bed. The elf went flying, falling to the floor in a heap of jingles. Oléfur lifted his head from the floor, staring up at Josephina as a hiss slipped from his lips. Her bedroom grew dark, dissolving into nothing-ness, leaving only her bed adrift in a black ocean beneath a dark moon.

"Oh Mishie." She squeezed him tightly. *What have I done?*

The elf appeared before her, only a giant this time. His hat now scraped the stars in the sky as he hoped from foot to foot. The bells on his feet were deafening, and she clasped both hands around her ears. She screamed as the elf laughed.

"Do you feel f-e-e-e-ar now?"

She squeezed Mishie with all her might. "Mother will stop you!"

"Your m-o-o-o-ther stands on the cusp of grea-a-a-tness... or great f-o-o-o-lly. Dark wings don't bring dark tidings, they *are* the dark tidings."

Oléfur's voice slithered into the Old Tongue, and Joseph-ina screamed again as her bed, now a boat, rocked violently among the midnight waves. His laughter erupted, high and shrill, twisting into a deep, roaring echo that filled the black ocean. The boat tilted precariously, the sea beneath it surging as a tidal wave of darkness consumed the horizon.

Josephina ducked beneath the covers, clutching Mishie as tightly as she could, and screamed her heart out. The roar of the wave grew deafening. She felt the spray of invisible water, the pressure building in the air, her bed sinking beneath the waves. The crushing force of the wave descended, and just as it was about to swallow her whole, a blinding light burst through the darkness.

"Josephina!" a voice called to her. She screamed louder.

"Josephina!" A sharp slap brought her back to reality. Her eyes flew open, and she found herself trembling, drenched in sweat. Her mother stood over her, frowning.

Josephina bolted upright, still shaking, her skin slick with cold sweat. In the corner, Oléfur stood idly, glaring out the window as if none of it had happened. "The wave... I saw it, and..." She trailed off, realizing it had all been a trick. "Just a nightmare..." Mother's side-eye to Oléfur cast doubt on her life, but Mother dismissed her ramblings.

"Do you know what day it is? Do you know how important this work will be to our *family*? Do you?"

"Yes, Mother."

"Then get out of bed and go downstairs. By the Trickster, it's far too hot in here. Say what you will about the sunshine, but this season's heat is damnable." Mother fanned herself, heading for the trapdoor. "No nonsense today, I mean it... from *both* of you."

Oléfur flashed Josephina a wicked grin before vanishing down the trapdoor. She wrinkled her nose in distaste as he disappeared.

Her room empty, Josephina sprang from bed. The air was sweltering now beneath the early morning sun. "Cursed season," she muttered, pulling on a red dress. Mother had sewn a pair of flames across the chest for this day, calling it a brilliant, swirling sun. Yet Josephina knew better. Her fingers lingered on the embroidery, a chill prickling her skin despite the heat. The pattern was no sun at all but two red swirls. *The eyes of the Trickster*. Goosebumps rose along her arms, but she swallowed her fear. She would greet her new sibling with pride, not dread. With a final glance at Mishie, she stepped from the safety of her room.

Downstairs in the kitchen, the familiar metal pot simmered over smoldering coals. Oléfur stood beside it, blowing gently over the flames as though coaxing them to behave. He pretended not to notice Josephina as she passed.

In the yard, Josephina's handiwork with the stone fire pit stood ready. The massive circle had been meticulously piled with logs and kindling from the forest, a small clearing left open for her new sibling's arrival. Beyond, in the fields, entranced thralls toiled mindlessly, tending to her family's crops under the watchful eye of her mother. She shepherded them like livestock, guiding them into the barn for safekeeping before the ritual began. Above, the sun shined brightly. *The solstice*. Nearly twenty-four hours' worth of sun. Josephina scrunched her brow. She missed the winter.

Everything seemed prepared, and with no further instructions from her mother, she returned to the kitchen. Oléfur had disappeared. Helping herself to a glass of sun tea and some salted goat meat, Josephina sat by the fire. The coals crackled softly, embers dancing upward as if struggling to grow, only to flicker out from lack of fuel. She felt a pang of sympathy for the fire. It was trying to become something greater, but Mother kept it intentionally weak. A dull ache spread from her chest, a quiet echo of what was to come. *Welcome to the family*. She stared into the embers, lost in thought until her mother's voice pulled her back.

"Josephina. It is time for us to begin."

"I am ready, Mother."

"I am happy to see that. Today our lives are going to change forever. Do you remember the prince I promised you?"

"Yes, Mother."

430

"A mere child's play compared to what's coming our way. Let your heart dream, Josephina. What is a man in the face of limitless power?"

Josephina straightened. "I'm excited to meet my new sibling, Mother. Tell me how I can help."

A smile tugged at the corners of her mother's lips—and was that a tear? Without a word, Mother walked to a nearby cabinet and retrieved a knife, *her* knife, and handed it to Josephina. "When the time comes, you must be brave." Her mother's voice softened as she leaned in, tucking the blade into Josephina's palm and closing her fingers around it. She planted a kiss on her daughter's forehead. A cold shiver swept through Josephina's body. "To the yard with you."

Josephina clutched the knife, her hands trembling, but she walked to the yard with a sense of triumph. She stood before the fire pit, waiting. The sun hung directly overhead; its rays harsh and fiery. She figured the heat was only going to get worse.

Oléfur appeared, shuffling before Mother, juggling a massive vase between his tiny fingers. He cursed in a language Josephina didn't understand, though his frustration was clear enough. She took the vase from him, following as he used a paintbrush to coat the ground around the fire pit in twisting spirals of blood. The smell was thick—iron and something else deeply unpleasant. Josephina held her breath, trying not to inhale the stench.

When the spirals were complete and the vase set aside, her mother emerged from the doorway. Sweat poured down her face, and in her hands large oven mitts gripped a smoldering cauldron. "Josephina," she whispered.

The command was silent, but Josephina understood. She rushed forward, grabbed her mitts, and took one handle of the heavy pot. Together, they walked through the carefully laid path of logs and wood and placed the cauldron at the heart of the fire pit.

"Do you wish to see?" Mother asked of her.

Josephina nodded.

With deliberate care, her mother lifted the lid from the cauldron. A cloud of smoke erupted from the pot, stinging Josephina's eyes. She coughed, instinctively raising a hand to rub them, but her mother grabbed the back of her neck, forcing her to look. Through the haze of heat and smoke, tears streaming down her face, Josephina saw it: a large, dark object sizzling inside.

An egg. Black, scaled, and enormous.

"Mother?"

"Your future sibling, Josephina. He will do great things for us."

"Oh Mother," she replied. Wisps of fire danced in her blurry vision.

Mother pulled her back. "I love you, Josephina. You are a curse upon me, but how we come to love our torments. You are loyal, my good girl, and soon the east will join the west. Fire will burn the world anew, finishing what the Ash Fall started. The age of man is at its end. Were you *normal*, I fear you would burn too. But alas, my monster daughter, we shall inherit what remains."

The coals whispered to Josephina, their crackling whispers strange and ancient: *A thurible for man. A sword of shadow that pierces the moon. A flame that bends the sea. Dark tides hide the singing voice. A path asunder.* She blinked through the smoky haze, registering her sibling's first words. Her heart leaped. "He's ready," she whispered to Mother.

"Of course he is!" she snapped, yanking her back.

Together, they stepped away from the fire pit, Josephina's eyes stinging from the heat and smoke as Mother lifted her arms to the sky.

"OHHHHHHHHHHHHH!" Mother's voice broke into a wail, raw and primal. She bent backward, her spine arching unnaturally, arms twisted behind her so far they nearly brushed the ground. It was the scream of labor—feral, unnatural like she was giving birth to something monstrous.

Josephina flinched, her mind swirling in the thick fumes. Oléfur began to dance wildly, the bells on his feet jangling in a discordant rhythm. The Old Tongue erupted from Mother's throat and the embers of the fire ignited:

"I gather the wood and spark your flame,
With ashen breath, I call upon your holy name.
But fire that builds can just as well break,
Creation and ruin in every spark you make."

Josephina's pupils widened as her vision warped. The mid-morning day still burned bright, yet the world around her darkened. Above her, the sky turned crimson.

"A bond of blood, a sacred flame,
Flesh and fire, bound by name.
In veins it flows, in flames it runs,
Blood and fire, we become one!"

Oléfur struck a match, igniting the first painted swirl around the fire pit. Flames leaped higher, one after another until the pit pulsed with deep crimson light. The world around them grew darker as the fire grew hotter. Insects joined Mother's singing. An owl hooted. Bats screeched openly in the crimson daylight.

"OOOOOOOHHHHHHH!" Mother screamed again.

Oléfur quickly joined her, his voice rising in a wild echo. Josephina followed suit, unleashing her own howl—howling at the blood moon.

"From your dawn, you brought the flame,
A spark to birth both time and name!
But blood once given, must obey,
It shall not turn from its master's sway!"

Mother struck another match as Oléfur rushed forward, torch in hand. The acrid scent of brimstone stung Josephina's nose as Mother raised the unlit torch high, then cast it into the dancing embers with a sharp cry. *"Zakaenys!"*

The sky split open as a crimson ray bathed the fire pit. Mother stepped forward, igniting the wood, and the entire pit burst into flames. Josephina started to dance; she couldn't help herself.

Mother passed her, thrusting her body, bobbing her head. Oléfur's bells jingled wildly, his feet thrusting into the air in a frenzy. Josephina jumped, clapping her ankles together. Smoke swirled in her lungs as she twirled, laughing, the knife raised high above her head. Mother's voice rang out in a piercing scream, and Josephina let out a shout of her own. Another crack split the blood moon overhead and more crimson rays joined their inferno. They danced around the flames, hooting and shouting in wild abandon.

Josephina spun, laughing maniacally, rejoicing in the crimson light, until she turned to find Mishie dangling between Oléfur's fingers. Oléfur leaped from foot to foot, a toothy grin on his face. She screamed as a crack shook the ground. The elf smiled as Mishie slipped from his grasp, flying into the inferno. Josephina screamed as she watched the cold button eyes of her only friend ignite in flames.

Oléfur circled the flames, laughter mingling with the crackling fire as the heat intensified, burning her eyebrows.

"He's coming! Oh, my child is coming forth!" Mother cried.

Another crack rattled the ground. Josephina could only see red. She ran forward, chasing the elf with her knife. Around the bonfire they ran, but the elf was always an inch away from the tip of her blade.

Blood for blood. The words of the Old Tongue echoed in her ears as the fire roared, consuming everything in its path. Josephina's heart raced as she caught sight of him. Her knife flew from her hand, slicing through the air before disappearing into the inferno. She screamed and fell to her knees before Mother, wailing as a final crack reverberated, throwing her to the ground.

"Do you see him? Oh, by the One Flame and the Five, the Nine and every other false prophet—behold his beauty!"

Tears streamed down Josephina's face as she fought to clear the smoke from her eyes. From the heart of the flames, a dark shadow emerged, wings unfurling like a shroud. Three heads broke free from the inferno, and Josephina blinked in disbelief. *Mishie?*

A horrific scream erupted from Mother. "What is it? What has happened to my baby?"

Josephina's heart thumped in pace with the lick of the flames. A dark shadow emerged from the fire. No larger than a dog, a two-headed dragon looked sheepishly around them. Tiny, bent wings flapped in the air. One of the heads unleashed a muted cry.

"Mishie?" she called aloud again.

Mother shrieked again. "What is this? What is this monstrosity!"

The baby dragon lurched forward with its three twisting heads. Its wings unfurled, batting at the flames and casting embers toward Mother. The dragon hissed.

Mother fell backward, raising her arm to shield herself from the embers. "By the Trickster, why am I cursed like this? Zakaenys! *Zakaenys!*"

Josephina flinched, clutching her ears as Mother barked at the creature. The dragon reared its three heads, poking through the flames of the bonfire's edge, and belched a fireball toward Mother. She screamed and ran.

"BETRAYAL! I have been betrayed!" Mother wailed.

Oléfur turned on his heels to run, but the bells on his feet gave him away. Mother was upon him in moments, beating him with her fists.

"Liar! Traitor! What have you done!"

The baby dragon looked to Mother, cocked its two heads, yet crawled toward Josephina like a scared puppy. With a trembling, outstretched hand, she brushed against its scaly back. It flexed its bent wings and blew smoke from its two heads. Josephina's mouth hung open.

"Mishie?"

Oléfur escaped Mother's grasp. He ran from her, jumping behind Josephina. He tried to grab her, but the dragon snapped at his hand. "A deal is a de-a-a-al. How could I kn-o-o-o-w the reason they left it undefended?"

"They are going to find out! Do you realize what this means?

We are going to die with all the others! You have brought forth an abomination! A *stolen* abomination!"

"Your blood... your abomina-a-a-tion."

Mother recoiled at his words. A crimson curtain hung over the world. The fire cackled madly beside them. All appeared as shadows beside its light.

"I will not suffer another curse. I will not!"

"The Trickster's blessing cuts both w-a-a-a-ys! We have all been dece-e-e-eived!"

Josephina stroked the malformed creature before her. *Brother? Or something else?*

"Kill it, we have to kill it!" Mother raised her arms to her head, twisting on her feet. "This can't be. This is unfathomable! The knights will surely send reinforcements. What will we do now? And the East... oh when the world comes to ruin, we are doomed now, do you hear? Doomed!"

The elf, however, only seemed to have heard one thing. "Kill it, y-e-e-s!"

"N-no!" Josephina turned and screamed. The fire roared. The elf reached for the dragon. Josephina closed her eyes. "No! *NO!*"

A bolt of fire erupted from the deformed creature. The elf screeched and stumbled backward, flaming.

"Josephina!" Mother screeched. She opened her eyes, finding the elf running away, patting viciously at his smoldering clothes. The dragon looked at her with one of its heads turned sideways. "Josephina! Kill it!"

Mother lunged forward, but Josephina managed to scoop up the creature. "Josephina, you must kill it. Do not let it suffer! Do not let it bring ruin!"

Mother lunged. Josephina dodged, rolling to her side as the creature's scales burned against her skin, landing hard on her ribs and knocking the wind from her. The dragon hissed, arched its back, and released a plume of searing smoke. Mother shrieked but lunged forward again. This time, a bolt of fire struck her square in the chest.

"You bitch! Do you know what I have done for you?" Mother screamed, dropping to the ground to beat out the flames.

Seizing the moment, Josephina pivoted on her feet, clutching the dragon tightly to her chest. The dragon seared her skin, but it only incited her to run faster. She burst into the kitchen, darted through the parlor, and pounded up the stairs toward Mother's room. Gasping for breath, she gripped the rungs of the ladder, but only sulfur and brimstone filled her lungs. Bursting through her trapdoor, she tumbled onto the floor, the dragon rolling alongside her. Josephina scrambled, trying to get back to her feet, when she locked eyes with the beast—three fiery-red eyes staring back at her.

Her heart dropped. The creature's fourth eye was malformed and shut, black and lumpy as a button. A tear came to her eye. "I'll love you forever Mishie," she said to fire incarnate.

The dragon looked back to her and snorted smoke through four nostrils. She smiled. Mishie was gone, but the dragon would take his place. The beast rose onto its rear legs and flapped its malformed wings as if to agree, belching fire with its two heads.

JAE VIII

Storm clouds rumbled overhead, and the wind howled through the streets, sharp with the tang of sea salt. Far out at sea, the moon glowed an ominous red, and the streets of Astrelaide lay nearly empty. Jae trudged forward beside Luke and Guard, their muscles straining under the weight of the litter. Inside sat the good master and his lady wife, their unexpected presence making the burden even heavier. Jae had never known Aeksilor to use his litter before.

Fortunately, fat droplets of rain began to fall, forcing the few remaining passersby to seek shelter, leaving the streets empty. Lightning flickered in the storm-tossed sky, sending a prickle through Jae's skin. His sandals slipped on the slick yellow bricks as he and Guard struggled to keep their footing at the front of the litter. For once, Jae wished Pete and Pate were there to help bear the load, but Aeksilor had sent them to a neighboring manse, buried deep underground, to guard highborn children. Astonishingly, Luke managed the back alone, his strength unyielding.

Gritting his teeth, Jae pressed forward, inch by painful inch, through the wide deserted grand promenade of the lower city. The sun had long since vanished behind the storm clouds, and above them, the grand stepped pyramid of the Temple of the Sun stood steeped in shadow. A brazier burned on its roof, its flames reflected in the swirling clouds. Jae felt Aeksilor pull back the curtain of the litter and lean out, his gaze fixed on the brazier's glow against the storm. "A damnable day for a damnable occasion," the good master cursed.

"My husband," the Lady Aril replied calmly, "sometimes we must make our own light, even on the darkest days."

As they reached the base of the pyramid, Jae's knees wobbled, his breath ragged. Spittle flew from his lips, and his legs trembled at the sight of the endless stairs ahead. He was certain his legs might give way beneath him.

"That will do," the good master called out. He stepped from the litter, extending a hand to his wife.

She emerged reluctantly, her gaze drawn to the uncountable steps leading to the pyramid's summit. "Let's be done with this formality," she said, not waiting for a reply. Gathering the ends of her black gown, she ascended as thunder rumbled through the city. Aeksilor hurried behind her, struggling to match her pace.

Jae, Luke, and Guard quickly deposited the litter among the other litters of the great masters. They dropped it without a second glance, avoiding eye contact with the Thorned Men patrolling the pyramid's base. They followed their master up the steps, careful to climb quickly, but not so fast as to outpace him.

Jae's legs burned as he reached the top, stepping onto the stone mezzanine behind Aeksilor. Thorned Men awaited them there, along with a host of household guards from the city's other noble families. Braziers flickered, their fires casting wavering light over the stone. Above them, the great brazier still crackled atop the temple, its flames reflecting off the storm clouds. Jae's skin flushed from the heat, his flesh prickling with the mingled sting of salt in the air and the oppressive glow of the false sun.

A trumpet blared, followed by the deep beat of a drum. The storm answered with a fresh round of thunder, shaking the pyramid. The Thorned Men dropped to their knees in a deep bow as a towering figure emerged from the temple's entrance.

"Announcing the High Priest of the Temple of the Sun, of the city of Astrelaide, and dedicated servant of the almighty Sun God," a Thorned Man declared, its voice deep and gravelly, like distant thunder rolling in over the ocean. Goosebumps crawled up Jae's arms at the sound.

The High Priest emerged, clad in resplendent red and yellow robes. His golden headdress, marked with the emblem of the sun, gleamed faintly under the overcast sky.

"And presenting the House of Aeksilor: Cato Aeksilor and his good wife, Aril Aeksilor, faithful servants of the Sun God's light," the Thorned Man continued, his words echoing across the stone.

Aeksilor and Aril bowed low. Luke, Guard, and Jae instinctively followed suit. When they straightened, the High Priest towered over them.

"Your Holiness," Aeksilor said, dropping to one knee. "Thank you for the invitation."

The High Priest folded his immense arms, thrusting out a clenched fist. Aeksilor shuffled forward on his knees, leaning in to kiss the ring on the priest's hand.

The priest gestured. "Rise, good master, and be welcome in the light of our Lord."

"An honor upon my house and family."

The High Priest nodded, a satisfied smile creeping onto his lips. He turned to Jae, Guard, and Luke. "Your slaves are well-trained. A rarity these days." His face suddenly darkened. "They may remain here in the presence of my Thorned Men."

Aril shot a disgusted glance at one of the Thorned Men beside her, then elbowed her husband sharply.

Aeksilor chuckled nervously. "Thank you, Your Holiness, for the compliment. I choose my slaves wisely…"

"Perhaps too wisely," the High Priest remarked, rocking back on his slippered feet.

Aeksilor blinked. "Your Holiness? I'm afraid I don't understand."

The priest's eyes narrowed. "There has been much talk of your decision to reduce your slave stock. It pains me to see such an ancient and noble house arrive with so few servants. But I digress." He sighed dramatically. "The price of slaves is high these days, and your reputation for business is well-known. I'm sure you made a handsome profit, no shame in that. And yet, some whisper it was done out of fear—fear of your slaves' growing defiance." He paused, his gaze shifting to Jae. "We are all servants in the end, aren't we, boy?"

Jae's heart raced. He spied the immense sculpture in the priest's hand and his throat tightened. He stammered. "Y-yes, of course."

"Your Holiness!" Aeksilor hissed, correcting him sharply.

The High Priest raised a hand. "I, too, am a servant. Fear is a useful thing. Fear of the master. Fear of God, for He is a vengeful spirit when His commands are ignored when pride grips a servant's heart." His eyes glinted dangerously. "I know you well, Aeksilor, and your lady wife. You'll replenish your slave stock soon enough, once things are set right tonight."

He turned toward the entrance of the temple, briefly casting his eyes upon the blood moon. "Come, let us join the other good masters. Your slaves will be safe here, under the watch of my Thorned Men."

But Lady Aril coughed loudly, glaring pointedly at her husband.

Aeksilor's grin widened, toothy and forced. "Ah, yes, Your Holiness, but you see—my wife is quite fond of her servants. And with the storm coming… well, a sick slave at these market rates? Who could afford to replace those my wife trusts?" He chuckled, glancing nervously at Aril.

The High Priest's gaze darkened, colder than the storm clouds overhead. He stared at Aeksilor, then flicked his eyes to Aril. "Very well," he said slowly, voice heavy with displeasure. "I wouldn't dream of upsetting the fairer sex. They may remain outside our meeting chamber... with the others." The High Priest sighed but allowed them to enter the temple. The other slaves watched them go with thinly veiled contempt. Jae offered them a friendly look, but received only scowls in return. Funny, he thought. He considered them the lucky ones.

The High Priest led them into the pyramid's antechamber. Inside, the air hung thick and oppressive, transforming the pyramid's immensity into a crushing weight. Massive stone slabs loomed just overhead, nearly scraping the High Priest's ornate hat. Only scattered torches provided light, their smoky haze adding to the growing darkness.

They moved quickly toward an immense stone staircase that plunged into a black void. At the sight of it, Lady Aril shivered and stepped closer to Luke, clutching his arm. Their descent went slowly as the steps were barely visible in the darkness, though the High Priest seemed untroubled. He folded his robed arms and smiled, humming a soft melody to himself. Goosebumps prickled Jae's arms as Lady Aril tightened her grip on Luke's arm. Their going went steady when light suddenly danced across the yellow stones above their head. The ceiling blazed to life.

Jae audibly gasped. It took a moment for his eyes to register what he was seeing, but as he blinked away the darkness, a patchwork of gold twinkled all round him. By his fingers creeping up from the darkness and inching along the walls of the stone staircase, golden vines shimmered in their torchlight. He recognized honeysuckles, lilies, and more etched in gold leaf, stretching upward for a sun that wasn't there. Instead, the ceiling had been consumed by roses. Beautiful petals covered the otherwise yellow stones, surrounded by symbols of a bountiful harvest. A cornucopia of fruits and foods, wheats and meats, served as tender soil for the flowers.

Jae's eyes followed the golden display, never mind that he almost lost his footing once or twice on the dark stairs. Above, the yellow stone bricks gave way to older stone—crimson, as they came to their first landing, and dark hallways stretched into the darkness. There were no torches here, only pale faces of Sun Priests staring back at them, and strange sounds coming from deep within: slamming doors, shuffling feet, human cries, and something... other. He shuddered. The slaves left above were indeed the luckier ones.

They went deeper, and as they did, the golden vines creeping along the walls grew thicker, while the mosaic above shifted. The roses gradually disappeared, replaced by men and beasts, sickles in hand, tending to the soil. There were no slave collars, but Jae spied the chains linking the figures together.

"Truly beautiful, isn't it?" the High Priest asked, his voice echoing through the chamber, though he addressed no one in particular. In his hand, the dark ruby of his scepter smoldered brighter than ever in the dim light.

"It truly brings a tear to one's eye, does it not?" Aeksilor pretended to wipe away a tear. "It speaks volumes about our grand city. Ah, I can hardly wait for this year's harvest to be complete and the coffers overflowing. The House of Aeksilor is long overdue for another contribution."

"You are most generous." The High Priest smiled and stopped at a landing illuminated by large braziers, casting long shadows across the stone walls. "Come, the other families have already gathered. However, your servants will need to wait outside. Honor forbids their presence in the Hall of Masters. You understand, Lady Aril?"

Aril only pursed her lips.

Again, the stone above changed, giving way from red stone to an ugly black. The air here hung heavy and moist, and Jae's ears popped from the pressure change. They were now deep within the pyramid, and yet the staircase stretched on forever, perhaps down into the Hearth itself. The golden vines transformed into stone carvings and reached their thickest here, but above, all the splendor had disappeared. Only crude drawings remained—ancient and partially eroded: lines and lines of figures, linked by chains, staring deeper and deeper into the pyramid. "Zakaenys," Jae thought to himself.

Finally, the High Priest led them onto a stone landing. The staircase stretched deeper still below, but Jae's gaze drifted back to the entrance. The sun, sky, and freedom lingered as a distant, shining star, seemingly as far away as those in the night sky. He sighed as Lady Aril trembled in her robes. Her husband handed her his cloak.

"This way, this way please. The others are gathering," the High Priest beckoned them. They went into a torch-lit corridor, the walls so thick and low the High Priest had to remove his golden hat to proceed. Behind them, they left the stone vines pouring up from further down in the pyramid, instead following a single vine carved into the wall beside them. It led them to the Altar of the Sun.

The High Priest ushered Aeksilor and Lady Aril inside, and it took not a word, but the most hateful scowl, to forbid them from entering. Jae was happy for this exclusion. Inside the room, a contingent of Thorned Men stood guard, surrounding an immense stone table. The other masters of the city had gathered, dressed in black. Aeksilor and his wife entered to muttered greetings as the High Priest took his seat at the head of the table.

Jae, Luke, and Guard took up position just outside the room, gathering among a handful of other slaves their masters refused to part with. Jae offered an uneasy smile to the other guards, though none returned it—save for a lone scribe, a woman stationed nearby, who met his glance with the same uncertainty. Her presence was unusual among the guards, where not even Lucien had been permitted. She clutched a worn scroll with ink-stained fingers that trembled slightly, but she met his gaze and gave him a playful smile. She pointed into the chamber toward the head of the table. Jae's gaze followed, finding a pair of glinting, red eyes staring back at him. Startled, he looked upon the Altar of the Sun—an immense depiction of the Sun Father above. A golden sun spiraled outward from the center of the room, and set in the center, a pair of ruby-red eyes glinted in the torchlight. This was where the single stone vine led.

"Moth," the woman beside him whispered, then smiled. Jae broke his eye contact with both the woman and the Altar. He didn't want this attention. He would be a good slave today, just like those carvings on the ceiling—*holy servitude.*

"Zovaesys," he whispered to himself but felt sick to his stomach.

"My esteemed fellows, nay, my *good* masters," the High Priest began, greeting his audience. "What dark days we have endured in our city of flowers. As I look across this room, I am reminded of the decay that plagues our beloved city. Aye, it is true. We wilt, my good masters."

He paused, clenching his fists, the weight of his ornate rings grinding together. "But I cannot help but ponder: When does the good flower wither? It happens, of course, under the rays of the mighty Sun—our Lord, our life-giver... and our life-taker." He leaned forward, the tension in his voice palpable. "Our Sun Lord gives life as easily as He takes it, and yes, He takes when He is angered. My good lady Amirose of House Balon," he said, turning his gaze sharply. "I look to you now."

Every head in the room turned toward Lady Amirose, cloaked in black, her face concealed by a heavy veil. She gasped, the sound piercing the stillness as tears slipped from beneath her veil.

"You were married to a good man," the High Priest called out. "A great man. A good master of our fine city!"

"Hear, hear!" cried the good masters.

"Oh, how I wept when I heard the terrible news. And how I weep for you now, my good lady, and your dear son, made a man far too soon."

A boy barely into puberty trembled in the seat next to his widowed mother.

"I am sure you must be asking yourself *why*? How could this happen? You served your husband faithfully, just as he served our city, and our Sun Father well. And so again, we must all be asking, yes indeed, *how* could this happen? A godly man. A good man. A loving father and husband. How could this happen?"

The widowed woman sobbed from beneath her mask. Silence enveloped the room; no one dared to move or speak. Jae held his breath.

"Well, my good masters, I will tell you why," the High Priest said, leaning forward, his knuckles pressing against the table. "Who is the enemy of the good master? The Sun Lord? He who only dares to show Himself when He must rest, as He grants rest to all?"

"The Dark One," the widow choked out, her voice trembling.

"Precisely. It is no coincidence your good husband died on the eve of the summer solstice under the full moon—a pure display of treason and *disloyalty*." The High Priest's voice grew more intense, his words spilling forth like poison. "This is what happens when we allow disobedience to fester. This is what happens when a man, free or not, forgets his place!" He slammed his palm onto the table, making it rattle. Jae's heart raced, and Luke jumped beside him.

"The Sun God is the embodiment of order! He is duty personified—sowing and nurturing life, bringing forth fertile fields and bountiful harvests. In stark contrast, the Dark One thrives on division, betrayal, pride, and deceit. He emboldens only those who dare to emerge from their shadows when His radiance fades." The High Priest's voice grew more intense, his presence looming over them. "His creatures flutter forth in the darkness, little moths drawn to the light…"

Jae was almost certain he could see Aeksilor's eyes upon him. He glanced away from the chamber, his face burning, knowing he was being watched. Indeed, when he lifted his gaze, he found the slave with the scroll watching him from across the way, her eyes wide and a smile stretched across her lips.

"Yet even the moth seeks the light. In its wickedness, it cannot escape His majesty and power. And do you know what happens when the moth finally finds the light and confronts its truth?" The High Priest paused, allowing the weight of his words to settle in the silent room. Suddenly, he brought his monstrous hands together with a thunderous clap.

"THE MOTH BURNS!"

Lady Amirose erupted into loud, hysterical sobs, her anguish echoing through the hall. Other high ladies in the room followed suit, their sniffles creating a chorus of sorrow. The High Priest observed the scene with a nod of approval before gathering himself, straightening his posture, and folding his arms before the gathered masters. He closed his eyes, his voice steady and measured. "I am but a humble servant, ever reaching toward your light and love."

"We blossom in your presence," the room responded, their voices uniting in reverence.

"And wilt without," he continued.

"Amen," they echoed back.

The High Priest opened his eyes, surveying the Hall of the Masters with a discerning gaze. What he saw, Jae could not tell, but he noted the priest's nod before he took a seat at the head of the table. He took a deep breath and asked. "So, what shall we do about this?"

A heavy silence fell over the room, then pandemonium.

Jae didn't know all the good masters' names, but he was aware that thirteen great families ruled the city. He suspected that the High Priest's influence was rivaled only by his imposing size. Voices and shouts rose out of the chamber. From the corner of the room, he caught sight of a man in a black robe shouting. "And what of the Ghost Bull? This monster who terrorizes our colonies on the Sea of Sorrows? It's said he commands every beastfolk of the plains! Why aren't we calling for help? The other cities of the Sun Coast must recognize the grave threat this poses!"

A voice boomed from deep within the chamber. "And who will come to our aid? My House of Trekilor has maintained close ties with our sister cities of Kaidney and Platyberra, but neither has the troops to spare. We'd be fools to meet this 'Ghost Bull' on the battlefield. Our strength lies within our city walls and the protection of the Stone Master—long may it stand!"

Another voice joined the fray. "I would be distraught if our city's prestige fell to one who cannot field an army against savage beasts. We can purchase more slaves, surely? Or make alliances?"

A wave of dissent swept through the room, with long shadows dancing along the chamber walls as masters leaped from their seats, shouting as their voices echoed deep into the tunnels of the pyramid.

"And where are these slaves to come from?" a deep voice bellowed.

Jae caught a glimpse of a man, his face contorted with rage, rising from his chair and flailing his arms wildly. "There are no more slaves to buy, damn us all! We pretend the Ash Fall is behind us, but I spit upon all our house names! A hundred years since ash darkened the skies! A hundred years since the fall of Makka! Our most prized institution perished that day, I tell you! The slaves no longer breed like they used to; they wither and die in our pens and fields like a vineyard succumbing to disease. We are cursed! I daresay, minotaurs and worse have ravaged our lands for a century! There is no satisfactory solution unless I propose war against our neighbors. Either we take their slaves, or the city of Astrelaide dies!"

The word "war" jolted Jae, and he brushed arms with Luke, who must have felt the goosebumps spreading like wildfire across his body. Luke said nothing, but gently placed a hand on Jae's shoulder to steady him. Guard stood emotionless. At that moment, Jae hated him for it.

The Hall of the Masters was aflame. More voices rose as others fell quiet. The High Priest watched from his golden seat, while Aeksilor looked wildly about the room, bewildered. Lady Aril sat next to him, entirely detached from the chaos.

"We declare war on our sisters, and we invite the full wrath of our Sun Lord! I say, let it be the return of the Lyonnians!" A woman's voice rang out, filled with fervor. "The other houses may have forgotten, but Remixae has not. Before the Makkans were the Lyonnians! For centuries they ruled us, and for centuries they have tried again! With their strange beliefs and traditions, my family still spits on their emblem to this day! If we go to war, we invite our own destruction. They possess a fleet; we do not."

"By all accounts, the Makkans rebuild their fleet as well. East and west, we find enemies closing in. To the south, we face monstrous hordes. Is there nothing we can do but look north? Good Lady Aril of House Aeksilor, you are descended from the famous corsair, Jax Amorae, yes? Surely he can lend us some ships! A fleet must lie at his fingertips!"

Jae watched as Lady Aril jolted upright at the mention of her name. Her eyes darted around the room as if she were struggling to orient herself before a sense of calm returned to her. Aeksilor began to rise, ready to speak for his wife, but she silenced him with a gentle touch on his arm, quieting the room.

Standing, she spoke softly yet firmly. "No, he does not have a war fleet for this city. Furthermore, I fail to see how a fleet could mitigate the threat of the minotaurs." She sat down, leaving the room to descend back into chaos.

Jae was not in the room, but he was exhausted by its mere proximity. The masters argued over everything and nothing. A thousand allies were promised to their cause, while another thousand threatened to bring war upon them. The Ghost Bull was a looming danger, yes, but were there not marauding beasts on every side? They spoke of forcing the slaves to breed, but that solution wouldn't resolve production issues for years. The nations of Verope despised their practices of servitude, yet could they be swayed with gold? Yet even at that proposal, little gold was volunteered from the good families of Astrelaide.

Shouts erupted, insults between families were traded, and above all, between the vile insults and the pleas of desperation, there was always the constant sound of weeping. Jae folded his head down, doing his best to ignore the shouting. Yet over the chaos, the widow wept, and it was all he could hear. For some reason, Jae's eyes burned alongside hers. She cried for her husband, for her family, lost to her forever. This high-born lady, to whom he was less than a person, shared something intimate that bound them together: their families were destroyed, their loved ones gone for eternity. He understood that pain.

Gradually, the shouting came to an end. Only whispers and half-arsed apologies were exchanged now. The pyramid shrank with an end to their vitality. The dark hallways grew quiet. The stones overhead grew heavier. And then like a dark curse, his name was shared, and the pyramid pressed in all around him, and he could not escape.

"The True Moth."

"A tamer of beasts! A creature of the night! Emerging in the dead of night, silent, spreading its foul treason under the light of the moon."

"Who was he? Was he a myth? Could he be found? Hanged? Mutilated beyond recognition?"

Jae's feet went numb as panic surged through him. Guard, of all people, sensed his turmoil and placed a firm hand under his armpit, offering silent support. Heat flooded his cheeks as he felt the weight of Aeksilor's gaze bearing down on him from the Hall of the Masters, the man pulling at his beard, staring directly at him.

No, not me, he wanted to plead. *I don't want this!* Tears streaked from his eyes. Luke turned, and quickly wiped the tears from his cheeks. The other slaves pretended not to notice. If he would have looked, he would have seen tears on their cheeks as well.

The meeting ended with no resolution. The twelve good masters and their families filed out of the chamber. The weeping widow, shrouded in black, walked past with her son in her arms. They did not make eye contact.

The few chosen slaves to come into the pyramid were collected. Jae did not watch the slave with the scroll go. Aril and Cato Aeksilor were among the last to leave, their movements slow and deliberate. Guard immediately took his place at Lady Aril's side, while the High Priest followed closely, guiding them toward the landing with the grand staircase.

"It was not much, but a start," the High Priest lamented to Aeksilor.

"I cannot thank you enough, Your Holiness." Aeksilor bowed. "If you ask me, this has been long overdue."

"Do you think there is any merit to this moth talk? It could be a thousand different slaves in the city, but we must pull at every thread."

Aeksilor was quiet for a moment, Jae refusing to so much as breathe. "Perhaps, though the slaves tell many tales. A moth is such a filthy creature; so many slaves bear its disgusting name."

"Yes, so many…"

They had begun their ascension up the grand staircase when a guttural cry came from deep within the pyramid.

Aeksilor paused halfway up the stairs. "My good friend, I dare ask, is there no way to increase the number of Thorned Men in the city? I do enjoy their unwavering loyalty. Perhaps they could be the answer to our problems?"

"Yes, a natural proposition." The High Priest nodded. "But alas, there are only so many second sons of freemen in Astrelaide."

They continued up the stairs as more screams came from below.

Jae kept his head down, heart pounding. Even freemen weren't safe in this city.

WARWICK VIII

He entered the garden, Wulford at his heels.

"My prince?" the knight huffed after him.

"If you're meant to protect me from flowers and bees, then I advise you to keep up."

Warwick was in his element today. A harpist strummed gentle lullabies from a nearby fountain. Young lords and ladies, no more than toddlers, waddled and laughed through manicured lawns. Bees and birds hummed through the trees, and high above them, the Falls of Ness flowed over the cliff side, ensuring a cool breeze wafted over the garden. After so much heartache and misunderstanding among the court, he was determined to turn things around today. He received the bows and gratitude of the guests frequenting the gardens with a smile upon his face. It also didn't hurt that Lysander was not invited to today's affairs.

Warwick wound his way through the gardens, eyeing the

spot near the cliff where he had first met Polina. Today, he was meant to impress her. Aye, the whole realm too! And he knew just how to do it.

In the far corner of the garden stood a greenhouse. Small and cramped, it was packed to the brim with exotic plants and flowers that could not otherwise grow at such an altitude. He barged inside, politely greeting the few ladies within, then waited for Wulford's brutish Esterian presence to drive them away. They took the cue, and free of their prying eyes, he turned to his prize. A magnificent Desert Rose, its petals cultivated in a bright shade of violet, with only a single bulb blooming from the plant. He went to it at once, picking up a pair of pliers and cupping his hand around the flower.

"Your Grace, should you really be doing that?" Wulford cautioned.

Warwick clenched the secateurs in his free hand. "Do you mean to tell me the daughter of Dymtrus is not worth such a rare and beautiful prize?"

"My prince, I only meant that such a prized possession of the castle—"

"Are you a botanist, Wulford?" he cut in.

"No, my prince."

"Have you spent years studying flowers in secret? Neglecting your skills with the sword?"

Wulford stood silent.

"Hmph." Warwick scowled. He would not have the sweetness of the day ruined by his guard. He was beginning to see why the rest of the realm regarded Esterians so poorly.

Careful not to nick his fingers on the thorns, he took the gardening tool and snipped the rose from its stem. The flower fell delicately into his palm. Running a finger over its petals, he counted.

... Eight, nine, ten...

He frowned, then plucked out a spare petal and tossed it behind him.

"Feeling auspicious today?"

Warwick at last smiled. "If Polina is to be an empress, Wulford, then of course she demands the best."

"I understand, my prince. By the Nine."

"By the Nine," Warwick echoed, feeling, for once, an ounce of religious spirit, before his smile faded. He turned to his guard with a glare. "And by the emperor as well. God's holy anointed ruler on this world, lest we all forget."

Wulford raised an eyebrow. "Of course, my prince and heir-to-be. Too many forget."

Warwick studied him, unsure why he felt such anger toward him. But his knight was stoic, his thick, bushy beard hiding the lines of his face. He was hard to read.

And by God, so backward, those Esterians...

Warwick shook it off, testing his coat pocket to make sure the flower was still safe, then nodded. "Let it be known, Wulford. I will earn my crown today and put to bed any rumors."

Warwick then spun on his heels, taking off in the closest thing to a run he had ever accomplished, moving quickly back through the garden and into the castle.

The interior of the castle was abuzz with life, but unlike in days prior, lords and ladies dressed in their finest clung to one another for balance, as if the entire fortress might tilt and send them plummeting down the mountainside. Whispers of Thane's corpse arriving grew louder by the day, threading through the halls like cracks forming in stone. Coupled with his father's retreat from public court, the castle itself seemed to wobble on the cliff side, as though one wrong step might send everything toppling. But Warwick, with a flower peeking from his coat pocket, intended to change that today.

His grandmother, the good lady of Esmerelda, had organized an Electors luncheon, and anyone who was anyone within the realm wanted to be invited. (Lysander, he giggled, had not received an invitation). Even the Rose Monts and Goldwoods were not invited, nor was his auntie. Grinning ear to ear, Warwick swept with ease through the crowds of the castle, the lords and ladies sweeping aside, bowing, as if the crown had already passed to him. He made his way toward the grand ballroom, where they would gather beneath the towering, long-vanquished feathered serpent of the Makkans.

Outside the doors, a loose line had formed, and a contingent of Demonbreun Guards stood at attention, gently pressing back any ladies who lingered too eagerly.

"Fools among fools," Warwick muttered under his breath to Wulford, who did not share his buoyant mood.

"I would be cautious, Your Grace, to not forget your manners. There are other meetings being held in the castle today."

Wulford had a habit of wiping the smile from his face. "Ah, yes. The Rose Monts host their own luncheon, but with lords who can barely fill their coffers, let alone field an army."

"Yes, but…"

Warwick dismissed him with a flick of his wrist just as they reached the line of Demonbreun Guards.

His grandmother Lady Layana stood outside the ballroom doors, dressed to the nines in a gown of flowing emerald silk. "Ah, if it is not the prince of the realm, Warwick, and proclaimed heir-to-be. I take great honor in welcoming you to my festivity." She bowed gracefully, her voice warm with court decorum, and Warwick broke into another smile.

"Thank you, Grandmother. I am humbled that you went through such trouble to gather the Electors of the realm. Where would we be without your guidance? Only Aethylios would know—praise the Nine."

"Praise the Nine indeed," Layana echoed with a knowing smile. She stepped aside to usher him in, but her expression faltered for the briefest moment. Warwick, ever the gentleman, paused at the notice of a woman's displeasure.

"Is there a problem, my good lady?"

Layana raised her chin, eyes narrowing at the hairy brute clasping the sword behind him. "Will your… ah, *guard* be joining us today? I did not prepare an invitation for him."

Warwick glanced over his shoulder at Wulford, who for

the first time appeared genuinely uncomfortable. He shifted his stance, suddenly aware of the attention, but said nothing.

Warwick sighed. "Grandmother, allow me to deeply apologize. My father, the emperor insists that he accompany me at all times. That said, I should have had the foresight to inform you. My rudeness is entirely my own, but I can promise you, my guard will not disrupt your festivities nor interfere in any way. He is here only to watch over me. Correct, Wulford?"

"Aye, my good lady, I will take post in the back. I will not be noticed."

Layana's lips pressed into a thin line, but she relented with a nod. "As the emperor commands, I must obey. Be welcome, Wulford of Esteria."

The knight gave a proper bow, and with that, having tested Warwick's patience enough for the morning, he slipped through the doors into the grand ballroom.

The chamber had been transformed for the luncheon. The gilded chandeliers, each a dazzling constellation of glass and flame, bathed the vast chamber in golden light, reflecting off the polished marble floors. Along the walls, an endless array of delicacies had been set out on silver platters: candied fruits, spiced nuts, sugared pastries, and cured meats for light snacking. At the far end of the room, directly beneath the gaping, fanged mouth of the feathered serpent, a quartet of musicians played a lively melody, spurring a few guests into dance.

Yet the true heart of the feast lay at the very center of the room, where Warwick's eyes drifted to an immense banquet table littered with goodies. Towering platters of roasted meats and exotic fruits were piled so high they threatened to obscure one's dining companions. Golden goblets gleamed beside intricately engraved silverware, while jugs of deep red wine stood at the ready, waiting to fill an empty cup. Around the perimeter, a contingent of servants remained poised, ensuring that no Elector would be left wanting.

Here, beneath the vaulted ceilings of the imperial palace, the realm's most powerful families had gathered. The Electors, the nine noble houses that held the passage of the crown in their hands. At the head of the table, Warwick's father, the emperor, sat in deep conversation with Edwin Battlebridge, the representative from the free city of Brattleboro. To his right, Warwick's mother, Melinda, and his grandmother the formidable Lady Layana of House Esmerelda held court with their usual poise, their words measured, their smiles calculated.

Across the hall, Wulfnoth of House Goldshire, the imperial secretary, spoke in hushed tones with Lord Lyon of House Valkirn. His son, Casimir, was present too, engaged in polite conversation with his betrothed, Torralin Rose Mont. His irritation spiking, at least Makepeace of the Goldwoods had not been invited, but her absence was little consolation when her kin had still managed to slither their way in. Young Fielding Goldwood, a snake in every sense, hovered near Edwin, eager to ingratiate himself, his marriage to the statesman's niece granting him far more influence than he deserved.

Near the musicians, Graham Fontaine had thrown himself into a lively jig with his cousin, Arrianette, their laughter ringing above the melody. Elsewhere, young Gael of House Alfair stood alone, a quiet presence amid the revelry. Sent in place of his father, who fought far away on the Isle of Fláimir, he stood awkwardly among a room of the elite, munching absentmindedly on a chocolate-covered strawberry. Grandma'am and Lyon Valkirn stood nearby, chatting near a window as Wulfnoth browsed the food selection. Only House Faelwood and its figurehead, Lord Cornwallice, the *supposed* voice of the Kaesnfolk, had yet to arrive at the Crownhold.

Yet, for all the power and intrigue gathered under one roof, Warwick had eyes for only one.

Across the ballroom, beneath the glow of the chandeliers, stood Lady Polina of House Seavíc. Draped in an embroidered gown of black and freshly cut white flowers sewn directly into the fabric, she looked every bit a vision of nobility. A delicate headdress adorned her raven-black hair, the diamonds woven into its design catching the light with every turn of her head, accentuating the piercing blue of her eyes. Had the name *Catelyn* been whispered in his ear at that moment, Warwick would not have spared a single thought for it.

Then, a voice rang out, echoing across the great hall—

"THE PROCLAIMED HEIR-TO-BE, WARWICK, FIRST OF HIS NAME, OF HOUSE HIERONYMUS."

He jumped, snatched from his daydream of his beauty by Norbert, who lingered by the door, proclaiming his arrival. The room turned as one, the string quartet faltering into silence, all eyes now fixed on him.

"A pleasure, one and all, to see you in such good health and spirits."

A polite round of applause rippled through the chamber, those standing dipping into bows and curtsies, save for Ernest, who staggered across the room, sloshing a tankard of ale.

"Aye, my prince! Especially to the spirits!" he bellowed, lifting his drink in a lopsided toast.

A few snickers sounded around the room. Warwick wrinkled his nose, exhaling sharply in disapproval. Huffing, he turned, intending to make a direct path toward Polina and her father, but before he could take a step, a light gloved hand settled on his shoulder.

He turned to find his grandmother standing beside him. Compared to him, she was a small, shriveled thing, but the weight of her presence far outmatched her frame. The ballroom doors clicked shut behind her.

"Rowdy dogs are often the most loyal. Remember that, my prince. I will whip him in private."

"Oh, my good lady, no, I did not take offense…" he stammered, but Layana saw straight through him. She merely shook her head and drifted toward the grand table.

The string quartet struck up again, this time with a more subdued melody. Gradually, the Elector lords, ladies, and their families began to move toward the center table. Warwick's eyes sought Polina's, and when they met, she blushed, casting him a sly smile. His chest swelled and lower, his pants stirred. He returned the smile, his fingers instinctively patting the rose in his pocket to ensure it was still there.

Assured, he made his way to the head of the table, taking a seat to the right of his father. To his surprise, neither his mother nor grandmother joined them. Instead, across from him sat Lord Dymtrus of House Seavíc, with Polina beside him. Warwick burned hot. Oh, if he were feeling scandalous! To stretch his foot beneath the table, to graze hers just once…

"Aye, boy, how do you fare?"

Again, he was robbed of his salacious dreams. The emperor leaned sideways in his chair, peering at him with a tired gaze. For the first time, Warwick took real note of his father's declining health. Though he wore his kingly robes, and the Crown of the Nine rested upon his head, the man beneath them seemed… weakened. His breathing was shallow, and the chair creaked loudly beneath him. His belly stretched out too, straining the silk beneath the robe. It pressed against the table before him. Startled, he looked down at his own belly, suddenly self-conscious that he was nearly of the same dimensions.

"The prince is well! Does he not glow with imperial authority?" Dymtrus answered for him. He raised a goblet of wine to him and then heaved it back.

Warwick couldn't help it, but his eyes drifted to Polina's. Their gazes met, and both of them blushed with the shared embarrassment of children suffering their fathers' theatrics.

"I am well, thank you, Father." Warwick looked away.

"Of course, just look around you…" His father leaned back in his chair, spreading his hands wide to gesture at the table's guests. "We're all here for you, Warwick."

Warwick turned, finding all eyes upon him. He smiled, nodded, and, feeling fully in his element, he felt compelled to rise and stand before the most powerful families of the realm. "I thank you all for your attendance, on behalf of both my father and myself. It is an honor to have all the electoral families gathered together under one roof… and by the Nine, within the same room!" He let out a forced chuckle, which was quickly followed by the laughter of his guests. "It is such a shame, though, that we come together only under the most tragic of circumstances.

"I know much has been said of my uncle, Thane, and much more will be spoken when his body finally arrives at court, but I believe it must also be said we are the good voices of the realm, from the humblest peasant to the highest lord and lady, from the borders of Gothonia to the shores of Isperia. We are the voice of Aethylios and his flame and I feel extraordinary tragedy should not be the only reason we gather. But please, do not mistake my words." His gaze swept the room before settling upon his grandmother. "Lady Layana of House Esmerelda, the mother of my stepmother, though I detest that title. For she is as blood to me as my own kin and I cannot thank you enough for organizing this luncheon, as well as for gifting the realm such a righteous empress. A woman, if I dare say, I call mother. Thank you." Warwick burst into a smile and struck up a round of applause, his large, fat hands deafening those beside him. Melinda broke into quiet sobs as the other lords joined in, and finally Layana rose, nodding to Warwick as he resumed his seat.

"I cannot thank you enough for those words, my prince. We are all here, each and every one of us, because we have a duty to not only the realm, I say aye, but to Aethylios, and the enduring legacy of his Nine Miracles. Since the foundation of our great empire, and the brave acts of the Phoenix King, who overthrew our oppressors, who was a Hieronymus no less, I can think of no better bloodline, nor individual, to bear that weight."

At this, Dymtrus led a round of applause, followed by the other lords.

Layana inclined her head. "I thank you, as I thank all the Electors gathered here today. Now, there will be much time for talk, but now is the time for food. Let us eat."

With a wave of her hand, the servants moved at once, clearing away the towering platters of food so the guests could see one another more clearly. In their place came fresh dishes: roast duck, suckling pig, and even smoked fish, rushed from the sea. The lords and ladies descended eagerly upon their meals, conversation turning into a lively din.

All except Warwick.

For once, his stomach knotted, the thought of food turning to ash in his mouth. Polina was so close, and their glances across the table continued to grow bolder, daring, even. His armpits began to flood and his tongue went dry. Never before had a lady, not even his cousin, stirred him so.

Abruptly, he rose, tossing his napkin onto the table. The motion snatched the attention of those around him.

"My good lady, my grandmother, if I may call you that in public." He turned to Layana.

She nodded, a little stunned, but smiled nonetheless.

"I find it a great title—greater, perhaps, than duke or baron or lord. Just like my Grandma'am, who has the unfortunate burden of that name!" Warwick turned to her, seated between Torralin and Arrianette, and gave a playful wave.

"You see, there are things that are so much more important than titles and castles and crown, but family, whether by blood or by bond, as Aethylios himself preached. And as we have discussed in private, Dymtrus, I am honored not only by your service to the realm through my father's council but by the way you have raised such a fine and noble young woman."

He turned now to Polina, and a hush fell over the table.

"Polina of House Seavíc, I would be honored if you would accept this gift from me..."

Warwick moved his fingers delicately to his pocket, withdrawing the rare rose and raising it in his hand. A wave of gasps, oohs, and aahs swept the table. "My good lady, this is a Desert Rose, a rare and fine thing, blooming even amid the treacheries of the Sun Coast, where beasts roam, where men live and die in chains, where droughts and sandstorms reign. And yet, it draws its strength from the sun, rising against all odds, to share a little of Aethylios's light with the world."

He lifted the flower toward her. "I can think of no one more deserving of this gift than you. Will you accept it?"

Polina's eyes gleamed, shifting between Warwick and her father. Dymtrus bore a huge smile and gave a nod. No words were needed.

Warwick moved around from his side of the table and Polina rose. Not a breath was drawn in the room. With delicacy and precision, Warwick appropriately secured the desert flower to Polina's dress. Polina looked down, still having not uttered a word, and curtsied.

"T-thank you, my prince," she managed.

"No, my lady," Warwick said, dipping into a graceful bow. "Thank you."

Then, knowing better than to press his luck, he straightened, offering the table a composed smile before returning to his seat.

Conversation resumed around the table, chief among them Dymtrus and his father, who placed a gentle hand upon his knee to signal a job well done. The younger ladies of the table, Arrianette and Torralin, sprang up at once, rushing to Polina's side, admiring the rose. Though she did not look at Warwick, he could feel her smile.

Feeling celebratory, Warwick poured himself a goblet of wine and leaned back, striking up a conversation with Graham beside him. They quickly fell into an animated discussion on the finer points of yachting, passionately debating whether a man should ever bare his naked chest at sea. Their words grew lively, laughter bubbling between them, the topic spinning further into absurdity, until a commotion at the entrance struck the wind from their sails. The great doors to the ballroom flew open with force, swinging backward on their hinges as Norbert, though not an Elector, leaped up in alarm from his position near the door.

"ANNOUNCING THE GOOD LADY CATELYN OF HOUSE HIERONYMUS."

There was a stir among the table, and though Layana said nothing, her eyes stretched as wide as possible. Warwick too felt a lump form in his throat as he dared not look at Polina. Catelyn entered the ballroom, wearing a radiant white gown, her dark red hair gathered beneath a delicate diamond net, just like Polina's.

No one moved to welcome her, and the poor girl stood before the whole room, petrified, like a marble statue. It was finally Grandma'am who rose from the table, quickly rushing to her granddaughter's side, and brought her to the table as a servant dashed for an extra chair.

Layana now rose from her chair, pressing both hands firmly against the table. "Lady Catelyn," she said coolly. "I was not aware you planned to join us today."

Warwick turned sharply to his father, his pulse hammering, but the emperor only stared forward, blank and helpless.

"I-I received an invitation," Catelyn stammered, lifting a small card between trembling fingers. "My mother and I were to have lunch with the Rose Monts, but she thought… I should attend both affairs."

"Well then…" Layana stepped forward and plucked the invitation from her hand, examining it. "I do see you were, in fact, given one."

"Aye, that was me," Edwin Battlebridge piped up. A few guests turned to him with raised brows. "What?" he scoffed. "The poor girl just lost her father. We're here for her, aren't we?"

"Indeed," Grandma'am said firmly.

"Quite," Layana echoed, though her tone was clipped. "Lady Catelyn, you are, of course, welcome to dine with us. Please, take a seat, though I fear you've just missed Warwick's wonderful speech and presentation to Lady Polina."

Warwick's gaze met Catelyn's for the briefest of moments. But neither of them held it. Both turned away, quick and clumsy. He could not bear to look at Polina now.

Catelyn took her seat, her shoulder colder than the far north. Dymtrus was visibly seething, already deep in his cups, muttering curses and slurs with increasing venom. Graham attempted to steer the conversation back to lighter matters on their discussion on boating, but Warwick could barely hear him. He couldn't swallow his heart. It thumped too loudly in the back of his throat.

It was a heavy hand to his shoulder that finally broke his trance. "Come, boy, let me get you a drink."

Startled, Warwick looked up to find Uncle Ernest looming over him, grinning lazily, a fresh tankard of ale in hand.

Around the room, the gathering had begun to shift. Lords and ladies were rising from their seats, drifting toward the musicians, falling into private conversations. For a fleeting second, Warwick caught Catelyn's gaze again, but they both broke their glances immediately. He turned instead to Polina, who sat rigid, arms crossed, head tilted sharply away, staring off into space.

"I will not drink," he said to Ernest, hoping the lords that heard would not think him unprincely, but as soon as he was away from the table, he took a mighty swig from his uncle's cup. Wulford watched on, shaking his head, but Warwick didn't care. He let the ale wash over him.

"Lady troubles? Aye, I've had my fair share of them myself. It's tough I tell ya, especially when they're aware of each other, yes indeed, no bigger headache." His uncle took another swig. "Of course, now I've got my firstborn, Hugo, and a second on the way. God willing, it'll be a girl… I don't need another son runnin' around causing as much fuss as I did as a lad."

He gave Warwick a hearty slap on the back, laughing until he noticed Warwick wasn't laughing with him. The smile faded from his face.

"Ah, sorry, boy. I didn't mean to… well, you know. With Lysander." He winced and rubbed the back of his neck, then tried again. "Ehh, take it from me, the boy isn't a threat. He looks Lyonnian. *You* got them sweet blond curls of the Kaesnfolk. These tests happen every time the crown is lookin' to pass…"

Warwick's heart dropped again as he looked to his father.

"Agh, I'm really not doin' you any good here, am I?" Ernest muttered. He took another deep drink, then suddenly brightened. "Say, boy, these functions were never my strong suit. Wanna sneak away? I know a place ripe for explorin'."

"No thanks… I really shouldn't…" Warwick mumbled, close to tears.

"What if I told ya it would really piss off the Goldwoods?"

Warwick's ears perked at the sound of that.

"Aye, that's what I thought!" Ernest grinned. "Here, take another swig, I'll fetch more. When the coast is clear with your guard over there, we'll slip out the servants' way."

Warwick didn't need to be told twice now. When all was set, they made their escape, darting through a servant passage deep into the interior tunnels of the castle. Warwick led the way at first, but once they reached the castle proper, Ernest took charge, guiding him through unguarded corridors.

"Where are we going anyway?" Warwick asked.

His uncle shot him a wink. "Aye, it's a surprise."

They moved quickly, darting through the halls and as Ernest expertly avoided both the guards and attention of guests. He led him to the far side of the castle, where the Crownhold jutted over the mountain's edge. Beyond, the realm stretched beneath them, dark peaks and winding rivers fading into the distant horizon. Ernest led him out onto a walkway, the wind rushing past them, and there, moored to a ledge over the cliff side, was the Goldwoods' airship.

"By the Nine," Warwick gasped at the sight of it.

"By the Nine indeed, kiddo," Ernest said, hands on his hips as he admired the massive contraption.

The balloon was a deep crimson, stitched with vertical laces of gold. A gilded phoenix spread its wings across the fabric, crafted in the likeness of House Goldwood's heraldry. Beneath it, tethered by shimmering ribbons, clung a golden carapace to the balloon like a bloated tick.

"You… you want us to *go in there*?" Warwick stammered.

Ernest grinned, looking to a sturdy steel door at the center of the carapace. "Do you see any guards?"

"Well, no, but…"

"Then what are we waitin' for? Quickly, boy! Quickly!" Ernest urged, racing toward the airship's hatch.

Warwick hesitated only a second before following. They scrambled up a short rope ladder to a narrow metal platform jutting from the gondola's side, a gold railing framing the edge. The wind howled around them as Ernest grunted, wrestling with a heavy metal wheel to unlock the door.

"Such… luxury," he muttered, straining. "The door alone must weigh a ton. How in the hell do they get this thing to fly…?"

With a groan, the steel door swung open. Ernest wasted no time. He grabbed Warwick's coat and yanked him inside, slamming the door shut behind them.

Warwick spun in a slow circle, his mouth slightly open. The floor beneath them seemed to move as the balloon hovered and jostled in the air. He had never felt such a sensation before.

"I don't like this," he muttered, gripping a nearby crate for balance.

Ernest didn't hear him or chose not to. They stood in a cramped lower deck, packed tight with crates, an ornate desk, a fireplace, and carved sofas. A chamber pot sat shoved into the corner, as if an afterthought. But what drew Warwick's eye was the massive glass window overlooking the ledge, the world beyond disappearing into a setting sun.

"Incredible…" Ernest whispered, running his fingers across the desk's polished wood before taking another swig of ale. His curiosity was insatiable. He turned, eyes locking onto a central ladder leading upward. "Upward, boy! Always upward!"

Ernest went first, grunting as he hoisted his bulk through the narrow opening. Warwick followed, barely squeezing his broad shoulders through the hatch. He had to remove the Crown of Knox before it scraped against the ceiling.

The second floor was larger, lined with four canopy beds, each positioned beside a porthole. Ernest wasted no time and jumped onto the nearest bed.

Perhaps from the alcohol, perhaps from the daring sense of exploration, Warwick relented and jumped onto the nearest bed. It creaked under his weight, and if the entire balloon didn't sway beneath him…

"We're big men! Proud men!" Ernest laughed as Warwick sat up abruptly, face red as he checked under the bed to see if he'd broken it.

"I don't know about this…" he lamented.

"Nonsense!" Ernest dismissed him, already eyeing the final ladder leading to the top deck. "There's still one more floor…"

Warwick begrudgingly followed, and soon they stepped out onto the upper deck of the carriage. The great balloon towered above them, its maw gaping like a beast meant to swallow them whole. Warwick inched forward, gripping the golden railing that surrounded the deck—its solidity a comfort against the howling wind. He craned his head upward, studying the balloon's vast opening. At the center, he spied a contraption designed for flame. It unnerved him and sent a chill down his spine. Shivering, he lowered his gaze to the deck: several telescopes stood in place alongside pots of flowers, and at the helm, a golden steering wheel shaped exactly like that of a sailing ship.

Ernest ran to the nearest telescope. "Good lord," he spat, squinting through one eye. "You can see the craters of the moon! And I'll be damned… it's red!" He pulled back from the device, then spun on his heels, letting out a childish giggle as he spotted the steering wheel. Shoving his tankard into Warwick's hands, he rushed to touch it.

Warwick, however, was finished. "No! No more, Uncle. I forbid it."

"You forbid it?" Ernest dismissed him. "Come on, boy, learn to have some fun."

"No. I gave my command. This isn't fun for me. We…" Warwick looked around at the balloon… the strange contraption… the stench of his rotten, extended family. "We shouldn't be here."

"Just for a moment, let me get my hands on the wheel and…"

"NO!" Warwick shouted. He threw the tankard of ale down. "I do not wish to do this anymore. Let us be away."

Ernest turned to him, startled. "Oh, I'm sorry, my prince, I can take you back..." But he stopped, noticing the tears brimming in his nephew's eyes, the heaving, short breaths. Quickly, he came to his side, guiding Warwick to a bench near the railing. "Listen, Warwick, I get it. Girl troubles have brought many men to their wits' end before. It's nothing new."

"That damn... whoever... Edwin... he invited her... at the behest of my aunt, no doubt. Everything... it was going so smoothly."

A chuckle erupted from his uncle, and Warwick wanted to punch him for it, but he kept his gaze to the floor as he sniffled.

"Do you know what my mother thinks of Edwin Battle-bridge?" Ernest said in a silly voice. "He isn't even a real lord... just a wealthy merchant representing a 'free city,' what-ever that means. He has no noble blood. So you know what that means? He goes wherever the money is. That lowly, cow-ardly dunce."

"So what? He's been paid off then? How does that make me feel better?"

"I don't know, my prince, but if he has... then there is one thing that would motivate him even more."

Warwick looked to his uncle with red wet eyes. "What?"

"Taxation. Trade embargo. Threats. It's really not hard, not for someone whose blood isn't noble, just wealthy. Bah! Don't worry about those false lords."

Warwick sniffed, wanting to feel better, but all he could feel was the balloon rocking beneath him. "And what if... what if they have noble blood... *and* money?"

Glancing at the Goldwood symbol, Ernest had no response. He rose, bending over to pick up the spilled tankard, using a handkerchief from his pocket to mop up the mess. He then tossed the handkerchief over the railing, standing over the stain as if it didn't exist.

"Come on, my prince. I'll take you back now."

Warwick went quickly, his uncle behind him. He couldn't wait to get off the balloon, especially when something in a crate near the door whimpered. Head swimming, he had Ernest slam shut the door behind them as he went stumbling back to the castle looking for Wulford.

LEAWYN VII

The war drums thundered, and her clan danced to life.

Leawyn's feet twitched, each *thump* of the drums reverberating through her chest. Saralyn drifted past, her gaze wild and unfocused, her body swaying as though caught in a trance. Leawyn nodded to her, but Saralyn did not seem to notice. She melted into the frenzied mob gathered around the campfire, disappearing into the pulsing mass of bodies.

As the leader of her small clan, the ritual fell upon her shoulders. She would be expected to join them soon, but first, she had to prepare.

Takoda had come to her earlier. Takoda, who even now swayed near the bonfire, his old bones aching yet unyielding. His hands had been steady as he passed her the sacred paste of the Hearth, green paint drawn from the mossy soil itself.

Over her heart, she traced the form of a stag. A tribute to Lahotka, her late husband and the love of her life. On her left biceps, she painted a hare for her eldest son, Nukhta, swift and nimble, who had loved nothing more than a bowl of rabbit stew. On her right, a bear for Kaelin, her youngest, who had stood unshaken in the face of the enemy. Together, they were her strength.

On her temples, she painted twin doves in memory of her parents. Bound together in this life and the next, their love had been steadfast, unwavering. She felt it still, guiding her even now. Around her ankles, she strapped beads that chimed softly as she moved. Then, over each foot, she traced a curved rune. A mark of strength, one for each of her grandchildren. They were her guiding step, the reason she had found her footing again.

At last, she turned her back to Takoda, allowing him to paint the centaur. They had not followed her, yet she imagined their unseen presence, watching over her and her people.

When he finished, she was a living canvas, her body adorned with swirling patterns, sacred runes, and the marks of those she held dear. Aside from the beads that jingled with her movements, she stood bare like the rest of her clan, unashamed, unburdened.

Through the trees, the drums thundered louder, pounding through the forest. It seemed the whole Isle of Fláimir had descended into revelry.

A fresh log was added to the fire in the center of their camp, sending flames high into the sky through a break in the trees. The fire hissed, a malignant thing, but whatever cursed words it wished to say were drowned beneath the pounding of the drums.

Testing her ankles, she hopped from one foot to another. Satisfied her aging body would support her, she turned her gaze to the sky and looked upon the twinkle of stars against the crimson glow of the full moon. She closed her eyes and took a deep breath, digging her bare feet into the cool soil.

Yes, she thought, *I can feel your pain. I can feel your neglect. Hearth, Nukhta, Kaelin—to all of you, I hear you.* She opened her eyes, again looking at the blood moon in the sky. The moon was a reflection of their world, and right now, it was seething.

She began her dance, jumping from one foot to the other. The rhythm of the drums pounded through her bones. Then Takoda hobbled by, a heavy tankard of hastily brewed ale sloshing in his hands. He stopped before her, tilting the flask, letting the bitter liquid pour over her waiting mouth. She drank the corrupted nectar of the Hearth, letting her inhibitions go, turning her blood hot with poison.

"Pollute me!" she cried out, steeling her tongue against the foul taste. "I will take your poison!"

Takoda emptied the flask and danced away. Leawyn swayed on her feet, her mind already beginning to swim. She jumped from foot to foot, finding the music melding with her body, the tempo surging through her muscles.

She turned, raising her arms to the sky, and joined her herd around the fire, dancing in wild circles around the roaring flames. She screamed, twirling, her heels kicking up a cloud of dust. Her beads clattered against her skin, her runes pulsed with firelight, and her voice, raw and untamed, rose with the inferno.

"Sip the poison, from the Hearth,
Feel Your pain, prove our worth.
Take the weight of every wound,
Offer all, in rhythm, tuned.
Flood our veins with fire, pain,
Grant us mercy, our tribe cries out the same!
If we have sinned, then let us pay,
But guide our steps, don't turn away."

She broke into song, the chant rippling from her lips as she moved. The drums pounded, her body flowed, and she was no longer just herself. She was part of the current, a thrashing tide of legs and arms, a single force among the herd. A hundred other clans would be doing the same tonight, their voices lifting to the same beat.

"Down, down, to the deep below,
Where the old roots twist and grow.
Sink through the Hearth, let it take hold,
The Hearth calls us, strong and bold.
We shall drown, no fear to keep,
Waters whisper, soft and deep.
Breath may fade, eyes may close,
But in the dark, only sleep we know!"

Her chant wove into another, then five, then ten, until the entire herd was singing. And beyond them, a thousand thousand voices echoed across the isle. If she dared to dream, she could imagine stranger people still, far across the Hearth, lifting their heads to the blood moon and knowing, as she did, that their world was enraged.

"Diving hearts, yet burning all,
YOUR POWER DAMPENS THE PYRE'S CALL!"

The fire flared violently, sending a massive spray of flames that shifted the logs in the bonfire, causing them to collapse. A wave of heat rushed over the dancers. Leawyn stumbled back, eyes wide as flames shot upward, consuming several branches above their heads.

"Fetch the water!" she shouted and her people scattered like rodents. They tossed water haphazardly up into the trees, dulling the glowing embers. Leawyn looked upward, her head spinning as she watched the flames turn to white smoke. A wave of relief washed over her, but she stumbled backward, unable to keep her footing. Saralyn was there in an instant, catching her before she could fall, steadying her with a firm grip.

"Old Bird, you should rest."

Leawyn shook her head in protest, but that made the spinning worse. The world tilted beneath her feet.

Saralyn, seeing the struggle in her eyes, signaled to the drummers. They resumed their rhythmic beats, their drums pulsing in time with the distant sounds of the rest of the clan's war camp. Slowly, the crowd returned to the fire, their dance and howls resuming under the eerie light of the blood moon. As the noise swelled, Saralyn gently pulled Leawyn backward, leading her to the edge of the clearing. She settled Leawyn against a sturdy tree, facing away from the glaring flames. The cool night air kissed Leawyn's skin, and she breathed in deeply, finding solace in the silence of the forest. Saralyn sat cross-legged beside her.

"How do the Outsiders do it? How do they consume this vile stuff?" Leawyn moaned and looked down at her blurry hands. The ground swayed beneath them.

"Their bodies must be accustomed to wickedness," Saralyn answered. "Probably helps them burn better, too."

Saralyn's comments came off as sour, but a moment later they were both laughing. Behind them, in front of them, and in fact through the trees and shadows, the beat of drums were everywhere.

Leawyn nodded along with the drumbeats. "I wonder if they can hear us now. What must they think?"

"I hear they do not regard the moon as we do. They have probably poisoned themselves into an early sleep. The blood moon must terrify them."

"Yes, as it s-should," Leawyn slurred. "But I didn't mean them."

"You... you mean centaurs? From your journey before the battle?"

Leawyn nodded. "I ate with them. I drank with them. They nursed me to health."

"I've heard you mention them before, but I must admit, I know little of them except they keep to themselves..."

"They saved us... my clan, after my son's great victory and death!" Leawyn bolted upright, her voice raised, as spittle drooled from her mouth. She swayed unsteadily, wobbling where she sat, before the dizziness overtook her and she slumped back against the tree. "T-then they vanished, back into the forest. And I went after them. Then they saved me again. Both times..." Her head lolled from side to side. "They never asked for anything in return. They are content in their narrow woods of the east. They won't help us."

"No one will help us. No one." Saralyn's voice was quiet, but bitter, her gaze fixed on the bloodred moon. "We lose, and the Outsiders take. Again and again. When will it end? I don't know… but if the Hearth itself burns with rage, then let the end times finally come. I cannot lose anymore."

"I remember the fear well." Leawyn licked her dry lips. "The day the War Maker's messenger arrived at our clan. My eldest granddaughter was barely a babe, and my youngest still swollen inside her mother's belly. I knew what the summons meant for my family. But boys will be boys, and they were eager for the fight."

"A tale as old as time," Saralyn echoed.

"Quite so. That was the second time I saw the War Maker's men come. The first I was but a girl myself, if you can believe." Leawyn snorted. "He was a different man back then, the War Maker. Chosen by the clan leaders for his skill with an ax, though less for his ability to hold us together. He came himself to our village, spewing nonsense about glory, riling up the men with talk of battle around the fire. 'The ash,' he would say, 'is a time of cleansing. A sign that rebirth is upon us, but the land must be cleared first.' Hah." Leawyn lifted her trembling hands, watching them blur before her. "He kissed me that night, right here." She tapped her forehead. "Told me to behave for the next several months. That was how long he thought he would be gone. That," she swallowed hard. "was the last time I saw my father… before he went into the bog."

Saralyn stared absently into the darkness. Behind them, the liquor was working its way through their herd, their ritual dissolving into drunken laughter and revelry. Even from the main war camp, the echoes of song, laughter, and merriment had overtaken the somber and serious nature of their ritual. Somewhere in the dark, a tree branch snapped, and the giggle of a man and woman could be heard through the darkness. Above, the blood moon glowed as bright as ever.

"It seems a natural thing…" Saralyn mused, "to want to forget."

"I wish it were so easy," Leawyn whispered. "I wish I could forget it all."

"Why is it that we are cursed then? To never forget?"

Leawyn stared into the darkness, feeling the drumbeats give the forest a dark heartbeat. "What is it that you wish to forget, then?"

"Loss, of course," Saralyn answered, her voice quiet but firm. She turned her gaze to Leawyn. Though her vision was blurred and her head spun from the poisoned water, Leawyn could still hear the weight in her voice.

"Tell me," Leawyn urged.

"Tell me about your home first. Then, perhaps, I shall tell you of mine."

"Hilly, with deep forests and swift, winding rivers…" Leawyn closed her eyes, letting the memories flood her mind. "The game is plentiful, and the sun… shy, always hiding behind mist or clouds. Our village is nestled at the base of a great hill, and at its peak, we built a lodge that could see for miles. My home was among the trees, where a little farm stretched along the edge of a forest brook. How I wish I could see it again."

"A place of pleasant dreams," Saralyn whispered with a half smile, but her expression darkened as her gaze fell downward. "My clan hails from the coast, where the gentle slopes of the Hearth meet the bitter salt of the sea. The land is rocky, the winds fierce and unrelenting. We fish rather than hunt, crafting boats from the trees and trading with the other clans along the shore. My village stands on a bluff, high above the waves that crash against the jagged cliffs. The salt air rises and pickles your skin, but I would not have it any other way. For the few days the sky is clear and the sun is bright, I can see to the very ends of the world…" She paused, and lifted her gaze to the moon. "And at night, I could witness the power of the moon as she commands the sea to rise. Nowhere else do I feel its strength so clearly."

"I see." Leawyn nodded, eyes still shut. "I would like to visit someday. There is so much to our people and our land, and we know so little of it."

"But as with all things... like the tide that surges in at night and must recede by morning, there is always a price to be paid." She coughed, pressing a hand lightly to her forehead as if to steady her spinning thoughts. Then, quieter, she admitted. "I miss my wife and my daughter. I fear they are forever lost to me."

The drop in Saralyn's tone was sobering. Leawyn looked down to her hands, her vision returned to normal. "To battle?" she asked, though she had little faith in her own question. Even in the crimson moonlight, she could see the tears streaking down Saralyn's face.

"The Salt Men," Saralyn whispered, pulling her knees to her chest. "They come for us while the men are at sea. They them... our boys, while they provide for us, but still that is not enough. Cowards, they are, sweeping in when the men are away. That's when they take the rest of us, the children especially..." Her breath hitched as she glanced at Leawyn's ankle beads. "I could never... never..." Her voice broke into a shudder. "The sound... it's too much like the rattle of their metal shackles."

"I'm sorry, I didn't know..." Leawyn immediately reached down to remove the beads from her ankle.

A firm hand caught hers.

"Do not remove them," Saralyn said sternly. "That is the tradition of your clan. That is your right."

Leawyn met her gaze. Tears traced silent paths down Saralyn's cheeks, but she did not sob. Her voice remained low but steady. "I am forever cursed to wonder if they're alive and where... should I ever see them again, in this life, or the next."

A cool breeze washed over Leawyn, prickling her skin. She looked up at the moon, swollen and red, hanging heavy in the sky. It seemed closer than before, as if it had doubled in size. She shivered.

"The Outsiders," she muttered. "Such damnable people. Will they ever leave us alone?"

Saralyn shook her head, sniffing hard. "Not the Outsiders." Her voice was thick but certain. "Others. They do not bear the flaming sigil of the bird, and their skin is darker." She turned her gaze to the forest, her eyes sharp, as if searching for ghosts in the darkness. "You'd think, for all the years my clan has sailed the salt sea, we would know what lies beyond. But the world is far stranger than any of us understand... than any of us *can* understand."

Leawyn followed her gaze into the dark.

"Sometimes, when I stare out at the horizon, I swear I see it just where the sky meets the sea. But no matter how far I sail, the edge only moves, always beyond reach, like some great elusive waterfall, pouring over the side of the Hearth." She exhaled, her breath shaky. "The moon, they say, fights against the current. That is why we have tides. And the Outsiders... I think they come from *there*, from the place that lies below. That is why they love fire, why they despise us so much. *Our waters rain on them.*"

A sudden sob tore from Saralyn's throat. She bent forward, burying her face in her hands, her shoulders trembling with the force of it. Leawyn instinctively reached for her, meaning to pull her close, but Saralyn lurched upright with a raw, wounded snarl, shoving her away.

"No!" she barked, sucking in a ragged breath, her whole body shuddering. A heartbeat later, she straightened, smoothing her expression as if her heart had never broken.

Leawyn hesitated before speaking again. "There is such diversity in our land," she said softly. "In our accents and beliefs, in our waters and our soil. And yet, I never imagined there would be such *variety* in our enemies. I thought the Outsiders were enough."

"That is the legacy of the War Makers." Her voice was dry now, distant. "They see the struggles of every clan. They *feel* the pain of this land. And they know... unity only comes through fire and war."

"But he won't come," Leawyn answered.

"No. He won't come."

They sat in silence, the drumbeats of their people fading into the night. Yet the land did not reclaim the quiet with birdsong or the hum of insects. Only the brittle crackle of a dying fire filled the Hearth beneath the blood moon's cold light.

Leawyn exhaled slowly. "I cannot imagine what you have gone through. I'm sorry." She hesitated, then added. "I am left with two healthy granddaughters, kin of my own blood… yet I doubt I will ever live to see them again."

"They are not lost to you," Saralyn added. "They will rise with you, when the time comes."

Leawyn nodded, but the words settled heavy in her chest, offering little comfort.

"You don't need the War Maker either," Saralyn continued. "We didn't follow you because of some promise. You saved our lives. You brought *hope*, Leawyn. Hope. Something our people have not known for generations. If you, one simple old woman, can turn the tide of battle against bottled thunder, just imagine what we could accomplish…. together."

"I will need more. *A lot more*," Leawyn added quietly. "If I am to make a true difference."

She planted her feet, hands pressing against the Hearth as she struggled to rise. Her knees crackled and popped in protest, but she gritted her teeth and rose, bracing herself against the tree.

"Your chieftain is coming, Chieftain Hunta said as much." Saralyn sprang to her feet beside her. "Numbers, maybe? Different clans coming together, just like the War Maker?"

"No." Leawyn shook her head, turning her gaze to the bonfire at the heart of the camp. "My clan is withered. He will bring nothing but the temptations of home. Help won't come from him." Her voice dropped lower. "We'll need the power of this land to win… and all those who inhabit it."

She looked to Saralyn as the rising cries of a woman being pleasured cut through the dark, and a moment later, Leawyn bent over and retched.

"Come on, let me help you get to bed," Saralyn urged.

Leawyn did not protest, leaning into Saralyn's steady grip, but not before she looked up into the night sky once more and watched the red swirls of the fire dance across the face of the moon.

Lady Aril

She lay awake until she heard the soft cries of her daughter gradually slip away into sleep. Yet it was only when she heard the gentle snores of her husband from across the hall did she dare to move.

Quiet as a mouse, she slipped out of bed, her slippered feet making barely a sound as she tiptoed down the hallway. Peeking through the satin curtain into her daughter's room, she saw the child sound asleep, Cato's arm protectively tucked around her. A single tear slipped from her eye, trailing down her cheek before falling silently to the floor. With a heavy heart, she drifted back to her chamber.

She lit only a single candle, bathing the master bedchamber in a dim, eerie light. She quickly dove into her closet, hiking through a forest of clothes. She batted away tree branches of gowns and dresses worn for only single occasions, or never worn at all. Priceless gems and jewels clattered like the chirp of birds as she made her way to the back wall, and only here, in the deepest recess of the forest, with only the twinkling light of her dim candle, did she uncover a leather bag hidden under a pile of yet more clothes. She seized it and ran from her closet, escaping from the suffocating thicket of her life.

Like a thief in the night, she ransacked her drawers and clothing, gathering only what seemed essential. Simple gowns with minimal embellishments, plain robes that could pass for a common woman's attire. The jeweled dresses hit the floor in discarded heaps—too elaborate, too eye-catching. Her jaw clenched as she touched one particularly extravagant gown, its bodice glittering with black diamonds.

A thousand slave lives. Fingers worked to the bone. She spat on the floor. The dress followed.

She selected a few plain robes. Nothing that would draw the eye. *Or can I not tell anymore?* She bit her lip. She held up a robe crammed into the top of her leather pack. It was dyed yellow and white like everything in this cursed city. Only a few small opals sparkled in its collar. She yanked it to her mouth and silently screamed into it. Tears stung the corners of her eyes. A fire crackled in her cheeks.

The dress I arrived in. The dress he bought me in.

She hissed, gritting her teeth as she gently put it back in the bag. She was not a slave to this city—or anyone! But she had been sold all the same, a hand in marriage bartered by her corsair father for favorable trade conditions. In a fit of rage, she ripped a priceless gown in two, a million jewels spilling onto the floor. Kicking many under her bed, she turned away from the mess.

Well, Father, I am coming home anyway.

With her bag now full, she reached for one final item: a well of black writing ink.

Settling at her makeup table, she tore a small piece from her husband's stolen stationery and scribbled a quick note. After tearing the remainder free, she burned the remaining parchment in the candle's flame, watching the ashes rise like smoke from her dreams. The good lady of the House of Aeksilor then stuffed the inkwell into her leather bag and returned it to the depths of her closet.

"God forgive me," she whispered. There was no choice now. Soon the match would strike, and the city would burn.

She emerged from her bedroom on her tiptoes again. She moved down the hallway, once again checking on her daughter and husband. They were still wrapped tight together under the sheets. She smiled, even though she knew could save neither one of them. Sirene sensed the coming fire, while her husband still lived in denial. They would both need each other.

She stuck her head in her eldest's bedroom. He lay sound asleep too, snoring quietly on top of his blankets. A cool breeze whistled in from the night air. A crescent moon hung over his balcony overlooking the city.

My first, my oldest. You are the future of this fated house. Cato will never let you go. She shed a tear here as well. She tiptoed on.

Lastly, she came to the bedroom of her middle child. He too slept soundly under a mound of blankets. A small candle burned in his room. He was afraid of the dark. *My dumpling,* she wanted to call out but knew better. *You and I forever.*

With a heavy heart, she left the owner's suite of her manse, a shadow gliding through the night. Clutching the note tightly in her hand, she slipped silently through the dim halls and into the kitchen, cloaked in darkness save for a thin ray of moonlight. There stood the old woman, gazing out the window. Aril entered quietly, but not quietly enough.

"These are odd hours to be awake, my lady. What can I do for you?"

"Old Mother... I seek your help."

"That is my station, my good lady. How can I serve?"

"No, not serve!" Lady Aril clenched her fists. "I mean I need your services. I have brought payment."

"Payment? My good lady, I do not require payment. I serve the House of Aeksilor with pride." The old mother did not turn from the window.

"I do not wish to be called that. I have never wished to be called that."

"It is the dream of many little girls in this city to be a good lady. Forgive me if I do not take your words as sincere."

"Please, Berona, we both know the game I play here. I masquerade as a good lady while tolerating this city." She spat on the floor. The whites of Berona's eyes shone as she finally turned to Aril. "I may wear jewels, but I was bought and sold all the same."

"And yet you have never known the iron grip of the collar." The old woman reached up and touched her neck. "Be direct, my lady, for the hour is late, and I do not have time for games."

Tears stung her eyes. "I need you to deliver a message to my father."

"The corsair? My lady, I recall he is far at sea… not easy to reach. How am I to possibly…"

But Lady Aril pulled a pouch from her robe. She tossed it in her hand. The unmistakable sound of jewels filled the night air.

"And what am I to do with jewels?"

"I have never berated you. I have never struck you. I have only treated you and the other slaves with kindness. Why can you not do the same for me?"

"Because I am a slave and you are free. What can a slave do with jewels except lose her head for theft?"

"Not for you then, but for your *sweetlings*."

The old woman turned sharply in the moonlight, her face shrouded in shadow. She moved closer. "And what do you know of my sweetlings?"

"I only want to leave," she answered.

"Leave? But why? What kind of mother would abandon her own children?" The shadow cocked its head as something dark darted in the corner.

"You know as well as I that Cato would never let his first-born leave. And Sirene… she was made for the life of a slaver. But Boros…"

"… is as sweet as a summer orange?"

"He is not corrupted. You feel the same as I."

At this, the shadow held silent.

"Please, take these jewels. Use them however you please: for your sweetlings, for the slaves, or the unrest building in the city below. I care not."

"You care only for yourself!" The shadow lurched forward, but Aril did not flinch.

"Sometimes we must do hard things to survive in this world. I will save whichever of my children I can, but I will not be here when the city burns. I am not a slaver. I care not for these jewels." She tossed them into the air. The shadow caught them.

"It will be difficult to arrange things…"

"You can get it done," Aril affirmed.

"Very well then. I will see to it, my dear lady."

"I do not wish to be called that anymore."

"We shall see," the shadow replied, retreating. "For when a fire is struck, it is up to the wind whom it burns."

Aril backed away as more shadows crept along the floor. She left the kitchen, turning to flee back to her bedroom.

WARWICK IX

The High Priest held a wriggling cobra in his hands. The snake twisted, hissing, desperate for a strike, slicing through the air as a gasp swept his congregation. Osbert feigned fear, dodging as the snake's fangs missed his robed arm by mere inches. The cobra, entangled within the priest's arms, grew frustrated. It coiled itself around the priest's chubby arms, and for the first time during the ceremony, Warwick leaned forward in the pew, suddenly intrigued.

Osbert, if he knew fear, did not display it. He slid his grip up the base of the neck, grasping just below its head, trying to regain control of the creature. The snake, however, had other ideas, and coiled its immense body around Obsert's chubby arm, giving it the leverage it needed. Women in the congregation gasped—to his far right Warwick even saw Catelyn throw her hands up to her mouth. The congregation frothed, incensed by the snake, as Osbert danced on the stage, flailing with the beast wrapped tightly around his arm. This had never happened before.

Warwick and his family sat in the front row. Hundreds, if not thousands, of nobles and other stately guests sat behind him. From here, he saw the feigned smirk of Osbert transform into fear. He watched Osbert's fingers slip on the snake's head, losing his hold bit by bit. The cobra, though likely drugged, was cunning, and Osbert, perhaps slightly drunk, was now at its mercy. It twisted its head again, this time striking its fangs straight through the cloth of his priest's gown. The congregation went mad, rising to their feet in shrieks and shouts. Warwick joined them, his heartbeat pounding in a frenzy. The priest, unlike the many fake snake wranglings of the past, was in real danger.

His aunt let out a wail as the snake recoiled for another strike. Osbert, panic-stricken, danced wildly as if to shake the tightly wrapped snake from his arm. He clutched the snake's head for dear life, the last leverage he had on the beast, when the cobra twisted free. Spinning on his heels, Osbert bought himself a few precious seconds as shrieks of terror shook the audience. The snake reared for another strike, and just as all seemed lost, Osbert shouted a word that shook the Church Hall like thunder. "Maeknys! Zoareyns!"

Warwick wormed in his seat at the sound of the words. Women around them threw up their hands to cover their ears. *"Submit. Obey."*

The snake froze, flicking its tongue up toward Osbert's sweating face, when he brought the snake down hard upon the podium. *Crack.* The snap of the snake's spine splintered through the congregation. Warwick stood on his feet, joined by a thousand others, sweaty, hearts racing, as not a word was uttered. The snake's body fell limp onto the floor.

"The beast of oppression... the icon of the Trickster... is nothing in the face of the Nine..." Osbert called out to his congregation.

His congregation erupted into applause. Warwick's stepmother burst into tears, Catelyn jumped madly on her feet, and from his periphery, he caught his love interest Polina on her hands and knees, thanking the Lord for the snake's defeat. Even his father roared with approval. Warwick turned back to the dead snake, a heavy lump forming in his throat. To his own surprise, a single tear traced down his cheek.

"There is nothing more powerful than the Nine. Nine Miracles, each a divine blessing more profound than the last. When our prophet Aethylios was born into poverty, without a penny or a title, and when he crossed the Soundwatch Sea to reach our shores, cast away by the proud lords of distant lands, it was the Nine who saved him. It is the Nine who saves us all!"

The congregation returned to its pews. Warwick was among the last to sit, even outlasting his brother seated on the other side of his father. "When Aethylios fled the tyranny of Lyonnia, our world was not as it is now. In those days, the prideful god-emperor of Lyonnia ruled with an iron hand, his laws and customs suffocating all who dared defy him. Yet it was not his soldiers nor his priests who pursued Aethylios with the greatest zeal. It was his pride. A pride so fierce it sought to consume even the workings of the divine itself."

Osbert paused, letting the words settle before continuing. "In his flight, Aethylios came to these lands, to the fledgling Makkan Empire. He sought refuge among us, finding fleeting kindness from our people. But even in this sanctuary, betrayal waited. He found himself in the company of a merchant, a man who, atop his mounds of gold, saw no reverence for the serpent his people worshipped. Amused by Aethylios's goodwill and his faith in the divine, the merchant betrayed him. He sold the prophet's location to the Lyonnians."

The congregation stirred. Even the mountain itself seemed to grumble.

"And yet, the merchant's treachery did not end there. He offered Aethylios a false promise—a guarantee of safe passage to distant lands. But when Aethylios opened the crate meant to carry him to freedom, he found not deliverance, but a viper. A deadly serpent, meant to seal his doom."

Cries of outrage erupted among the congregation. Osbert raised a steady hand, silencing them. "Yet even in the shadow of betrayal, the hand of our Lord moved!" His voice swelled, filling the chamber. "Blessed with divine power, Aethylios worked a great miracle. Before the merchant's eyes, before the blades of the Lyonnians, he raised the serpent high. It writhed and stiffened, its flesh transforming into wood. It became a staff, an instrument of divine power." Osbert's voice crescendoed, echoing off the vaulted ceiling. "With this sacred staff, Aethylios struck the ground at the Hearth and split the sea itself! The waters parted, and he forged a path to the Holy Isle, escaping his enemies to continue his divine mission."

"Amen," answered the congregation.

Osbert continued. "In the coming days, the body of our late Master of War, cherished brother to the emperor, and beloved husband and father, will arrive at court for his final rights. I have spoken today of a great miracle, even put on a fantastic display of faith over sin. Yet nothing I do will ever come close to the power of the Ninth Miracle—the power of fire. When our prophet was recalled to heaven, he did not go into the ground to rot and be devoured by worms, no! He went into the fire, turning to ash, rising into the sky, joining with our Lord within the very sun! And so we will all follow in his wake. The body of Thane will be burned, as we all will, and we will witness the greatest, most final miracle of all—salvation. Amen."

The congregation broke and the Church Hall broke into a thousand conversations at once. From the front row, Warwick watched as Osbert slipped behind a side curtain, only to drop heavily onto a seat. A tankard of wine was delivered to him a moment later.

"What do you think?" Lysander whispered, appearing beside Warwick with a skeptical look toward the priest. "Think he was drunk with wine for the spectacle?"

"Such things shouldn't be joked about. Really." Warwick shook his head.

"I do not jest. He got lucky today. It would have been a bad omen for us all if the snake's strike had been true."

"Have some faith," Warwick snapped at his brother.

Lysander turned to him, eyebrows raised, and a tinge of pain hit Warwick's gut. "I guess you would know about false strikes." Lysander's voice cracked, then he turned on his heel and strode toward Derrick, who was back on his feet, though his arm still hung in a sling.

Warwick lowered his head. The lump in his throat was still there. *This is the house of forgiveness, after all.* He pushed past his father, entrapped by his auntie who was seeking an audience, and greeted Catelyn.

"Good morning," he said, offering a slight bow. "Did you enjoy the sermon, my lady?"

"I found it moving. Snakes are disgusting creatures, and I feel this entire castle is tainted with their presence."

"Do you not feel safe here, dear cousin? Perhaps I could keep you company sometime? I know these walls well, and though I understand you may still be cross with me for the unfortunate tourney strike with your brother, I have been training with the sword."

Catelyn's stiff upper lip may as well have been an upper-cut. "I would feel safer with a cobra than with you with a sword." She paused, letting the words cut deeper, before continuing. "Do you know why Osbert's story was so moving today? Because it is a story about power and a bully. And a humble man, tearing down those without remorse or shame. No, I think not with you."

Catelyn turned on her heels, sauntering off into the congregation. Derrick and Lysander now looked at him. He blushed, feeling the sting, and tried to speak to Derrick, but the lump in his throat grew and he could speak no words. His cousin then turned as well, brushing against his shoulder as he left, leaving only Lysander behind.

"I'm sorry, Brother. I know you care for her. When our betrothal is announced, I promise to treat her well, and know this, you will have an ally in me." Lysander placed a gentle hand upon his shoulder, even as fire burned away the lump inside him. He walked away and Warwick turned, ready to spit fire, when Lysander stopped to speak with their auntie, freeing their father, forcing him to swallow his bile.

To my own betrothed, then, he thought bitterly. He stormed through the crowd, pushing past the Rose Monts, until he halted abruptly, locking eyes with Polina across the hall. She stood beside her father, Dymtrus, one hand absently fingering a nine-pointed star pendant against her chest. She glanced at Warwick, her gaze flickering away just as quickly. Dymtrus noticed him and broke into a broad smile, giving his daughter a gentle nudge, but Polina held her ground, refusing to budge.

Am I stained with sin? Or am I meant to suffer? The questions haunted him as he turned away, his mind clouded with turmoil. Blinking back a swell of tears, he looked up to find Lacius watching him from the shadows behind a pillar, a sly, knowing smile on his face. Warwick quickly averted his gaze, but the confessor's eyes bored into him, compelling him to look back. With a grin, Lacius beckoned, his fingers curling in invitation. And though he couldn't explain why, Warwick felt himself drawn, step-by-step, toward the court confessor.

"Be welcome! Be welcome, young prince," Lacius greeted him.

Warwick, however, merely hung his head down.

Lacius stepped forward, placing a trembling hand upon his back. "I am so glad you have finally come to see me."

Lacius guided him away from the congregation, drawing him out of the realm fellowship's loud chatter. The bright morning light spilling through the stained glass windows dimmed behind them, replaced by shadow as they moved past the main stage. In the dark, Osbert stumbled forward, already heavy with wine.

"A shame," Lacius shook his head, glancing at Osbert's swaying figure. "o see a holy man indulge so heedlessly. But you, my prince... you've made the right choice."

Warwick barely heard him, his thoughts circling back to

Polina. He wondered if she had seen him leave and if she might think better of him for it.

"Your father comes to me. His council comes to me. Even your brother has come to me."

"My brother?" Warwick perked up.

"Indeed so."

"To discuss what?"

Lacius laughed. "His sins of course."

Warwick's face scrunched and he shook himself free of Lacius's grip. "If it is a matter of state, then I have to know."

"I am afraid that is between me and the good Lord, my young prince."

"It would be treason not to tell me."

Lacius laughed again. "I am the emperor's confessor, anointed by his High Holiness in the city of Incendrium, where our good Lord burned. I am entrusted with the confessions of the highest nobles in the land, and with me and the good Lord, and no one else, those words lie."

"The pope is not of our realm. Why should I entrust my sins to you?"

Lacius's eyes gleamed. "Does the Lord Himself not reside within our realm?" He tilted his head, watching as Warwick searched for a retort but found none. "I thought so."

"I still do not trust you."

"When you are finished, and your guilt is relieved, and your soul feels so light you could float right up to God himself, we shall see how you feel then." Lacius turned and smiled at him.

Warwick frowned but held his gaze, unwilling to let his unease show.

Confession could occur anywhere within the castle, but Lacius maintained a small, private chamber connected to the main Church Hall. He led Warwick inside, closing a thick wooden door behind him, and barred it shut with a steel latch. Warwick watched him with one raised eyebrow. The air in the room was cold and still with nothing but a single candle burning on a small, rickety table.

"Over here." Lacius beckoned.

He walked toward a booth of sorts with two flaps of cloth on either side. He held back one of the flaps, gesturing for Warwick to step inside. Warwick swallowed hard, eyeing the booth with suspicion. The door was bolted—*odd*—and he was unsure if anyone had seen him go. He thought for a moment to cry for Wulford, but suppressed the urge. *How would the realm react to hear I cried for my guard at confession? I would never have Polina.* He sighed and took a step forward. "I will do it for her."

"Oh?"

Lacius tugged the flap of cloth again and Warwick slipped inside. The flap slid shut as he adjusted himself within the cramped space. There was only a wooden bench to sit upon, which groaned heinously under his weight. It was nearly impossible to see, and next to him, he heard Lacius climb into the booth as well. A narrow window in the wood divider slid aside beside his head. "Do you wish to confess your sins, my son?"

Warwick was quiet for a moment before answering. "I do."

"Speak, then, and all will be forgiven."

A flood of thoughts rose in Warwick's mind: his brother, Catelyn, his father, the crown, the tournament, Polina. But his thoughts tangled and stalled, each one twisting back on itself until he could only bite his lip, twiddling his thumbs in silence.

"Have you been to confession before, my son?" Lacius, after some time, finally asked.

"No."

"Not even as a child?"

"I had a whipping boy when I was in the wrong as a child."

"Hmm, I see. Have you ever professed your guilt then? Relieved your conscience of any wrongdoing?"

"I suppose—at times."

"Such as when?"

"Well, when I was on my tour in Sanguinia, and there were many very pretty women and much wine to be had, and many nights where we were alone to stare at the stars or lie in the gardens."

"So you did not lie with these women?"

"No. Never."

"You mean to say you did not spill your seed, even with the pretty girls of the realm."

"I am too much a gentleman, sir!" Warwick's voice rose. "I respected all my suitors and friends. We lay awake drinking and talking of poetry and politics and longings for this world. Perhaps a kiss or two here, I do not deny it, but I never soiled my spirit or the bodies of my courtiers."

"I must say I am most surprised. It is rare to see a noble, or I daresay even a prince, who has not given himself over to fornication with so many women, or men, to tempt him."

Warwick's eyes narrowed. *I see your trap, old man.* "No, I have not spilled my seed into the young ladies of the realm. Is that so hard to believe? Or is it common among princes? Tell me then, does my brother have a bastard running around the north?"

"You know I cannot divulge the confessions of others, but if he were to have a bastard, would that anger you?"

"It would be yet another slap in the face."

"Explain, child."

Warwick's voice grew bitter. "He leaves the imperial palace in Aberness just to reach my father before me. He takes our family sword. He sits on the emperor's throne. He garners the attention of the realm, and..." Warwick's stomach did a flip. "He means to take Catelyn away from me as well."

"Ah, and do you think he does these things with malice?"

"What other option is there? He has half the realm whispering of a *better choice.* I injured my cousin in a tourney, and ah! I am becoming the detractor to the realm. Well, I say to the lords and ladies of the realm, see the true steadiness of my hand, for I could have my brother thrown into a deep dungeon, and all those whispers for his claim, and throw away the key. Simple treason, that's all it is," Warwick spat, his fist slamming into the wood panel.

"You are angry," Lacius replied.

"How could I not be?"

"It is a sin."

"So is to covet. Now tell me, which is worse?"

"You mean your brother covets your crown?"

"He covets my everything." Warwick became teary-eyed.

Lacius's tone softened. "She means a great deal to you, doesn't she?"

Warwick felt a tinge of pain in his heart. He knew he referred to Catelyn. "She is family, a cousin, but family. It would be wrong for me not to care for her."

"I see. And Polina? Do you think she is not a fine match?"

"She is... pretty," Warwick lamented. "Though I suppose we lack for much in common. Catelyn and I grew up together. She comes from the good stock of the family and... she just understands me." He shook his head, anger flaring again. "But my brother... he claws at everything my father and I have built. Derrick deserves Aberness in honor of his father. Catelyn could be wed to me, which would pacify my aunt. Lysander could take the family sword and run off to war for all I care... but now, even the succession of the crown itself feels at stake. I am their heir of our house, but how easy it could be to twist our birth order to take everything from me."

It was Lacius's turn to sit in prolonged silence. "I had not heard your father intended to pass Aberness to your brother Lysander."

"He has not spoken of it... publicly."

"Do you think it is a challenge to be twins?" Lacius asked.

"Excuse me?"

"Twin boys—twin heirs, born only minutes apart. Some lords try for years to divorce their wives over the blessing to have a son, and here the emperor is blessed with twin boys! Two firstborn heirs. A curse perhaps? This must bother you."

"Lysander has not been my brother since he returned home from his accursed trip through the north." Warwick tried to dismiss his feelings, but Lacius waited patiently. Warwick shifted uneasily on his bench, pulling at the sleeves of his tunic as the tight walls of the booth seemed to press in around him, squeezing him for the truth. "I suppose my heart fills with jealousy, to speak the truth of it."

"Jealousy now? But you are the crown prince. The firstborn. You wear the crown of your ancestors. Lords and ladies fight for your attention. In your station, are you not satiated? Or do you demand more?"

Warwick's teeth clenched. "Do you think me greedy?"

"Power is a form of greed," Lacius countered.

"Have I painted the portrait of a tyrant for myself? No, you have asked for my confession and I have spilled the truth. My heart fills with jealousy. It was I who was sent by my father to the south of the realm to treat with the lords and ladies of the court of a different culture and tongue. I secured the allegiance of the houses of Sanguinia, while my brother went north where our blood and tongue runs common with the Kaesnfolk. There was no challenge, and yet I return home, and my brother is hailed the hero only because he grew an inch and sprouted muscles." Warwick shook his head in the dark. "I can wield a sword and shoot an arrow, too."

"You feel your brother has surpassed you, is that so?"

"Yes... a better choice, I suppose." Warwick lowered his head. "Sometimes I feel we are not even twins, we have always been so different..."

"What do you mean to suggest, my son?"

"I suggest nothing, only how much easier it would be if he could be proclaimed a bastard or illegitimate. He lacks my father's and my gold curls... a simple whisper at court could do it..."

"That is indeed a very dark confession. Betrayal of family is frowned deeply upon by our Lord. Think of your mother, too, looking down upon you boys. What must she feel? Lysander sports her same brunette hair."

"I never knew my mother," Warwick answered.

"True, she died doing a mother's duty. No greater act of sacrifice than to give life."

"It would have been nice to know her."

"Aye, I knew her well back in the day."

Warwick pressed the nails of his thumbs into his palms. "What was she like?"

"Fair, very fair." The shadow of Lacius nodded next to him. "She loved your father deeply and was committed to the faith as well."

"So no wayward love affair?" Warwick jested, a lump in the back of his throat.

"None. She was the very image of virtue. The realm adored her, and she brought great wealth and power back to House Hieronymus following the Diet of Blood. No, my child, I daresay Lysander is indeed your kin. Never a stain on her honor. She left a legacy for your family to uphold, especially after the Rose Mont scandal."

"I thought you said confessions were private."

"It is not a confession. Charles's illegitimate child was a public spectacle, no?"

Warwick shifted uncomfortably on the wooden bench. His rump thumped with a dull ache. He wondered if his father or Wulford might be looking for him by now.

"Thank you, Priest of the Nine, for hearing my sins today, but I really must be going." Warwick started to rise, but a sharp lash of Lacius's tongue bid him to sit.

"*Kahaese!*"

Warwick slammed back onto the bench. The same urge he felt earlier in the Church Hall returned to him. He lifted up his hands to his ears ready to claw them from his head.

"How dare you speak the Old Tongue to me!" he screamed, but Lacius ignored him.

"The realm sits at a crossroads, young prince. You were smart to confess your sins to me and before God, but I am yet to know if you are wise, for a wise man will take what has transpired here today and learn from it. Tell me! Does your heart feel lighter?"

Warwick sat in the dark, struck speechless.

"*Zoareyns,*" came the command to obey in the Old Tongue.

"N-no," Warwick stammered.

"No?" The confessor's voice was shocked.

"No!" Warwick answered again, rising from the bench, heart pounding. "No, my heart does not feel lighter, if anything it is weighed down by the actions of others! Like a ship anchored at port with a tsunami coming, I am trapped when I know the best course of action is to strike out for sea. I cannot let the realm fall to pieces. People think me weak? I will show them my strength! The realm depends on me to take my father's crown. You hear me? Damn the Goldwoods or Lysander or any who would take up a sword for power—if Aethylios hear me, know me well. I am an agent of good, not greedy nor lustful. I will be the protector of our great empire!"

He burst forth from the confession booth. His eyes stung with the brightness of the single candle flame, but it did not stop him from tearing his way to the bolted door. He threw open the latch with a bang and tore from the room.

Blessed be the Nine. I will be weak no more!

LEAWYN VIII

The flags and banners of Clan Laehosha fell onto the Hearth. The battle ramparts and barricades took to the torch. Black smoke coiled into the sky. From the cover of the forest, Leawyn watched. Chieftain Hunta was taking his people elsewhere. The war's front was shifting.

She was not alone. Saralyn stood at her side, breaking off small bits of bread and offering them to her. Leawyn took them reluctantly, knowing she would need the strength. Behind them, the sharp crack of twigs and the rustling of branches told a familiar tale. Her followers were leaving too.

More rustling, footsteps. Leawyn and Saralyn turned to find Nayawyn approaching, a heavy sack slung over her shoulder. A bow and quiver were clutched tightly in either hand.

"I wanted to thank you, Old Bird," Nayawyn said. "For your hospitality... and for the glimmer of hope."

Leawyn nodded, her throat tightening, eyes stinging with

unshed tears. She parted her lips to speak but felt the crack in her voice before a single word could form. She swallowed it down, unwilling to appear weaker than she already felt.

Saralyn spoke for her. "You cannot be convinced to stay?"

Nayawyn looked from Saralyn to Leawyn, the weight of resignation settling heavily on her brow. "The war moves on. This land will return to nature. I cannot abandon my people."

"It's not abandonment," Saralyn answered sternly.

"Of course, Saralyn. We have known each other since we were children. I will pray for you under the light of the moon. I only ask, please, that you do not become lost to us as well."

Saralyn nodded. "As I pray for you. As I do for all our people."

The two women looked to one another, eyes stern, before flying into each other, locking into a strong embrace as kin does with kin.

"You will take care." Nayawyn smiled. "Watch over our people. And should the day come, whether in a week or in our next lifetime, I will see you again."

Saralyn stepped back, and Nayawyn turned to Leawyn.

"I wish I could have offered you more," she found the strength to say.

"You spared all our lives. The Outsiders will curse your name. If nothing else, Clan Laehosha will not forget. Thank you."

There was no embrace for Leawyn, only a nod of respect. Then Nayawyn hoisted her sack higher over her shoulder and set off toward the dismantling war camp, her bow and quiver rattling softly with each step.

Saralyn and Leawyn remained at the forest's edge, watching as more left their camp. One by one, they said their goodbyes, until at last, when the thinning herd had dwindled to only a handful of shadows, Leawyn turned to Saralyn, defeat heavy in her voice.

"You can go too, if you wish."

"The Hearth has not yet made that decision for me."

"I do not have a plan."

"A plan can be made for you. Trust by the rise of the moon tonight."

Leawyn sighed. "My clan are good people, but they are tired, and their hearts are heavy. My chieftain will not offer help."

The distant whinny of a horse briefly interrupted their conversation.

"He is your kin," Saralyn urged gently. "You must go and speak to him."

"Should I go, I am afraid I will become lost myself."

"Don't use that word," Saralyn said curtly. "We will never see them again."

Leawyn averted her gaze, unable to meet Saralyn's hardened expression. Instead, she turned toward the distant field, where a lone figure stood waiting for her.

"I wish you had told me sooner," Leawyn whispered. "Perhaps then I could have offered a plan—had the urge to move to action again."

"You are a wise old bird, Leawyn of Terrwoniwyn, you did not act because there was not yet a course. Like the bird flies south in winter or the moth emerges under the moon, the Hearth will speak when it is time to move. There was nothing to be done against the salt sea, anyway."

Leawyn wrinkled her brow, fixing her eyes on the white horse circling the figure in the field. "Tell me their names again, please. Before I go."

The wind rustled through the trees, setting the branches to whisper. Birds called to one another in the fading light. "There was my wife, Emmalin, and my daughter, Aya, lost forever to the shackles of the Salt Men."

"Thank you." Leawyn nodded. "I will do my best to honor them."

"Honor us all." And with a gentle nudge, Saralyn pushed Leawyn from the edge of the forest.

Her chieftain waited for her in a field of rustling grass, the reins of her stolen horse held loosely in his grasp. As she drew near, she watched his mouth fall open.

Finn, her lifelong friend and kin, looked at her as if she were a spirit.

"It is you…" he stammered.

"My chieftain," she said softly. But she did not look at him. Instead, she circled wide around him, her focus drawn to the stallion. The beast eyed her with wide, wild eyes. "Shh," she cooed, and placed a gentle hand upon his body. The horse jerked and stomped its feet, pulling on the reins. Finn held on for dear life, but Leawyn could see the weakness in his stance, the way his knees threatened to buckle.

He was looking at her as though he still thought her a ghost. "We thought you were dead."

"I felt dead… for a time."

Leawyn ran her fingers through the stallion's ghostly white mane, her touch light yet firm. The horse stomped once but relaxed beneath her hand.

"Leawyn, my dear friend, I just don't… I don't understand."

"Then ask your questions."

He studied her, brow furrowed, before dragging a hand across his forehead, wiping away sweat despite the cool breeze that swept through the field. With a sharp breath, he released the reins, letting them drop to the grass. "I don't know where to start. If it weren't for the horse reacting to you, I'd swear I was speaking to a spirit." The stallion snorted, tossing its head, testing the freedom Finn had reluctantly given. "Why don't you start with what happened that night? We woke to find you gone!"

There was anger in his tone, and at last, Leawyn met his gaze. The horse stood between them, a living barrier.

"I went to die, old friend," she said simply. "And instead, I was rescued."

Finn said nothing, his expression dark. The stallion shifted, eager to move, and Leawyn walked with him, her hand never leaving his back.

"I had grown tired, Finn. I am still tired, I suppose, of the same old thing. Day in and day out, week after week, year after year. Generations pass, and nothing changes. Only death. Our people are born, handed a bow or a sword, and marched to the front lines." She exhaled, patting the horse's flank. "It never ends. It's madness."

"We fight for survival," Finn countered.

"We fight for the illusion of survival," Leawyn corrected. "We do not change, Finn, and we are worse for it. How many generations have given their lives, and what do we have to show for it?"

"Do not dishonor the dead," Finn snapped.

"Do not dishonor the living," Leawyn fired back.

He kept pace with them, hobbling slightly, the weight of years hanging from his shoulders. He looked as if he had aged a decade in mere months.

"There is so much we don't understand about the Outsiders," she continued. "I know they are of many races. I do not yet understand them, but I understand what they want."

She glanced toward the horizon, where the rolling stretched into the horizon.

"Our land. Our people."

Finn flinched.

"We are lucky, believe it or not. Tucked away in our hills in the north of this great island, where the salt sea is just a story we tell our children. But there are other clans, Finn. Those who pull fish from the waters and live by the sea. And others come too… not bearing the flaming bird sigil of our current enemy, but still, they come. They take. And they carry away our kin to lands far stranger than we can imagine… or perhaps beneath the waves themselves."

"Leawyn, your clan needs you. Our time on the front is over. Each clan has its own responsibilities to this land. Though I curse those who take our people, that is not our fight. We cannot fight on two fronts; we cannot fight the salt sea. But what we can do is fight for our home, for our people, for our family."

"You don't understand. No one seems to understand." She shook her head. "Again, we refuse to change." She exhaled sharply, gripping the stallion's mane. "You didn't see them, Finn. But I did. When I rode into battle on this very horse, I saw the Outsiders wield weapons that roared with thunder, silver barrels flashing in the sun. They struck down Clan Laehosha with them. And if not for my guidance, none of them would have lived to see another day."

Finn stared at her across the horse's back. The stallion, sensing the tension, picked up its pace, leading them away from the departing battle encampment and toward the distant tree line.

"Listen to yourself, woman. You have gone mad."

"You have spoken with the chieftain of Laehosha, haven't you?"

He said nothing.

"Then you know my words are true."

"I do not withdraw my statement. Your actions were brave, yes, but also mad. I fear your mind may be slipping, old friend." He sighed. "Please, come home, be with your family and kin. Come home to Arianwyn and Layita while there is still time."

Leawyn froze in her tracks, gripping the reins of the stallion with a steeled fist. The horse came to an abrupt halt, whipping its head from side to side, but she held firm. "What do you mean?"

Finn's lower lip quivered. "Little Layita has grown increasingly ill. She has not shaken a cold since the night you left. I fear her days are numbered. It is time you came home. If what this clan says of your actions is true, then you have already won a great victory for our people. Waste no more time. Be with your family while you still have them."

Leawyn planted her feet firmly on the ground as the stallion jerked wildly against the reins. The beast tossed its head, nostrils flaring, eyes locked on the shadowed edge of the forest only a few paces away. Leawyn refused to let go, however.

"Leawyn, this is the duty given to our people. We are to fight for our land. And in turn, we are honored for it. We are chosen to rest beneath the soil in the cold bogs, so that one day, when illness and war and the Outsiders are all gone, we may rise again. By the Hearthsea, they burn their own dead!"

Finn's voice wavered, nearly breathless. "I know the loss of your second son was more than any mother should bear, but we will be victorious... in the long run. In the grand scheme of things, these battles, this war... they will be nothing more than forgotten memories when we all rise together."

Finn looked to her, eyes pleading. All color drained from his face. "Now please, come home, comfort your little granddaughter. She is afraid. I do not want her to go into the Hearth without you."

Her stallion reared back, kicking its hind legs into the air. Finn stumbled away, startled, but Leawyn did not flinch. She only tightened her grip as her horse looked to the treeline. With new determination, it dug in its hooves and pulled toward the forest. Leawyn, no more than an old woman, did not have the strength to stop such a creature. She dug in her heels where she could, but the stallion barely noticed, pulling her along.

Finn followed, keeping a wide berth from the reach of the horse's hooves. "Leawyn! This is madness!" he cried. "Please!"

They were almost inside the forest.

"I... I..." Leawyn looked down at her free hand, watching it tremble. Words wouldn't come. Her mind was clouded, spinning. The horse wouldn't stop moving.

They stepped over a fallen log, dipping beneath the first set of branches. Finn lagged behind, struggling to keep pace. She stumbled over a stone, nearly falling, but with a surge of strength that surprised even herself, she placed both hands on the beast's back and hoisted herself onto him.

The stallion halted.

Facing the dark shadows of the forest floor, it lowered its head and whinnied softly, but it yielded. Leawyn sat still, breath unsteady, before gently taking hold of the reins. She pulled, commanding the horse to turn, and slowly, it obeyed.

When they faced Finn, she saw the way he stared up at her, mouth slightly open, knees trembling beneath his weight. The deep lines on his face were etched in shadow against the sun's golden light.

His voice, rough with age and battle, barely carried across the distance between them. "You look like one of them."

A jolt of fear and fury snapped through her. Leawyn sat straighter on the stallion's back as she realized what he meant. He wasn't speaking of the Outsiders.

"I have treated with them, you know."

The look upon Finn's face did not falter. He already thought her truly mad.

"When I went into the forest to die, one found me. They brought me to their camp, nursed me back to health. They saved me, Finn. The other natives of this land, and we treat them like outsiders all the same."

"Leawyn…" His voice cracked, weak and worn. No more words followed, only a deep, exhausted sigh as he buried his face in his hands.

"They spoke no different than you," she continued. "Or the chieftain of Laehosha or even the War Maker. At least he has kept some unity across our land. If there is anything I have learned in all my years on the Isle of Fláimir, it is that we are born of stubbornness. Perhaps we have to be to survive. To refuse to be destroyed by so many threats. Like stone, like the Hearth itself, we remain defiant. A blessing… and a curse."

"Do not curse our land!" Finn spat. His frail hands curled into fists before he threw them skyward with a bark of bitter laughter. "If anyone has fallen to a curse, damn it, I say it is you! You have lost your way. Your mind, even. You speak as though the end times are upon us." He shook his head, laughing again, but it was empty, weary. "Perhaps you *did* die and rise again. Bah! Or more likely, you've become an old fool, driven mad by grief, by loss… the kind of woman who would turn her back on her own dying kin!"

Leawyn's breath quickened, rising to match the stallion's beneath her. "There is no easy decision here." She wiped pooling tears from her eyes. She thought of Saralyn's lost family. Of her new clan. Of their chance, however slim, at change.

"Damn you, woman! There *is* an easy decision!" Finn's voice cracked like a whip. "Take your victory and push fate no further! Nurse your granddaughter back to health. Give her a chance at life. Or at the very least, be there for her before she slips into the long sleep."

A tear streaked down Leawyn's cheek. The horse snorted.

"Perhaps… perhaps you are right." She blinked and looked off into the far distance. The war camp of Clan Laehosha was disappearing. The site of her great victory would be nothing more than another scar, another wound that nature would heal in time.

"Of course I am, Leawyn," Finn pressed. "It is the right thing to do. Now, come down from that horse. You know the superstitions of riding an animal. Not with the centaurs so close."

Lightning again struck her veins. For a moment, she feared she had been struck by one of the Outsiders' silver weapons. "What did you say?"

She heard all the breath go out of him. "You mad woman! Whatever you did, whatever you think may have happened between you and them, it has only provoked them! They have been closer than usual. They are *watching* our clan. And unless I am mistaken, they have tracked *me* here."

Leawyn's eyes fell to the forest floor, darting back and forth.

"Oh no, no, no, do not fall prey to my words. Our kind live separate for a reason. Do not lead your madness to—"

But she cut him off. "Thank you, Chieftain, for making the journey here, and for bringing me word of my family. But it is with a heavy heart that I must decline to return home. There are people who count on me now, people willing to fight and die for all of us. For *our* land."

She exhaled, steadying herself. "I am old… close to death. I *should* have died that night. The centaurs, the good moon, fate itself—call it whatever you will, but something gave me a second chance. Maybe I *am* mad, but I think true madness would be returning home and pretending none of this happened." She swallowed hard. "I'm sorry, Chieftain. I cannot go with you."

Finn stood there, silent for a long moment, his weathered face unreadable. "It is not me you need to be sorry for."

"Try to explain to her... to both of them... what it is I am trying to do."

"Sure, I'll do my best," Finn said quietly. "And when the time comes... I will send her into the bog myself." Tears streaked his cheeks, but he said nothing more. He simply turned and walked back into the open field to return home without her.

Leawyn remained in the forest. Her shoulders trembled, and then, at last, she broke. Her sobs spilled freely into the silence. The stallion beneath her shifted, snorting softly, but did not move away. It stood still, letting her grief fall upon its ghost-white coat like rain.

She stayed there until the sun bled into the horizon, until the crescent moon above glowed with the light of the Hearth. Her tears had dried, but her heart remained heavy. At last, she turned her horse back across the field. The sky burned with streaks of red, orange, and deep blue, while firebugs flickered along the grass stalks, lighting her path home. When she reached the hill by the tree line, her people were waiting.

The war camp of Clan Laehosha was gone, packed up and moved west. All that remained were her people, fewer than forty souls, standing together in the dying light.

She stopped before them, gazing up at their expectant faces. The stallion whinnied, the only sound in the hush of twilight. She let the world speak first: the birds, the crickets, the whisper of wind through the grass. She listened to the voice of the Hearth itself.

Then, and only then, did she speak.

"Gather your things," Leawyn said. "We are going west."

Bancroft IV

The ring was cold against Bancroft's skin. He turned it over in his hands, its black metal unknown to any smith or craftsmen, remaining icy even in the grip of his pudgy hands.

Was it like this for you in the end? Silent and cool, just like the ring?

He tightened his hold, his knuckles blanching. He closed his eyes and tried to imagine his brother's final moments. The shouts of valor, the taste of blood, the blare of trumpets, and the beat of drums. But no visions of knights with shining swords came to him, nor of familial banners snapping in the wind. Instead, he saw only the Opal Throne, surrounded by lords and ladies, their whispers needling his ears.

Land grants... taxes and levies... marriage pacts...

Wrapped in a regal silk cloak, his kingly body shuddered.

His eyes shot open as a stench took hold of him. He wrinkled his nose as he stared down upon the black ring. The smell had lingered day and night, ever since a priest had given him the ring the day before, alongside his brother's corpse.

"Khalidron Aeither."

He said the words aloud as his fat finger traced the engraved runes along the ring's surface.

The words were ancient, just like the ring. It was the oldest of family heirlooms, one that predated the Crown of the Nine, Empyrean Flame, and even the Crown of Knox.

He pondered whether the legends were true. The ring had been in their family for over a millennium, since long before the House of Hieronymus had ever come to this land—even before the Makkans and the fall of the Lyonnian Empire. Back then, his bloodline was nothing more than small-time merchants, their fortunes tied to the trade winds.

"Khalidron Aeither," he whispered again. "A covenant of fire."

He lifted the ring into a shaft of sunlight streaming through the window, watching the light dance across its engraved surface. Veins of a red mineral pulsed within the dark metal.

You've seen nothing but our rise... I pray you do not witness our fall.

"Are you ready, Your Imperial Majesty?"

Bancroft startled, nearly dropping the black ring as Strammond appeared in the doorway. He turned to his old friend, seated alone in his family's private dining hall. The table lay strewn with half-rummaged plates of breakfast foods, though his family had long since departed, each coming and going at different hours of the day. Warwick and Lysander refused to break bread together, even in the name of the Nine.

"Can any man be prepared to say goodbye to his kin?"

"No, Your Grace," Strammond answered, his voice low but steady. "I suppose not."

"I have always thought you as a man of wise counsel, Strammond." Bancroft threw down a crumpled napkin. He tried to rise, but his body betrayed him. His heart *thumped, thumped, thumped* in his chest. Strammond moved calmly to his side.

514

"My emperor?" He slid a gentle arm under Bancroft's own.

"My brother, Thane… now there was a man truly ready to meet death face-to-face, and bravely, I might add. And he did so in the end, of that I am certain."

Strammond helped hoist Bancroft to his feet. They took a few unsteady steps toward the door when Bancroft wavered.

"Have the corridors been cleared?"

"Yes, Your Grace. I've stationed my best men at every corner. You will not be disturbed."

"Good. Then let us make haste. I do not wish to grow so weak that I cannot rise from the mountain's depths."

"I would never let that happen."

They reached the main foyer of the imperial family's private wing of the castle. They descended slowly down a grand oaken staircase, the only one of its kind in a castle of white stone. Above them, the foyer chamber soared to a pitched roof adorned with glass panels like the world's grandest greenhouse. Higher still, beyond the glass, the castle's towers rose, blotting out even the peak of Mount Ness.

Bancroft paused to look up. Strammond stopped beside him, his boots scuffing against the polished wood. The private towers above were a haphazard sprawl of stone and glass, connected by covered archways and crooked turrets jutting at odd angles. He wondered if Lysander or Warwick was up there now, lost in the patchwork of grandeur and disorder, or if they would do their duties, not as princes, but as sons for once…

"Your Grace? Do you require assistance? Shall I fetch you a fainting couch? Or perhaps a chair?"

Bancroft let out a breathy laugh as he wobbled into the adjoining passageway. "Strammond, always testing my judgment. We both know I'm far too fat to be carried, especially through those narrow, dark tunnels."

He managed a smile, but Strammond's expression remained solemn. "I would do anything for you, my lord. As would any man of the Demonbreun."

"I appreciate that… truly." Bancroft nodded, but at the same time, he withdrew his arm, finding the strength to stand on his own as they descended into the castle's public halls.

"You've always been so proud." Strammond forced a half smile. "You'd think by now I would have learned to laugh at your jokes."

"You are a stern man, ah!" Bancroft raised an arm to his forehead, winking. "I could never…"

"You could never?"

"Serve in your order. The Demonbreun. The strict hours and training. The selfless dedication. No, my good man, I was born to be a fat emperor, tended to by better men, Aethylios willing."

Strammond's half smile lingered. "The order is not so hard, especially when the privilege is to serve you and the imperial family."

"Aye, and I half robbed you of that duty."

Strammond's nose wrinkled. "Regrettable, yes. I would have liked the chance to mold your boys, not those two… Wulford and Dyrebane."

"They are good men. Strange… but good men." Bancroft panted.

"Esterian. From the fringes of your realm. I don't like them."

"There was a time when my family was considered foreign too. There are still those in this realm who see us that way."

Strammond frowned, placing a careful hand on the emperor's shoulder as they approached a turn in the hallway. The castle was abuzz with activity as lords and ladies of every corner of the realm filled every guest room available, though true to Strammond's word, his guards maintained a carefully cleared path to the mountain tunnels. Bancroft moved largely undisturbed, offering only a few weary hand waves and strained smiles to distant lords.

"Try not to worry about those who still doubt your bloodline," Strammond cautioned. "Take refuge in the support of all the lords and ladies who come to pay tribute to the House of Hieronymus."

"Ah, that is easy to say when these low lords do not control the succession of the crown."

"Your Grace, you worry too much, and too often, I fear."

"An emperor who forgets his subjects is the one who loses his head, Strammond."

"And as I said, I would never let that happen, Your Majesty."

Their voices echoed faintly as they passed the threshold of the modern castle. On the heels of loyalty and its dangers, they stared down into a dark opening. The grand white stone gave way to rough-hewn rock, marble veins thinning like blood drawn too long from the heart. Beneath their boots, polished floors dulled, then vanished altogether, swallowed by jagged gray. Ornate sconces became iron brackets. Gilded moldings gave way to chisel marks, old and uneven, carved by hands that did not know symmetry.

Following the ancient, sloping path, they descended into the bitter, still air. Dampness clung to the walls, beading like sweat on stone skin. A sour smell drifted up from the deep, faintly metallic, like rain on rust. "The mountain remembers." Bancroft recalled the saying, and here in the dark, that felt true.

They passed through a gate of crude granite, its arch hunched and timeworn, not built by the same civilization that crowned the heights above. Pillars emerged, broken and eroded by the eons, their glyphs and art eroded to near-nothing. Strange grooves too curled along the walls, neither decorative nor natural. Tunnels branched like roots. Some led nowhere. Some were sealed with stone darker than the rest, like tombs that did not want to be disturbed. This was the base of their power. Upon the mountain and their pedestal of granite, and so much of it was unknown to them.

"Much can be said, Strammond, of where loyalty lies," he muttered, his voice soft as the dust underfoot. "It is amazing how quickly it can shift... A shame it's not like the mountain. Solid, and *eternal*."

But even as he said it, his boots struck worn grooves in the stone and he knew it was a lie. The mountain was ancient, her rock gnarled and chiseled away by hands even more ancient than the Makkans or the Lyonnians. Before fire came to this land.

"The Demonbreun serve the Nine. We serve God's chosen sovereign. You and your family. Never doubt that, my lord. Never."

"I don't doubt you, old friend. I never have. But your order follows the crown, not my family."

Strammond halted midstep, his heels digging into the worn stone of the staircase, but Bancroft did not notice. He focused on keeping his balance, on reaching his brother.

"Should even the Archon of Incendrium, the holy leader of our faith, order the Demonbreun against you, know I and many more of our guard would march to war for you and your blood. Call me a traitor then, my lord."

The weight of Strammond's words hung between them as they reached the base of the ancient stairs. His heretical oath seemed to echo in the mountain's hollow core, fading much too slowly into silence. Following the dark path, they rounded a bend in the rock, coming before the entrance of an ancient mine shaft, its maw gated by a curtain of black. The air here was heavy, tasting of damp stone and iron, compressed by the low stone ceiling a finger's width from their heads. Above, countless tons of stone and timber, the weight of bloated lords and silk-clad ladies, and the countless white spires that soared into the clouds—all of it resting here on the shoulder of the mountain. And yet still the patch stretched farther down, a gaping scraggle-tooth crevice that led down into the dark, straight into the depths of the Hearth itself.

This is where the first Priest of the Nine met them.

"Your Imperial Majesty… and knight… Sir Strammond of the Demonbreun…"

A bald-headed man in a flowing red robe greeted them, a single torch burning in his hand.

Strammond tightened his grip on Bancroft's arm, gently signaling him to stop. Beneath a castle teeming with thousands of lords and ladies, deep among the miles of dark tunnels, with no protection but the wavering torchlight, Strammond's breath caught. "Good sir, might I inquire what you are doing here? These corridors should be off-limits…"

The priest bowed, his gaze shifting between Strammond and Bancroft. "Your Grace, we tend to the body. I assure you, your brother lies safe under our watch."

Bancroft smiled, even as a draft washed over them from the deep. "All is well. I thank you for your dedication. Not only to my brother but to our faith as well. The Nine bless you."

"And may the Miracles bless you as well." The priest bowed again. "May I bestow upon you the last flame? A light of our divine Providence?" The priest extended an arm, gesturing for Bancroft to take the torch.

It took him by surprise. "Oh my good priest, I couldn't... I could not ask a man to stay in the dark. Strammond will fetch a lantern..."

"Your Majesty, I have sworn my soul to Aethylios and his flame. I am never in the dark, not truly."

Bancroft looked to Strammond, but he only shrugged and took the torch. "Thank you. Reside here so that no one else is to follow us in, lest they are of the imperial family."

The priest nodded. Strammond took a step forward, holding the torch to illuminate the mine shaft. It did little to dispel the dark. Instead, it made the black curtain peering upward at them from ancient, chiseled stone all the more intimidating. Against his better judgment, the emperor went first.

Bancroft hunched low, entering the sloping passage into the old mine shaft. The Makkans had widened and smoothed these tunnels when they built the castle, but even so, Bancroft was a large man, forcing them to proceed single file. Strammond followed closely behind, his hand a steady weight on Bancroft's back.

"Oh! And, Your Majesty," the priest called after them, his voice echoing down the stone corridor. "your brother has been at rest for many months now. I trust you understand... there will be a smell."

Bancroft froze, half-bent in the dark, his eyes fixed on the distant torchlight flickering at the end of the tunnel. His heart thumped—*thump, thump, thump*—growing louder, the sound trapped within the stone.

"Thank you, Brother. The emperor understands his late brother's circumstances well."

Bancroft swallowed, forcing his feet forward. Though large and lumbering, he moved with surprising speed through the tight corridor. As they reached the next torch, the tunnel widened, giving way to a natural crevice beneath the mountain.

The room opened into a grand dark canyon, its shadowy expanse stretching for unknown miles deep under Mount Ness. Despite many expeditions, no one knew how deep the tunnels truly went.

"To your right, Your Majesty." Strammond gently tapped him on his shoulder.

Bancroft was slow to move. He kept his gaze fixed upward, staring at the jagged rock formations that loomed overhead. Some reached only a few feet above his head, while others disappeared into the endless black above.

Few torches lined the way here. The air was cold and damp, and voices and sounds carried for miles, limited by nothing less than the sounds of the shifting rock deep beneath their feet. Distant whispers, grumblings, even words, perhaps lost to time, forever echoing in the dark, tickled his ears. One could easily go mad down here, and despite having lived nearly his entire life within the castle, only a few times had he ever ventured, or been *permitted* to venture, down into the subterranean labyrinth that lay below the castle. It was so deep, unexplored... Bancroft tried not to think of the implications. High Ness was meant to be impregnable, but here, deep below the imperial court, lay a whole network of tunnels disappearing deep into the unknown, where perhaps a whole army of Makkans still remained, breeding in the dark, stealing from their vast food stores, waiting for the right day to rise up and retake their castle. He knew the wives' tales spoken by the kitchen staff whenever a pot of flour would go missing... It was not uncommon for the serving staff to become lost in the tunnels.

Creeping through the chasm, their footsteps scraped against the stone, echoing deep into the dark. They passed vast rooms, some lined with heaps and heaps of grain, others lingering with the smell of smoked meats. Others still were lined with bottles and vats, filled to the brim with beer, ale, wine, and spirits. These were the vaults of High Ness, the true power of her seat. During a time of siege or war, the castle could eat for years while foreign armies withered on the single mountain road... But now the entire realm gathered within their walls. There were thousands of mouths to feed every single day. Their food stores would not last forever.

Directly ahead, the roof of the crevice rose once more, pressing dangerously close to their heads as they made their way through the narrowing passage. Two narrow points of light emerged, and at the end of the crevice, they came to a small room carved entirely from stone. Two priests of the Nine stood guard outside, each holding a flickering torch.

"Your Grace," they said in tandem and respectfully bowed. Their voices carried into the dark.

"Thank you both," Bancroft said softly, nodding in acknowledgment. He turned to Strammond. "I believe I will be fine inside alone. Allow me this moment to grieve in private."

Strammond raised an eyebrow, but after a beat, he reluctantly stepped aside. "I will wait with these holy men. I will come at your call."

Bancroft nodded to him, then ducked through the low, crudely cut doorway of stone. As he entered the small crypt, the air grew colder. There, upon a stone slab, lay his brother, mummified in cloth, and at his side, a dark figure still as death itself waited in the shadows.

"Your Grace," said the shadow.

Bancroft blinked, unsure of how to proceed.

"It is most kind of you... to come and see him," the figure continued.

"Elizabeth." He sighed. She wore her mourner's outfit, black as night even here.

She said nothing, only cradling her deceased husband's bandaged arm.

"I have come to pay my respects."

"That is most kind." The shade gently placed Thane's arm into a resting position over his chest. The shadow then hovered silently beside the body. From beneath the veil, he could see the faint glint of her blue eyes from the torchlight outside the room.

Footsteps came from the hall, loud and clumsy. Bancroft and Elizabeth both looked, and there within the doorway, Warwick appeared with a lantern. He froze at the sight of his father, his gaze shifting uneasily between Bancroft and the shadowed figure beside Thane's body.

"S-sorry, Father," Warwick stammered. "I... I will return." His words stumbled from his lips, and before Bancroft could respond, Warwick spun on his heels and fled, the sound of his footsteps fading rapidly into the corridor beyond.

"My boy." Bancroft tried to laugh, but the sound was hollow. "I wish Thane could have taught him a thing or two."

The shadow hovered, silent. Bancroft could feel the scowl from beneath Elizabeth's veil.

"Do not worry, Your Grace, you have denied a private audience with me for months. Or am I the dead one, cursed to drift in silence, my own kin lost to me?" she spat. "Never mind, you do not bother to court the dead. I will leave you to him now, for why should death be any different for us? I learned very long ago how to be apart from him." And before Bancroft could even begin to respond, the shadow flew from his brother's side, flying through the narrow doorway as if to chase after Warwick.

Yet he was not truly alone.

He walked slowly to the stone slab, his eyes adjusting in the low light to the pile of bandages that had once been his brother. The stench of lime hung heavy in the air, thick and sour. A breeze, whipped up somewhere deep within the mountain's core, wafted slowly over his brother, rustling the bandages. Even in death, Thane refused to be still.

He sat down beside the slab, his hand hesitating before resting on the body. The texture was wrong. The bandages were stale, almost crunchy to the touch. As he shifted his weight, the sound of his brother's body breaking beneath the pressure sickened him. He jerked his hand away, staring down at the malformed, crumpled heap that had once been his brother. The greatest living symbol of Hieronymus power, now reduced to this.

"I'm sorry, Thane," he whispered as he took out his ring. The dark, metallic object seemed to belong here, its red mineral veins faintly glowing in the dimness.

He wanted to place it back upon his brother. The public spectacle that was coming, done for the good of the realm because Thane always served the realm's best interests, would be to burn it, reducing it to flame and ash to satisfy the lords and ladies.

He sniffed and took a hold of his brother's hand. He clenched it, never minding the crunching sound from beneath the bandages. *My brother!* He wanted to wail, but the words wouldn't come. Instead, he took the dark ring and tried to slide it onto Thane's finger, but the corpse was so stale and decayed that he feared forcing it. With a heavy sigh, he chose to gently return his brother's hand to rest over his chest.

"I'm so sorry, Thane," he whimpered. "You should have been emperor."

"Father?" came the voice behind him.

Bancroft turned slowly to find Lysander standing in the dim doorway. His son, *a man now*, stood in the thin light, his face heavy with shadow and beard.

"My boy," Bancroft whispered, tears slipping freely down his cheeks. He turned back to where his hand had sunk into the corpse of his brother.

Lysander moved quickly to his side.

"Look at what those savages did to him."

Lysander placed a gentle hand on his father's back. "He was a great man. Filled with duty and honor. Sacrifice was no stranger to him."

Bancroft exhaled. "Our family is doomed for sacrifice, my boy. It's in our blood."

"Father..."

But Bancroft shushed him, raising his hand from Thane's chest as a fine dust of calcified remains drifted from his fingers. "I know. It's in poor taste to dishonor his sacrifice before him."

"The months have dragged on. And it is a long, long way to the front lines from here." Lysander eyed his father's hand warily, then took it, brushing away the last of the decay.

"My boy," Bancroft muttered.

"Yes, Father?"

Withdrawing his hand, Bancroft reached into his pocket and pulled out the dark ring. He held it up in the thin light, a dark circle, crisscrossed with veins of deep red. "This was his. Bestowed upon him by my grandfather before he passed."

"What is it?"

"The Seal of Oxcál."

Lysander studied the object. "I've never heard of it."

Bancroft grunted. "A lesser-known family heirloom, but no less important. It is older than this castle, older than the Makkans, older even than the Lyonnians. Its true origins are lost to time, but its journey to us is not. It comes from our original homeland... at a meager castle in Oxcál in the east, before Aethylios spread his light and the Lyonnian inquisitions chased us here. This ring has only known our rise, and now, I must entrust it to you."

Lysander's dark eyes widened. "Father... once Warwick hears of this... that I took another family heirloom from him—"

"Nonsense," Bancroft cut him off. "Warwick will have the crown. Besides, this ring is not truly for you." He took Lysander's hand, uncurled his fingers, and placed the ring in his palm. "It belongs to Catelyn."

Lysander didn't look convinced. "Father, not even a peasant woman would want a ring so ugly."

"Her father wore it her whole life. She will recognize it. The ring will mean more to her than gold or jewels."

Nodding, Lysander closed his fist around the ring. "So you mean it? I am to have her hand?"

"Yes, and it must be soon. Warwick will hate you for it, but I hope only for a time. We must unify the family... and soon. Catelyn will cherish it, and I pray..." Bancroft's voice wavered. He could picture Thane standing beside him, arms crossed and his eyes narrowed. He gulped. "... that Elizabeth will find peace."

"I will do it, Father. I will marry Catelyn."

Bancroft rose from the stone slab, pulling his son close. He kissed Lysander on the forehead, fresh tears shimmering in his eyes. "I cannot believe it... Soon, Aethylios willing, I will be a granddad!"

Lysander embraced him. "I am grateful, Father. I am glad we could do this before my uncle. It feels right... that he should be present when the decision was made."

Bancroft and Lysander pulled apart, turning to look back upon the mummified corpse. "Indeed," Bancroft whispered, kissing his hand and gently placing it on Thane's bandaged face. "He would have been proud."

Lysander's voice came low. "I wish I could have known him better."

"That is the sentiment of every lord and lady within the realm." Bancroft sighed.

"Such sacrifice bears a legacy, Father. I hear there is already talk of a grand monument to him by the lords. Not here, in High Ness, but in Aberness, and in other public squares throughout the realm. What he died for... it will not be forgotten."

"Forgotten..." Bancroft echoed. His hand rose to Lysander's face, fingers threading through his son's dark curls. He felt the bristle of his beard, the strength in his jaw. Dark eyes. *Lyonnian* eyes.

Not blue, like the Kaesnfolk, or Warwick's...

"Father?" Lysander steadied him as Bancroft began to sway. "Are you unwell?"

"I fear much has been forgotten." He looked away from his son, his gaze drifting to the faint torchlight beyond the chamber. "Tell me, has there been any word from Lord Faelwood?. He is the only Elector yet to arrive at court."

"Not that I can recall."

"I see..." Bancroft's head began to swim. Suddenly, the stench was back and it clawed at his senses. He broke into a coughing fit and doubled over.

Strammond came running as Lysander yelped. Together, they steadied him as he was dragged from the chamber.

"No, no, no," Bancroft protested, twisting in their grasp. His brother's corpse receded into the dark, swallowed by the shadows beyond the doorway. "No! It isn't right. A man shouldn't be left in the dark. We need to burn him! Please!" Bancroft roared as his lungs heaved. "He must burn! He needs to burn!"

JAE IX

A cool breeze wafted through the manse, heralding the close of summer. Soon, harvest would be upon them.

Jae stood in the courtyard, enjoying the cool evening air. Hex had just retired for the evening. Together with Petra, they had tended to the gardens, pruning leaves and branches to prepare the lawn and flowers for the changing seasons. It had been a long day, but the sun's heat had lessened. Clouds drifted slowly inland from the ocean, while flocks of birds took to the sky, heading south. Their raucous squawks filled the air, a song of a hundred thousand—maybe even millions—moving with the clouds to lands unknown.

Jae spread his arms out, gazing up at the night sky and watching their silent silhouettes cross the glare of the moon. He closed his eyes, imagining he was up there with them, feeling the wind brush against his face. He could turn and dive, summersault and glide wherever he wanted. He could even turn south, into the vast expanse of untamed land where rules and responsibilities ceased to exist—only wild beasts, their primal instincts, and their freedom. But like a wild creature driven by hunger, his stomach growled, and the wind suddenly died under his wings, and he plummeted all the way back to the house of Aeksilor.

"Dark wings," he muttered, kicking at the grass under his feet. "Or whatever bullshit they call it." He turned from the moon, though its radiance was hard to escape. He moved down the side path of the manse to the slave quarters, ignoring the glow of the city underneath him. Inside, he nodded to Petra as she emerged from the bathroom, her hair damp and wrapped in a makeshift towel.

"Any good food today?"

"For me, nay. But Old Berona always has something saved for you, her little man." She smirked.

Jae smiled as she passed, rubbing his stomach, and quickly ascended the hidden stairway into the kitchen. He emerged with a smile, but the old mother was nowhere to be found. Disappointed, he left the kitchen and entered the dining hall, which was equally dark and empty. He sighed, his stomach growling in protest. He had barely eaten today.

"Is everything not to your satisfaction?"

He froze, his blood running cold. He stood precariously, balancing on one foot, the other half-extended back toward the kitchen.

"M-master?" he called out.

"Do I mean so little to you that you cannot meet my eyes, *boy*?" His words came slurred. His good master was uncharacteristically drunk.

"My good lord?" Jae asked again. He took a step back into the dining hall. A dark shadow at the end of the table finally registered with his eyes.

"Am I meant to be served or not!"

A fist slammed clumsily against the table. Jae heard the clink of porcelain in the darkness. Without hesitation, he quickly walked to the far wall, locating a gallon of wine before making his way to his master. Aeksilor leaned back in his chair as if the weight of his head were too much to bear. An empty chalice lay before him alongside a half-eaten meal.

"I apologize for my rudeness, Good Master. Of course, I will serve you."

"You will?" He hiccupped. "My every wish? Where is my wife? Where are my children? They need to hear this! I am the proud lord of this city! An ancient line of a thousand years! But I'm so glad you will serve me…" He hiccupped again. "As if you even had a choice."

Jae poured the wine and took a step back.

"You think I'm a weak fool? Bah! I wield more power than you can imagine! At my height, I had thousands of slaves—tens of thousands! My manse bustled with their busy hands. And in my fields, toiling away like the good little boys, girls, and monsters they were. And godly—oh yes, I was very godly, for the Sun God blessed me well. By God!" Aeksilor cried out, leaning forward onto the table.

Jae took a step back, struck by the raw emotion in his voice.

"… If my ancestors could see me now—drunk and acting a fool! They were real men. We had a hundred thousand slaves, all to the east of us. Back when the Sorrows were less sorrowful, and the beastfolk knew to fear us. Then those damn Makkans came, and then the Ash Fall… and now everyone is dead!" A sob escaped his lips.

"And soon you will be too."

Static filled the air. Dry lightning crackled in the background. Had Jae said that, or had the good master?

Jae's grip on the jug of wine tightened. Tears filled his eyes, his stomach swam with pit vipers. His muscles, ripe with the raw power of a man entering his prime, constricted uncontrollably. The night was so dark, so quiet. Jae felt anything could happen.

"Water."

Water. The spray of the ocean. The rhythmic tumble of the waves. His mother, face obscured by the sun.

"Water."

Coco, his pet coconut crab. She slept with him in a hammock and followed him everywhere—in the jungle, across the sand. His little sister laughed as Coco chased a small hermit crab. His big brothers... what were their names?

"Water!" Aeksilor slammed his goblet down, and Jae heard the wine splatter on the floor. The ocean receded as Jae quickly grabbed the jug of water. He poured.

"Blessed be," his master cried, drinking deeply from the elixir of life. "A good master should not need to drink like this. Oh, what a lowly life it is now. The days when I had proper help—I had a servant for every whimsical need. Now look at me... how cowardly and small I have grown..."

The good master leaned forward against the table, spittle dripping from his chin. Jae lost his appetite then and there. He set down the water jug, turning to leave.

"Agh! And have you been dismissed!" Aeksilor cried out. "Nay! I think not!"

Jae froze again. A good thing, for his blood boiled.

"Aye, boy? Have you eaten today?" Cato whistled as if to summon a dog. "Boy! Boy? Are you there? Come here, boy!"

He patted his thigh, whistling as if for a dog. Jae took a slow step forward, the water jug trembling in his hands.

"Ah, so you can listen. What a good boy, though you did not come on the first command." Aeksilor tsked. "But what can be said? You are not a dog? No! You are a moth!"

A bolt of lightning arced over the ocean, casting a sudden, fleeting glow across the dining hall. "A lowly moth! A foul creature." Aeksilor shook his head. "Attracted to the light, only to die."

A single tear rolled down Jae's cheek.

"... but I am a good master..." Aeksilor choked through a sob. "So I feed everyone. Now come here and eat, boy. Take your fill. Grow strong and healthy under the sigil of House Aeksilor."

Aeksilor fumbled for the plate before him. He grabbed it and set it loudly upon the floor. "Come, boy, eat."

Jae did not move. He started to cry.

"EAT!"

He did as he was bid. He got down onto his knees and crawled over to Aeksilor's feet. Before him lay a plate of half-eaten food. "Good... good..." the master muttered, stroking Jae's head from above. Jae lowered his face to the floor and began to eat.

"That's right, lick the plate clean..."

Jae did as commanded, licking his tongue across the porcelain.

"Oh! You remind me of this cat I used to own. A sweet thing. Always drinking wine from my cup... What was her name? Mimi? Or was that your name?" Aeksilor hiccuped. "It was something ridiculous, foreign..."

Cato suddenly slumped heavily against the table. Jae slowly rose from the floor, trembling. His master only muttered incoherently, clanking his empty chalice against the table. Jae went to fetch more water, watching Cato chug before his head fell flat against the table. He turned to leave, when Cato called to him halfway out the door.

"Boy! I remember now..." he pointed an unsteady finger at him. "Your name isn't the Wilted Moth or the Bull Sssslayer," he slurred dismissively. "It was Jae... *Jae'eli.* An uncivilized name from an uncivilized island. I'm glad I took your name. I did you a favor!" Aeksilor tried to lift his head but managed only another wet hiccup. Wine dribbled down his chin as he spoke. "You're much better off here—much happier! And I'll never give it back either. Never!" He jabbed the air clumsily. "It's mine! Belongs to... to the House of Aeksilor!"

His words began to run together. "You'll never repay me for what I've done... And don't think I haven't started to piece it together..." A giggle escaped him as his cheek pressed against the table. "The True Moth... I know who you are..." His eyes rolled back. "I know..." Then, with a heavy thud, his head struck the mahogany surface. Within moments, loud snores filled the silence. Jae seized the opportunity to bolt from the room.

He burst into the kitchen, slamming the door behind him. The tide had come in, and there was no stopping it. He bent over, leaning onto his knees, and sobbed. Wet crumbs still clung to his mouth as he doubled over, his cries escaping into the night sky. Great teardrops fell from his eyes. He watched them fall to the floor and glisten against the moon.

"Death!" he called out. He could see the moon through the reflection of his tears. "Take me!" To his surprise, the moon answered.

"No."

Startled, he jolted upright, tears still pouring down his cheeks. A dark shadow stood in the corner.

"Old Mother?" he cried out.

She came forward and wrapped herself around him. He broke into loud sobs. He fell to his knees and the old mother came with him. She held him tightly there on the kitchen floor as he cried into her. Soon, her own warm tears joined his.

They held each other, rocking back and forth—a lifetime gone to servitude, another young life chained and shackled. They cried for their mothers and fathers, their grips tightening on one another beneath a beam of moonlight streaming through the window. A few shadows darted past them, but he was oblivious. In Old Berona's arms, he was back in his own mother's arms at a time when Coco crawled across the sand, eager to snatch the strips of grilled pork from his hands. The sound of his sister's laughter filled his ears, but it quickly morphed into her cries. He saw her clearly as if she were right in front of him—chained and beaten, powerless to help her once again. His tears began to dry, the sorrow settling into an aching stillness.

The old mother stopped too, slowly pulling back from him. They both stayed on their knees, looking at each other in the dark.

"You will do great things," she whispered, her voice not yet clear of sadness.

"I do not know how," he replied, voice trembling.

"Speak to Lucien. Talk with him."

"How is it he knows so much?"

"He doesn't, boy!" Old Berona gripped his shoulders. "He doesn't, but he tries—just as you must. I am old... my time is nearly at an end, but great forces are moving in this world—some good, some terrible. You must be among the great ones, if I may call you my child!"

"You can."

A sob escaped Berona's mouth. "That is good... for you remind me so deeply of him."

Jae wiped the last of the tears from his eyes. "What is to happen? What am I to do?"

"To happen? My son, oh my boy, to protect you from this..." She pulled on her own slave collar. "The world is complex. Humanity tears itself apart at the seams. Creatures and beasts claw for an existence on decent land. You are pure—a very, very good boy. Now please, Jae!" She gripped him feverishly. "Do the right thing!"

Jae looked into her eyes. They were dark and shadowed, and yet, the moonlight twinkled in her tears.

"I will try, but I am afraid."

"Be wary of everyone, even Lucien. Trust your heart, but not your head. Pride will fill it and is the worst sin of all. Now go to him. A path has been laid as years of planning are coming to fruition. Go, Jae. I believe in you."

"I believe in you too, good mother."

"...You're so much like him. I wish there had been more time... with the both of you."

Jae reluctantly rose to his feet and gave her one last smile. Old Berona returned it and silently dismissed him. He went, but not before she turned to whisper to her sweetlings.

Silently, he slunk through the manse and stepped outside, climbing the garden trellis up onto the roof. There he found Lucien in his usual spot, gazing into the void just above the ocean's dark horizon.

"What do you suppose is out there?"

Jae followed his glance. "Freedom... and drowning."

Lucien huffed. "Those are very different things, I fear."

Jae took his place beside him. "After seawater fills the lungs and the burning subsides, it is said to be a peaceful death—a gentle release into eternity. Many of the elderly and the sick from my island would slip into the waves, called by the void. They now rest beneath the sea, their bodies scattered among the fish, crabs, and mermaids."

"Oh, a nice existence, I suppose."

"After the struggle, yes, the long rest is nice."

They sat together, staring into the black abyss hovering on the far horizon of the ocean.

"I am afraid, Jae."

"Me too."

"Talk is one thing, and yet when you see the spark before you... I have to stop and wonder..."

"Will it burn?"

"Exactly."

"I say let it burn."

Lucien turned to him in disbelief. "You do?"

"I thought my station here was a blessing. I had a bed, good food, and good people," he nudged Lucien with a smile. "But I realize now I am still just a slave. A commodity and nothing more. And besides, I have been named a moth by our good master. What else is there for a moth to do but flock to the flame?"

Lucien chuckled. "Better than what was once my slave name."

"Oh?"

"The *Rancid* Bull." Lucien smiled at him.

Jae blinked in surprise. "A bull? Really? Perhaps you were the one I was meant to tame..."

And then Lucien was on top of him. Jae pushed himself back from the edge of the roof, the thrill coursing through him. Off came his cotton tunic, then his sandals, discarded without a second thought. Lucien reared upward, his pale skin shining in the moonlight. Jae gripped him tightly, pulling him close, their breaths mingling in the cool night air.

Above the master's house, they found solace in one another, desperate to feel each other's skin—their *full* skin. Lucien produced a metal wire from the pile of his clothes, and with a *clank*, his metal collar fell from his neck, followed by Jae's. Jae clutched at his neck, overwhelmed by the sudden sensation of liberation. He looked up at the moon, watching birds, noting them crossing the moon's gaze. Pure, unabated *freedom*.

Together, they lay in temporary freedom. Yet in the distance, at the lowest part of the city, a flicker of light began to grow. Soon it engulfed the entire slave pens, and as Jae and Lucien finished their intimate act, cries rose from the city below. They sat up, feeling each other's bare skin, when they saw that the match caught fire below.

The city burned. The time for harvest had come.

Leawyn IX

"We will go west," she declared to her herd. "And follow the trail of the sun."

A murmur of unease rippled through the few who had chosen to remain with her.

"That is a bad omen," Rowan, the man-child, insisted. For once, others agreed with him.

Leawyn met their apprehension with calm resolve. "And tell me, have you seen any good omens worth chasing?" She let the silence settle before turning her gaze to Saralyn, who stood at the forefront of the gathering. "It is my desire to follow the sun, east to west. I wish to gaze upon the great salt waters and stand at the edge of the world, where sky meets the sea, and most of all, I long to witness the flames of the sun as they are snuffed out by the roiling waves, its power surrendered to the majesty of our moon."

A wave of nods and approval swept over her followers.

Saralyn started a round of applause. Even Takoda, feisty despite his old age, stepped forward, hobbling as he did.

"If there are no good omens to find, then we will make our own! Tell us, Wise Mother, how shall we proceed? We are at your beck and call!"

Behind her, her stallion snorted and stamped its hoof upon the Hearth. Leawyn held his reins, but the beast did not fight her.

"We will travel by night," she commanded. "No torches. No bonfires, save for what is needed to cook our food and boil our water. We shall be guided only by the stars, the firebugs, and if the good moon blesses us, her silver light as well. The less the flames know of our approach, the better."

She straightened, stepping atop a bundle of gnarled roots, her head held high. The creeping shades of night enveloped them, yet even in the thick darkness, their pale faces glowed under the moon's burning gaze. The Hearth, at least for now, had been satiated.

"I did not choose you. I did not come to you by design. No, I went into the forest to die, and when I emerged reborn, it was fate that led me to your clan in the moment of your greatest need."

"She is truly reborn. She is risen!" An excited whisper escaped from one of her followers.

Leawyn did not dismiss the claim. "None of us fear death. None of us fear the war that has raged for centuries. You chose this path. You chose me. And, most importantly, you chose to bring an end to this war."

A flurry of excited voices rose up.

"Lead us, Wise Mother!"

Even Saralyn, ever reserved and quiet, lifted her voice. "Lead us, O Wise Mother." In her hands, she carried a bow and arrow.

"You are no longer in the hands of your chieftain. You are no longer in the hands of the War Maker. You are not even in my hands. It is only the Hearth that guides us now, and its great reflection. The moon above."

"Amen," the crowd answered as one.

Leawyn stood upon her small hill, surveying her herd. Her horse breathed warmly against her neck, and as she looked beyond them to the dark trees, pressing ever closer to the forty-odd souls gathered before her, the urge to leave took hold. There was nothing more to say. Without another word, she turned, swung atop her horse, and set off.

The Isle of Fláimir was not wide. The War Maker and his messengers traversed it in mere weeks. But Leawyn was a stranger to all that lay beyond the rolling hills and babbling brooks of her home village. The only truth she knew was to chase the dying of the flames. And in her advanced age, she prayed the chase would be swift. They were long overdue for action.

Their first night's journey passed without trouble. She guided them out of the woods and into the open fields, traveling beneath the cold gaze of the stars. Progress was steady, but an hour in the saddle left her withered legs aching, while Takoda struggled to keep pace on foot. When the others paused to hunt for game, Leawyn dismounted and coaxed Takoda toward the stallion. It snorted and stamped its hoof, meeting Takoda's wary gaze with wild-eyes. Laewyn laughed at the spectacle. "Oh Takoda, does your manhood resemble a scared turtle?"

At that, Takoda scowled, placing his foot in her clasped hands. She boosted him up, and he swung onto the horse's back. The stallion begrudgingly accepted him and they made better time. They walked until dawn, when Takoda finally dismounted, and Laewyn's flock returned to the trees to rest.

Leawyn was among the first to wake that evening, her legs aching, her thighs rubbed raw. She rose quietly, careful not to disturb the others. But Takoda sensed her movement and followed her to the edge of the forest. Together, they watched the sun sink beyond the horizon, and as the first firebugs danced above the swaying grass, they stood in silence, watching the spectacle.

"In all my years, never did I think I would be on such a journey..." he spoke quietly.

Leawyn kept her gaze fixed on the horizon, watching as the sky shifted from red to orange to deepening purple. Then, unexpectedly, a peculiar smile spread across her lips, and she began to laugh.

"Are an old man's words so amusing?"

Still chuckling, she pointed across the field toward a nearby tree. A purple vine crept up the base. "See there."

The last rays of sunlight bled over the horizon, casting a golden haze across the land. He shielded his eyes with a hand before nodding. "An orchard—blossoming before autumn."

"It goes its whole life waiting," Leawyn mused, her voice softer now. "Just for the perfect moment to bloom."

They stood in silence, watching the pink and purple blossoms sway gently in the evening breeze. The sun behind it winked at them one last time before sinking away, leaving the sky awash in the same violet hues as the flowers.

"Incredible," he whispered at last, turning to Leawyn with a rare smile.

They returned to camp, building a small fire to cook a quick meal, then doused it thoroughly, leaving no embers, no smoke, no trace. When night fell, they set out once more, guided by the stars and the silver glow of the moon, tracing the path of the sun in reverse. They crossed meadows where sheep grazed undisturbed, crept through forests so dense they had to slow to a crawl, and climbed towering hills that swallowed the landscape beneath them. They even stumbled upon a waterfall, its crystalline waters spilling over a sheer stone cliff.

That night, the entire clan stripped bare, laughing and singing beneath the open sky, splashing in the cool water like children. Leawyn even allowed a fire to be built for warmth. By dawn, it was nothing but damp ash, buried beneath the soil. They retreated to the shelter of the nearest grove to rest.

And so they carried on, wandering by night, passing through abandoned villages and weathered stone strongholds, their walls crumbling under time's relentless hand. In the distance, they glimpsed the glow of other clans nestled in their ancestral lands, their sacred bogs surely only a stone's throw away. Yet, it became curious that they did not encounter another soul until a week into their journey, when two girls stumbled upon their camp.

Laughter, high and unguarded, shattered the quiet. The camp stirred, bodies jerking upright as eighty pairs of wary eyes, plus two from the stallion, turned to find the source. Two young girls stood frozen at the clearing's edge, clutching bundles of firewood and wildflowers meant for their braids. For a moment, no one moved. Then, as if struck by the same realization, the girls screamed.

They spun on their heels, dropping sticks and petals in their haste to flee. Rowan started after them, but Leawyn's sharp voice cut through the tension.

"NO!"

He halted, lowering his head as he slunk back to gather his belongings. Then the entire herd sprang into motion, tearing from the woods in the opposite direction. They sprinted through fields and brush, driven by fear and instinct, until at last, Takoda's legs gave out. Two others collapsed beside him, and though Leawyn hated to admit it, her own strength had failed her, too.

That night, they made camp in a small patch of forest, though she forbade a fire. They gnawed on salted meats and nuts, but their bellies remained unsatisfied. Sleep beckoned, but the night crept upon them too quickly. Leawyn permitted only a half-day's rest before they would need to move again, but even with her aching bones, sleep did not come easy.

Every rustling leaf, every distant howl made her pulse quicken. Even as exhaustion pulled at her, her mind wove stories of foreign clans lurking in the shadows, their hunters and hounds closing in. When she finally succumbed to fitful slumber, it was not long before she woke again, only to find Takoda missing from camp.

Rising quietly, she slipped past the sleeping bodies, stepping lightly over tangled limbs and discarded packs. At the edge of the grove, she spotted a dark silhouette hunched against a tree, staring across the field they had fled from.

"Have we been followed?" she whispered.

"Nah, not that I can tell."

Even in the dim light, she saw him struggling to straighten his back. Her gaze drifted lower, catching the dark rash creeping down from his groin, an ugly souvenir from too many hours in the saddle.

"You cannot continue on like this." She reached out, resting a hand on his shoulder, but he stiffened, and she withdrew.

He let out a breath, rough and tired. His gaze never left the horizon. "A man my age should be in bed, tended to by my children, surrounded by my grandchildren. Life should be easy. Porridge aplenty for me. Not this."

"I am sorry," Leawyn said. Her voice was raw and head clouded with exhaustion. "You deserve more."

"Yes," he muttered. "That I do."

A shooting star streaked across the sky. Above them, the half-crescent moon lingered, casting its pale glow over the land.

"Make a wish," she said, though her words held no heart.

"I have my wish," he replied. He tried to straighten, but his back resisted. A grunt escaped him as he slid deeper into his stoop, his fingers digging into the rough bark of the tree.

"You're hurt."

"Yes."

She looked at him, but he would not meet her gaze. His eyes remained fixed on the distant fields and the endless sprawl of stars.

"I know I am meant to be wise," she said softly. "But I find myself wanting to ask... what is your wish?"

Takoda let out a strained chuckle, but it quickly turned to a cough. "Leawyn," he said, shaking his head. "We have not known each other long, but surely, by now, you must know."

She exhaled. "I see. Do you wish to speak of them, too?"

Shifting his footing, he winced, swallowing his pain. "No," he muttered. "It is a story as old as time. You need not trouble yourself over me." His fingers flexed against the tree. "There is no warm bed waiting for me. No grandchildren eager for my return. I followed the War Maker and our chieftain's call for a reason. I do not wish to die lonely and cold in some forgotten room. This," he gestured vaguely to the darkened world around them. "will be my last adventure. And I am content."

"May I be honest with you?"

"Of course." He nodded slowly.

"I am tired of hearing that story."

"Oh?" He tried to turn his head, but she caught the flicker of pain in his back. This time, when she placed a hand on his shoulder, he did not pull away. "You get to our age, and you've heard it all."

Leawyn grunted in agreement and looked upon the moon. She watched the stars twinkle, and the black void between the stars shrink and expand. Something stirred within her stomach, something that would not sit right. The moon was waning. The sun would rise again. The moon would wax. The stars would shine and dull. The endless cycle, as old as her own bones.

"No," she said at last. "I reject that statement."

"Wise Mother?"

"Something has to change… why else are we doing this? No," she asserted again. "I refuse to believe our story has been told. We do not know the ending."

Takoda regarded her carefully. "I follow you, Wise Mother," he said.

She narrowed her eyes. "But do you believe that?"

"Hmm. I know this much. We are lost, of course. Something as trivial as running into a fellow clan, our own people, was enough to throw us off course. We have drifted south, not west, toward the Great Bog. Would you call that fate?"

Leawyn studied him, then searched the sky as if it might answer. "I did not realize you knew the land so well. South, you say? To the edge of our people's domain… to the Outsiders' border?"

"It would appear so." He nodded and closed his eyes. When

he opened them, they seemed dark and cold. "Do you know about the marshes, Wise Mother?"

"Only what is spoken about in rumor."

"Hmm. And rumor is all we have…" Takoda looked away again. "A unified land, hah! We know little of each other, and even less of the world beyond our borders. Too afraid to come this close, lest the flaming bird loose its arrows." He trembled, and she tightened her grip on his shoulder, firm and steady. "The Hearthsea… salty and ancient, twisted with tides and swamp, quicksand and death. How many of our ancestors rest there, swallowed by the shifting waters? No one can say. Only this—we do not rule those paths. The Outsiders do. And beyond them, past the bogs they guard, lies land that was once ours. Cleared of trees and marsh, now home to a great foreign family who conducts their reign of terror. That is where I sense the Hearth guides us."

Leawyn looked south, where the land sloped downward into darkness. Even straining her eyes, she could see nothing beyond the horizon. "We keep moving west…" she said half-assuredly. "And slower too." Her gaze dropped to Takoda's thighs. He was barely holding himself together, and she fared little better.

"At your command, Wise Mother," he answered, and she turned her hand into a hug, and then helped him hobble back to camp. They went to wake their kin, when the first bolt of thunder shook the Hearth.

Leawyn's heart plummeted from her chest. She looked wildly to Takoda, who shared the same exasperated look. *The Outsiders—their silver barrels.* Leawyn sprinted back to the edge of the forest, staring south back over the horizon, but saw no sign of movement, no banners, no drumbeats, nothing indicative of their plan of attack. Frowning, she ran a bit farther out into the field, and catching a flash of light from behind her, she stared upward, over the tips of the trees, and spotted another bolt of lightning streak through a wave of encroaching clouds.

Autumn had come, and with it, the rains.

For three days, torrential downpours battered them. They threw up their canvas tents, seeking shelter beneath thick branches and tangled leaves, but it was impossible to keep everyone dry. Water seeped through the fabric, dripping in slow, ceaseless rhythms. Branches above funneled buckets of rain onto their heads at random intervals. Fallen twigs and logs, once promising kindling, became useless, swollen and soaked. They could not even light a fire.

The rain did not abate until late afternoon on the third day. For a brief moment, the sun broke through the churning clouds. Leawyn and her people emerged from their damp shelters, their clothes heavy with moisture, their feet numb and cold. Together, they stood at the forest's edge, looking eastward at the fleeting light, and collectively they raised their arms, Leawyn leading the charge, and cursed the sun.

They could not linger. To sit still was to die, in spirit and in flesh.

Takoda had developed a cough he could not shake, and the endless damp had drowned what little hope bound them together. The youngest among them, the man-boy Rowan, along with two young archers, Ciara and Dierdre, were already second-guessing the journey. Huddled with the old and the sick, gnawing on days-old rations of meat and berries, they had lost the rosy optimism that had carried them this far.

Leawyn could see it in their eyes. The doubt. The weariness. So she made them leave.

They made it as far as the next clearing before another rumble of thunder foretold more rain. The sun itself, whether out of fear or malice toward the power of the Hearth, slipped behind the clouds once more. Her herd scrambled to make shelter again.

The rain came, but not like the maelstrom of the day prior. Instead, a cool drizzle settled in over the land, a haze that penetrated everything—their tents, their clothes, and even their lungs.

Takoda's cough worsened. By the next night, he had developed a shiver he could not shake.

Leawyn and Takoda were not the oldest among their chosen herd, but together, they may as well have been the wisdom of their people. Now, one of them was dying.

Perhaps the true elder among them was Eabha, an ancient woman who had long lost count of the moon cycles since her birth. She rode atop her grandchild's haunches, too frail to walk the journey herself. It was Juukta, one of the few men still strong enough to carry a battle ax, who insisted they stop.

Leawyn listened, though Takoda protested weakly.

They made camp in a dense patch of trees beside a rare stony cliff face. The thick canopy shielded them from the rain, and the rock wall dampened the howling wind. Miraculously, they found enough dry wood to coax a small fire to life.

A sturdy tent was raised for Takoda to rest. Two others were sacrificed, their fabrics layered for a watertight seal. To account for the lost sleeping space, Leawyn dispatched hunters to scour the forest for small game. She also sent Juukta and a handful of others into the countryside to gather more firewood, though she knew the effort would be mostly in vain. In truth, she needed to keep her people occupied, giving them something to do while the inevitable took place.

Eabha, with her untold years of healing wisdom, tended to the old man.

Leawyn stayed beside Takoda as she worked. The fire burned just outside their tent, radiating a warmth that reached her bones. She felt selfish for relishing it, only now realizing how deeply the cold and rain had settled in her joints. But Takoda did not want her to leave. In his waking moments, he clung to her hand, mumbling nonsense as the fever took hold.

On the second night, huddled around the fire with a few others, Leawyn finally asked. "Will he make it? Be truthful with me, Eabha."

She saw the others' ears perk at her words. There was no point in hiding it; there were no secrets among them anymore.

The old woman fixed Leawyn with large brown eyes, clouded and worn by the weight of too many years. Her fingernails were long and cracked, like splintered bark, and tufts of white hair clung to her spotted scalp between patches of bare skin. Worst of all was her toothless smile, her withered tongue lingering behind her last remaining tooth like a dying worm.

"No," she croaked, the first word Leawyn had ever heard from her. Then, without another glance, she turned back to the fire, stretching her gnarled hands toward the warmth and immediately slumped to sleep.

"I understand," she answered quietly. She looked up to those seated by the fire, but none would show her their face. Their eyes were lost in the flames, faces flickering between light and shadow. For a brief moment, anger rose in her throat. She wanted to kick the fire out, to scatter the embers into the wet soil. But she knew better than to provoke a mutiny. So, with her head low, she turned and retreated to her sodden tent.

Dawn broke with muffled screams.

Leawyn jolted awake and stumbled into the dim morning light, pushing through damp canvas to find Eabha crouched over Takoda, a knife trembling in her frail, wrinkled hands. A thin trickle of blood ran down from the wound she had made.

Eabha looked at her calmly. "I need to drain the bad blood."

Leawyn's stomach turned. "Go on, get!" she barked, shoving the old woman aside.

Eabha made no protest, only slinking away on all fours, like a scolded dog. Leawyn dropped down beside Takoda, pressing his shaking hands between hers. His skin was clammy to the touch.

"Mother... Wise Mother!" he called.

"Yes, good friend, I am here."

He licked his cracked lips, his gaze darting wildly. Sweat poured from his brow. It took her a moment to realize. He had gone blind.

"Wise Mother," he said again. "She's waiting for me."

Leawyn patted his hand. "Who waits for you, Takoda?"

"She's speaking to me... like when I was a child, but..." His breath hitched. A violent shiver racked his body. "She is so sad."

"Shh, shh, it's okay, it's all going to be okay..." she cooed to him.

"No... no!" Takoda's body jerked as if gripped by unseen hands. His sightless eyes darted across the tent. "I can hear her... and my father... and my father's father... but..." His breath caught. "I can't hear *him*."

"Who?" Leawyn asked. Pity swirled in her stomach. This is how Finn must have felt, tolerance for madness.

Takoda's fingers dug into her wrist. "W-where is my son?" His voice cracked. "Why can't I hear his voice, Wise Mother?"

Tears welled in his unseeing eyes, sliding down his face, mixing with the blood on his wrist. Leawyn swallowed hard, unable to answer.

A terrible stillness overtook him. Then his whole body tensed, his grip crushing hers. His ears twitched, as if straining to hear a distant cry. "They are lost, Wise Mother! Lost to us forever! Taken from our land!" His voice rose in a wail, terror gripping his breath. "Find them! Find out where they take them! And if you can, bring them home to rest! The Hearth wants them, Wise Mother. It wants them back!"

A clap of thunder shook the sky overhead. Outside the tent, she heard the gathering of feet.

"Go!" Takoda gasped. "Go! And do not lose faith! Find them all. Save this land, and, oh... oh no..."

"Takoda, good friend." She tapped his hands, desperate to call him back, but he shook her free.

Shaking so fiercely, his spine arched and he clawed upward like a cat, staring at something beyond the walls of the tent. "It blinded me, Wise Mother! It blinded me so I could see. Wah? No... No!"

Outside, the herd gathered to watch.

"Takoda! Stay with us, please! I am here! We can protect you."

"Oh, Old Mother, have we been fools? I... I..."

"I will find them, Takoda," Leawyn swore. "I will find them and bring them home. I promise you that."

Takoda froze. His body hung rigid in midair, caught in the final grip of something unseen. "Leawyn," he grunted.

"Yes, good friend."

"… I taste ash."

His body then collapsed back to the Hearth, his spirit departed.

BANCROFT V

The stench of death lingered heavy in the hall.

Bancroft tore a handkerchief loose from a passing servant. He blotted his face and neck, insufferably hot. *Damn this vile day*. The sun hung high in the sky, piercing through the castle's windows, broiling the cramped and confined hallways loaded with lords and ladies of the realm. In the entryway to Church Hall, the imperial herald, Norbert, announced the entry of every landed lord and lady. It had been a long day.

"Could your brother not have passed in the winter?" Melinda muttered under her breath. She fanned herself incessantly, occasionally swatting at the swarming flies drawn to their sweat. Her efforts did little to deter them.

"My brother gave his life for our family and realm," he moaned. His voice cracked, croaking like a frog under the stress and heat of the day.

His wife turned to him, sweat pouring from her brow as

she forgot both herself and station. "Forgive me, husband, it is only the heat. You know how it gets to me."

"Aye, but a good omen. The sun burns brightly for my brother. God shines brightly on my brother's life, and soon, his pyre." Bancroft dotted his forehead as his wife nodded to him. He gave her a slight smile in return, the most he could do to agree with her at the moment.

Elizabeth stood behind them, silent, draped in black from head to toe. Even in mourning, she seemed more like an apparition than a woman, with her two youngest children, Dalia and Manford, clutching her hands. Derrick and Catelyn also stood at her side, dressed in the same somber attire.

A mousetrap, Bancroft thought, the tension between them coiled and ready to snap. He quickly glanced at Elizabeth, and for a fleeting moment, the specter of his brother stirred in her shadow. He blinked hard and looked away, fiddling with his handkerchief. There was a conversation coming, one he dreaded but knew must happen. In memory of Thane, in honor of his sacrifice, he would face it today.

He glanced at his children, hoping for some semblance of comfort. A simple smile, perhaps. Yet instead, he found only a shudder. He slid his hand over his chest, groaning as he watched his two boys refuse to look at one another, idling coldly on their feet. Lysander bore the family's ancestral sword upon his belt, Warwick the family crown. They did their best to ignore one another, Warwick's eyes desperately trying to creep behind him to Catelyn, and Lysander standing with his arms folded, staring intently at his cousins before him.

Warwick, you fool, keep the peace, he wanted to say and swat the boy to turn him from his cousin. *Few wed for love in this world,* he wanted to growl, yet it only took a slight pivot of his eyes to spy his wife before pain swept his chest again. He clenched his fist, receiving a gentle touch from Melinda as he waited for the pain to pass. *It's not fair, I know.* He wanted to weep for Warwick. *For both my boys.* He looked to his wife, his *second* wife, and nearly shed a tear. He had been

552

given two great loves in this life. He prayed his boys would experience similar love.

"Or simply care for each other," he found himself unexpectedly saying under his breath.

Lysander pivoted on his feet, confused, and bumped Warwick on the rump with his sword. Warwick yelped and fell into his stepmother. Bancroft's face went red as a barrage of snickers came from those around him. He unclenched his hand from his chest and covered his face to shield his embarrassment.

"I daresay, how the boy beat my own in the practice tourney is a guess as good as the Nine." Charles Rose Mont drawled, turning to face them from his place in the procession line.

Bancroft slowly lowered his hand from his face, the burning of his embarrassment no worse than the incessant heat and shine of the sun.

"It was a fair jest," Lysander spat back.

A giggle of laughs came from the Rose Mont cluster. Charles's son, James, danced on his feet, imitating the fanciful footwork of a jester pretending to fight. "I lost, aye, I admit it," the boy quipped. "A gentleman knows how to lose with honor."

"Please, Son, you were hardly the loser of that day."

A faint rumble, like a boulder tumbling down a mountainside, echoed through the hall, though it may have been the shifting floorboards beneath his unsteady feet. Bancroft rocked back on his heels, desperate for air, keenly aware that the ghost of that day would forever scar his nephew.

"My brother competed with honor," Lysander barked back, his voice rising. "I will not suffer an insult to our house, especially on this most holy and mournful of days."

"Yes, please, let us all show love to one another on this somber occasion," Melinda pleaded.

"No, no, the boy is right." Charles held up a hand. "This is a terrible day. A dark day! Thane was my cousin too. Distant, yes, but still blood. What would the realm think of division between our houses? I can only offer my most sincere apologies for any... unintended slight." Charles smiled, but not to Bancroft nor his wife nor even Lysander. Instead, his gaze settled behind them. The specter remained quiet.

"Must you prattle like a noggin over a trough of ham?" The sharp clack of a walking cane against stone silenced the mutterings. Alexander Goldwood rounded the bunch of Rose Monts, his wife Hollace taking her place beside them.

"Please, of all days to stir the pot," Melinda pleaded.

"Dearest me." Alexander pulled a handkerchief from his front pocket and dabbed his round face. Sweat poured from his greased hair as their distant cousin struggled to compose himself. "An auspicious day, indeed. This sun, this suffocating heat. Surely, our family has been honored enough by God's radiant attention?"

"Then let us speak with honor," Lysander snapped. "instead of shrouding jests and insults in half-truths."

"Like you would know of honor," Warwick muttered, rolling his eyes.

A smile spread across Alexander's lips. "Yes, is there no honor among our family? Our poor Elizabeth, to see her family bicker on this sacred day. This should be about her and her now fatherless children. And you, poor cousin…" His gaze settled on Bancroft as he twiddled his thin mustache. "You've lost your brother and the sword of the realm. Yes… the sword."

An uncomfortable silence gripped the huddle. Bancroft's chest tightened as Alexander's gaze slid away from him and toward Lysander. His gaze fixed on the family sword resting at Lysander's hip. Slowly, dreadfully, Lysander followed his distant uncle's gaze. Realizing the implication, he stiffened, his hand instinctively brushing the weapon's pommel as though shielding it from view.

"Our family sword. *My* family sword."

"I did not realize it had returned," Alexander answered.

"It was my uncle's," Lysander growled. "The sword remained at Aberness before his noble demise. My father has bestowed it upon me."

"Upon you, ah. But not the son of our fallen Master of War? If only… for appearances?"

"Oh, by the Nine!" Bancroft exploded, his voice cracking as he raised it. The words tore from him, red-faced and livid, his fury trembling at the edges. Melinda rushed to his side, her hand a soothing weight on his shoulder, but it did little to calm him. Bancroft inhaled sharply, ready to dismiss these fools, these vagabonds… these pompously dressed bastards!

But Warwick stole the breath from him. "I think that would be a fine idea, Uncle."

The words sliced into the air like a thunderclap. Lysander spun on his heels, his face a mixture of disbelief and betrayal. Melinda gasped audibly, her composure slipping, while Harriet, barely containing herself, let loose an impolite giggle.

"Brother… how can you… are so cross with me as to side with *them*?"

Warwick merely stuck up his chin as if to bear the brunt of a punch with pride. "Let Derrick wield the sword, just for today. In honor of who wielded it before him. The man, and *father*, who gave his life in the name of our house, our faith, and our realm."

"The sword was bestowed to my son and that is where it shall stay," Bancroft growled. "The crown wears heavy upon me, and I daresay to all of you, heavier is the sword that will swing if such talk should continue…"

But talk no longer needed to continue.

The slow, deliberate clack of heels on stone silenced the whispers as effectively as a thunderclap. Bancroft froze, his breath catching in his throat. The hairs on the back of his neck rose as the shadow swept past him, a cold silk brushing his fevered skin.

Elizabeth.

She moved with the weightless grace of a specter, her veil a shifting mass of black pooling around her like spilled ink. She did not issue a command nor speak a word, but by the trembling of Lysander's fingers, she stripped the boy of his standing, and Bancroft's second son unsheathed the sword from his hilt and placed it into his aunt's hands.

"To family," the specter said.

She turned without another glance at the boy as she knelt before Derrick, who took the sword with a proud hand.

"What have you done?" Bancroft demanded, his voice barely audible as he turned to Warwick.

Lysander stood motionless, his entire frame quivering. Bancroft couldn't tell whether it was from rage, humiliation, or some mix of the two. Warwick, by contrast, remained composed. He crossed his arms and locked eyes with his brother.

"To family," he repeated, his tone resolute.

From farther down the hall, Royal Herald Norbert announced the entry of another noble family. "DYMTRUS OF HOUSE SEAVÍC."

"It seems fate is nearly upon us, tah tah." Alexander fluttered his handkerchief. He turned around with Hollace, resuming their position in line ahead of the Rose Monts.

Charles smiled faintly, his eyes flicking between the brothers before he, too, turned away. "A generous move, dear cousin," he remarked, voice laced with sly amusement. The Rose Monts realigned, and the line took a collective step forward, closing the distance to the chapel doors.

Bancroft stared forward, dazed by the glare of the sun. He swallowed hard, cocking his head, blinded by the light, deafened by the growing roar of what sounded like a swarm of bees. *No! Flies!* He swatted at the air with his hand, desperate to chase them from the hall. *Flies! Come for my brother's corpse!*

Or my sons?

The thought seized him, and he clawed at the air as if to banish the vile creatures. He swatted at the air, pawing like a cat, nearly knocking Warwick's crown from his head.

"Father!" Warwick yelped, stepping back, clutching his crown.

"Dearest, you must stop!" Melinda grabbed hold of him and yet still he made another pass at the air.

"I hear them!" He choked. Tears pooled in the corners of his eyes. He was numb all over. He didn't understand what was happening.

"Yes, dear, I know," Melinda soothed, leaning into him as she tightened her grip on his arm. Her embrace was firm, her voice steady despite the tremor in her breath. "We're almost there."

He moaned softly, his chest rising and falling in shallow, ragged breaths.

Lysander turned back, his face taut with concern. A man grown now, tall and broad-shouldered, he looked almost a stranger to Bancroft in the haze of his unraveling.

"Father, it's all right," Lysander pleaded, his hand resting on Bancroft's shoulder in reassurance.

"Leave him be," he heard Warwick command. "His tears will be a good thing for the realm."

The procession continued as the hour grew later. The lords and ladies of the realm had been lined up since the crack of dawn, but only now as the sun reached its hottest in the day did the funeral procession finally reach the imperial family. The Goldwoods were summoned first and announced to the realm, followed by the Rose Monts. At last, the core of House Hieronymus approached the great white doors of the Church Hall. Norbert stood here, completely and utterly drained of life from a day of announcements, and yet at the sight of the emperor and his son, the will to live returned to his pudgy face, and with the blast of trumpets, the realm rose from thousands of pews, ushering in the imperial family.

"OF HOUSE HIERONYMUS, LYSANDER, AND THE PROCLAIMED HEIR-TO-BE, WARWICK!"

The sound of his boys' names recalled Bancroft's sanity. He shook his head, clearing his thoughts, blinking hard as the light receded from his eyes and his two boys, the only living remnant of his first wife, took off before him, parading for the realm amid an aurora of silence and remorse. The twins, the entirety of his world, marched in silence, side-by-side, yet not a notion of love or comradery was shared between them. They marched as if soldiers, merely doing their duty, obedient yes, but compassion all but burned away.

"AND NOW TO THE LORDS AND LADIES OF THE REALM, WE GREET THE EMPEROR, HIS IMPERIAL MAJESTY, BANCROFT HIERONYMUS, IN ESCORT OF HIS WIFE, EMPRESS MELINDA OF ESMERELDA."

Melinda pulled his arm tight as they began their procession. Bancroft braced as if to prepare for a barrage of applause, but there was none. He forgot he stood in a funeral hall. He marched slowly, leaning on his wife for support, blinking rapidly, unaware that tears clogged his eyes and fell upon his cheeks. Lords and ladies nodded at his passing, but this was only an afterthought to him. Before him, at the very end of a long, long row of pews, lay his brother, nothing more than a rotten corpse, concealed beneath a carved coffin of the most ancient oak. His bottom lip wavered. A sob nearly escaped his lips.

Brother.

For the first time since his sons were born and his first wife died, his heart truly broke. It was not the familiar clench of muscle or shortness of breath, but something deeper. A savage, wordless urge rose in him to fall to his knees and cry out to God, to the Nine Miracles, to reject the wisdom of powers greater than any emperor, and to feel, with certainty, that all was lost.

By the Nine Miracles, they somehow made it to the front of the Church Hall as the realm looked upon him. Bancroft and Melinda took their seats among the front row of pews, joining their sons, as well as Grandma'am and Alden, deemed too old to make the customary walk. Only Osbert stood before them, standing silently with his arms clasped over his red robes. When the imperial family was settled, he gave Bancroft a gentle nod before raising his arms.

A piercing blast of trumpets shattered the late afternoon stillness, their echo cascading through the vaulted hall. All eyes turned toward the grand white doors. Catelyn and Derrick emerged first. Catelyn, dressed in black but unfathomably beautiful for a girl her age, clutched her younger sister, Dalia, with one hand. Derrick stood adjacent to her, one hand clutching Empyrean, the other his younger brother, Manford. Bancroft swallowed hard. A few bursts of moans and weeping overtook the weaker women of the realm.

"PRESENTING CATELYN AND DERRICK, DALIA AND MANFORD OF THE LATE THANE OF HOUSE HIERO-NOYMOUS, MASTER OF WAR TO THE REALM, AND LOVING HUSBAND TO ELIZABETH."

Catelyn moved with a quiet dignity, though a few tears slipped silently down her cheeks. Halfway through their walk, Dalia's composure gave way to loud, heart-wrenching sobs, her cries echoing in the stillness. Derrick stopped, turning to comfort his brother as Manford, too, began to whimper in distress. But Catelyn, ever composed, scooped Dalia onto her hip with a practiced ease. She brushed a stray strand of hair from her sister's tear-streaked face and kissed her gently on the nose. Bancroft pushed down the lump in his throat at the sight. They resumed their march and, upon reaching the front row, Derrick passed Manford to Catelyn. She quietly ushered the younger siblings to sit beside Bancroft. As she approached him, Bancroft bent forward, whispering a soft blessing over her and her family. She nodded in return, her eyes glistening with tears, and took her seat.

Derrick now approached his father's casket. He walked slowly up a row of stone stairs before dropping to his knees. He unsheathed Empyrean, presenting it upward to his father. No one heard what he uttered, but the gesture was felt throughout the realm. From somewhere behind Bancroft, Charles's voice slithered in a whisper to Alexander. "Ah, a third claim to the throne?" A jape, but one he would have his tongue for when the time was right.

Derrick remained kneeling in solemn silence before his father's resting place, then returned to his family moments later, his movements unhurried, his head bowed. All eyes then turned back toward the great white doors at the far end of the hall. Once more, the trumpets sounded, their fanfare cutting through the air, ringing out until their final notes faded into a hushed, reverberating echo that seemed to linger beneath the arched roof.

"PRESENTING THE WIFE OF THE LATE THANE HIERONYMUS, THE LADY ELIZABETH OF INVERNESS!"

The white doors pulled back to unveil the grieving form of Elizabeth. She was a dark stain amid a tapestry of white and sunlight, and the crowd gasped at the sight. She stepped forward, slowly, so that each of her footsteps echoed through the cavernous and crowded space.

Elizabeth took her time.

Each step was powerful, a poem, a statement. Bancroft found himself tilting his head as the minutes passed by, his crown, the crown of the realm, tilting on his brow as she stepped forward. Women burst into tears. Men nodded and bowed. Children turned away, burying themselves in their mother's skirts, too afraid or too overwhelmed by the specter making its way through the chapel.

Beside Bancroft, Catelyn's composure crumbled. She broke into sobs, her slender shoulders shaking. He extended a hand to the poor girl, but Lysander was quicker. He coddled his cousin, taking her hand and patting it. He reeled, watching Warwick turn away. Then young Dalia also burst into tears, and red of face, he watched Warwick leap forward and take her from Catelyn's side. He picked her up and patted her on the back like a wet nurse. It was at least a decent gesture.

Elizabeth made her way through the Church Hall. Not a single footstep was wasted. At long last, she reached the front row, and like her son before her, she climbed the stone stairs to her late husband's casket but fell to both knees. No one could hear what words she whispered to the carved wood of the casket, but the sight of her there, crumpled upon the stone, spoke volumes. The black silk of her mourning gown billowed and settled around her, a shroud that seemed to swallow the light. Then came great wrenching sobs that broke the stillness and echoed through the hall. She lay there before the entire realm, her anguish raw and unyielding. Not a single eye remained dry.

At last, her strength waning but her resolve unbroken, Elizabeth rose. She lingered for a moment, her head bowed, her voice carrying a final, inaudible farewell to the man she had loved and lost. Then, with the composure of a woman who bore the unbearable, she turned and made her way to her children. She took her seat beside them.

Osbert stepped forward, his crimson robes catching faintly in the golden light. The ceremony proceeded with measured dignity, a stark contrast to the spectacle of snake handlers and divine theatrics the realm had seen in other rites. This was solemn, by the book, deeply traditional. Aye, much of the realm nodded along with the High Priest's recitations. Some were in quiet agreement, others with heavy-lidded eyes as the hours stretched on. Even the most pious among them began to feel the toll of the heat and time.

The mountain air of Ness, usually crisp and cool even in the summer months, sweltered mercilessly under the midday sun. Lords and ladies simmered in their finery, sweat pooling beneath layers of velvet and brocade. Even the grandest among them seemed diminished, their noble dignity reduced to damp discomfort. Bancroft felt the sticky weight of his own robes and caught the faint, acrid stench that hovered like an omen. The thought struck him suddenly and grimly: *The flies will come soon.* Drawn to the stench of sweat, sorrow, and the inevitability of rot. The flies always came.

Then came his summons.

With a subtle tug from Melinda, Bancroft rose, his legs shaky beneath him, the crown threatening to tilt further. Together, they marched forward and up the steps to where his brother lay. Melinda gave him a gentle kiss on the cheek and resumed her seat. Standing now before the coffin and the assembly, Bancroft turned. His heart hammered in his chest, and his voice, when it came, trembled. Before him lay not just his brother but the weight of everything he had fought for and everything he had left behind. He cleared his throat and began.

"My brother was a good man. A great man. A man of"—Bancroft's voice faltered, the words catching in his throat, his chest tight and breath shallow—"much dignity and honor." He paused, swallowing hard before continuing, his voice growing stronger. "From childhood—nay! From babes, we were the best of friends. We trained with swords together, we studied together, we stole sweets from the kitchen together."

A light ripple of laughter echoed from the audience. Bancroft drew in a shaky breath, gathering himself. "But most importantly, we prayed together. Here, in this chapel, beneath this hot, hot sun. For we understood one thing, more than family, or duty, or honor, but faith. Aye, yes, faith, but a word with so much weight. Much like this crown, faith does not come easy. It comes from sacrifice, hardship, doing the right thing, and in my brother's case, the *hard* thing, in the heat of the moment. It was my brother's faith, you see, that drove him to his great merits.

"Osbert behind me here has spoken greatly of the many hardships the followers of Aethylios and his Miracles have endured. It is, by far, the only thing in this room that unites so many peoples of different tongues, cultures, and traditions. And despite the forces that pull at our realm, despite the divides that threaten us, it is our faith that forever binds us together.

"Forged in the fires of the Ash Fall, our realm was born, wrestled from the twisted snake of Makka. But before that, before the Makkans and the Ash Fall, before this crown and this castle, there were the Lyonnians, and from its most humble of farming villages, a child, a boy, a little younger than my boys now, who displayed something remarkable. You see, he was blessed by God. And so, he spread his gifts, and his blessings, and his Miracles, and all of mankind was better for this. Yet the old emperor of Lyonnia did not like this, and so Aethylios was persecuted and he fled, and he came to these lands, and so did my family after him, killed and tortured, hunted and raped, and together, among all of you—among beer or wine, beef or ham, cloak or jacket, we were bound together under God."

Bancroft took a moment to breathe. His heart swelled.

"Thane understood that better than anyone. He fought heretics. He fought treason. He even fought, yes, centaurs, for the good of our realm. Our religion. Our faith. He... he... he..." Bancroft's voice wavered, and he stumbled, his chest tightening, his breath shallow. He stepped back, raising his hand as if to grasp the very air for the words, but his body betrayed him. He gripped his chest in agony, stumbling forward as he brought his fist down on his brother's casket with a resounding *BANG*. The crowd gasped, and a wave of silence followed the sharp, echoing sound.

Spittle flew from Bancroft's mouth as he stood, breathless and red-faced, his hand pressed over his heart. Slowly, he composed himself, his voice a hoarse rasp. "He did everything for you. For our realm. Honor his legacy, please. Honor what he died for. Thank... you..."

The realm rose to its feet in a round of applause. Lysander rushed forward as he hobbled down from the stone steps, clutching his chest with extreme pain but finding his footing with Lysander's help. Slowly, they made their way under the thunder of applause back to the pew, where he was seated. There he smiled, wiping the spittle from his mouth. Outside, the sun began to wane. Dusk approached.

Elizabeth was called to speak, and as the crowd settled back into their seats, there was not a soul who did not watch her closely. She stepped to the front and stood before the assembled lords and ladies, holding herself still for a long, breathless moment. Silence gripped the hall, the stillness only broken by a coughing fit overtaking Bancroft. Lysander tended to him, and only then did Elizabeth move to pull back the black veil from her face.

"Thank you, my dearest brother-in-law, for those kind, kind words. My husband, true to the emperor's words, was a believer in all of those things. He loved the Nine—cherished them. He prayed every morning as he broke his fast and confessed his sins every night before bed. As a husband, he did his duty, showering me with the greatest blessings of my life. Four healthy children, including a beautiful young woman, and a son who wields the family sword with strength and honor. My late husband was a great man who carried that sword with pride. And pride is a sin, yes, but I want you all to know there was a purpose to his sin."

Elizabeth paused, allowing the awkwardness of her accusation to settle over the realm. Many lords and ladies shifted uncomfortably in their seats. "My brother-in-law has neglected one key word, the very *essence* of who Thane really was. I want you to know he was a very prideful man but was also deeply, deeply selfless. There were years I went without seeing the greatest love of my life. Countless nights where my children did not see their father. Derrick grew into a man before all our eyes, except his own father's. Catelyn became a courtly woman, and yet she would be a stranger to him if they were to meet unannounced. And perhaps most grievously of all, my youngest has only heard of him in passing. There were nights when they were both very young where he doted on them, gifting them candies and sweets and kisses, but then the call of war would summon him back to duty, and our hearts would be empty."

Elizabeth's voice faltered, and she paused, overcome with emotion. The audience hall hung on every word. "It was not easy being married to Thane. It was not easy at all. So many lonely nights. So much worrying. So much unknown. He gave so much…"

Elizabeth broke into a barrage of tears. A hundred women joined her. Bancroft even sniffed, his coughing fit and chest back under control.

"He gave so much for all of you! A truly, truly selfless man, who heard the call of duty, kissed his wife and children on their foreheads, and then rode off for war! Fighting for you! For me! The Nine! For the legacy of our children and everything we hold near and dear. He carried *pride* with him. By Aethylios himself, he was a *prideful* man." She shook her head.

"And now he is dead. He gave his life fighting for everything we believe in. Faith. Realm. *Family.* He built a legacy that I daresay cannot be matched." Elizabeth turned her gaze to Derrick. "My boy, my poor, sweet boy, Derrick. You are your father's oldest. A man grown before my very eyes. Your father loved you. He cherished you. He fought and killed for you. Most importantly, he selflessly built a legacy for you."

Oh no. Bancroft, finding the strength, rose back to his feet, joining the rest of the realm.

"As his heir, you have much to live up to, but as your father's son, and with good Catelyn beside you, and your siblings, and the great blessings of our emperor, I know you will match your father's legacy, if not exceed it. I love you. I love all my children. You will all do so well in this life, for you are every bit of your father. Selfless, but strong. Fight for what is right in his honor. And to the realm, thank you for joining us here today. I know Thane would have been honored, if not embarrassed over all the fuss. Thane, I love you and I await the day we are joined together again in heaven. Thank you."

A round of applause overtook the chamber. Thunderous, loud clapping, joined by tears of sorrow and joy as Elizabeth bent over to kiss the casket of her late husband and then rejoined the rest of her family. Bancroft clapped along, smiling and beaming, but inside his guts were twisting and churning. She had all but declared war on the will of the emperor.

The late afternoon sun was in danger of setting before the ceremony could be completed. To the relief of the realm, Osbert ceased the call for any additional tributes to Thane. Instead, he thanked the realm for attending and called for the pallbearers to rise. Bancroft rose, alongside Lysander, Warwick, Derrick, Charles and James Rose Mont, Alexander Goldwood, Dymtrus, and Strammond. Nine pallbearers—a holy number, enough men to bear the weight as Bancroft struggled to merely lift the casket, again short of breath.

They begin their procession to the funeral pyre. Osbert led the way, stopping before a pair of Demonbreun Guards who pushed open a pair of mammoth oak doors, unveiling a large, outdoor ceremonial space. A gust of cool wind flew in from the mountains, but the sun was intense, burning nearly at eye level as it prepared to sink below the distant mountain range to the west.

They moved forward in silence, guided only by the steady rhythm of the High Priest's chants. Slowly, a shadow stretched over them, and Bancroft's vision cleared. Before them stood a towering funeral pyre, and as they drew near, he began to make out the various offerings tucked between the logs and branches.

Articles of fine clothing, once worn by his late brother, were draped over the stacked wood. New garments, tunics, cloaks, frocks, and curled shoes had been gifted by the lords and ladies of the realm. Parchments and letters were carefully tucked into the gaps, though these were not meant for kindling. They were love letters between husband and wife, words of affection between father and daughter, notes detailing battles fought and victories won, religious verses, and articles of faith. Thane's favorite bread and cookies, sweetened with memories of home, sat beside clay jugs of wine and spirits. What was absent were jewels, precious swords, and golden trinkets. None of those could ascend with the body to heaven, for only what could burn or boil could accompany the soul. These were the final vestiges of a life well-lived, bound for the flames alongside his brother's body.

Bancroft, breathless and struggling under the weight of grief, helped lower the coffin gently onto the pyre. One by one, the pallbearers took their turns to say their goodbyes, each man silently offering his final respects. Bancroft was last. He leaned down, kissed his hand, and placed it reverently upon the lid of the casket. "Goodbye, Brother," he said solemnly. "You represented the best of the realm."

He stepped back and returned to his family, who stood at a safe distance from the pyre. Knights of the Demonbreun then stepped forward and pushed the coffin deep within the stacks of logs and branches, the sight of which sent Catelyn into a burst of tears. A thousand lords and ladies crowded the outcrop, forming a disordered circle around the pyre. The gathering and assortment of lords and ladies took so long the sun threatened to disappear entirely behind the mountains, but at long last, the final lord sauntered just into position as the sun ejected its last but most brilliant rays of light, purple and red. The light danced across the summer sky, joining in harmony as Osbert struck up a torch. Melinda held Bancroft tight as he approached the pyre. Grandma'am stood before them all, quiet as a mouse, a mother burying her child.

WHOOSH.

The act itself was swift. Fire, a divine gift from God that separates man from beast, soared upward toward the heavens. Its flames quickly licked the sky, reaching out to kiss and bid farewell to the final rays of light that sparkled over the distant mountain's edge. Then, in the blink of an eye, his brother was gone. The sun dipped too far below, and while the light would return, this day was forever lost.

House Hieronymus stood quietly together. Even the Rose Monts and the Goldwoods stood nearby, quietly holding hands or offering quiet embraces. A band with a string quartet entered the space, followed by servants bearing platters of food and drink. Gradually, the hushed offerings of respect gave way to the sounds of a gathering, a celebration of life, and shared drinks. Thane burned quickly, and apparently, so did his memory. Bancroft stared absently at the fire, wondering how long it would take before the realm forgot him, too, when his time came.

"He was a good man," Melinda said softly, cradling him gently.

Bancroft did not have the strength to answer her.

The flames would burn all night, but not his constitution. When the fire died to an acceptable level, the family began to depart for their social arrangements. Grandma'am, consumed by grief, allowed herself to be escorted to a private chamber by Alden. Bancroft thought to go after his mother but opted instead to be placed on a private bench overlooking an immense cliff beside the castle. The light here was low, and the warmth of the fire was soothing but not overpowering. Here he dismissed his wife, requesting to be left alone. Melinda abided, not realizing it was finally time.

Like a moth to a flame, Elizabeth came minutes later.

"Bancroft," she greeted him quietly.

"Elizabeth," he answered in return. There was a long pause between them. Then, a brief, unsaid understanding passed as they embraced, for all the tension between them, they had both lost Thane. For that, civility in his memory was due. Elizabeth settled beside him, and once more, they both simply watched the flames in silence.

"Time is fickle," she said at last.

"Have you grown to possess the powers of a witch?" he jested, but she did not laugh. No matter, for he did not care to usher in a laugh, but only spoke from the cusp of his tongue. "It is only you can read one's mind. Many would give much for such a power—to know what the emperor was thinking."

At that remark, Elizabeth did laugh. "Were it so, would I be here now?"

"No, I suppose not." And again, they fell silent.

"Derrick is not to inherit Aberness?"

"No." Bancroft was firm in his answer.

"I see." Elizabeth looked away from the fire. "Please then, tell me, do you know what it is to be a woman?"

"I cannot say so, no my lady."

"It is to live in a world that is entirely not under your control. You watch as things… happen to you, but you have no agency. I am nearly an empress, you see, and no, do not accuse me of treason or of coveting Melinda's role, for I know she feels this evening more keenly than I—I am among the most powerful in the realm. But without a man by my side, or worse, one to verify my words, I have no cause for action. No real authority, even… even…"

"Over your own family?" he added.

"Precisely," she tried to smile. "I never got to see my husband. He was always off fighting some war. When he did come home, the moments were tender and soft. He blessed me with many children, but then, as things became comfortable, he was gone. Just like that. And then there were the suitors. Oh yes, Bancroft, the suitors, for the realm knew, they *knew*, he was going to die. He was at war for twenty years, it was inevitable I suppose. And each one of them, *every last one of them*, promised me this or that. 'I give you my word,' they said. And it became so clear to me that I had no agency at all… I have been a widow in waiting a long time." She sighed, staring coldly into the diminishing funeral pyre. "To have power and then so little of it, to care for my family without the backing of a man to secure alliances, promises, all the political shite…" She waved her hand in frustration.

Then, she turned to him, her eyes glistening with more tears than had ever fallen for her late husband. "This is not about me, Bancroft. Understand that. It is about my family. I know what the realm expects of me. I know what the texts and God say of me. But I'm also a mother, and as civilized as we pretend to be, a mama bear will tear apart anything that threatens her cubs. I cannot stand by while Derrick is denied what is his. And Catelyn, what of her? Is she to be empress, or is she to be second fiddle? To inherit a great realm, or marry some minor lord who will dismiss her as a whimsy? I don't know. I've spent my whole life not knowing, and you, Bancroft, my dear *emperor*, and dare I say *brother*, you've only poured more fuel on that fire."

A long silence hung between them, each listening to the crackling of the bonfire.

At last, Bancroft spoke, his voice low. "I am but a man."

"By the act of your pants, I account so," she curtly answered.

"I am but a man," he replied again. "I am *only* a man. I am not God. I am not a prophet. I am just a man! A mortal! Filled with the same blood and guts as any other here!" He waved his hand and spat, finally consumed with rage. "I do not possess divine powers. Every last man, woman, and child here wants something, Elizabeth, do you understand this? You speak of a woman's lack of power? Then imagine a man—an emperor for the Nine's sake!—who is helpless to watch everything fall apart beneath him. My grandfather served at a time of great calamity. Of civil war and great unrest. The first spring of a great harvest since the Ash Fall and the first thing man wants to do is kill. Well, we killed, as cousin fought cousin, and the realm only just stayed together. And here I sit, a man torn in every direction, appeasing every lord and lady of east and west, until my chest splits in two! Do not question me, woman. I say then, the mama bear may worry for her cubs, but I worry for every cub in every county under every lord! By the Nine… my own boys wish to annihilate one another." He shook his head and rested it on his hand. "A thousand, thousand, thousand cubs."

Elizabeth rose slowly, her tears choked back as she whispered. "Then do what you must." Her voice trembled as she continued. "But know that I will fight with all the authority a woman can." She curtsied, bowing deeply to him, before gathering her black dress in her hands and disappearing into the crowd.

Bancroft sighed, sick of the court, sick of the flames. He looked away from the fire, staring coldly at the stone before him, before at long last he stuck up his hand and twisted it madly in the air.

Strammond appeared almost immediately, ever at the ready. "Yes, my lord?"

"Bring me Lysander," he ordered. "And be quick about it."

"Of course, my lord." Strammond was gone in a flash.

A single tear fell from his cheek. It joined with the stone, and thus, he surmised, the mountain. His decision would be final. It was for the good of the realm. Lysander appeared beside him a few moments later.

"It is time, my boy. Go to her. Content our two branches of the family. Let neither hell nor whore stop you in your matter."

"You mean…?" his son stammered, but Bancroft waved off the question with a gesture. He watched his boy pull the dark ring from his pocket.

"Go. Now."

And so he did, as Lysander was born to serve. He moved toward the serving staff, whispering urgently in one of their ears. The string quartet began to play, their fiery tune swelling as he approached Catelyn. He bent to one knee before her and produced the dark ring.

From across the crowd and through the flames, Bancroft watched. He saw her hands fly to her mouth in astonishment, her eyes wide with disbelief. He heard the collective gasp of the realm, followed by the laughter and joy that rippled through the gathered lords and ladies. Catelyn jumped up and down, her friends rushing to embrace her in a joyous frenzy. Lysander rose, sliding the Seal of Oxcál onto her finger. He then took her and gently placed a kiss upon her lips.

Bancroft wanted to smile. He wanted to rise and wipe the tears from his eyes. But instead his focus turned to Warwick, to the blank expression upon his face, and the way he turned, storming from the occasion.

Elizabeth wasn't far behind him.

LEAWYN X

Takoda's corpse slipped beneath the murky brown water, only to resurface a moment later.

"A curse," someone whispered.

"An ill omen," another added.

Leawyn stared at Takoda's body bobbing in the water. The corpse drifted in a lazy turn, his face rounding toward them with faded blue eyes. The same sickly shade as his bloated cheeks.

"Saralyn?" Leawyn turned to her most trusted comrade, but Saralyn only watched the body, her brow creased, her eyes darting back and forth.

Leawyn turned back to the body, fingers clenching and unclenching. She didn't know what to do.

A tug on her arm provided the answer.

Eabha, the impossibly old woman, stood beside her, clutching the same knife she had used to drain Takoda's blood on the morning of his passing.

No. Not again. Leawyn swallowed hard, but Eabha only nodded and tugged her arm once more. It had to be done.

Leawyn dropped to her knees, stretching over the water to grasp Takoda's cold, clammy arm. She hauled him toward solid ground, and Juukta, Eabha's grandson, moved to help, heaving the corpse into the bog. Eabha then hobbled over, a knife clenched in her fist, when a collective gasp of horror swept over the gathered flock.

"The Hearth has rejected him!"

Leawyn didn't know who had spoken. It didn't matter. Some recoiled, running in disgust. Others stood frozen, watching in mute terror. Eabha slowly worked her bony fingers down Takoda's burial gown, and then delicately brought the knife to the base of his stomach. Leawyn braced herself, though not for the sound, but for the smell. With a wet pop, the body split like an overripe fruit, and his foul juices coated the soil.

Leawyn turned and gagged, her eyes stinging in shock. Many more of her herd ran, mouths covered. Even Saralyn turned away in disgust. Eabha tugged on her arm, her son bent down next to the corpse. Together, holding their breath, they pushed Takoda back into the bog, and finally, as the waters of the Hearth spilled into his ruptured body, he sank, disappearing quietly into the cold, dark depths.

"Rest easy, new friend," she whispered, bowing her head in respect. She held the position for a long time and was prepared to hold it even longer, to outlast his clanfolk and kin, but the ceremony had been soiled.

Those who had known and loved Takoda most lingered only briefly. Their tears were silent, muffled, and they left without a word.

"At least you are here, among your people, forever." She nodded, about to turn away, when a bubble gurgled up from the bog.

She froze. Her eyes darted over the water to the swaying trees, to the branches shifting in the wind. Her mouth parted, her lungs swelled with breath when the clouds parted and sunlight spilled through the canopy, painting the forest gold.

She looked down at her hands, watching them tremble, tracing the bruised, tattered skin of an old woman. She closed her eyes, feeling the wind run its fingers through her hair.

I saved him. I saved Saralyn. To go forward is to be greedy. I will not waste this gift.

She left Takoda to his long rest.

Turning from the bog, she followed the narrow forest path back to the open field, where the remainder of her clan waited. Saralyn stood with hands on her hips, a deep scowl etched across her lips.

"Shall we return to camp?" Leawyn asked loudly. She didn't want to have this conversation here. Not so close to him.

Saralyn started to answer, but Rowan's voice cut through first.

"Old Mother, there's trouble. They're blocking our way back to camp, on top of the far hill, look!" Rowan pointed, and Leawyn's heart fluttered. She followed his finger point, scanning the ridgeline, searching, when she found them.

A line of soldiers and archers standing firmly across the hill.

Flairnish, not Outsiders, she understood, but the sight did not bring comfort. An unknown clan of her people barred their path.

"I will go alone," Leawyn announced.

No one protested.

She set off across the damp, grassy field as the sky began to drizzle again. Behind her, moving like a flock of wary hens, her people followed. Huddled together, yet keeping a respectful distance.

At the base of the hill, she halted. Above her, silhouetted against the storm-heavy sky, warriors and archers stood in an unbroken line, their brown tunics blending into the gray backdrop with the wind at their backs. In front of them, their chieftain stepped forward, his heavy cape billowing in the rain. The great antlered helm he wore loomed dark as night against the churning clouds.

"Who walks upon the ancestral land of Clan Falómeir?"

"My name is Leawyn of clan…" The wind slapped her in her face. She didn't know how to answer. "…We mean you no harm!"

The grizzled face of the chieftain gritted his teeth as he chewed over her words. He was a middle-aged man with a great red beard and bushy eyebrows. He reminded her of Finn in his younger years. "Who has sent you? Why do you camp on our lands?"

"We have answered the call of the War Maker," she lied.

The chieftain grunted. "We have received no word of battle approaching our lands." He stepped forward, nearly slipping on the slick grass, and cast a glance over her shoulder. "I see no warriors. Only old men and women. You wouldn't lie to a man on his own land, would you?"

Leawyn swallowed. "W-we chase the sun. That is our order. That is where fate guides us."

The chieftain took a step back, staring down upon her. "You must all be craven… or cowards and turn-cloaks fleeing your duty. Or worst of all, *mad*."

Leawyn lifted her chin. "I am Leawyn, known as the Wise Mother or the Old Bird. We struck victory against the Outsiders many moons ago. I pray word of our feat has reached even here in the west."

"My clan's service was given a generation ago. We will not offer lives until the War Maker himself calls for them."

"Treat with us," Leawyn countered. "So that I may tell you of our victories against the Outsiders, so you may see the honor in our duty. We are many clans come together! Unconventional, yes, but that is our strength."

The chieftain studied her for a long moment, then shifted his gaze past her, toward the patch of forest where her people had emerged.

"You just held a funeral, didn't you?"

"Yes," she answered truthfully.

"A wound?"

Leawyn blinked hard. "Illness."

"Hmm." The chieftain grunted. "No strength, but at last, the truth." He nodded, then took a step back. "I know nothing of your clan, your people, or the War Maker's plans. What I have heard is of a band of rovers terrifying children and disturbing villages. Of strange happenings in our woods. I came prepared to fight, but before me I see only a pack of insane elders and their lackeys." His lip curled. "Go now, Old Mother, and be gone from our land."

He turned to leave when Leawyn blurted out. "The Hearth belongs to us all, does it not?"

The chieftain froze, slowly turning back upon his heels.

"You share no blood with me, and I have already shown you a great deal of common cause by allowing you to rest your dead among our ancestors. Leave! Before my respect for the resting is tested."

He turned again, but Leawyn took a step forward. "We are all of the Hearth," she insisted. "And only together can we drive the Outsiders from this land."

The chieftain ignored her, walking back to join the ranks of his warriors atop the crest of the hill. "Go now, Old Mother, before you invite more trouble to our people, and you come to rest among my ancestors."

The chieftain raised his arm, signaling for his men and women to turn and leave. They went without another word, disappearing on the other side of the hill. Leawyn stood in the rain, watching them go. Water trickled down her face, mingling with the taste of salt on her lips. She prayed her people had heard little of their conversation.

She led a silent herd back to their miserable camp. Rain drizzled down through the trees. Leawyn paused by the fire, somehow still burning low but hot, hissing each time a raindrop found its way through the tree canopy into its embers. She looked to her people, but none of them looked back. Quickly, they tore their moccasins from their feet and slid into their tents and shelters, eager to escape the cold and wet.

"Should we talk?" she said to no one in particular.

It was Saralyn, opening the flap to her tent, who looked at her in defeat, who told her no.

Leawyn lowered her eyes and looked into the fire, kicking a clump of wet soil into the flames. The embers hissed and the flames nearly died, and she immediately regretted her action. The fire, and the rain, were the only things keeping her herd from bolting in the night.

She turned, slipping into what had been Takoda's tent. No one stopped her. Inside, she stripped off her soaked clothes and lay down upon the warm bed of furs. She left the tent flaps open, letting the fire's heat seep inside, and rested her head nearest the flames.

She awoke standing in a field.

A blue moon hovered overhead, reduced to nothing more than a narrow crescent, and dark clouds raced across the sky. She held out her hand and stuck out her tongue as snowflakes flew through the air. She lifted her hand up into the sky, trying to chase one, and felt the snow brush against her ankles.

No. Not snow. *Ash*.

She spit the taste from her mouth. She whipped her head around, screaming, calling for Saralyn or Juukta or whoever would come to her.

"Leawyn," came her name on the wind.

She spun toward the sound.

There stood Takoda among a field of blackened ash. His figure wavered, hazy in the dim light. Behind him, shadows swirled, lost in the smoke.

"Leawyn," he called again, lifting a hand. There were other figures, shadowy and black, standing farther behind him. Reluctantly, she followed.

Her footsteps cascaded through rock turned to dust. A wall of ash rose from the horizon, meeting the Hearth at a point

578

of impossible darkness. Still, she went forward, trailing him. Voices swirled in the air. The figures, impossible to discern on the horizon, spoke to her. Some were impossibly tall, others exceptionally tiny, horned or with tails. She wanted to scream and bolt, but her legs carried her forward, heedless of her will.

"Where are we going?" she called out. The voices frightened her. The void was growing darker. The ash, thicker.

"To the resting place," answered the voice.

"But I am not ready to die."

"Even the flame goes there. The red ember turns to black ash."

"And feeds the Hearth," she answered.

"NO!" the voices all cried out as one.

She fell to her knees, shielding her ears. On the horizon, the black void disappeared, growing redder and redder, until it exploded in fire, and a yellow curtain of flames reached for the sky.

"It feeds new flame!"

Leawyn raised her arms to shield her eyes. The flames kicked dust into the wind, burning her skin and eyes, filling her with the black substance. She tried to scream, clawing at her burning throat, desperate to breathe.

"Those who rest do not need to breathe."

Leawyn tore at her throat. When she felt she could take no more, she looked into the curtain of flames and saw Takoda standing, clear as day, beside a monstrous beast, with hooves for feet and horns upon its head.

"I don't understand..." she gasped, but the words came easily. Her lungs no longer burned. Blinking in confusion, she lowered her hand from her throat and straightened. The pain was gone. Slowly, almost weightless, she stepped forward—toward the fire, toward Takoda, and the strange, foul creatures gathered at his side.

"Stare upon the seed of destruction," Takoda commanded.

She nodded, trudging through the ash up to her knees now. She walked toward the flames, toward a point of burning light, and stopped before a burning sword, composed entirely of flames.

"Grip the sword," Takoda commanded.

Leawyn trembled. The heat of the sword could alone burn all the Hearth. "I do not trust the flames!"

An echo of thunder shook the world. All around them, the flames danced, casting orange light on the swirling black ash.

"This is why I died," Takoda answered.

"I never intended for that!" she screamed back.

"And yet it happened anyway."

Leawyn looked upon the shadowy image of her friend, upon the swirling ash and shadows of the beasts and monsters standing beside him. They were everywhere.

"D-do you… must I slay them?" she asked.

The world answered with another crackle of thunder. "If you feel that is right."

She looked around, staring upon the shadowy images, finding their eyes igniting with embers of red, when she heard the whinny of her horse, and the flames receded.

"Where is he?" she demanded.

"Make your decision, Wise Mother, and be fast about it. A single flame does not burn forever."

Leawyn turned her attention back to the flaming sword. The curtain wall of flame behind her rapidly extinguished. It became cold so quickly.

Ash swirled in the wind, blowing the monstrous shadows away. Even Takoda, her new friend, lost his color, blackened by the ash, and in turn, disintegrated into nothingness. She looked to the sword, to its hilt made of flames, the burning, twisting yellow of its heat. She heard the whinny of her horse again, and she stuck a hand out.

Agony.

She screamed. She screamed as loud as she ever had. The pain was unbearable. Fire surged up her arm the moment her fingers closed around the hilt, searing flesh, peeling skin. Still she held the sword high, watching its flames lick at the sky, even as the flames crept to her torso. She continued to scream, until even her lungs burned, and only embers shot from her mouth, and before her appeared her granddaughters.

Bathed in silver moonlight, they appeared untouched by the fire. "Grandmother," they said in unison.

She tried to answer, to warn them, but her vocal cords had burned away. "NO!" she wanted to scream, but she felt her muscles turning to ash and her grip on the sword slipping. The sword fell and their heads rolled, and the whinny of her horse pulled her from sleep.

Leawyn jolted upright, gasping, her body slick with sweat. The fire burned nearby, reduced to nothing more than hot embers. Rain still drizzled from the sky.

"Curses," she whispered, and wiped the sweat from her brow.

This tent is cursed, she thought, when she heard the whinny of her horse again, and at once her heart was in her throat.

Springing to her feet, she yanked on her tunic and slipped into her moccasins, then darted out into the rain. The camp lay undisturbed, shrouded in the silence of deep sleep. She picked her way through the dark, weaving past slumbering bodies and smoldering hearths, until she reached the tree where her stallion had been tied. Instead, she found only its reins, lying limp around a tree trunk.

Her heart sank, but she couldn't even be mad. The creature was born to be free.

A twig branch snapped in the woods and her poor heart leaped again. She laughed, nervously, feeling mad, and crept forward in the dark. "Here pretty, pretty," she cooed.

A head rose in the darkness. She squinted her eyes. She heard her horse pant, and her hands balled into fists.

"Of all the low, no-good things you have done, you are a simple-minded man-boy," she cursed.

She looked upon the shape of Rowan, his torso bobbing beside his horse, ready to flee back to his people—then his torso rose, impossibly high for a human, and her mouth fell open.

A centaur stepped forward.

"Hello, new friend."

Her throat tightened. Her body refused to move. She clenched her palm, trying to grip the flames.

More figures emerged from the shadows. Seven centaurs in total. And among them stood her stallion, its pale coat gleaming under the shifting glow of the rain-heavy sky.

"Y-you came," she finally managed to stammer.

"We heard a creature in distress."

Laewyn looked from Om to her horse, unsure who he referred to. "He has been ridden, first by the Outsiders, then by me," she admitted. "But I want him to be free."

The centaur nodded, turning to face the stallion. The great beast pawed at the Hearth, its breath misting in the cool air, then snorted, shaking its mane, but otherwise did not move.

"The horse has made its decision," her new friend answered.

"So it has," she agreed.

Om smiled, and without thinking, she ran forward, wrapping her arms around the base of his torso. He was solid, steady, *real*. A moment later, his hand rested lightly on her shoulder. From behind him, she heard the other centaurs snort.

After a brief pause, he gently pushed her back. "So, Old Bird, what is your plan?"

Leawyn stood in front of the centaurs, stammering, trying to form a word.

She couldn't believe it.

The centaurs had come!

WARWICK X

Warwick lay slumped against his fainting couch, staring coldly into the fire. Only a few embers remained, casting the room in an eerie orange-and-red glow. The crown prince, the heir-to-be, watched the shadows squirm, for without the light they did not have the power to dance.

To dance, he thought bitterly, swallowing the rising bile in his throat. *I wouldn't even think of it!*

His hateful gaze shifted to the piles of clothing sprawled out on the floor before him: silks, velvets, and brocades in shades fit for royalty. A gilded tunic caught his eye, its fiery-gold threads of his family's sigil glinting in the dim light. The garments had been brought by his stepmother earlier that afternoon, during one of her many visits. Melinda, the only mother he had ever known, had arrived with a hopeful smile and soft-spoken assurances, arms laden with clothes as though finery alone might lure him out of his chambers.

"Please, my love," she'd said. "Come down. The realm misses you. Join us, won't you? Lysander and Catelyn wish to see you. It breaks their hearts that you hide away in your tower."

But the mention of Lysander—and Catelyn—only sent him into a worse mood. *How I wish I could sink through the stone floor and vanish into the castle's deep, cold cellars!* She tried, again and again, to persuade him to join the others, stroking his curly blond hair as if her touch could smooth away the tension. But even her patience, so often endless, had begun to wear thin.

"It's for your father. For you! We all have our duties, Warwick. Do you think I loved your father, the great man that he is, when we first became betrothed? I hardly knew him then. You're putting us all at risk by acting like this. You are breaking your father's heart. And Lysander's as well!"

He had finally snapped. "And what of Catelyn's heart?"

She didn't know what to say. For a time, they sat in uneasy quiet, watching clouds drift past the arched windows. She stroked his hair, but gradually her fingers lost their gentle rhythm through his curls and she rose, speaking softly one last time.

"A sickness of the heart." She kissed him upon the head. "I understand now. There's no easy remedy. But think of the love of your family, Warwick. That is all I ask of you."

By evening, the servants arrived. They were to help him select clothing.

"A ball, my prince, in honor of your brother's engagement!" one said, draping a rich navy cloak over the back of a chair.

"You love dancing, don't you? You love fine clothes! Try this. Oh, it's perfect for you!" another chimed in, holding up a tunic embroidered with silver thread.

The flattery grated at him. They tried to appeal to his manliness and handsome features. Lies, all of it. He was too fat for half the clothes brought to him even with half the stitching redone.

"Gifts from the Goldwoods and Rose Monts, wills of good gestures. The good lords are paying for the ball themselves. And look here, my prince! A hat from the south, a tunic from the north! You'll love it, I promise!"

Eventually, the servant girls fled as well, so bothered by his behavior they did not mind themselves with the heaps of clothes strewn across the ground. Warwick sat alone, thinking of love, thinking of *her*, sick to his stomach.

And yet, his stomach growled.

He rose from the couch, his hand clutching the soft curve of his belly as he stared into the dwindling fire. A sharp spitting sound broke the silence as he hocked a loogie into the embers. They hissed in protest, and the last flicker of flame on the first log extinguished, leaving only the faint crackle of dying sparks to light his chambers.

"To love, to getting what I want." His face twisted as a tear rolled down his cheek. He wiped it away with a swift, angry swipe. Sick of his room, he fled from his chamber, disappearing down his staircase and slipping into a servant passage before any of the guards could see him.

He followed his nose—or his heart, he knew some would jape—toward the kitchens. The passageway, though dark and twisting, was as familiar to him as the back of his hand. Sparse candles cast flickering light, their flames painting restless shadows as he crept through, weaving between the servants occupied with their late-night tasks. It was a sport, perhaps the only one he was good at, and before long he emerged from the passageways a stone's throw from the kitchens.

The late-night fires and smell of soup and sweets still lingered, and again his stomach growled, but oddly he did not find himself in the comfort of the dough and sugar. Instead, he turned on his heels, drawn elsewhere. He approached cautiously but found the servant's entrance to the throne room abandoned either by miracle or invitation. He slipped inside.

A chill greeted him at once. Shadows cloaked the vast chamber, broken only by the faint, silver gleam of the harvest moon hanging low in the night sky. Its light was pale and insufficient, lost in the enormity of the space. Even his footsteps did not make a sound. The throne room stood like some long-forgotten chamber or attic, locked away and forgotten by people and fate and time. It even included its own ghost—a dark shadow standing before the base of the Opal Throne. Warwick approached, numb.

"Coincidence, or fate?" he said aloud, his voice echoing throughout the chamber.

Lysander turned in the moonlight, broken from thought, but not at all surprised. "I find little in our lives is ever a matter of coincidence and not fate."

Warwick stopped a few feet from his brother. They looked over one another before turning to the throne. It glistened, as it always did, no matter the time of day. "What little choice we have. In all things."

"It is much to rack the brain. To be a dullard, I suppose, lost in drink or ignorance—aye, that would be the life I choose."

"Then choose it."

"Were it so simple, so easy." Lysander's voice fell.

They turned together, now shoulder to shoulder, and stared at the base of the throne. Warwick felt a verse stir within him.

"Should time stand still
And the knife born to kill
Never drops
All men get what they want."

"A poem from Sanguinia?" Lysander asked.

"Yes." Warwick twiddled his thumbs. "The original translation is much better. The flow in the Monteclecian follows a different beat. But I wonder, if the meaning is still conveyed, does the prose even matter?"

Lysander gave a soft chuckle. "A question for you, Big Wick, not me. You always did enjoy those lessons in poetry and arithmetic. I, on the other hand, could hardly keep awake."

"Yes, the education and training of the noble and finer arts is a challenge I suppose. It is what separates us from the peasants. Those *born* to rule and those meant to follow."

The wind howled outside, a sharp, mournful sound. They both stared at the throne. A lump worked its way into Warwick's throat. Lysander stood taller, stronger, faster, but suddenly he seemed a hundred miles away, dwarfed by the significance of the throne. He curled his fists, recounting the verse. It was time to let the knife drop.

"Why have you come here today, Brother?"

"I am to become a man, Warwick."

He turned his head with a half smile. "What? You mean to say your privates have only just dropped to your undergarments?"

"No, Big Wick." Lysander frowned, dismissing the joke. "I am to become a man in a few days' time. I thought I understood what that meant once, but now I am not so sure."

"Catelyn?"

"Aye, I thought turning six-and-ten made me a man. I thought wielding a sword made me a man. No, foolish thoughts of youth." He shook his head. "I am to become a husband, and most likely within a year, a father as well."

The sound came before Warwick realized what he'd done: a sharp crack as Lysander hit the stone floor, the impact reverberating through the chamber like a boulder crashing down a mountainside. Warwick stood over him, chest heaving, with his balled fist aching.

"By the Nine!" Lysander shouted, clutching his jaw. Blood darkened his lips, and he glared up at his brother, wild-eyed. "Are you mad?"

"What is your plot? What else do you mean to steal from me?"

Lysander looked up at his brother, eyes wide. "You idiot, do you think I had any choice in claiming her hand?"

"You've always been jealous!" Warwick spat, jabbing a finger at his younger brother. "Covetous! That's what you are! A sinful, hateful little boy!"

Lysander was on his feet in a flash. Warwick took a step back, aware of a new look upon his brother's face. Lysander had dark hair and features, and within the scarce moonlight, his brow hid his eyes, except for a faint, reflective twinkle of the Opal Throne upon his irises. "Do not dare to name me sinful, glutton. You have no clue about the trials and tribulations I have endured to prop this family up."

"You cannot stand to live in the shadow of your eldest, aye? You see my gaze and follow? Covet my love? My crown? My sword? Step forth from my shadow and forge your own path, *younger* brother."

"I would if I could, but the shadow you cast is large, Big Wick!"

Warwick's cheeks burned hot. "I have told you not to call me that!"

He lurched forward and pushed his brother. Lysander stumbled backward but kept his balance. Warwick was strong, surprisingly strong, but Lysander was quick. In an instant, he returned, their noses nearly touching, his breath hot and sharp.

"You've done nothing to outgrow that name," Lysander growled. "You're still just a boy, a foolish, foolish child who would rather study words than war!"

"Why should I study war? I thought my brother was always loyal, but a curse onto me for suspecting treason from within my own house!"

"Think, Warwick!" Lysander struck the sides of his temples with both hands, his frustration boiling over. "Our house stands divided. Can you not see it? Aunt Elizabeth, the Goldwoods, the Rose Monts! How can you be so blind as to spout such stupidity?"

"It's not them I fear," Warwick shot back. "It's a usurper, someone with just enough ambition to tempt the votes of the realm. You name me gluttonous, but I say it is you who wishes for a second Diet of Blood."

"You really think I am so craven as to claw at your inheritance? To defy everything our family has built? No, Warwick, I am doing my duty as I have all along! Damn you for your wanton heart! I had no choice in the matter!"

"You can shout that claim all you like, but it is as weak as all your others."

"Then tell me, Brother! What choices have I had in this life!" Lysander took a step back, tears sparkling in his eyes, arms cast wide aside, making him bare and vulnerable.

Warwick sneered. "Look at you, little brother. A master of theatrics. But I've dined with enough stage performers to see through your play. You're no different from them."

Lysander opened his mouth to speak, but Warwick rushed forward, again pressing their noses together in a heated stance, and silenced him. "Aberness! You fled before my procession! Rushed to our father's side and sat beside the throne at my arrival. Do you understand how weak I looked to the realm? My own brother, scrambling for the throne while our family lay broken!"

"Warwick…" Lysander's voice softened, his shoulders slumping. "Perhaps you're right. Perhaps that was a grievous slight on my part." He let out a shaky breath. "But you don't know what I've seen. Father sent us on those tours with me to the north and you to the south. You had the easier path. How many angry lords did you have to face? How much treason and rebellion simmered beneath the surface in your domain?"

"You had the easier path! You treated with blood and kin! To say so little of my progress through the south to lords and ladies of different tongues and cultures! What did it take to impress them? Ha! You know nothing of my travels or deeds!"

"Then you are a fool, Brother, for your ego clouds your judgment! Who among the northern lords sit on our father's council? The Kaesnfolk, *our people*, are dominant in our realm, and the crown ignores them to placate the fringes of our empire. Lord Faelwood feels as much!"

"The ego of you—to see common kin and think it a threat. You're weak." Warwick spat upon the floor. "But not surprising, given your actions."

"My ego?" Lysander's voice rose, sharp and incredulous. "Look to yourself, Brother! I was forced to grow muscle, wield a sword, and win tourney after tourney, lest our family appear weak. While I fought for our name, you ate and drank your way across Sanguinia! Yes, you are talented in learning and language. I won't deny it. But when words fail, a sword must suffice."

"So you've taken the family sword, then? Another symbol of legitimacy to take my crown?" Warwick's eyes narrowed. "I should call the guards now and have them remove your sword hand for theft!"

"For the love of God, Brother, how thick of skull are you?" Lysander spun around, gesturing wildly as Warwick stood with a quivering upper lip. "Father gave me that sword for you. To protect you! I wield that sword *for you*. You are the future of the crown and our family."

"Like a noggin is to a wordsmith, you are to a stonemason," Warwick growled.

"What?" Lysander shook his head.

"Your words are empty and hollow. You claim to have built a solid foundation for our house, yet you've gone and planted the idea of a *second choice* in the realm's mind. There can only be one choice, Lysander. Had you studied the histories, you'd know this."

"Brother, *please*," Lysander pleaded, his voice raw. "Hear me! Or at least open your eyes. Look at Father! The realm already sees him as weak. God forgive me for saying it, but it's true. He grows weaker by the day. The man can barely stand! When I heard of Uncle's death, I rushed to Father's side because he needed me. The north knows his frailty, Warwick! You and I may have been sheltered as children, but we can't deny it any longer. Father needed me, and more importantly, you needed me, should the worst have happened and the throne sat empty."

"Ah-ha!" Warwick jumped back, his finger stabbing through the air like a blade. "The truth is at hand! You meant to sit on the throne. No longer content to be the second choice."

Before Lysander could answer, the heavy doors at the far end of the chamber slammed open. The brothers' shouting had drawn the guards, their torches casting jagged shadows as they hurried forward.

"The throne means nothing, Brother. I meant to sit upon it for you. The crown is our power and belongs to you." Lysander nodded.

Warwick only shook his head. "You have stolen, or meant to steal, every symbol of legitimacy from me. If Father and I are seen as weak, it's because you've given the realm the *choice* of another. Spit your venom all you like, Lysander. I only pray you didn't poison the poor girl with this marriage."

"Brother!" Lysander reached out a hand, but Warwick spurned him.

The guards slowed, their armor clanking as they came to a stop. "Your Highnesses," one ventured, his tone cautious. "What are you doing out of bed at this hour?"

But the brothers ignored them. A gust of wind suddenly swept the chamber, flickering the light of the torches as the mountain beneath the castle gave a groaning shudder.

Warwick glared at Lysander. "Do you feel that, Brother? Time moves on and the knife falls." He then turned, storming from the hall.

JAE X

The fire was the first star to emerge that night, flickering in the backdrop of the city. Above, the crescent moon hung high, veiled by drifting clouds. Far off, heat lightning flickered over the ocean, casting brief flashes of light. The night air buzzed with anticipation, like the charged pause before a lightning strike. Jae and Lucien rolled apart, their chests heaving with labored breaths. Another star appeared in the city below.

They lay together on their master's roof, panting, fingers intertwined. Jae closed his eyes, his body humming as if floating on the ocean's surface. He sighed, a wave of memory washing over him. He could almost hear his sister's laughter or the crash of waves. His mother's face—always just beyond focus—lingered in his mind. He could almost see her face this time… before the chains came. The shackles, the scream—always the scream.

His eyes fluttered open, the sound still echoing in his ears. Instinctively, he reached for Lucien, but found him already sitting up, their fingers still entwined, Lucien's gaze fixed somewhere in the distance.

"Do you see it?"

Jae slowly sat upright, his gaze drawn to the flashing clouds above the city, now tinged with hues of yellow. In the far corner, the Slave Quarter was ablaze. "The match has been struck," he said in disbelief.

Flames danced in Lucien's green eyes as he scanned the city below. "Harvest has come early."

"I thought… you mean you didn't plan for this?"

"I've been playing with fire Jae… It can be so hard to predict."

Jae scrambled to his feet, tearing his hand away from Lucien's grasp. Whirling around, he stared up at the ridge that towered above their manse. His mouth dropped open as massive plumes of black smoke billowed into the night. Overhead, the clouds reflected the fierce blaze spreading in the fields far beyond the city walls.

He stumbled backward, bumping back into Lucien. He whipped Jae around and clenched his shoulders tight. "Jae, listen to me. I do not know what is going to happen. No one does. Only that this is a long time coming. Come dawn, the city of Astrelaide will be either a city of free men or a city not at all. There is no middle ground."

"I am ready." Jae looked into his eyes. "I am ready to fight."

"Yes, but are you ready to *lead*? Are you?" Lucien's voice cracked, his expression torn. "I'm sorry, my love, but this is your role now. Not because I chose it. Not because anyone did. Fate has handed it to you!"

Jae's heart fluttered. "But to lead? I don't understand—"

Lucien shook him again, harder this time. "Listen to me! This was going to happen, with or without you. People will die—men, women, children. The price of freedom is steep! And you… you have a gentle heart. You need to be ready for what's coming. Many are already looking for you, Jae. Some are probably on their way right now. Friend or foe, they seek the True Moth."

Jae's heart raced as Lucien's words sank in.

"The match has been struck, and the fire has a will of its own," Lucien continued as his voice dropped. "I pray it's in our favor."

"Lucien…" Jae began, but before he could finish, Lucien leaned in and kissed him.

They embraced passionately, Jae's hand cupping Lucien's face. Perhaps this would be the last time or the first of many, but Jae wanted this moment to last forever, a single reward for all the misery he'd taken on the chin in his life. But it was not meant to be.

A ghastly cry pierced the night—a mother screaming for her child. Jae knew that sound too well. It echoed from the manse next door. Lucien and Jae broke apart, eyes darting toward the ridgeline. The neighboring palace loomed in darkness, like an iceberg adrift in the sea, but flickering torches moved through narrow windows. The masters were waking.

"We don't have much time! Come!" Lucien grabbed Jae's hand. Together, they fled from the roof, the cries from the city rising like a tidal wave beneath them. They jumped from the roof just as Hex emerged from his small hut. Jae wasted no time.

"Hex! Hide!"

The faun obeyed instantly, vanishing into the shadows.

Jae and Lucien burst into the servants' quarters below. Jae heard rustling from the sleeping chambers and moved to wake them, but Lucien caught his arm. "Armor. Weapons. We don't know who we can trust tonight."

A cold knot formed in Jae's stomach. He hadn't considered that.

In the darkness, Lucien collided with a row of metal spears, sending them clattering to the floor. Swearing under their breath, they scrambled to arm themselves. Jae hastily fastened Lucien's leather armor, then slammed a metal helmet onto his head. A torch flared to life in the hallway, and Jae barely had time to grab a shield and sword as Luke and Petra stormed into the storage room.

"Just what in the hell is going on here?" Petra demanded.

"It's time. It has begun," Lucien stated.

"Finally." Petra shook her head. She marched past Luke and grabbed a leather torso piece. "I will see to Hex."

"Hex is already in hiding," Jae replied.

"Then that is good. He can scale the rock face to safety. What about the old mother, will she need…?"

Guard and Luke wandered in sleepily from their bed chamber. "Just what is the meaning for all this noise," Luke demanded to know. He rubbed his eyes sleepily when Guard suddenly gasped. Quick as a flash, he bolted past Luke, nudged Jae aside, and snatched a knife from the table. He was gone in a heartbeat, thundering up the stairs.

"What the… Somebody better have answers for me! Just what in the world is going on!" Luke shouted. Neither Lucien or Jae answered him, and with a suspicious glance to the both of them, he cautiously approached the window. The moment his eyes landed on the scene outside, his breath caught. He gasped, dropping his torch, and bolted across the room. He shoved Jae and Lucien aside in a frantic rush, scrambling to equip himself. Jae's hand instinctively tightened around his sword hilt.

"The masters! We have to protect the masters!" Luke's voice trembled. "Why are you all just standing there? Do you want to lose your heads!"

Jae and Lucien pressed close, watching Luke's massive frame tremble uncontrollably. Behind them, Petra melted into the shadows, slipping away unnoticed.

Valeana, Pete, and Pate finally emerged from their sleeping chambers. Valeana took one sleepy look at the chaos, gasped, and then bolted up the servant staircase still in her nightgown. Pete and Pate, twins of chaos, broke into a run for their armor, Pate tripping over Pete as they scrambled for weapons.

"Tell me! Tell me all that you know!" Luke shouted. He fumbled with his steel chest plate. He couldn't get the straps to tie. "One of you! Help me! Now!"

But Jae and Lucien didn't move. They backed away slowly from him. Pete and Pate were still tripping over one another.

"What's wrong with you two?" Luke's voice cracked, desperate. "We have to protect the masters! They'll kill us if we don't!"

Jae and Lucien exchanged a glance. Under different circumstances, Jae might have laughed at the sight of Lucien trembling in ill-fitted armor, his hand gripping a knife. But now, the weight of realization settled over him—for the first time, he had control over his own life. The feeling was terrifying, yet exhilarating. Slowly, Jae's hand moved to the hilt of his sword, his glare fixed on Luke. His resolve solidified. He didn't budge.

Luke looked at them, sweating profusely. "I see now," he stammered. He tied his chest plate together, threw on his helmet, and grabbed his sword. "Understand I cannot save you." Without another word, he barreled up the staircase to his master.

Jae and Lucien met each other's eyes again, a flicker of relief passing between them. They almost felt the urge to kiss, but a loud crash from upstairs stole their attention. Sirene's piercing cries followed, followed by a vase shattering and hurried footsteps stomping through the hall above.

"What do we do?" yelled Pete.

"I don't know!" cried Pate.

"We can't just stand here," Lucien stammered. "This is the hour of decision. We have to make a move!"

Jae's thoughts turned to running, but there was no way out of the Rose that didn't lead to the Thorned Men. Old Berona was upstairs too, and the good master. He needed to save the old mother, and given the chaos, maybe he could even strike a bargain with Aeksilor to let them go without trouble—*or fighting Luke.*

"The kitchens!" Jae exclaimed, grabbing Lucien's hand. They dashed toward the hidden staircase, pounding upstairs into the kitchen, only to find it dark and empty. Old Berona was nowhere to be seen. "We have to find her!" But Lucien grabbed his arm.

"We won't be able to save everyone."

"We have to try!"

Jae's heartbeat was in his ears as he burst through the kitchen door into the hallway that led to the dining chamber. A few torches now burned in the house, and damned if he could believe it, the Lady Aril walked calmly toward him, her hair cut short and dyed solid black.

"M-my lady?" Jae bowed, instinctively, but she only looked to him in passing. She dragged her middle child, Boros, behind her as he cried silently to himself. Guard walked behind her, followed closely by Valeana.

Jae and Lucien stepped aside as Aril brushed past them. Guard held up a knife as they passed, glaring at them with cold eyes. Valeana quickly acknowledged them, whispering urgently to Jae. "Be safe. Thorned Men are in the house. We're heading toward a better future. Fight for your own." She pressed a quick kiss to both Jae and Lucien before disappearing into the shadows of the kitchen.

Jae and Lucien could only exchange wide-eyed glances with one another.

"Stop them! My son! My son has been stolen!" The sound of Aeksilor's shouts filled the house followed by Sirene's shrieks. He staggered into view at the far end of the hall, half-drunk and fully furious. Spotting them, he pointed an accusing finger and let out a roar. Two Thorned Men appeared from behind him. Even from this distance, Jae could see the hate burning in their yellow lives. They charged him, brandishing their iron rods as if to ram him.

Lucien fumbled for his knife, but Jae grabbed his arm, shoving him hard into the kitchen. Jae planted his feet, bracing himself as the Thorned Men closed in. At the last moment, he leaped back into the kitchen doorway. The Thorned Man skidded to a halt, pivoting to follow him. With a fierce clash, Jae swung his sword down hard, the sound of metal on metal reverberating through the house. One of the Thorned Men dropped his rod, and Jae seized the opportunity, lunging forward to catch the second off guard. He drove his sword into the man's abdomen, blood erupting from the wound. In shock, Jae lost his grip on the sword and stumbled backward.

The disarmed Thorned Man tackled him, sending Jae crashing to the ground. His head struck the floor with a dull *thud*, the leather helm offering little protection as his vision blurred. He barely registered Lucien's terrified scream before a spray of warm liquid coated his torso. Dazed, he rolled over, just in time to see the Thorned Man slump to the side. Jae rose to his knees to find Lucien repeatedly stabbing him. It took a soft hand from Jae to get him to stop.

They rose together, panting heavily. Jae wanted to embrace him, but another scream from Aeksilor sent his heart racing into his throat.

"Your sword, you idiot!" Lucien shouted.

Jae glanced down at his empty hands in disbelief before sprinting to the still-gasping Thorned Man. He yanked the sword free just as another one lunged at him. Pivoting on his heels, Jae deflected the Thorned Man's iron rod upward. The Thorned Man stumbled, and Jae seized the moment, launching an offensive of three swift strikes that knocked the weapon from his hands.

The Thorned Man stared at him with wide yellow eyes, but before he could react, Jae drove the sword into his belly, falling into the hallway. As the man crumpled to the ground, Jae yanked the blade free, blood splattering across his clothes.

Luke emerged behind the fallen corpse, panic etched on his face. "What are you doing?" he cried.

"Don't do this, Luke!" Jae pleaded with him.

"Don't you understand? There are too many of them! You're doomed and you'll take us all with you!"

"Don't be a coward," Lucien said as he emerged from the kitchen. He was drenched in blood.

Luke stood frozen before them, mouth agape. Jae and Lucien slowly pushed past him, all three gripping their weapons tightly.

"You fools," Luke whispered as they brushed by. "They'll kill her."

Aeksilor screamed when he saw them approach and bolted into the foyer. Jae and Lucien broke into a sprint, rounding the corner only to come face-to-face with Aeksilor and Sirene. Old Berona was backed into a corner, a knife pressed to Luthor's neck as he squirmed, wide-eyed, held captive in her lap. Ten Thorned Men stood in the doorway, blocking their escape.

"Traitors! All of you! I bring you into my home! The good House of Aeksilor and this is how you repay my kindness! I should have let you all rot in the fields! Your skin burned raw by the sun and then scalped by the beastfolk of this world. You horrendous fools! You are worse than devils! To betray a family—it's unfathomable!" Aeksilor foamed at the mouth.

Jae's eyes shot to Old Berona. She held Aeksilor's oldest child in a death grip, her face twisted in fury. A chill ran down Jae's spine; he had never seen such rage in a human being before. Behind them, Luke trudged down the hall, his head hung low.

"Luke! Kill them! Kill them all! Show your loyalty!" Aeksilor stamped his feet, pleading.

Luke's hand went slowly to his sword. He unsheathed it, the steel glinting ominously in the flickering torchlight. Old Berona unleashed a blast of curses in a language no one understood. The Thorned Men inched forward, rods extended, as Luthor whimpered in terror.

"Luke, no! Listen to me—they don't know how to fight!" Jae pleaded.

"There are simply too many…" Luke muttered, slowly inching toward him.

"No! We can take them! Their rods are meant for punishment, not for fighting. You saw us kill three, easy!"

"Oh, Jae…" Luke sighed, shaking his head. "I'm so sorry I have to do this…"

A loud crash stole everyone's attention. Pete and Pate stumbled out of a hidden staircase, colliding directly with the huddle of Thorned Men. One of the creatures let out a guttural scream, as if choking on mud, and stabbed Pate straight through the throat. Pete screamed. Sirene broke into fresh tears. Aeksilor dove for cover. Four Thorned Men moved for Old Berona. With a chilling smile, she sliced Luthor's throat from ear to ear. Two iron rods then pierced her upper chest.

Jae didn't recall moving, but the next sound he heard was the sound of his sword against a metal rod. He thrust upward with all his strength, sending the rod high into the air. His sword then found its way across the accursed man's neck.

Luke's sword joined his, hacking the head off a Thorned Man with a clean, decisive swing. Pete, seemingly forgetting his own weapon, tackled one of the abominations. Out of nowhere, Petra slid from another hidden compartment and sliced a Thorned Man's neck with a butcher's knife.

Three Thorned Men fled outside, Aeksilor and Sirene hot on their heels. The others were butchered in seconds.

"Aeksilor is getting away! We can't let him escape!" Lucien shouted, darting for the door, but a firm hand from Luke stopped him.

"We don't know how many more are out there!"

"Let's secure the household," Petra urged. "We can hold here and wait for help."

Jae ignored all of them. With the Thorned Men dying around him, he dropped his sword and sank to his knees next to Old Berona. She was bleeding heavily, but still alive. "Old Mother..."

"Jae," she coughed, her voice fading. "Do not be sad. I enjoyed more years of freedom than you've been alive. Now it is your time to know that feeling. I have seen to it that you will find success. The world will know of your deeds. Please, no, do not be afraid." She cupped his sobbing face. "End this evil practice and beware the East. And last of all," she choked out, "be wary of his lies."

Jae held her hand as she slumped backward. Tears fell from his cheeks.

The survivors shouted around him. More torches were lit. A Thorned Man gave a dying cry. Footsteps surrounded him.

Pete let out a guttural scream. Petra turned to him forcefully, shouting something directly to his face, and then disappeared. Jae couldn't hear anything except the crash of the ocean. The Old Mother's face became blurred by the sun.

Lucien brought him back to reality with a kiss on the cheek, wrapping his arms around his waist to help him to his feet. Dazed, Jae blinked and surveyed the room. Luke stood nearby, his shoulders slumped but still alive. Hex had made it into the manse, and Petra was tending to him. Pete silently wept over his fallen twin, while Lucien regarded him with feverish eyes.

"Listen, they'll be coming for us now. I need to give you this." Lucien held in his hands a red tablecloth, quickly tying one end around his neck to fashion a makeshift cape. "They need to see you as a figurehead, but not as a master. It's time."

With one hand gripping Jae's shoulder, Lucien placed his sword into Jae's other hand. Together, they stepped out of the manse and crossed the courtyard. The mermaid fountain in the center of the courtyard had been toppled in the excitement. Jae looked downward, seeing the decapitated head of the sea creature lying in the dirt. Lucien didn't let him stare. He pulled him toward a flickering gathering of lights, with other survivors trickling out from the manse behind them.

"Be brave. Embrace the legend. Acknowledge the tall tales. Your image will be everything."

Jae let go of Lucien's hand. His two hands gripped the sword and lifted it upward. The city burned below. A strong wind whipped the makeshift cape behind him.

A mass of torches ascended the hill toward them. The neighboring master's manse became engulfed in flames. Voices and shouts filled the night air.

"Here he comes," Lucien whispered.

The bricks underneath them thundered. A hulking shadow emerged from the blaze of the torches.

The minotaur. The very one that forged his namesake.

Bull Slayer.

The beast approached him, two massive sickles clutched in either hand. Behind it, humans, other minotaurs, and creatures moved in unison, their voices fading into an eerie silence. Blood coated everyone.

The minotaur emerged from the pack, stepping forward until it stood just feet away from Jae. Lucien instinctively shrank back, and Jae felt a chill run down his spine. The creature was larger than he remembered.

"Yes, I recognize you." The minotaur glared down over Jae. "They say you killed me."

It took Jae a moment to find the courage to speak. "More lies from the masters. You may be a beast, but I saw you as a brother that day. I still do."

The minotaur snorted, then lifted its head to survey the remaining survivors of the House of Aeksilor.

"I see then, you are the True Moth who seeks the light. Then come, let us finish our harvest. You walk with me, Crassius, and together we will embrace freedom by dawn."

Crassius.

"Let us welcome the dawn together," Jae nodded.

MELINDA IV

"You did what?" Melinda stood tall over her husband, hands planted firmly on her hips. Her scowl deepened as she felt the fresh powder on her face flake. The ball had yet to begin and her happy facade was already crumbling.

"The boy wouldn't budge otherwise. You tried reasoning with him yourself." Bancroft sighed. Seated in his imperial uniform crisscrossed with medals and badges, he looked every bit the ruler, except for the absent crown and the weariness in his posture. Without it, she noticed a slight bald spot forming on the back of his head.

"That didn't mean you should indulge his childish whims," she snapped at him but immediately regretted it. The lines under his eyes had never appeared deeper.

"He is heartbroken." He looked away from her. "An immature boy, yes, but heartbroken nonetheless."

"Oh Bancroft, look at me." She teared up. His heavy eyes

obeyed, lifting upward. "I am dripping in jewels, burdened by this massive strawberry-brunette monstrosity of a wig, reeking of opulence and grandeur, and yet I am still robbed. Despite all my riches, I am poorer for it. You've taken my boy from me, just as the other becomes a man."

"Warwick becomes a man too, my good wife." Bancroft would not keep his eyes trained on her. "Childish as he is, this is a step toward manhood. He'll enter the ball with Polina tonight, and soon they'll be formally engaged. Then what? Grandchildren, I suppose." He forced a smile, faint and fleeting.

"Grandchildren…" Melinda's heart fluttered at the thought. *A granddaughter, perhaps, to dote upon.* "But still, I should have been consulted. The scandal of it all! The realm will notice if the heir gives his brother the cold shoulder."

"Scandal?" Bancroft scoffed. "My court is built on scandal. Do you forget Alexander and Charles are hosting tonight's ball? I assure you, tonight will be no exception."

"All the more reason we should present a united front as a family. Warwick must be brought to heel."

Bancroft shook his head as if too tired to even sigh. "Must we argue, tonight of all nights?" His voice grew weary. "My youngest debuts as a proper prince, and we're already late."

"You are the emperor and I the empress. We arrive precisely when we mean to."

That drew a smile from him at last. She leaned over, careful not to topple her wig, and kissed him upon the cheek.

"To think, this is almost over," he whispered.

"My dear?"

"The boys married, the succession settled. By the Nine, I pray Warwick has a son within the year. How contented my heart would be!"

"Then let us rise, my husband," she said, offering her hand. "Let the night proceed, and we shall be one step closer to such a goal."

He took her hand and rose with some difficulty, his growing belly making the effort more taxing than he cared to admit.

Together, they descended the grand staircase from their private chamber, Melinda steadying him while carefully managing the precarious weight of her towering wig. Their progress was deliberate but steady, and soon they reached an ornate hall linking their family's towers to the quarters of only their most distinguished guests. Waiting for them was Strammond, his usual black-and-red knightly attire replaced with a well-tailored suit and bowtie. His thinning gray hair had been carefully combed over, though not without effort. He looked more the servant than guest, but she figured such an occasion was beyond his warrior demeanor, and she found his effort endearing.

"By the Nine," Strammond gasped at their descent. "Now the realm will truly see your nature, my lady, for your guise is ruined. An angel in human form!" He nodded to his wife and she blushed. "And you, Your Grace, as regal and splendid as ever."

"I may as well be a centaur turd compared to my good wife," he jested. "but aye, I have done the best I can to compete with her beauty."

Strammond blinked, momentarily stunned by the emperor's crass humor. "Your Grace, you sell yourself far too short. The realm will be in awe of their lieges tonight."

"Your courtesies are noted, my good man, but tonight is for once not about my good wife or me. Pray tell, how fare Lysander and Warwick?"

Melinda's stomach tightened, and her heart gave a nervous flutter. *How I wish I could be with them.*

"Lysander remains under the close watch of his cousin, Derrick," Strammond reported. "He will not see Catelyn until their grand entrance this evening. The same is true for Warwick. I understand he is spending the evening in the company of Lord Dymtrus until his debut with Lady Polina."

"By Aethylios!" Bancroft shook his head. "A whole evening stuck with that man. Perhaps you were right." He elbowed Melinda.

She forced a smile but could not bring herself to join in their laughter. Slipping her hand free from her husband's, she left him and Strammond to their banter. Her gaze wandered and landed on Harriet Rose Mont, who stood idly nearby, lost in thought. Wishing to bite her thumb in frustration at Bancroft, Melinda instead plastered on a beaming smile and made her way toward her. *Compliments, compliments only,* she reminded herself, but her steps faltered as Harriet suddenly let out a startled squeal. Melinda froze, heat rising to her cheeks as she assumed the excitement was directed at her. Yet, a moment later, Harriet dashed to a nearby staircase, where her daughter, Torralin, was descending.

Melinda's breath caught. Torralin, only five-and-ten, glided down the staircase like a rose petal unfurling in bloom. Her mother burst into tears, rushing to the girl's side and falling to her knees. Torralin flushed but fought back tears of her own, determined not to let them mar her carefully applied makeup. Instead, she extended a gloved hand, which Harriet kissed reverently, dotting it with affection.

"My baby! Look at my baby!" Harriet cried as she rose to embrace her daughter. Torralin blushed, now betrothed, standing on the threshold of womanhood. "Everyone must see my baby!"

Melinda watched, her heart ripped in two, as Harriet stroked her daughter's long, curled black hair, teasing it gently over her shoulders. Torralin's gown, with its scandalously exposed bosom, signaled an undeniable truth: childhood was over. Like Warwick, like Lysander, the girl had crossed the threshold, and her parents' role was complete. She pivoted sharply, biting her thumb to stifle a sob, and hurried to a nearby bench. She collapsed onto it, clutching one hand to her womb as tears burned her eyes. Memories surged unbidden—her screams of agony and terror, the echoes of the court physician's frantic cries.

Too soon, too soon! She could hear the court physician shout, barely over her own sobs. No babe had ever been cradled in her arms.

"Empress?" came the soft voice of a boy.

Melinda blinked hard, stunned to find an angelic figure standing before her. A little boy with blonde hair and green eyes looked enigmatically up at her. "Little thing, where do you come from?" she whispered.

"Up above," he gestured, and her heart fluttered.

Were you one of my own?

"Empress, are you all right? Shall I call the guard?"

The boy's question pulled her from her reverie. She followed his gesture upward and realized her mistake. He was pointing to the imperial guest chambers. This was not a vision, not her child, but Gael, her husband's cupbearer.

Not her own.

"I am fine, boy. I am fine."

Still, she extended her hand. He took it without hesitation, and together they wandered back to her husband.

"Oh, what a fine sight!" Bancroft beamed when he noticed them. "Melinda, I can think of no better guardian for you than the boy whose family guards the Isle. You are in safe hands."

Yes, safe hands, she thought, allowing herself a faint smile.

Strammond stepped forward and escorted them toward the throne room. Melinda clung to her husband's arm with one hand and held the boy's small, firm grip with the other. Gael's fingers tightened around hers, perhaps unconsciously, as though reaching for a mother's hand he had not held in far too long. For the moment, they could both pretend.

From across the castle, the strains of strings and triumphant horns echoed through the halls, the music carrying the life of the party underway. Servants bustled past in a blur, balancing trays of sparkling wine and gleaming decanters of spirits. The air was alive with the intoxicating aromas wafting from the kitchens. Melinda's nose twitched at the scents of roasted pigs and golden-brown ducks, steaming bowls of whipped potatoes, and bubbling pots of richly spiced stews. Sweet notes mingled with the savory: honey cakes, cinnamon buns, lemon tarts, and sugared cookies were paraded past, destined for the tables of the finely dressed guests slowly making their way to the festivities. Melinda smiled softly, imagining Warwick reveling in such delights. She paused midstep and snapped her fingers, summoning a passing tray of sweets. Offering it to Gael, she watched as the boy delighted in the treats, his small hands sticky with honey and dusted with sugar. She allowed Gael to have his fill until he became caked in honey and sugar.

"Oh, honey," Melinda said with a soft smile. She licked her thumb and gently wiped the sticky sweetness from the boy's cheeks. Strammond grew visibly impatient at their slow progress, but it was known that a lord or lady never arrives late, and for an emperor, nothing could be truer. When they finally arrived at the entrance of the throne room, Norbert awaited them, his grin stretching from ear to ear.

"Your Grace! A fine occasion, just fine, I say. You must be so proud of your boy."

"Both boys, I daresay," Bancroft replied with a chuckle. "By chance, you haven't seen either, have you?"

"I cannot say we've crossed paths."

"No, I suppose all is well then. Speaking of wellness, how is your voice?"

Norbert sheepishly reached a hand up and touched the base of his throat. "I am healing very well, thank you, Your Grace."

"Then let us be prompt about it." Bancroft smiled and looked to her. "Ready?"

She nodded, and Norbert's grin returned, wider than ever. "An honor, as always, to announce you."

At Strammond's signal, two Demonbreun knights rushed forward, their heavy boots echoing in the corridor as they swung open the grand doors to the throne room. Strammond gently took the boy's honey-coated hand from Melinda's, the sticky separation drawing a tinge of sorrow from her.

"PRESENTING THE EMPEROR, HIS IMPERIAL MAJESTY, BANCROFT OF HOUSE HIERONYMUS, AND HIS GOOD WIFE, THE EMPRESS MELINDA."

A band struck from a raised plinth beneath two pillars of the throne room as the lords and ladies of the realm burst into applause. Melinda blushed, catching her husband smiling as they made their grand entry. The aisle was long, reminiscent of their entry at Thane's funeral, though the occasion was a world apart. Lords and ladies, already deep into their cups, cheered and toasted with goblets of wine, their faces alight with merriment. Smiles and laughter were on the face of every attendee, and where Melinda's bones tended to rattle from the chilly air of the Opal Throne room, a warm breeze welcomed her, perfumed with wine and honey.

"A splendid occasion," she whispered to her husband.

"One that is most deserved," Bancroft replied, raising a hand to acknowledge the crowd.

Their grand procession ended before a long table erected at the base of the Opal Throne. Two Demonbreun knights approached, their faces alight with pride as they handed Melinda and Bancroft each a goblet of wine. The applause swelled as the imperial pair separated, circling the long table with stately grace before reuniting at their seats.

"To the realm and all those who celebrate this grand day for my family!" Bancroft's voice rang out as he raised his goblet high.

Melinda watched him sweep the hall, his gaze settling upon his mother seated with Alden at the nearest front table. The Dowager Empress held herself with quiet dignity, her silvered hair crowned with modest jewels. She nodded in response to her son, raising her goblet in return. Melinda's heart nearly broke for the second time today. Grandma'am was passing the mantle to a new generation; her dedication to family was unwavering. Melinda could only hope she could live up to such a legacy.

The realm's energy quickly ebbed, wearing off after another long series of introductions, but certain honors and expectations were due. Alexander and Hollace Goldwood came next, followed by Charles and Harriet Rose Mont. They made the long procession through fierce applause and joined Melinda and her husband at the long table as sponsors of the event.

Melinda raised her goblet in a toast to the new arrivals, a gesture of respect and camaraderie, and greeted them formally. "To my esteemed cousins," she proclaimed, her voice resonant. "Your gold and faith bring blessings aplenty to the realm and our family!" A fresh wave of cheers followed, but the night's true spectacle was only beginning.

All eyes turned to the great doors of the throne room, their twin panels adorned with the two-headed phoenix of House Hieronymus. With a slow, deliberate motion, the phoenix emblem split down the middle, revealing Elizabeth at the threshold. The room erupted in applause, yet Bancroft and Melinda exchanged startled glances as another figure stepped into view.

"ELIZABETH OF INVERNESS, ACCOMPANIED BY... EDWIN BATTLEBRIDGE, TREASURER TO THE REALM."

The applause faltered briefly, replaced by whispers rippling through the crowd. Melinda's fingers tightened around the stem of her goblet, her practiced smile freezing in place. Bancroft's expression betrayed no more than mild surprise, but his eyes darted toward Melinda, wide with unspoken alarm. *This will be the night of scandal,* he reminded her without words.

Elizabeth and Edwin arrived at the head table, and Elizabeth gracefully kissed the hands of Alexander and Charles before bowing before the emperor. Edwin followed suit, though his eyes would not meet Bancroft's. When Elizabeth turned to Melinda, she greeted her with a kiss on the cheek. As the pair settled beside them, Melinda subtly shifted her chair away from Elizabeth, her cheeks flushing with heat. The loud applause was a blessing, for it drowned out the curse whispered under Melinda's breath, which, had it been heard, might have sparked further scandal.

A pair of trumpets blared, commanding the realm's attention as the herald of House Hieronymus approached the throne room doors. They swung open with a gust of wind or perhaps the collective gasp of the realm, for Melinda nearly tumbled out of her seat. Applause faded to astonished murmurs. Derrick entered the room, and to Melinda's shock, he was accompanied by none other than the princess of Isperia, Vipra. The sight of them together struck the crowd silent, and Alexander and Charles were the first to rise, applauding them as they made their way toward the high table. With little choice, Melinda and Bancroft followed suit, begrudgingly standing to welcome Derrick and the princess of a foreign and hostile power to their banquet table, the family sword still hanging from Derrick's hip.

Melinda smiled. She smiled until her cheeks were fit to burst. Derrick and Vipra joined them at the high table. *Oh, the swears that bubble inside!* Her tongue flicked like a snake, judging the perfect moment to strike at Elizabeth beside her when the realm quieted, and once again they took their seats. She turned, ready to unleash hell before the realm, but Elizabeth simply looked past her. She nodded to Alexander, who then waved to the Demonbreun knights. The trumpets sounded once more, and Warwick entered the throne room, Polina, daughter of Dymtrus, at his side.

Once again, Bancroft and Melinda were forced to rise. Melinda applauded, tears welling in her eyes, while the lords and ladies looked to her, blushing, bashful, watching the empress welcome her adopted son and his betrothed. She played the part well, smiling through her tears, but her heart clenched with a quiet fury. The moment was not hers to savor. Again, she was robbed of any inkling of motherhood.

"Mother, Father." Warwick arrived at the high table. He dropped to one knee and kissed both of their hands with an air of solemn respect. Polina followed, a striking young woman draped in a dark gown, a diamond necklace accentuating her neckline, her bosom visible in the deep cut.

Melinda forced a tight smile, accepting the girl's curtsy as she and Warwick took their seats. Warwick, ever the gentleman, pulled out Polina's chair with a flourish, earning yet another round of applause.

The realm settled for a moment before the guests of honor were to make their formal appearance. Watching as the eyes of the realm shifted away from her, she fluffed her skirt, gulped wine, and leaned in close to Elizabeth. Her voice was low, carrying just the right amount of venom. "So soon, you mean to remarry? Your husband's ashes have barely cooled."

Elizabeth did not look at her but simply picked up her goblet of wine. "A woman without a man by her side is as good as invisible in this world. Surely, you cannot blame a widow for finding a potential match?"

"That is precisely the issue—for you not to ask for a blessing or even consideration from the crown. To promote subterfuge within our own house!"

"I'm giving away my daughter's hand to your son." She sipped on her wine. "How can you accuse me of treachery?"

"And the foreign princess who agitates our borders? You would take such a risk without the emperor's approval? Do you not see the scandal brewing? Does the inheritance of a single city really justify the threat of a war?"

Elizabeth turned toward her with a sly smile, her words coming smooth as silk. "Pray tell, my empress, how could an alliance with the Kingdom of Isperia be anything but beneficial for all of us? Especially with your current troubles with the Isle of Fláimir?"

Melinda sharpened her tongue, ready to unleash a further lashing, when Elizabeth stole the blade out from under her.

"Mind you, my son nearly died at the hands of Warwick. The crown may have downplayed his injury, but it was Princess Vipra who saved both Derrick's arm and his life. This gesture serves as much as a thank-you as it does a sign of goodwill from a kingdom that could easily turn against us. Polina, seated beside her, understands the danger, and this is merely a bridge to her estranged kin. I have brought Isperia to our side." Elizabeth leaned in close to Melinda, her breath warm against Melinda's flushed skin. "And speaking of alienated kin, let the sword be my needle and the house our torn cloth. Watch how I stitch us whole again."

Melinda recoiled, her eyes widening as the deep rumble of a drumroll reverberated through the throne room, followed by the blaring sound of trumpets. Almost instinctively, she rose, her gaze still fixed on Elizabeth, her breath caught in her throat. The grand doors to the throne room swung open with a mighty creak, and the air was suddenly alive with deafening applause. A herald's voice rang out. "WELCOME THE NEWLY BETHROTHED, LYSANDER OF HOUSE HIERONYMUS, AND THE GOOD LADY OF HOUSE HIERONYMUS, CATELYN, DAUGHTER OF ELIZABETH AND THANE!"

Melinda applauded, trying to smile as she watched Lysander and Catelyn make their long procession toward the throne when Derrick rose from his seat, sword in hand.

Bancroft VI

There was an initial moment of shock. All eyes turned from the newly betrothed couple to Derrick. The knights of the Demonbreun shifted uneasily, gauntleted hands twitching near their blades. Bancroft's gaze swept the room and found Dyrebane. The knight struggled fiercely to reach Lysander, restrained only by his brother.

"Husband…" Melinda desperately pulled on his sleeve.

Bancroft kept up his applause even as the realm drew quiet. "Let us watch."

Lysander and Catelyn, walking hand in hand, stopped halfway down the aisle. Derrick marched forward, gripping the family sword Empyrean.

Charles leaned over and whispered into his ear. "A fine spectacle."

A ruse, Bancroft knew, and he ignored the jest. As Derrick reached the center of the hall, he stopped and, with a deep breath, dropped to one knee before Lysander and Catelyn. The blade rested flat across his palms, its ancient steel catching the flickering light of the chandeliers. The realm fell silent.

"Before you, Cousin, I present the family sword, forged in the fires of the Lyonnian Empire. For a millennium, this blade has stood with our house against man and beast alike. It has safeguarded our family's honor, never knowing defeat. Through this sword, the Phoenix King united this realm from tyranny and ash, and by its steel, my father gave his life defending our family and land. Though its balance feels natural in my hand, I cannot deny its rightful master." He bowed his head, arms extending as he raised the sword toward Lysander. "Lysander, I offer this legacy to you. To protect our honor, our family, and, above all, my good sister."

For a moment, the hall held its breath. Then, Catelyn gently touched Lysander's arm, and her eyes filled with tears. She gave him a slight nudge, urging him forward. Lysander stepped toward Derrick and took the sword, raising it high above his head, the blade catching the room's light like fire. "To House Hieronymus," he declared, "and the honor of our realm!"

Bancroft's wife unleashed a torrent of breath as the realm again broke into loud applause. Bancroft nearly collapsed, the relief so grand his bladder leaked slightly into his trousers. He slunk to his chair as Catelyn broke free from Lysander's side and rushed forward, throwing her arms around Derrick in a deep, tearful embrace. Her whispered words of gratitude were lost in the roar of the crowd. Moments later, she returned to Lysander, and together they resumed their grand walk, crossing the hall to the high table. As honor demanded, they approached the emperor first. Lysander bent the knee at his feet. Bancroft sat forward, placing a firm hand upon his boy's shoulder. A tear fell from his eye as he whispered. "I am so proud of you, boy."

"Thank you, Father. I promise I will do you proud."

"You will do us all proud," Charles interjected. He stepped forward and gently ran his fingers along the blade. "A spectacle, truly a fine spectacle! You are destined to serve your family well."

"I will serve all of our family, and the realm, greatly and as one. Especially with my future wife by my side." He slipped an arm around Catelyn's waist and pressed a light kiss to her cheek. A burst of surprise swept through the audience, and a moment later Melinda crashed through between them, completely red of face.

"Catelyn, and my love, do not give the ballroom any further scandal." Melinda blushed.

Despite her words, she kissed them each on the cheek. Bancroft, for all the merriment surrounding him, did not dare look upon Warwick.

Lysander and Catelyn, though betrothed, were not allowed to sit together. Lysander took his place beside his father, a deliberate barrier between himself and Charles, while Catelyn sat with her mother and Melinda. Around them, guests filled the hastily arranged maze of tables and benches, voices swelling with chatter. Servants poured forth, carrying every manner of dish and drink known to the realm. Feasting and revelry consumed the hall, and the vibrant symphony of music, laughter, clinking knives, and goblets rose to fill every corner of the throne room.

Amid this commotion, few noticed Dymtrus striding purposefully toward the high table until he appeared beside the emperor. "A moment of your time, *Your Grace*."

Bancroft froze, his knife and fork paused above a half-carved roast duck. A familiar weight pressed on his chest, and with a resigned sigh, he rose, gesturing for Dymtrus to follow. They moved toward the shadows near the Opal Throne, but even in the dim light, Dymtrus burned bright with his ire.

"My lord, in anticipation of your fury…"

Bancroft raised his hand, having neither the patience nor strength to politic. "My fury? You cannot even begin to comprehend my fury!"

Dymtrus spat. "I have held my tongue while my stomach churned at the thought of that *creature* sharing the same walls as me. And now she sits at my table next to my daughter. It is *unacceptable*!"

Bancroft raised a subtle hand, trying to quell both his irate Master of Laws and the malaise mounting in the pit of his stomach. "Her attendance, alongside my nephew, is merely a gesture of goodwill. She aided in healing the boy, after all."

"Healing?" Dymtrus's voice rose to a shout. "Healing! Do you know what her family is capable of? By the Nine, her sister rules Isperia through an incapacitated man. You are lucky the boy still walks! Now I will not have this, I simply will not!"

"And what would you have me do?" Bancroft looked back to his plate of food. "Do you wish for war?"

"I fail to see your point."

"If it is a war you want, then so be it." Bancroft shrugged. "I will throw the princess from this hall, humiliate her before the court, and shun diplomacy. Are you prepared to raise your war banners, Dymtrus?"

"What other choice do we have?" Dymtrus bared his teeth. "Either you slight both myself and my daughter, or you are so stupid to allow her to remain. The venom within her!"

Bancroft suddenly took a step forward, pressing into his subject. "Caution your tongue, Dymtrus. I would hate to take it from you on the eve of your daughter's betrothal."

Dymtrus's eyes darted wildly. "Wulfnoth! Where is he? Our secretary, perhaps he will speak some sense to you about this border debacle!" His head snapped from side to side, searching frantically.

Lysander tried to look casually over to them, but Charles followed his gaze and gave them both a sly smile. Unable to locate Wulfnoth, Dymtrus turned his frenzied attention to another target: Edwin Battlebridge, seated at the high table.

"Edwin! Edwin, come here at once!"

Edwin froze midsip, his shoulders hunching like a dog caught with its snout in the larder. His sheepish expression grew more pronounced as he rose, stammering an apology to those around him. Bancroft lifted a hand, ready to intercede, but Dymtrus bellowed again, louder this time.

"*At once!*"

Reluctantly, Edwin shuffled forward, shoulders slumped as he came to stand by the emperor's side. "Your Grace," he bowed, "I assure you, I meant no disrespect to your brother. Elizabeth came to me just yesterday, distraught, requesting a male escort for the evening..."

"Another *unexpected* guest?" Dymtrus snarled as his brow furrowed and spittle flew from his lips. "How many unexpected guests sit at the high table, when I, the father of Polina, have been denied such a privilege!"

"The matter of Elizabeth's choice in escort is neither for debate nor reproach," Bancroft assured him, though he was becoming short of breath. He tugged angrily at the neckline of his tunic.

Dymtrus ignored him, rounding on Edwin again. "Edwin, speak some sense into our liege! The princess of Isperia should not be here, and seated at the high table, no less!"

"Perhaps, like myself, she is simply a victim of polite obligation. Imagine attending a foreign court and declining an invitation from the imperial family. Surely, her hands were tied..."

"Is the prospect of Elizabeth's *hairy doughnut* so enticing that..."

Edwin's hand ripped across Dymtrus's face.

"ENOUGH!" Bancroft yelled. He lurched forward, pushing forward between the two men. "You commit a hostile act before me on such a holy day!" He started to shout but took notice of the high table and felt all eyes fall upon him. The heads of lords and ladies poked above the table, desperate eyes searching for the next scandal.

"Father!" Lysander pushed up from the table, darting to his side. "Gentlemen, please, on such a blessed day? Can we not work out whatever plagues us in the morning? Perhaps a hunt in the mountains, my treat?"

Dymtrus's cheek flamed red as he stepped closer to Lysander, his eyes locked on Edwin with venomous intensity. "An assault on a lord demands a life. But in recognition of your service to the realm, and your pitiable state as a recent widow, I will settle for your hand!"

Edwin took a step back, also burning red, but no less indignant. "A worthy price to pay for an insult to the imperial family! So we shall take off your tongue while we're at it... to utter such profanities about the emperor's sister-in-law..."

The tension thickened like smoke until the sudden blare of trumpets cut through the hall, silencing all. Heads turned toward the dais as Charles rose from the high table, a sly smile playing at his lips as he gestured for attention.

"ANNOUNCING THE ARRIVAL OF TORRALIN ROSE MONT OF HOUSE HIERONYMUS AND HER BETHROTHED, CASIMIR OF HOUSE VALKIRN."

A stunned wave of applause rippled through the throne room, leaving the four men momentarily frozen. They exchanged bewildered glances before joining the realm in polite, uncertain clapping. Seizing the opportunity, Edwin slipped away, retreating to his seat beside Elizabeth with the grace of a man escaping a battlefield.

Dymtrus, his face flushed crimson with anger, shot a final glare in Edwin's direction and spat through clenched teeth. "The Spider Queen ensnares you in her web. Watch for her poison." Without a chance of rebuttal, he turned and stormed off.

"Father, what is the matter?" Lysander turned to him.

Oh, my poor boy. Bancroft's heart ached for his son. They stood eye to eye now. Lysander, no longer a child but a man. His son's broad shoulders stretched the fine fabric of his suit, the dark stubble of adulthood shadowed his jaw, and his olive skin and dark hair carried the unmistakable mark of their lineage from Lyonnia. A pang of sorrow struck Bancroft's chest. *A shame he was born second.*

"I fear the phoenix is nearly at its end, my son," he said to his boy, gently grabbing his shoulders to scoot him aside. He walked back to the high table, spotting Torralin and Casimir making their way down the center aisle. Charles stood from his seat, clapping. An intermittent crowd of lords also clapped, but none joined from the high table.

"A welcome distraction from the theatrics backstage."

Charles winked at him, but he knew better. This was always planned.

Bancroft turned to the realm, his hands coming together in applause as he remained standing. Gradually, the entire hall followed suit, rising to their feet in a thunderous ovation. Torralin and Casimir took their seats below with Harriet, while Alexander stood, raising his goblet. He clinked it lightly, and the hall began to quiet, the lords and ladies turning their attention to him. Bancroft sank back into his chair, nearly collapsing under the weight of the evening.

"Esteemed lords and ladies, honored guests, and most venerable of nobles, be welcomed to this grandest of celebrations. We gather here today to celebrate the betrothal of His High Imperial Highness, the emperor's beloved son, Lysander, to Catelyn of the late great Thane of the same house, the realm's most recently dearly departed."

Applause filled the throne room, but Alexander raised a hand to quiet the hall. Lowering his voice, he forced the audience to lean, straining to hear his words. "Many in this realm forget that I, Alexander of Goldwood, am also of the Phoenix's blood, as is my dear cousin, Charles of Rose Mont. We share the same lineage, bound by ties of blood and destiny. My children and Charles's children carry the same noble legacy. And so, it was only natural that we would lend our support to this most auspicious occasion." He turned toward the high table, his gaze resting on the two young men. "Warwick, Lysander, your presence represents the greatest blessing of House Hieronymus.

"Our house symbol, the phoenix of two-heads, is no mere adornment. It is a reflection of our unique heritage. The Phoenix King himself bore three sons: an eldest heir and a pair of twin boys. From that legacy, the Rose Monts and the Goldwoods were charged to build and expand the empire, to serve as its two heads. And it is a legacy we uphold to this day."

Alexander lifted his goblet higher, seemingly in time with the rise of Bancroft's heartbeat. "The Rose Monts and the Goldwoods—two heads of the phoenix. Warwick and

Lysander—two heads of the phoenix. Even the late Thane, though not a twin to our emperor, shared a bond so deep he may as well have been. He fought valiantly for faith, country, and family. And tonight, we toast in his honor and in celebration of the union before us." Alexander raised his goblet high. "To faith, to country, and to family!"

The hall echoed his words, lifting their goblets as one. Hundreds of gallons of wine disappeared down the gullets of the nobility as the band resumed. Rising from her seat, Catelyn moved gracefully toward the center of the room. Lysander, lingering briefly beside his father, cast Bancroft one last concerned glance before joining her. Together, the couple began a rehearsed dance, their steps drawing admiration from the realm.

Bancroft tried to watch, tried to smile, but the inevitable caught his eye. Warwick rose from his seat and disappeared into the shadows.

Melinda V

The band played a graceful tune, and a crowd gathered around her stepson and Catelyn, forming a dense circle. Melinda rose from the table, her arms clasped across her chest, and shared a fleeting, heartfelt smile with Elizabeth. But her gaze soon fell upon Warwick, sulking in the corner, his bride-to-be left alone, tears threatening to spill from her eyes.

Poor dear, Melinda thought, her heart softening. She moved toward the young girl. "Don't fret, my dear. If I know Warwick, he's got something special planned for you." She winked, but the girl only blinked rapidly, tears continuing to pool.

Perhaps she does not mourn Warwick's departure... The thought sent a chill through her. She ran her hand gently through the girl's hair, then lifted her skirt to stride toward the high table, a fire kindling within her as she pushed through the lords and ladies, all clamoring for a better view of Lysander and Catelyn's dance.

A dance I should be watching. She caught her stepson just as he noticed her and tried to slip away. Melinda was quick though, snatching the back of his collar and pulling him behind a massive pillar.

"Ow! Mother!" Warwick twisted in her grasp. There were still a few guests situated this far back into the room, but she figured the family was long past hiding its woes.

"The pain I have caused you is nothing compared to the torment I carry in my heart!" She shoved him against the pillar. "How dare you slink away from your brother's big day? How could you leave that poor girl all alone at the high table for all to see?"

"I can't stand it, Mother! I can't!" Warwick stamped his foot. "Let the realm see my contempt, or let me hide where my image is safe!"

"Safe?" Melinda reached forward and seized his jaw, her fingers digging into his cheeks. She twisted his face toward Polina, sitting alone at the high table, her eyes glassy with unspilled tears. "How does that look 'safe'?"

"I will return, just in a matter of time!"

She jerked him back behind the pillar. "Do you have any idea the stakes that ride behind your betrothal to that girl? The fate of the realm could rest upon it!"

"I cannot abide my heart, Mother," Warwick said defiantly.

Melinda blinked, her mind suddenly blank of words, before a slap whipped across Warwick's cheeks.

"You cannot!" he screamed.

"What I have just done is nothing compared to what our enemies will do to your rotting body in some dungeon. Listen to me, you little boy, you will learn to do your duty and you will do it tonight. Take this ring from upon my hand!" She ripped a fire red ruby from her finger and shoved it into his trembling palm.

"I do not understand," Warwick stammered.

"What is there to understand? Propose to the girl!"

Warwick chuckled, a sound Melinda had not expected. "You want me to steal the attention from my brother?"

Melinda's gaze hardened as her eyes locked onto his shimmering dark-green ones. "Your brother, of all people, is in service to you. Now go. Secure your crown, unless you have no ambition to be emperor." She forced his fingers closed around the ring, then shoved him out from behind the pillar.

The first dance of Lysander and Catelyn was drawing to a close, and a wave of applause swept through the room. Warwick paused, turned back, and winked at her.

"I will do it, *mother*, and let the knife fall."

Melinda raised a hand to her head, ready to faint, when she saw Dymtrus elbow aside a fat lady, making a beeline for her. In a flash, she turned, just as the room erupted into chaos. The band struck up a lively chord, and the floor flooded with lords and ladies eager to dance. Melinda pushed through the crowd, keeping to the shadows, her thoughts consumed by one prayer: *Please, Warwick, be quick about your duty!*

"Empress! Empress!" voices called to her.

By the Nine, I detest my station! She kept moving, drawing farther into the crowd, when an arm grabbed her and she let out a startled yelp!

He's caught me!

"Empress!" A gloved hand shook her, and Melinda spun to find her closest friend, Arrianette, standing behind her. "Darling, whatever is the matter?"

"Dymtrus," Melinda said breathlessly. Her eyes darted toward the approaching lord, but then her gaze snagged on something. *The charm.* It hung from Arrianette's neck, the same peculiar symbol she had seen earlier: the shrouded flame, entwined in a web, an unblinking half-open eye glinting at its base. The realization hit her like a cold wave. *Elizabeth.*

"Understood." Arrianette nodded and, with a swift motion, released her. She staggered backward, then pretended to faint directly into Dymtrus's arms.

Melinda didn't wait to see the result. She dashed across the dance floor, weaving through twirling lords and ladies, bowing and smiling politely to her subjects as she made her way toward the row of pillars. There, she took refuge behind one, breathing heavily, her heart racing. Her fingers trembled as she gripped the fabric of her gown. *What does this mean? My Arrianette? In league with Elizabeth?*

"Something amiss, Empress?"

The voice, low and cold, slithered into her thoughts like a shadow. Melinda jumped, a sharp gasp escaping her lips as she turned, finding a thin, skeletal figure standing before her, dressed in plain priestly robes that hung loosely from his gaunt frame.

"Oh pardon me, I didn't see you there…"

"Are you well, Empress, or is something the matter?"

She racked her brain, knowing she recognized the man when it clicked. Her husband's confessor.

Lacius. A snake in human form… but a man who could get things done.

"Warwick… family trouble… he needs to get it done…" she muttered, barely able to focus.

"Empress?" He tilted his head.

But before she could answer, the sound of Dymtrus's voice cut through the air. "It seems I have finally found you, Your Grace."

Melinda forced a smile, though her stomach churned. She leaned in close to Lacius, whispering urgently into his ear. "Help the crown prince get it done. For the realm."

Lacius nodded, and with a swift, graceful bow, he disappeared into the crowd.

Melinda then turned to Dymtrus, forcing a smile upon her lips. "My lord, you're not dancing?"

"We need to discuss my daughter's station." Dymtrus ignored decorum. "Matters have come to a head. Your husband allows open enemies of the realm at his high table…"

"Darling… oh dear, had a bit too much of the wine, have we?" Melinda's voice dripped with mock sympathy. "There's a plan to everything if you trust the Nine. Everything will be well."

"The future of my daughter, I daresay, is not well. We cannot continue with the betrothal, not under these circumstances."

"Dymtrus, please, you are not one to break an oath before the Nine."

"Empress, no oath has been made. I am free to revoke my word at any time I please..."

Suddenly, the orchestra cut its music, and the swirling dance floor stilled. A ripple of audible gasps swept through the crowd. Dymtrus turned toward the high table, his mouth agape in disbelief. Melinda smiled inwardly. She watched as Warwick dropped to one knee before Polina, a gesture that elicited a dramatic gasp from the room. Bancroft rose from his seat, overcome with emotion. Polina threw both hands into the air with a small shriek, and the crowd erupted in applause as the young couple embraced. The orchestra resumed their music.

"My dear," Melinda breathed a sigh of relief. "An oath has indeed been made."

Dymtrus, now overshadowed by a palpable darkness, said nothing. He slipped away into the crowd without another word.

Alone, and unbothered for the moment, Melinda sank to her rump. The cold stone floor of the throne room felt like ice beneath her, but she didn't mind. She fanned herself, laughing erratically through tears as lords and ladies rushed to her side, lifting her to her feet.

"No, no, I'm fine. Just a bit too much wine and twirling on the dance floor," she jested to passing lords. Fitting, it was Ernest who finally came to her, laughing to himself about her having finally had too much to drink. He helped her regain her footing, and woozy, she glanced back toward the high table, where she witnessed Bancroft and Warwick, Catelyn and Polina, embracing one another. Her heart swelled with pride. The two halves of the phoenix had rejoined.

Ernest helped escort her back to the high table, but halfway there, Alexander Goldwood rose once more from his position and clinked his glass. The room fell partially silent, for much drink and merriment was underway, and the throne room was much too rowdy to command full attention. Melinda giggled, arms crossed, half-expecting Alexander to announce another feast in honor of Warwick.

"Lords and ladies of the realm! What a night… Two betrothals to celebrate now, indeed!" He raised his glass, and the realm shouted in celebratory cheer. "A celebration for the ages! And for such an occasion, a gift," he continued, grinning widely. "All the way from the Sun Coast, I bequeath unto the newly betrothed Lysander and Catelyn, and Warwick and Polina, a treat most eyes in our dear realm have never seen. A dancing noggin!" A concealed door dropped from the crate and from within the darkness, a small dog-like creature hobbled forth.

"Dear God!" Melinda cried aloud. The realm's reaction was no less. Shouts of horror and amusement, intrigue and disgust overtook the court.. Lords and ladies rushed forward; others darted backward.

A beast! Melinda's mind screamed. *High treason! The Reisonic Order would declare war on us for such an act!*

One of the men who'd wheeled out the crate revealed a flute and broke into song. The lord who had been carrying her almost dropped her in his own shock. Trembling on stage, no taller than Melinda's shin, the creature began to dance, dressed in a striped jester's outfit. The noggin worked its tiny, malformed legs comically in tune with the bells strapped to its feet. The creature drew every eye in the hall.

She saw Strammond charging through the crowd. "Get that beast out of here!" From the high table, Bancroft looked away in disgust, while Warwick tucked his betrothed into his chest. Catelyn ran to her mother, but Charles and Alexander laughed at the sight. Aye, much of the realm laughed, entranced by the spectacle. Melinda, horrified and angry, shoved her way forward, reaching within an arm's length of the table when an ear-splitting cry overtook the room.

All froze, even the noggin.

Bancroft rose from the high table, a sob rising high from his throat.

Lords and ladies scattered. Melinda rushed forward.

There, in the center of the throne room, Lysander lay twitching on the cold stone, frothing at the mouth. A spilled goblet of wine and a piece of uneaten bread lay beside him.

Melinda dropped to her knees beside him, cradling his head in her hands, and before the entire realm, she screamed. She screamed as loudly as any mother ever could for a beloved child.

JOSEPHINA VII

Josephina's room filled with thick smoke. Each breath burned, her lungs screaming for air as she stuffed her few belongings into a leather sack. Time was running out.

A sharp crack echoed from the bonfire outside, followed by a crash. Flames shot past her window. Her head throbbed with the rising heat. The little dragon lumbered toward her, puffing smoke, and nudged her leg.

"We have to go! It's not safe for us here!" she said, gently pushing it aside. But even as the crimson curtain of morning rose, the fire raged, turning her room into an oven. Heat shimmered, and shadows danced madly across the walls. Any of them could be Oléfur. Or Mother.

"Mother," she whispered, staring at the half-packed sack. A wave of nausea overtook her. She fell to her knees and vomited, sweat pouring down her face as her body shook. Everything she knew was going up in flames.

She collapsed onto her side, the world spinning. She tried to cry, but the tears wouldn't come. "Oh, Mishie," she breathed, bile on her lips. Smoke filled her lungs. She didn't move. She was ready to burn.

A soft nudge brushed her hand. She ignored it, drifting, but then two small heads pressed against her. She blinked.

The dragon sat before her, staring.

"Oh," she muttered, struggling to move. Her skin stuck to the straw mattress.

The dragon turned, lumbering away from her. The poor creature could barely walk, swaying on two hind legs while its malformed wings, long and crooked, served as its front legs. The dragon waddled over to the trapdoor and clawed at it before it sat down and looked back at her. Three glowing eyes looked at her from two inquisitive heads. The right one had one long horn twisting behind the other, while the left head bore two straight horns, sharp as knives. Josephina sniffed, finally wiping the dribble from her mouth. Her head felt like it was going to explode. This was simply too much for her to process.

A crack from the bonfire split through the silence. The window splintered, and the dragon's two heads jerked in unison.

Mishie. The thought of him returned, sharp and painful. *Dead. Gone into the flames. His sacrifice—the egg, cracking because of him.* Her heart leaped into her throat, but this time it was a good kind of ache. A tear welled up in her eye. She would do this for Mishie. With a deep breath, she pulled herself from the bed and immediately hit the floor with a *thud.* The dragon squawked, startled.

Groaning, Josephina shook off her fall and crawled along the floor, staying low beneath the smoke. She grabbed her duffel bag, slung it over her shoulder, and clawed her way to the trapdoor. Her breath came in ragged gasps as she descended, the dragon's two heads peeking over the edge a moment later. Reaching up, she grasped it—it was heavy, but she managed. Together, they made their way down into her mother's room, where a blast of cooler air filled her lungs. Strength returned to her limbs, enough to lift the dragon as she fled from the room, rushing toward the kitchen, desperate for water.

She found the kitchen empty, save for the flickering glow of the bonfire outside. Stumbling, Josephina scoured the shelves for supplies, shoving excess meats into her bag. Her eyes landed on a pail of water. Desperate, she flipped it over, gulping it down and splashing the rest across her body, sending the dragon into a squirming, hissing fit. She set it on the floor, breathless, only to freeze when she saw Mother standing in the doorframe, arms and legs splayed wide like a spider.

"Josephina." Her mother's voice roared over the flames of the bonfire.

Josephina dropped the empty pail, and the dragon hissed again. Mother's hair stood wild and frayed, and her red dress smoldered with embers, scorched in multiple places.

"Do you have any idea how much trouble you are in?"

"Mother," she gasped, water dripping from her chin.

"I am going to destroy you, Josephina."

The dragon snorted, squirming on the floor between them.

"No, Mother. Let me go."

"It will be a mercy, Josephina."

"A mercy for you!" she shouted.

Mother tried to creep forward, but the dragon hissed.

"Zakaenys, my child!" she screamed.

The dragon in turn belched a bright flame from its two mouths. Mother hissed back, climbing the wall above the door like a spider, perching in the room's only shadow, her eyes dancing with firelight.

"You stupid girl! You have no idea how much trouble we're in now. The end of the world is at hand! I wanted us to stand as equals, and instead, I've been betrayed!"

"Then go chase Oléfur!" Josephina shot back.

"No, not just Oléfur!" Mother's voice rose, sharp as the flames around them. The dragon reared up on its hind legs and screeched. "By the very Trickster himself! I've played with a double-edged sword and paid the price. With you, with this monster, it seems all I'm doomed to produce is ruin."

"You are the monster," Josephina replied coldly.

Mother pulled inward on her limbs as if ready to strike. The hair on the back of Josephina's neck prickled, but she held her ground, refusing to look away.

"How dare you," Mother croaked. "You have no idea the sacrifices I have made for us. What has become of me!"

"I have only suffered, Mother!"

"You have been nourished and clothed and loved, Josephina. Have you not seen how the world treats you?"

"I am a monster, I know. But I think it takes one monster to make another."

The shadow on the wall recoiled. "Born of desperate love and now I reap the consequences."

"Mother?"

"A mother's love is not always easy, Josephina, but I do love you. That is why I must end you now. I will not allow you to suffer in the final apocalypse."

"You stay back."

Mother's shadow limbs retracted, gathering for a pounce.

"Let me go, Mother." Sweat poured from her brow. She took a step back.

The shadow leaped and a burst of flames shot through the air. Josephina stumbled backward as she threw her hands up from the heat. A loud *thud* came from the floor in front of her. Mother screeched, rolling on the floor, engulfed in fire. The little dragon stood across from her, unleashing bolts of fire—one head aimed at Mother, while the other unleashed fury upon the house itself.

"Curses," she said to herself.

She sidestepped her mother, grabbed her duffel bag, and lifted the dragon, flames dripping from its mouth.

"Joooosephinaaaaaa!"

Mother's wretched cry followed her out the door. She did not hesitate, though. She stepped into the sun, the *natural* sun, and a cool breeze greeted her. She closed her eyes, tasting smoke in the air, but also something else. Something sweet.

She ran for the barn, lumbering through the field with the dragon tucked against her chest. The fields were a golden brown. Tomatoes, wheat, potatoes, and more neared harvest time. She made a mental note to snag a few vegetables as she reached the barn, carefully opening the door.

"Here donkey, donkey," she called softly. She didn't want to spook any of the animals as she walked slowly toward the donkey's stall. It was dark inside the barn. Only a few streams of sunlight filtered through the ancient, cracked wood beams. Dust hung thick in the air, swirling gently in the light. The dragon snorted beside her.

"Please behave," she whispered to the dragon, then whistled gently, so the animals would not be startled by her presence. She didn't want any of them to die. They all deserved freedom too, and she could give it to them. She whistled louder, approaching the donkey's pen, and with a gentle hand, opened the stall, her whistle rising into a sharp squeal.

Her hand slammed over her mouth, suppressing a scream. Inside the stall, the thralls her mother had brought to work the farm were huddled together, their vacant blue eyes staring up at her in eerie silence. She flew back against the barn wall and bit down upon her hand, dropping the dragon. The thralls stirred, startled from their stupor, but they did not approach her. The dragon released a small burst of flame from one of its two heads, warming the air around them. Quickly, she choked down her fear and reached out with her free hand to stroke the dragon's two necks.

"There, there, I've got you. It's all okay." Her heartbeat hammered in the back of her throat. She prayed the dragon didn't sense it.

The thralls hunched low, trembling in her presence. She didn't know how much of their humanity remained, but she couldn't bear to witness what Mother had done to them. Hand trembling, she crept forward and pulled the donkey's gate shut.

The dragon growled softly but didn't belch fire, and for that, she was grateful.

"Here donkey, donkey," she squeaked, and this time heard it bray from a different stall. Biting her tongue, she opened another stall door and found it, no further surprises. "Blessings," she said aloud and grabbed its reins.

The donkey took one look at the twisting mass of necks and glowing eyes in her arms and decided to obey. It followed her from the stall without issue.

"Okay, we're going to need my tent and supplies. Where did Mother put them..." She opened the door to the storage room and collided with a cold, clammy gray corpse. Stumbling backward, she fell onto her rear as the dragon slipped from her grip.

Dazed, she blinked, staring up through the swirling dust at the lifeless body hanging from the ceiling before her. There was no stopping the scream this time. It came loud and from the pit of her stomach.

Franz. His body dangled from a chain from the ceiling. Josephina screamed with all her might, and as if the knight were still alive, his body swayed in the air, revealing three other gray mummified corpses dangling from the barn's rafters. The dragon instinctively roared, unleashing a jet of fire that shot upward. One flame struck Franz, another hit a different corpse, and the last collided with the barn wall, igniting both hay and wood. The storage cabinet erupted into a blazing inferno.

Josephina crawled backward, gasping for air. Franz went up in flames, his gray withered skin igniting in an instant. The dragon pressed against her, nuzzling under her arm as she lay in the hay, oblivious to the approaching flames. Her eyes shifted from Franz's haunting gaze to his chest, where two dark-red swirls carved into the flesh began to glow, radiating a fiery heat as the corpse burned. Despite the heat, Josephina had never felt so cold.

The donkey let out a frantic scream, kicking a fence post beside it. Josephina shook her head and pushed herself to her feet. With no time to waste, she allowed the dragon to chase after her—there was no sense in holding it back now. Working among a torrent of smoke, she tore her tent from the wall, barely saving it from the licking flames. She quickly scavenged a pot, a blanket, and a small carving knife, gathering what she could.

The rope supporting Franz's body was the first to snap under the heat of the flames. Sparks flew from the storage cabinet as the chickens went mad. Poop ran down from the rafters as she rushed forward, the donkey right behind her, and shoved open the barn doors. Fresh air rushed in and the fire roared, but she didn't look back. Grabbing the donkey's reins, she yanked the creature to a halt. She flung her supplies over the donkey's back and secured them tightly. Behind her, a frantic flock of chickens burst forth from thick, billowing smoke. From the growing inferno, a small black figure emerged, crawling along the ground.

"We have to go, now!" she screamed at the creature. Rushing forward, she scooped up the dragon, tucking it under one arm. Her muscles screamed under its weight, but she fought to maintain control, steering the donkey with the reins as they pressed onward.

Together, they sprinted toward the edge of the forest. At the tree line, however, she came to an abrupt stop, digging her heels into the ground to stop the donkey's momentum. She didn't know where she was going, and feeling a tug in her heart, she turned to take one last glance at her home.

Her twisted house, the place of Mother and Mishie, of love and comfort, and treachery, beatings, and *worse*. She tried to think of Mishie, cuddling together on a cold night during a blizzard, or sitting with Mother in the parlor before the fire, enjoying a delicious pot of porridge. She recalled her first memories of running through the green fields during springtime, or Mother letting her hide in her bed during a fierce thunderstorm. But she also recalled darker memories, like Oléfur and his toothy grins and those dark nights in the cellar as he took from her. Mother would vanish, or worse, pretend not to hear.

"Joooosssseeeeppphhhinnnaaaa!"

The call sliced through the air. At first, she dismissed it as a dark memory echoing in her mind, a fleeting, dark daydream, but then the call came again, very real.

"JOOOOSSSEEEEPPPHHHIIINNNAAAAA!"

Her blood turned to ice. The dragon wiggled and snorted in her arms. From afar, she watched as a black figure emerged from her burning home. She whipped around, grabbing the donkey's reins, and bolted into the woods.

She ran as far as she could through the trees until exhaustion forced her to stop. The smell of smoke still lingered in the air. *Too close,* she thought, but she couldn't run forever with the dragon in her arms. It was simply too heavy. Thinking quickly, she arranged her supplies on the donkey's back, creating a cozy spot for the dragon to rest. The donkey whined, but a quick snap in the air by the left dragon's head forced the donkey to reconsider.

They walked all day. She didn't know where they were going, only that they had to move. They only came to a rest when the sun slipped below the mountains and deep shadows engulfed the forest floor. Fearing her weary legs would give out, she stopped for the night and set up camp. She pitched her small tent, laid out the blanket inside, and tied the donkey to a tree. The donkey snacked on nearby plants while she snacked on salted meats. She allowed the dragon to start a small fire before the tent, but as much as she tried to feed it, it would not take the meat.

"You are going to be a lot of trouble," she said to it. The dragon merely sat down by the fire, staring at her with its four eyes.

"Mishie was a handful too, but he always stood by me when things got tough. He even rode on the donkey, looking out for us." Josephina smiled. "You did well tonight."

She patted one head as the other yawned and lay down in the dirt. The left head pushed into the fire and fanned the flames. Josephina's brow scrunched.

"You're a lot like him, but what do I call you? Are you one or many?"

The right head rested on the dirt, watching her. The left went to sleep.

Josephina racked her brain for a name, but the pull of sleep soon overwhelmed her. She crawled into her tent and closed her eyes, not tasting ash or smoke on her tongue, but the strange, enticing elixir that only sweet freedom could bring.

She drifted off, the dragon curling into her arms not long after.

JAE XI

From his childhood, Jae remembered the sandcastles he'd built by the shore. No matter how big or how thick the walls, the ocean always came. High tide or low tide, a wave always found its way up the shore to melt away his handiwork. Nothing lasted forever.

Now, he walked amid a tide of humanity and beast, surging down the extravagant streets of the Rose. His gaze remained fixed ahead, while beside him, Crassius the minotaur thundered with each step. In either hand, the giant gripped massive sickles—tools meant for harvesting wheat, now slicing the air with every stride, dripping with blood.

Behind them, the House of Aeksilor went up with a *whoosh*. The survivors from Jae's former master were swallowed by the crowd, swept away in its currents. Only Lucien remained at his side as the revolution spread like wildfire. Mansion after mansion went up in flames. In a courtyard, an execution unfolded as they passed: the lady wife of a master, dressed in her finest jewels, shrieked as the blade fell. Her severed head joined the remains of her family, tossed into a growing pile of the dead. Lucien had to push Jae forward to keep moving.

Surviving slaves stumbled from the charred ruins, gathering in courtyards where they once served. Some stood in shock, staring at the flames or searching each other's faces for answers. Others whooped and ran mad in the streets. One man, waving an iron rod of a Thorned Man like a prize, was struck down the moment he startled the crowd.

We sweep like the tide, lifting everything with us!

He wanted to believe it—*needed to*—but doubt gnawed at him. He watched the man be butchered. Ash and blood tainted the air. Grit coated his tongue. Bodies littered the streets while corpses mounted in courtyards, fuel for more fires. Flames reached toward the sky, transforming mansions into funeral pyres. Through gaps between burning estates, he glimpsed the dark ocean retreating toward the horizon.

The taste of ash filled his mouth.

"Look at these poor slaves," Crassius' voice boomed over the chaos. "Cowering in fear. They don't even recognize their own liberation."

"All they know is burning," Jae answered, wincing as Crassius's blades sliced the air.

"The winds do not ask the grass if it's ready to bend. Change comes whether they recognize it or not," the bull responded.

"I have never heard such a saying before."

"Of course not, bull slayer."

"I thought you no longer believed that."

"No, but humans are creatures of deceit. When this night ends and the sun brings clarity to the land, perhaps then I will make my final judgment."

"The sun," Jae spat, his voice bitter. "I've rarely seen it shed truth here."

Crassius snorted—a deep, throaty sound that could have been laughter. "The real sun, the true sun!" he bellowed, raising his massive arms to the sky. "Not the falsehoods these men preach. We shall gather beneath it, at the heart of their lies, and burn this city to the ground!"

A roar erupted from the crowd behind them. Another minotaur let out a fierce yell, and soon everyone was shouting, cheering, swept up in the rising fury.

Crassius led the crowd to the gates of the Vanilla, where a heap of Thorned Men lay. A freed slave ran forward and took a torch to their bodies. They went up in flames like dried leaves in the height of summer. After their bonfire, the streets sloped sharply downward, and Jae allowed himself to be carried away by the surging crowd, grateful to escape the stench of burning flesh.

They swept into the Vanilla like a torrent, flooding the quiet streets. The district lay still, draped in darkness. Few freed slaves lingered outside; most homes and shops were tightly sealed. Shadows darted through narrow alleyways, and somewhere in the distance, a baby cried. A handful of torches flickered on street posts, but otherwise, the Vanilla seemed lifeless. Above them, the fires still raged in the Rose, casting an orange glow on the clouds, just enough for Jae to make out the three dark figures blocking their path ahead.

"Friend or foe?" Jae called, hand to his sword.

"Correspondents," Lucien cut in before Jae could step forward. He pushed past him, but Crassius easily outpaced them both, his long strides forcing Lucien to swerve to avoid the sickle in his right hand.

"What news do you bring of the lower city?" Lucien called out.

The figures stepped forward, shedding their cloaks in the gloom. Jae moved closer, squinting to make out their faces: a middle-aged woman with sandy hair, a young girl no older than twelve, and a man who was clearly an Islander.

Jae's heart leaped. *I know them.* The woman—she had held her master's scroll in the Temple of the Sun. The Islander he'd encountered in the fields, right after...

Jae's breath caught. It was her. The same girl from the field and the auction block. The one he had struck.

"Chaos grips the city. The docks are burning. Looters have taken over…"

As if on cue, the crowd behind them broke from its thin restraint, surging into nearby shops and homes. Windows shattered, doors were kicked in, and possessions were dragged out onto the streets. Through the frenzy, Jae spotted Petra, clutching Hex tightly as they navigated the chaos.

"Then the city has indeed fallen." Lucien nodded.

"Not yet," the Islander corrected. "The Thorned Men have retreated to the Temple of the Sun. They're preparing for a final stand atop its steps."

"I have been inside the temple. I can't say how deep the tunnels and passages go, but I worry they could give an advantage to the good masters."

The woman in the center looked to Jae. "Crassius, is this him? Is this the *correct* one?"

Crassius grunted. "You stand before the *Wilted Moth*. Annihilator of the House of Aeksilor. The *slayer* of bulls."

The woman smirked. "Then we'll deal with the other false prophets in the city. It seems every moth has been drawn out into the light."

"Aye, *polecat*, I promised you I watched the True Moth," Lucien added.

"I'd caution certainty on a night like this."

"Our work brought down the House of Aeksilor and the so-called good masters. Why deny him now? Even the great bull sees him as true."

The woman's grin widened. "That's the beauty of tonight, *Rancid Bull*. We're no one now—free of the masters! We can choose new names or reclaim old ones. In these fires, we're finally free!"

"No," Crassius boomed again. "We are not free. There is still work to do."

"Then let us join the others at the Temple of the Sun. By the time their Sun Lord rises, this city will be bathed in blood."

The roar shook the streets, freezing the rioters in their tracks.

Heads turned, eyes wide with shock. The minotaurs behind him echoed the call, raising their weapons to the sky. As if under a spell, their ragtag followers poured out from homes and shops, some clutching stolen jewels, others with priceless vases or paintings strapped to their backs. Through the mess, Jae spotted Luke and locked eyes with him. He motioned toward Petra and Hex. Luke nodded, though his shoulders sagged, and he moved sluggishly as if weighed down by more than just fatigue.

"Freedom!" Cassius bellowed. "It is almost within our grasp! We march to the Temple of the Sun, where we will join our brethren! And tonight, the masters of this cursed city will have their reign *crushed*!"

The crowd roared in response. Jae's heart pounded in his chest, the beat thrumming in his throat. He glanced at Lucien, whose wide green eyes mirrored the terror inside him. Two hulking minotaurs, one with fur the color of hay, the other a deep brown, stepped forward to flank Crassius, forcing Lucien to step behind Jae.

"Let us go now, good brothers. Tonight, we end this." Crassius pounded his fists.

The brown-furred minotaur snorted. "I ache to see the plains again as a free bull. Let us smash this city and be done with it."

Crassius nodded and turned, leading the mob into the lower ward. The two minotaurs flanked him, their broad shoulders forcing Jae back, though Lucien was close behind. Lucien dug his fist into Jae's back, shoving him forward.

"Be. Their. Leader!"

Jae stumbled, struggling to keep pace with the minotaurs as they barreled down the steep, narrow streets like a living battering ram. The mob surged behind them, crashing through the streets without restraint. The dense buildings of the Ivy blazed like a raging wildfire, while the madmen, freed of civility, scattered through the chaos like animals fleeing through a brushfire.

Ahead, a house erupted into flames, the crackling fire devouring everything in its path. A woman's shriek echoed from a dark alley, but before Jae could react, a glass facade exploded in a violent burst, showering the street with shards.

Lucien jabbed his fist into Jae's back again, urging him to move. They ran alongside the minotaurs as mothers clutched their babies and homes burned to the ground. Drunken men tore through the streets, smashing anything in their path, their slave collars discarded and forgotten. Above them, the bodies of Thorned Men swung from signposts like grisly ornaments, while a minotaur's corpse was trampled beneath the frenzied mob.

Crassius halted at the sight. Without a moment's hesitation, his fellow minotaurs charged forward, their massive weapons cleaving through four humans with brutal efficiency. The remaining rioters scattered in terror.

Jae's mouth fell open in shock. He watched as Crassius took a step forward, as though to give chase, but the sudden collapse of a burning home nearby stopped him in his tracks. The building fell with a deafening roar, a sea of screams erupting from within. A wave of searing heat rushed over them, causing Jae's makeshift cape to billow wildly in the wind.

Lucien was knocked away from him by the force of the collapse. Before Jae could react, the sandy-haired woman known as Minerva appeared beside him, gripping his shoulder and pulling him close.

"If you are indeed the Wilted Moth, then raise your sword and charge before this mob decides to kill one another!"

She shoved him forward. He stumbled but quickly regained his footing. Bewildered, he turned to face the flames of destruction, their glow casting eerie shadows, and raised his sword high into the air.

"To me, the free people of Astrelaide!" he cried. "Let us bring an end to tyranny!"

Those who could hear him cheered, their eyes glowing against the flames, not unlike the Thorned Men. A chill swept down his spine and he lowered his sword. Crassius gave him a long look, then pounded his chest with closed fists, a primal call to battle. This time, Jae didn't wait for Lucien's signal. He planted his feet firmly on the pavement and charged forward. The mob surged behind him. The minotaurs came too.

The streets were choked with bodies, but the path ahead was clear. The Temple of the Sun stood tall over the city, its brazier still burning the brightest of all, casting its glow into the burning clouds of ash above. Jae sprinted forward, a thousand footsteps pounding behind him. The ground trembled underfoot as the minotaurs followed, crashing through the human and beastly tide. Women were knocked to the ground, men were swept up in the frenzy. A faun scrambled frantically up a burning building, trying to escape the madness. Little noggins darted into the shadows, having no other defense.

Jae rode the surge of the mob like a mighty wave, and for a fleeting moment, he saw his homeland again. He was back on the shore, watching the ocean consume his sandcastle. Now, it was his turn to be the wave, to crash down on the city and wash away its resistance—or so he hoped. The Temple of the Sun was made of stone, not sand, after all.

He reached the Plaza of the Sun. Corpses lay scattered like refuse: Thorned Men, slaves, beasts, and freemen alike. His feet splashed through blood, pooling like water at his feet. Rioters and freedom fighters wandered among the fallen, some dazed, half-dead themselves, staring blankly at the burning city. Others were looting, robbing from the dead with practiced cruelty.

A wave of nausea rose in the back of Jae's throat at the sight, but this wasn't the time to administer justice for those who wronged the dead. He had to reach the top of the temple. He stared upward at the steep mountain of steps before him. Thorned Men lay scattered around him, dying or choking on their last breaths.

Jae took a glance behind him. Lucien was still with him, winded but close by. The minotaurs, led by Crassius, surged forward, the mob in their wake. The looters and dazed survivors in the plaza either scattered in fear or joined the growing horde, pushing forward toward the temple. Jae took his first step onto the pyramid's base, his legs burning with the effort, but he could feel the energy of the mob building behind him.

Lucien appeared beside him, gasping for breath, and shouted. "Go!"

So Jae climbed. He tore up the pyramid steps, dodging the bodies of the fallen Thorned Men. Behind him, Crassius and the minotaurs climbed as well, their heavy breaths echoing in the night air. Jae put distance between himself and them, his ears filling with the sound of clashing steel and angry shouts from above.

He used all his strength to ascend the pyramid, leaping the final step onto the top mezzanine. He unsheathed his sword as he did so, but found the last Thorned Man dying with a scream at the hands of a ragtag bunch of slaves.

Jae stopped in disbelief, pain ripping through his calves. Around him, humans, minotaurs, greejees, fauns, satyrs, and even a few noggins were present. Some lay dead or dying, tended to by loved ones or friends. Others cheered as the last Thorned Man fell, their triumphant cries ringing out into the night. Near the temple's entrance, a group of survivors pressed desperately against the temple's barred doors.

Crassius and his companions emerged a heartbeat behind him. They too stopped to survey the scene. Crassius snorted, his nostrils flaring, then shoved Jae aside with a rough push as he leaned back and bellowed at the top of his lungs. "They have robbed us of the good fight!"

The minotaurs beat their chests in fury that there was no fight left for them, but Jae knew better. He stepped forward, shaking his head. "No, Crassius, the High Priest and his lackeys still live! Look!" He gestured toward the gate. "Our fellow slaves are tearing down the doors!"

Crassius's mad bull's eyes flashed with an unsettling excitement. He grinned, baring his teeth. "Then the final victory shall be ours to take. Brahmulis! Bullion! To me!"

With a roar, Crassius charged ahead, his two minotaurs in

lockstep. The crowd behind them erupted in a cheer, running toward the gates, scattering the slaves in their wake. Lucien, panting and red-faced, climbed the final steps of the pyramid, the crowd surging behind him.

"Lucien?" Jae called out, but he didn't stop. Lucien, panting, brushed past his shoulder, running for the temple's entrance.

Jae broke into a light jog, blindly chasing after him, when a loud crash split the air. The minotaurs, their massive arms driving forward, smashed through the barred doors of the pyramid. Jae's heart pounded as he raced after them, knowing that if he fell behind now, he would lose them in the maze of dark corridors within the pyramid. But when he arrived at the entrance, the minotaurs had stopped, frozen in place, staring into the black void ahead.

Jae skidded to a halt. "What's the matter? Why aren't we moving?" he called, his voice echoing off the stone walls.

The minotaurs didn't respond, only peered deeper into the shadowy abyss, their eyes narrowing in suspicion. Lucien wormed his way between them, and Jae followed suit. He joined their gaze, his own eyes adjusting to the overwhelming blackness.

The pyramid had always been dark, but this—this was different. The Temple of the Sun, the heart of this place, stood silent and cold. No torches burned within.

"Do we dare?" Brahmulis, the tan minotaur, called out.

"Do you mean to call me a coward?" Crassius growled in response.

"No, but we're not fools either..." His gaze looked down upon the dark corridor. "I didn't fight my way here to die flailing in the dark. It could be full of traps."

Jae spoke up. "I have been in there, and I have a suspicion where the priest may be hiding."

Brahmulis spat a large wet loogie onto the ground. "You know of this house of pain? Maybe you are the True Moth, drawing all to the light." The bull snorted. "Or maybe you are in league with the masters, luring us to our deaths."

"Good intel does not mean he is a traitor." Lucien elbowed his way forward. "We can find them and end this—tonight."

Crassius for the first time looked at Lucien. "Then by all means, you lead."

"We need a light source first…" Jae added.

"Are you fools just going to stand there?" Minerva's voice rang out, sharp and breathless as ascending the pyramid's steps. She didn't waste a second though. Snatching a torch from a man beside her, she pushed through the group. "Onward, my good fellows. Let us put an end to this madness."

Jae nodded, springing into motion behind her. Lucien followed, with the minotaurs close behind. Jae took the lead, charging down the grand staircase. Behind them, the mob they had rallied came crashing forward, their cries echoing deep into the dark heart of the pyramid. A hundred torches flickered like stars in the hands of the freed men and women, lighting the way into the labyrinth.

They reached the Hall of the Masters, and Jae's heart surged. The chamber ahead was bathed in torchlight. *The monstrous priest,* he thought, hands moving to his sword, but before he could act, Lucien tugged on his arm. Jae slowed, allowing Lucien to pull him into a recessed alcove in the wall. Minerva flattened herself beside them as the minotaurs and the frenzied crowd stormed past. Jae could hear the inhuman screams of the Thorned Men, followed by the brutal sounds of slaughter.

"What are you doing? I am missing the fight!" Jae protested.

"That is not the fight you need to concern yourself with! Now please," Lucien restrained Jae from rushing into battle. "we need to find the High Priest."

"You don't think he's in there?" Minerva raised an eyebrow.

"No," Lucien said, shaking his head. "But if I know him—and I *don't*—his pride and lineage wouldn't allow him to die in the Hall of the Masters…" Lucien paused as a gut-wrenching cry of a man being stabbed to death echoed through the dark.

"Okay, then where?"

"There's only one place a man like him would go. The heart of this pyramid, the heart of this city—the Altar of the Sun."

"Then let's go." Jae tried to brush past him.

"No!" Lucien grabbed his arm, stopping him. "You've seen the man! He's enormous, and well guarded. We'll need the others."

"Then let's go get them." Minerva nodded. She swept away into the Hall of the Masters.

Jae hesitated, glancing back at Lucien. "I thought you said I needed to be the one to lead them..."

"You do, but it won't matter if you're the one who does it if no one's there to see it—or worse, if you die before you get the chance. Follow Minerva, let's gather the others, and then we'll lead them to victory."

"Lucien, do you know her? Can she be trusted?"

"Can any of them?"

Jae frowned.

Lucien shifted uneasily on his feet. "I don't know... She's from another great house and helped organize this whole thing, but listen..." He grabbed ahold of Jae's shoulders. "When the others fight, stay back. Let them take the blows. Then you can deliver the final strike."

"I'll try."

"You'll have to do more than that. Now let's go."

Lucien whipped away from him. Jae shook his head but followed him into the hall. What he saw paralyzed him in his tracks.

More blood. Everywhere. Its crimson hue stained the walls and dripped over the furniture. A golden table stretched the length of the room, now a makeshift graveyard for the Thorned Men and red-robed priests. The massive murals, ancient relics likely centuries or millennia old, were splattered with yet more blood. Human and minotaur alike tore into the remaining priests, their brutal hands leaving a trail of carnage. Brahmulis himself seized a screaming priest, tearing him in two, the man's flailing body crashing against the tapestries depicting the sun, turning their yellow rays red.

"This... this is what we wanted?" Jae's sword fell from his hands. It landed with a *clang* against the pyramid floor.

Lucien only glanced at him, then nodded toward Minerva.

"Freemen! Hear me well! For a great enemy still lives!" Minerva's voice rang out, sharp and commanding.

Lucien's voice boomed, overtaking Minerva's, filled with fervor. "Follow us! Follow the Wilted Moth to the flame! Let us extinguish the false flame once and for all! Earn your freedom in a show of blood!"

"Let's go!" Minerva waved.

"To battle!" Lucien beat his chest with a shout, rallying the mob.

The minotaurs, consumed by their bloodlust, turned at the sound of Lucien's charge. Crassius bellowed, tossing a decapitated head behind him, and with a primal growl, lunged onto the table, snapping it beneath his massive weight. He charged forward, barreling past Jae as Minerva and Lucien disappeared into the darkness of the pyramid, leading the blood-hungry crowd deeper into the abyss.

The crowd roared past him, screaming for more blood, yet Jae stood still. Only when the last freedom fighter—*freed man... rioter... looter?*—ran past him, arms filled with priceless goblets and ceramics, did he turn to follow. He left the dim chamber, a helpless moth following the last vestiges of light slipping farther into the pyramid.

Blood dripped from the ceiling, muffling his footsteps as he slipped into the dark.

Leawyn XI

The clop of hooves on the damp ground roused her herd from sleep.

They emerged from their tents, rubbing the sleep from their eyes, when they collectively froze, rooted to the soil.

Seven dark shapes emerged from the forest, tall and imposing, their bodies an amalgamation of horse and human. Beside them, Leawyn walked, her smile beaming through the dark. Her grin matched the stallion's bared teeth, gleaming as if touched by starlight, the creature walking willingly at her side. They came as one. A new herd.

"Attack! Attack!" The cry broke the silence.

Someone scrambled for a bow and arrow, but most remained motionless. Her people, tired, defeated, cold, and hungry, had no fight left in them. Several lowered their heads, surrendering before battle could begin. Only Eabha, alone among them, gripped her grandson's hand and met Leawyn's gaze with a smile that matched Leawyn's own.

Leawyn pressed forward, the centaurs towering beside her, their immense forms brushing against the lowest branches. They stopped at the dead embers of the bonfire, with centaurs on one side and humans on the other. Saralyn, the only one who had found her bow, dropped to one knee, her arrow trained on the centaur at Leawyn's back. Om did not flinch.

"My people, we have chased the sunset, and see how we have been rewarded!"

No one moved. The taut hum of Saralyn's drawn bowstring was the only reply.

Leawyn turned to Om. "Show them."

The centaur snorted and stepped forward, unclasping the burlap sack slung across his torso. Her people tensed. If Saralyn were to loose her arrow, now would be the time.

Om stopped just before the fire and turned the sack upside down. Berries, nuts, fruits, and vegetables spilled forth from the sack. For a single breath, silence held them all captive. Then the spell broke. Her people lunged, scrambling for the food. Om took a stunned step back, staring at Leawyn with an arched brow, but Leawyn only smiled. Her gaze swept over her people, then found Saralyn at the edge of the crowd. She nodded to her friend, who slowly lowered her bow.

"Another victory," Leawyn proclaimed.

Juukta was summoned, and before long, a roaring bonfire bathed their camp in flickering light and warmth. Nuts roasted over the open flames, their rich scent mingling with the damp earth. The trees above swayed and crackled in protest against the rising smoke, but her people no longer cared. They feasted, stuffing their hollow bellies, stripping nearly naked to shed their soaked clothes. Damp garments hung on makeshift drying racks near the fire, steam rising as they dried. A small drum was produced, and Om fetched a flute from his bag. Few words were exchanged, but a chorus of beast and man's music filled the night.

The crack of dawn, however, brought a sobering reality. Their bellies stuffed, their feet weary, and their clothes warm and dry, malaise and the precariousness of their situation gripped them as the sun's rays swept the land. One by one, her people gradually took to resting around the fire, their eyes drifting toward Leawyn and Om as the centaurs retreated behind their leader, until it was again human and centaur, divided by fire.

"I would like to start... with a prayer." Leawyn stood before her flock. She bowed her head, and the others did the same, even the centaurs. "Let us pay homage to this occasion, when kin and blood of different clans and races have come together and broken bread and shared in merriment. And let us also pay homage to those that we lost, to my sons, to my ancestors, to kinsfolk of Clan Laehosha, who have suffered in battle, and to the centaurs, who have no doubt made sacrifices of their own. We are a strange people, of different accents and blood and form, yet we have all come together for common cause. Liberation. Freedom. Peace.

"Let us honor those that we lost, and those who will be lost. The fight is not yet over. The war is still yet to be fought. Let all our ancestors watch over us as we continue on the path to victory! Amen."

They raised their heads, and for the first time in the light of day, human and centaur looked upon each other. Not a soul spoke; not a being moved. Even their horse, lingering at the edge of camp, watched the two races with a cautious side-eye. Leawyn let it linger, standing before the fire, arms folded, swaying slightly on her feet as the fog of dawn slowly burned away.

It was a young girl, the youngest of their flock, curled in her mother's lap, who blinked sleepily at Om and said. "Are you a horsie?"

Om snorted and stamped a hoof. "No."

"Why do you know our language?" asked another.

"Why do you not know mine?"

"Do you eat humans?"

Leawyn flinched at the audacity of the question. It came from Saralyn of all people.

"We do not eat meat," Om answered sternly.

"H-how... how did you find us?"

Om turned, looking to his centaur companions. Leawyn herself unfolded her arms, looking at them with a raised eyebrow. Her heart fluttered.

It was a new centaur, one that Leawyn did not recognize, who stepped forward, clopping his front hoof upon the soil. "When the old bird came to our people, we thought she was mad, and like all mad things who jeopardize a herd, she needed to be put down."

A gasp rippled through the humans. Saralyn, seated against a tree, shifted, her hand creeping toward the bow resting just behind the trunk.

"It is true what my friend Annenmednon says." Om bowed his head.

Annenmednon snorted. "And so we hunted your old bird, but it was Om... who spoke kindly of her, and her plea for help. And so we turned to watching. From your victory to your march to your death and mourning, we have been there."

"And your verdict?" Saralyn asked, arm halfway behind a tree.

The centaur tilted his head. "Pardon?"

"Your verdict? On madness," she clarified.

A weighty silence settled between them. Then, in unison, the centaurs stomped their hooves, glancing at one another in silent understanding. Leawyn shot Saralyn a heated look, though she sensed no hostility among her own kind.

"She is of a strong heart and sound mind," the centaur declared at last, nodding to Saralyn and then to his kin. "We have come to join you."

Leawyn broke into another toothy grin.

"We are two clans. Two races. And with what we accomplish together, many more will join us."

A few heads nodded.

Saralyn finally eased, releasing her grip on the bow, but she did not stay seated. Instead, she rose to her feet. "Do we have a plan, then? Or will we keep chasing the sun and rotting under the rain?"

Leawyn met the gaze of her most trusted companion. Her heart sank, though she kept her smile in place. "We will... figure that out together."

There was nodding and agreements. She turned to Om, her eyes hopeful.

"I cannot say that I know your actions, Old Bird, but we have followed you west regardless. A wise move, if our scouts are to be believed. Your War Maker has summoned his forces east, where the Outsiders have concentrated their forces."

"We have missed the fight then?" a worried voice called out.

"No, we have merely found an opening," Leawyn countered, and moved to the side of the fire, dragging her foot along the soil. She quickly set to work, tracing a crude map in the dirt, then stepped aside so both factions could see. "The Hearthsea lies in the midlands. A natural barrier between us and the Outsiders. In the past, our homeland. To long-forgotten clans. Perhaps even to centaurs." She glanced at Om before continuing. "If the Outsiders have moved east, and we have moved west, then we are free to cross through the bogs and swamplands to enter the south. With time, we could strike deep into their territory."

"And then what?" Saralyn said sharply.

Leawyn's composure at last broke. "We'll achieve a great victory, something that demonstrates our power... and our unity. We will return home, and we will demand the War Maker and the other clans take audience with us."

Saralyn scowled but did not take a seat. Juukta chose to speak in her place.

"The late summer is upon us, and with it, the rains. We are all of Fláimir here, but never in my life have I seen such weather. How do you expect us to cross the bogs? It's a dangerous trek at the best of times, and then expect us to be ready to fight? Look at my mother!" He gestured to a frail old woman beside him. "She cannot fight."

There were many nods in agreement with him.

Annenmednon stepped forward, pounding his hoof atop Leawyn's dirt drawing. "Our people have rarely ventured beyond the Hearthsea, but we know of a few routes through. And on the other side, with the Outsiders gone east, there are great stone towers these people use for shelter and attack. They have been the bane of us centaurs for centuries. But... built by you humans, you could seize one, and hold it for yourselves. As to what humans hold sacred, I cannot say..." He stepped back, looking at Leawyn.

"Fate and determination have driven us this far, let us not turn our backs on victory again. We stand on the precipice of great change! Of liberation! And safety... for all our peoples!"

Eabha quickly rose to her feet, helped by her grandson. She stood no taller than a small child. "To the ancestors! To Fláimir!" she squeaked, thrusting her bloodstained knife high into the air.

The entire camp followed. "FOR FLÁIMIR!"

The sun fully breached the horizon and the camp went into a frenzy, packing their bags, gathering supplies, and deconstructing their tents. They were tired and sleep deprived, but with full bellies, Leawyn felt they could at least trek through the midmorning. Besides, she wanted to be respectful of Clan Falómeir, and knowing they were probably still watching them, she wanted to see them marching into the lands of the Outsiders, centaurs by their side.

As they readied themselves, Leawyn's stallion came to her willingly, but one sharp look from Annenmednon made her hesitate. She quickly understood riding the beast would not be well received. Instead, she offered the horse to Eabha and another elderly woman, who accepted eagerly. The centaurs still shot her wary glances, but they did not protest.

They set out in the early morning, marching back east into the rays of the rising sun. Leawyn did her best to keep pace with the seven centaurs leading them, but their long strides outmatched her own. Despite her calls for unity, they whispered among themselves in their private tongue, their camaraderie reserved for each other. Even Om, her friend, offered only a half smile before falling back in line with his kin.

Like morning dew burning away beneath the sun, so too did the fragile warmth of their bond.

Two herds, human and centaur, moved as one in name only.

By midday, as the sun reached its zenith, Saralyn finally broke the uneasy silence. She stormed up to Leawyn, her frustration barely contained. "We are heading too far east," she said sharply. "We've already covered this ground. Where are the bogs? Where are we supposed to cross?"

There were mutterings of agreement, and Saralyn's harsh eyes told Leawyn she was not the only one whose emotions, fears, and mood were running volatile. Leawyn waited until an opportune moment to call upon the centaurs to stop. She ran forward, careful to not damage anyone's pride, and spoke up.

"New friends, perhaps we stop here and rest. My people have been through much, and we feel safer traveling under the cover of darkness."

She held her breath as her people dropped their bags and belongings at once, grinding the centaurs to a halt. Om flicked his ears, his gaze sweeping over the weary humans.

"Very well, Old Bird," he said at last. "We shall resume under the light of the moon."

He lingered as the others dispersed into the trees, waiting as Leawyn watched over her people. When they were alone, his voice lowered.

"Your herd is not what I expected."

"We have been through loss and hardship," she remarked, looking upon her people scattering into the trees. "Their own kin have died for me."

Om made a quiet, thoughtful sound. "A hard thing." He turned to her, eyes dark and unreadable. "And what about you, Old Bird? Has your blood joined you?"

Leawyn jolted as if struck. She took a step back from her new companion, her heart thudding in her chest.

"I must tend to them," she said quickly. "We all need rest... If you'll excuse me."

She fled into the trees, taking a second to at least smile again as she watched her people settle in. Fires were lit, tents pitched, and sleeping rolls unfurled. She wanted to go to them, to sit and share in their warmth, but exhaustion crashed over her like a falling boulder. Under the cool shade of the trees, she found a quiet patch of soft soil, spread out her furs, and before shutting her eyes, whispered softly into the night.

"Arianwyn, and Layita, good health... and happiness."

Sleep took her before she could say more.

When Leawyn awoke, the full moon shone through the tree canopy overhead, silver light spilling between the trees. Saralyn sat beside her, arms crossed, her expression unreadable.

"Good," she muttered. "You're awake."

She sat up, rubbing her eyes. It took a moment for her to remember all the events of the day prior. "Saralyn... wah?"

"I do not trust them."

Leawyn blinked, her body still heavy with exhaustion. "You mean... our new allies?"

Saralyn turned sharply toward the distant campfire, where low voices drifted through the night. "Our kind have never coexisted. And now they lead us back east and south. Into swamps, bogs, and disease. Straight into the heart of our enemies." She exhaled sharply through her nose. "I think it could be a trap."

Leawyn shifted, trying to sit upright, but the weariness of travel and age weighed her down. With a sigh, she leaned back against the tree instead. "You never believed me, did you?" she asked softly. "When I told you I went to them. That they gave me a second chance at life."

Saralyn's head jerked away from the fire, her gaze vanishing into the dark. "No."

"Why not?"

Her answer came quickly. "Because I believe in you. In *your* message. But we have accomplished little, and a great and old friend of mine died following your words. I still believe in the cause, every day I awake praying to never hear the cries of children, mothers, and men being abducted into the sea… or have war horns and foreign clans telling us how and when to fight. Yet…" Saralyn held her breath, and finally turned to her. "you have mourned Takoda not even a second. You have only worn a smile upon your lips. It is my fear, Wise Mother, you care not for us but for your little alliance, and you will eagerly march us to our doom should it please the centaurs, or your ego."

Leawyn listened intently, nodding along with her most trusted friend. "Thank you, Saralyn, for sharing your concerns with me. I trust your advice, and your thoughts, more than any other. It is true I have not had time to mourn Takoda's passing. No one has. I am sorry. I am sorry for you, and all your people." She sighed, looking back toward the firelight. "I forget… sometimes, that I must still be seen as an outsider to you and them, with my strange accent and devilish thoughts of glory." She smiled wryly, and though Saralyn turned away, Leawyn caught the faint flicker of amusement on her lips.

"I don't know what I'm doing, Saralyn," she admitted. "I don't. All I have is faith—faith in the cause, and in the Hearth. Perhaps we are fools, myself the greatest among them, marching like moths drawn to the flame. But look at what we have done. We turned the tide of battle. We have brought two peoples together. Maybe we are walking toward death. Maybe. But I will die soon anyway. I'd rather go with glory and honor, having tried. If you would like to turn back and return to your people, I will not fault you. I ask an impossible task."

Saralyn stiffened. "You think me craven?" She shot to her feet. "I will fight for my clan. I will fight for my lost family, and for those who rest beneath the Hearth. But I only wish… no, I *demand* that you do not treat us like cattle in the trials to come."

Saralyn strutted off, leaving Leawyn to breathe a sigh of relief. Slowly, and with great pain, she lifted herself from her sleeping spot, collected her belongings, and joined her people for breakfast under the glow of the full moon. Before long, they set off again. This time heading south, toward the Hearthsea.

It took only an hour before they reached its edge. A dense wall of trees loomed before them, stretching across the horizon as they descended a low hill. The ground beneath their feet grew soft, shifting from firm ground to treacherous muck.

"Single file," one of the centaurs commanded.

They obeyed, stepping cautiously into a world unlike any other. Towering trees, their limbs heavy with moss, draped over them like silent sentinels. Half-sunken logs the size of homes lay scattered in the gurgling, brackish water. The centaurs moved carefully, seeking the safest path, but every step was slow and treacherous. One misstep could mean sinking beneath the Hearth's murky embrace.

How many bodies rest here? Leawyn wondered. *How many ancestors?*

For some reason, a shiver shot through her.

They moved in silence, the only sound the slow, sucking pull of mud against hooves and feet. Even the stallion, usually willful, followed without protest, subdued by the weight of this place.

Still, despite the centaurs' careful guidance, there was no avoiding the damp. The cold seeped into their bones, and thick mud clung to their skin and clothing. Leawyn shivered as an eerie presence seemed to linger in the trees, the darkness stretching long fingers that refused to yield to the coming dawn. Perhaps for this reason the centaurs sought a small hill deep in the bog, and when they reached it, everyone threw themselves down upon the ground, kissing the solid Hearth. They made camp swiftly, huddling around a fire as the first golden light bled into the sky.

Then, the Hearthsea stirred, and they witnessed the true power of this place.

Water flowed past their refuge, funneled by a tangle of roots at the hill's base. The bog came alive with the gurgle of shifting currents and the sloshing of unseen depths.

"What is happening?" Rowan, the man-boy, called out.

"The power of the moon," a centaur responded, nodding toward the sky.

Leawyn's herd lifted their gazes, mouths agape. Though the sun's rays had begun to dull its glow, the moon's power remained undiminished. Even this far inland, with the last vestiges of night fading, it exerted its final revenge, recalling the tides to its domain. Huddled together, they fell asleep to the slow filling of the Hearthsea.

The following night unfolded much the same. They trudged through the cold, damp bogs, feet sinking into half-solid ground, sometimes battling the moon's unseen current as brackish water bled through shifting channels of mud. Their second night in the bog mirrored the first.

By the eve of the third night, their food stores had begun to dwindle.

"Worry not," the centaurs assured them. "We are nearly through. Where the Outsiders twist the Hearth to their liking, food grows in abundance."

Saralyn looked to Leawyn when they said this. Leawyn didn't want to admit it, but it sounded too good to be true. Yet just before dawn, when only the faintest hint of light breached the horizon, they came upon an impossible clearing and looked upon the south for the first time.

"By the Hearthsea," Leawyn whispered, standing in awe of the great stretch of fields before her. Rows upon rows of wheat, vines sprouting with tomatoes, and flowering stalks of vegetables rooted in the ground. It was nearly time for harvest.

"And there," a centaur gestured toward a distant tower, its flickering light barely visible against the dark horizon. "That is where the enemy hides."

"It must be destroyed before dawn," Annenmednon added. "While darkness is still on our side."

"Do we have a plan? Uhh, Annen?" Juukta asked.

Om looked to Leawyn. "The Outsiders practice ways foreign to the Hearth, foreign to us. Their towers are designed with stone, with ladders and steep stairs we cannot ascend. Your people will need to lead the battle within, but we can grant you the inside."

Leawyn nodded. "This is our first true test. Harder than the trek, harder than hunger, harder even than the long slumber of our kin. Now, we must prove ourselves. We will take the tower and strike a victory upon their land. Our land! And show our people what we can accomplish together!"

Her people went for a cheer, but the centaurs shushed them. "Back into the woods, quickly. We will formulate our attack."

They returned to the forest just as a lone rider galloped past atop a thundering warhorse. They straddled the bogs as they moved closer to the tower. The sun was nearly over the horizon; the time for action was now.

Her people readied for battle. The youngest and eldest remained behind, tending to Leawyn's horse. Nearby, Rowan trembled, his breath ragged with fear.

Leawyn thrust a bronze sword into his hands. "Earn your manhood today."

Her voice was steel, but the boy only shuddered harder. The old woman, Eabha, walked forward bearing a toothy grin and sliced the air at him with her knife. Leawyn didn't know if it helped the boy find courage, but he certainly hightailed it to Leawyn's side.

"Enough words, enough waiting, let us secure another victory. For our people!" Leawyn's whisper carried like a command, and her warriors raised their swords and bows in silent agreement. They stood behind her, clad in leather, armed with bronze and iron blades, quivers lined with bone-tipped arrows. Leawyn herself gripped a spiked bludgeon, copper nails jutting from its head.

The centaurs took the lead.

"No words," she reminded her warriors. "Not a sound."

There were fewer than thirty of them fit to fight.

The centaurs bolted from the woods. Leawyn and her people came charging after them. They ran fast and silent, cutting through trimmed grass, bolting toward a tower of stone. They said nothing; there was no horn or beat of the drums. Only their hearts, pounding with fear and pride, forwarded their feet.

They reached the base of the tower with no alarm just as the sun breached the horizon. Two of the centaurs reeled around, facing their hind legs to a barricaded wooden door, and unleashed a series of powerful kicks. The thud of the wood cut through the early dawn, oddly in time with the *thump, thump, thump* of her heart.

Shouts went up from within the tower. Leawyn looked up, spying a portcullis above the doorway. *Hurry,* she thought, as the door splintered.

The door cracked. Another kick. Wood splintered.

With a final, shattering blow, the barricade collapsed inward.

The fog of war was lifted. Led by Juukta, a great shout went up among her people, and wielding a battle ax, he sliced through the remains of the door as the centaurs bolted. He burst into the tower, followed by the other men, then the archers. Leawyn jostled her way forward, snatching Rowan by the collar, leading him through the door. They crashed into a cavern of darkness.

The room stank, filled with the stench of smoke and blood. Leawyn stumbled forward as an arrow was loosed next to her ear. She saw Saralyn standing atop a table, screeching a war cry, and loosing an arrow toward a shadow atop a staircase. The arrow met its target, followed by a loud crash. A tapestry on the wall shot up in flames. The two-headed flame bird caught fire. In the burning light, Juukta roared, lifting his ax high before bringing it down with a sickening crunch. Blood splattered across Leawyn's face, hot against her skin.

She blinked, and the battle surged up the stairs. Leawyn followed, moving as fast as she could. On the landing of the second floor, the clash of metal rang out. She saw a man dressed in only a sleep gown raise a sword in desperate defense, when three arrows pierced his chest. Leawyn witnessed the young archers Ciara and Dierdre meet their mark. The Outsider slumped over just as a door crashed open, and the flow of battle surged inside.

"Secure the doorway!" she yelled, but like the water against the power of the moon, she only flowed with the tide of battle, and was swept down a hallway.

She reached for a door, grasped the handle, and yanked it open, dragging Rowan inside with her. They came to a small room lined with wooden beds. Two men, naked and trembling, stood frozen. One clutched a knife; the other was defenseless, wide-eyed with terror.

"I will take the one with the knife," she told Rowan. "Let us be quick about our work."

Rowan trembled but followed her advance. She raised her club and brought it down upon her target. Outside a narrow window, the centaurs charged in circles around the tower, distracting the archers on the highest floor.

Minutes later, Leawyn emerged onto the tower's top floor.

The sky stretched open above her, streaked with the first rays of dawn. "Simply incredible." She exhaled, her chest heaving, and turned to her warriors. They stood blood-splattered, exhausted, but victorious. A few even bore wounds, but none had fallen.

She wiped the blood from her brow and looked to the horizon.

Before them, the sun cast a bronze glow across the land, unveiling rolling hills coated in golden wheat and more vegetables than she could have imagined. In the distance, a cock's crow drew her attention to the lights of a small village, and beyond that, even more fields of fruit and vegetables and barley.

"A world of abundance," she smiled at Saralyn.

Saralyn did not answer. Her mouth hung open, speechless.

Below, the centaurs spoke for her, screeching in victory. One sported an arrow lodged in his back, but did not seem bothered.

The elderly and children emerged from the woods. They came cheering, though Leawyn barred them from the tower until the bodies could be hauled from the structure and piled out of sight. While this work occurred, she barked commands, knowing they had precious little time. "Gather all the vegetables you can. All the food! Be quick about it, before the village wakes!"

Every able-bodied person took to the fields, keeping low, picking every piece of food they could carry, depositing the food at the base of the tower before returning for more. Leawyn kept her eyes trained on the village the whole time, noticing figures emerge from their homes in the far distance.

"What shall we do?" Juukta eventually asked her.

Leawyn did not hesitate. "Bring me a torch."

Her people were recalled to the tower and each given a piece of flaming wood. As the sun crested the horizon, they set the fields ablaze.

Smoke billowed into the sky, thick and blinding, curling over the land in an ashen veil. Under its cover, Leawyn and her clan turned toward the village.

They took the tower. Now, they would take the entire south.

Bancroft VII

Strammond supported Bancroft up the tower's spiral staircase, each step a struggle. Bancroft dragged his weight upward, the endless stairs coiling high into the clouds above the mountain. His breath came in ragged bursts, his body racked with pain.

"Damn them," Bancroft moaned, trembling. He paused mid-step, leaning heavily on Strammond. "Damn them all to hell."

The light from a narrow window cut through the gloom, slanting across his haggard face. His breaths came in ragged bursts, and his head swam as the staircase twisted upward, higher and higher, an unrelenting spiral.

"My lord, we're nearly there," Strammond urged, but Bancroft's head spun as the staircase twisted upward, farther, and farther…

Bancroft stumbled. His foot caught on the edge of a step, and he pitched forward. For one desperate moment, his arms flailed in search of balance. The cold stone met him instead, jarring his bones as he fell and rolled onto his back.

"Your Highness!" Strammond's voice rose in alarm.

Bancroft lay sprawled, his chest heaving. He was no emperor, no sovereign to millions. Just a man, mortal and frail, undone by gravity and time. "My wife," Bancroft whispered, his voice cracking. "My boy…" A sob escaped him, and his trembling arms reached for the stairs below as if to retreat. "I should've saved them. I should've done more…"

"My liege, let me aid you!" Strammond knelt, looping his arm around Bancroft's girth, heaving him onto his back. "You cannot stay here. I'll summon the guards…"

"NO!" Bancroft's cry was sharp, more desperate than commanding. He stared upward, a single tear falling from his eye. He did not wish for more guards. He did not wish for more obligation, only rest.

"I cannot leave you here. Please, you must rise."

"Leave me to rot like my son. I wish to rise no further."

"Your Grace, please. Lysander lives. You must fight, just as he fights," Strammond pleaded.

His worn face appeared over Bancroft's own. Streaks of worry, decades in the making, stretched into a deep frown.

"He is not long for this world," Bancroft replied cold as stone. "The poison will finish its work."

"That is not true, my lord. You must keep faith! He opened his eyes this morning. You witnessed this blessing yourself!"

"The House of the Phoenix falls not in fire, but in ash," Bancroft muttered.

Strammond's voice rose. "You are the Phoenix! And from your ashes, your son will rise. Keep the faith!"

"The same was said of my first wife. Long did she toil, and to our surprise, a blessing. Twin boys." Bancroft licked his lips. "But her bleeding continued, and she drifted in and out of sleep for days. She held my hand moments before her passing, aye, she did. Told me all was well, though I saw all color slip from her eyes. A lie for my comfort, as told then, as told now. I thank you for your words, Strammond, but this is a story as old as time."

"My emperor, please rise..." But Strammond's face slipped away from his own. "I will go get help now. Do not move, my lord, or you may risk more harm..."

Bancroft's grip on Strammond's arm was like iron. "No guards. No help."

"And I swore to serve you, as I did your father. Even if you strip my title, my knighthood binds me to protect you."

A weary smile tugged at Bancroft's lips. "No more knights, Strammond. Just... help me to the top."

They made slow time. Bancroft braced for pain, from his chest or his legs, but it never came. A numbness found its way inside him. He no longer felt the steps beneath him nor the strain of Strammond's grip under his armpit. He rose slowly, gliding into the clouds, and upon reaching the top landing to his chamber, found the sunshine magnificent above the Hearth.

"Let me assist you, Your Grace," Strammond urged, pulling at his attire, but Bancroft waved him away.

"Fetch my Groom of the Stool," he commanded quietly.

"Your Majesty, you were firm earlier that you wanted no additional staff to see you..."

"My Groom of the Stool," he commanded again. "M-my stomach, I need to make."

Strammond disappeared back down the staircase. Alone, Bancroft wrestled with his tunic, his swollen fingers fumbling uselessly. By the time the groom arrived, he was drenched in sweat, stripped to his undergarments.

"Quickly," he gasped. His groom assisted him, guiding him to the chamber pot. The emperor strained, his breath shallow and ragged, but no relief came.

"Shall I prepare a drink, Your Grace? Prunes will do wonders..."

But Bancroft waved him away. He pushed and pushed, yet it would not come. Finally, as he began to sway in his seated position, his groom lifted him from his chamber pot and helped him to his sleeping chamber.

"No, not the bed," Bancroft pleaded. "My chair... the chair..."

He was seated nearest a window overlooking the castle

below. From his periphery, he could see Warwick's tower beside his own.

"You are dismissed," he commanded. His groom nodded and disappeared.

The clouds were below him now. They drifted by quietly. There was little wind today. The sun shined brightly, stinging his eyes from the sun's reflection upon the clouds. Yet he did not look away. Instead, he scooted his chair closer, exhausting the last of his energy as he looked below. The castle, aside from a few towers, slipped from view. Even the mountain, Ness and her domineering mountaintop, lay shrouded in mist. Only Warwick's tower remained visible, standing defiantly above the shroud. His eldest son. His boy. Locked away in isolation, whether for protection or punishment, even Bancroft wasn't certain anymore.

No, he thought fiercely. *Not Warwick.*

His mind turned to Lysander, his youngest. Bancroft's hands trembled as the memory surfaced—his eyes opening this morning, blood-streaked and haunted, pupils burning crimson. Lysander had tried to speak, his lips forming soundless words before sinking back into silence.

"Speak, boy," Bancroft whispered, his voice cracking. "Free the realm of your brother's suspicion. Free us all…"

But there is a price to be paid for hope. A tinge overtook his heart, the numbness vanquished with pain. He gripped his chest, looking to Warwick, when he too disappeared beneath the drift of the clouds. He whimpered, reaching one last hand out for his family.

The sun bore down on him, and Hearth disappeared beneath the mist. Alone, Bancroft's heart faltered, and with his final breath, he thought only of his family.

Jae XII

The grand staircase of the Temple of the Sun flickered with moving light, where the mob's torches swayed like distant stars. The sight stirred memories of his homeland—nights spent on the beach with his family, watching shooting stars streak across the sky.

He descended slowly, the air grew cooler as the pyramid's stone heart pressed against him. Screams rose from below, some human, others not. A group of humans ran past him, arms filled with stolen treasures. Jae didn't meet their eyes, but he followed them as they raced toward a distant point of light at the top of the pyramid. They could go anywhere. They could do anything.

Jae stopped in the dark, his hand rising to touch the cold iron of the slave collar still locked around his neck. He pulled on it, feeling the weight of his makeshift cape caught in its clamps. For a moment, the idea took hold—he could turn around and follow the looters into the night. Slip onto a boat bound for anywhere but here. Disappear anywhere in the world, and no one would ever know what happened to him, but the collar wouldn't budge.

With a breath, he let his hand fall. He kept walking—wading deeper into the dark.

Torches lay scattered across the grand staircase the deeper he descended, their flames flickering out as if surrendering to the dark. Blood pooled in the crevices between stones. Bodies appeared—Thorned Men, freed men. But no minotaurs. No Lucien. The golden walls shimmered faintly in the dying light, adorned with ancient images: the sun, the harvest, an enormous fruit ripening, light falling from the heavens, fire spreading like a storm. Jae kept descending, wading farther out to sea.

Finally, he reached a new level of the pyramid. Humans lingered here, some tending to their wounds, others clutching stolen treasures, wide-eyed and silent. The mob's torches went no farther. The air had thickened, a musky scent filling his lungs. A sound echoed up from the depths—low, guttural, and inhuman. The others heard it too. They glanced downward, exchanged uneasy looks, and quickly retreated to the surface. No one met his gaze. No one spoke as he passed.

The pyramid branched out into countless passageways as it had above, but here, it was easy to see where the chaos had left its mark. Bodies of Thorned Men lay sprawled, blood staining the stone beneath them. Freed men too, their brief taste of liberty ending here. A poor satyr's corpse lay decapitated. Shouts and the clash of weapons echoed from nearby. Jae followed the sound, drawn by the void on the ocean's horizon at midnight. He waded deep, deep into the waters, and hoped the ocean would take him away.

He entered the Altar of the Sun. The chamber was gargantuan, supported by huge stone columns. High above, the ceiling shimmered with a gilded sheen, and below this false sky, a column of Thorned Men held the final line of defense from their revolution. Behind them, a gilded altar rose on a slab of white marble where the High Priest's scepter rested, and above this, a depiction of the Sun God with His many rays twisting outward like the tentacles of some ancient sea beast. Worse still were His eyes—crimson jewels glimmering for irises, heated and watchful. Jae immediately looked away.

His gaze fell to Lucien and this Minerva woman lurking behind the fighters. Bodies filled the chamber, a mix of Thorned Men and free slaves alike. The minotaurs were naturally leading the assault. Lucien, as if sensing his gaze, spotted him enter the chamber. Without hesitation, he came running as Minerva shouted something incoherent.

"Where have you been? I was so worried when I didn't see you at the front! I thought they got you!" Lucien's breath came quickly as he struggled to form words. "We need to get you up there now. The last of them are about to fall…"

But Lucien's voice was quickly drowned out by another—a booming, boisterous hymn that filled the chamber. Jae's blood ran cold as the High Priest emerged from behind the golden altar. He stood as tall as any minotaur, and in his hands he wielded two massive swords glimmering with embedded jewels the same color as the Sun God's irises.

The High Priest sang. His voice rang out, coming from every direction, in the hideous language of the Old Tongue. Jae winced at the song clogging his ears as the priest sang. Jae didn't know all the words of the language, but its meaning was felt deep inside him.

"If the sun shall fade, His flames undone
In the shadow's grasp, the night is won
From light to ash, all things will turn
And in the dark, the world shall burn."

The High Priest pushed through the last line of Thorned Men and cleaved the head of a slave fighter clean off.

Jae broke into a loud sob. Tears stung his eyes. He tore at

his collar, no longer wanting this. "Lucien, please, we can leave all this behind if we go now!"

"Are you out of your mind? We have to end this now!"

"No, I don't want to be the *True Moth* anymore. Listen to me, I am Jae..."

He stopped as his mind reeled and tongue searched for the right vowels... *the Bull Slayer, Moth, Jae...* but he still could not recall his full name!

"I am sick of this, Lucien!" Sweat poured from his brow as he tore at his makeshift cape. He was burning up on the inside. "I... I just want to go back to the ocean... where nothing is known of fire!"

Lucien gripped his arm so tightly it hurt. "We have no chance of survival out there in the city. No ship is going to dock at our ports. The Ghost Bull is real, and he has an army. The city will crumble into chaos without a leader." His voice dropped to a hiss as another decapitated head flew through the air. "And who do you want that leader to be? One of the false moths?" He spat the words. "Or one of those damn minotaurs? You don't understand, Jae. It has to be you. You must be the figurehead."

"Me? For your own cause, you mean."

Lucien blinked as if Jae had slapped him. "We can't fail tonight, Jae. I did this for us. *For us,*" he repeated.

Jae merely looked at him and replied. "Okay."

"Jae... my love..."

But Jae ignored him. He stepped forward, prying a steel sword from the grip of a fallen freedom fighter, his eyes fixed on the last of the slavers of Astrelaide.

Only a handful of Thorned Men remained. Their line fractured, splintering into pockets of resistance. Jae's fellow fighters were carving through them, but the chaos was to the High Priest's advantage. The minotaur Bullion took a blade across his belly, roaring as he collapsed to the stone floor. A few slaves fled the melee. Three Thorned Men fell in quick succession. The High Priest's voice rose again, breaking into another hymn.

"The man released from duty's weight,
Swims to the ocean's escape.
Yet the Moon, with chains unseen,
Keeps him bound, away from sunlight's gleam."

The minotaurs roared. The High Priest descended upon a fighter, cleaving him in two. A Thorned Man shrieked and died. At that moment, the priest pivoted and found Jae's sword in his belly. The chamber came to a standstill. The High Priest's voice fell quiet. The last Thorned Man died. Jae pulled the sword from his stomach.

He sank to his knees, face now level with Jae's. A moment of recognition flashed in his eyes followed by a warm smile. "Ah, the True Moth, I had a feeling we would be seeing each other again."

Jae held the sword to his neck. "D-do you have it?"

"Oh, and what would that be?"

The tip his sword pressed into the priest's skin. "My name!"

"Ah, my boy, still so prideful," he tsked. "I'm afraid that still lies with Aeksilor. You do remember what I first told you? *Zovaesys.* Your master always knows best."

Blood sprayed across Jae's face as the priest's head rolled across the stone floor.

His world blurred. He couldn't hear. He couldn't see. His stomach twisted, and he retched. Someone slammed into him, and he rolled onto his back, gasping for breath, wiping spittle from his mouth. His eyes opened, and there, above him, the Sun God smiled upon him.

Lucien then fell upon him, screaming. He was pulled onto his knees and then shoved to his feet.

"Go," he saw the word form on Lucien's lips.

He blinked, trying to clear the blood from his vision.

"Go!" Lucien screamed and this time the word registered.

He jolted awake as something heavy was shoved into his hands. He looked down to see the priest's severed head resting warm and slick between his fingers. His body jerked. He dropped the head, but Lucien was there in a heartbeat, forcing the head back into his hands.

"Go now! To the top!" Lucien shouted, shoving him forward with all his strength.

Jae stumbled, the bodies of the fallen underfoot, Lucien pushing him from behind. The survivors of the battle screamed. A fire engulfed a tapestry. He tripped, sending the head sliding across the blood-drenched stone. Lucien's hand was under him in a heartbeat, pulling him back up. Somehow, he was running again, the severed head back in his hands.

They charged up the grand staircase, the heavy thunder of Crassius's steps echoing behind them. Something inhuman shouted at him from below.

Lucien didn't allow him to stop. They sprinted to the top. On the mezzanine, the light of dawn broke across the horizon. The sun's first rays blinded him. Lucien surged ahead, clearing the way, shoving humans aside.

"Come!" Lucien screamed.

The sound of shouting rose around them. A woman dove away from him at the sight of the head, while others cheered. A satyr snarled in his face, but before Jae could process it, humans were running toward him, patting his shoulders, clapping him on the back. Wine was splashed into his face, mixing with blood and salt.

He spit the taste from his lips. He stumbled around, looking for Lucien. A crowd surrounded him, screaming. His knees trembled. A minotaur roared nearby. Then Luke appeared. He pushed the crowd apart, Lucien at his heels.

"Give it to him, now!"

Luke's fingers trembled as he looked upon Jae. He unsheathed his sword and gave it to him.

"One in each hand! Now go—earn your right to lead!" Lucien gave him one final push.

Jae staggered toward the steps of the temple. The entire city screamed below him. A sea of humanity and beast, churning together in an ocean of depravity. Jae blinked through the blood and wine dripping from his brow. The city burned in the pale light of dawn, smoke rising in thick black plumes, choking the sky.

Jae trembled as he lifted the High Priest's severed head with his left hand, brandishing his sword in the right. He held them high before the city of Astrelaide, his cape billowing in the wind.

The crowd roared as the sun's rays burst over the horizon, his cape tugging at the collar still tight around his neck.

Vipra

The doors of the castle were barred the night the boy was poisoned, and with the emperor's death, the realm descended into lockdown. Roads to High Ness were closed, while the city watch enforced a strict curfew. Demonbreun Guards took position at every junction within the castle, and servants were forbidden to move through the hallways unsupervised. Merchants, artisans, musicians, and others of low birth were pressed into service as food tasters. Every meal and drink was feared to be laced with poison.

Panic gripped the lords and ladies of the castle. Lord Landstride and his wife Ruby were caught the night after the emperor's passing, scaling a window with a rope made of bedsheets. Both were dragged off to the dungeons for questioning. Another minor lord from the north tried to assault a guard at the main gates. His lifeless body was thrown into the dungeon, his blood staining the stone in a stark red line, marking the realm's so-called order.

Law and order, Vipra thought with a bitter laugh. *How feeble a concept.*

She paced about her room aimlessly until a servant, escorted by a guard, brought a simple meal to her door. Stew and ale, nothing elaborate, but she accepted the meal, for she knew supplies in the castle must be running low after the feast. She ate in silence, seated by her window, gazing upward at the imperial family's tower.

My time will come, she knew. Her royal blood, *foreign blood,* bought her some dignity, a little time, but the inevitable must always come to pass. She would be questioned, *sharply.* Her only hope, she thought with a rueful smile, was that she would not be showing when they came for her.

She finished her meal and, hearing the wail of some weak-willed noble below, closed the window. She struck a match and lit a candle. A bitter chill had swept down from the mountains with the emperor's death, and firewood was scarce. Though she shivered, she opted instead to undress. She removed her yellow lace gown, shedding it as she stripped down to her human self. Standing before the flickering flame, she spread her legs wide, touching herself as her sister's doctors had instructed.

"Yes, I'm sure of it," she whispered to herself. "Absolutely sure. I'm with child."

She dressed herself again, placing one hand gently upon her belly. *One half of the plan is complete, now the other half lies with you.* She prayed for a boy. *Give me a boy.* She understood the consequences if she failed. She knew her sister's wrath.

She returned to the window, thinking, for there was little else to do in her room. The boy had the sword, snatched away in the chaos of the prince's poisoning. *Would we marry? Could we seal a union between the two realms?*

She liked Derrick. The boy was strong and handsome. She had enjoyed willing him to her advances. Long tender nights of healing the boy's arm, of stripping his bandages, peeling away his clothes as he sweated, finding his muscles...

A shudder overtook her, followed by a flush of heat. She

opened the window again as tears pricked at her eyes. It was the child, she knew. Her body and instincts would begin betraying her. She longed for the boy, for the father.

Derrick. She whispered his name aloud, turning to the candle's warm flame. *Why wouldn't he make a fine emperor? He held the sword; Warwick has no goodwill with the realm, and Lysander rots in his bed. And those muscles... the firmness of his hand gripped on my thigh...*

"CAW! CAW!"

The warmth of her thoughts evaporated. She whirled around, finding a crow perched on her windowsill.

"Shoo! Shoo!" she hissed, rushing toward the bird, flailing her arms. But the creature wasn't afraid. It fluttered into her room, darting wildly, before landing on her mantel. It looked at her inquisitively, before she came to an understanding.

"A moment, then," she said softly. She snatched a quill and a piece of parchment, quickly scribbling a message in the tongue of the Kaensfolk to avoid suspicion if intercepted.

I am gone. I am but five, perhaps six weeks away. Much trouble befalls these lands, though I ward the web. With a hopeful heart, I look forward to our reunion.

She set the quill down and reviewed her words. Simple. Coded. Satisfactory. She approached the crow, attempting to tie the note to its foot, but the bird squawked loudly in protest.

"Quiet, you scoundrel!" she glared at the creature. "Do you want the guards to hear you? My sister will have both our heads!"

She tried to tie the note again, but this time the bird took flight, flapping wildly around her room.

"Damn my sister's servants!" she screamed, swiping at the bird in frustration. She missed and tumbled over the chair. As she fell, she cried out, muffling the sound quickly as she landed hard on her side. A sharp jolt shot through her abdomen, and tears filled her eyes. "No," she whispered, her hand resting gently on her belly. After a moment, the pain subsided. The bird watched her from its perch, head cocked.

"Fine then, no note. Tell her... the Webwarden is gone. Two, maybe three weeks. The land is in turmoil, and I've done my part. I await further guidance." A tear slid down her cheek as she crawled onto her knees, still clutching her baby. The bird tilted its head, cawed softly, then flew from the room.

Vipra closed her eyes, breaking into a soft cry. *This is not me. I am not myself! Damn this babe...* But she stopped herself. *I didn't mean that... I only wish to feel myself...* And she sniffed, opening her eyes, finding a small mouse at the base of her feet, watching her from beneath the chair.

"Oh!" she cried out and kicked at the wicked thing, but the mouse was quick and scampered away. "Filthy thing," she cursed and rose to hunt like the spider she knew herself to be. She moved furniture, flipped cushions, and searched high and low, but the mouse was gone.

"Very well," she said at last, glad for the sport of it. "Let us play the waiting game." She placed a hand on her belly. "I can be patient. I can spin a web."

She took her seat by the window again, gazing at the towers above.

"Do we climb, young one," she whispered. "Or do we knock them down?"

With a final glance at the flame, she tossed the note into the fire.

Appendix
The Holy Empire of the Nine

The Imperial Family of the Holy Empire of the Nine

His Imperial Majesty, Bancroft Hieronymus
Holy Emperor of the Nine and All Its Realms.

Her Imperial Majesty, Melinda of Esmerelda
Second wife of the Holy Emperor.

The Imperial Heirs:

- **Warwick** (*Crown Prince and Heir to the empire*)
- **Lysander** (*Second Prince of the Realm*)

The Dowager Empress Sylvia (Grandma'am)
Mother of His Imperial Majesty, a revered figure in the imperial court.

The Late Brother of the Emperor and His Family

Thane Hieronymus (*Deceased*)
The emperor's late brother and former Master of War.

- **Elizabeth** (Auntie) of Fláimir (*Sister-in-law of the Holy Emperor*)
- **Derrick** (*Nephew, Firstborn of Thane, and heir*)
- **Catelyn** (*Niece of the emperor*)
- **Dalia** (*Niece of the emperor*)
- **Manford** (*Nephew of the emperor*)

The Immediate Extended Family by His Cousin, Milton of House Hieronymus

Milton of House Hieronymus
Governor of High Ness and cousin to the Holy Emperor.

- **Jayne** (*Wife of Milton*)
- **Mayflower** (*Daughter of Milton*)

The Cadet Family of House Hieronymus of Rose Mont

Charles of House Hieronymus
Patriarch of the Rose Mont branch of House Hieronymus.

- **Harriet** (*Wife of Charles*)
- **James** (*Son of Charles*)
- **Torralin** (*Daughter, betrothed to Casimir of House Valkirn*)

The Cadet Family of House Hieronymus of Goldwood

Alexander of House Hieronymus
Patriarch of the Goldwood branch of House Hieronymus.

- **Hollace** (*Wife of Alexander*)

- Makepeace (*Daughter of Alexander, betrothed to Wallace of House Faelwood*)
- Fielding (*Son of Alexander, betrothed to a merchant of House Battlebridge*)
- Emerson (*Son of Alexander*)

HOUSE ESMERELDA

His Lordship, Fermi of House Esmerelda
Husband of Layana, patriarch of the Elector House Esmerelda.
Her Ladyship, Layana of House Esmerelda
Wife of Fermi, matriarch of the household.

The Heirs of House Esmerelda:

- Her Imperial Majesty, Melinda of Esmerelda (*Daughter of Fermi, Empress of the Empire*)
- Ernest of House Esmerelda (*Son of Fermi*)
  - Adeline of House Esmerelda (*Wife of Ernest*)
  - Hugo of House Esmerelda (*Child of Ernest and Adeline*)
  - Unborn Child (*Awaiting birth*)

HOUSE FAELWOOD

His Lordship, Cornwallice of House Faelwood
Patriarch of the Elector House Faelwood.

- Packard (*Son of Cornwallice*)
- Wallace (*Son of Cornwallice, betrothed to Makepeace of the cadet house of Goldwood*)

HOUSE VALKIRN

His Lordship, Lyon of House Valkirn
Patriarch of the Elector House Valkirn.

- Casimir (*Son of Lyon, betrothed to Torralin*)

Knights of the Demonbreun Order

A holy order tasked with the protection of the Crown of the Nine and the ruling imperial family.

- **Strammond Ligard** (*Head of the Demonbreun Guard and knight to the emperor*)
- **Lyfford Lemont** (*Personal knight to Derrick Hieronymus*)

Other Employed Knights to the Imperial Family

- **Wulford** (*Personal knight to Warwick Hieronymus*)
- **Dyrebane** (*Personal knight to Lysander Hieronymus*)

Members of the High Council

The Castellan
The Castellan serves as the chief advisor to the emperor, entrusted with the governance of the imperial household and strategic counsel in matters of state. Current Castellan: Alden.

The Governor of Ness
The Governor of Ness is charged with overseeing the administration and governance of the imperial city of Ness, ensuring its prosperity and security. Current Governor: Milton of House Hieronymus.

The Treasurer
The Treasurer holds responsibility for the financial stewardship of the empire, managing the imperial treasury and ensuring fiscal stability. Current Treasurer: Edwin of House Battlebridge.

The High Priest of the Nine

As the spiritual leader of the realm, the High Priest of the Nine advises the emperor on matters of faith and religious observance. Current High Priest: Osbert of the Holy Isle.

The Master of Laws

The Master of Laws oversees the judiciary and legislative functions of the empire. Current Master of Laws: Dymtrus of House Seavíc.

The Secretary of the Realm

The Secretary of the Realm acts as the principal diplomat of the empire, managing all matters of internal governance and external diplomacy. Current Secretary: Wulfnoth of House Goldshire.

The Master of War

The Master of War commands the strategic and operational planning of the imperial military forces, safeguarding the realm from external and internal threats. This position is currently vacant, previously held by Thane.

The Grand Admiral

The Grand Admiral commands the imperial navy, overseeing maritime strategy and the defense of the empire's coasts and trade routes. Current Grand Admiral: Graham of House Fontaine.

The Chief Confessor

The Chief Confessor serves as the spiritual confidant to the emperor and the imperial family, providing counsel and absolution in matters of conscience. Current Chief Confessor: Lacius.

The Cupbearer

The Cupbearer serves the emperor within the imperial court, attending to ceremonial duties and ensuring the sovereign's needs are met. Current Cupbearer: Gael of House Alfair.

The Herald of the Realm

The Herald of the Realm is entrusted with delivering proclamations, decrees, and important messages on behalf of the crown across the empire. Current Herald: Norbert Noherth.

The Commander of the Demonbreun Guard

The Commander of the Demonbreun Guard leads the holy order sworn to protect the imperial family and uphold the faith of the Nine. Current Commander: Strammond Ligard.

The Nine Voting Families of the Holy Empire of the Nine

The Nine Voting Families form the cornerstone of the Empire's governance, each holding the right to vote on the succession of the Crown of the Nine. These ancient and illustrious houses are bound by their oaths of service to the Holy Emperor and their shared stewardship of the realm.

House Hieronymus

The ruling house of the empire, renowned for its storied lineage from Lyonnia and the forging of the holy empire following the Ash Fall. House Hieronymus serves as the current seat of imperial power.

House Seavíc

Bordering the Queendom of Isperia, House Seavíc represents the only major house of Vayern blood. Unlike their kin in Isperia, House Seavíc and their people are fiercely devout to the Nine.

House Goldshire

Renowned for its diplomatic prowess, the house thrives as a master of statecraft, deftly navigating the shifting tides of the Empire of the Nine and neighboring kingdoms.

House Fontaine
Masters of the seas, House Fontaine oversees the empire's naval strength and its dominion over maritime trade and security.

House Alfair
House Alfair holds the tide against the savages and heathens of the Fláimir. Their holy task grants them the utmost regard throughout the realm.

House Battlebridge
Custodians of the empire's treasury, House Battlebridge has a long history of trade and merchants, overseeing the famously independent and wealthy city of Brattleboro.

House Valkirn
House Valkirn, known for its closer ties to Isperia and foreign lands than to the empire, their house thrives on wine, music, theater, and a tenuous adherence to the faith of the Nine.

House Esmerelda
House Esmerelda, renowned for its mastery of gemcraft and engineering, controls vast mines rich in precious stones and metals. Their innovative designs and intricate craftsmanship have earned them great wealth and influence throughout the realm and abroad.

House Faelwood
House Faelwood, representing the Kaesnfolk, the realm's largest common blood, wields immense influence through their fertile lands and deep adherence to tradition. To maintain order and stability, House Hieronymus claims common blood with the Kaesnfolk.

The Isle of Flaimir

Clan Terrwoniwyn

Chieftain, Finn of Terrwoniwyn
Chieftain of Clan Terrwoniwyn, ruler of his people.

Notable Members:

- **Leawyn** (*Widow of Lahotka*)
- **Lahotka** (*Deceased*) (*Husband of Leawyn*)
- **Nukhta** (*Deceased*) (*Firstborn son of Lahotka and Leawyn*)
- **Kaelin** (*Deceased*) (*Second son of Lahotka and Leawyn*)
- **Arianwyn** (*Granddaughter of Lahotka*)
- **Layita** (*Granddaughter of Lahotka*)

Clan Laehosha

Chieftain, Hunta of Laehosha
Chieftain of Clan Laehosha, leader of his kin.

Notable Members:

- **Takoda** (*Respected member of the clan*)
- **Rowan** (*Member of the clan*)
- **Eabha** (*Esteemed elder of the clan*)
- **Juukta** (*Grandson of Eabha*)
- **Ciara** (*Member of the clan*)
- **Dierdre** (*Member of the clan*)
- **Saralyn** (*Member of the clan*)
- **Emmalin** (*Fate unknown, Wife of Saralyn*)
- **Aya** (*Fate unknown, Daughter of Emmalin*)

- **Omnageddenon** (Om)
- **Annenmednon** (Annen)

The City of Astrelaide

House Aeksilor

His Lordship, Cato of House Aeksilor
Master of the household, a respected noble.

Her Ladyship, Aril of House Aeksilor
Lady of the household and wife of Cato.

The Heirs of House Aeksilor:

- **Luthor** (*Eldest son of Cato*)
- **Boros** (*Second son of Cato*)
- **Sirene** (*Youngest child and daughter of Cato*)

Slaves of House Aeksilor:

- **Guard** (*Soldier*)
- **Hex** (Faun) (*Groundskeeper*)
- **Berona** (Cook)
- **Jae** (*Soldier*)
- **Lucien** (*Errand boy*)
- **Luke** (*Soldier*)
- **Pate** (*Soldier*)
- **Pete** (*Soldier*)
- **Petra** (*Servant*)
- **Valeana** (*Servant*)

House Balon

His Lordship, Palo of House Balon
Master of the household.

Her Ladyship, Amirose of House Balon
Lady of the household and wife of Palo.

In the Far East

On the Homestead

- **Mother**
- **Josephina** (*Daughter of Mother*)
  - **Mishie** (*A toy of Josephina's*)
- **Oléfur** (Elf) (*Servant to Mother*)

Knights of the Reisonic Order

A holy order of knights sworn to protect the realms of men from the horrors that dwell in the untamed wilderness to the far east. For millennia, their five great fortresses, collectively known as the Fist of Men, have served as bastions against giants and darker threats. Each fort was built to honor one of their five sacred prophets.

The Five Fortresses:

- Eisvach
- Dreadfjord

- **Prophetenfyst** — *The capital and base of operations for the order*
- **Hammersford-en-berg**
- **Mannenhalvara**

The Bestiary

A collection of sapient races known to the realms of men.

- **Brownies** — Humanoid, ugly creatures, they are relatively unknown and rare to the realms of men. They are known to be crafty and intelligent, but few in number. Occasionally, a band of them will sneak through the Fist of Men only to be hunted down later.
- **Centaurs** — Half man, half horse, these nature worshipping beasts inhabit the far eastern forests of the Isle of Flàimir.
- **Dwarves** — An incredibly mysterious race, their skin is said to be as dark and as thick as the stone caves they live in. They are only known to inhabit the desert mountains west of the Scorch Grass.
- **Elves** — Small, humanlike creatures known to inhabit the far north. They rarely interact with humans, aside from the Krithinian port city of Aelfryne. They are known to be followers of ancient, darker beliefs, and are believed to have enslaved a subset group of humans known as the "Snow Men."
- **Fauns** — Half man, half goat, their numbers were once plentiful across the world of Hearth. Now, their numbers grow rare, fighting for survival in the Scorch Grass. The slave cities value them for very little, except for their ability to climb and work with their hands.

- **Gardners** — Closely related to brownies, these creatures are exceedingly rare but highly prized among the slave cities for their ability to work with plants and agriculture.
- **Gargoyles** — A long forgotten, potentially extinct race of humanoids. They were rumored to have helped build the Fist of Men with the Knights of the Reisonic Order before betraying mankind.
- **Giants** — Massive, humanoid creatures of the far east, they warred against the Knights of the Reisonic Order for millennia. Since the Ash Fall, they have rarely been seen outside of their whaling ships, confined to an isolated island in the Shiverloch Sea.
- **Greejees** — Small, demonic apelike creatures with devilish eyes. They come from the lands far south of the Scorch Grass and are valued among the slave cities for their intelligence, manageable size, and ability to climb. They are also prized for the wide variety of colors their fur coats come in.
- **Mermaids** — Mysterious, aquatic creatures, said to be half-man, half-fish. Little is known of them except for their disdain of humans.
- **Manticores** — With the face of a man, body of a lion, wings of a bat, and tail of a scorpion, they are known to be highly intelligent, but live like beasts, roosting in the hills and mountains of the Scorch Grass. Considered a delicacy among the slave cities, their numbers have dwindled due to excessive hunting.
- **Minotaurs** — Large, intimidating bovine-like creatures, they inhabit the lands of the Scorch Grass. Highly prized for their strength and work ethic (if they can be brought to heel properly), their numbers are plenty among the slave cities.
- **Noggins** — Tiny, dachshund-like creatures that wobble on two legs. The slave cities value them for very little except for their ability to fit into tight spaces, keep pests at bay, and serve as jesters.

- **Satyrs** — Smelly, intimidating goat-like creatures, they come from the lands of the Scorch Grass. They are valued among the slave cities as a fair alternative to human labor.
- **Trolls** — Nasty, vicious creatures, good for little more than frightening the enslaved beastfolk of the slave cities from fleeing back into the Scorch Grass.

Author's Note

Thank you for embarking on this journey with me. Whether your heart lies with Laewyn's courage, Josephina's sweetcakes, Warwick's pantaloons, or any of the other characters who have captured your imagination, I hope you found someone worth cheering for.

Portrait of Fire marks the beginning of an ambitious nine-book saga, and I couldn't be more excited to share what lies ahead. Your support means everything to me as an author, and I can't wait to continue on this epic adventure together.

I hope you will join me in the next installment in the series, *Pyre of Blood*, where the world is truly set on fire.

Author's Bio

T. G. Clark is a professional fund-raiser, helping nonprofits secure support for causes that strengthen communities. A lifelong writer and world-builder at heart, he's the type of fan who will happily lose hours to a wiki, chasing down the lore of immersive universes. That love of fantasy, intrigue, and dragons led him to write *Portrait of Fire*, his debut novel. When he isn't writing, he's trying to rekindle his relationship with his estranged cat, Neyland. He lives in Nashville, TN.